AERON DUSK

THE VARCROSS KEY

Ordering Information:
Quantity sales. Special discounts are available on quantity purchases by corporations, associations, and others.

Cover Design and Artwork: ZeForge

www.patreon.com/zeforge

Cover Design: Tania

www.miblart.com

Editor: Caroline Barnhill

www.fiverr.com/carolinebarnhil

The Varcross Key/Aeron Dusk. -- 1st ed.
ISBN (Paperback) 978-1-7378433-3-7

There were a lot of hands and eyes on this book from start to finish, more than I can acknowledge on a sheet of paper. To all my followers and beta readers, thank you! This story was made better with all of your help.

My loyal readers that have been supporting me from long ago, you're why these books exist. Those of you that have gone above and beyond, offering to read through these manuscripts multiple times, your attention to detail has helped more than you know.

To Forge: The support and help you've given has done just as much for me personally as it has professionally. It's been fun bouncing ideas off of each other.

The last four years have changed my life for the better, and I look forward to writing new stories while continuing these series well into the future.

The Road To Nowhere

Dawn set the surrounding mountains aflame, painting the snowy peaks vermilion as my packed SUV emerged from the Eisenhower Tunnel. Steady streams of tears cast a rippling haze over my vision, which made weaving between traffic even more reckless. Caution signs for steep grades coupled with flashing amber exits for runaway truck ramps had me giving every semi I passed a much wider berth.

After another mile of descent, I pulled off of the busy Colorado interstate and onto a scenic outlook, cracking the driver's side window to let in a rush of late-autumn air. At eleven thousand feet, I had expected something fresher than what actually filled the cabin. The stench of burning brakes from the passing convoy made me roll the window back up.

I leaned forward, wiping my face with the collar of my shirt. Sitting alone for hours gave me nothing to do but watch the road and dwell on every decision that led to this moment. In my mind, everything was still the way it was when I left home at eighteen.

As a teenager, I would look in the mirror and imagine with doe-eyed fascination what my life would be like if I could live somewhere far away, but those eyes were often black and blue. It was like I had blinked and eight years had passed, only to now see the same tired and bruised eyes but on a grown man's face. All the sterling dreams I thought would be realized by now were tarnished by falling in love with the wrong person.

I was too young to be this jaded.

My cell phone buzzed against the middle console, and with it came a rush of nausea. Had Ben discovered I was gone? He was supposed to be in Georgia visiting family, but I knew what he was really doing behind my back—and who he was doing it with. I wasn't as clueless as I pretended to be, and I had been waiting months for the perfect opportunity to finally disappear.

The caller ID flashed a different name, but the nervousness didn't abate.

"Hey Joe," I said, trying to speak more through my mouth to hide the stuffy nose.

"Today's the day, Leo. Are you on your way?"

"Yeah."

"You did remember the key, right?"

I picked up the heavy, ornate object that had been rattling around the cup holder the entire trip. It looked more like a beautiful antique novelty than anything used to open a door—about four inches long and obviously spray-painted gold. Its texture was that of pitted cast iron, and it had crescent-shaped teeth with runes carved into the stem. Its strangest feature was the chaotic, beast-like pattern at the top. Whenever I'd spend a while staring at it, the pattern would give off an optical illusion, seeming to dance and change.

"Why do I need this?"

"If you want to get into Varcross, you'll need to have it in your possession," he said, trying to disguise a stilted accent he'd let slip out occasionally. We'd been talking to each other on and off for a few months, and I still couldn't tell where he was from by the way he spoke. "You sound upset."

"I'm fine, but I'd feel better if you gave me an address."

"Are you having doubts again?"

"That's the understatement of the year. I'm about to drive over a thousand miles to a place I'm not even sure exists."

"I understand your trepidation, but I did send the first payment, and you have all the information on the town."

"Yeah, about that. I expected a check, not ten grand in cash. This looks sketchy as hell."

"Given your current situation, I thought it would make things easier. The money is yours, whether you choose to live in Varcross or not," he said calmly. "I know you'll have a change of heart once you arrive."

"Where do I go when I get there?"

"Just follow the instructions. The right people will find you."

"This is really making me nervous." I looked over at the folded sheet of thick, coffee-stained paper lying on the passenger's seat with hand-written directions to the town. It had arrived stuffed in the same envelope as the money a few weeks ago.

I should have been more discreet about my dwindling savings and my desire to leave an abusive relationship, just in case he was feeding on the desperation I often exuded. There was a slim window of opportunity I had to seize, and with my soon-to-be ex-boyfriend being away for a few days, the stars aligned almost *too* conveniently.

Glancing up at the visor mirror, I gently rubbed the mostly faded bruise around my right eye. The abuse had gotten so bad that I was cut off from friends and hadn't been allowed to hold a job for a few years. I didn't want to be homeless, but I also didn't want to live the rest of my life as someone's punching bag.

"I know you're concerned, but sometimes you have to take a leap of faith to get what you want. If you decide to back out of this, I can't stop you, but remember, this is an opportunity few people will ever get."

"How much is the stipend again?"

"Three thousand monthly, tax-free—once you sign the contract."

Though we'd been through this multiple times, I often asked the same questions to check his consistency. The website for Varcross was legit and professional. It was an experimental town, not yet incorporated, and investors were paying qualified people to move there. I'd done so much research on this that I knew each investor by name. I'd even called a few of them but never could get anyone other than secretaries on the line.

The application process was rather straightforward, but Joe was the recruiter who'd interviewed me. His questions were thorough—to an unnecessary degree. I had to disclose everything from my age to my mental and physical health while providing pictures of myself from different angles. They wanted to make sure the population was young and healthy, but all it did was give off vibes I wasn't comfortable thinking about.

All the more reason to be extra cautious when I arrived.

"Before I sign anything, I want to get to know the locals and see the place, and any meetings that occur will happen in public. Got it?"

"Of course. Put your mind at ease. You're going to fit in just fine. You may be one of the most important people in town."

"What does that mean?"

The phone chirped, and the call ended. Signal had been going in and out through the mountains, but I wasn't moving. I hit the call-back button, and instead of a ringtone, I got an automated operator message stating the number was no longer in service.

Red flag after red flag. This *opportunity* was once-in-a-lifetime, but it seemed like an outright scam. If the town turned out to be something other than what was advertised, I wouldn't take my chances by stopping to look around.

Minutes passed, and I kept playing out different scenarios in my head. What would happen to me if I went back to Ben? What would happen if this turned out to be some kind of Jonestown death cult? I had ten thousand dollars, and everything I owned was in the back of an eight-year-old Subaru Forester. If I wanted, I could take the money and start over anywhere, but that choice was also risky. Either way, I had to get as far away from this place as I could feasibly go.

While working this out in my head, I put the car in gear and pulled back onto the interstate. If I was going to get to my reserved hotel in Boise before nightfall, I'd need to stop wasting time.

Two Days Later

The only radio station I picked up out here began to crackle, fading in and out until I finally turned it off. I kept my dry eyes trained on an endless ribbon of cracked gray asphalt, winding around emerald hills of evergreens with dots of golden bigleaf maples. Weathered utility poles lined the right side of the road, some of them slanted, their lines dangling lifelessly in the gusty winds. When the last of those disappeared, the voice in my head telling me to reconsider what I was doing grew louder.

As the wind died, I relaxed my grip on the steering wheel, letting my right arm rest against the middle console. My fingers traced along the sun-warmed edges of the antique key. I doubted they would deny me entry to the town if I lost it, but Joe was adamant about its importance.

A flood of texts brought my phone vibrating back to life in the cupholder.

"Thank God," I whispered, reaching for the only lifeline connecting me to civilization. That was the first noise the phone had made since I'd left the last rural town seventy or so miles ago, and I had been in a knot of anxiety ever since. I never knew how empty Oregon was; in fact, I didn't know much of anything about the state. It would have been an exciting adventure had I not been so terrified.

I held the screen close to my face, splitting my attention between it and the narrow mountain road. After swiping away the lock screen, his text popped up like an unwanted ad, putting an end to the very brief moment of repose.

where the fuck are you leo—

A surprising gust caught the car before I could read more, causing me to swerve as the road rounded a sheer rocky face. The phone fell from my hands, landing between the seats, and I tapped the brakes, gripping the steering wheel again with both hands. The rational side of me wanted to leave the phone down there, but there was also a part of me that was still in his grasp. I could hear the tone of his voice in that sentence, and I wanted to vomit.

The man had invaded every facet of my life like a metastatic cancer, making me believe I couldn't do any better than him. When I found out he was cheating on me on top of everything else I'd endured, it was as though someone had turned on the lights for the first time in years. I had talked myself into believing that even a bad relationship was better than being alone, but I was no longer that naïve.

The phone being out of my reach gave me time to contemplate and calm down. There were moments when I could feel the end of Dad's belt snapping against my bare back when Ben would strike me with random objects. Moving to Colorado was supposed to be my escape from all the physical and emotional trauma, but like a moth in darkness desperate for light, I flew too close to the humming blue glow of gentle affection, not realizing what it actually was until the zap.

I was supposed to be smarter now, so why was I here?

Slowing the car while making sure no one was behind me, I pulled off the road along the shoulder, careful not to go too far since there was a steep drop beyond that. After putting the car in park, I took a moment to admire the beauty of this place as the trees along the mountainside rippled like water in a pond.

This would never happen to me again. I was twenty-seven years old, and I knew better than to do what I was doing. Signing binding contracts with suspicious terms could make my life even more of a living hell. There was another town further along the highway past where Varcross would be, and I'd make a stop there for the night before heading north to Washington.

I felt around under the seat for my phone, and the first thing I did was swipe Ben's message away before I could read anything more. The next thing I did was block his number like I should have done a couple days ago. This part of my life was over, but instead of mourning the loss, a surge of exhilaration pricked at my skin, making me smile. For the first time since I'd started this journey, I felt relieved. Whatever would come to pass, I would start the next chapter of my life free. Maybe I would finally find a home.

The clock on the dash read five, and the late afternoon sun poured in through my windshield as the road curved west again. With no traffic to avoid and no sound in the cabin save for the drone of the engine, I'd lost track of the day. Another hour had passed, but I could have sworn it had only been five minutes.

Worry settled back into my stomach when I examined the fuel gauge. I was already at a quarter of a tank, and there were no road signs for fuel stops. I had underestimated the distance, and since my navigation app had been disconnecting out here, all I could do was follow signs. But where had they gone?

The phone had been sitting silent in the passenger seat, no signal since the text I'd received from Ben. If I ran out of gas out here, would anyone find me? I had enough food for a few days, but no one knew I was here except Joe, and I hadn't been able to contact him at all.

"Everything's fine," I whispered, paying closer attention to my surroundings for anything I may have missed, but every mile took me further into nowhere. It was too late to turn around, and the road here was in a state of disrepair. After hitting another shallow pothole, any remnant of collectiveness morphed back into a bunch of terrifying what-if scenarios on which I would reluctantly dwell. What if I got a flat tire? What if I broke down? What if it started snowing?

"I'll be fine," I said through clenched teeth, trying again to center my thoughts. I had to keep repeating that mantra out loud, especially since Varcross was close, and now I had no choice but to discreetly stop there for gas.

In the distance, I caught sight of something that had me actually thanking God for the second time. Blinking white lights appeared over the road, just as Joe wrote in his directions, and as I got closer, the flashing intensified. Whatever these were, they hovered like tiny UFOs, not emanating from any source I could see. There also weren't any power lines out here. The moment I passed under them, a jolt of energy tore through my hands from the steering wheel, causing my skin to tingle and my hair to stand on end. Another stronger shock made my muscles lock up, and all I could taste was metal as a thousand white flashes blinded me. The car shuddered and dipped as I veered off the road.

Was I having a stroke? My body went numb, and all I could feel was my disembodied head as it floated around the car. The paralyzing sensation didn't last as I regained control of my body, and in a series of adrenaline-fueled reactions, I slammed on the brakes and turned the wheel slightly, my car sliding sideways on what may have been sand before coming to a stop. Bright halos lingered in my vision, but after a few breathless moments, the terrain faded back into view.

Somehow, I had ended up on a dirt path surrounded by giant Douglas firs. It was only a few seconds; how had I ended up here?

I opened the door and nearly fell out of the car, my legs still trembling like I'd just gotten off of a rollercoaster. A frigid, still air nipped at my skin, my breath now visible in the chill. It had been in the fifties most of the day, but now there were patches of frost on the grass. When I turned toward the direction I'd come from, the scene confused me even more. This narrow road I'd somehow swerved onto went on for miles through the trees in both directions. Where was the highway?

"This can't be right," I whispered to myself, tears welling in my eyes. I was so disoriented and confused that I began to wonder if I had died a moment ago or was stuck in some kind of dream. There must have been a rational explanation, but I couldn't think of one at the moment.

It was nearly twilight, the sun no longer visible through the dense canopy, and I shivered, crossing my arms before catching sight of a wooden sign ahead. As I stumbled closer, my shoes crunched through the icy blades of dead grass, and I held up my phone's flashlight to get a clearer look. Though crudely carved and barely legible, the word Varcross appeared.

"I'm going nuts," I muttered while ambling blankly back to the car. "What the hell happened?"

It was as though my body was on autopilot, and I slid behind the wheel, slamming the door shut before starting the engine. "I should try to find a hospital or clinic in town…if I even make it."

The further I drove, the more I couldn't shake the feeling I was missing time again, and another staticky tingle traveled up my arm. The road went from dirt to solid and bumpy, like cobblestones, and the dreamy feeling returned, my head swimming.

I cornered the narrow path, which was no longer wide enough to drive on fully, but there was enough space between the road and the trees. The tires on my right began slipping on gravel, and warm-colored lights ahead led to a clearing with the town now visible in the distance, like a beacon holding back the sinister shadows of this strange forest I'd somehow driven into. In the dark, Varcross didn't look at all like the pictures Joe had sent me. From what little

I could make out at this distance, the buildings had a worn, classic appearance, as if they were hastily constructed as a movie backdrop. The website said the town was new, but that clearly wasn't the case.

My foot left the accelerator, and I let the car move on its own at a languid pace while trying to get a better view, but out of nowhere, an enormous figure stumbled onto the road. Thinking it was a large man, I rolled down the window, preparing to ask for directions. However, when my headlights fully revealed him, I hit the brakes, my body lurching forward. My knuckles were white and the blood drained from my cold face as I tried to come to terms with what was staring back at me with glowing, ice-blue eyes.

Ashy fur covered the hulking beast, its maw agape in either anger or fascination, revealing a jagged set of long, pointed teeth. It staggered as if drunk to the front left of my car, intense curiosity in its features as it slid a claw along the hood while inching closer to my open window.

I threw the gear in reverse and slammed the accelerator to the floor, the left tires sliding while throwing gravel up into the wells before finally gaining traction enough to put some distance between me and whatever the hell that thing was. The vehicle stopped hard as I made a rough turn, the car halfway onto the grass. I punched the gas again, sending the old Subaru into a fishtail as the traction light flashed on the console. The town and the monster disappeared quickly in the rearview mirror, but I had to slow back down as the road began to wind. This didn't seem like the same road I was on earlier, but there were no others I could have turned down.

Once again I was buzzing with terror and adrenaline, my breathing rapid, almost matching tempo with my pulse as I pushed the accelerator again when the stone road straightened before turning to dirt. I reached into the cup holder to grab my phone, but instead of a smooth case, my fingers crushed a soft, sooty substance where the heavy key had been earlier. I held my blackened fingers to my face, not noticing the path disappear in a thick fog until I looked back out to see white.

The car shook on the rough path again as the town I'd just left popped back into view. The massive creature I'd escaped from also appeared, but I couldn't stop in time to avoid hitting it. Instead, I swerved left, the vehicle sliding sideways in the icy grass. Realizing I'd overcorrected, I braced as the headlights revealed a huge spruce mere feet ahead of me. With a glass-shattering crash, the side of my head slammed against the frame of the window before jerking forward as the airbag exploded outward.

My vision blurred and frantic rapping came from the passenger window, but that was all I could register before everything went dark.

I didn't know how badly I was injured, and I felt myself being lifted and pulled. A grunty voice spoke, but it was so distant and muffled I couldn't understand the words. There was a heady scent of dog and strong liquor as I struggled to keep conscious. Two points of blue light pierced through the darkness, leering at me before turning orange. As I felt myself slip back into unconsciousness, reality disappeared into an inky morass.

I didn't know how badly I was injured, and I felt myself being lifted and pulled. A grunty voice spoke, but it was so distant and muffled I couldn't understand the words. There was a heady scent of dog and strong liquor as I struggled to keep conscious. Two points of blue light pierced through the darkness, leering at me before turning orange. As I felt myself slip back into unconsciousness, reality disappeared into an inky morass.

Something heavy landed on my chest, shaking me. My eyes blinked open, and an immediate stab of pain spread from the left side of my head down to my neck.

"Yer okay." The voice growled from overhead, and as my hazy vision cleared, a large, gray snout and sharp canines were inches from my face.

I screamed and pushed the monster away before rolling off a leather sofa and smacking the old wooden floor with a painful thud. A giant hand wrapped around my lower leg, pulling me back as I tried in vain to crawl away backward.

"Now, you just calm down," the beast said in a thick southern drawl. Despite how deep his voice was, he spoke like a human would. "I ain't gonna hurt ya."

The only movement I could manage was uncontrollable trembling as I locked eyes with the creature's, held in place as he hovered over me. My back slid against the frigid floor when he pulled me closer to him. The other hand that wasn't holding my leg reached for my face, and I flinched as the top of his furry finger stroked my cheek.

"There now." The gentleness of his tone didn't match his feral appearance, but it did calm me down, if only a little. This all seemed so real, but there was no way it could be. This was a dream. A very vivid dream.

But if this wasn't real, how could I be feeling pain? How could I smell the beast's doggy odor and hear the rumble in his voice? Maybe this was all a hallucination caused by the head injury, and I needed to go to the hospital.

Despite the monster in front of me, the house he'd carried me to was cozy with unusually tall ceilings. There was a stone fireplace to my right, its dying embers radiating warmth to the small room, and there was a ragged leather couch with rips in the cushions to my left. A buckskin rug in the middle of the floor dressed up the dusty wood surrounding it.

At the far end of the living room, an animal skin drape covered a window, and on a crooked log table in front of it sat a transparent rectangle with a dark screen. It looked like a television, but there were no visible wires or circuitry. Whatever the device was, it didn't seem like it belonged in such a primitive-looking place. My focus shifted back to the high ceiling as I tried to avoid further eye contact with the wolf-like creature whose intense stare I could almost feel. A dim, flickering crystal in the shape of those Himalayan salt lamps gave everything a warm hue.

"Where'd you come from?" he asked.

My attention snapped back to the beast. He was dressed sort of like a half-naked man, wearing nothing more than a pair of black patched shorts with frayed edges and a tear above the right leg.

As I tried to answer, the jumbled words caught in my throat. I couldn't believe how enormous he was. His arms were thicker than my thighs, and just one of his hands could easily crush my head. At least his hooked claws were neatly trimmed and ground to a smooth finish.

There was an uncanny placidness about his movements and his voice, but what was more striking was his appearance. Now that I got a good look at his dark gray fur, I noticed blackened tips that got darker toward his chest. A thick, jet-black mane covered his head, and it shortened to hackles at his neck, trailing his back and chest before narrowing at his broad abdomen.

Some of his fur had human hair characteristics, especially along his face. There were what appeared to be softer mutton chops growing through the coarse gray that covered the rest of his features. His long, pointed ears fell downward as he waited for my response, and a necklace of bone and teeth clattered around his neck as he released my leg and nervously scratched his head.

"I ain't nothin' to be scared of," he said, the intense glow of his blue eyes dimming as he sniffed the air. "Them stories ya heard on the outside, they ain't all true." His ears folded back. "Okay, maybe they's true, but I ain't like that."

"What are you, and where am I?" Even though I could finally speak, the shaking didn't stop.

"Yer an odd fella," he said, a soft smile exposing a couple longer canines. "Kinda weird that they's throwing humans in Varcross now. I thought only us vargyrs was in here." He leaned back and sat cross-legged, his tail pattering against the floor behind him. The beast's feet were just as enormous as the rest of him, the soles black and padded, and in the place of toenails were shorter claws that weren't as neatly trimmed as the ones on his fingers. "You musta done something pretty bad to end up here."

"If blindly trusting people makes me bad, then sure. I'm awful," I said, groaning in pain as I pushed myself into a sitting position. We were both on the floor, staring at one another for an uncomfortable moment. "I just wanted a place to live."

"And you chose here?" His head tilted. "How'd you even get past them wards?"

"What the hell are wards?" I shook my head, mumbling *Jesus Christ* under my breath. "I just followed the directions and drove here."

"Directions?"

"To the town," I said, trying to dial down my frustration. "There's a road leading here."

"Yer talkin' nonsense. Ain't no road into Varcross. You musta really took a nasty hit to that noggin."

I paused and rubbed at the painful bruise along my temple.

"Now I'm seeing monsters," I mumbled to myself. "I need to go to a doctor. I think I have a concussion."

"I ain't a monster." The creature huffed, gritting his sharp teeth as he faced the floor. "I was human, just like you...kinda." The light of the room danced in his big, glassy eyes as he looked back up at me. "*They* treat us like monsters, but we ain't always that." He leaned forward and gently rested his rough hand on my arm, but the gentle gesture turned to a strong grip before he let go and pulled away. "*I ain't that. I swear.*"

The way he'd grabbed me moments ago made me nervous. I still had no clue what he was talking about, but he was obviously upset at what I'd said. There was a dumb part of me that wanted to pat his head like I would a dog, but the rational part of my brain sent a stern reminder that this was an actual werewolf—or vargyr as he called himself.

"I'm sorry," I said, giving him a fake, reassuring smile. His ears perked up, and his tail pounded the floor again. "I'm really tired." I rubbed my temple again and remembered the accident. "My car!"

"What's a car?"

"What's a—are you for real right now?"

He cocked his head and I let out a sigh.

"It was the thing I was in that hit the tree." The vargyr didn't respond, and I slowly stood up, feeling a little less light-headed than earlier. That was a good sign. "I hope it's not too bad."

"Where're ya goin'?" he asked before jumping to his feet. Now that he was upright and so close to me, I felt like a child in front of him.

"I didn't even want to come here, but I need to get gas and drive to the next town—if I can even figure out where the hell I am."

"Gas? What the heck 'er you talkin' about? I'm startin' to get a little worried about you now. Ain't got no doctors here."

"I'll be fine." I walked to the door, but his hand caught my arm.

"You can't leave."

The strong grip made me lock up in fear. He seemed so nice at first.

"Are you—are you keeping me here?"

The beast's eyes grew wide, and he shook his head, holding up both hands in a defensive gesture.

"I don't mean ya can't leave my house. I'm tellin' you there ain't no leavin' the town." His arms dropped to his sides as he sighed. "I don't know what you've been told, but Varcross is a prison."

I turned toward the freshly varnished antique door to leave but stopped as his words caught up to me.

"I didn't see any guards. The only person I saw when I got here was you." I looked back at him. "And if you're a guard, I'm sure you can look away just this once."

The vargyr stomped across the room, passing me before blocking my way.

"There ain't no guards; they're wards. Magic wards."

We both looked at each other, and I turned away, letting out a shaky laugh.

"Look, nothin' would be more fun than watching you try to leave this place, but it's dark out. Ya ain't got no place to go, right?"

"I'll get a hotel."

He shrugged and opened the door, waving me through.

"You sure are stubborn, but I'll take ya to yer...car. You ain't goin' nowhere, though."

Hungry Eyes

I trailed the monster at a distance for the first ten minutes of our walk, neither of us speaking to the other. Despite the endless questions buzzing around in my mind, I wasn't sure where to start.

"What's your—" we both asked in unison, cutting each other off.

He grunted, and I cleared my throat as we passed what looked like an old-fashioned pub. Wolfmen of different fur colors and sizes stumbled in and out of it, either howling, laughing or—

My focus shifted to the far side of the property, but it was hard to tell exactly what was going on. I squinted as a much larger vargyr pressed a smaller one against a tree, his hips ramming so hard I could hear it from this distance. The act was violent, yet both of them seemed locked in some kind of drooling trance, their eyes burning a deep crimson. It was like watching a bad accident, and I couldn't look away.

"Ya ain't gotta walk so far back," he said, startling me a bit. "What's yer name?"

I turned toward him. "I'm sorry, what?"

"Yer name," he repeated louder.

"Leo."

"Nice to meet you, Leo. I'm Axel," he said, turning playfully on his heels. Though he wagged his tail and politely extended his hand to shake mine, his sheer size made me want to slink away.

I shoved my hands deeper into my pockets.

"Do ya hate me?"

"I don't even know you."

"Well, let's fix that," he said, his giant, heavy hand landing on my shoulder. I met his eyes, expecting him to be angry; instead, his sharp grin softened to something a little less forced. "'Round here, when you meet someone you don't know, it's polite to shake hands." Axel gave me a nod and extended the gesture again. "Even though I got the teeth, I ain't gonna bite ya."

I reached for his hand, and the thick, rough pads of his palms scraped against my skin like old calluses.

"Sorry, you're just...really big," I choked out as his grip tightened. Axel stood still, his eyes glowing an intense amber as a bit of drool seeped from the sides of his mouth.

"Axel?" I squeaked out. The vargyr shook his head and jerked away, his irises fading back to a gentle blue.

"We should probably hurry," I said, my chest tightening. Everything inside of me wanted to sprint away as fast as I could, but I also needed to keep my head.

"Yup," he replied as though nothing happened, turning away before continuing along the uneven cobblestone path. I decided to trail him a little further away this time.

As the road took us the rest of the way out of town, all I could make out in the blackness were different colored eyes dotting the way. There really were no other humans here, and the once rowdy laughter and howling died to silence as many began following us, their stares trained on me like hundreds of laser sights.

"Are they stalking us?" Ignoring my discomfort, I quickened my pace until I was standing at Axel's side again.

"Many of us ain't seen another human in years. The closest we got to humans is the wilkyrs."

The silence gave way to growls and incoherent chatter as even more of the shadowy beasts leered from every direction.

"Wilkyrs?"

"Hard to believe you ain't pullin' my leg right now," he said, shortening his strides so I could keep up with him. "You really don't know nothin' about us, huh?"

"No." A loud snarl came from the right side of the path, and I jumped closer to Axel.

"Don't worry. They ain't gonna do nothin'," he said, patting me on the back. "Wilkyrs is vargyrs that ain't fully turned yet. They look kinda funny; ain't got a full body of fur yet, but you can definitely see the wolf in 'em. They got sharp teeth, pointy ears, claws, but they ain't grown yet, and they still look closer to human than we vargyrs do."

"You don't turn back human?"

He let out snorty laughter.

"There ain't no going back. Once the curse has us, we turn into this," he said, letting me go before pressing his thumb into his broad chest. "Wilkyrs can sometimes shift to full vargyr, but it don't last. It's kinda dangerous, cause it only happens when they're really pissed off." He let out another deep chuckle. "Everyone knows not to cross that line. Eventually the body stops changin', which is good, 'cause it hurts like hell."

"That's terrible."

"The physical part ain't that bad." His gruff tone turned effervescent. "Had it in my blood since birth. We're faster, stronger, we don't never get sick and we don't get old. I ain't sayin' everything about it is perfect, but it could be worse."

As we left the path and cut through some trees, the headlight beams of my car lit the rest of the way. Thankfully, the battery hadn't died...yet. From this distance, the damage didn't seem so bad, but as I jogged closer to get a better look, I couldn't see past the wide spruce-like evergreen I had plowed into.

"Crap." I circled the car to fully assess the damage, looking in through the windshield. The driver's side airbag had deployed. I wondered if it would even start. "Can you help me push it away from the tree?"

"Course I can," he said, brushing past me to the front of the vehicle before cracking his knuckles. "Stand back; I got this."

Vice-like hands gripped the front bumper, the vehicle groaning as Axel's huge arm muscles flexed. The front tires lifted from the ground, and he pulled the car away from the tree before turning it. He let it drop and hurried to the back. With very little exertion, he pushed against it, and the car rolled the rest of the way onto the road.

"Shit," I whispered, watching a grinning Axel as he folded his arms proudly against his chest. They all looked strong, but I got the feeling this particular vargyr was an outlier since I hadn't yet come across anyone else as large. If he could lift a thirty-five-hundred-pound vehicle like it was nothing, what would he do to me if I made him angry?

My attention shifted from the cocky beast to the tree trunk-sized dent that had just missed the wheel but damaged the door where it was hinged to the frame. I pulled the handle, and the door clicked, but I couldn't open it further than a crack.

"Well, my door is fucked."

"Here," Axel said, tapping my shoulder to move me out of the way. "I might be able to fix that."

"I guess you couldn't possibly mess it up worse than it already is."

"Uh...yeah," he said, grabbing the edge of the door with his right hand. "Listen, I'm just tryin' to show off fer ya, but I'm probably gonna end up breakin' this."

The way he said that, and the silly look on his face, made me actually smile for the first time. His personality certainly seemed more human the longer we were around each other. I still couldn't shake that distant, predacious look he gave me earlier, and I didn't want to find out what was lying just beneath the surface of this *friendly* beast.

He pulled the door, bending it a little before trying to shut it. Of course, now that he had done that, it didn't rest all the way against the frame. "Oops," he said, pushing the door back in until it clicked. "Hmm." He pulled again, opening it halfway before closing it easier. It was like watching someone bend aluminum until it was more pliable. "Yeah, that'll do it. It ain't gonna open all the way, but you should be able to get in now."

I stepped over to the driver's side door. "Thanks, Axel."

His tail wagged, making him look more like a German Shepherd excitedly waiting by the front door than the blood-thirsty werewolves I'd seen portrayed in movies.

"So yer really gonna try to leave?"

"I'm not trying," I said as I climbed behind the wheel, pushing the deflated airbag out of the way.

"You seem pretty sure of yerself, so how 'bout this: when you get back, you gotta agree to go with me to the pub and let me buy you a drink, 'cuz I wanna hear more of yer story."

"Sure," I said dismissively, looking toward town. "Where's the closest gas station?"

He tilted his head in response, giving me that signature look of canine confusion, one ear falling to the side.

"Are you serious? There's no gas station around here?" I asked, shutting the door all the way, shattered glass rattling around inside of it. The keys were in the ignition, and the car was still in drive. After resetting the gear, the old Subaru miraculously sputtered back to life.

"Don't know what that is, but I'll be right here when you get back."

Perhaps I'd make it to highway twenty-six before running out of fuel. At the very least, I'd be on a road that had cars on it, and breaking down on a highway was less of a nightmare than being stuck here.

"Thanks for all your help. Really."

"Mmhmm," he grunted with a nod. "I'll wait right here fer ya."

"Now you're just being annoying," I said, absentmindedly trying to roll up the broken window. This was going to be inconvenient while driving in the bitter cold. After making a shaky U-turn, I sped away, staring into the rearview mirror as the lonely wolfman in the middle of the road disappeared into the darkness. The only part of him that remained visible were two glowing blue eyes. I wondered how long he'd wait there before returning home.

The road wound around thick trees, and I lost visibility as a fog rolled in again out of nowhere. I put on the high beams and let up on the gas, but the lightheadedness from earlier returned. There was still an injury I had to contend with, and I wondered if I should have taken my chances back at that town rather than possibly passing out behind the wheel. The pain wasn't as bad now, and aside from a couple new bruises over the eye and temple, it could have been much worse considering how fast I was going on impact.

The fog cleared, and when Axel faded back into view, his arms still crossed with that shit-eating grin plastered on his face, my blood turned to ice.

"There's no way," I muttered, shaking my head as I stopped and made a three-point turn, pulling back onto the road. "I must have gotten turned around somewhere."

This time, instead of looking at Axel, I watched the digital compass in the rearview mirror. It read east, the direction of the main highway. I alternated between watching the road through the fog and eying the compass to make sure my heading remained constant.

The swimming in my head returned, and the digital compass went from east to west in an instant. The mist cleared again, and there was Axel, standing in the same spot.

I put the car in park and cut the engine, gripping the steering wheel tightly as the dim lanterns from the town glowed through the windshield. None of this could really be happening. Was I trapped in some kind of lucid nightmare?

Axel strolled up to the driver's side door and stuck his head in through the open window.

"You okay, buddy?" he asked. "Bet yer ready for that drink now, ain't ya?"

I blinked a few times, trying to focus on his calm expression before responding.

"I don't understand."

"I'll explain it when we get into town." Axel reached in and gently rubbed my shoulder before circling to the other side of the car. After a few failed attempts, he opened the passenger-side door with a cracking sound and crammed himself into the seat, the entire vehicle tilting to one side under his weight. Contorting himself so that his face was against the windshield, he pulled his tail inside and slammed the door shut. "This is neat."

"What the hell are you doing?"

"I wanna ride in this thing," he replied, barely able to turn his head.

I wanted to laugh at how hilarious he looked, but tears welled in my eyes instead. "I'm not supposed to be here."

"It's gonna be okay." His hand patted mine against the middle console, giving it a reassuring squeeze. "Worry 'bout it tomorrow, and let's get shit-faced tonight. Whaddya say?"

I used the sleeve of my shirt to wipe my eyes, and I smiled at the uncomfortable monster sitting in the seat next to me. Despite his looks, his presence made me feel a little less isolated. All I could do was hope I'd somehow wake up tomorrow, back to reality.

A Night To Forget

"A hard cider," Axel bellowed over the disturbingly quiet patrons surrounding the bar. I watched on as a stocky, silver bartender poured cloudy yellow liquid into a tall stein. "Put some extra hard in it, Tobes."

"Keep calling me Tobes, and you won't ever get another drink here again." The older-looking vargyr wrinkled his nose into a snarl. He had a slight gut and stood about a foot or so shorter than Axel, but like all the others, he packed on a lot of natural muscle. His face was broader as well, and the scraggly furry beard on his chin and below his nostrils was a little longer than the rest of his fur. He wore a faded black vest with a pair of ripped dress pants, as if he'd torn them while putting them on. Though he was shorter than Axel, he was still way bigger than me; in fact, I was probably the smallest living thing in that bar, aside from the occasional flea that would crawl on my arms before disappearing onto another furry host with questionable hygiene.

Axel howled with laughter, and I looked around nervously. When we got there, most of the vargyrs were outside, but the moment we entered the bar, they all filed in behind us, not making a sound. It was disturbing how fast their behavior shifted from foggy and careless to razor-sharp focus.

The pub was small, and aside from some *really* drunk patrons passed out in the corner, there wasn't a lot of jovial banter. An eerie mood settled on top of everyone, almost like they were all waiting for something to happen.

Flickering crystal lanterns dangled from black chains beneath gothic-style arches supporting the high ceilings, and there were shackles and goat-like animal skulls adorning the blackened walls. Mysterious carved runes decorated most of the faded wooden surfaces, each one painted a different color. It was then that I recognized one of the patterns; it was the same symbol on the key Joe gave me.

A hand settled onto my back, startling me out of my thoughts.

"You gonna be okay?"

I stared down at the stein resting on the claw-pocked bar in front of me.

"I don't know." My thumb pushed down on the top of the handle where the hinge was, and the pewter lid pulled away from the mug. A powerful vapor hit my nose, causing me to cough and tear up. I let go of the container, the lid slamming shut as I pushed it away.

"What the hell is this?"

"Hard cider—well, we call it cider, but I ain't sure if there's a lick of fruit in it. It's Toby's special brew, and he don't tell anybody his secret." Axel eyed the barkeep before sliding the mug closer to me.

"I can't drink this."

"It ain't that bad, trust me. We gotta make our own liquor here, and this stuff'll get you right tanked."

I looked around again and lowered my voice to a whisper.

"I'd rather not get drunk in this place." I rested my elbows against the bar, and the silver vargyr Axel called Toby gave me the same odd stare as everyone else. "Why are you guys looking at me like that?"

He shook his head and wiped a glass with a stained white cloth before turning back to Axel, ignoring me completely.

"You're a complete idiot."

"What?" Axel muttered, picking up his own stein before guzzling the entire drink in one go. "I ain't gonna let nothin' happen to him."

Another huge, lumbering vargyr stumbled through the bar and plopped down on the stool next to me. Though I wasn't looking directly at him, I could almost feel his stare. Hot, alcohol-laden breath moistened my face as he leaned close. He had the same powerful odor about him that everyone else did.

I scooted closer to Axel. "Something doesn't feel right. I don't think I should be here."

"Of course you should! Toby's is fer everyone. They're just real friendly, is all." He flashed me a grin before it shifted to a bare-toothed snarl that made me slink forward against the bar. A low growl vibrated the surrounding air, and his eyes flashed blue. He and the other vargyr locked stares in a wordless show of dominance, but no one else seemed to care what was happening. Even Toby rolled his eyes at the display.

The overbearing presence dissipated when the unwelcomed beast stood and stumbled to a stool at the opposite end of the bar. Axel smiled as he nudged my stein closer.

"You gotta relax."

"That was friendly?" I asked, my eyes wide as I slowly lifted the mug to my lips, stopping as the vapors burned my nose, taking my breath away.

"You gonna drink it, or just admire the aroma?" the barkeep asked, seeming unusually interested in my reaction as he leaned in.

I took another sniff and gagged.

"I hope it tastes better than it smells."

Toby and a few other vargyrs sitting at the bar broke into fits. I should have taken that as a warning, but I went for it, tilting the stein just enough to get a mouthful of the stuff.

"Oh God," I choked out in a high-pitched voice. My mouth and throat were on fire as I stood from the stool and heaved. The sensation was akin to that time I downed a cinnamon whiskey shot, only ten times worse.

"Maybe I really should have gone easier on the...*secret* ingredient," Toby said as I struggled to catch my breath.

Axel's hand patted my back, and watery vomit launched from my mouth.

"Damn, you okay buddy?"

"Yeah," I squeaked out, my face burning hot as the bar erupted into more howling laughter.

"Uh, let me drink this one." Axel grabbed the handle of the stein and gave Toby a nod. "Can you get him somethin' a little lighter?"

The barkeep shot me a grin before placing a pink ceramic teacup on the bar with a squiggly daisy painted on the front.

"Here you go," he grunted. "If you hold your pinky out when you sip on it, it'll go down a little easier."

I tried to laugh it off, but I never took being the butt of a joke very well. It wasn't like I couldn't hold my liquor, but this was dreadful.

"That's funny," I said, looking down at the sad-looking cup.

"Ya still have it," Axel said, turning the teacup so he could see the flower on the front. "I didn't know you cared that much about me."

"I kept it because it's the stupidest-looking thing I've ever seen. Stop making me ugly shit!"

The larger vargyr wiped his eye and laughed again before inhaling the cider from the stein I tried to drink from. He belched before slamming it down on the bar, shooting me a cross-eyed stare.

"Toby's a real sweetheart," he slurred, before looking back at the annoyed vargyr. "Ain't ya... sweetheart?"

Toby huffed and set to work pouring a drink for another patron.

I put the cup to my lips, throwing caution to the wind as I chugged it as fast as I could, this time holding my nose. The *weaker* alcohol tasted like what I could only describe as watered-down lighter fluid, but at least it didn't burn that much. Toby and Axel shot me wide-eyed stares as if I'd done something wrong.

"What?"

"Are you insane?" Toby asked, the volume of his voice growing louder. "Humans aren't supposed to drink it that fast."

"What do you mean?"

"You might actually die," he continued, seemingly more concerned than before.

"Die?" My voice got louder as I stumbled to my feet, the booze hitting me a lot faster than it should have. Or maybe I'd actually been poisoned. "Why the hell would you give me this?" The floor seemed to wave at me as I paced in front of the bar. "What do I do? Do I induce vomiting? Should I drink water?" I dashed back over to the bar. "Get me some water, please!"

More howling laughter came from all around me, Axel now slamming the palm of his hand repeatedly against the counter, barely able to catch his breath.

This time, I didn't pretend to go along with it as a crush of embarrassment weighed heavily in my guts—or was that the disgusting booze?

"Fuck both of you!" I turned toward the door but stumbled as the room spun. Before I could grab onto anything, I slipped on my own vomit from earlier and fell face-first onto the floor. Vargyrs were falling out of their seats as I lay there, wishing that that drink actually had killed me.

A pair of brawny arms wrapped around my waist, lifting me with no effort before setting me on a stool. As he let go, Axel's grin faded.

"We was just jokin' with ya." He draped his arm over my shoulders, leaning in close. "You know how many times I've fallen on my ass in front of everyone?" He nodded at Toby, who poured more into my cup. "If you care, you ain't drunk enough yet."

I simmered for a moment longer, and instead of gulping down the cider, I nursed it like I would any drink.

"Talk to me," Axel said, his wet nose briefly touching my cheek. "What's yer story? Where're you from?"

I took a sip and squinted at the black and gray wolfman.

"I drove here from Colorado, but I was born in Kansas."

"Ain't heard of those places. How close are they to Stellous?"

"Stellous?"

The bar went dead silent as everyone stared. This time, they seemed to be genuinely interested in what I had to say instead of ready to rip me to shreds.

"This is ridiculous," Toby muttered from behind the bar, wiping another glass. "You're stuck here now, so you may as well tell the damn truth." He sat the glass on the counter. "I wanna know why the mages are throwing humans in here. This shouldn't even be possible given how the wards work."

I finished the cup and placed it on the counter, pushing it away, but Toby sneered and filled it back up again before setting it firmly in front of me.

"You're gonna keep drinking until you either die of alcohol poisoning or start telling the truth."

"I am telling you the truth." My words were starting to slur. "I don't know what you're talking about. What is Stellous?"

Toby lifted the cup, pushing it toward my mouth. "Yeah, sure. You've never heard of the most powerful nation in all of Eqiros."

I sighed and threw my head back before downing the drink faster than the first cup.

"Alright, now you gotta slow down a little," Axel said, pushing the cup away and holding his hand up as Toby went to pour more. "So why was you lookin' for a place to live?"

I swayed a little on the stool while looking down at the floor. "Cause I'm a failure and an idiot. I should have paid attention to all the warnings."

Axel's hand slipped under my chin, pulling my face up. "I can tell just from lookin' at you that ya ain't no failure. Yer also lookin' at the dumbest guy in town. I'll fight ya if you take that title away from me."

He made me smile again. Axel seemed so different from the others, going out of his way to cheer me up while everyone else was more interested in staring at me, some drooling as they did so. Thankfully, I was drunk enough that it no longer disturbed me as much as it probably should have.

"I'm here because I needed to get as far away as I could. Some guy named Joe told me how to get here." I picked up the teacup and handed it to Toby. "You know, it's an acquired taste, but it's growing on me."

He grabbed the cup and exchanged it for a much larger stein. "Here," he said, filling it to the top. "I was only kidding earlier about drinking yourself to death, so take it easy."

I nodded and continued. "Joe left out the part about being trapped in a town full of monst—" I paused, reconsidering my words as everyone glared. "I mean, vargyrs. Should have gone with my gut and headed to Washington when I couldn't contact him again, but I was desperate." I shook my head. "And being desperate makes you do stupid shit like hope for a better life."

"It'll get better, Leo." Axel gave me another pat on the back. "So how long was you together with yer mate?"

I shot him a puzzled stare.

"Aw, don't look at me like that. You ain't that hard to figure out. Hang around any pub for long enough and you start to pick up on things. Plus, it's a tale as old as time."

"That part of my life is over. I don't want to talk about him."

"Him?"

I looked down at the stein, forgetting I wasn't back home. There was no telling what the social dynamics were here, but I'd already let too much slip.

"Uh, forget I said anything."

"Naw, you done said it, and it's interesting," he said, prodding me with his elbow.

"What the hell's so interesting about it?"

Axel pulled away and held up his hands.

"You get defensive real easy, even when yer drunk."

"I'm gay, okay?"

The vargyr narrowed his eyes. "No you ain't."

"Excuse me?"

"You got that sourpuss look." He shoved his thumb into his chest and smiled. "I'm much gayer. Hell, even Tobes is gayer than you right now."

"Axel!" Toby shouted.

"Sorry. To-by."

It took a moment before I understood what he was implying.

"I think we just confused each other again. There's a double meaning where I'm from. It means I'm into guys."

Axel's tail swayed from side-to-side behind him, and Toby remained quiet, save for the loud grin on his face as he poured another drink, sliding it toward a brown vargyr at the end of the bar.

"Ah. That is confusing." He nodded toward the back of the room, and I turned toward two vargyrs licking each other's faces. "Most of this town's shacked up with each other, so that's kinda normal for us."

"Are you for real?"

"No choice. There ain't no women here, and most of us ain't exactly picky."

"Now that you mention it," I turned on the barstool and leaned in, "what's up with that?"

"The curse only affects men, and it's passed down from the dad if he's a howler himself. That's what happened to me. I grew up in foster care on the outside, and didn't find out what I was until my mid-twenties. This is a town full of vargyrs, and there ain't no women vargyrs."

"You didn't grow up here?"

"Nah," he said, shaking his head. He slid his stein across the bar toward Toby. "Need more of this."

"We can talk about something else if you want."

"It's all good. Can't expect you to spill yer guts if I ain't gonna follow up." He raised the drink to his lips, smacking them loudly. "Plus, I got all the cheer right here." Axel tilted the liter-sized pewter stein before slurping down what must have been his fourth round of the stuff. Another belch growled from his throat, followed by a satisfied moan.

"My twenties wasn't all great after I found out. The moment I started seein' the hair get thicker, I knew I was on borrowed time. It's the same story with a lot of us. The change don't happen overnight. You get thick body hair, then yer ears get all long and pointy—same with yer teeth. Then ya get the claws." He laughed. "Them damn claws. I remember wipin' my ass and forgetting about 'em." He shoved me with his elbow and leaned into my ear. "You only make that mistake once."

I laughed, and his smile turned into something more somber.

"Years go by and it gets harder to ignore, even though you want to. Then one day, yer lookin' at some half-turned beast in the mirror you don't recognize. The moment I couldn't hide what I was, I had to give up the comfortable life. Lucky I wasn't seein' no one, but I had to quit my job and go on the run before the mages found me. As scary as it was at first, I started to like livin' out in the woods."

He paused and turned to me, his ears against his head.

"I'm talkin' too much, ain't I?"

"When are you not talking too much?" Toby said before looking at me. "Three drinks, human. That's all it takes, and he never shuts up."

"I don't mind," I said, smiling at Axel. "So, what do the mages do to you when they find you?"

"Are you thick?" Toby interjected. "Look around. You think we're in this miserable shithole for the good times?"

"Don't mind him," Axel said, waving the short-tempered barkeep away.

"They give us a little trial, fasten a deritium collar to us, and shove us through the wards," the black vargyr who sat next to me earlier interjected, holding his head up with his right fist as he downed his alcohol. He seemed more exhausted than drunk. "Isn't that what they did to you?"

I shook my head. "I literally drove into town. One second I'm on a highway in Oregon, and the next, all I can see is white light. I can't explain it any better than that because it still doesn't make any sense."

The rest of the bar stared at me as though I had gone insane, and maybe I was considering how comfortable the crazy had become sitting in that bar.

"How long does that stage last before you turn?" I asked.

"Depends," Axel said. "I spent three years hiding in the woods with no one, trying to hunt fer my meals before the wilkyr phase ended. It was pretty damn painful, but I'll never forget my first night under the stars as a full vargyr. It was the night I finally felt complete, and hunting got a lot easier. I wasn't a freak no more—at least, I didn't feel like one."

He let out a heavy sigh.

"But you know how the story turns out. Ya can't run from 'em once you hit yer full turn. Their magic finds you easier, and they threw me in here where I've been livin' fer ten years."

"I'm sorry," I said, as he stared blankly into his empty stein. Maybe it was the booze or the sad story, but I wanted to console him the only way I could. Slinging one arm around his neck, I leaned in for a friendly hug.

Toby let out a sharp gasp, and Axel went rigid. Taking a hint from the uncomfortable responses, I recoiled, then exhaled in relief when his thick arms wrapped around me. Why did they react that way?

Though brief, it was as though they were frightened of me—which was rather ridiculous.

"This place ain't too bad, and I got company." I pulled away from him and he wore his usual grin. Again, I took note of his eyes, which were usually blue, but were now a darker gold color. The significance didn't seem to matter as he continued his story in a much lighter mood. "I got reunited with my best friend from when I grew up in the foster home. Turns out, we was both howlers. I kinda had a feeling there was somethin' deeper that bonded us."

"You're really not what I expected," I said.

Gradually, his eyes faded back to baby blue, and one of his canines peeked from under his lips as he gave me a wink.

"I hope that ain't a bad thing."

"Not at all. Thanks for taking me here. This really helped." I started to enjoy talking to him. The bar was starting to get rowdy, like it was before I came in. Many of them were still leering, but with a friend like Axel, I wasn't as afraid. A second wind of energy coursed through me as I finished my third drink...or was it my fourth?

"It's a pleasure, Leo." His arm draped around my neck as he pulled me in for another drunken hug. Toby's head snapped toward Axel, and his eyes grew wide. "Get a few drinks in someone, and ya might have a friend fer life."

Warmth flushed my face, mostly from the booze, but admittedly, some of it was him. Being held by friendly monster was a strange experience, but not at all unpleasant.

"I'll pay for the drinks," I said, reaching for my wallet. "I'd say it was worth it."

He grabbed my hand. "Don't you dare."

I pulled out a one-hundred-dollar bill and slapped it on the countertop. "Too late."

"What the hell is that?" Toby asked, holding the bill up to examine it closer. "Is this a joke?"

I'd felt so at home that I'd completely forgotten what a strange place this was.

"Oh," I said, nervously thumbing through my wallet. The silver vargyr didn't seem that upset, but he was getting impatient as he placed the bill back on the bar before tapping his clawed pointer finger against the wood. "You take credit cards?"

"We take money," he growled, baring his teeth while leaning forward. "Silver, gold, and platinum." He paused and shook his head. "Actually, not platinum. I don't have enough in the till to make change for that."

"I got him," Axel cut in, dropping a misshapen silver coin into Toby's palm. "Cut him some slack. He said he ain't from where we're from."

"Yeah, and I think he's full of shit." His eyes narrowed on me. "We use the same currency on Eqiros."

"Well, he ain't got none." He glared at Toby before a friendlier stare settled on me. "What do you normally do fer money?"

"Well, I went to school for front-end development. I started working on web design."

His eyes glazed over.

"Don't spiders already do that?" He scratched his head. "I don't think we got a need for spider-wranglin'. I mean, unless you enjoy killin' 'em. They creep me out."

It took me a moment to figure out what he was rambling on about.

"Never mind. It's definitely not whatever the hell you're thinking." The concept of getting a job was irrelevant because I'd expected to be paid to live here. However, as I sat on the stool, holding useless currency, I wondered how I was going to survive. "Do you guys have computers?" I was really slurring now, my eyes harder to keep open.

Axel scratched his head again, and with that gesture, my prospects for gainful employment got a lot worse.

"What else are you good at?"

"I—I don't know."

"He'd make a killing working for Gar." Toby tossed the coin into the till and nodded, looking me over. "You know that's what everyone here's thinking, right?"

"No!" Axel bared his teeth.

"A human in this place isn't going to be able to do more than that. You know this. In fact, it's only a matter of time before you—"

Axel's fist hit the counter, making me jump. "Stop," he said, trying to hold back something more than anger. The larger vargyr looked down at me and smiled. "Why don't you come stay with me, and uh, we can talk 'bout work once yer settled in."

"Idiot!" Toby shouted, slamming the register shut. "I've been watching you struggle to control yourself all night. Take him to the wilkyrs."

"It ain't yer business what I do with friends." The grimace returned to his face, his eyes glowing a brighter blue as the hackles along his mane shot up.

Toby held up his hands and shrugged. "You do what you want, Axel. All you're going to do is hurt yourself when he ends up like Orryn."

"I don't wanna hear this no more."

"Too bad. Remember what you had to do? This is a gamble you don't want to make."

"No more. Not tonight." The gray vargyr stumbled to his feet and grabbed my hand, pulling me off the shaky stool. Being upright so suddenly made me realize just how blitzed I was. Everything spun like a wild carnival ride, and I had to lean against Axel for balance. "Let's get you to bed."

I wanted to ask so many questions after what I'd just heard, but I was having trouble speaking. My vision clouded as Axel led me out of the bar. Gravity pulled me downward, but his arm wrapped tight around my waist, keeping me from falling.

"Now that's not fair," a huge brown vargyr said as we walked out the door. "You're not gonna share him either, are you?" He followed us outside but kept his distance as Axel looked back at him.

"Did I not kick yer ass hard enough last time?" Axel pulled me away faster, and the angry vargyr at the entrance of the pub began shouting.

"Your luck's gonna run out one of these days, and I'll have that inbred pelt of yours covering my bed." As we got further away, he shouted louder and pointed to me. "And I'll make him scream while we're on top of it."

That last part made me nauseous.

"What the hell is he talking about?"

"Don't worry about him. Just stick close to me, okay? It'll be fun havin' a roommate again."

It took us twice as long to get to his house than it did getting to my car earlier, and *that* was about the same distance away. We were both having trouble walking, and at one point, we ended up at someone else's front door. Luckily, the resident wasn't home when Axel kept trying to jam his key into a lock that wouldn't fit, all the while mumbling curse words before finally figuring it out with a hearty, drunken laugh.

When we were inside, I took one look at his couch and was about to fall onto it when Axel pulled my arm toward the hall.

"You can sleep in my bed. Yer the guest."

"I couldn't impose like that."

"Shit, you ain't imposin' at all."

He led me into a small corridor before entering a cramped bedroom with dirty old shorts and what looked like animal pelts in the shape of large underwear strewn about the floor. There was a musky smell coming from everywhere, and the stench made me reconsider the sofa. There was also a layer of fur and sawdust coating everything—from the messy, oversized bed to the corners of the room where it piled up along the paint-chipped baseboards.

"Didn't expect company. Sorry 'bout the mess. It's comfy, though. Well, more than the couch is."

"I'm actually fine sleeping on the couch."

"I won't hear it. I can sleep anywhere."

I sat on the firm, lumpy bedding and used my feet to slip off my shoes. My eyelids barely stayed open, and the weirdness of this situation wasn't something I cared to dwell on at the moment. It only took a second of me sitting there for my head to hit the mattress, my legs still hanging over the side of the bed. There was no way I'd be able to move them; I just wanted to sleep.

My body went weightless before landing softly on the pillows.

The Dungeon

The sun poured in through the window, drenching my face in painfully bright light. Every time I tried to open my eyes, a stabbing pain would shoot like an arc of electricity through my head. My fingers brushed against a heavy, fur-covered arm holding me in place.

"Axel?"

I thought nothing of it at first. Falling asleep drunk next to a stranger was something I'd gotten used to before I met Ben, but when I tried to roll out of bed, those powerful arms would pull me back.

"Hey, wake up," I said louder, trying again to scoot away, but he'd effortlessly drag my body back across the bed like a giant child holding a doll. As I fully came to and struggled more, his hold only grew tighter—so tight I thought he might suffocate me.

He was still fast asleep which made the situation even more terrifying. When I went limp against him, his embrace loosened, but when I tried to move again, his claws would dig in a little as he clutched my abdomen. I resigned myself to being spooned by this huge beast as warm slobber dribbled down the back of my neck. The vargyr's odorous and overbearing presence reaffirmed that I hadn't dreamed the events of last night.

I stayed in that position for what must have been half an hour, sweating as his long, wet tongue lapped against the top of my head, occasionally going into an ear. When he wasn't licking me like a frozen treat, he snored, giving me a hit of some of the worst morning breath I'd ever smelled.

His hold loosened, and he finally let me go before rolling over, leaving me lying still and wide-eyed, afraid to make any sudden movements or he'd turn around and snatch me again. Making certain I was in the clear, I carefully rolled out of bed before my sore bare feet met the freezing floor.

I couldn't remember much from last night, just pieces of the conversation at the bar and a lot of disturbing stares. The last thing I recalled was slipping off my shoes while Axel watched me with almost red-colored eyes, not saying a word. Had we talked anymore? I certainly couldn't recall him crawling into bed with me.

Letting out a groan, I reluctantly pushed myself off the lumpy mattress before stumbling through the hallway, my mouth like dirty cotton. The rest of the house was tidy, and it looked like Axel had swept the floor while I was asleep. There was still a faint scent of sawdust, but I had become nose blind to everything else.

As I entered the bathroom, I stood in front of the sink and looked around. There was no toilet, and half the space was devoted to a showering area. It had concrete flooring and a grated drainage barrier, separating it from the rest of the wooden floors. The sink had a rough texture, similar to cast iron, and there was rust around the drain. When I turned one of the spotted brass knobs, nothing but air raced through the faucet at first. After a few seconds, murky orange water shot through in spurts before gradually flowing clear.

There was no way I'd drink it, but I had to wipe the crust from my face and Axel's slobber from my neck and head. The icy water pricked at my skin as I splashed it all over my face, the shock of it making me gasp. At least it didn't have that lingering sulfur smell of well water I'd grown accustomed to as a child growing up in rural Kansas.

After turning off the tap and patting my skin dry with the long sleeve of my shirt, I stared at my face. Dry, irritated eyes squinted back, the redness of my sclera starkly contrasting the hazel at the center, and the bruise on the left side of my forehead where I smacked into the door during the accident had darkened. The older injury around my right eye had now faded to a greenish-purple, and staring at it conjured up familiar yet unwelcomed feelings.

I hadn't shaved in a week, and the black, thicker stubble made my face and neck itch. Black tufts of hair stuck out in all directions, and when I went to press them down, I got a handful of Axel's drool. I shuddered, remembering the grunty moans as he lapped at my head with that huge tongue. Cupping my hand under the faucet, I held as much of the icy water as I could before wetting my hair, diluting the slobber into something manageable.

Worrying about my appearance seemed silly since I was stuck in a town full of monsters. I smiled at the reflection, examining my teeth before frowning again. When I thought about all the ways Ben criticized my appearance while sleeping around behind my back, I had tortured myself nonstop by thinking there was something wrong with me.

Though I never wanted more than earrings, Ben insisted on me getting more...exotic piercings. I rubbed at my chest, the hard studs in my nipples poking through the thick fabric. He wanted me to go more extreme, but that was one of the few times I grew a spine and refused. During the trip, I thought about removing the steel rods and letting the holes close, but I'd grown rather fond of them. The reason I went through with it may have been wrong, but after experiencing something I never thought I'd do, I was proud of myself.

The longer I stood there looking at that mirror, the more flaws appeared. I was never self-conscious when I was younger, but over the years, the back-handed comments here and there wore me down. No matter what I did, I could never be perfect.

An hour in the bathroom each day had become my daily dysmorphic ritual, almost compulsive when I lifted my shirt. I had been in the best shape of my life, though I wasn't quite as lean as I was months ago. With all the planning in secret lately, working out wasn't exactly on the top of my list of priorities.

The water trickled to a drip as I turned the knob and backed away. Why was *this*, of all things, what I was concerned with given my current situation? I was the only human here, and I still didn't understand how I'd ended up in what I could only assume was another world.

Toiletries and clean clothes were still in the car, which I had parked behind the pub, out of sight. The floorboards groaned as I crept around the place, now able to see it clearer in the natural light. The house was tiny. Axel meant well by offering me a place to stay, but there was no room. I didn't want to sleep on a couch for however long it took for me to find work, and there was no way I'd sleep in that bed again. In fact, after the way I woke up, I got this uneasy feeling. Was I safe anywhere?

I tiptoed back into the bedroom, and the huge vargyr was now lying on his stomach, his long, brawny limbs sprawled out on the bed while his clawed feet hung over the end. A bushy wolf tail stuck out through a hole ripped in his frayed shorts, and it moved slightly with every heavy breath he took. For a very brief moment, I actually found him kind of cute while in that position, especially as his long tongue hung out over the pillow.

I slipped into my socks and shoes before hobbling to the front door. It was going to be an exhausting walk while hungover, but one I needed to take if I wanted to feel less gross. After opening the door, I slipped outside into the late-morning sun.

There was only one dirt path leading from Axel's house, and the trees along the sides of the road in the distance were too thick to see beyond. Quaint log cabins with smoky chimneys were staggered throughout the woods close by, including the one we unintentionally tried to break into last night. Every house was somewhat close together, except for Axel's, which was the last before the road narrowed to a weedy path that disappeared into the wilderness.

It was clear and cold, and there was a briny scent in the air. Being closer to the ocean was one of the perks of living in Oregon—but this place definitely wasn't Oregon. Now that I could see my surroundings in the daylight, I didn't know what to think.

Everything was more alien than familiar, and not just because the area was new to me. The trees, though much taller, resembled the Douglas firs I drove by along the hillsides yesterday, but they also grew alongside trees I'd never seen before. Oddly-colored leaves covered gnarled branches that arched over the road, like haggard witches with spindly arms draped in shaggy purple robes. The seeds that had fallen to the ground were black and S-shaped, rattling when I kicked them.

There wasn't a toilet in Axel's bathroom, so I had to hold my bladder until I could find a private place to relieve myself. Since the trees were thicker here and there wasn't anyone around, I decided the brush ahead was a suitable spot.

A few twigs fell from above, landing on my head as I unzipped my fly. The rustling leaves had me looking around for the source, but I couldn't see beyond the first set of branches.

Goosebumps pricked at the back of my neck, and I hurried things along, fumbling with the zipper of my jeans as I picked up the pace toward town. A crashing thud in the distance made me jump, and as I turned toward the disturbance, reddish-orange eyes leered back at me from the shade. Though he was rather hard to see from here, the vargyr's silhouette was somewhat familiar. He was brown with a lighter fur pattern along his chest and an almost auburn mane covering his head and neck.

I turned away, trying to ignore the creature, but leaves rustled and crunched behind me as eager footsteps sped closer. I swallowed hard and kept my eyes forward, hoping he'd leave me alone. There was no Axel here to keep them away this time, and it was then I'd realized what a huge mistake this may have been.

"Hey," his bassy voice called out, uncomfortably close. I stopped and turned again, now recognizing the face. It was a brief interaction, but his violent threats from last night were unforgettable.

"Uh, hey," I said, trying to keep a solid composure. Now that I saw him up close, I started panicking inside. The beast was nearly Axel's size, and Axel was already freakishly huge.

"You sure had fun last night." He leaned over, his snout now inches from my face as he sniffed between sentences. "How'd Axel treat ya?"

I stepped back, but that didn't deter him from getting closer. He wore a similar 'outfit' the other vargyrs did: a simple brown pair of ridiculously short ripped shorts that had darker patches of new fabric stitched over tears.

"It was fun, and Axel treated me fine," I said quickly. There was a lump in my throat I couldn't swallow. "I need to grab a few things from my car." As I turned around and continued along the path, the vargyr ran to my side, his clawed hand settling on my back.

"I'll walk you there." Ropes of spittle seeped from the sides of his mouth. "It's dangerous out here. Never know what might get ya." He turned and licked away the drool, his breathing heavier than before. "You sure are small..."

"Maybe I should go back—"

"You smell like Axel, but I can work with it." I locked up as he sniffed me again. "Did you like it?"

My trembling worsened as he reached lower. "Like what?"

In a swift motion, he grabbed my arms and held me still. "He didn't do anything to you. Did he?"

"Please," I said, looking around to see if there was anyone else on the road who could help, but if there were more vargyrs, would that have been worse?

"Oh boy this is good." The vargyr's free hand traveled to my crotch, his sharp claws ripping at the front of my pants. "I've never gotten to do this with an actual human, not even when I was human." His irises turned blood red, and he tried to speak again but could only manage grunts and whines. "Nnngh..." His throat rumbled as he pressed his nose into my neck, and a warmth dampened my shirt where his shorts rubbed against me.

As his right hand continued to work my pants off, his diverted attention gave me a brief opening. In a swift motion, I reared back and sent my fist barreling into what I thought was his stomach, but as he let out an ear-piercing whine and shuddered before crumpling to the ground, I knew I'd done something much more effective.

When he looked up and bared his teeth, I knew that I had only moments to run before he recovered. The trees whipped around me as I sprinted from the path, holding my ripped jeans in place. Every few seconds, I'd glance back to see if he was following, but thankfully, I was alone. The scent of smoke grew heavier as I pushed onward, now completely out of breath.

My legs buckled, and I gasped for air, my arms scraped and bloody from running through a few briars when I wasn't paying attention to the path. I was so terrified that I didn't even feel it. Every time I blinked, I'd see flashes of that vargyr's red gaze—which seemed familiar to how Axel had stared at me before I passed out. I reached down and zipped my jeans, but since he'd torn the button off, I couldn't fasten them.

The way ahead was clear, and I could make out the blackened wood buildings of town; however, none of them looked familiar. When I emerged from the woods, the vargyrs walking the path around town and those sitting on back decks froze, their eyes following me as a last kick of adrenaline pushed me to a brisk walk.

They were all predators, but it wasn't food they were after. Knowing I'd likely survive a vargyr attack in this town brought little comfort, considering what I now knew they wanted to do to me. What if Axel—

No. I likely wouldn't have been able to walk, much less run if he did, if I could even survive something like that.

Up ahead was a tight alley between buildings, too small for any vargyr to fit into. I squeezed my way through and sat on the ground, raising my knees to my chest. Padded footsteps surrounded me, and I put my head down, closing my eyes while hoping I'd wake up from this at any moment.

As minutes passed, most of the commotion faded.

"Are you okay?"

I opened my eyes, and a small gray vargyr stood in front of me, his icy-blue stare reflecting a bit of the sunlight. He stood less aggressively, his ears off to the side and tail tucked.

I was too frightened to respond. Here I was, this twenty-seven-year-old man huddled like a child in an alley. What could I do? One of them would get me, eventually.

"It's okay," he said, sitting cross-legged on the ground. There was a larger vargyr standing behind him, his fur unnaturally black on the side that was shaded, while the other side turned an oily cobalt blue in the sunlight. I'd never seen such an interesting fur color before.

"Where are you going?"

"I—" Something Toby mentioned last night could've been my salvation. "The wilkyrs. Do you know where I can find them?"

He extended his hand toward me. "Come out, and I'll point you in the right direction."

I was scared, not stupid.

"Can you get one of them?"

"We're not allowed in their part of town," he said, waving me forward. "Come on. Nothing's going to happen to you out here, I promise." He smiled and crawled forward until he couldn't go any further, keeping his hand extended. "You can trust me."

I backed away.

"Did something happen to you?"

"You're all trying to get me."

The vargyr nodded, his ears lowering to the sides of his head again. "We are, but not always."

"I don't understand."

"The town is safer than the woods. If one of us attacks, another will help. We were all human, and we know how you feel, but don't take that for granted. The curse affects all of us the same way."

"How do I know *you* won't attack me?"

"Look," he said, pointing up at his face. "If a vargyr's eyes turn the color of blood, then you'll know to run. The lighter our eyes, the safer you are."

"Is it something you can't control?"

He nodded, and his honesty gave a bit of comfort.

"This curse is really twisted," the other vargyr behind him said. "Everyone in town struggles with it, but it's not like we all go nuts at the same time." I examined his eyes, which were an amber color.

"What about his eyes?" I said as the smaller vargyr looked up at his partner.

"He's okay for now."

Swallowing the fear, I took my chance and extended a hand toward him. He grabbed onto me, his palms like sandpaper against mine. What choice did I have? I couldn't stay in this alley forever.

"You're pretty close to the wilkyr part of town. Most of them live and work together over there." He pointed to a row of longhouses in the distance, walled off from a larger black building at the end. "That's the hub of the town, Gar's Dungeon."

"A dungeon?"

"It's not a real dungeon, it's just a theme." He trailed off and smirked, one canine poking over his lower lip.

"You uh...you gonna work there?" the black vargyr asked, his eyes darkening to orange as slobber dripped from the sides of his mouth.

The gray vargyr shook his head and cut in. "Ignore him. When you get there, ask for Cole. He runs the place when Gar's not around, and he'll be able to help you out."

"Maybe...he can get you a job...workin' at the dungeon," the black vargyr said slowly, his words coming out in breathy growls.

"Go stand over there," the gray vargyr snapped, pointing to a small tree near the road.

"I wanna see—" With a snap of his friend's fingers, the black vargyr took on a more submissive stance, his ears pulling back as he sauntered toward the tree. Though he was further away, he still stared, his eyes more crimson.

"Thank you." I reached to shake hands, but he didn't return the gesture; instead, he backed away.

"Human," he said, his voice lower than before. "Don't make any stops. Get to the dungeon as fast as you can and avoid the woods." He took another step back. "What's your name?"

"Leo," I said, nervously moving away from him. His eyes slowly faded from blue to gold, and though I didn't understand all of this curse, at least he'd explained the warning signs.

"I'm Mikael, and that's Gavin—my mate," he pointed to the other vargyr. "It's a relief to see a human again after so long." He cleared his throat and looked away. "Remember, keep to the road and don't stop for anything."

With that not-so-subtle warning, I nodded and turned toward the direction of the black building in the distance, my heart about to explode as I pushed myself through another sprint. Running through town like this reminded me of when I was a kid, turning off the light in the basement at night before making a mad dash to the safety of the hall light, only this time, the monsters I ran from were very real.

As I neared the building, I slowed, my legs wobbly and sore. Sweat soaked through my long-sleeved shirt, making the already bitter breeze unbearable as I ascended the wooden steps to what I hoped was a safe place to hide out. There were empty tables and chairs in neat rows along the covered deck near the entrance. A large wooden sign hung next to the double doors with what looked like a list; however, the letters were those runic symbols I couldn't read. I thought back to the sign outside of town with 'Varcross' written in English, and that only added to the mystery of this place. How was everyone speaking my language if this was another world?

Three more heavy-footed vargyrs strolled by the building, slowing to gawk, none saying a word at first, but as I reached for the knob, the brown one spoke up.

"Heeeey," he said, his voice dripping with a flirty inflection. "When's your shift?" He stepped closer, sniffing the air, but stopped at the stairs as if he were afraid to go any further than that.

"I don't work here."

"Really?" he asked.

The silver and black vargyrs with him stepped forward as well, each one sniffing feverishly.

"I saw you at Toby's last night. Are you gonna start workin' here?"

The other two eyed me with anticipation, all three of their tails wagging in unison.

"Maybe if they're hiring. Is this a bar?"

"It's the dungeon," the silver one said, grinning excitedly. "Best place in town—even better if *you're* gonna be working here."

"O–kaaay," I said, looking back at the sign. "Can anyone read this?"

"You can't read?" the brown one asked.

"I can. I just can't read...whatever *this* is."

"Those are Gar's rules. They're for the vargyrs, so you don't have to worry about it." He licked his chops, casting a quick sideways glance at the beasts standing next to him. "If you start working here, can I be your first customer?"

The silver vargyr next to him wrinkled his snout while baring his teeth.

"That's against the rules!" He looked back at me. "But...if you were to take requests, I run a store in town with lots of Stellous goods. I'll give you anything you want."

"You can't bribe him!" The black vargyr raked his claws across the silver's face and roared. In seconds, the area erupted in what sounded like a monster dog fight—growling, snapping, ripping. Bloody gashes on all three were visible through fur, and I took that as my opportunity to get the hell away before I was pulled into it like one of those old-timey cartoons. The speed at which they turned aggressive was alarming, but not at all a surprise anymore.

I turned the knob and threw the door open before slamming it shut behind me. The fight outside raged on, but the brick walls and heavy door muffled the violent commotion. I looked around, and the place reminded me of a gothic nightclub. There were multicolored lights from crystals along the high ceilings. Chains and unlit candles in black iron holders were fastened to the walls. A long bar took up space on the far left with log stools lining it, and two large kegs with taps on their sides sat on shelves behind the counter. There weren't many tables or chairs around, but there was a stage.

A matte black dancer's pole in the middle of it unraveled the subtle, gross hints I'd been given about this place. Dangling from thick chains and pulleys around the room were six cages that hovered around five feet above the floor. There were three doors, one next to the bar, one next to the stage and one on the far right that was open, leading into a darkened corridor.

So that was what the vargyrs thought I'd be doing. I thought back to earlier this morning when I stared into the mirror wondering if I was still attractive, and I would have laughed if I weren't in such a terrible situation.

You're going to fit in just fine. You may be one of the most important people in town.

If only I had known the significance of Joe's words. Who the hell was he really, and why put me through this?

"That's enough," a voice shouted outside, and the rabid snarls and roars suddenly ceased. I hurried toward the door closest to me, which turned out to be the closet next to the bar. After slipping inside, I kept the door slightly cracked just in time for the entrance to slam open, two human-like figures stomping inside.

Thick, fur-like body hair covered them both—the taller of the two was brown and the shorter one a light blonde. They looked almost like men in the dim light near the door, but as they walked through the empty room, they were exactly as Axel described.

Hooked, black claws poked from where fingernails would have been, and their feet were larger, with shorter toe claws. The taller one had wild brown hair, tamed by a red and black bandana which kept long bangs out of his eyes. It was similar to a vargyr's mane since it went down his neck, but it didn't go beyond that. As he spoke, his clean, white canines were longer and more pointed but not long enough that they stuck out as much as Axel's. His facial hair had been trimmed into a connected beard with thick sideburns, and his furious amber eyes glowed as he held a black bag in front of him. All things considered, he was incredibly attractive, especially his multiple helix piercings working stylishly with his gorgeous gold, gemmed necklaces and choker. The beast-like qualities mixed with his ruggedly handsome human features gave him a clean, hyper-masculine appearance.

The blonde wilkyr had similar facial features, but his hair wasn't as thick, and his eyes were a faded hazel without the glow. There was another difference between them: the larger guy had a brown, stubby tail that hung from a hole in his pants while the blonde one didn't have anything. If it weren't for the ears and claws, he'd easily pass for human.

"What the hell got into them?" The brown-haired wilkyr tossed the bag he was holding behind the bar.

"Good thing Gar wasn't here to see that."

"The last thing I want to see is a damn vargyr right now. Can't believe I have to work on my night off." The taller wilkyr climbed onto one of the log stools and rested against the bar. "I swear, if Vince doesn't get the hell off my couch..."

"How many times are you gonna kick the guy out before he learns his lesson? And how many times are you gonna fall for that cute face and empty promises?"

"That cute face will be my downfall. It's bad enough he sits there like a corpse playing with that stupid box, but—" He sniffed the air and snapped his head toward the closet. "I can smell you, Axel. We need to have a talk about Vince." He jumped off the stool and dashed over to the door, jerking it all the way open. "And you're not even supposed to be here—" The rage on his face immediately shifted to wide-eyed disbelief. "Unbelievable. How in the hell?"

"I heard the rumors," the blonde said, looking over the other one's shoulder. "I thought they were just being horny."

"I'm looking for Cole," I said, backing away, but the bigger wilkyr grabbed my hand and yanked me out of the closet.

"You're looking at him," he said, shutting the door before scrutinizing me further.

"Well, that explains the fight outside." The blonde wilkyr adjusted his vest and shook his head. They were both wearing the same outfit, a pair of clean, frayed denim shorts and black leather vests, their hairy chests left bare. "Gar's going to freak. Are you gonna work here?"

"I'm really sick of everyone asking me that." I pulled away from both of them and crossed my arms.

"Why do you smell like Axel?" Cole asked.

"He let me crash at his place and gave me his bed for the night. Vargyrs don't bathe very often, do they?"

The blonde one gasped.

"You slept in a vargyr's bed? Are you thick or insane?" Cole's voice got louder and more unhinged. "Did he do anything to you?"

"No! Ew."

"Okay, I don't know how you don't know this, but don't ever—" He paused and grabbed my arm again, forcing me toward the hall on the other side of the stage "EVER go alone into a vargyr's house, and definitely don't sleep in his bed."

The smaller wilkyr put his hand on my shoulder. "Cole knows all about this."

"Shut up, Feran. I feel shitty enough as it is."

"Listen," I said, following them into a darkened room in the middle of the hallway. Cole slapped a switch on the wall, and the crystals on the ceiling hummed to life, casting a magenta hue on what appeared to be a dressing room. "This is going to sound crazy, but I'm not from here."

"No, really?" Cole asked sarcastically, pointing toward the tawny leather loveseat in the middle of the room. I walked toward it and collapsed, more exhausted than I thought I was. "Humans can't get into Varcross. It's literally impossible."

"I don't know, man," I said. With my hands crossed in my lap, I leaned forward, staring at the floor. "I just drove here, and now I can't get out. I'd never seen a vargyr before I met Axel, and I thought they were pretty nice until one of them attacked me."

Cole sighed and sat next to me before taking my hand.

"I'm so sorry. That must have been painful." He studied me closer and furrowed his brows. "Well, you're not showing any signs. How are you feeling?"

"What are you talking about? This whole town looks at me like I'm a steak dinner."

"Hold on. What happened when you were attacked?"

"He tried to either eat me or fuck me, I'm still not sure. I ran away from him."

"How the hell did you get away?"

"Let's just say he won't be walking right for a while." I gave him a confident smirk. I sounded a lot braver than I actually was, but I couldn't help but flirt with him a little. Now that he was so close to me, that man-monster thing was really working in his favor. I had to pull my shirt down a little more to hide the discomfort.

"Damn." Cole returned the smile. "You're one hell of a lucky guy. That could have ended so much worse." Cole narrowed his eyes and sniffed the air before clearing his throat. "Well, you know my name." He pointed to the smaller wilkyr. "And this is Feran."

"Hey," he said with a wave, blushing while looking down at the floor for some reason.

"I'm Leo."

Feran padded toward a wooden crate in the corner. "A customer gave this to me yesterday. You hungry, thirsty...horny?" He mumbled that last part.

"You're not supposed to take bribes from them," Cole snapped.

"Says the walking display case."

Cole looked down at his jewelry, clutching one of the larger ruby gems. "These were in lieu of payment, and Gar said it was fine."

"Sure," he said as he tossed a bottle of red liquid to Cole before staring at me expectantly.

I put up both hands and shook my head. "I'm good, thanks."

"Did you accept gold?" Cole continued.

"Yeah, so? What is Gar gonna do? Fire me? I didn't break the rules; Remmy did."

Cole sighed. "It's a stupid rule, anyway." His judgmental eyes rolled back to me. "You look atrocious."

My face boiled with embarrassment. I wished Axel had warned me how hot the wilkyrs were, I'd have freshened up a lot better while at his house. "It's been a trying few days."

"I didn't mean it like that. You just look really roughed up. I can't believe you got drunk with a bunch of vargyrs and nothing happened to you."

"Axel didn't seem like the type."

"They're all the type. All of them. That's why this place exists. It was the only way to stop the spread."

"The spread?"

"The curse." Cole uncorked the bottle he held and gulped down whatever juice was inside. When he finished, he wiped his mouth with the back of his arm. "Man, you weren't joking about not being from here, were you?"

I shook my head. "That's what I've been trying to tell everyone."

"Well, *someone* wanted you here. The only way to get in is if a mage throws you through the wards. At least as far as I know. And even then, I think you have to have the curse for the wards to activate and not spit you back out."

"I keep hearing about these wards."

"It's a lot to explain, and I don't even know exactly how it all works. But the most important thing you need to understand is that the curse makes it impossible for vargyrs to control themselves in the presence of humans."

"I think I know where this is going."

"It gets so much worse," Cole muttered, clearing his throat. "Vargyrs *need* to fuck—all the time. They'll get human women pregnant if given the opportunity, and those women will have male vargyr children that will spread the curse to others if they aren't captured first. Most of the time the children are given up for adoption, and the mothers never tell anyone what the father really was, for good reason. Even if it wasn't their fault, women who give birth to a vargyr's offspring are...not treated very well in society. So, their children sit in foster care, no one knowing who's got the curse and who doesn't until later on in life."

"If the curse is congenital, why were you worried I had it?"

Cole clenched his teeth. "What they do to men is far worse. If one gets you under him, the curse will spread to you in the most awful way, and the change happens painfully fast—sometimes in a few hours or days."

I felt sick again.

"The curse gets a lot more messed up than that, but I don't want to stress you out even more than you already are."

"I think that ship has already left the port, Cole," I said, realizing just how fucked I was—literally. "What do I do now? I can't go back out there."

He gave me a pat on the back and a reassuring smile. "Don't worry. As long as you're here, you're safe. I'll talk to Gar when he gets back from wherever he disappears to. He'll let you stay in the wilkyr part of town, but he'll probably put you to work."

I thought back to those hungry expressions from earlier. "No way, man. I am not working here."

"We'll find you something, okay?" Cole wrapped his arm around my neck and pulled me close to him. There was a hint of that familiar beast smell on him, but it wasn't nearly as strong as the others in town. He actually smelled good, like spicy cologne. "Everything will be fine if you stick with me."

"That's what Axel said."

"Well, I'm not Axel, and I'm not a full vargyr yet."

"Is Gar a vargyr?"

"Kind of. He's different. The curse didn't affect him the way it did the others, so he looks really weird and he doesn't lose his mind. He's been around longer than any of us, and he's the only reason any order exists at all. I don't know how he does it, but he's working with Stellous to keep the goods flowing and the lights on."

"Stellous is the country we're in?"

"No, we're not in any country. This is a different world entirely."

"If that's the case, why would Stellous trade with the very people they trapped here?"

Cole shrugged. "Probably cheap labor. The stuff we get isn't exactly premium quality."

"So how do they trade if no one can leave and no one can get in?"

"No one really knows how the trade portals work, but they are very well regulated."

I looked down at my hands and sighed. "This is confusing. If they aren't giving you quality, why do the vargyrs keep working? You're all wolf people. Can't you do your own hunting?"

"You sound just like Axel." He shook his head. "Gar's made it very clear that all vargyrs have to work for Stellous, or they'll be denied services."

"What services?"

The entrance to the dungeon slammed open and heavy footsteps quickly approached.

"Leo? Buddy?" A deep, frantic voice echoed through the building.

Cole gulped down the last of what was in the bottle and chucked it into a basket next to the door. "Well, *buddy*, sounds like Axel finally tracked you down."

Not-So-Safe Space

Axel's rapid footfalls slowed as he got closer to the door before stopping. Though I couldn't see him, I could almost feel his trepidation. Cole crossed his arms while tapping his clawed foot on the fur rug next to the sofa.

The door slowly opened, and Axel strolled in with a soft smile, though there was a bit of anxiety in his low and careful posture.

"Ah, here you are. Was lookin' everywhere fer ya."

"He's safe, no thanks to you." As if he'd been waiting to tear into the guy, Cole jumped from the couch and stomped up to Axel.

The huge vargyr winced, giving a whale eye while tucking his tail. He sort of looked like a nine-foot two-legged dog that had gotten caught rummaging through the trash.

"What the hell were you thinking? The moment you saw him, you should have brought him here."

"He was safe with me," Axel whispered.

"You put him in danger." Cole clenched his fists. "You didn't warn him or anything! You just took him home like a lost pet knowing what could happen."

Axel looked away, his ears folding against his head. "He's safe with me. I swear."

"He is?"

The wilkyr grabbed Axel's snout, tugging it so they could lock eyes again.

"I swear, Cole. He's my roomie now." He broke from Cole's grip and turned his head toward me. "Tell him how much fun we had last night."

As much as I wanted to defend him, Cole's warning put everything into stark perspective. I didn't know how to respond.

"You don't feel scared around me, do ya?"

"I...I don't..." I didn't want to hurt his feelings more, but I had to be honest. "Yes. When I woke up, you were holding onto me and wouldn't let go. Now that I know what you were trying to do—"

"You didn't tell me you slept in the same bed," Cole interrupted, grabbing Axel's snout again.

"Now hold on a minute," he whined out, holding up his hands. "I wasn't awake. I—I don't remember none of that."

"Why did you get into bed with him?"

"Cuz I couldn't sleep good on the couch."

Cole slapped Axel's nose, and the vargyr let out a sharp whine.

"That's a lie! I've seen you passed out naked on the ground outside of Toby's more times than I can count. You were fine on that couch."

"I got control, but I did think about it," Axel said remorsefully as he rubbed his snout, his tail still tucked between his legs. "It was like being hungry and knowin' you still got leftovers in the kitchen. But I stopped."

"If you had control, you'd have stayed on the couch. Don't you understand?" Cole's tone was gentler this time as he reached up and rubbed Axel's head. "You were able to stop yourself last night, but what happens when it's all you can think about?"

Axel leaned into Cole's touch. "Then I'll come to you, like I always do."

"He's not going back to that house, so put that out of your mind." Cole took a step back and they both fell silent.

"I ain't Vince." Axel bared his teeth and met the wilkyr's glare with his own. "I ain't careless like him. I'm sorry it happened to you, but one mistake don't mean we're all like that."

"Don't you dare bring up something you know nothing about. And don't call it a mistake so casually."

"He didn't know—"

"He knew! Everyone knows, but he thought he could control it. Sound familiar?"

The vargyr took a moment before responding.

"Ain't a day goes by that he don't regret it. He won't let it go, and you won't forgive him."

"It must be nice to have the luxury of doing nothing but sitting on the couch feeling sorry for himself, while I have to do *this* every day. He gets to waste away while the responsibility of keeping everyone sane falls on my shoulders. If he wanted to make it up to me, he could start by cleaning the house once in a while."

"Ya think it's a luxury to keep reliving the moment you hurt your lover over and over again?"

"It happened to *me*, not him."

"It happened to both of you. He's just as much a victim of the same curse. Vince loves you more than anything..." Axel trailed off, his low voice cracking as tears welled in his eyes.

Cole shook his head and calmly put his arms around Axel. "I'm sorry."

The vargyr looked up at me, his irises beginning to turn blood-orange as drool roped from his mouth, the sign I was warned about earlier.

"Uh oh," Axel said, digging his claws into Cole's arms. "I—I think I need...to talk to you alone fer a little while." He forcefully prodded the wilkyr toward the door.

"How long's it been?"

"Don't remember."

"Damn it, Axel." Cole glanced at me nervously. "I've gotta take care of this. I'll be back." He barely finished speaking before Axel yanked him the rest of the way out of the room.

"Well," Feran said from the corner chair, startling me. He hadn't made a sound since Axel arrived. "It's just you and me now."

"What the hell just happened?"

The blonde wilkyr stood from the chair and peeked out into the hall before shutting the door all the way.

"They're *talking*," he said, walking back toward the crate in the corner. "They'll probably be *talking* for a half hour at least, maybe more. Want anything to eat? We've got lots of good stuff in here."

"I'm not really hungry," I said, looking back toward the door. "So that's what Cole does?"

"It varies, but that's kind of what we all do," Feran said, fishing around the container for something. "What Axel just did is the reason they're so dangerous. You could be laughing and joking around with each other one second, and the next he's got you pinned to the floor. It's random, but the longer they go without satisfying the conditions of the curse, the less control they have over it."

That cold, clammy feeling returned to my hands as the blood rushed from my face. This was exactly what Mikael had warned me about earlier as well, but that wasn't what made me sick to my stomach. Cole was right about how lucky I was. How many opportunities had I unknowingly given Axel to 'satisfy the conditions of the curse?' I was in his bed. I may as well have put my ass in the air while lying there like a pork roast on a dinner plate.

"This place is really important to the town. We provide a lot of the services Cole talked about earlier. Here." He stood upright and tossed me a bottle with red juice. My palms were so slippery, I nearly dropped it. "You're hungover and dehydrated. You need to drink something."

"Thanks," I said, staring into the bottle. "What are the exact conditions? Is it just sex?"

"Cole only half explained it. A vargyr exists only to spread the curse to as many people as he can. That's like, the entire purpose."

"And what happens if they don't?"

"They become feral monsters, losing their minds," he said, sitting next to me on the loveseat. "No one really knows a whole lot about the curse's origins, but because of how it works, scholars think it's likely an act of revenge or some kind of demonic cult looking to cleanse the world. If the mages didn't lock us away, it would keep spreading until there were more vargyrs than humans. Human females would eventually die out, and with no humans or wilkyrs to satisfy the conditions of the curse, the vargyrs would turn feral, and all civilization would collapse. It's terrifying to think about."

"But wilkyrs aren't human."

Feran nodded. "A convenient loophole Gar figured out. It was either intentional or an oversight by whatever entity started this. It's the only reason Varcross exists, otherwise all the vargyrs would have just split off into packs and disappeared into the wild within weeks of turning."

"I thought they couldn't leave the town."

"Oh, we can leave; we just can't take the portal back to our world. The portal is hidden by wards further along the road leading out of town. That road used to lead to Eqiros, our homeworld back when this place was used for resources. This world is a lot bigger than you think it is, and Varcross is just a tiny part of it."

I pulled the cork from the bottle and took a sip. The juice was perfectly tart and not too sweet, a bit similar to raspberry.

"If there's an entire world out there, why does everyone stay here?"

"We're afraid," he said, lifting one of his legs before crossing it over his knee. Now that I got a good look at his feet, he had black pads on the soles, similar to the vargyrs. "Gar's dungeon is the most important place in town. If a vargyr is out exploring the world and the curse takes over, he won't have much time to get back before it takes his mind."

"Why don't they just take a wilkyr with them?"

His nose wrinkled, and his warm stare turned cold.

"It's bad enough that we're forced into being glorified sex toys the moment we're thrown into Varcross, but now you're saying we should just give up what comfort we have here to follow a group of horny beasts into the unknown?"

"I didn't mean to upset you."

Feran sighed. "I know you don't get it yet, but you will. Plus, Gar would never let one of his precious wilkyrs out of his sight. There's not a lot of us left. Eventually, wilkyrs turn into full vargyrs, and there hasn't been enough new blood coming through the portal to replace the ones we lose. The town dies without us, and Gar makes all of us drink his new potion that slows the transformation. Cole should have already turned a while ago, but he's still hanging on. We aren't supposed to have tails, but Cole does. He's trapped right on the edge of turning, and it's kind of painful for him."

I looked down at the bottle in my hands, choosing my words more carefully now. "Is anyone trying to find a way to break the curse?"

Feran shrugged and patted my shoulder before standing. "They've been trying for almost eight hundred years." He walked over to a table with a mirror before picking up a pair of shears. He examined the thick hair on his face and began trimming it. "It's probably best not to think about it that much. Before you came, I was the new guy in town; the mages threw me in here about a month ago, so I'll be doing this for a while. Everyone puts a lot of trust in Gar since he's the oldest. I just hope he'll figure something out before my time comes, because there probably won't be anyone left by then."

I took up the blonde wilkyr's offer of odd-tasting dried jerky from the crate, but whatever it was did not agree with my stomach. I had to wander around the hall looking for a bathroom, hoping they weren't all like Axel's. Fortunately, there were toilets here, and they were flushable. Compared to all the other buildings in town, this place seemed to be a much newer construction.

After Feran left, I lay on the couch trying to force my mind to go blank, but it wouldn't stop racing. Not only did I have to contend with being in a different world, but I also had to worry that I couldn't come out of this without getting the same terrible affliction everyone else had. Though I'd only been here a day, this situation had seemed so temporary last night, but I knew now that I'd likely never be able to escape this place. Even though I didn't have much to return to, being the only human in an entire world was terrifyingly lonely.

Then there was Axel. He seemed so sweet, but when he dragged Cole away like that, I kept picturing myself in a similar situation. I didn't know if it was fate or if I was just insanely lucky, but for whatever reason, it was Axel who found me. Even though he lost control earlier, he didn't do anything to me. Mikael and his partner turned so fast, so there must have been some truth to Axel's claim that he could control it...at least somewhat.

Slow, uneven footsteps creaked along the floorboards before stopping at the entrance to the room. The door squealed open, and Cole stepped inside. His hair was slightly damp, and he smelled of soap and leathery cologne.

"Our conversation took a lot longer than I thought." He limped over to the couch and groaned as he sat next to me.

"I know what happened."

"Feran filled you in on all the sordid details, huh?"

I nodded.

"How much did he tell you?"

"Enough to know I'm probably screwed." The queasiness from earlier returned. "Curses, mages, portals, huge wolfmen. It feels like a nightmare I'll wake up from at any minute, but…" I sighed, pinching the skin on my arm.

"You never really explained how you got in." Cole shuffled around and winced as he lifted his shirt. There were crusted-over claw marks on his back.

"Damn, Cole."

"We heal really fast, so it's not a big deal," he said, holding his hand up in front of me.

"Axel did this to you?"

"Don't let this sour your opinion of the guy. He's the sweetest person I've ever known, but he's not exactly the brightest crystal in the box." Cole let out a laugh but stopped when I didn't join him. "He means well, but the poor guy's lonely and a little delusional."

We both smiled as he tried to keep the conversation light-hearted, but his physical and emotional pain was hard to mask as he winced again.

"How'd you two meet?"

"Vincent," he said, grabbing a rolled-up bandage from a case next to the couch. "He and Axel grew up together but fell out of touch after they left foster care. Vince and I ended up in Varcross six years ago, and when they were reunited, they recognized each other right away.

"Vince introduced me, and I adored Axel from the start. I'll always have a soft spot for him. When he gets lonely, we'll invite him to stay with us for a while, but he never sticks around. He's not interested in pairing off with someone, and there's no one quite like him in town.

Vince told me stories of Axel's wanderlust when they were kids, and he still prefers to be out there than here."

"It sounds like you love Axel more than Vince."

Cole frowned and shook his head. "I complain a lot, but I've loved Vince for a decade now, and I'll keep loving him until the curse takes us. Axel's a sweet guy, but he's not for me. I just hope he finds someone who really makes him happy and enjoys all the weird shit he does."

I chuckled. "What kind of weird shit?"

"Axel loves being a vargyr, and he's the only one in town who fully embraces it. He never buys food or relies on Stellous supplies." Cole unwrapped the bandage before soaking it in a solution with the strong smell of pine sap. "He doesn't really work; he just makes things and sells them for a little coin so he can drink and socialize at Toby's. Then there are times we won't see him for almost a month."

"So how did you turn into—" I stopped myself mid-sentence when I felt him go rigid. He didn't look at me as he struggled to wrap the bandage all the way around his chest. "Never mind. Do you need help with that?"

"Nah. I do this all the time, and I'm tougher than I look. Also, I don't mind telling you what happened. There's no way someone like you should be here, and bringing any person from another world is reckless and forbidden. You're at a lot of disadvantages right now because you don't fully understand how things work. You could stand to learn from my mistakes."

The bandage fell again.

"This is driving me nuts," I said before grabbing one end of the bandage, holding it in place while I reached around him with my other arm to wrap it. A lump formed in my throat as I leaned into him, his thick body hair brushing against my skin. Even though he was slightly shorter than me, he was stocky, just like the vargyrs in town.

"Thanks," he said, flashing me a handsome grin.

It was hard not to be a little aroused, and I was trying my best not to make this weirder than it was. There was something strange about the way he smelled. It wasn't just soap and cologne; there was a subtle note of earthy spice that made me want to bury my nose in his neck.

"Vince and I met when I had just turned eighteen, and he was twenty-six." I stopped wrapping for a moment and raised an eyebrow. "I know what you're thinking. I was going through a rebellious teenager phase. After we got to know each other, I started sneaking out every night to be with him. Him being a wilkyr was something different, and a little dangerous. Plus, it didn't hurt that he was the sexiest man I'd ever met, both in looks and personality."

I resumed dressing his wounds. My hands worked lower toward his abdomen, but my upper arm brushed against a metallic hoop piercing on his nipple.

"Thinking back on it, I was a real idiot. I didn't fully understand the curse, and we'd had sex so many times, it was just a natural thing. That insatiable side of him was addictive, and we'd go all night sometimes and into the morning. And after we were done, we'd talk about everything and fall asleep in each other's arms.

"We fell in love, and I stayed with him for three years while also studying at the athenaeum—the grand library and magic school at the heart of Stellous. I wanted to know as much about the curse as I could so that maybe I could help Vince, but most of that knowledge required a higher rank to access. One day, he turned, and I knew what that meant. I couldn't hide him anymore."

I finished wrapping, pinning off the end of the bandage to itself, and Cole leaned back, getting more comfortable.

"We wanted to say our goodbyes at the place we met: the old stables near my parents' estate. We were both in tears, and he didn't want to leave me, and I sure as hell didn't want him to go. Even though he had turned into something that only slightly resembled who he was, I still loved him more than anything." He cleared his throat and wiped his face with the back of his arm, his tone becoming shakier. "But the true nature of the curse came out. His eyes turned red, and when I tried to talk to him, he wouldn't say anything back. He just stood there, looking at me with that cold emptiness."

"Cole—"

"It was the most painful thing I'd ever gone through, both physically and emotionally," he continued, interrupting a sentence

I had no idea how I would finish. "Vargyrs don't stop until they're done, and they're so strong that a human can't fend them off alone." He let out a weak chuckle while wiping his eyes. "Maybe I should have done what you did."

"I was lucky I could move at all. Whenever I get scared, I lock up." I wanted to say anything to turn the conversation away from where it was going. "We should talk about something else."

"No," he whispered. "It's not often I get to talk about it, and it kind of helps."

"Okay," I said with a nod. "It must have been devastating for both of you."

"It was, but I wasn't thinking about him at the time. After he finished, his eyes went back to normal. It was like he saw me for the first time. I couldn't pull away because of how different his anatomy had become, and we were stuck together, staring at one another in horror.

"He let out this howl, and it was the saddest thing I'd ever heard. He kept apologizing over and over, but it was too late. I knew it wasn't his fault, but when he was on top of me back then, I wasn't thinking like that. He was a monster."

I rested my hand on his bare shoulder in response.

He smiled, the visible skin on his face turning a light shade of pink as he leaned forward, wrapping me in a firm hug.

"Thanks for listening to that," he whispered before letting me go. "Most wilkyrs don't understand, and the ones that do don't want to talk about it. They just keep it to themselves and hate everything until they turn. They end up not being very well-adjusted vargyrs, and I don't want to end up like that—if I'm even still aware of who I am then."

"What do you mean? Why's it different when a human gets the curse instead of being born with it?"

"Scholars have been trying to figure it out for centuries. You won't meet many vargyrs in this town who weren't already predisposed for it. There are only ten living here, one of them wilkyr, aside from me. The rest went feral right after their full turn, and some had to be culled." His voice broke as he lost more of his composure.

"Whoa! What do you mean *had to be*?"

"It's a rare condition. Sometimes the part of the curse that makes a vargyr crave sex goes haywire, and they crave blood instead. Once a wilkyr like me starts showing signs, we're locked in a cage until we make the full turn. If we're normal, they let us continue living in town. If we're feral, they release us into the woods. If we're blood-crazed, it's up to the strongest in Varcross to put us down. That means Axel has to do it."

"There's no way in hell I could picture him doing that. The poor guy nearly broke down when you yelled at him earlier."

"He shouldn't have been forced into that responsibility." A catchy beat thudded through the walls outside, and Cole let out a sigh. "It's almost time for work."

"Do you have to? You can still take the day off."

"What else am I gonna do? I'm already here, and I have to talk to Gar when he arrives."

I thought back to what he said moments ago. "Has Axel...killed anyone before?"

He nodded. "Twice."

"Jesus Christ."

"Jesus Christ?"

"It's a..." I trailed off, thinking of how to explain it. "Religious thing. Never mind. How did Axel handle that?"

"About as well as you're probably thinking. The first one was five years ago, a year after I got here. There was an older wilkyr named Lucas that no one could ever talk to. I tried to be friends with him, but he hated everyone. He didn't like the dungeon at all, but Gar still made him work, which made everything worse.

"Then along came Axel one day, back when Gar actually let him in the dungeon." He paused and laughed through his nose. "That's a funny story for another time. Axel overheard me talking about how difficult this guy was, so one day he set a reservation for Lucas without me knowing, and of course, the poor guy was scared out of his mind. Most of the wilkyrs were scared of Axel because he's so huge. But he showed up with several bottles of booze, meat he'd killed and butchered himself, and a pretty little lockbox he made.

"They were in that room for hours, and we all thought Axel was still going. But the door eventually opened, and they were both laughing, piss drunk. Come to find out, Axel never did anything to him. He just wanted to talk to the guy, and Lucas really opened up after that. He and Axel got close, but Lucas had been here for longer than any of us, and Gar hadn't started us on his elixir regimen. When the curse finally took over, he turned out to be the rare case.

"Axel wasn't the same after that, and he disappeared for about a month. We all thought he turned feral, but sure enough, he wandered back into town again one day, completely naked, his fur covered in dried blood, dirt and burrs. That was when Vince and I started letting him stay with us, but it would happen again a couple years later."

Cole's reaction to this conversation was so different than before. He was swallowing a lot more, his eyes wider and more focused.

"Orryn was a weird one. Axel didn't know him that well; in fact, none of us did. He just showed up out of nowhere and never spoke a word. On the few occasions I saw him wander around town, he didn't look or smell like any of the other wilkyrs. It was almost like his bones were kind of messed up. He didn't work in the dungeon either, and Gar, for whatever reason, kept him close and away from everyone. It didn't take that poor guy long to turn, and sure enough, he went blood crazy. He didn't look like a normal vargyr either, since he had paws on his feet just like Gar. Even though Axel didn't know him, he left town in tears again."

"I don't understand why he has to do it. There are a lot of other vargyrs in this town that would probably be better suited." I thought back to my encounter this morning. "I could think of at least one."

Cole shook his head. "Trust me, not even the most deranged vargyr wants to do that. Granted, not everyone gets along, but there's a deep bond between us all. Since Axel doesn't contribute much to the town, Gar gave him an ultimatum: he either takes on the responsibility, or he won't be allowed back. After Lucas, he told me he wouldn't be back, but he found out the hard way that vargyrs can't be alone for too long. He may be able to resist the curse more than anyone, but he still can't be alone."

Cole swallowed hard again and rubbed his forehead. "He might have to do that to me."

"You said it was rare, right?"

"I don't know. I just...have this feeling. I'm scared and tired. Half of me is terrified of dying, but the other half hates having to live like this. Sex lost its pleasure a long time ago. It's just a transaction now, nothing more."

"I hope I'm not being too forward, but—" I took his hand in mine before wrapping my other arm around him. "When I'm anxious, sometimes this helps."

While embracing him, his heart thudded as though he had run for miles. At first I thought he was having a full-blown panic attack, but then I noticed the rose-like color of his face.

"You're a sweet guy, Leo," he whispered into my ear. There was a throaty growl to his voice. "I need to be careful around you."

I pulled away from him. "Why's that?"

He chuckled but didn't respond. Instead, he pushed himself from the couch and stretched.

"Gar's back," he said, turning toward the door. I'd forgotten his senses were much more acute than mine. I couldn't make out any other noises aside from a faint drum beat. "Stay here. I'll be back in a bit."

I nodded, noticing him limping toward the door. "Are you gonna be okay? Is your leg hurt?"

"No," he responded. "Axel's a lot to handle, if you know what I mean."

"Oh!" This wasn't exactly a shocking revelation, but I was still getting used to how different these creatures were. "Guess I'm lucky you were here."

"I probably saved your life." He gave a wink and turned back toward the door. "You owe me."

The door to the dressing room swung open, and a black vargyr ran inside, his face lighting up when he saw me. He was a foot taller than Cole, but there were so many things physically off about him. The beast didn't have a lot of the lingering human characteristics that the others had. There was no thicker fur on his face, no mane on his head, chest or back. His fur was shorter, and his face lacked some of the muscles that allowed him to make more complex expressions, at least from what I could see. He also had paws instead of flat feet, just as Cole had described earlier.

"Aren't you a lovely sight," he said, staring at me in amazement with his blood-red eyes. They weren't blue, green or golden like the others, and his tongue was longer and more pointed. "When did he arrive?"

"Last night. You didn't hear the rumors?"

"I wasn't in town." Gar learned forward, his nose probing me. "Smells like someone's been with Axel." I went to push him away, but he caught my wrists with his hands, scrutinizing my body further.

"Don't worry, Axel didn't do anything to him."

Gar nodded and took my hand in his, giving it a shake. "You're a very lucky young man," he said through a sharp-toothed grin, "but no one stays lucky for long in Varcross, unfortunately. What is your name?"

"Leo," I answered as he let go and stood upright.

"It's nice to meet you, Leo, but I'll be frank. Your situation is a lot more dire than you think. Humans are not meant to be here."

"He'd be safe with the wilkyrs," Cole said.

"Yes, but for how long?" Gar asked, all three of us turning to the door as howling erupted from down the hall. "You all have so many responsibilities as it is, and it's impossible to watch him every hour of the day."

Cole didn't respond.

"There has to be something you can do," I interjected, scrambling to my feet.

Gar lifted his forefinger under my chin and shook his head. "Your fate was sealed the moment you got here. All I would be doing is prolonging the inevitable, and you'd be living in fear every day. That's no life."

"And you think this is?" Cole asked. "Just what are you saying, Gar?"

"It would be better for him to contract the curse in a controlled and comfortable setting than suffering the horror of it being forced upon him. Vince is small, perhaps he would be suited for this."

"Absolutely not," Cole shouted. "Vince is messed up enough, and this would be his push over the edge."

"I know how you feel, but I don't know of any other way."

"You're the most brilliant alchemist I've ever met, and I've met a lot of them. You're telling me there's nothing you can do?"

The old vargyr stroked the short fur under his muzzle. "Cole, it took me centuries to formulate that elixir you all take, and all it does is merely slow the transformation. Do you honestly think I can come up with a vargyr deterrent for this human in just a few weeks or months? He likely won't have that long, and this curse is so complex that it could take several human lifetimes to come up with anything that works even temporarily."

"What about the lotion you gave me that takes away my scent? Couldn't you do something with that?"

It was hard to tell what Gar may have been thinking, since his facial expressions rarely changed. However, his tail swayed and eyes widened.

"I forgot about that creation."

"Do you think you could do something with it?"

Gar rubbed his chin again, staring pensively in my direction.

"Maybe," he said. "I can try something, but you both need to understand that this goes against the very tenets of my craft. There's no way to test this, and we wouldn't have enough time even if there was."

"We could keep him safe, Gar. The vargyrs know they aren't allowed in the wilkyr part of town."

Gar crossed his arms. "You know better than that. With Leo here, the line becomes even more tempting to cross. If a vargyr wants this human bad enough, nothing will stand in his way."

"Couldn't I just stay here?" I asked. "This place is pretty fortified."

Gar opened the door and stepped into the hallway, waving us over. "Come, both of you."

Cole walked out into the hallway, but Gar put his hand up, stopping me from following further. "You stay here, out of sight."

His paw-like feet seemed to trot along as he made his way to the end of the hall to open the other door. As it slowly cracked, a flood of multicolored lights poured in, and the live tavern music echoed through the solid block corridor. I got a peek at the crush of vargyrs practically standing on top of one another, each one looking around anxiously. The double doors to the dungeon entrance were held open, with a crowded line leading outside. Every vargyr in town must have been trying to cram into the place.

Gar shut and locked the door, peace returning to the hallway, save for the muffled music and howling from the other side.

"They know you're here."

"Shit," Cole whispered under his breath as he sauntered back into the dressing room, pulling me away from the door. Gar followed us inside.

"Now do you understand why you can't stay? I've got to gather everyone tonight to handle this, and even that won't be enough. They've got your scent, and they are expecting to see a human. They're not going to be too happy when they don't get that chance. All that stands between you and that mob of randy beasts is a flimsy door and a buffer of exhausted wilkyrs. This is not sustainable, and I'm not going to work everyone into the ground to buy you a little more time when we're not even sure of success."

I turned to Cole. "What do I do?"

The three of us stood silently, and I gave Gar's stern response more thought as I noticed the dark circles under Cole's eyes. He was right. This wasn't fair to anyone. Simply existing in this place brought terrible consequences, and that feeling of hopelessness returned.

"You'll stay with me," Cole said, hesitantly at first. "I could have Vince stay at Axel's, and have Axel watch the house while I'm gone."

"You're going to trust Axel to watch him?" Gar asked.

"The guy slept in the same bed as Leo and nothing happened, so he's really the only option. He'd stay outside, of course."

"And what about you?" he asked. This time there was a flash of something disconcerting in his eyes.

"What do you mean?"

"You'll be alone with this human, and what happens when the elixir no longer works? There's no way to predict when that will happen."

Cole took a deep, shaky breath, but Gar was as unmoved as a stone.

"Then Axel will have to take care of it."

The old vargyr nodded and turned to me. "Alright. This could work for now, but there are no guarantees. Do you understand?"

"Yes," I answered, but Gar held up his hand.

"I don't think you truly do." He turned toward the door. "I'll get to work on a repellent, but I make no promises about its long-term effectiveness."

"It's better than nothing," I said as Gar walked out into the hallway.

He turned around, his crimson eyes glowing brighter. "Perhaps."

A Life Of Regret

The warmth of the dungeon dressing room kept lulling me to sleep, but I'd snap awake with the occasional creak or thud. I lay on the couch waiting for Cole's shift to end so he could escort me safely to his house. I couldn't get his story out of my head. The fear and exhaustion in his eyes retold his past trauma, and gave an even bleaker account of everything to come.

The door slowly creaked open, and dread billowed into the room, swallowing me like a black mist. I could tell from the deep, heavy breathing that my visitor wasn't one of the wilkyr.

"Leo?" Axel whispered, through the narrow opening. "You awake, buddy?"

I shot upright, relieved it was Axel and not one of the others, but this didn't completely allay my concern. "You shouldn't be back here."

"I know," Axel said, his snout poking through. "You was asleep earlier when I snuck by, and I didn't wanna wake ya. I, uh…" He took a deep breath, seeming to contemplate his words. "I'm really sorry. Thinkin' things through ain't what I'm good at."

"You didn't do anything. You saved me last night."

"Gar said I can't stay long. I'm kinda shocked he didn't kick me out," he said, slinking the rest of the way inside, not able to make eye contact as his ears lay flat against his head. He kept his distance and leaned against the wall next to the door, his left hand keeping it from closing all the way. "I just wanted to tell ya that even if you can't be my drinkin' buddy or my roommate, we can still be friends—if Cole's around." He balled his hands into fists, his posture slouching forward. "That's if ya want to. I'll understand if you don't."

He was so sweet the way he stared like a sad puppy, but I couldn't shake that image of him earlier. Still, if Cole could trust him enough to guard the house and buy me time, I had to trust him a little with this.

"It'd be great to have more friends here, and I'll need them. You're a hell of a fun guy to talk to." His tail thudded against the wall. "But only when Cole's around. I can't trust you alone."

"I know, and I get it. It's why I'm not stayin' long." A look of excitement replaced the hesitation from earlier. "I really did like havin' you fer a roommate, even if it was only a night. It gets lonely in that house, and knowin' you was there made that place feel homey."

"Why do you live by yourself? There's plenty of people in town."

Axel crossed his arms, giving my question some consideration as he let the door gently fall against the frame.

"No one wants to have to sleep on a couch, and the bed's not big enough for two vargyrs just wantin' to be friends. I thought about building an addition onto the house, but that's a lot of work when I could just be drinkin'."

"What about someone more than a roommate?"

He shook his head. "Nah. The one's I was interested in, well, they's already mates with someone else." His cheerful attitude made the sad conversation seem a little less so, but I had to maintain eye contact with him. If they started to change color, I'd have to react fast to get away from him. "I don't need no one all the time, you see. Whenever I need someone in that way, I go to Cole's. It's nice sharin' a bed with two of my best friends. It's warm, and sometimes I wish I didn't have to leave."

"Which one are you in love with, Cole or Vince?"

Axel's smile faded. "That obvious, huh?" His eyes shifted downward. "I love both of 'em, but Vince and me had a history when we was younger and human." He shook his head. "It ain't right, though. They found each other, and I'm happy for 'em, even though I wish they was happier."

The door slammed shut, and I jumped up from the couch. A startled Axel grabbed the knob as a white glow spread outward through the wood and along the walls like the surface of a swimming pool reflecting moonlight. The strange light distorted the room, like the entire building had been completely submerged. Axel pulled on the door, but it wouldn't budge.

I ran my fingers against the wall, and the glow undulated under them. There was a familiar electric sensation against my skin, like when my car drove through those lights. "What is this?"

"I don't know, but the door's stuck," Axel said calmly, turning the knob with so much force, he should have broken it, but it was jammed tight. "Gar's gonna be so pissed when he finds out what I'm about to do."

He took several steps back, then leaned forward and charged, right shoulder first. The flimsy wooden door wouldn't stand a chance against Axel, and I braced myself, expecting it to explode open. However, as soon as he hit it, the light rippled into an arc, and he bounced backward, flying across the room until he crashed into one of the dressing vanities, crushing it and shattering the mirror.

"Christ, are you okay?" I ran over to help him off the floor, but he stood and rubbed his head, shaking the glass out of his fur as though he'd merely tripped over something.

"This ain't good." His voice wasn't as calm as it was earlier, and I backed away from him. Axel looked around the room, probably having the same thoughts as me. There were no other doors or windows. "I don't know much about magic, but that's kinda what this looks like."

I ran to the far corner, scanning the room for any narrow areas to squeeze into in case I had to crawl out of his reach. Unfortunately, I wasn't as lucky as I was earlier today when I found that alley.

"Magic?" I asked. Axel was about to respond, but I cut him off. "I guess I shouldn't be surprised about that."

He turned his attention back to the door. "Actually you should be. Aside from all the doodads we get from Stellous, ain't nobody can actually use magic here. Varcross has these wards, but I don't know how any of this stuff works. Cole explained it to me a while ago, but I forgot like ten seconds after he told me."

My eyes never left him as I watched for the signs.

"You okay, Leo?"

I shook my head.

"I know yer scared of me." He sauntered to the other side of the room and sat against the wall. "Wish I wasn't so scary."

"You're a nice guy, but I don't want you to do to me what you did to Cole. You really hurt him."

A heavy gasp, followed by an uncomfortable minute of silence made an already tense moment even worse.

"I–I did?" he asked, his quavering voice increasing in pitch. "I never notice when it's over, and Cole always leaves in a hurry. I ain't me when it happens, and it's hard to explain. My body wants to feel pleasure, but I don't wanna lose control. The more you feel for the person yer doin' it to, the worse the pain is, which makes your body want more. I always wanna throw up when it's over."

"Is that why you disappear for so long?"

The vargyr wiped his snout with the back of his arm and smiled. "Ya know about that?"

"Cole had a lot to say about you."

"Hopefully it wasn't too bad."

"It wasn't. You sound like a really good friend."

Axel's ears drooped again as he looked around at the ripples of magic along the walls. Though he was keeping the conversation calm, I was still looking for any way out, but there wasn't an inch of the wall the light didn't cover.

"Sometimes...I hear these voices when I'm out in the woods all alone. They're always tellin' me to let go, and it's hard not to."

"What do you mean?"

The claw of his pointer finger tapped the floor nervously. "It's hard to talk about, and the others think I'm weird enough, so I don't say nothin'. But I don't think we're supposed to live like this. We ain't human no more, and we ain't supposed to hang onto that kind of baggage. I wanna let go and be what I am. But if I do that, I'll leave the ones I love. Going feral don't scare me, but not being there for my family when they need me does. I don't wanna hurt Cole no more, and I don't wanna hurt you neither."

The stress and exhaustion of the last couple days finally came to a head, and tears streamed from my face, though I tried to hold them back. Axel's raw emotions didn't help, and I'd have given anything to have someone to hold onto. I'd have loved to comfort him as well, but I couldn't even do that.

"I didn't mean to make ya cry." The vargyr grabbed tufts of his mane and pulled. "Sorry. I ain't usually like this."

"It's not your fault. I'm just really tired."

"*That's* my fault. I shouldn't have gotten you so drunk and let you wander the town alone."

"I'm tired in a different way." I wiped my eyes with the sleeve of my shirt and examined him again. His glowing irises were still sparkling blue. "Even as a child, I never had a safe place to call home. My parents used to beat the shit out of me, and I ran away from that to spend seven years of my life in the same situation with someone who—" I let out a resentful laugh, "*loved* me. Varcross was supposed to be a place to start over and call home." I tilted my head up, watching the white, translucent ripples gently move across the ceiling. "I'm never going to have a home."

"You sure as hell will. I'll see to it."

"You just met me yesterday."

"Yeah? And I consider you a friend. I care about my friends. They're the only family I got. I'm not gonna hurt you, Leo. I swear."

"You can't swear something like that in this situation."

"Don't worry," he said right before the crystal in the room went dark. "Kinda freaked out, but I'm good. You?"

I slinked across the room, and every step made the ripples of light pulse bright before dimming. Though eerie, the magic was beautiful, like being at the bottom of a clear lagoon while looking up at sunlight diffusing through a wind-swept surface.

"Leo. You don't gotta—"

Sooner or later, Axel would start to succumb to the curse. Every day I'd live like Cole and the others until finally turning into a beast myself. My only choices lay in front of me: I could live in fear for the rest of my life never getting close to anyone, or I could try one more time to trust someone, even though trusting strangers never seemed to work in my favor.

"On a scale of one to ten, how much control do you really have over the curse?" I asked, stopping in front of him. "Be honest."

"Eleven," he said, his eyes a little wider. "I ain't like the others for some reason. Each time I satisfy it, I go a little longer, building up a tolerance. I know what Cole said, but he doesn't know me deep down—really deep. He doesn't know what I can do."

I knelt in front of him.

"Leo—"

"I need someone strong that I can count on in this place, because I'm scared to death," I said, falling into him, my arms gently wrapping around his fluffy neck. He went rigid for only a moment before melting into my arms, almost as if he'd been waiting for someone to do that for years. "You're a good guy, Axel." I pulled away and sat on the floor next to him. "How do you feel?"

His tail swished along the floor. "Was just feelin' sorry fer myself, but I guess I shouldn't. I'm lucky."

We smiled at one another, then tittered before turning away at the same time.

"What's it like where you come from?" he asked. "You done said that you ain't from Eqiros, so I've been thinkin' about it since we talked last night."

I took a second or two to consider how I'd respond. "It's a lot different, but kind of similar in a way. It's strange how much Earth has in common with this place, especially since you all speak English. Like, that shouldn't be possible, should it?"

"English?" Axel scratched his head. "Don't know what that is, but yer speakin' Meterin right now. Everyone in Stellous-controlled territories does."

Sweat beads formed on my forehead before running down my face. "Damn, it got hot in here all of a sudden."

"It feels a little cold to me."

I used my shirt collar to soak up the sweat, but the rest of my body was on fire. The long-sleeved shirt I wore made everything worse. Axel began sniffing the air, and when I tried to shuffle away from him, something held me in place.

"What is this?" I whispered, trying again to stand but kept being forced back to the floor by something invisible. "I can't move." A low growl cut me off, and I turned toward Axel as his eyes shifted from blue to orange then back to blue. It was too good to be true after all.

"You smell..." His giant clawed hand rested against my abdomen as he turned, his snout pressing into my neck. I helplessly braced for the inevitable, but with a dog-like whine, Axel jerked away. Jumping to his feet, he dashed to the other side of the room, covering his nose.

I was wrong again. He really did have control over this—or at least enough control for now. There was a fiery sensation where my skin touched cloth, and I cried out in pain while slipping out of my shirt.

"It hurts," I yelled, going for my pants next. The button was still missing, so I unzipped them and began pulling them off. The heat seemed to pour into me from the wall, but when I tried to get away, it would pull me back.

Axel ran across the room and knelt next to me, stopping my hands.

"Yer okay," he said calmly.

Gripping both hands, he pulled me free from the invisible restraints before lifting me to a wobbly stand. He pointed at the rippling green glow as it traveled from the walls to the floor, creeping toward us. "We gotta get off the floor."

I held my pants up with one hand, and we both ran for the couch before he fell onto it first, taking up all of the space as his legs dangled over the armrest. "Sit on my legs and keep yer feet off the ground."

As the light crept closer, I started to panic. Hesitation locked me in place as I looked down at the vargyr lying on the sofa. If the curse hadn't taken him while we were both sitting next to each other, surely sitting on him would push him over the edge.

"Leo!" he shouted, grabbing my arm before pulling me on top of him as the light flowed like sludge under the couch. We were face-to-face, but Axel turned away. "Don't get too close to my nose."

Scrambling backward, I sat upright on his shins as far away from his face as I could get.

"Do you think it can get up here?"

"Don't know," he said, looking back down at the light. "It's just a guess."

"I know I keep asking, but how are you feeling now?" I asked as he shuffled under me.

"I don't wanna worry ya, but this is bad. Yer sweat smells pretty strong."

Embarrassment should have been the last thing I was feeling at the moment, but I couldn't stop it. "Sorry. Didn't get a chance to take a shower yet. It felt like my clothes were burning me."

"It ain't a bad smell."

I looked around the room, and the light receded to the walls. "Looks like you were right. It couldn't get up here." I struggled off the couch, allowing Axel room to reposition himself before sitting next to him. "You were right about the other thing, too."

"I told you," he said with a grin. "I always know the signs when it gets too much, and I ain't even close to that. Yer safe around me, but we gotta get out of this room."

"I'm too afraid to go near the walls now." The light faded from green back to white. "So that's what magic feels like."

"Let's take our minds off of it. It can't get us now, and Cole should be done workin' soon," Axel said, turning slightly on the couch to face me. "Got any hobbies?"

That was something I hadn't given much thought to in a while.

I shrugged. "Haven't really done anything but play video games to keep my mind occupied."

"You gotta have somethin' you like doing."

"I like nature and hiking; it was one of the reasons I moved to Colorado." Things that brought me joy started trickling into my thoughts. "I guess I like singing, and I played the piano for church when I was a teenager."

"Singing, huh?" Axel mumbled, fidgeting with his fingers. "I'd like to hear it."

"We'll have to ask Toby for a few steins of cider before I'll do that."

We were both too tense to laugh.

"I love nature, too. I'd like to take you out there one day," he said.

"Have you ever been to the ocean?" The moment I asked that, I could see every tooth in his mouth as his face lit up like a match.

"Only gone there a few times, and it's pretty. Never seen a shore like that before, all rocky with lots of cliffs. If it's really clear, you can see the volcanoes far in the distance. But I don't go there too much cause somethin' never smells right, and there ain't no animals around. Probably ain't safe for me either, considering we don't really know what's in this world."

"You think it's a monster or something?"

Axel shrugged. "I dunno. Maybe one day, you, Cole and Vince can come explorin' with me. Cole don't get much free time anymore. Should probably beat the shit outta Gar until he lets Cole have a few days to himself, but then I really wouldn't be allowed back in town." He threw his head back and laughed.

"You don't like Gar?"

"Not a lick. Cole trusts him, though. He gives the wilkyrs potions to keep 'em as human-like as possible fer the dungeon, but I think it might be messin' with their heads. When Cole does finally hit his full turn, that'll be it fer me. There won't be no one left to keep the curse from making me feral."

"But there's other wilkyrs."

"I ain't allowed. That's a long story. Kinda embarrassin' too. I'll save that fer another time." He fidgeted more. "I meant what I said earlier. I'm yer friend now, and you can talk to me 'bout anything. I'll listen."

"Thanks," I said, patting his hand before looking up at the glow. "This may be too much of a coincidence."

"Why do you mean?"

"Some weird guy lured me here, and I don't know why. He told me I'd be one of the most important people in this town, and it didn't make sense until today. Wilkyrs keep this town alive, and there aren't many left. What if someone's luring humans in here to replenish the supply?"

"That's not gonna happen to you," Axel said.

"You can't promise that."

"I'm a real stubborn bastard."

"You just said earlier that without Cole—"

He squeezed my hand. "Listen. We can do anything with enough determination. This curse ain't gonna keep me controlled, and neither is Gar."

"I know you don't like Gar, but he's right about this. I'll always be looking over my shoulder."

"It's gonna work out somehow. No one's gonna find the cure for this, and I don't think anyone really wants to. I ain't gonna sit in this shitty town and be miserable for the rest of my life."

The light around the room disappeared, and the crystal in the ceiling flickered back on. Seconds later, the door slammed open, and seven sweaty wilkyrs sauntered into the room before gawking at us, their mouths hanging open.

"Axel!" Cole pushed his way inside, wiping his face with a towel before letting it fall to the floor. I pulled my hand away from his.

"Nothing happened," I said as Axel and I jumped off the couch, putting some distance between us.

Cole turned back to the others. "Go home. It's been a long night."

"What about the cleaning?" Feran asked, looking away when I met his eyes.

"Oh, don't worry about that." His voice dropped to a growl. "I've got someone to punish."

The wilkyrs filed out of the room, whispering to themselves before shutting the door. Cole dragged himself to the couch and collapsed into it.

"I'm too tired for this," he said, his tone airy as he rubbed the stubble on his face. He had shaved hours earlier, but the hair was already growing back. "Axel, you know you're not supposed to be here. You just can't help yourself, can you?"

"Gar let me in."

"Sure, he did."

"Cole, I—"

"No more excuses, Axel."

I walked over to the door and examined it. "It's not his fault. He came by to apologize, and someone locked us in."

"Someone...locked you in?" Cole's angry glare shifted to me. "Leo, look at the door knob and tell me what side the lock is on."

"I'm not an idiot, God damn it! There was magic or something." Cole raised an eyebrow. "Axel, tell him what you told me."

"It *was* magic, I swear. I tried to break down the door, but it wouldn't budge." He knelt next to Cole. "Please don't be mad. I didn't do nothin'. We was just havin' a good conversation while trying to stay away from the light."

"The light? You both had better start making sense, and soon."

"I had good control—"

"You're full of shit," Cole interrupted. "And now you're tricking Leo into thinking he's stuck in a room with you just so you can prove something. You know no one can use magic in this world. You lied to him so he'd let you near him." His eyes darted back to me. "And where the hell is your shirt? Do you want this to happen to you or something?"

Axel's ears fell, and he shook his head faster.

"Hold on a minute," I cut in. "Axel hit the door *hard*, and it threw him across the room." I turned and pointed to the broken furniture and mirror. "There was some kind of light covering everything, like water. Whatever it was pinned me to the wall. My shirt felt like it was on fire, so I had to take it off." I let out a sigh. "God, this sounds so idiotic, but it's true, I swear."

Cole's expression went from angry to worried. "You just described Lo'rim, but that's impossible."

"What's that?"

"Something that shouldn't exist in Varcross, or anywhere. It's magic that's only practiced by deva'kohs—and they were either wiped out or locked away for contracting demons."

I peeked out into the hall before lowering my voice.

"Maybe we shouldn't put too much trust in Gar."

"I don't like what you're insinuating." Cole stood and shoved the large vargyr. "Just because you don't like him, Axel, doesn't mean you have any right to spread lies."

Axel snarled. "Open yer eyes, Cole. You think he's some kind of savior, but there ain't nothin' about him that's right. He don't even smell right."

"And that's what you're basing all this on? The way he smells?"

"Jeez, it's more than that. It's my gut."

Cole rolled his eyes.

"Maybe you shouldn't be too quick to dismiss Axel," I whispered. "You said that you trusted Axel enough to watch over me, and he's known Gar for longer than you have."

"This doesn't make any sense." Cole walked over to me and shut the door before lowering his voice. "If Gar could use that type of magic, he'd have gone insane centuries ago, like all deva'kohs eventually do. He knows more than anyone here; plus, he's been trying to find a way to break the wards. If what you saw was real, that means there might actually be a way to break the wards if it came down to it. But Lo'rim is dangerous and unpredictable. Gar needs to know what you saw."

I grabbed my shirt off the floor, slipping it on. "Let's hold off on that until we know more. I'm going to trust Axel's gut on this."

Cole tossed a suspicious glance at the vargyr before narrowing his eyes on me. "You and I need to have a serious conversation later because I'm seeing an alarming pattern here."

"Now what are *you* insinuating?"

Cole didn't answer; instead, he pointed to Axel.

"Get your ass up and go clean the floors."

"I can help." I looked over at Axel who was wrinkling his nose. "What's wrong?"

"You sure you wanna help? I mean, I done grosser things before, but I don't think you got the stomach fer this."

"What the hell's on the floor?"

The vargyr stood and cleared his throat. "Go grab a mop, and I'll get us a couple shots of somethin' strong."

"That was the most disgusting thing I've ever done." My voice was distant as I stared blankly at the tree-covered path in front of us, trying to push tonight's chores out of my mind.

"If *that* was the most disgusting thing, then I envy you," Cole said, slinging his arm around my neck.

"I've never seen so much in my life, and I used to clean bathrooms at gay dive bars." I took in a breath through my nose, and gagged. The scent seemed to linger.

"Are you going to be okay?" Cole asked, picking at the shiny black vest he gave me to wear. "You look good in that. I'm glad you and Feran are about the same size."

I was freezing in that skimpy outfit, but it was all there was to wear after my unfortunate slip and fall earlier.

"I look ridiculous."

"A vargyr designed these, so you're lucky anything's covered at all."

Cole and I laughed, but Axel remained quiet for most of the walk. We both kept checking on him to see if he was getting any urges, but he'd keep his eyes forward and tell us he was fine.

"What did you do with your clothes?" Cole asked.

"I buried them."

That time, Axel snorted.

"I'm sorry, Leo, but it was kinda funny...until ya threw up," Axel said. "Ah hell, even that was kinda funny."

"Glad I provided the entertainment." I sniffed a few times. "I still smell it."

"Ya smell fine." Axel took a few deep sniffs in my direction and stopped. "Wait, I don't smell nothin'."

"De-scenting lotion," Cole said. "I gave it to Leo after his shower so we could get home without having every vargyr in town trailing us."

"This stuff really works. No one's even approached me, and I'm half naked."

Cole gave a nod to the huge vargyr at our side. "That's also because of Axel."

"It's a good thing everyone hates me. At least I can keep my friends safe."

"They don't hate you," Cole said before correcting himself. "Well, maybe only Loken does."

"Fuck that guy."

"Who's Loken?" I asked, watching as Axel's entire sweet disposition shifted to a toothy snarl.

"The second biggest vargyr in town," Cole replied. "He used to boss everyone around before Axel got here. Loken and Axel actually got along for a little while, but one drunken evening, they both tore each other up, with Axel breaking just about every bone in Loken's body."

"I should have torn him up again after he threatened Leo last night."

"Wait, *that* was Loken? He's the one who attacked me!"

"I'll fuckin' kill him!" Axel roared, veering off the path, back toward town. Cole ran after him and grabbed a handful of his mane.

"Alright, calm down," Cole said, gripping the fur tighter. "I had to do a lot of damage control last time to keep Gar from making good on his word when he threatened to kick you out of town."

"He started it. And it ain't like we can't heal fast. He needed that ass-kicking."

"It was the curse," I said, grabbing Axel's arm, Cole and I pulling him back to the dirt road. "You guys told me the curse makes you do things you don't have control over."

"Oh, that bastard knew exactly what he was doin'," Axel said, his voice low as he followed me.

"At least he's a lot more tolerable now," Cole said, pointing to a rustic, mid-sized house along the road, nestled between two giant evergreens. It had a bit of a run-down appearance from what little I could see in the faint glow of the crystal on the front porch. "Home-crap-home."

"I guess I should be headin' home myself," Axel said, with an overexaggerated wistfulness. It was obvious he wanted to come inside, but Cole didn't even acknowledge it.

I tapped his shoulder.

"Maybe Axel could stay and visit a while." The wilkyr's eyes narrowed, giving me that same suspicious look from earlier. "He did most of the cleanup tonight." There was a pulsing breeze hitting my back as Axel's tail sprang into action.

"I know you two were fine together earlier, but I'm going to have to say no to this." Axel's tail stopped moving, and he gave Cole a wide-eyed look, his lower jaw quivering. "Stop that. I need you to get Vince out of the house. He's gotta stay with you until we figure out what to do with Leo, and he's probably going to put up a fight."

"Don't worry, I know how to handle him."

We climbed the steps of the porch, and Cole grabbed the knob. "Maybe you can smack him around for a little while in front of me before you leave."

"I ain't doin' that. You two need to do more talkin' and work things out."

"Sure, I'll fit being a therapist in with the other million things I already do," Cole muttered before pulling the door open, a flood of colors washing over him. The three of us filed into the house, and a dark brown vargyr sat on a faded leather sofa, his glowing, light hazel eyes unblinking as they locked onto the screen in front of him. It was the same glass object I saw at Axel's house. The images on the screen were nothing more than weird symbols and flashing colors. However, Vince couldn't seem to look away from it, even with all the noise we were making.

The vargyr barely moved, appearing almost catatonic. He was much smaller than the others, probably not much taller than me. Though he had the typical vargyr physique, there was an emaciated look about him.

"Hey, brother," Axel said in a flirty tone before tackling the brown vargyr, jarring him out of whatever trance he was in.

"You fucker!" Vince's scream was muffled under Axel's heft. "You killed me. Now I gotta start over." He pushed against the larger vargyr. "Why do you always smell so fucking awful."

Axel pushed himself off of Vince but pulled the smaller vargyr into an embrace. Vince snarled, snapping his jaws.

"You play them games too much. When's the last time you ate somethin'?" Axel asked.

"I dunno. Yesterday?"

"I'm makin' you eat tonight."

"I ain't hungry," he said, his eyes widening as they snapped to me. "W—what the hell is that?"

"*That* is going to be living here," Cole muttered. "And you're living with Axel."

"He's human!" Panic tore through his voice, but that turned to rage when he realized what Cole said. "Yer kickin' me out again? Make *him* stay with Axel."

"Nah, he ain't safe livin' with me."

"That's not my problem." Vince's breath quickened, and he looked away from me before whining like a dog. "You coulda warned me."

Cole grabbed Vince's snout and squeezed. "You and I need a break. You don't leave the house anymore, you barely eat, and we don't talk. This might do you some good."

Axel gave the smaller vargyr a playful shake. "Ya get to hang with me. We haven't hung out just the two of us since we was kids!"

Vince opened his mouth to protest, but all that came out was a defeated sigh.

"Still got yer LCR?"

"Never use it that much, but it's there. You can bring yer games, but I'm gonna drag you outside once in a while."

I walked toward the couch and extended my hand to the smaller vargyr. He glared at me before gripping my hand tight, giving it an angry, single shake. "It's nice to meet you, Vince."

"Yeah," he muttered, releasing me.

Axel got off the couch and grabbed my hand with both of his, vigorously shaking it.

"I loved talkin' to you, and I wish we could talk more."

"Same," I said, a bit of warmth flushing my face as we locked eyes. Vince sniffed the air and jumped up from the couch, making as much noise as possible as he stomped across the room.

"Let's get the hell outta here. I gotta restart that level," the small vargyr muttered, grabbing a clear hexagonal device from the table next to what must have been the LCR. The console wasn't that big and could be carried in one hand. It also didn't have any wires attached. Whatever technology their old world had was lightyears ahead of Earth's.

Axel let go of my hand and padded excitedly to the front door before disappearing outside with Vince following close behind. He stopped and glared back at me.

"Hey, idiot," he sneered. "Don't you ever fall in love with a vargyr."

With that, he ran outside, and the door came to a forceful rest against the frame.

"Wow, he really liked me," I said sarcastically, but Cole didn't respond. "What?"

"You need to be careful, Leo," he said, plopping onto the sofa before crossing his legs.

"What did I do wrong now?"

"He likes you."

I let out a forced laugh and sat down next to him. "That certainly wasn't the vibe I was getting, especially when he called me an idiot."

"Not Vince, he obviously hates your guts. I'm talking about Axel."

"Yeah, I know. He wanted to still be friends, and I didn't see any harm, as long as you're around."

"You're really not getting this. There's a scent vargyrs give off when they find someone they're interested in, and Axel stinks when he's around you. That's why Vince said what he did."

I felt like someone dropped a safe on my head.

"Oh...OH! Shit, did I give him the wrong idea?"

"I'll have a talk with him tomorrow."

"Alright," I said, now a little more nervous. "I don't want to hurt his feelings, but even if I was attracted to him, how the hell would that even work?"

"Just watch what you say; otherwise, he'll start taking risks. Since he thinks he's got a handle on everything, this could get out of hand fast. He'll convince himself of anything if he thinks he has a chance with you." Cole turned his head and yawned loud enough to be somewhat obnoxious. "So what do you wanna do now?"

"Well, I crashed my car last night and afterward got drunk off what I can only assume was kerosine. I got chased by a rapey vargyr this morning, and now I've given the wrong impression to Axel."

"You also slipped in a shallow puddle of spunk earlier," Cole added.

"Thanks for reminding me of that. I'm going to bed."

Cole let out a tired laugh and put an arm around my neck. "I think you and I are gonna get along great."

A Matter Of Trust

ole's exhausted smile was the last thing I saw before closing my eyes. He mumbled while he slept, and there were a few times throughout the night when he'd jerk around or snap half-awake before falling back into what seemed like nightmares.

The curse took such a heavy toll on everyone, but somehow, Axel and Cole still had it in them to look after me. It hadn't completely broken them, but their stories made me realize how close everyone in this town was to the edge. I also couldn't stop thinking about Vince. Meeting him in person put everything I'd heard into perspective, and the physical signs of his ailment clung to his small frame. The more I learned about this place, the more desperate I was to leave it.

The chill of the room rushed across my exposed skin as I pushed away the covers and sat up, looking down at Cole once more. We were strangers, but he gave me shelter and protection when he could have just looked the other way. Axel did the same, though he had a different motive in mind.

I slid off of the mattress, being extra careful not to stir too much. It was awkward sharing a bed with a man who wasn't Ben, and even though I was physically attracted to Cole, there was no way I'd act on it. I needed friends I could depend on, but in this world, I wondered how long those friendships could realistically last.

Then there was the misunderstanding with Axel I needed to clear up. With Cole's warning still fresh, I doubted we could really be close, despite the connection we both felt in that room. I also wondered if he really liked me or if it was the curse pushing him closer to its next victim. I couldn't think of him like that. There were monsters everywhere I looked in my old life, and they were all human. Axel was the furthest from that.

As I tiptoed through the house, a miserable scene I hadn't noticed last night appeared in what little light trickled in through the curtain-drawn windows. The kitchen was in a disgusting state with dishes stacked on top of one another, covering the counter tops and filling the sink. Dried puddles of a black mystery fluid looked like they had fused to the wooden floor with drizzle lines along the warped cabinets that wouldn't close all the way. Pans full of charred grease straddled X-shaped guards covering the burner openings on the stove, and a whiff of rotting food from the overflowing garbage bin made it a challenge to breathe through my nose without gagging.

Vince's brown fur covered the hallway floor leading to one of the bathrooms. Like in Axel's house, the guest bathroom looked like it hadn't been used in decades. There was another room at the end of the hall, but it had no furniture. Instead, there were piles of firewood stacked against the far wall.

The house had very little natural lighting, since there were so few windows and the purple canopy outside blocked most of the sun. The filth and neglect only added to the despair. If their living conditions were any indication of their mental health, Cole and Vince had given up a long time ago.

Healing had to start somewhere, and a clean house used to always put me in a better mood. Even if I was barely scratching the surface, a little happiness in a town this dreary was a net gain.

It took most of the morning, but I got the kitchen as clean as I could. There wasn't any dish detergent, so I grabbed a bar of soap and a scrub brush from the master bathroom and made do. The closet next to the back door had a straw broom but no mop, so after sweeping, I had to crawl on my hands and knees to scrub away the more stubborn messes.

"Whoa," Cole said, startling me. "There's a kitchen in here!"

"Good morning." I climbed to my feet, using the counter as leverage. "How'd you sleep?"

"Jeez, Leo." He ran his fingers along the tile next to the stove. "I forgot what this counter looked like."

Before I could respond, Cole threw his arms around me. "I'm in shock. I don't know what to say."

"How did it get so bad?"

He pulled away. "Everything kept me so busy that I never had time to clean, and on my rare days off, it was the last thing I wanted to do. Vince wouldn't help, and everything got so gross that when I was finally feeling up to it, I didn't even know where to start."

I threw the dirty cloth I used to clean the floor into the sink. "I'll get to the rest of the house after you leave. I wanted to make you breakfast before you woke up."

"I took you in because I like you. You don't have to clean up our messes, and you definitely don't have to cook." He leaned back against the counter and sighed. "Plus, there's no food, anyway. I haven't used this kitchen in almost two years."

"You're letting me live here rent free, so it's the least I could do. Plus, I'm a bit of a neat freak, so this was bound to happen."

"I know it probably seemed like I didn't want you living here when we were negotiating with Gar, but the truth is, I didn't want you seeing the house."

"You guys can't keep living like this." I didn't want to come across as preachy, but I had to say something. "And Vince looks terrible."

The melancholy from last night returned, turning Cole's stare distant.

"Shit. I'm sorry if I overstepped."

"You didn't, and you're right. Vince hasn't cared about himself or anything else since the mages got us. As bad as it was for me, I think it affected him much worse. He may not show it, but he's probably the most sensitive person here, even more than Axel. It's made him so angry all the time. When we first got to Varcross, he said he'd rather die than live like this, but each time he tried to hurt himself, instinct took over. I tried to help him, but I couldn't be there for him all the time. It made me sick knowing that one day I'd probably lose him forever, and I'd be powerless to stop it.

"But killing a vargyr is hard to do, and suicide is nearly impossible. When he did manage to hurt himself badly enough, he'd just heal in seconds or minutes. He's tried to break up with me, saying he wants me to find someone better, but once a vargyr makes a bond like what we have, they can't leave. Plus, I don't want anyone else; I just want my Vince back."

Cole's eyes shifted from me to the kitchen window. He grinned before pulling aside the curtain. "I thought I heard something out there."

I joined Cole in peeking through the window at an ashen-gray vargyr sitting cross-legged on the ground with a paper sack next to him. He was staring out at the road, his tail gently disturbing fallen leaves.

"What's he doing out there?"

"This would be cute if it weren't so damn creepy. He's either standing guard outside the house, or he's waiting for you to wake up. He used to do this to me after he found out I liked him."

I turned away and got that weird feeling in my stomach again. "What do I do? I really don't want to hurt his feelings."

"Leo, I don't want you to take this the wrong way, but this is kinda your fault."

"How the hell is this my fault?"

"You were holding hands with him last night."

I opened my mouth to protest, but I had no defense. That's exactly what I did, even though it was just me being supportive.

"Oh, you thought I didn't see that, did you?" he continued.

"I just wanted to comfort him, and it was comforting to me too, considering we were trapped in that room."

"Well, now you have to break that big, innocent heart of his."

"Don't say it like that."

"I can talk to him, but Axel gets super clingy unless you tell him to back off."

"How clingy are we talking?"

Cole threw his hands up before pointing back out the window. "That clingy."

I looked back out the window, and this time, Axel turned around, staring at the door for a few seconds before visibly sighing and turning back toward the road.

"I'll talk to him, but later. I don't want to start the day off like this."

"Fair enough," Cole said, slapping my upper arm. "It's kind of sweet how much you care about him."

"I don't care about him—I mean, I do care, but not the way you're thinking.

"Well, you say that, but there's something else."

"Now what am I unintentionally doing wrong?"

Cole pointed to his nose. "You remember what I told you last night? Vargyrs and wilkyr can tell if someone's a little turned on."

"You're full of shit."

"It's true. I caught a little something when you were with him."

"I am in no way turned on by Axel! Jesus Christ, listen to yourself."

Cole gave me a frigid librarian's stare. "There's no lying to a wilkyr."

"I'm not fucking lying!" I was on the verge of losing my temper. Cole seemed to know exactly what buttons to push, and accusing me of borderline bestiality was the big red one.

"And neither am I. You give off a particular scent when he's close to you." His eyes narrowed, and he gave a sly half-smile. "It's not as strong as when you're close to me though."

My face flushed as I remembered what I felt while wrapping him in that gauze yesterday. How many times had I bombarded him with whatever scent he was picking up on? Hell, even in bed last night...

"Christ..."

"Jesus Christ?" He flashed his brows, and I rolled my eyes. "I'm flattered, by the way."

"I can't look at you right now."

"It's no big deal. It happens all the time. It's not like the same thoughts don't cross my mind. If I weren't with Vince—"

"Okay, we should get off this subject," I said, walking across the living room to the front door. "I really hate this. It's like a major invasion of privacy."

"Well, we can't help it, so you're just going to have to deal with knowing that Axel and I *know* what's happening down there." He tented his fingers. "It's one of the few perks of our condition."

"Ugh," I groaned out before jerking the door open. Axel jumped to his feet and grabbed his paper bag. "I really hope you haven't been sitting there all morning."

"Hey," he said excitedly, padding up to the front step. "Ain't been that long, only an hour or so. Wanted to make sure anyone walkin' by on their way to the mines didn't bother ya."

"That's really sweet," Cole said, waving Axel inside before raising an eyebrow at me. "What did you bring us?"

"Breakfast," he said, his tail wagging through the torn hole in his shorts.

Cole eyed the bag suspiciously. "Wait, is this something you killed?"

"Don't worry, I cooked it this time."

"That certainly doesn't put my mind at ease."

Axel made his way to the dining room and set the greasy bag on the table. "I swear, yer both gonna love it."

"How's Vince?" I asked.

Axel's smile faded.

"Sleepin'."

"Did something happen?" Cole asked, plopping down on the sofa. Axel shrugged and sat next to the wilkyr while I took a seat on one of the dining room chairs. That turned out to be a painful mistake as I shuffled around, trying to get comfortable.

"I just don't know what to do for the guy. He shuts me down or ignores me whenever I try to talk to him. We used to talk all the time, but now it feels like we're strangers." His eyes went from his lap straight to me. "Why you sittin' all the way over there? There's room enough right here." Axel scooted toward Cole, shoving the poor wilkyr against the edge, leaving about six inches of space between him and the arm of the sofa. Cole didn't look at me; instead, he bit his lower lip and stared straight ahead, trying not to laugh.

"That's okay. I like this chair," I said, pretending to be comfortable on what was essentially a crooked log frame with rattan partially woven over it to form a seat. My ass was already going numb.

Axel beamed, and Cole struggled to hold back more of whatever the hell it was he found so funny.

"Ya really like it?" He jumped off the couch and strutted over, pulling another crooked chair out from under the splintery dining room table. "I made this table set fer Cole and Vince on their anniversary last year." Cole's reaction earlier started to make more sense, and I needed to stop lying before this got out of hand. "Vince always says his ass falls asleep right after sittin' in these."

"About that..." I gauged Axel's reaction. "It's really not that bad for a first attempt. I wouldn't say my butt's asleep."

"This was actually my fifth set. I talked Toby into buying one, and he paid me twice just to get it out of his house the next day." Axel started laughing. "I got to drink a lot that week." He paused for a moment, and his eyes widened. "I'm gonna make you a bed. How's that sound?"

A snort from the couch caught a quick glare from me as Cole lifted his knees to his chest, burying his face in them.

"That's really nice of you, but I think the spare room is for firewood." Axel furrowed his brows, cocking his head slightly. "And Cole was nice enough to let me sleep in his bed. I wouldn't want you to go through the trouble when you don't need to."

"What's firewood doin' in the house?"

"Uh..." I looked at Cole again, who was about to fall off the couch. "It's to keep it dry, right?"

"There's a bin outside fer that," Axel said.

"I think Vince was just lazy and didn't want to have to go outside to grab any." Cole's feet hit the floor, and he scooted toward the edge of the seat before slapping his knee. "I've got a great idea. Why don't you take that bedroom, Leo? This way, Axel can make you your very own special bed."

I wanted to kill him.

"That's *really* not necessary. I like sleeping in bed with you." When I said it, my face immediately got hot.

"Leo, I know you have feelings for me, but I'm taken," Cole said, the shocked tone of his voice clearly over-exaggerated.

Axel looked even more confused, and I couldn't blame him after Cole's performance.

"I don't want him to go through the trouble," I said, articulating each word slower through clenched teeth.

"Ain't no trouble at all. I'll make ya a big bed with plenty o' room." He paced in front of the hearth, growing more excited as he spoke. "An' I'll make ya a chest of drawers, and a wardrobe, and, oh! You might need a nightstand—maybe two. Maybe some lamps to go on those nightstands. I can buy those from the traders."

"Axel, hold on. We need to talk," I said, trying to figure out how to stop this before he took up knitting just to make me an ugly sweater for each day of the week.

"Sure buddy, what's on yer mind?"

My heart sank as I thought about how to let him down gently. Those huge puppy-dog eyes, that friendly smile, the way his tail wagged—this nearly nine-foot-tall killing machine melted my heart.

A defeated sigh left me as I looked up at him and smiled. "I don't really need a wardrobe. A dresser's more than enough."

His giant hand fell onto my shoulder. "Then I'll make ya somethin' extra special. It'll be a surprise. I can't wait to see the look on yer face."

"I can't either," Cole said, that malicious grin returning.

"Gotta run home and get my measurin' tape, then I'm gonna get that wood out of yer new room." He sprinted to the door with me following before looking back. "I'm gonna get you all settled in, make it feel like yer home." With that, Axel ran from the house like a toddler on a sugar high, forgetting to close the door behind him. "This is gonna be perfect," he shouted while running down the dirt path toward his house.

"You're an asshole," I shouted at Cole after closing the door all the way.

"What? Don't get mad at me because you don't have a heavy enough set of balls. At least he'll woo you with a bunch of lovingly hand-crafted stuff."

"How the hell do you say no to *that*?"

"I'll let you know when I figure it out."

I dragged my feet before sitting on the loveseat next to Cole. "Will you at least let me still sleep in your bed if this turns out to be a disaster?"

"I'm not a sadist." He laid his head on my shoulder. "Plus, I like sleeping with you."

"Yeah, you're an asshole," I said, pushing him away.

"What is this thing?" Cole asked, sliding his fingers over the faded, scratched-up hood of my car. I needed to drive all my stuff to the house, but this time I had the sense to bring an escort. Even though he wasn't a full vargyr, no one in town messed with me while Cole was around. Axel offered to come with us, but since he was happily moving firewood out of the house, Cole insisted he stay behind and finish.

"It's a car." I examined the damage, which looked a lot worse in the daylight, especially where Axel bent the driver's side door to get it to open. Thankfully, the vargyrs hadn't gotten curious enough to mess around with anything. "It's how I got to Varcross."

"You don't have gateways?" Cole asked while jogging around to the passenger's side.

"Like portals?"

"What else would they be? It's the only way to get anywhere quickly in Eqiros. I mean, we have exploration vehicles, but they're more for primitive areas outside of the portal network." He gave the roof a tap. "At least these are fun to fly. I got to do that once."

"Uh, this doesn't fly."

His brief excitement quickly turned to disappointment. "Oh. Well what does it do?"

"It's got wheels. What the hell do you think it does?" I pried the stubborn driver's side door open before sliding into the front seat.

"Someone's in a mood," Cole muttered on the other side of the window, cupping his hands to look inside. "How do you get in?"

I cranked down the passenger window. "Lift handle. Then pull."

"I don't like your tone right now," Cole said with a smirk as he struggled with the handle. "This thing's not working."

"How are you finding this difficult? Axel got it right the first time."

"Oh, he did? Judging by this giant hand-sized dent in your door, I'm guessing he probably didn't get it right the first time either."

"What?" I leaned over the seat and pulled on the handle, but nothing clicked. "God damn it! Axel fucked up the only working door."

Cole lithely jumped in through the window, feet first, before falling into the seat.

"How the hell did he even fit in here?"

"He didn't. He just crammed himself in."

"Yeah, that sounds like something Axel would do."

He said that so casually that it nearly went over my head.

"I'm deleting this conversation from my brain."

It was late afternoon, and Cole was in a much more revealing uniform than yesterday, standing in front of the bathroom mirror while trimming his facial hair. This time he wore a glossy leather thong with his vest, and my eyes would instinctively travel downward. It was hard not to look, considering how little was left to the imagination since he barely fit.

He inhaled deeply through his nose and set the sheers on the counter next to the sink before turning around.

"Excited?"

"Ugh, Christ."

"Jesus Christ?"

"That's starting to get old," I muttered, forgetting there was no hiding anything from him. "What time do you have to be at the dungeon?"

"Sunset."

"I can help you clean up tonight, if you need me."

"We spent most of the day staying out of sight so no one would see you. You're not fucking that up by leaving the house."

"As much as I deeply cherish the idea of never cleaning vargyr jizz again, I promised I'd help you. I could just as easily stay out of sight with the lotion."

"We need to save that." He shook his head. "And what you saw last night wasn't a normal thing. It's never been that bad, and it was all because you were there."

We both fell silent, and I looked away.

"Sorry."

He wrapped his arm around me. "I didn't mean for it to sound like that. It's not like it was your fault. This is all uncharted territory." He let me go and stepped into the bedroom before sitting down on the mattress.

"Wolves aren't like this, and neither are people. Why is this curse so sexual?"

"No one seems to know. When I was studying to be a mage, this was all glossed over, like the curse barely existed. It's part of the reason I let my guard down around Vince. I never understood why he wanted sex all the time; he just did. Being a teenager, I thought that was normal."

"So wilkyrs have to deal with this too?"

"Kind of. It's different for us. We can actually control ourselves, and we can't spread the curse. But we do have similar libidos." He sniffed the air again and grinned.

"Oh, come on!"

Cole laughed. "If you think about it, it's a rather brilliant way to spread a curse. If they were all bloodthirsty killers, they would have either killed their victims before the curse could set in, or there would have been so few of them that the mages could have taken care of the problem centuries ago."

"I didn't think about that."

"I hope that when I turn, I go straight to being feral. I heard you lose the human part of your brain and all your memories. It must be great not to have to worry about any of this anymore."

"Well, I hope you don't," I said, grabbing his arm. "You're literally the only person in town I can talk to alone."

"We'll see what happens when it happens."

After Cole left, I spent the evening cleaning the rest of the house. I finally got around to eating the food Axel brought over, which was basically just an entire bag of charred mystery meat. It was edible if I scraped off the burned bits, and I was so hungry, I'd have eaten just about anything.

I'd occasionally peek through the curtains to see if Axel was sitting outside, but he hadn't been back since he cleaned the logs out of the room. He was fun to talk to, plus I had nothing to do now but sit on the couch listening to the pops and crackles of the orange embers in the hearth.

Being so bored made me paranoid, and I remembered again that Axel wasn't guarding the house...

Every creak and groan of the place made me wonder if we hadn't completely gone unnoticed today. Were there any vargyrs outside stalking around, looking for a way in? Would they even need to look since they could just as easily break down the door?

My phone sat on the small living room table, fully charged, but of course, it had no signal. Earlier, I'd had the bright idea of scrolling through pictures, only to be reminded of everything I'd left behind. I deleted the albums, save for a few photos of old friends while making space for new memories. As long as I started the car once in a while and didn't let the battery die, I could keep the phone charged—at least until I ran out of gas. There was still a quarter of a tank.

It may not have been what I wanted or expected, but this was my new life, which was the entire reason I left Colorado. I'd always wanted to start fresh, and it couldn't get any fresher than leaving Earth completely. I had to try Axel's way of thinking, focusing on the positives rather than feeling sorry for myself, which often morphed into more anxiety.

There he was again. Axel kept creeping into my thoughts, and maybe Cole had a point. Actually, he may have been somewhat right, but the thought of that scared the shit out of me. If he were human, I wouldn't hesitate to see where it went; after all, I'd never met anyone quite like him before.

A knock at the front door cheered me up until I remembered unexpected company in this town could mean sexual assault and a lifetime of being a mindless monster. The only other person who knew I was living here was Axel—at least I hoped so. I didn't breathe or make a sound, hoping the visitor would think no one was home and leave.

"Relax, it's Gar."

The rush of relief made me want to skip across the room. After unlocking the deadbolt, I pulled the door open and gestured for the old vargyr to come in.

"I'm glad it's you," I said, noting the small leather satchel he carried. "Did you already finish?"

"I sure did," he said, extending his hand toward the sofa. "I wouldn't be here if I hadn't."

Gar may not have been physically expressive, but from the tone of his voice, he seemed less than ecstatic to see me again.

"Is something wrong?"

Gar took a seat next to me, setting the bag on the table. "Do you trust me?"

"I—" The odd question with no lead-in had me scrambling to find a suitable answer. "Maybe, I don't know. We don't really know each other."

He reached into the leather satchel and pulled out a long vial. Inside was sanguine fluid with the viscosity of blood. He swished it around, and the thick serum coated the sides of the glass like cough syrup.

"I know Axel probably had a few things to say about me, but he needs me just as much as the rest of the town does. We're all hanging on by a thread, and I'm trying not to lose any more to the curse's full effects, especially Cole." He stopped fidgeting with the vial and held it in front of me. "He's like a son to me."

I reached for the elixir, and Gar let it fall into my hands. "That vial may contain your salvation, and a solution to our problem as well. It's something I've been working on for over a hundred years, and I need you to test it. It's an elixir that gives the imbibing human temporary immunity to the curse, like a vaccine. You could fool around with as many vargyrs as you wanted and nothing would happen."

"Just what the hell are you suggesting?"

"The wilkyrs need more help, Leo."

The excitement moments ago turned to cold dread.

"I'm not doing that," I shouted before realizing something else was off. "Wait a minute. If you already had something like this, why didn't you mention it last night?"

"This is not something I want to disclose just yet, especially in front of Cole. This needs to be your decision, free of anyone else's influence."

I looked into the glass tube and swallowed hard. "That doesn't really make much sense. If you have a possible cure, why wouldn't you want anyone to know?"

"What part of 'temporary immunity' did you not understand? I never said it was a cure. It's a preventative." Gar's eyes shifted to the side. "And I am not entirely sure it will work." His tone grew increasingly irritated. "I haven't exactly had humans to test this on, and you both insisted I rush this. Am I wrong?"

"You don't know if it will work, and I'm supposed to literally put my ass on the line to test it?"

"I'm not suggesting you go out pleasuring the town. You only need to see if they no longer react to your presence. That's how we'll know it at least partially works. So, will you trust me?" He gently placed his hand on my knee. "I only want to get rid of this curse so we can be free, and if this works, it's one more step toward a cure— or at the very least preventing it from spreading without needing to imprison the vargyr. You've seen the miserable state we're all in. Don't you want to help us?"

"Well, yeah, but what if it doesn't work?"

"Then I'll tweak the formula again, and have you keep testing it."

"What if it kills me?"

"I've been doing this for too long. I know what will kill you and what will not, and I promise this will do no such thing."

"Any side effects I should worry about?"

"The usual. Headache, nausea, dizziness. You may feel ill for a few days, but it won't be anything you can't handle. We also won't know if it prevents sexual transmission unless something happens, so hopefully dulling the vargyr's to your presence is enough for now." He nodded to me, seeming anxious to rush this along. "Your answer?"

"Gar, I—"

He picked up the leather sack and placed it in my lap. It was heavy, full of what felt like small ingots.

"The platinum there is worth more than a small country's economy back on Eqiros. If you decide to drink it and help us with this crisis, you'll live like a king when they open the wards and let us back home." He stood and slowly walked toward the door, but stopped and turned back around after he opened it. "If you decide not to do this, you know what fate awaits a human in this world. The curse will find you, and you understand what that means."

My eyes were dry from barely blinking, but I nodded as he disappeared into the night, letting the door click shut behind him. I dropped the bag onto the table and ran to the entrance, fastening the bolt and chains. With my back against the door, I slid downward. Gar was right. Eventually, someone was going to get me. A flimsy deadbolt and Axel being the only one guarding the house wouldn't be enough to stop creatures who could lift entire cars off the road.

I stared at the red vial lying on the table. Drinking that potion terrified me, but so did the alternative. If he was telling the truth, I could actually do something meaningful, but if it was a lie—what then? I couldn't make this decision tonight, and I likely couldn't make it alone, despite Gar wanting to keep this secret.

The Truth In The Vial

"You're not listening to a word I'm saying, are you?"

Cole's voice yanked me out of my thoughts for the third time that morning. Though I'd been watching his eyes, Gar's proposition weighed on me, drowning out his voice. Keeping the vial out of sight didn't help, but neither did keeping Cole in the dark about my sketchy late-night meeting nearly a week ago. I didn't want him pressuring me, especially since he had so much trust in the elder vargyr.

"I am," I said, leaning back against the arm of the couch, my feet resting on the living room table.

"Then what would you choose? One wish for anything you want or to be supernaturally lucky for the rest of your life?" He squinted and waited for a response.

"Well, wishes can backfire if you don't get the wording right, so I guess I'd take the luck."

A throw pillow slammed into my face.

"Damn it, Cole! Why?"

"That was a trick question and had nothing to do with what I was talking about." He placed the pillow back behind him and leaned forward. "Are you really okay? I know I've been too busy to keep you company lately, but you seem more out of it than usual."

I rubbed the side of my face while spitting out some of Vince's fur that had gotten into my mouth. "It's just the usual. You know, being trapped in a different world surrounded by rapey monsters."

It wasn't just Gar's meeting, or the fact that I was rolling the dice every day I delayed taking that potion. Locking myself in a dark house with no one to talk to was starting to affect me in weird ways. There were times I'd clean something three or four times while continuously holding debates with myself about absurd topics. The best was when I talked myself into believing fruit-based currency could work.

"I haven't smelled fear on you in a while." He scooted closer, studying my face. "No, that's not what I smell. I wonder what else you could be thinking about."

"I feel like we've had this conversation before."

"Could a nine-foot-tall, sweet-talking monster be occupying your thoughts?"

I rolled my eyes and pushed him away. For how little time we'd known each other, he seemed to understand me better than most of my friends did back home. It was as endearing as it was annoying. I'd never met anyone who was so interested in me, and he was fast becoming someone I could trust more than anyone.

My stomach made an embarrassing gurgle, and I turned toward the kitchen. "I'm thinking about making some lunch. Axel brought fresh meat yesterday."

Cole pulled me back down on the couch as I tried to stand.

"Give me an actual answer, please."

"I'm fine. I'm adjusting," I said, sitting upright. "And I'm really grateful you let me stay here, but I feel like a pet waiting anxiously by the front door for you to come home every day."

"Well, I got Vince a collar years ago when he was wilkyr. Maybe it'll fit you."

"I'm serious," I said, though it was hard not to crack a smile at that mental image.

"If you wanted to go outside, why didn't you just scratch at the door?"

"You usually fall asleep before I do. Just thought I'd make you aware of that in case you wake up completely bald one day."

Cole slapped my leg and laughed. "It would all grow back before I woke up."

"I will draw dicks all over your face."

"That would probably work with the uniform," he retorted smugly. "You know, I've actually been wanting to take you for a walk, but with how traumatized you were, I didn't think you'd want to risk leaving the house."

"You told me that you didn't want to risk other vargyrs finding out where I was, remember?"

The wilkyr scratched his head. "Oh yeah. Well, things have settled down, and I have a secret weapon in case anyone tries anything."

"A secret weapon? You're like five-foot-eleven."

"Hey now, size doesn't always matter." He paused and looked away nervously. "Well, it does in this case, but I'll only use it if things go south—which they won't."

"You don't seem so sure about this," I replied, noting the uneasiness in his tone.

"As much as I would like to keep you hidden away, this isn't good for you."

I leaned back and sighed through my nose. "What's worse? Going a little stir-crazy or getting a curse that actually makes me crazy?"

"We could have sex."

"I'm being serious, Cole. When I'm dusting, sometimes I'll draw faces on the wood with my finger just to pretend like someone is listening to me."

He slapped my arm. "Damn it, Leo."

"You're so busy and tired, and I didn't want to bother you with this."

"You need to start speaking up for yourself or no one's going to know," he scolded, but his voice was more concerned than angry. "I should have pried more the moment you let Axel design your room without stopping him."

"Speaking of Axel, he doesn't say good morning or anything when he's out front watching the house."

The moment I said it, Cole smirked. "Aww."

"I swear to God."

"I'm only working with what you give me. You've been bringing him up a lot lately. Plus, there's a good reason he's not coming up to the house to talk to you while I'm gone."

"Why's that?"

"Because I told him not to come up to the house to talk to you while I'm gone."

"Oh..."

"And, you know, the whole rapey monster thing. Remember? It's the whole reason you're going 'stir-crazy' as you say," Cole continued.

"I guess I have a hard time imagining him doing something like that. Ever since that night in the dressing room, he's been like this earworm stuck in my head." My eyes wandered to the torture chair sitting under the crooked dining room table. "I'm worried about what he's going to end up bringing over."

"He made that a few years ago. Maybe he's gotten better?" Cole examined the dining set and shook his head. "I've wanted to get rid of all of that for so long, and I've even gone as far as considering burning the house down just so that I wouldn't hurt his feelings."

I stood and stretched my arms over my head. "I'll take you up on your offer. Let's go for a walk."

"Axel's house is close by if you want to see him."

"Stop it," I muttered as he followed me outside. A strong, chilly gust of wind hit me, and I turned back around.

"Hold up. I need to grab my coat."

I slowed as the road curved toward town, but Cole didn't seem fazed. Everything ahead was disturbingly quiet.

"You okay?" Cole asked, slowing beside me. "We can go back if you want."

"I forgot to wear the lotion," I said, my pace quickening to a brisk walk to get away from the trees. "Why's the town so empty?"

"Everyone's still asleep. They usually go to work at the mines from late morning to early evening, then stay up all night drinking after having their fill at the dungeon." Cole grabbed my arm and guided me toward another path. "We'll stick to the outer road. Believe it or not, you're safer in town than anywhere near the woods."

"One of the vargyrs told me that. Wouldn't town be the worst place to be?"

"Nah. They keep each other in check. We have rules, and they all have a responsibility to each other. No one wants to be exiled or killed. But in the woods, all bets are off. Freshly turned wilkyrs don't go near them alone because a vargyr's prey drive is even more powerful out there. Being in civilization tames the beast for some reason." Cole chuckled once through his teeth. "Maybe that's why Axel hates the town."

It was nice to breathe fresh air, and I did feel safer with Cole next to me, but as we got closer to the tavern, the uneasiness came racing back. A pair of wide yellow eyes were all I could focus on in my peripheral vision. I pulled up my hood and kept my head down.

"Why can you walk through the woods alone, then?" I asked. There was a quick shuffling from behind us that faded abruptly.

"I'm a bit of a special case. We should change the subject. You've got that fear smell on you."

I breathed deeply through my nose and remembered something from the other day. "How far is the ocean from here?"

"It's a little cold for a swim, isn't it?"

"I just wanna see it. I've only seen the ocean a couple times, and it's been on my mind since Axel mentioned it."

"I've never been. It's too far out of town, and on my days off, the last thing I want to do is trek through those woods for hours." Cole seemed more concerned as footsteps scuffed along the path out of our vision. "Axel goes out there all the time, so maybe we can talk him into coming with us when I have another day off." The shuffling behind us grew nearer. "We should head back to the house."

"Should I be worried?" I asked, glancing back to see a lanky brown vargyr following at a close distance.

"Not with me here."

"Hey," the vargyr grunted.

"Not now." Cole didn't look back at the stalker. "These are not business hours."

"What about the human?"

He was so close that his stale panting pulsed against the back of my neck.

Cole snarled, whipping around to swipe at the unwanted stranger with his claws. The vargyr whined and took a step back.

"You know better."

"I know." His voice turned from threatening to an almost suffering whimper. "Please. This hurts. I need that human."

Cole stepped in front of me, pushing me back. The thick, fur-like hair on the back of his neck stuck straight out, and his stubby tail stood at attention.

"Hold your nose and back away. That's the last warning. You know what's going to happen if you act on this. Do you want to take that risk?"

The trembling monster put his hand over his nose but couldn't back away.

"I can't. This hurts." And with that last growled-out word, his eyes darkened to crimson.

My attention went from the vargyr to Cole, who was now growing actual fur, his glare a piercing yellow with red around the edges of his irises. He pointed to the tavern a few hundred feet away.

"Run to Toby's."

Bones snapped, and his claws grew longer and sharper.

"What about—"

"Leo!" His voice wasn't the same, and his skimpy clothes ripped as he grew larger.

A shot of adrenaline took over, and my feet nearly flew over the gravel road toward the tavern. Snarls, snaps, rips, and whines beckoned me to look back. Two vargyrs fought, and one of them had Cole's fur color and facial hair. He was much larger, about as tall as Loken but not quite as thick.

They moved so fast I could barely tell who was injuring who as they lunged for each other, roaring like demons, their claws ripping through flesh. In a sudden, powerful maneuver, Cole knocked the other vargyr to the ground with him on top. After pinning him, Cole's maw clamped around his rival's neck. The beaten monster whined in submission, and the fight was over. Both of them were covered in so much blood, their fur turned auburn in the sunlight.

Cole stood and shifted his glare toward me as the other vargyr limped away, bloody drool roping from his shredded maw. I felt sick. Cole was my closest friend in this world, and now he might have turned feral...or worse.

As he stalked closer, the emptiness faded from his eyes, and he shook himself back to his senses. His fur receded, and his body shrank, returning to the humanoid wilkyr I recognized. His clothing lay in tatters on the ground, and he fell to his knees, holding a deep gash on his left side.

I scrambled away from the tavern and rushed toward him.

"Shit," I whispered, kneeling next to him. After removing my coat, I gently draped it over his upper body. "What should I do?"

He grabbed my hand, panting. "Stay next to me." He let out a howl I'd never heard from any creature before. It was wolf-like, but shaky and high-pitched. "Help's coming."

"Alright." I placed my other hand over his, the warm slickness of his blood coating my palm. "This is really bad."

"Not as bad as it looks, trust me," he replied. "This was my way of testing the waters, but I'm afraid you won't be able to leave the house from now on. I'm sorry, Leo."

"It's okay. Don't worry about it." I couldn't go back to isolation, but I also couldn't let this happen again. The only logical option lay hidden among my belongings.

A group of vargyrs emerged from the tavern and sprinted toward us.

"Stay away," I shouted.

"Take it easy," Toby said, and I closed my eyes for a moment in relief. The silver vargyr kneeled in front of Cole before leaning in. "Who did this?"

"It was Aiden, but—"

Before he could finish, Toby stood and turned to the others. "Anyone who attacks a wilkyr dies. Those are the rules." He turned to a smaller, black vargyr. "Get his scent, and track his ass down. We'll let Gar decide. This is gonna kill Axel."

"No," Cole gasped out before stumbling to his feet, his arm around my neck for support. "He tried to fight it. He was struggling; it wasn't his fault."

"You know that doesn't matter. Once this happens, it'll happen again," Toby replied.

"No, it won't." Cole cast a worried glance in my direction. "I'm the idiot here. Catch Aiden, but don't kill him—and please don't tell Gar."

"Damn it." Toby pushed me away with enough force to make me fall over before pulling Cole into his arms. "This was the human's fault, wasn't it? You should have let nature run its course instead of putting yourself at risk. We need more wilkyrs, anyway."

"Don't say that! I mean it," Cole hissed through his teeth. "I need Axel here now because I don't trust anyone else to keep him safe."

"And you think that dumbass will?"

"Just get Axel," the wilkyr demanded, now struggling to breathe normally.

"If this is what you want, but your safety comes first before his, though." As he lifted Cole to his feet, he turned to the group. "Norris." A smaller black vargyr nodded and sprinted along the road. I'd never seen one run at top speed before, but he disappeared into the trees within seconds. Toby pulled Cole along, but he protested.

"Can't leave him alone." His voice quavered as the freezing wind whipped up dust from the road, some of it sticking to the blood on his naked body. The only thing keeping him somewhat warm was my light coat.

Another vargyr dashed toward us with a plush fur blanket, draping it over Cole's shoulders while two others dabbed the wilkyr's lacerations with wet cloth. The scene reminded me of images in my mother's bible. Cole seemed almost Christ-like, and given how important he was to the town, it made perfect sense.

Each of them, even Toby, seemed to shrink away into submissiveness. Tails hung between legs and ears flattened against heads. Even Axel, as big as he was, often slumped in front of Cole, showing a lot more respect than I would have ever thought. Cole was like their *alpha*—at least, it seemed that way.

"I'm sorry," I whispered.

"Don't." He smiled at me. "We heal fast, and this isn't anywhere near life-threatening. It just hurts, that's all."

Rapid, heavy footsteps approached, and I turned to see Axel's barreling into the crowd.

"What happened?" Axel shouted, looking at me, then Cole.

"Get the human out of here," Toby said, finally lifting the wilkyr into his arms.

Axel held my arms and sniffed before turning his attention back to Cole.

"He'll be fine," Toby said. "We're going to get him to Gar, and hopefully, the geezer doesn't lose his temper."

"I'm trusting you," Cole said, pointing at the giant vargyr. "Do you think you can handle this?"

"You know I can." He stood behind me, his massive hands grabbing my shoulders. "What the hell was you guys doin' out here without me?"

Just as Cole was about to explain, Toby whisked him away. "Take him home, Axel," he shouted. "And don't stay around too long."

Axel nodded.

"Oh, and keep close to the house. Don't let anyone near it."

"Don't worry about nothing," Axel called back, watching on as the group made their way to Gar's dungeon. After the commotion died, we stood alone with each other in the middle of the road until he gently prodded me forward. "C'mon. I gotta get you home."

❦

Axel and I were cautious as we traveled side-by-side along the road, not saying a word. My stare would occasionally shift toward the lumbering vargyr every time he started breathing funny—which was often. Each time he'd hold his breath, his mouth would open as if wanting to say something, but nothing ever came out.

"Axel." He was already looking at me, but not in the way the other vargyrs often did. "Holding up okay?"

"I should be askin' you that," he replied.

"Cole was the one that got torn up. He protected me."

"Wilkyrs are tough, but their bodies just ain't like a full vargyr's, even when they shift."

Axel had gotten too close, and I had to move away without making it seem obvious. When I widened the gap between us, his ears flattened. I wasn't as subtle as I thought.

"Yer still scared." His voice cracked, and he moved to the other side of the road. "It's okay. I don't blame ya. That's the second time somethin' almost happened to you. Guess I need to come to terms with this."

"That vargyr who attacked didn't stand a chance against the curse, and as nice as you are, I don't know if you can control it the way you think you can. Seeing it happen like that was a huge wake-up call."

Axel didn't look up from the ground.

"It's weird to love what you are, but hate yerself at the same time." Though I couldn't tell from his voice, the tears that fell to the ground gave him away. "That fantasy I have in my head, it's always gonna be just outta my reach. Ain't nothing to feel sorry for, though. I'm still gonna be there for you guys." He balled his hands into fists. "When I saw you covered in blood, I almost threw up."

We both stopped walking and turned toward one another.

"I'm—"

He put up his hand to stop me.

"When I smelled you, I knew it wasn't you that was hurt. Cole may heal fast, but you can't. I never want you guys to go anywhere without me again."

"This shouldn't be your problem, Axel. I feel bad enough that Cole has to deal with this."

He stepped closer to me.

"If only you knew what I felt," he whispered, trailing off.

"I do," I said with a sigh, shoving my hands into my pockets. Cole told me I'd need to be direct with him, and this had gotten too dangerous to mess around with. "I've known for a while. You're not exactly subtle."

His eyes wandered to the woods, almost as if he were looking for a path to escape.

"It don't matter." He struggled with the sad grin he wore. "I don't need nothin' more than friendship."

I debated pressing him further or letting it end there, but this had been nagging me for days.

"How do you know this isn't the curse pushing you closer to me?"

He drew in a deep breath through his flared nostrils. "Because I felt somethin' similar a long time ago when I was human. That first night we met, you took me by surprise. Then when we was locked in that room, I remembered those human feelings."

I tried to interject, but he let the words come out louder.

"Yer all I been thinkin' about lately. I play out these scenes in my head where we're just walkin' through the woods, talking about anything. Sleeping under the stars, climbing them mountains no one ain't never been to." His dreamy smile faded. "But that ain't you. The person I know is a fantasy version of you I keep creating in my head. It's embarrassing now that I'm sayin' all this stuff out loud, but it makes me feel better."

I didn't know how to respond. We couldn't even look at each other, and when I'd try to say what I needed to, I'd choke. The few minutes that passed seemed agonizingly long.

"I'm glad I met you," I said.

We could look at each other again, and his sad, goofy grin was contagious. He understood the subtlety of my words. Perhaps he could smell the sadness on me.

"I'm glad I met you, too."

The distance between us narrowed, and we continued onward toward the house.

❦

Hours passed as I sat alone on the couch in the cold living room with the curtains open, holding the corked vial of warm liquid in front of my face. Dusk turned the sky a gradient of pink and navy blue, and Axel had set up his usual camp in front of the house. Though I was suffering in silent deliberation, having him nearby brought me some comfort.

I hadn't bothered lighting the hearth; in fact, my indecision kept me from doing anything other than sitting and staring. Should I throw caution to the wind and drink whatever this was, or should I wait for something worse to happen? The events of today only foreshadowed how bad things were going to get. When Cole looked at me with those blood-tinged eyes, he ceased to be the person he was. That was the fate that awaited him, and if Gar was being honest, that fate could be circumvented.

It was impossible to make a potentially dangerous decision alone.

I leaned forward and placed the vial on the table before making my way to the window, letting the orange glow of Axel's campfire burn away the dreariness. With a click, I flipped the crystalline switch to my left, turning on the warm lights in the ceiling. After unlatching the three locks, I opened the door, catching Axel by surprise.

"I need you."

His tail wagged when he leapt to his feet and trotted toward the front door.

"What do ya need?"

"To talk."

His eyes shifted. "I thought we already did?"

"Not about that," I said, grabbing onto his hand before pulling him inside. "You trust your gut, right?"

He nodded before following me into the house. I walked over to the couch and sat down, grabbing the vial.

"And how often is your gut right?"

"Ain't never been wrong, as far as I know."

I nodded. "I know you don't like Gar, but do you think he has everyone's best interest at heart?"

Axel stood next to the door, appearing to give my question a lot more consideration than I expected.

"Everyone trusts him."

"But do *you* trust him?"

Axel examined the potion in my hand.

"What's that?"

"My dilemma," I said, giving the liquid a shake. "A week ago, Gar came by when I was alone and gave me this." Axel crept over the groaning wood floors and sat next to me. He held out one hand, and I dropped the small bottle into it. "He told me that this might make me immune to the curse."

"That's kinda convenient."

"That's exactly what I thought," I responded with a nod. "He also said that the results could get him one step closer to finding the cure, and I can save Cole. Since I'm the only human in this world, I'm the only one who can test this. Maybe this was why Joe led me here, to help you guys."

I studied his face for any more doubt, but when his ears pointed upward, I felt like I could finally breathe.

"I had this talk a while ago with Cole," he said. "He was the first one who tested the potion all the wilkyrs take. I told him not to, that I didn't trust Gar, but in the end, he didn't listen. Thinkin' back on it, I guess I'm glad he didn't listen to my gut. I might not like the guy, but those potions of his work."

I held my hand out, expecting him to return the vial, but he locked up, holding the glass tube tightly.

"What's wrong?"

"Just 'cause he got one right don't mean this is gonna work. Did he tell you what the side-effects might be?"

"Yeah. They didn't seem too serious, but I got this feeling he was playing it down because he didn't really know." After a few tense seconds, Axel dropped the vial into my hand. "He did make this my choice. I mean, he could have just as easily forced me to drink it."

We both said nothing for a moment, likely thinking the same thing.

"If you really want my opinion," Axel continued, "I wouldn't want you to risk yer health for us."

"It's not just for you. I can't keep living like this." I uncorked the bottle with trembling hands. "I don't want to be alone, Axel. I want something to feel like home, and not live in fear all the time—always afraid of either getting the shit beat out of me by an angry dad or drunk boyfriend, or...this curse."

He grabbed my wrist before I could put the potion to my lips. "I'll beat this curse, Leo. Everyone should have a home, and you can be home with me. I'll never let anything happen to you."

"You don't know that, and what if it's the cure? I'm going to pour out everyone's hope, including yours? If this curse didn't exist, we could get closer. Maybe it would be possible to see if whatever this is between us could actually work."

He fidgeted, barely able to keep still after that, but I could tell he was waging an argument in his head.

"What if it ain't? What if something bad happens to you? I won't even have you fer a friend."

I stared deeper into his eyes. "What happens next time when the blood covering me is mine?"

Axel let go of my wrist and let his arm fall limp at his side.

"I don't like this," he whispered. "But my gut's been wrong once before."

Before I could talk myself back out of it, I pushed the rim of the vial to my lips and tilted my head back, gulping down every drop of the tangy liquid. The metallic taste lingered on my tongue, and for a moment, it felt like acid dissolving my esophagus and stomach. Before I could complain about the pain, it vanished.

Axel's eyes widened, but he remained silent as we both waited anxiously for the worst. Alchemy was pseudoscience and fantasy back on Earth, so all I had to go on were video games and movies. Would this take effect immediately, or would this play out over the course of several days?

"You feelin' anything weird?"

I shook my head. "I don't quite know how we're going to test this. Are you always suppressing the curse when you're around me? Do you feel any different? Do I smell different to you?"

"I'd have to get a good sniff, but if I get too much…"

"How about a little sniff, and if your eyes start to go red, get the hell out of the house."

He pressed his nose near my armpit and sniffed once before pulling away.

"Oh boy…" he said, leaning back while rapidly tapping his foot on the wooden floor.

"I didn't think you'd put your nose there!" My face got hot as I examined his eyes, which were glowing a dull blue. "Do you need to go?"

"Nah." His tone was just as rigid as his body language.

There was definitely something different, but I didn't notice at first until my skin warmed and tingled. Every scent I took in through my nose had a slight ammonia-like odor, causing me to tear up. As the scents sharpened into something different, my stomach tightened and my heart raced, like I was on a roller coaster that had taken the first plunge.

"Leo?" The sound of Axel's voice was like hammers to the head.

"Okay, I feel weird now." This wasn't just weird; I was painfully aroused.

Axel sniffed the air and jumped off the couch, darting toward the door, but stopped. This wasn't a cure at all. The longer the vargyr stayed in the room, the more I craved him.

"You've gotta go," I yelled, running toward the hall. "That sick son of a bitch."

"What if somethin' happens and yer alone?"

"Something's going to happen if you don't leave right now." Every muscle in my body ached, and as if by instinct, I undid the button of my jeans, letting them fall to the floor. Axel's eyes had a tinge of red to them, and he stepped forward. "Get out of here, Axel!"

The vargyr jumped in surprise, slamming face-first into the door with a whine before pulling it open and disappearing into the night. As soon as the scent dissipated, I could regain control of my body—somewhat.

This shouldn't have surprised me, and there was no doubt in my mind now. I'd allowed myself to be manipulated by guilt once again, and it had become crystal clear what Gar wanted. The curse was going to be even harder for me to avoid now.

I had to force myself away from the door, and every step I took in defiance sent jolts of electricity through my body. Sweat beaded on my face, drenching my shirt, so I stripped down to nothing, leaving a trail of clothing to Cole's bedroom. My salvation was there on Vince's side of the bed. As I dove face-first into the pillows, I knew there would be no sleep until the effects wore off—if they even would.

CHAPTER 9

Denial

The relief of sleep was short-lived as the sun seemed to sit directly on my face. Even in my dreams, I couldn't escape the puissant effects of Gar's potion as I lay in bed, covered in sweat. My lower half stung, still slick from an almost unending orgasm. While that might have sounded amazing, after the first thirty minutes of no relief, I was screaming. After two hours, I was nearly catatonic, alternating between silent screams and wide-eyed stillness.

It didn't matter how much pain I was in, when I'd smell Vince on the bed covers and pillow, the response was instant, violent, and involuntary. I thought for sure I'd die of dehydration before it was over, but after a few hours, it ended, leaving me a weeping, quivering mess, unable to move. My body felt as though I had pushed an entire house up a hill by myself, and my tongue had a sooty texture. I was so thirsty, but I couldn't get up to drink.

The front door clicked open before squealing shut, rattling the walls of the old house. Steady footsteps crept along the floor before stopping at the entrance to the room.

"Whoa, Leo," Cole said, averting his eyes from my naked body sprawled out on his bed.

A soft groan escaped my throat as I tried to cover myself with the blanket.

"Hey, Cole. I'm glad you're okay." My voice was so hoarse that I could barely hear myself.

Heavy sniffs came from the entrance, and Cole dashed to the side of the bed. "Did Axel do this?" He pulled away the blanket before I could stop him.

"No. I'm just a little sick." That was an understatement. After what Cole had been through, and with how exhausted I was, I didn't want to keep this conversation going at the moment.

"There are no scratch marks," he mumbled to himself before pulling the blanket back over me.

"I just need to sleep." My tone hit a nerve with him as he pulled away. "I didn't mean—"

"Fine," he interrupted, backing toward the door. "I'll be in the living room. You better explain this."

Before I could say anything more, he firmly shut the door.

There was no more moisture in my eyes as they peeled open for the second time, and I could finally roll over without wincing. The golden-red late afternoon sun combined with the wind made every trembling shadow dance against the wall. As much as I dreaded confronting Cole, I needed to salvage what was left of the day. It took me a few minutes to hobble out of bed, my sluggish gait uneven as I balanced along the walls until I got to the sink. The first thing I did was cup my hands under the icy water to drink.

It took ten or fifteen gulps to soothe the sting in my throat, and after I was done, I leaned over to support my upper body with the palms of my hands, catching my breath. After limping to the tub, the rust-speckled lever squealed when I lifted it, releasing a rush of steam before scalding jets shot from the shower head. I wasn't sure what heating mechanism was used for this, but there was never any gradual warming. It took me by surprise the first time I put my hand under to gauge the temperature, only to burn myself.

When the water cooled, I stepped through the warm veil that billowed toward the ceiling while gritting my teeth, waiting for my clammy skin to adjust to the heat. A stinging in my groin made me turn away, the flesh so raw that I couldn't touch it, and the pressure of the water made the pain worse. The thought of seriously killing someone had never crossed my mind before now, and I couldn't wait to hear what excuse Cole would come up with for the monster that poisoned me with what was essentially a potent aphrodisiac spiked with viagra on steroids.

As the comfortably warm torrent trickled to a stop, I stepped out and wrapped myself in a towel hanging on a hook next to me. After gently patting myself dry, a terrifying realization took hold. What if the potion physically altered me somehow? I studied my face in the mirror, but nothing seemed out of the ordinary.

A shadow rushed through the room, and my attention snapped to the locked window, but there was no one looking in. This feeling happened with enough frequency that paranoia would set in, and I would circle through the house, repeatedly checking the locks. Perhaps it was Gar spying to see if I had contracted the curse yet, or worse—a vargyr biding his time. I pulled the curtains shut and unzipped one of my duffel bags, my breath turning to mist in the freezing room as I grabbed a few articles of clothing.

It took some careful maneuvering to slip on my boxers. Silk may as well have been steel wool against my chafed skin, but I couldn't exactly walk around the house naked, though I had given it consideration. I threw on one of my black long-sleeved shirts and made the walk of shame, limping through the hall toward the warmth of the living room hearth.

The *LCR* was on with no sound as Cole sat shirtless on the loveseat, glaring at me without saying a word. There wasn't a scratch on him; it was as though yesterday had never even happened.

"I need to wash the sheets," I said, clearing my throat.

"We have a tub in the back. Do you want some help?"

"I've got it."

"Do you want to talk?" His voice got louder as he shuffled toward me.

"Not right now."

He grabbed my arm and pulled me until we were face-to-face. "I don't want to live with another Vince."

"What do you mean?"

"Vince keeps everything to himself and never talks. He just suffers in silence."

"I'm not suffering, Cole. I'm just angry, but not at you." I continued toward the bedroom, silently debating if I should convince Cole that Gar was a monster, or wait until I had more proof. If I didn't handle this right, I could lose a friend.

"Let me do it," he said, walking ahead of me before snatching the blankets and sheets off of the mattress, lightly shoving me out of the way as he left the room.

"I didn't mean to upset you," I said, limping after him. He dropped everything on the floor next to a shallow wooden tub, and after plugging the drain on the bottom, he cranked a spigot with a short black hose attached. "And you're still recovering."

He grabbed a cloth bag dusted in powder from the shelf and turned back to me.

"I made a full recovery last night." He opened the cloth sack and sprinkled what looked like detergent into the water before setting it back on the shelf. "We haven't known each other long, but I'm closer to you right now than anyone. Vargyrs and wilkyrs take that seriously. Friends are like family." He eased up on the angry stare. "I took you in, and you're my family now. So don't keep important things from me, especially in this place."

A family? Hearing those words took me by surprise. None of my friends ever considered me family, but Cole did, and he'd only known me for a fraction of the time. Wolves were pack animals, and I supposed vargyrs were no different.

However, as much as I wanted to embrace the notion, I couldn't allow myself to get too emotionally attached. There was no telling when Cole would turn, and I was already going to be devastated enough.

"I promise I'll tell you, but will you hate me if I don't want to talk about it right now?"

"I wouldn't hate you over something so stupid." His brows furrowed. "I'm just going to be pissed off."

"I can live with that." I held out my arms. "I could really use one of these, and I think you could, too."

The anger clinging to his face faded to laughter as he pulled me into a rough hug. The sudden motion made me yelp.

"Sorry," he said, letting go before taking a step back to pick up the sheets, tossing them into the half-full tub of suds.

"I'm glad you're okay. Yesterday, when you turned, I thought you were gone."

"That's not the first time that's happened. Gar's elixir has this weird side effect the longer we take it. Since it keeps us in this form for much longer than normal, some of us older wilkyr can shift in extreme circumstances, especially if our lives are in danger or if someone pisses us off...or if the sex is *really* good." He stirred the contents of the tub with a wooden oar before throwing the blanket and pillowcases in with the rest. "Lately I've been shifting more, and it's definitely not because of the last reason." He finished stirring and cut off the flow of water. "I thought they wouldn't get that close with me around, but that cute little ass of yours is just too much temptation. I guess the test was a failure."

"Well, up until that point, it was good to get out of this house."

Cole leaned the paddle against the wall and walked back toward the living room.

"Let those soak for a while," he said as I followed him back into the living room. "I've got a hypothetical question, and if you don't want to answer it, that's fine."

I let out a sigh. "We're doing this again?"

"Suppose vargyrs couldn't spread the curse, and you really liked one. Would you date him?"

"You don't take hints well, do you?"

"I'm really bored. Entertain me." He smiled and sat on the sofa, and I took a seat next to him, propping my bare feet up on the table. "Could you look past the claws, teeth, bad breath, and funky body odor?"

"If I really liked him, maybe." Cole's face lit up, and I recoiled. "I'd have to be so blindly in love that there would never be another man alive that could compete with his personality or charm."

"Well, you do live in a place where you're the only man alive," he said, picking up what looked like a smooth piece of glass. It was square with rounded edges. As his fingers traced along its surface, tiny arcs of light refracted through it. "How far would you go with him?"

"Why are you doing this to me?"

"Morbid curiosity. It's not like you can date one, so what's the harm of answering a simple hypothetical?"

"After yesterday, I'd rather not talk about this."

Cole nodded, studying my face.

"What?"

"Nothing." Cole waved the glass device at the crystal screen to turn up the volume. He kept his gaze fixated on a weird soap opera.

"If Varcross is closed off from Eqiros, how do you guys watch shows from there? Don't you need some kind of network?"

"We're not completely closed off since Gar works with the mages outside to keep the trade portals going. All of the stuff we watch on the LCR isn't broadcasted." He held up the crystal remote. "We pick out the programs we want, and they're loaded onto these."

"That's really cool."

We didn't say anything more, and I became fascinated by the alien culture playing out on screen. Though the story was too confusing to find interesting, the technology on set, the futuristic skyline of the city, and the obscure references to Stellous's pop culture had me so engrossed that when the screen blackened, I threw up my hands.

"I was watching that."

Ignoring my frustration, he continued. "Okay, let me rephrase this."

"Let it go, Cole."

"Come on, this is gonna drive me crazy. Can you at least tell me what happened between you and Axel last night? Did he try to do something to you?"

"He didn't do anything, and nothing happened. Drop it."

"Uh huh," he said dismissively. "The poor guy was so shaken up, he nearly tripped over his own feet when he packed up and left the yard this morning. He didn't say anything, which as you know, is not like Axel at all." A knock at the door made me jump, but Cole looked like he had been expecting it. "We have a visitor."

"Christ," I muttered.

"Jesu—"

"Stop it. I need to put on pants."

Cole stood and looked down at my boxers. "What's wrong with those? You can't even tell they're underwear."

"I never said they were underwear, which means you could tell they were."

He ignored me and threw open the door. "Hey you," he said with an overexaggerated inflection. Axel nervously scratched the top of his head, keeping his eyes averted.

"Uh, hey. I brought somethin'. Finished it yesterday, but with everything that happened..." The vargyr lowered his ears and looked up at me. "Hey Leo. You feelin' okay?"

Cole turned to me, and that heat from last night started to come back.

"Alright. Let's see what you came up with," Cole said as he followed Axel into the yard with me at a distance. Two polished spires peeked up from a large wooden cart the vargyr had pulled close to the porch.

Dumbfounded, the wilkyr climbed onto the wheel to get a better look at what was inside. From where I stood, it appeared to be a bed frame, elegant and smooth with a swooping headboard that lay detached against the back wall of the cart. The bed's fancy spires stood tall, and elaborate runic carvings decorated everything else.

"I hope you like it," he said softly.

"I'm absolutely speechless," Cole said, running his fingers over the waxy finish.

"I've been practicing. Been meaning to make you guys another dining set at some point."

"It's beautiful," I said, studying the painstaking detail. This was on another level, completely different from Cole's table or that little flower mug he made for Toby. He was an actual artist. "How did you make this so fast?"

"Once I put my mind to somethin', I don't focus on nothing else." He took a few steps closer, and a breeze blew in from behind him. "I still gotta get to work on yer other stuff."

The burning sensation from earlier snaked through me, the heat all concentrating on the one area that thin underwear couldn't hide. The feeling wasn't as potent as last night, but it made me lightheaded enough that I almost fell forward. Both Cole's and Axel's nostrils flared as they breathed in what I was giving off.

"This is amazing," I said, stepping backward toward the porch steps. "Sorry, I've got laundry to finish." My shaky steps turned to a full sprint as I dashed up the steps and threw open the door.

The strongest effects of the potion may have worn off, but it still lingered. Was this permanent? I needed to confront Gar, but after yesterday, I couldn't take the risk without Axel's escort—which I could no longer depend on now.

I knelt next to the tub, dipping a hand into the dirty water to pull the drain cord as Cole ran into the room.

"Alright. Start talking."

When I didn't respond, he grabbed the collar of my shirt, pulling me upright with ease.

"When did this start happening?"

"I need to talk to Gar," I replied.

"I don't think he has a potion to fix this."

"Oh he does, considering he's the one that did this to me."

Cole raised his brow.

"About a week ago, he gave me a potion he claimed would make me immune to the curse. I sort of got this gut feeling when I was talking to him that maybe this was a bad idea, but after what happened to you yesterday, I had to do something."

My explanation didn't seem to satisfy the skeptical expression he wore.

"I asked Axel to stay with me because I didn't want to be alone while testing it. At first, nothing happened." Just talking about this was humiliating. "But then all I could think about was having... relations with the first vargyr I saw, which unfortunately happened to be Axel." I smacked the wall with the side of my fist. "I took my pants off in front of him."

"So Axel did something after all!"

"No, he didn't. The potion altered my sense of smell, and Vince was all over your bed. It was scary. I felt like I was going to die." Now that I was saying it out loud, there were startling similarities coming to the surface, but I wouldn't dare make those assumptions in front of Cole.

"I'm sure *Gar* didn't mean for this to happen, but you should have filled me in. It's a new potion. Sometimes things go wrong."

"This is why I didn't want to say anything to you." I knocked his shoulder with mine as I stormed into the living room.

"Don't be pissed off." He followed closely, and Axel brushed by me in a hurry toward the room. Those feelings quickly returned.

"I've got to get the hell out of here," I muttered, pushing open the front door. As soon as I made my way around to the back of the house, I froze, knowing I couldn't go too far into the woods.

"Gar's always protected us," Cole said, casually following close. "I owe him my life, and you owe him yours, too."

"I don't want to argue with you. You're not going to listen, anyway."

We stood silent as the sound of Axel's hammering thudded through the wall.

"That bed was really big," Cole said, trying and failing to lighten the mood.

"It's too big for me. You and Vince should have it."

"You didn't see your name in huge letters on the headboard?"

"I can't read your letters."

"He's never made anything like that before." He walked the conversation back when I grew more frustrated. "I'm sorry. Please don't be mad at me. I didn't mean to dismiss you like that, and I'll talk to Gar tomorrow when I go to the dungeon."

"Thank you," I whispered, feeling a little less angry. "I'm sorry I didn't tell you about the potion. I just needed to decide without anyone else's influence."

"You thought I was that selfish that I'd guilt you into drinking it?"

I shook my head, holding my hands up. "No!"

"But Axel's influence was okay?"

"Only because I nearly got you killed."

His smile faded.

"I think you're blaming other people for the way you've felt about Axel since day one."

His words pelted me like a fistful of gravel. "Here we go again."

"You liked him before drinking that potion, and I think you're trying to find an excuse because you can't admit it."

"So you think I'm lying?" My voice carried, but I didn't care. "Also, how many hypotheticals do I need to answer before you get it through your thick head that I don't like Axel, and I'll never like him like that. He's a dumb, smelly monster, and I'm not into him!"

The sound of rustling caught my attention as a devastated vargyr stepped out from around the corner, his head down and his ears off to the side. My heart shattered the moment all the anger drained from me.

"I finished yer bed. It needs a mattress though. I—I got a friend who makes 'em." His voice trembled as he turned away.

"Axel, wait!"

"I should head home," he said, looking up with a forced smile, tears welling in his big blue eyes. "Vince is probably hungry. Been meanin' to hunt today."

He took up the leather straps of the cart and tossed them over his shoulder as he pulled, speeding up when he got close to the road.

"I guess that's one less thing to worry about," Cole muttered, turning the corner toward the front door. "You destroyed the poor guy."

"I didn't know he was there," I said, chasing after Cole. "And you still think I'm lying. I can't win."

"It's better this way." We stepped into the house and took our usual spots on the sofa. "Regardless of what Axel says, this was never going to turn in anyone's favor."

"I don't know why I said it like that."

"Because you're in denial." Cole folded his hands and looked out the window. "I have to admit, the thought of you two together was kind of cute. If the curse didn't exist," he glared at me, "and if you weren't such an ass."

"I'm not in denial. I was mad because you don't believe me about Gar."

"That's because you've been keeping important stuff from me."

"If I were falling in love with anyone, you would make more sense."

Cole let out a forced laugh through his teeth. "Oh, please."

"Are you a mind reader too?"

"No, you're just obvious. You think I don't notice you staring out the window at Axel's camp when he's not there, or how irritable you've been lately when I bring him up in conversation? There's also a different scent you give off when you look at me and when you look at Axel."

"That's the potion."

"It predates the potion, Leo. You and I are good friends who happen to be attracted to one another. There's nothing more than that, and there shouldn't be. You look at me and see someone you'd like to fuck and hang out with, but that's where it ends."

"Do you have to say it like that?"

"Well, it's true, and it doesn't make you any less of a friend. But when you look at Axel, there's more than that. You find him interesting and both of you light up around each other."

"I was never attracted to him, though."

"Maybe not physically, but there was something there." He slapped me on the back. "Vince, one of the biggest idiots when it comes to emotions, knew within five minutes of meeting you."

"How do I fix this?"

Cole shrugged, standing before gazing out the window. "I don't know how much I can really protect you anymore."

"I like him, but he's still a vargyr."

"Too bad there's no cure." The wilkyr paused and scratched his head. "I bet he and Vince were really handsome when they were human. I know Vince was unnaturally attractive as a wilkyr."

"I need to apologize," I said, dragging my feet toward the door. Cole put his hand up to stop me.

"Yes, you do, but not in your underwear."

"I thought they didn't look like underwear?"

"I guess I'm a liar, too. I can see every bulge, outline, and detail." He ran his fingers over the slick fabric. "Where did you get those? They look amazing."

"Axel saw this."

"He probably appreciated the view up until you called him an ugly monster."

"I never called him ugly!"

"It was implied."

"I'm a terrible person," I said as my knuckles hovered over Axel's front door.

"I believe we've already established this."

"I feel bad enough as it is," I said, turning away from the entrance. "What do I say to him?"

"How about 'I love you, and I want to ride you like a wild hyukan.'"

"A wild...what?"

His voice trailed off into the overdramatic. "'But it's not meant to be, for you are cursed, and I am not.'" He pressed the back of his hand against his forehead. "'But if we can't be together, then perhaps we can share one long, sloppy vargyr kiss, my beloved Axel.'"

We both stared at each other without saying a word.

"Are you done?" I asked, biting my lower lip.

"Yeah."

I rolled my eyes and knocked on the front door.

The knob jostled, and the door swung open as Vince stood in the doorway. Judging by his furious expression, he wanted to rip me in half.

"You two gonna keep flirtin' in front of me or come in?"

"You're in a much better mood," Cole said, pushing him aside. "Where's Axel?"

"He ain't home yet. I thought he was over there puttin' that stupid bed together." He glared at me. "Don't know why he's wastin' his time making you shit."

"Because he's been sleeping in bed with me," Cole said, taking in Vince's jealousy with a sense of pride.

"Didn't he say he was going to go hunting?" I asked, derailing the hostility.

Cole turned toward the woods. "Oh, that's right."

"I'm sure he's out there somewhere. Should be able to smell him for miles if the wind holds," Vince muttered, about to close the door when Cole caught it.

"Come with us."

Vince shook his head. "Not with the human."

"My name's Leo."

"Yer name should be bait."

Damn, he was infuriating.

"Then you come with me, and Leo can stay here."

The small vargyr crossed his arms and leaned against the door frame. "You ain't been to see me in about a week. Yer obviously fucking *him* now."

"While Leo is definitely an upgrade, you're still my guy." Cole reached for Vince's face, but the jealous vargyr pulled away.

"It's too cold," he said, turning to saunter back inside.

"Too cold to have some fun in the woods?"

Vince froze. His tail wagged before he turned back around and rushed outside.

"It ain't that cold. Let's go."

"That took a lot of convincing," I mumbled.

"We'll be back as soon as we find Axel." Cole looked around before turning back to me. "Don't leave the house, okay?"

"I'll be fine. Take your time," I said, waving back at him.

Vince tugged on Cole's arm before pulling him into a deep kiss, his eyes wandering to me as he made sure I watched. It was the first time I'd seen a vargyr kiss a wilkyr, and while it was passionate, their mouths didn't quite fit together.

I took that as my cue to step into the house and shut the door. Despite the blanket and a few dirty plates lying around the couch, it was just as clean and cozy as I remembered. After picking up the itchy comforter and shaking Vince's loose fur out, I folded it neatly against the arm of the sofa. The vargyr's scent, thankfully, had no effect, and I wondered if the potion's effects had completely worn off by now.

Balancing as many dirty dishes as I could carry, I brought them to the sink, which was already full of plates and bowls soaking in cold water with a grease film over the top. It seemed even Axel struggled to keep up with Vince's laziness. I drained the sink and ran what I could under hot water.

The front door creaked open, and heavy footfalls slowly made their way inside. There was a wall separating the kitchen and the rest of the house, but I knew it was Axel when his voice called out from the living room.

"Yer actually doin' dishes? What's got into you?" There was a slight nasal quality to his voice. "Wanna come have a drink 'er six with me?"

I turned off the water and dried my hands on my shirt before slinking around the corner. As I stepped into view, the vargyr wiped his face with his arm before clearing his throat.

"Hey, Axel."

"You ain't supposed to be here alone."

"Cole walked me here. He and Vince went out into the woods to look for you, but they probably got sidetracked."

He wiped his nose again. "I wasn't huntin', so I don't got much in the way of food fer ya, but I can go get some. We'll have a barbeque."

I sat on the couch, leaving space for him. "Do you want to talk for a bit?"

"That ain't a good idea. Not with that potion—"

"It's gone," I interrupted. "It wore off, I think."

I expected him to look relieved, but he seemed even more disappointed.

"That's good. One less thing for you to worry about."

"I am so sorry. I didn't mean to say those things about you." I stared at the scratched wood floors, trying to think of a way to put this without making it worse. "I was pissed off because Cole was under the impression that my feelings for you were making me blame Gar."

Axel padded over before sitting next to me, the couch dipping enough to slide me closer to him. The warmth of his body sent a rush of heat to my face, and I tried to push the feeling away. Axel pretended not to notice, but his muscles tensed.

"I guess it hasn't completely worn off yet," I muttered.

He shuffled away, but I grabbed onto his arm.

"You don't have to get up. It's not as bad as last night."

"You sure?"

I nodded.

"Do you really think I'm a dumb monster?"

"No, but I'm apparently a complete idiot." I looked up at him. "I really like you, Axel."

His tail brushed against the cushions.

"You were right about me being smelly, though," he said, folding his hands nervously in his lap.

"You could stand to bathe a little more."

The mood between us shifted into something a lot more familiar and light-hearted.

"This morning, Cole kept annoying me with hypotheticals about you, and I can't stop thinking about them. You're the first guy ever to make an actual bed for me, and I can't give you anything in return."

"That's not why I did it."

"I know. The curse scares me, but I'd still like to get to know you better."

His eyes shimmered. "You sure this ain't the potion talking?"

"I sort of wish it was, so this way I could have something else to blame."

"It don't gotta get physical, Leo." Axel's giant hand slipped over mine. "I'll be happy with bein' friends. We could stand to talk more, ya know?"

His hand snapped away from me, and he let out a gasp.

"What's the matter?" His eyes darkened to red as he stared down at me, ropes of drool dangling from his chin. When I saw that look, all the warmth vanished from the room.

"Leo," he snarled, his body quaking as if it were priming to give chase. "Run..."

I jumped from the couch and backed away, nearly falling over the small table in the middle of the room.

"Something's wrong. I ain't got no control this time."

It happened so much faster than usual, and whether by luck or pure will, Axel clung onto the last strands of his sanity long enough to let me escape. I threw open the door and leaped down the steps, my legs pumping hard as they sprinted toward the dirt road. When an ear-piercing howl rattled the open windows of the house, leaves rustled from all around me. Large figures raced between trees, and more howling echoed from everywhere.

My luck had just run out.

The Anomaly

The pounding in my ears grew so intense that it competed with the howls of the predators hunting me. My chest burned with every rapid breath of freezing air I took in, and I didn't dare look back, despite claws on gravel approaching faster than I could outrun them.

How many were chasing me? Five? Ten? I felt like a mechanical hare on a greyhound track. The beasts approached from every direction, and the only reason I still hadn't been tackled to the ground was because of their aggression toward one another. When one would get close enough to grab me, another would kick or punch him away before taking his place.

Gar had warned that something like this would happen eventually, but the circumstances were too coincidental. Something had lured these vargyrs from their usual evening activities, and the moment they saw me, their eyes flashed red in an instant, like Axel's had earlier.

I made the mistake of looking back to see two of them in a bloody scuffle on the road, not paying attention to the one on the side darting toward me. When he appeared out of the corner of my eye, he bared his teeth, using his hands and feet to pounce from the ground to the trees before rebounding off the trunks, launching himself in my direction. His powerful arms snatched me up like a child, and he threw me over his shoulder. When I gasped a scream for help, all it did was attract the attention of even more of them.

The vargyr carrying me veered off the road and into the woods, but not before two landed on the ground in front of us. The force of the attack caused him to stumble, throwing me several yards before I slid to a stop, sharp twigs and stones rubbing dirty gashes into my skin. Aside from some bloody scrapes and getting the wind knocked out of me, I wasn't seriously injured. Even if I was, there was enough adrenaline to push me to my feet, allowing me to stumble back toward the road.

There wasn't a shred of humanity left in any of them as they fought, snarling and tearing at one another. Going to Cole's was out of the question, and the only one I could turn to was the monster likely responsible for all of this. The town was about a mile away, and I kept up my sprint while trying not to puke.

At last, the road curved toward town, and a strong tailwind whipped up, making running a lot easier. However, as more deafening howls echoed from the direction I was heading, the mystery was solving itself. Was this a latent effect of the potion? Whatever was different about me now turned me into a drop of blood in a tank full of sharks.

As expected, vargyrs from town leaped onto the road with me in their sights as some fell to all fours like animals. They could only maintain that for a moment before they were back on two legs again. When I turned to run the other direction, a few of them that had broken free of the fights earlier had already caught up. Around fifteen of them circled me, each one seemingly daring the others to go first until one finally lunged, setting off a frenzy of teeth and claws.

They snatched at what they could—arms, legs, clothing, anything their claws could hook into. Fighting broke out, and a pain stabbed my right calf as one swiped at the other, catching me by mistake. I fell to the ground, trying to crawl backward, but there was no getting away. They hadn't even noticed I was injured, and all that went through my mind was being mauled to death before anyone came to their senses.

A dark-gray blur tore its way into the circle, prying the fighting vargyrs off of me. The pile of beasts thinned, and I could make out

Axel's face, still wild and distant, eyes glowing that familiar blood red. One by one, he snatched them by the neck, tossing them to the side of the road until there were only three left. When they went to attack, they were met with teeth, muscles and more aggression than I'd ever seen. One flew a good twenty feet into the woods while another doubled over in pain where Axel had rammed into him, shoulder first. The last one standing gave up and backed away, and the rest watched the larger vargyr's movements as he orbited me. No one could match Axel's strength, and once he was on all fours, his nose probed my body.

His warm tongue lapped at the torn flesh of my leg before he lifted me in his arms and dashed into the woods. The red in his eyes flashed to blue momentarily, and he jolted, but the glassy, feral expression returned as bloody drool roped from the corners of his thin, black lips.

When we approached a clearing, he lay me down on the leaves, but the others followed at a distance, their crunching footsteps circling out of sight like hyenas waiting to scavenge the kill. The momentary reprieve gave me a chance to assess my injury. The middle of my calf had four deep gashes in it. Even though I couldn't feel much at the moment, I knew that when this was over—if I survived, the pain would be intense.

Axel's gaze shifted upward, and he shivered as a glimpse of humanity came over him again.

"Leo." His voice wasn't the same. It was slurred as he struggled to get control of his tongue. He was still in there, still somewhat aware of what he was doing.

"Can you hear me?" If Axel was still in there, perhaps a calming voice would bring him out of it. "Remember how to control it? You gotta let your mind go blank."

"Sorry." That word came out in a whine as he crawled on top of me, his claws gently ripping my pants from the front.

What hurt worse than the injuries was knowing the sweetest guy I'd ever met was about to do something that would destroy us both, and he'd do it without being able to stop.

"No," he shouted, pushing himself away while clutching the wild mane on his head. He lurched forward and jerked back, as if he were in the throes of a violent seizure. He howled and screamed before the yellow of his irises dimmed back to red.

He hovered over me, and I didn't bother to struggle. There was nothing I could do but swear to myself that whatever happened next, we were not going to end up like the rest of this miserable town. If I had to be a wilkyr, I'd escape with Axel into the woods as far away from this place as possible. I'd much rather turn into a feral animal after a few years than spend decades being used up until I was nothing more than an exhausted, resentful husk.

"If you have to," I whispered, holding back tears as his snout fell against my neck, "then I'm glad it's you. We'll go sleep under the stars and climb the mountains, just like you wanted."

With that, he pulled back again, his defiant eyes flashing a radiant blue. He clawed violently at his head, moaning and snarling. The episode soon passed, and he reared back, letting out a roar of an emotion I couldn't quite understand.

"We'll climb the mountains," he shouted, shuddering as whatever malevolence that had taken him earlier drained away. "It ain't strong. I'm strong!" He laughed and took me by the hand. "I'll beat down anything and anyone that hurts you."

I dabbed the wet fur around his watery eyes with the long sleeve of my torn shirt.

"I know." Though I didn't fully believe what I was saying, this was the final test. Whatever strength of will Axel had against the curse, I had to rely on it going forward. He not only saved my life, he was in every position to give up. It was so easy. I was injured and helpless.

His forehead pressed into my shoulder as he inhaled through his nose, but he remained resolved.

"I'm gonna get you back home, and then we're gonna have that barbeque."

"I can't go home until I talk to Gar." He stood and reached for my hand, but I looked down at the small puddle of blood in the dirt. "I can't stand up."

He glanced at the injury and nodded.

"We'll go see Gar." He reached down to grab me, and I instinctively flinched. "It's okay. I gotta rip yer shirt."

I pulled the black shirt over my head, letting him shred it into strips of fabric he carefully wrapped around my leg to stop the bleeding. After he finished tying off the makeshift bandage, he examined his work to make sure it was secure.

"I'll get you another one from the dressing rooms. I'm sure Cole ain't gonna mind."

He lifted me in his arms and started toward town, and as more of the fear and excitement faded, the throbbing in my leg got worse.

"Are you okay?" I asked, noting the threatening scowl he still wore.

"I might actually kill him when we get there."

"Don't do that. He's the only one who can fix this."

"I shoulda never let you drink that shit," he muttered before stepping back onto the path. The vargyrs were still around, their glowing red eyes following us from the trees. When I looked over Axel's shoulder, several of them trailed us at a distance. "Shoulda stuck with my gut."

The steep roofs of the longhouses slipped into view, followed by the imposing, black-bricked building everyone in Varcross called the most important place in town. To me, it was an actual dungeon neither the vargyrs nor the wilkyrs could escape. Perhaps that was the reason Gar called it that.

As we neared the door, Axel's foot slammed against it, and the wood exploded inward, ripping from its hinges.

"It's usually unlocked," I said, stroking the back of his neck to see if that would calm him.

"It was an ugly door," he said while stepping over the splintered remains. Even though the sun had begun to set, the place was empty since most of the vargyrs had gone insane.

"What's going on out there?" Gar's furious voice called out from the back as Axel carried me into the dressing room. He gently sat me on the couch before dashing out into the hall. All I could make out after that were choking noises as the huge vargyr returned holding a spindly Gar by the throat, slamming him against the wall.

"Axel, I'm warning you," he sputtered, pounding his fists into Axel's forearm.

"Why?" he asked, his sharp teeth dangerously close to Gar's face. "Why shouldn't I kill you?"

"Because," the black vargyr coughed and tossed me a glance as Axel's grip tightened. "If I die, Leo's done for, and the whole town dies...you might have to...kill Cole."

It may have been a trick of the eyes, but an arcing white light engulfed Gar's hands for a moment before he fell to the floor, gasping for air.

"You're in real trouble this time, you idiot," Gar hissed while rubbing his neck. "How dare you come in here—"

"You think I care about yer rules or this shitty town? You ain't really helping anyone, are ya? Yer just making everyone suffer for longer, like a sick game."

"You know nothing!" He pushed himself from the floor and took a step toward me before Axel went to grab him again. "I wouldn't do that," he said with startling confidence, holding up his hand to stop the huge vargyr. "I smell blood."

"What the hell did that potion do to him?"

Gar actually seemed surprised. "The potion did this?"

Axel's hand caught the back of Gar's neck. "Don't play dumb!"

"Alchemical effects on humans from other worlds...it's all uncharted territory," he said, swatting the hand away. He took a few steps closer and undid the torn shirt from around my leg. "This is nasty. How did it happen?"

"Do you really not know?" I asked, clenching my teeth as he peeled some of the stuck-on fabric away from my flesh. "The vargyrs go crazy when they smell me now."

"I swear, that wasn't my intention, and it was unusually reckless of me to let you imbibe it without my supervision." He grabbed the first aid kit next to the couch that Cole had used the other day. "Since this wound is becoming infected, and you aren't showing any wilkyr signs, I'm going to assume you've managed to evade the curse yet again." He looked up at the ceiling and sighed.

"So this wasn't just some side-effect."

"Yes and no," he said, pulling out a dark bottle and a clean white cloth. As he uncorked the container, my eyes watered from the sulfur-like stench. "The potion was only supposed to make vargyrs irresistible to *you*, not turn the whole town into slavering animals. The fact that you're still human means it failed."

"That's because I was with him," Axel said, his voice dripping with rage. "As long as I'm around, the curse ain't getting him. Makes you angry, doesn't it?"

Gar's eyes narrowed. "I don't know what your secret is. You should have turned feral over a year ago, and now, a human practically throws himself at you and you can't even—"

"What do you mean you don't know? Didn't you also beat the curse?" I asked as Axel cracked his knuckles.

"Look at me, Leo. You've probably noticed something's not quite right about my appearance."

I nodded as he held the bottle of medicine up in front of him.

"When I contracted the curse, I had precious little time to try to counteract its effects. I'd been studying vargyrs in secret for years, only getting as far as being able to concoct an elixir that stops the part of the curse that affects the mind, but it has to be administered within an hour of infection. I didn't know what that would do to my physical body once I made the full transformation, but here I am, still sane but at a cost."

He sat the soaked cloth aside and pulled out another one to wipe the excess blood from my leg.

"No one's ever been able to beat the curse."

"Well, I can," Axel hissed through his teeth. "So don't think you'll be gettin' another wilkyr anytime soon."

Gar furrowed his brows and turned away from the larger vargyr. "I'm ashamed to admit that I underestimated you. However..." He leaned in and sniffed me. "He is giving off one hell of a scent. How did you resist?"

"I just let my mind go blank." He smiled at me.

"So what you're telling me is your idiocy makes you resilient," Gar snapped, picking back up the cloth he'd doused in medicine. "All I wanted was to speed things along. He's going to get the curse eventually, and Cole can't protect him forever. Also, the curse will adapt to whatever technique you've figured out, Axel. I hoped I could make it enjoyable for him, instead of how it usually goes."

"I was in pain," I said. "It wasn't enjoyable."

"The pain was your own doing. If you had listened to your desires and allowed yourself to be taken, that would have gone away. Pleasure, pain; they're the same." He pulled in close and whispered, baring his teeth. "If there's one thing I know how to do well, it's inflicting both at the same time."

Axel snarled.

"He's going to kill you if you keep this up," I said, a bit creeped out by how he said that.

Gar grunted and straightened his posture, moving the cloth above my leg. "This will help close the wound and heal you fast, but I've been told the pain is similar to being set aflame." He tossed Axel a glance. "You may want to restrain him."

"Wait," I shouted, but it was too late. He pressed the dampened cloth onto the open wound, and at first, it was just cold, like rubbing alcohol. That lasted a fraction of a second before a boiling pain raced through my lower and upper leg. Screams tore from my throat, and my muscles convulsed as my back slammed against the arm of the couch.

Axel pulled my shaking torso against him, holding me in place as he nuzzled the nape of my neck. I squeezed his forearm so hard that my fingernails sunk into his fur, digging into flesh as Gar poured more of the powerful liquid onto the wound.

"Yer okay," he whispered. "Hold onto me as tight as you want."

Everything around us, the room, Gar, the pain—all of it faded to a single point until I could only see blue, just like the night I crashed into the tree. Axel was so gentle as he pulled me closer.

Though his eyes gave off a supernatural glow, the longer I stared into them, the more human he seemed. It could have been wishful thinking, but he was different somehow.

"I'm done," Gar said, his pompous tone shattering the mood. "If you both need privacy, there are plenty of beds in the back."

Axel let me go and stood up, towering over Gar. "It drives you crazy, don't it?"

"Your stupidity?" he asked, folding his arms. "Of course it does!"

Neither of them spoke.

"You can't keep fighting this. You will go feral, and then what? You'll turn him, or someone else will." Gar broke away and pulled up a chair before sitting next to the couch. "You want him, Leo. I smell it all over you. Just tell him so this nightmare can end."

"End one nightmare only to jump headfirst into another? You think that life as a wilkyr in this town is better?"

"It's an endless pleasure. Do you think I keep the wilkyrs here against their will? Of course not. They crave it just as much as full vargyrs do, and that could be you. With my potions, I could make it last for as long as you want." He folded his hands in his lap and crossed one leg over the other. "Now, doesn't that sound better than hiding in a house every day, alone?"

"Cole sure as hell doesn't look like he's having the time of his life. Just who are you trying to fool?" I asked, sitting up straight. "I'm not stupid, and I'm not going to let you have your way."

"You think I'm the enemy, but I only want what's best for you and everyone else in town."

"You want another slave," Axel muttered. "You ain't foolin' me, and you never have. I piss you off because you know I don't need yer town or yer *services*. You wanna keep us dependent for some reason, and I'm gonna figure out yer game."

Gar stood and pushed the chair back against one of the wooden tables. "On the contrary, you imbecile, I want us to be free from this place, not roaming the wilds as witless beasts."

"We ain't human no more. This ain't how vargyrs are supposed to live."

"You speak as if this is a natural way to be. Whatever nirvana you're tricking yourself into experiencing out there is not how you're supposed to live." He glanced down at me before turning away. "I'm so close to getting us out of here."

"I thought you were close to breaking the curse?" I said, making him stop in the doorway.

"It's been eight hundred years, Leo. Nothing's going to break this curse, but at least we'll all be free." He stepped into the hall and shut the door behind him.

Axel sat next to me in silent contemplation before finally saying something.

"He scares me. He's small, but somethin' scares me about him."

"He seemed desperate. Did you notice?"

"It was hard to notice anything when I was more interested in lookin' at you."

Though he didn't mean it to come across as funny, it made me chuckle. "You sure lay it on thick."

"Don't know what that means, but you ain't pullin' away." He took my hand in his. "I know we can make it work. If I could control that, I could do anything."

Even after what we'd been through, I was still unsure how to respond.

"At Cole's earlier, I didn't thank you properly. No one's ever made me something so beautiful."

"I loved doin' it. All I could think about for days was you sleepin' comfortable and safe in it." He lifted my chin with his forefinger. "You got such a warm smile."

"You're such a cheese ball," I said, running my fingers through the fur on his hand.

"I miss cheese. Ain't had it in ten years."

He made me laugh again.

"Cole's probably worried sick."

"He'll be here soon enough. There's a trail to follow, and as soon as he sees the blood, he'll come runnin'."

I thought back to Vince kissing Cole. "It sucks they didn't get to spend much time together. I guess this will be one more reason for Vince to hate me."

"He don't hate you. He's just got a real mean jealous streak in him. Don't pay him no mind, though."

I shuffled to the edge of the couch.

"What's the matter?"

"I've gotta pee," I said, rocking to the side.

"Need me to carry ya?"

I put some weight on my leg, but amazingly, there was no pain.

"I don't know what the hell Gar wrapped my leg with, but nothing hurts."

Axel's ears pressed against his head. "He better not have done anything else."

When I stood up, there was a slight throb, but it was merely an odd sensation. Still, I took care not to walk too fast.

"Holler if you need me."

I nodded and limped gingerly out the door into the dark hallway, remembering the path I took the last time I was here.

✦

Gar's voice echoed softly from the other end of the building, and I followed it after flushing the toilet.

"This one you sent is promising."

When he resumed his conversation, I was able to breathe again.

"Have you prepared the ritual as written?" a familiar voice asked as I leaned against the wall, being careful to stay as silent as possible. It was Joe, and he was working with Gar for some reason.

"Until I know how the curse will affect him, I'll not risk wasting more magic like last time."

"He's still human? The other one I sent didn't last a day before the curse got him."

"He didn't have Axel watching his every move."

"I thought you took care of him?"

"I am running out of patience, Josiah, and I can no longer be discrete. I've done what I can by keeping that...anomaly away from the dungeon, but his friendship with Cole puts a damper on that." Gar let out a growl. "Something is happening to him, and it worries me. Everything is unraveling, and we may not get another chance after this."

"You can't let anything happen to that human. I don't know if my body can handle another trip to his world. Your curse is unpredictable with them, but I'm quite sure Leo is the one."

"I made a miscalculation with the other, but I've got eyes on Leo constantly. The moment he contracts the curse, I'll prepare the ritual. The timing is where things get tricky. I don't know how long he will last before everything is complete. Everything has to come together perfectly, or it will fail. I just hope your confidence is not misplaced."

"Your elixirs," Josiah said, his tone a little more desperate than before. "They keep Cole in a halfling state. Can they do that for Leo?"

"I tried that, remember? Curses are unpredictable with these other-world humans, and my potions seem to be a wild card as well. The potion I gave Leo nearly got him killed, and I should have been more cautious. I do not have the time needed to study him fully, and you and I are on borrowed time."

The room went quiet.

"If I need to make another trip, I will. But please, let my sacrifice be atonement for the sins of my ancestors."

"You know the deal. The contract has not yet been fulfilled. Stellous still stands, and I remained trapped in this purgatory, hobbling around in this wretched form. I should make your entire bloodline suffer ten thousand years for every day I have to look at myself in the mirror."

"But the agreement—"

"Is me being merciful," Gar interrupted. "I am still bound by contract and have no obligation to abide by an agreement, but I am making an exception. The treachery I suffered will not be forgotten, and your ancestor's hubris ensured his torment in X'eeva the moment I am free. One cannot seal a Devah away forever, and the imprint of a soul-pact cannot be undone by me or the other deva'kohs. I will see justice doled out as it should be, even if it takes hundreds of thousands of human lifetimes."

Gar's tone reminded me of his earlier desperation, but something was different. He was scared, though there was no way I could know why given how little information I had. All that mattered was that my life was probably in danger.

"I swear, Atorien, you will be free, but please do not forget our agreement. I only wish to atone for the sins that were committed against you."

"You had better hope you got it right this time, because mortals are fragile—you even more so."

The conversation ended in a brilliant flash of light that turned the dark hallway into nothing. I spun on my heels and stumbled forward, feeling my way through the corridor while trying to keep quiet. After blinking a few more times, the haze over my vision lifted, and the dressing room door was a few yards away. I limped through to see Cole and Vince sitting on the couch with Axel, each one wearing a worried look.

Cole jumped to his feet and threw his arms around me.

"I swear, you're like a toddler getting into everything."

"I'm really lucky I have you guys," I said as Vince leered at me, red-eyed with drool stringing from his mouth. "Uh...Axel?"

"Oops." The larger vargyr grabbed his friend by the scruff of his neck, lifting him from the couch like an angry puppy. "I'll take care of this and be right back," he said, dragging Vince out the door.

"So that's what Axel was talking about earlier. Vince was just talking normally a minute ago. I've never seen it happen quite that fast."

I nodded and looked toward the open entrance of the room.

"We need to talk later," I whispered. "And you need to believe me this time."

Welcome Back, Roomie!

Cole lay next to me in bed, and I stared at the ceiling, exhausted but unable to sleep, the events of today replaying in my head. I knew what needed to happen now, and it seemed to go against all common sense.

I turned to Cole and poked him, "You awake?"

"I've been awake," he replied, now looking directly into my eyes. "What's wrong?"

"I probably should go live with Axel."

Cole sighed. "Leo."

"It's not as stupid as it sounds, and after what happened today, I'd feel safer with him. If everyone goes nuts again, you won't stand a chance."

"You should probably give this more thought." Though he seemed apprehensive, he knew I had a solid point.

"I'm thinking of survival, Cole." I lifted my leg and pointed to the bandage still tight around my lower leg. "Axel saved my life. He had every opportunity to give in to the curse, but he didn't."

"That doesn't mean you're safe with him."

"He was literally on top of me, and his eyes were red. Before he lost control, he was able to fight it enough to let me escape. If those other vargyrs hadn't attacked, he would've let me go. I think he may have beaten it."

The wilkyr gave me a glazed look before shaking his head. "Not one person in the almost thousand years this curse has been around has ever beaten it. Axel's really strong, but one day, he's not going to be."

"And if that's the case, what's the difference between me living there or him camping in your front yard? You think a locked door is going to stop him?"

Cole didn't respond.

"There's literally no one else in Varcross I'd be safer with." I turned toward the ceiling again, so I wouldn't endure that anxious stare. "You and Vince need to be together, and I need to see if any of this is going to work out."

"You're in love with him, aren't you? Was I right?"

I shrugged. "I don't know. This feels more like desperation." I looked back at Cole. "If it's not him, then who? A wilkyr? I don't want to be anywhere in the vicinity of Gar."

"I was going to ask you that earlier. Do you know if he did this on purpose?"

"He admitted it." When I said that, Cole seemed to shatter. "I overheard a lot of disturbing shit, and I still don't really know what to make of it all. Gar said he's a Devah or something, and he was talking with the guy that lured me here. Somehow, I'm the key to Gar getting out of Varcross, but I have to be cursed for it to work for some reason."

"A Devah," Cole whispered. "We usually call them demons."

"You don't seem quite as surprised as I thought you would be."

"There've been rumors based on his appearance, but I assumed they were lies. Everyone assumed that."

"Does Atorien ring a bell?"

That time Cole's mouth opened in surprise. "How do you know that name?"

"That's what the mage called Gar."

Something broke in him as his stare turned glassy and hollow. He was so defeated he couldn't even cry.

"I need to sleep," he choked out, turning away. "I'll help you pack tomorrow."

"Alright," I replied, not pressing him further.

Two Days Later

"Are you really sure about this?" Cole asked while helping me pile my bags onto the couch. Today he was in better spirits, though I wondered how much of it was an act. He never brought up our conversation about Gar again.

I slipped my black hoodie over my shirt before giving Cole another hug.

"Yeah. Plus, me staying here is not winning any points with Vince."

"If you're okay with the risk—"

"I know I'm making the right choice," I said, cutting him off. "It's a gut feeling."

"You really do sound like Axel sometimes."

Cole had been unsure about this decision since I told him, but we both eventually agreed that Axel's house was the safest place.

"He won't hurt me." I rested my hand on the doorknob. "And if one day I end up with the curse, we'll just deal with it. I should be terrified right now, but I think I'm dumb enough to actually feel relieved."

"I'm gonna miss my clean house," he said, faking a sob, his forehead resting against my chest. "You know I do have ulterior motives for wanting to keep you here."

"I'm going to miss the way you lighten the mood."

"Leo," he said as he placed his hand on my shoulder, "I'm literally going to be right down the street."

"I know. It just seems like I'll never be able to come over when you're home."

"I'll make time," he said. "And I'll kick Vince out for a bit while you're here."

"I think Vince might be ready to make some changes, and if he's not, you can always turn into that huge monster again and beat his ass until he cleans up after himself." I picked up a couple of bags and opened the door in time to see Axel disappear around the side of the house.

"That is a fantastic idea, except I might accidentally kill him, and then I'll be sad."

"But you'd have a clean house."

Cole grabbed two bags and followed me outside. "Damn these tough decisions."

I popped the hatch of the car and tossed both duffel bags into the back. "When whatever this potion did to me wears off, maybe I can talk to him."

"Ooooh no," Cole clicked his tongue and looked away. "That's not a good idea. Vince sees you as competition."

"Gee, I wonder why?"

He winced. "I only wanted to make him jealous so he'd straighten up, but I did kind of overdo it."

Axel wandered back into the front yard, holding a small black piece of metal.

"Uh, I looked at yer thermal pipe 'cause you mentioned hot water issues, and I—" His ears fell off to the side. "I guess I ain't so good with this stuff."

"Did you break my hot water?" Cole snatched the metal piece out of Axel's hands.

"I'll get someone out here. Don't worry."

"Axel!" He rubbed one of his temples while silently mouthing something I couldn't understand. "I was going to take a nice hot bath tonight to keep from killing Vince when he gets back."

"You can still take a hot bath! You, uh, might wanna let it cool fer about a half hour before you do."

"You broke my *cold* water? How in the hell did you do that?"

His tail hung between his legs. "Don't worry. I'll find someone who knows what they're doin'." He looked over at me and smiled. "You guys need some help?"

"Go grab the rest of the bags off the couch," Cole muttered, pointing toward the door. "And try not to break the couch." He paused. "Actually, don't touch anything but those bags. You can break Leo's things."

"Hey!" I shouted.

"Yes, Cole," Axel said with a heavy sigh, slinking toward the half-open front door. When he got to the top of the steps, he looked back at me and smiled before catching Cole's eye and turning around.

"Man, this is really happening, isn't it?" he asked.

"We'll have to see where it goes, but you were right. I like him."

"So it's your fault I won't have cold water."

"You're blaming me?"

"Damn right, I am. When Axel gets nervous about something, he tries to *fix* stuff to take his mind off of it." He chuckled and leaned against the car.

Axel emerged from the house with every bag in his hands and under his arms, including two sets of straps in his jaws. The goofy way he hobbled down the steps while trying not to drop anything made Cole and me laugh.

"I got these," I said, grabbing the straps in his mouth.

"It's gonna be nice havin' you fer a roommate...again."

"Just a roommate, huh?" Cole asked as Axel's gaze shifted downward. "I already know about you two. Leo can't keep a secret to save his life."

Axel handed me more bags. "You havin' second thoughts?"

It took a few seconds to try to think of a light-hearted response. Instead, I blurted out the serious truth. "Maybe a little, you?"

"No way," he said enthusiastically, his tail springing back to life. "I been lookin' forward to this, but if yer havin' second thoughts..."

After repositioning the last bag, I turned toward him, kind of relieved that he had said that.

"We'll take this slow. Just friends, okay?"

"We'll go as slow as we need." His huge grin nearly cracked his face. "And I love havin' more friends."

We locked eyes for a moment, and Cole cleared his throat.

"Adorable." Axel turned away, and my face burned. "Have you two kissed yet?"

"What part of taking it slow confuses you?" I asked, shoving him away from the hatch so I could close it all the way.

"I'm a wilkyr; 'taking things slow' is an alien phrase to us."

"Well, I'm a weak and fragile human at risk of a mind-altering curse—and possible internal injury. I have no choice."

Kissing Axel—*really* kissing him—was something I had only considered briefly, but the thought of even the slightest bit of intimacy with him sent me into a panic. I warmed up to the idea of possibly having a vargyr boyfriend, but when I thought about everything that entailed, the giddy feelings turned to dread.

Oddly, knowing he could spread the curse gave me some comfort because there was only so much we could do with each other. Healthy relationships didn't need to involve sex, did they? It would certainly be a first for me, but even if we had to remain friends, would that be so bad?

"You guys should do it," Cole said. "Like, right here in front of me."

"What the hell is wrong with you?" I tossed him a disgusted look.

"I meant kiss him!"

"Why do I get this creepy vibe from you all of a sudden? Where did pervert Cole come from?"

"Pervert Cole had amazing sex with his mate interrupted by you being chased around by the town, so I'm just frustrated." He wet his lips and continued. "Call it morbid fascination."

"I'll call it what it is: you being horny, and I wasn't being chased around for fun, you know."

A mortified Axel slunk backward. He hadn't been saying much of anything, and I wondered if I upset him again by being so weirded out at the thought of his long, canine tongue in my mouth. Perhaps I could kiss him on the nose later on to make him feel better.

"I'm gonna get a head start cause I gotta peel Vince off my couch." His tone shifted to annoyance as he mentioned his best friend's name.

"Already sick of him, huh?" Cole asked.

"Naw. I ain't never sick of ol' Vince. He's like a brother to me."

"Leo and I were just saying earlier that if Vince is doing so well at your house, Leo can stay here for another week or so."

"No!" the vargyr shouted, his eyes wide as he backed further away. "He ain't stayin' in my house no more!" His feet hardly touched the ground as he sprinted toward the road, disappearing into the trees.

"Vince finally broke him," I said, pulling open the dented driver's door before sliding behind the steering wheel. "Don't let him mess up the house."

"Don't worry. There won't be many dirty plates left when I smash them over his empty head."

I pulled up to the house in time to see Axel carrying a very pissed-off Vince by the nape of his neck, with the gaming console under his other arm. After cutting the engine, I kept the windows rolled up as they went by, Vince glaring at me with his ears flat against his head like a cat being forced to take a bath.

"I guess everyone's gotta make room fer *him*." Vince's tone was slightly throaty before Axel put him down.

"Come on now. Ain'tcha happy to be goin' back home to Cole?"

"That ain't the point," he said, opening his mouth to say something else, but he looked away instead.

"Then what is it? Ya mad at me?"

"Nobody wants me around. Cole don't want me back, and you didn't even tell me you was kicking me out today."

"I told you Leo was comin' to live with me yesterday. You was playing yer game and said *okay*."

Vince shot me another cold stare before turning back to Axel. "I can't believe, after seein' what Cole and I went through, yer gonna make the same mistake." I cracked the window so I could hear them better. "You're gonna end up just like me."

"No, I ain't. I care too much about him to let that happen."

Silence took them both as Vince reared back and sent his fist flying into Axel's jaw with a loud thud. The larger vargyr staggered backward and held his face.

"Yer sayin' I didn't care?" Vince screamed, tears welling in his eyes. "I'll tell you this only once: what Cole and I had back then was realer than whatever the hell this is. You just met the guy, and you have the balls to talk like you know anything about this. I never loved anyone more in my life than I did Cole, and I never will. What chance do you think you have when the curse takes you too?"

"Vince, I didn't mean—"

"Yes, you did," the smaller vargyr snapped, leaning in closer. "You think yer just too good, that you can't do no wrong. Just wait, though. One day yer gonna be lookin' down at his face when he screams while knowin' you can't stop. You'll want everything to go back to the way it was, but it won't. You get to live with it for the rest of yer miserable life. That smile you keep flauntin' around me? It ain't gonna be there no more. That's what that human's gonna do to you."

"Cole still loves you, Vince." Axel's voice shook as he lost more of his composure. "He don't blame you no more, but yer suckin' the life out of him. You don't know how long he's got, and you ain't makin' his life any better with how you treat him." He stood straighter, towering over Vince while glaring into his best friend's eyes. "I used to care how you felt, but I don't no more. I been makin' too many excuses for you, and that's gonna change today. Go home. Hold onto what you got while you've got it."

"I ain't—"

"Get yer ass home!" His booming voice echoed through the trees like a whip snap, sending black birds fluttering away from the hidden branches. He snatched the gaming console out of Vince's hands. "And you ain't getting this back until you're a better mate."

"You can't—"

"I'm gonna count to three before I start kickin' yer ass down the road."

The smaller vargyr hunched forward, and he turned toward the path, his ears hanging low as he sauntered onward, occasionally looking back.

"And keep that damn house clean!"

I opened the door and climbed out of the car, creeping up behind Axel while he continued staring down a demoralized Vince, his hackles raised.

"I feel just awful," he said with a slight whine, not looking back at me. "I never yelled at him before."

"He needed to hear that from you, though." My cheek rested against his back, and I slipped my arms around his abdomen, not able to reach all the way. "He knows you care about him."

"I love all my friends." He playfully pulled me next to him, wrapping his arm around my waist. "Including you." His sad smile twisted into a slight grimace. "What he said, though…I kinda forget sometimes just how messed up that was for them both."

"I know the risks. Cole didn't fully understand back then, but I do."

"But you don't know how it'll affect you."

"You're right, I don't, but I also know the real you. If you lose control, we'll deal with it. We don't really have a choice anymore because you know what will happen if I stay with Cole."

Axel breathed deeply through his nose and held me a little tighter. We stood together in the front yard listening to the rustle of wind through leaves, and I thought about the few men I'd dated over the years, including my ex. I'd often think that maybe my mother was right. Maybe I'd be happier trying to be someone I wasn't. Anything would be better than feeling so empty—so cheap.

The gentle giant standing next to me was still a man inside, but he was nothing like my ex. Instead of telling me things I wanted to hear, he'd show me real affection without expecting anything more in return. Axel was the type of person who would give someone everything he owned if it meant he could bring them joy. He didn't deserve to be marred by this affliction, and he didn't deserve to be written off because of it.

Axel started toward the front door with me on his arm.

"I can't fit another bed in the house, so I'll sleep on the couch until yer more comfortable around me."

"I'm smaller; let me sleep on the couch."

"You already know how this argument's gonna end," he said with a grin. "Oh! Maybe I can make two smaller beds fer us."

I let out a laugh at how excited he was getting. "How about we see how tonight goes."

"What do ya mean?"

I'd been sleeping in the same bed for a couple weeks with a wilkyr I was extremely attracted to, but we didn't do anything, and it never seemed awkward. If I couldn't sleep in the same bed with Axel without him losing his mind, then what chance did I have sleeping in his bed alone or on the couch?

"If we can spend the evening close together and nothing happens, then let's try sharing a bed."

Pulsing air rushed behind me as his tail wagged.

"No being all grabby this time," I added.

"If I feel anything strange, I'll go away. I promise."

I pointed to the gaming console still under his arm. "What are you gonna do with that?"

"Guess I'll just set it with the LCR. Kinda want to throw it away, though; these things come with warnings for a reason."

"Warnings?"

"They ain't toys," he responded, holding the device up in front of him, giving it a look-over. "The mages designed these to copy real life, but they put you in a fantasy. I think."

"So it's like VR?"

He scratched his head. "What's that?"

"Sorry," I said. "So with the games, you actually feel like you're there, in real life?"

"That's what I been told by Vince. I ain't never fooled around with it, though."

I hummed in contemplation, giving Axel a half-grin. "I think I know how we'll spend the evening."

※

"Holy crap," I said, glancing at the dark, open window on the other end of the room.

The sun was out when Axel and I settled on the couch to give Vince's games a try, but I understood then why the poor guy was so addicted to them. It was much more than virtual reality; in fact, at some point, I could no longer tell the difference between reality and what I was experiencing. I thought the small, fuzzy screen of the LCR wouldn't be enough to draw me in, but the screen did nothing more than display sequences of hypnotic patterns. Before I could even question what was happening, a beautiful world melded around me with different symbols I couldn't read popping up in random places.

Thankfully, Axel could read them, and the place we'd ended up in was only the menu. There were thousands of different scenarios and games to choose from, so we randomly picked one that sucked us in from the start.

"That was fun," Axel said, shifting underneath me as I lay against his chest. "Got kinda sweaty when you poked that Gantabeast, and it ate you."

"That was horrible, but you just respawn again. I'm so glad we didn't feel any pain." I looked over at the window while standing to stretch my legs. "Where the hell did the day go?"

"At least we'll sleep good tonight. Ain't like we got anywhere to be tomorrow." The vargyr let out a loud, contagious yawn as he climbed off the couch.

"You don't work like the others?"

He laughed. "Oh, hell no. I get by just fine makin' stuff to sell every now and then." He waved me over before kneeling to pull a hefty trunk from under one of the end tables. When he opened it, there was a mound of silver and gold coins inside. "This is the most useless trunk 'o pretty shit I've ever owned. The only thing I buy is booze."

"How'd you get all this?"

"When I first started woodworkin', no one wanted to buy anything I'd make, so I'd just sell it to the trade vendor at the Stellous portal. Turns out, the wood I use is pretty damn valuable, and only I know where to get it. Since they wanted more of that soft black wood, and I wanted to practice, I kept selling my failures to the trade guy. Now that I'm good, they're actually paying me top coin for my craft and not just the wood. All the gold I make ends up in here, but I ain't got nothing to spend it on 'cept booze since I ain't allowed in the dungeon no more."

"Jeez," I muttered as he closed the trunk and slid it back under the table. "That's more gold than I've ever seen in my life."

Axel patted my head. "It's all yers if you want it. I don't buy nothin' from Stellous anyway."

"Why not? You could get anything you want."

"Everything I want is already here. I hunt fer my food, and I make my own things. No point in havin' teeth and claws if ya ain't gonna use 'em to feed yerself." He looked back at me and slapped his forehead. "I forgot about food. Humans and wilkyrs don't eat things raw." Axel frowned while shaking his head. "Even Vince don't eat things raw, and I hate washing dishes. Since when's a howler too good to get on all fours and eat dinner off a fresh carcass?"

"Don't worry about that. You do the hunting, and I'll cook it and do the dishes, deal?"

"You got it, buddy." He grinned excitedly. "We got some nice fat caribou outside of town, and the game's pretty easy to come by. There's nothin' that quite describes the feeling of sinking yer teeth into muscle and guts." Drool poured from the corners of his mouth, and he sopped it up with the back of his arm. "We didn't eat today, did we?"

I shook my head. "That sounds, uh, delicious," I said, trying to mask my revulsion at the mental image of him on his hands and knees, gorging on dirt-covered guts. "I've never butchered anything before, though."

"Ya ain't gotta do that, but if you wanna learn, I'll teach ya."

"That...sounds nice."

Axel's left ear fell off to the side, and his smile faded.

"What's wrong?" I asked.

"Ya don't gotta force yerself. We'll find somethin' we both like, and there's all kinds of stuff. We can camp around a nice fire under the stars, and I'll keep you warm." His eyes lit up as he turned toward the hallway. "Oh! You said you liked the ocean, right?"

"I've wanted to go there since I got to Varcross," I said, following Axel into the bedroom.

"I can take you to my second favorite spot. You can still get a decent view of the mountains." He tapped on a lantern near the bed, and it flickered awake.

"Second favorite?"

He pulled down the blanket and paused. "Remember that bad feeling I told you about? That place don't ever seem right. Always creeps me out, but it is my favorite place."

"Oh yeah," I said before sliding into the freshly laundered bed. Axel really had been preparing for my arrival, since everything was so clean. "The monster?"

"It could be my imagination, but I trust my gut. We're built to survive just about anything, and if my gut tells me to run away, I ain't too proud to do just that." The nervous vargyr paused, looking down at me. "Well, sleep tight," he said, turning to leave.

"Axel."

He stopped, his tail betraying him. I could tell he was already expecting me to call him back.

"You sure?" he asked.

"I practically sat in your lap for hours while we played that game. Did you feel anything?"

"Besides comfortable? Nah."

I patted the right side of the mattress.

"Then get over here."

He skipped across the room before pulling down the covers on his side.

"You like the left side of the bed?"

"Oh, sorry," I said, climbing off the mattress. "I didn't even ask which side of the bed you liked. I just assumed since that's how it was last time."

Axel sat down before scooting onto the bed. "And yer right. I always sleep over here. See? It just comes natural to us."

We both laughed nervously, and I shuffled back into bed, settling into the fresh down-stuffed pillows.

"How far are the mountains?" I asked.

The vargyr folded his hands behind his head as he stared up at the ceiling. "Pretty far north, and I ain't been to 'em yet. The furthest north I've gone was to see the ferals. People might think this place is a prison, but it's only a prison if you stay in town. The world's a lot bigger than Varcross."

"Isn't visiting the ferals dangerous?"

He turned toward me, his eyes shimmering with that same excitement from earlier. "Nah. Remember when I told you that I ain't scared of being what they are? There's a reason fer that. I got lots of old friends out there that used to live here. They don't talk no more, but I know how to communicate with 'em without sayin' a word. They still remember me somehow, and they love it when I come out there and hunt with 'em. They let me sleep in their dens until it's time for me to go back home.

"That's why I know goin' feral ain't the end. They're still in there, and they know who I am. They just think differently now, and they look happier without the worries of town or the curse. I hear 'em howlin' some nights when they all get together. Even the ones that go it alone for a while always come back to the pack, and they're always welcome. It's sad that no one but me goes out there to visit, and I don't know why."

"They're scared," I said, remembering what Cole told me.

"Vargyrs don't need to be scared of other vargyrs."

"They aren't scared of the vargyrs. They're afraid of looking at what's going to happen to them eventually. They'll lose most of who they are to be something else."

Axel swallowed hard. "Maybe, but considering the alternative, it's a great way to end up. The humans that get turned sometimes ain't so lucky."

The light mood of the room turned heavy in an instant. I could see it in his eyes: that flash of regret.

"I'm worried about Cole," I whispered, pulling the black blanket to my neck.

"Everyone loves him, and he'll be missed if he turns feral right away. I'll miss hearin' his voice, but I'll visit him like I do the others."

"But what if—"

"Please," he interrupted, his voice trembling as he struggled to hold back tears. "Let's not talk about that."

"I'm sorry." I sat up and rolled over until I was almost on top of him. My fingers traced along the thick fur on his cheeks, my thumbs wiping the tears from around his eyes. "It's sweet the way you care so much about everyone. You have a way of taking the worst things in life and finding the good when other people can't."

His eyes widened as I leaned in closer.

"I ain't that good."

"That's a lie," I said with a smile, thinking back on all the guys I could compare him to. "I want to kiss you, is that okay?"

"Kiss...me?" He whispered those words like someone had sucked the air from his lungs. "You wanna—already?"

"It's just a kiss," I said, holding a finger to his lips. "A small kiss."

I didn't want to think too much about what I was doing, and I wanted to do what I'd thought about earlier while at Cole's. He had to know that I liked him, and I wanted to see if he could handle something small like this.

Axel's breath coated my lips as I pressed them against his, and while the shape of his mouth felt strange, there was still an odd familiarity to it. It was gentle, and it was over fast as I pulled away.

"How was that?"

Axel didn't speak, and I watched his gaze for any signs of discoloration. However, instead of turning red, his eyes glowed a brilliant blue.

"You look worried. Are you okay?" I asked.

The vargyr touched his lips with his fingers and closed his eyes as if he were savoring what we just did.

"Yeah," he whispered. "That was nice."

He opened his eyes again, and we stared at each other, not saying a word. There was a scent that I didn't recognize at first, but it got stronger as the seconds passed. Before I knew it, my lips were pressed against his again, and his rough hand slid up my back as he gently turned me against the mattress. He was timid at first as he looked down at me, supporting his weight with his arms so that he wouldn't crush me under him.

Everything went by in a blur as my tongue slid into his mouth. He soon realized what I was doing, and his own thin, wet muscle eagerly met mine. This wasn't the 'sloppy wolf kiss' Cole had mentioned earlier. It was strong and clean, our tongues slipping easily against the other, Axel's thin and flexible enough to almost envelope mine in a blanket of taste buds.

Though there was a bestial quality to it, the emotions were distinctly human. There really was a man in there, and the beast he was now only enhanced that part of him. The way he kissed me was genuine and thoughtful—vulnerable, yet rough enough to light a fire that sparked a reaction I didn't expect.

He pulled away, his once watery eyes now dry and wide.

"I," he whispered, struggling to find his voice, "didn't think you'd actually do that."

"You're still you," I whispered back.

Axel let out a breath of relief and nuzzled my neck with his cold, wet nose.

"I'm still me," he said, scooting over a bit before pulling me into him.

We lay there in silence, neither one wanting to say anything more, though I wondered how I'd be able to sleep with so much buzzing through me. I couldn't believe I'd just kissed him so passionately. I also couldn't believe how turned on I was after that, but since consuming that potion, was it any surprise?

I kept blaming the potion, but there was a lot more here than physical attraction.

"It's weird how natural this feels," I said as he held me close, every heavy breath rocking me in a steady motion.

"I feel weird," he whispered. "I know the feeling when I hold back the curse, but I didn't even have to try."

"Maybe it's gone."

"I wanna think that, but let's get through tonight. If I don't end up runnin' out of the house, then I know something changed. Nothin' feels the same anymore."

"Is that bad?" I asked.

"No," he replied. I turned toward his smiling face. "I've never felt so...normal."

A rapid knock on the front door jostled me awake. Axel was still asleep, holding me against him, his fur keeping me comfortably warm in the frigid house. I didn't want to get out of bed. Perhaps whoever it was would get the hint and go away, but as the knocking became more frantic, I moved away from the cozy vargyr and threw off the blankets before stepping onto the painfully cold floor. Nothing seemed to wake Axel as he slumbered, despite the racket coming from the living room.

After stumbling half-asleep through the house, I peeked through the window to see Cole with tears running down his face.

I threw open the door and pulled him inside. "What happened?"

He plopped down on the couch, exhausted.

"I'm sorry to wake you up like this, but I'm glad you answered the door and not Axel."

"What's going on?"

"When you told me who Gar was, a part of me didn't want to believe it. But I don't think he's trying to hide it from me anymore."

"Cole," I said, grabbing him by the arms so he'd face me. "What did he do to you?"

"He stopped giving me the potion. He told me you'd know what to do if I wanted it again. I'm scared now."

I pulled him into my arms.

"I'll take care of it."

"How? He's not just any demon, Leo. There's nothing we can do. He's got everyone deceived."

"How much time do you think you have?"

"I get it every few weeks." He shuddered against me. "I've got a week, maybe two."

Even though there were two choices I could make here, Gar threw down his hand. He wasn't hiding anymore, and he was more dangerous than ever.

A Friend In Need

The floorboards in the hallway groaned as Axel stepped through the house, and the back door squealed before clicking shut. I thought about waking him when Cole left, but I'd let him try to enjoy the morning, even if I had to pretend.

Five minutes later, the front door opened, and Axel trotted back inside with the biggest grin.

"Mornin'!"

I noticed something different about him. He stood straighter, with a lot more confidence. His mane was wet in what I assumed was an attempt to style it using the hose outside.

"Good morning. Sleep well?"

"Like a baby. You've got a cute snore."

My chest tightened at that statement. Ben had often told me how cute my snore was when we were first dating only to have it be a source of annoyance several months later. Axel immediately picked up on my mood shift.

"It's just a little snore," he said nervously. "I like it." He stood in the middle of the living room, eying the place next to me on the couch. "Ya mind if I sit next to you?"

"I think after last night, we're past this part."

His ears went from flat to straight up. "Oh, right!" He trotted the rest of the way over to the couch before plopping down next to me.

"You don't think this is too fast, do you?"

"Maybe a little. Last night really shook me—in a good way. But I worry you might have a change of heart if I don't get rid of the old habits."

"Old habits?"

He hesitated.

"I suppose I should start showerin' now and brush my fur."

"Wait, when's the last time you took a shower?"

"Hmm." He looked down at his lap. "I usually go fer swims in the river when it's warmer."

I gave him a sniff, and there wasn't anything too off-putting, but then again, I'd gone rather nose blind to it lately.

"You don't smell bad, and you don't have to change for me." I picked a couple small twigs out of his tail lying between us. "Bathing more often would be nice, but don't worry so much about what I think."

"You sure 'bout that?"

I ran my fingers through his damp mane. "I spent most of the time with my ex trying to change myself to please him, but it was never good enough. If you can't be yourself around me, then I'm not the right guy for you."

He didn't respond to that like I thought he would.

"What's wrong?"

"Just thinkin' about kissing you again."

"How about a little kiss this time?" I asked, leaning close to him. "We've both got some powerful morning breath."

He smiled, lowering himself to eye level, meeting my lips. It was sweet and quick, but no less intense. Either Axel was really good at kissing, or I never really had feelings like this before. Perhaps it was a bit of both.

"How did *you* sleep?" he asked.

"Pretty good, all things considered."

My mind quickly wandered to Cole. Gar held all the cards, and without that potion, it wouldn't be long before he turned. If he went feral or if the worst happened, this little house of cards we built would fall. I'd lose someone who, in such a short time, became my best friend. Axel would probably fall into depression, and Vince would lose the only person keeping him tethered to reality. I could only see one solution to this, but even that was awful.

"Leo?"

"Hmm?"

"Did I do somethin' wrong?"

I shook my head. "What gave you that idea?"

He pointed to his nose. "Yer scared of me still, ain't ya? I can smell that, you know."

"Of course not."

His eyes narrowed as he put more space between us. "Yer not lyin' are you?"

"I'm just worried about things, but I'm not scared of you."

Axel's hand gently fell onto my back. "You can talk to me about the curse. I know it's still a scary thing, but I'm sure I got this under control."

"If I wanted to be a vargyr, would you do it?"

The silence was deafening as the atmosphere of the room tensed.

Axel's eyes widened. "You don't want this."

"If you can control it, why can't I? It's going to happen one day, like Gar said. I'd rather you give it to me."

"No," he snapped. "You ain't bein' honest about something."

"Wouldn't it be better? We could do all those things you talked about last night."

He jumped from the couch and bared his teeth. That was the same look of disappointment he gave Vince yesterday, and that alone made the sick feeling worse.

"Didn't you just tell me I didn't have to change fer you? Do you think that don't apply to yerself?" He opened his mouth to say something else, but instead, he backed away and ran for the door, nearly breaking it.

"Axel," I called out as he disappeared into the trees before the door swung back against the frame, not shutting all the way.

Regret quickly took the place of fear, and as well-meaning as it was, I did lie to him. However, there was a small part of me that wished I could be like him so I wouldn't be so afraid of getting closer.

I stood and grabbed the jar of scent-masking lotion Cole gave me. There was more than enough to last, and I'd need to apply it each time I left the house or risk drawing every vargyr to my location.

After dabbing a little on the places Cole showed me, I waited a minute for the effects to kick in. Grabbing my black hoodie from a hook near the door, I pushed my way outside.

"Axel?" I called out, just loud enough that he'd be able to hear me if he was near. There was no response, and I walked a little further from the house. If Axel didn't want to be found, there wasn't anything I could do but wait for him to return.

"You ain't supposed to be outside alone." Axel's voice came from the branches of the broad, purple tree next to me, its canopy concealing him surprisingly well.

"I'm stupid, and I'm sorry." I scanned the tree. "Where are you?"

"You ain't stupid, yer scared—which I guess kinda makes you say stupid things. I wanna know why you want me to give you the curse." The leaves rustled, and he dropped into view before landing deftly a few feet in front of me. "You don't really want it, Leo." His hand slipped under my chin, tilting my head upward as he stood tall.

"I don't know what to do," I whispered, my vision hazy from watery eyes.

Axel gently caressed my face, wiping a tear away with his rough, padded thumb. "Start by being honest. What's going on?"

I nodded.

"Alright. Let's go inside," I responded, grabbing his hand. "But don't overreact."

Axel leaned against the unlit hearth, his stare distant at first as I explained the situation, but his expression quickly settled into furrowed brows and bare teeth.

"We're backed into a corner now, and getting the curse is the only thing I can do to help Cole, unless you know of a better way."

Axel's jaws snapped shut.

"If I kill him, we'll be free."

"What exactly is that going to do to help Cole? Gar's the only one who knows how to make those potions, and I'll at least have some leverage to trade. My cooperation in return for the formula might be our best last resort."

Axel let out a frustrated groan. "You know how to make potions?"

"Of course not, but there might be vargyrs in this town who know what they're doing. Cole said some of them used to be mages."

He sat next to me, the couch dipping downward under his weight as he settled his hand on my back.

"Gar ain't gonna play nice, ya know. You don't have the leverage you think you do."

"I *am* the leverage. If anything happens to me, whatever ritual he talked about with Josiah won't happen." He remained stoic, and the more I talked about this, the more I started seeing Axel's point. "It's better than doing nothing at all."

"Let me take care of him." His tone had an unsettling candor to it.

"Remember when you told me that something about Gar scares you? There's a good reason for that, and your gut was right. He's a demon, and a really dangerous one according to Cole." Axel's eyes flashed blue, and murderous intent hardened his expression again. "If he can use magic here, he can kill you. Who's going to protect me then?"

"Demons..." He folded his hands in his lap and looked down, but his ears perked up. "I remember somethin' about demons."

"Really?"

He gently tapped the sides of his head with his fists. "Things back then was real hazy cause I didn't spend a lot of time sober, but years ago, back before I met Cole and got reunited with Vince, I had another drinkin' buddy named Silas. He was an older vargyr, and one crazy son of a whore." He chuckled.

"That's kinda mean," I said with a slight laugh.

"No, he actually was the son of a whore. Came up in one of our conversations. Anyway, we got close, and he'd always tell me stories. Most were funny, but some were disturbing. The story that stuck out the most was about a wilkyr mage named Xavier who talked to demons."

"Cole told me about this. He called them something weird."

"Deva'koh," Axel said. "Ain't a lot of 'em left, but Silas told me about all the weird shit he'd heard from Xavier during his trips to the underworld. Did you know some demons get their power from sex? Xavier apparently made a contract with one of 'em to get revenge on his landlord. The demon put a curse on the guy, makin' him fuck himself to death."

Axel snorted, but I didn't find the story particularly funny, given the current situation.

"Cole didn't tell me what type of demon Gar was, but if he's responsible for the curse, it would explain a lot," I said.

"You think he is?"

"It sure seemed that way when I overheard him talking. Cole also mentioned the curse was demonic in origin, so it doesn't take a genius to put two and two together."

Axel was quiet at first, but the realization hit him hard as he scratched his head.

"I suppose that makes sense, especially since he's the only one who never suffered any of the really bad effects."

"So what happened to Xavier? If he could talk to demons, did he know about Gar? Did Silas know?"

"Silas didn't say nothin' about Gar, and no one really knows what happened to Xavier. The story goes, he was up on stage, but he didn't look so good. A few minutes later, he went full vargyr, but turned feral and ran away. That was the last time anyone saw him."

This wasn't much of a helpful recollection, but there may have been something more that was missing.

"Do you know if there's anyone else in town who might know about Xavier? What about Silas?"

Axel shook his head. "No one's seen Silas in years, and that story he told happened over twenty years ago."

"What do you think happened to Silas?"

"Dunno, but probably ain't all that complicated to figure out. Vargyrs go feral all the time if they're tired of livin' like this, and Silas had been in Varcross fer fifty-odd years. Sometimes they just wander out into the woods and don't come back. I never see him when I visit the ferals, so he's probably in a pack farther from town than I can go."

"There has to be someone around here who was close to Xavier."

"Our best bet is Toby, but even if someone knows where he is, he's feral. Ain't gonna get a feral to talk."

"What if it's possible?"

"I've been around 'em for a long time, and I don't think it is. When I talk to 'em, they just stare like they don't understand. They don't think the same way they did when they had human brains."

I jumped to my feet and scrambled toward the front door. "We have a week or two, maybe less. If we don't find any leads or valuable information, I won't have a choice but to do what Gar wants."

"I ain't gonna let you do what yer thinkin', and you've always got a choice. Cole's been my friend for years, and this should be my and Vince's problem, not yours. Remember, that potion ain't a permanent fix. He's had a tail for months, and that ain't natural." Axel rubbed his forehead. "Suppose I give you the curse, and Gar keeps his word and gives you the formula: what happens when it don't work no more?"

"It can still buy us time."

"Yer gonna take this on, and it won't amount to a hill 'o beans. You'll suffer the same thing he's going through, and I'll have to watch you. And if you go blood-crazed—"

"Alright," I said, holding up a hand to stop him. "I forgot about that."

Axel pulled me back into a hug. "I don't wanna lose no more friends, and I don't wanna lose you or Cole that way. If I go through it with him, I don't wanna do it ever again."

"I don't think the curse is as ironclad as everyone thinks. You may be proof of that," I whispered, turning around so I could return the embrace. "And Gar mentioned something about it all unraveling. He's on just as much borrowed time, and that might make him more dangerous."

"We'll go talk to Toby and see where that takes us, okay?"

I nodded. "We need to visit Cole first. I'm really worried about him."

I had expected more vargyrs to be prowling the roads, but everything was so quiet. There were no birdsongs, and even the wind wasn't blowing. Sometimes it seemed we were the only ones around for miles, but I also knew that was far from the case as many were either sleeping or stalking through the woods around the house, hopelessly waiting for an opportunity. There were brief instances of shadows darting between the trees, vanishing before I could fully see them.

The lotion I wore worked to keep most of town away. Despite Gar being a looming presence in our lives, the demon knew how to make things that worked. A few dabs along the groin and under the arms were enough to replace my scent with a strong, turpentine-like odor before all scent vanished.

Axel and I walked along the dirt path toward Cole's house, my hand in his. It may have been too forward of me to offer, but it was nice to have someone like Axel so close. The touch was tender, but still so alien with how rough his palms were. I ran a finger along one of his smooth, hooked claws I once feared, but now I knew they'd keep me safe. There was a strange sense of exhilaration knowing I could now walk these roads without fear with him next to me. However, when I looked over at Axel, his tail slipped between his legs and his body went rigid as though he were nervous about something.

We approached Cole's cabin and ascended the porch steps before I knocked lightly on the weathered door. There was no answer, so I knocked a little harder.

"Maybe they're not home," I said, turning back.

Axel folded his arms and leaned over to whisper in my ear. "I smell Vince on the other side listenin'." He gave me a light nudge out of the way before rearing back and giving the door one loud bang with the side of his massive fist.

There was a muffled yelp from the other side before the door slowly creaked open, revealing Vince rubbing the side of his head.

"Didn't you get the damn hint when I didn't answer?"

"I just thought you was hard of hearin' all the sudden."

Vince kept his posture low, but looked up at his best friend. "You gonna yell at me again?"

Axel stepped so close, their chests touched. "Been cleanin' up after yerself?"

The smaller vargyr huffed and walked back into the living room with us close behind. "Ain't like there's nothin' better to do since you took my games."

"Then I ain't gonna yell at you." Axel pulled an unsteady Vince into his arms before dragging him the rest of the way to the couch. The way he strong-armed his friend was kind of cute, and I could tell they really loved each other. Vince, despite his abrasive personality, had a lot of respect for Axel—probably even more after that discussion yesterday.

"I need to talk to Cole," I said, making my way toward the hallway.

"Leo," Vince mumbled. "I uh, like what you did with the place." I turned to see him staring at the floor while rubbing the back of his head.

"I'm glad."

His demeanor seemed less gloomy. A calm, slight smile pinched at the corners of his thin black lips, replacing the anxious, glassy stares he'd given me the night we met. Vince stepped closer to me and extended his hand, not able to make eye contact. I met him with mine and gave it a shake.

"I still don't like you." He paused for a moment before rubbing his head with his other hand. "But maybe I don't dislike you as much as I did." He let go of my hand and folded his arms. "But I still don't like you enough."

"Apology accepted," I said, turning back toward the hallway. "I like you too."

"I didn't say that, and I sure as hell ain't got nothin' to apologize to you for." His footsteps started toward me, but stopped abruptly when Axel grabbed him. "Hey! Ya ain't invited in our bed no more now that I'm back. Keep that little dick to yerself."

It was a brief victory, and I had to take those when they came. Especially dealing with Vince.

After giving the bedroom door a few knocks, I cracked it open. "Cole?"

There was no response, so I tiptoed into the room, shutting the door behind me. The wilkyr lay on his stomach, his right arm tucked under his pillow. He seemed peaceful at a glance, but the tear stains along his cheek told a different story.

I sat on the mattress and placed a hand on his broad, hairy arm. "I'm here."

He snorted and cleared his throat, letting out a light groan as he pushed himself upright.

"Everything I thought I knew…" He trailed off, leaning back against the headboard. "I thought Gar really cared about me—about all of us."

"I know," I said, scooting closer to him, but he shuffled away.

Cole examined the longer claws protruding from his fingers.

"You're not going through with it. I wouldn't be able to live with myself. Even if you bought me more time, I'm still going to turn soon. Every week, urges get harder to control. My body is screaming for release because it wants to change, and there's nothing anyone can do about it."

Cole swallowed hard, and his watery, amber-colored eyes were so empty. He had already given up before we started, but I couldn't exactly fault him for that. His entire world turned against him without warning, and I understood that hopeless feeling well.

"I don't want your help if it comes with knowing you're going to end up like me. If we're born human, the stakes are too high, and this is not a fun thing to go through. You and Axel should get as far away from town as possible and leave me to whatever happens."

"You already know I won't do that."

The wilkyr let out a sigh. "Yeah, I know, but I had to say it anyway."

"I'm also not going to do what he wants," I added.

Cole wrapped his arms around me. "Thank you."

"That still doesn't mean we're leaving."

"You're really going to be stubborn about this, aren't you? You're just like Axel."

"You know that's a compliment," I said as he pulled away. "There's got to be a way to beat this. Axel's proof of that."

"There is no proof. We don't know as much as we think we do."

"Have you noticed the difference in—"

"Axel can still turn on you. I hope it doesn't happen, but don't be surprised if it does. I don't know how he controls himself for so long, but I know what happens when too much time passes. He gets violent during sex when it happens."

"Cole, you're only twenty-eight, and this isn't the end of your life. If Gar's the demon that was contracted to create this curse, then he knows how to reverse it."

"I didn't get very far in magic, but what I do know is once a demon's curse has been unleashed, even the being who created it can't take it back unless his or her contract is fulfilled. It's why deva'kohs were feared so much throughout history."

"Axel said there was a deva'koh in town years ago, but he went feral. There may be more to the story, and Toby might be able to give us information."

"What is that going to do? You already sound like you've given yourself false hope instead of thinking about this rationally. Deva'kohs are secretive and hard to find. And even if there are some in town, none of them will be able to use magic or make a pact with Gar to stop him."

"True, but if they find out that he's a demon, they might give us some insight into how to handle him without magic."

"That's a reckless idea. Don't tell anyone what Gar really is, because as far as he knows, we don't know. If we back him into a corner, there's no telling what he'll do." He scratched his head and let out a quiet hum of contemplation. "This is all so confusing, and there are more questions than we'll ever likely get the answers for. The biggest mystery is how a demon ended up in this place, especially Atorien. These are lords of their realm, way too crafty for most mages to handle. The only time they ever get *trapped* anywhere is if that's what they intended. Plus, the only ones with the magic to seal such a powerful being away are powerful deva'kohs. Given what you overheard, I'm guessing Josiah's ancestors must have played a part in sealing Gar in here."

"I thought you didn't know that much about this stuff?"

Cole smiled. "I said I didn't get very far with magic, but I studied as much as I could where I was allowed. I probably wouldn't have made it as a mage, even if Vince hadn't done what he did, but it was a fun dream." He scooted toward the edge of the bed before standing. "Let's go to Toby's."

"Feeling more optimistic?" I asked.

"No. I'm just curious now."

The door flew open, and Vince jumped into the room.

"Ah ha!" He paused and closed his mouth as Cole and I stared at him.

"Well, go on," Cole said. "What were you going to say?"

The small vargyr's tail slipped between his legs. "Nothin'. Just wanted to see if you both needed anything."

Footsteps stomped quickly through the hall, and a burly arm reached in before wrapping around Vince's neck, pulling him out of the room before Axel peeked in. "Sorry, had to pee, so I wasn't watchin' him." He disappeared and the door slowly shut against the frame.

"His jealousy's made him way more attentive. It's nice."

"Axel's still holding his video games hostage, which might be helping as well."

"Damn, I love that big guy." His eyes widened. "Oh! We never did get to talk about last night. Seeing as how you're still human, I take it everything went okay?"

I nodded. "We played Vince's video games for hours, and then we talked for a little while in bed." That serious look returned to his face.

He sighed and shook his head. "You're a grown-ass man, and you know the risks. I don't need to keep beating you over the head with it."

"We kissed, Cole."

His mouth opened wide. "Already?"

"I don't know what came over me. It wasn't some little peck on the cheek either, and I'm still not sure how to feel about it."

"And he didn't do anything to you? Even after that?" Finally, there was a bit of optimism to his tone. "How long was this kiss? Tongue? Slobber?"

"It was *really* good." The skin on my face flushed as I relived the moment in my mind. "I was so turned on. Sounds gross, doesn't it?"

Cole grinned, this time with a lot more relief. "Maybe Axel did beat the curse, and you get to embrace that forbidden vargyr love. He's good, isn't he?"

I nodded.

"I don't know where the hell he learned to do that. We've kissed a few times, and he knows how to use his tongue better than any other vargyr I know." Cole leaned closer, whispering into my ear. "He's a better kisser than Vince. Don't ever tell him I said that because I *will* deny it."

"Don't worry, I'm probably the last person he wants to talk to."

Cole turned the doorknob and stepped out into the hallway. It was good to see his usual personality shine through again.

"Give him time. He'll come around."

Monster By The Sea

"Are you insane?" Toby shouted as I followed Axel into the pub. Cole and Vince slowly made their way in behind us, looking around at the remains of broken tables and chairs. "The whole town lost their damn minds the last time he was anywhere close. Everything's destroyed." His voice cracked as he glanced over at a pile of ornate ceramic shards swept into a dusty pile in the corner. "My beautiful steins are all gone."

He pointed to the crooked boards hastily nailed to the windows as sunlight poked through inch-wide cracks. Deep claw marks wrapped around pillars while also ruining the intricate runes along the walls, some of them punctuated with blood spatters.

"He ain't gonna make anyone crazy now."

Toby gritted his sharp teeth and threw open the half door separating the back of the bar from the rest of the pub.

"He's supposed to be your responsibility, right?"

"Actually," Cole cut in. "He's mine."

Toby's ears fell to the sides of his head. "Well, I'm blaming Axel." He snapped his attention back to the larger vargyr. "You were the first to bring him here, and you're not getting another drink until you pay for everything."

"Don't worry; I'm good for it."

"Yeah, sure you are." He pointed at me. "*He* should be the one to do it. One night in the dungeon would replace everything and get me a month's supply of goods from Stellous."

Axel grabbed the thick fur on Toby's chest. "Don't ever suggest that again." Blue flashed in his eyes before he regained his composure, releasing the now furious barkeep.

"That does it!" Toby roared, shoving Axel back.

"I'm sorry. I didn't mean to do that."

He held his clawed finger to Axel's face. "You come into *my* destroyed bar, and you threaten *me*?"

"I—"

"Get out! All of you! None of you are allowed back—except Cole."

Axel's posture slumped forward, and I carefully approached Toby, who snarled at me.

"I didn't mean for this to happen." He ignored what I said, still gesturing to the door. "How much is it going to cost to replace everything?"

"A lot. All those steins alone were worth about a platinum."

I turned to Axel. "I've got platinum."

"Sure, you do," Toby said with a sarcastic laugh. "You're both the richest bums in town."

"Where did you get platinum?" Cole asked, but before I could answer, Axel interjected.

"I'll pay." He darted across the room and threw open the door before looking back at Toby. "I got somethin' that'll—"

"So help me, Axel, if you come back through that door with more ugly shit you made, you're done."

"Don't worry," Axel said before disappearing, the door slamming loudly behind him. It cracked and hung slightly off the hinges. "Sorry! I'll pay for that, too," he shouted from outside.

"Do you mind if we wait here?" Cole asked. "You don't have to worry about Leo causing trouble."

I opened my mouth to object to that, but Cole gave me a look I'd come to know well over the weeks. We were all on a tight wire with Toby, and he was the best chance we had for information.

The barkeep turned to me, his snout inches away from my neck as he drew in a deep sniff.

"Well, he doesn't stink anymore. Fine." His demeanor softened when he turned back to Cole. "Do you want a drink?"

"I could really go fer one." Vince salivated as he pointed at the two kegs behind the bar. "Is that yer new stuff?"

"You're not getting shit. Did you forget your little bar fight a few weeks ago?"

"Now you know fer a damn fact I didn't start that one."

"You threw the first punch. I'm old, not blind."

"He called me short."

"You ARE short," Toby snapped. "You're the puniest one here, and you need to know how to handle yourself better. I've told you over and over, they're just trying to get a rise out of you 'cause it's funny as hell."

Vince looked away and huffed.

"How about just one cider?" Cole asked, his seductive eyes working Toby over.

"You can't keep covering for him all the time."

"Please? I'll pay for the damages Vince caused." He walked his fingers along the side of the bar. "You know you're my favorite client."

"You're awful," Toby muttered, grabbing a wooden cup from the shelf.

⛧

Axel's heavy, ornate trunk slid across the bar toward Toby.

"This is everything I've earned in seven years. It's yours."

The silver vargyr shot Axel a wary stare before opening the trunk. "How in the…" He trailed off, running his fingers through the coins. "This is a hell of a lot more than seven years of work, and you don't even do anything!"

Vince belched, pulling everyone's attention to the slightly intoxicated vargyr who was on his third round thanks to Cole's sweet-talking.

"What?" Vince asked, nearly falling off the stool.

"I do a lot more than ya think, Tobes." The barkeep growled, and Axel's ears fell. "I mean, Toby."

"This is too much."

"It's not just fer the damages," Axel said.

"Now I really don't want all of it."

"It's not like that," I said, speaking up for the first time since Axel left to get the trunk, but I was met with a dismissive snort. "Hopefully you can give us some helpful information."

"Why are *you* talking to me?"

"Come on, Toby," Cole said, snatching the cup away from Vince when he burped again. The smaller vargyr went to say something but stopped when Cole bared his teeth. "There was nothing Leo could have done to prevent this. This could have been a lot worse, you know."

Toby closed the trunk and pulled it behind the counter.

"He's living with Axel now, and everyone's pissed about it. Half the town got pretty banged up, and no one knew what happened. I was in the woods naked, and the last thing I remembered was a smell."

"Can't smell nothin' no more," Axel cut in.

Toby slammed his palms against the bar. "If he's going to live in this town, he needs to be a wilkyr!" His eyes widened as he glared at me again. "He's dangerous! I've never seen a human turn everyone within smelling distance feral all at once. What if the next time it's permanent?"

"It's why we're here," Cole said calmly. "A potion Gar gave Leo had an unfortunate side effect, and now we need to ask you some questions since you know everyone pretty well."

"And you don't?" Toby sneered. "You get more business than I do."

"Really, Toby? You know damn well my job isn't social."

The silver vargyr lowered his head. "Sorry. That was out of line. What do you want to know?"

Cole looked over at Axel and nodded.

"You remember a wilkyr named Xavier?"

"There are four Xaviers in this town. Be more specific."

"He was a crazy deva'koh. Went feral years before I got here." Though Axel tried to keep his tone soft and posture low, Toby's hackles were still raised from earlier.

"Ah, yeah, *that* one." The older vargyr rolled his eyes. "I hated the guy. Why are you asking me about him?"

"Toby," Axel said, laying his head on the bar. "Please stop what yer doin'. I don't want no fight, and I didn't mean what I did earlier. Yer my friend, okay?"

The barkeep put his hand on the submissive vargyr's head, and the fur that stood rigid on his neck moments ago fell back into his bushy mane. This was a curious interaction, and it added a layer of unspoken communication between them. Though everyone in Varcross tried to hold on to their humanity, they couldn't escape the instinct that seemed to dominate their social hierarchy.

"Alright," he muttered. "Get off of my counter; you're drooling on it."

Axel smiled and lifted his head.

"You know anything about him? I only heard stories, and I need to find someone who knows more about him than I do."

Toby scratched at the thicker fur on his face. "All the wilkyrs he worked with are vargyrs now. Derrick was the one he was closest to. They were...mates." He chewed on his lower lip when he said that.

Axel turned to gauge Cole's reaction, but he shrugged in response.

"Ain't heard of no Derrick," Vince slurred, pointing to a small keg on the floor that was almost out of sight. "Oh shit. Is that what I think it is?"

"No!" Toby shoved the keg the rest of the way under the bar with his large foot. "And you're not getting anything else today."

"C'mon. Axel just gave ya a lifetime of gold."

"*Axel* did." He glanced at Cole and gave a sly smile. "But I might be persuaded to give you free booze if Cole tells me you're done being a sad, worthless sack of shit."

Vince's tail wagged as he stared at his mate expectantly.

"He's been good to me these last couple of days." Toby grabbed the wooden cup and started to fill it when Cole stopped him. "But..."

Vince let out a high-pitched dog whine. "Come on, babe. It's free booze!"

"I've got conditions."

"Anything you want, I'll do it."

"You know that thing you did last night, and remember where you did it?"

"Oh…" Vince's tail batted the stool. "Is that it? I can do that any time. I can do it right now on the bar if you want."

"The hell you will," Toby snapped.

"You're gonna do that all the time now. You're also going to treat Leo better, and you're going to keep the house clean."

"Deal," Vince said, licking his lips as Toby slid a full cup in front of him. He went to lift the cup, but Cole placed his hand over the top.

"Don't just say 'deal' and be done with it. Look me in the eyes and promise me."

The smaller vargyr leaned in and slipped an eager tongue into Cole's mouth before backing away. "I promise."

"Alright then," Cole said, removing his hand, and Vince slammed the cup back, gulping the entire thing.

"Does Derrick still come here? I ain't never talked to no one with that name." Axel sounded more serious as he moved the conversation forward.

"He hasn't been back in about a decade, and he wasn't the same after Xavier went feral. He started spouting nonsense about demons to anyone who would listen. The last place he lived was in a cabin close to the beach."

"All alone?" Axel asked, taken aback by the revelation.

"Yeah. That's what happens when you fuck around with deva'kohs," Toby growled. "Sane vargyrs can't live alone like that. So either he went feral, or something else happened to him. I stopped caring a long time ago."

"You sound like you knew Derrick pretty well," I said, but jumped when Toby hit the counter with his fist.

"This is the last I want to hear of his name. Got it?"

I nodded, hesitant to ask the next question.

"Do you know where on the beach his cabin was?"

"I'm not a damn map, human," he said, throwing a dirty dishrag into the sink behind the counter. "If you guys want to find that cabin, your best bet is to take a hike." He pointed to the door. "And I mean that literally. Get the hell out of town before everyone goes crazy again."

Axel nodded, leading me by the hand to the door. As we stepped outside, we caught a few wandering vargyrs off guard. They froze before scrambling away.

"Damn, ain't that a switch," Axel said with a laugh.

"I don't blame them. The way Toby explained it, they could have probably killed each other because of me."

"C'mon babe, just one more." Axel and I watched as Cole pulled a stumbling Vince from the pub by the arm. "I ain't had a good drink in weeks."

"Fine. If you wanna stay, we'll just go without you." Vince rubbed his hands together and gave the group a drunken salute before climbing the steps back to the pub's entrance. Cole hooked my right arm in his. "At least I know Leo cares about me."

My jaw dropped as I felt a glare bore a hole through me from Vince's direction.

"That ain't fair," he growled, scuffing along the gravel toward Cole with his ears back against his head before pushing me away.

"We should leave now," Axel said, shielding his eyes as he examined the position of the sun. "We don't want to be at the beach too late in the day."

"What exactly are we going to be looking for?" Cole asked. "Even if we find his cabin, what then?"

"Derrick definitely knew about Gar, so there might be something there that'll point us in the right direction," I replied.

"You're makin' a lot of dumb assumptions," Vince muttered. "I don't like you gettin' Cole's hopes up while draggin' us all around creation like we got all the time in the world. I agree with Toby. You need to be a wilkyr so Cole can get some rest."

Cole slapped Vince across the maw. "Stop that!"

"Babe—" Vince whined. "You know I'm right. I don't wanna lose you yet, and payment for yer potion's standin' right there."

"I'm not in the right state of mind to have this argument." He pointed west. "Let's go to the beach and see what we can find. It's better than sitting here waiting for the worst."

I tapped Axel's shoulder. "If you get that gut feeling, we'll turn back," I said. "This isn't worth it if something eats us."

"Eats us?" Vince asked, his squinty eyes a little wider. "Just where the hell are we goin'?"

"Don't worry about it," Axel said, rubbing the smaller vargyr's head.

"Now I'm even more worried about it!"

We spent hours wading through dense, prickly brush, Axel and Cole groaning every time Vince opened his mouth to complain. The strange lichens on the boulders at the base of the hills glowed red when the sunlight hit them. There were so many different trees along the way, but I wouldn't have been able to name any of the species. Some looked like the familiar pines and firs I was used to, but others were different versions of the knobby purple trees of Varcross. The most stunning were the fat-trunked evergreens with enormous canopies that stretched three times wider than the tree was tall. They kind of reminded me of baobabs.

Sea spray filled the air, and I'd been smelling brine for the last half hour. The distant crashes of breaking crests followed by moments of peace painted a serene picture in my mind. The familiar screeching of seabirds caught my gaze as they flew overhead.

"We have those on Earth," I said, pointing skyward as the birds disappeared. "We call them seagulls."

"In this world, we call 'em annoying," Vince muttered. He held hands with Cole and was surprisingly quiet now that he had sobered up.

Axel gave the air a few quick sniffs. "Still ain't got nothin'," he said, pointing his nose windward.

"The coastline is pretty big, so we should probably split up. Vince and I'll head south, and you guys go north," Cole said, pushing a low-hanging branch out of the way. "If either of us sees anything, we'll howl. Well, Vince and Axel will howl."

"What if we're too far away to hear you?" My question prompted an expected jeer from Vince.

"Then you won't hear shit, will ya? We will, 'cause we ain't pathetic."

"Heh, right," I muttered, looking at the ground. "Guess I'll leave it to Axel."

Cole's elbow rammed into the smaller vargyr's ribs, eliciting a whine.

"Did you forget the deal already?"

"Sorry, babe." He turned to me. "Sorry...Leo," he said through his teeth.

Axel pushed ahead, snapping limbs out of the way as I continued along the trail behind him, but he stopped and turned toward Cole. "Only stay to the south. Oh, and Vince?"

"What?" the smaller vargyr asked, picking briar thorns out of his tail.

"If you smell anything weird while yer out there, you both turn back. Got it?"

"Why're you lookin' like that? Is there somethin' out there? Is this about what you said earlier?"

"I dunno."

Vince shook his head and backed away. "Fuck that. I ain't splittin' up if something's scaring *you*."

"Just be cautious, and you'll be fine. Trust yer gut."

"Come on, coward," Cole said, pulling a reluctant Vince in the opposite direction. "Is a big, strong vargyr like you afraid?"

"I ain't big, and I ain't that strong," Vince muttered.

Cole pointed to my backpack. "Do you have your lotion?"

"Yeah," I said, unzipping the front pocket to double check.

"Keep a nose on Leo, Axel. If you can smell him, anything can."

"Don't worry, he'll be safe with me."

What started out as an exciting adventure into the unknown now felt like a family day trip with two worried parents and a sibling who hated my guts. I kind of wished I was a vargyr just so that I'd feel more included and not some burden everyone was obligated to babysit.

As Axel and I continued west, the grass disappeared, giving way to rockier ground littered with empty mollusk shells. He stopped near a clearing and turned toward me, his eyes brightening with his smile.

"I can't wait for you to see this." He held his hand out, and I grabbed it, taking my place next to him as we continued toward the sounds of waves crashing into rocks.

The sunlight blinded me, but after my eyes adjusted, a sparkling, endless blue stretched into the horizon.

"Wow," I whispered, catching my breath as I scanned the shore, looking north along the gray granite cliffs. The land bowed into a bay of snow-capped volcanic peaks far in the distance, taller than I'd ever seen. What the ocean hadn't gobbled up, the vast mountain ranges dominated.

I'd never taken a moment to really look at the sky in this world, since I spent most of the time inside a house or in areas shrouded by thick trees. The sun seemed smaller than it was on Earth, and the sky was a darker shade of blue. It had a rich, sapphire hue and the bright, smaller sun barely made a difference. Even as beautiful as Colorado was, there was nothing there that could rival this scenery. No haze lingered in the air, and I could almost see for tens or maybe even a hundred miles.

"Pretty, aint it? This here's my secret spot."

I turned to Axel, his eyes shimmering in the light reflected from the sea below.

"I've never seen anything like this."

"Not a lot of people have. Now you know why I want to see what's really out there. There's a whole world like this: beautiful and untouched." He squeezed my hand. "One day, I wanna take ya—just you and me. We'll go far away where we ain't gotta worry about the curse. We'll get to see things we ain't ever seen before. All I been waitin' for was someone to see it all with; that is, if you ever wanna take a chance with me."

"That sounds scary," I said as we continued along the cliffside, following the sloping terrain down to the shore. "If something happened, it would just be us."

"Look at me," he said, puffing his chest out. "What have you got to worry about? I could take care of you real easy out there. Huntin' ain't nothing to me."

"What if I get sick or injured?"

The excitement he exuded moments ago faded. "I traveled all over my old world, but there was always a portal somewhere close. It never felt big because you could go just about anywhere in the blink of an eye."

"Is your old world as beautiful as this one?"

"It's got its pretty parts, but there's also a lot of people. Everything's been explored, from the highest mountains to the deepest oceans. Even the most remote places have people livin' there. Everywhere I went to see was owned by someone. Was it beautiful? Yeah. But I didn't get to enjoy it.

"Here, the world feels big because there ain't no magic to take us anywhere we wanna go. There's no people, so no one owns anything. And no one's been too far from Varcross, so nothin's been explored. When you have to work to get to where yer goin', it makes the destination all the more worth it."

We neared the frothy water as it lapped and swirled along the jagged shore, some of it soaking my shoes as it washed further in than I was expecting. Though the air had a chill to it, the water was strangely warm.

"We don't have portals or magic in my world, but we have cars like the one I drove here. Oh! And we can fly on planes."

"Humans fly in your world, too?" His jaw dropped when I nodded. "I always dreamed of being up there in the clouds."

"Why didn't you fly?"

Axel shrugged. "Was always too poor. Have you flown?"

"A few times," I said, eying something small and black further up the shore. "What is that?" I asked, walking a little faster, but stopped when Axel pulled on my arm.

"Let's go back." He gave the air a few rapid sniffs, the fur on his mane sticking straight out.

"Is it that feeling?"

"That's a dead garvok," he said, pointing to the black mound lying still on the rocks. "They're delicious, but something ripped it apart without eating it."

Thick brush rustled further inland, the noise vanishing in one spot, only to rustle again ten or fifteen yards away almost instantly. Whatever was out there was fast—impossibly fast.

We stayed still, neither of us making a sound as Axel's head followed something so quiet that I could no longer hear it. The vargyr gave the air another sniff and pushed me behind him, his eyes scanning the forest's edge. A black blur tore from the woods, and Axel shoved me away before running head-first into the beast. As it flew into my line of sight, it appeared to be a vargyr, but he was different from the others.

He had a slight hunch and ran on four legs, his eyes black with two beads of glowing crimson in the centers. Even the simplest living creature had something in its expression that gave it life, but this monster seemed hollow, almost dead in a way.

Axel tackled the monster, but was bucked back by unusually powerful legs as it righted itself, its feet digging into the sand for leverage as it lunged back toward the other vargyr. It wore no clothing, and its fur was so matted and filthy I could smell the fetid stench from yards away. I was powerless to intervene as I watched them go at it, blood splattering from both as they tore into one another, their movements so rapid my eyes couldn't keep up.

It was then I heard Axel's gargled howl of pain as two-inch-long claws raked across his chest and down his abdomen.

"Axel!" I screamed as the beast shoulder-rammed him into a tree, his body going limp after sliding to the ground. My feet moved on their own as I ran toward them both before leaping into the air and landing onto the monster's back. With one arm around its neck, I braced it with the other, squeezing as hard as I could to choke it.

It pulled away from Axel, reaching to claw me off, but I held tight. If I lost my grip, I was dead for sure; however, as it bucked and slashed at me, it became all too apparent that all I was doing was pissing it off more. The beast turned, and I got a good look at Axel lying on the ground unconscious, blood oozing from the deep gashes along his chest. I wanted to help him, but I was too preoccupied with struggling in vain against this creature. I had no exit strategy here, and eventually I'd be too exhausted to hang on.

The monster froze and sniffed the air, his posture now upright and rigid. He could smell me, which meant the lotion had worn off at either the most opportune or terrible moment.

As if the creature was regaining some of his senses, he grabbed my legs, which were locked around his waist, and pulled them before shaking like a wet dog. I lost my grip and dropped to the rocks, the hard fall knocking the wind out of me. Without giving me enough time to gasp, his powerful, dirt-caked arms tore me from the ground and tossed me over his shoulder.

⁂

Each slam of my fist against the tall but slender vargyr's back did little more than elicit a grunt as he continued along the path toward wherever he was taking me. Eventually, I had become too exhausted to keep struggling, and I let myself go limp against him.

Was this what feral vargyrs were like? This creature wasn't at all how Axel described them; however, as with any other of his more aware kind, he was still driven to spread the curse despite his more bloodthirsty nature.

After another few minutes, the vargyr halted and dropped me to the ground, which thankfully was softer than the shore was. The monster's huge hand pressed against my abdomen to hold me in place as his nose probed my chest before wandering to an armpit. The cold, wet sensation against my skin was replaced by a warm, wet one as his tongue lapped, spreading thick saliva along the side of my torso to my back. That combined with his horrible smell made me retch.

I stayed focused on those knife-like teeth now inches away from my neck, still tinged with Axel's blood. His stale breath hit my face with every pant. All he did was stare at me, and I wondered if there was a part of him that was in any way intelligent. Now that I could see his face better, he had the same features as others of his kind, though his facial fur was longer and matted like his mane.

"Can you understand me?" I whispered, my lips shivering as his snout drew closer. "If you ca—"

His clawed hand gripped my pants, and his maw traveled downward. It was worth a try, but the beast was too far gone. His claws ripped at more fabric, as if by instinct, and I crawled backward before kicking him in the face. I soon regretted that as he roared and lunged forward with all of his weight.

A burning sensation registered as a wetness dripped down my forearm, and my muscles spasmed as rows of nasty teeth tore into my upper arm. I screamed, trying to push his massive head away, but he held firm. A howl erupted from the trees, and the wild vargyr released me and lowered to all fours, as if preparing to fight. Axel leaped from the brush, going airborne before landing on the creature.

With incredible agility, the black vargyr slithered out from under Axel's grasp, leaping backward before standing upright. Although he was still fast, there was a sluggishness I noticed right away. The blackness around his irises lightened, and the redness of his pupils dimmed. The beast snarled, but Axel stood his ground, preparing to go all in as he lowered himself to a pouncing position.

The gashes in his chest and abdomen had closed, and all that remained was blackish-red blood that had dried into his gray fur. As his clawed feet dug into the dirt, he took off toward the monster, but the other vargyr darted away, disappearing into the trees.

Axel started after him, but my cries of pain halted his pursuit.

"Oh no," he whispered, dropping to his knees next to me. "He got ya good, but you'll be okay once I stop the bleeding."

"This really hurts," I said, groaning as Axel ripped my hoodie away, shredding it. Given the pain I was in, I wasn't about to protest him destroying my favorite article of clothing. With a quick jerk, he tore away the shredded sleeve of my shirt and wrapped a makeshift tourniquet under my arm and over my shoulders, tightening it into a knot that made my already cold arm go numb. He then wrapped the puncture wounds in the rest of the cloth before lifting me off the ground. "I gotta get ya home."

"You saved me again." I squinted at Axel, his face blurring in and out of focus. I wasn't bleeding that much anymore, and the feral vargyr hadn't hit anything vital, but I couldn't keep my eyes open. "The backpack," I whispered. "I need that lotion..."

"Don't worry. I'll get it." Axel dashed through the woods, his muscles trembling. "You gotta stay with me, okay?"

His voice was miles away, and the world around me turned to soot.

I awoke, freezing in a strange bed, its blankets smelling of mold, lightly covered in black fur and dust. My body wouldn't stop shivering as I pulled the covers over my head. It did little to help warm me. This was a cold that went much deeper than flesh.

"I don't like this." Cole's tone was harsh, but quiet. "Are you sure what you fought was a vargyr?"

"Kind of," Axel replied, his voice was closer to me. "He looked like a vargyr, but somethin' wasn't right."

A rough hand braced my head. "He's cold," Vince said before pulling away. "He's probably gonna die, you know."

"Vince," Cole snapped.

"What? I'm bein' realistic here. The only bodies that cold are in morgues."

"Give him the curse," Cole said nervously, clearing his throat. I could barely move, and my teeth chattered so much that I couldn't get a word out.

"He's barely breathin', and you want me to do *that?*" Axel asked.

"We have to do something," Cole whispered. "If he's wilkyr, the curse won't let him die."

The room went silent for a moment.

"Well, don't ask me to do it," Vince mumbled.

"Wasn't gonna," Axel growled out before a thud shook the floor.

"Ya ain't gotta get violent!"

"Axel," I whispered, pulling the blanket down enough that I could see part of the room, noticing the glow of the fireplace along the wall. All three turned to me. "I'm cold."

"I gotcha buddy. I'm gonna warm ya right up, okay?" He picked Vince up off the ground by the nape of the neck. "Go put more wood on the fire."

The smaller vargyr slapped Axel's hand away. "Now yer gonna boss me around?"

Axel crossed his arms and met Vince's glare.

"Fine," he said, his tail clinging between his legs before walking toward the door. "There's more wood in the bin out there, right? Cause I draw the line at choppin' it myself."

"There's plenty," Axel responded before inching toward the other side of the bed. The mattress dipped as he shimmied under the blanket, scooting closer until my bare back lay flush against the heat of his furry chest.

"Still cold, huh?" he asked, draping his heavy arm over my midsection.

"Yeah."

Cole pulled the blanket up and scooted against me. "I'll get your front."

Vince walked back into the cabin with a bundle of logs in his arms. He threw the wood haphazardly into the hearth before dashing toward the bed. "Why're you layin' with him like that?"

"He's freezing, Vince." Cole paused and looked up at the annoyed vargyr. "Actually, I have a better idea." He stood and pointed to the empty spot on the mattress.

"Hell. No." Vince snarled and shook his head.

"Please?" Cole gave him a light shove toward the bed. "I don't have much fur, and he needs to get warm."

The short vargyr looked down at me, then back at Cole, before letting out a sigh. "Yer lucky I love you," he muttered, lifting the blanket to crawl under. His body was just as warm as Axel's, which calmed some of the shivering as he cautiously scooted against my chest. "Don't get any funny ideas back there."

After a few minutes, it became harder to keep my eyes open. If heaven existed in this world, it was at that moment, snuggled between two vargyrs. I buried my face in Vince's back fur, remembering that scent from the other night, only this time, the situation was a little more pleasant.

"How's that, Leo?" Cole asked.

"Warm."

"Can't believe I gotta do this fer *you*," Vince complained, giving me a quick glance before turning back around. The side-to-side movement of his tail against me betrayed what he was really thinking.

Cole stood over the bed, watching us. "Well, this sucks," he said, trying to keep the mood a little more light-hearted. "Now *I'm* cold."

"Why don't we scoot this way and give Cole some room," Axel said, maneuvering himself and me toward the other side of the cramped bed.

Vince followed, and Cole jumped onto the mattress before scooting against his mate. He turned back and whispered to Vince.

"Thank you."

The smaller vargyr wrapped his arms around Cole and nuzzled the crook of his neck.

"This is a cozy cabin," Axel said, his nose against the cook of my neck.

I looked up at the crude logs lining the ceiling, thick cobwebs along the corners and in the gaps of the walls. "Where are we?"

"We ain't far from where that vargyr attacked. Found this cabin hidden in between a circle of trees. Don't look like no one's been inside fer years." Axel rubbed the injury on my arm, which was numb to the touch. "With how cold you was, we had to get you somewhere warm. We got lucky."

"Looks like we found what we were looking for. Derrick's cabin," Cole said. "I haven't looked around yet for any clues, but at least we know where this place is now."

"That vargyr," I whispered, quickly losing consciousness. "I wonder if that was him. What if he comes back?"

"Then I'll be better prepared," Axel said, holding me tighter. "I've seen blood-crazed vargyrs before, and he didn't look like that. He also didn't look like the ferals. I couldn't make him out; he just seemed like somethin' different."

"We need to get Leo back to town," Cole said. "I have medicine at my house."

"The cold's too dangerous for him. We gotta wait this out 'til tomorrow," Axel said before tapping me on the shoulder. "How's yer arm?"

"I'm not in pain; I'm just really tired."

"We'll let you sleep," he whispered back, his thin lips pressing against the back of my neck. "If you need us to get ya anything, just ask, okay?"

I nodded and drifted back to sleep.

The cabin door slammed open, tearing me awake, and Axel scrambled out of bed much faster than someone of his size should have ever been able to. A bewildered black vargyr stumbled into the room from outside, his fur sopping wet.

"Oh! Visitors," he said with an almost child-like excitement, smiling warmly at Axel who was snarling and primed to attack. "Not that I mind, but what are you all doing here?"

CHAPTER 14

A New Friend

"Derrick?" Axel asked, falling into a less protective stance. Vince jumped out of bed behind Axel to join in fending off the intruder while Cole remained next to me.

"Do I know you?" the black vargyr asked, pushing past Axel toward the fire burning in the hearth. "I am wet, and it is rather cold outside, so if you don't mind, I'd like to warm myself by the hearth." He gave me a quick glance before sitting cross-legged on an old skin rug in front of the fire, water dripping from his outer coat. "I was a disgusting mess. How unbecoming."

"Uh," Cole said, clearing his throat before sliding out of the bed. "Everyone thinks you went feral."

Derrick glanced down at himself and shrugged. "That would explain the horrible stench earlier, but it certainly seems not to be the case anymore. How curious."

Axel stepped closer, his ears pulled back. "Yer eyes is green."

"My eyes *are* green, yes," Derrick corrected. "Why am I the one answering questions when you are the ones in *my* house?" He looked over at me again as I pushed myself up from the pillows. "Not that I mind. I never get company out here. My cabin is rather cozy, is it not?"

"Yeah," I said, confused as the monster that tried to kill me earlier spoke with an elegant accent while making pleasant conversation.

"Oh, you're human!" Derrick's eyes widened as though he'd just noticed me, and he jumped up from the floor.

Axel stepped in front of him, pushing back against the slender vargyr's chest. Though Axel was bigger, Derrick was almost as tall.

"Don't you get near him."

Derrick swatted Axel's hand away before leaning all the way in, his snout nearly touching my face. "How is this possible?" His ears twitched as he looked back at Axel. "I have so many questions."

"That makes five of us," Cole said, sitting on the bed next to me. "If you answer our questions, we'll answer yours. Deal?"

Derrick stood straight and smiled while rubbing the long, scruffy fur under his chin. "Of course," he replied. "What is it you wish to know?"

"We need to know where Xavier might be. Toby said he was your mate, but he went feral and left town."

Derrick froze, and his eyes watered a bit as he glanced at an old wooden cabinet at the far corner of the room.

"Why do you want to know about him?"

"We need to know how to deal with a demon," Cole said.

Derrick winced. "If you know he went feral, then you also know he won't be of much help."

"Well, can you help us?" I asked.

"I believe I can," he said with a sad nod. "Let me dry, and we will take a nice walk along the bluffs."

"I can stay with Leo," Axel said while checking me over.

"I'm feeling better." I jumped out of bed and rubbed my arm. "I guess all I needed was a good sleep. My arm doesn't hurt anymore."

"Does it hurt when I do this?" Cole squeezed where the injury had been wrapped, but aside from slight numbness, there was no pain.

"That's weird," I said, as Cole pulled at the dirty strips of cloth. When cool air grazed my bare skin, he let out a gasp.

"What is it? What's wrong?"

"How in the hell?" Vince asked, looking me over suspiciously. "Since when do humans heal that fast?"

I ran my fingers over the smooth skin where the bite marks used to be, making a fist before letting my hand hang loose.

"What did you do, Axel?" I asked.

He held his hands up, scrambling. "All I did was stop the bleeding. I swear."

"Another side-effect of Gar's potion?" Cole asked.

Derrick wrinkled his nose while baring his sharp teeth. "Keep the human away from that monster."

"What do you know about Gar?" I asked.

"Enough," he muttered, tying his long mane into a ponytail with leather strips before grabbing rusted shears from one of the wooden shelves nailed to the wall. "I suppose since you're all seeking answers from a deva'koh, the fiend has revealed what he truly is. Am I correct?" Derrick began trimming his facial fur, leaving the slightly longer beard untouched. As he finished, it hung off his chin in a wedge that curled back slightly, giving the vargyr a scholarly and handsome look.

"I overheard some of the things he talked about," I said, still rubbing my arm. How had such a serious wound healed so fast without Gar's medicine—unless Cole was right. "We know everything."

Derrick shook his head and opened the front door.

"You've likely only scratched the surface. I want to show you all something."

❦

A tall mound of stones sat neatly atop a tall hill overlooking the ocean. Though no words were spoken, the solemn atmosphere was deafening as our attention shifted from the pile to Derrick, who knelt next to it.

"Here he is," he said, pulling loose some of the thorny overgrowth covering the grave. Though tears welled in his eyes, he gave a gentle smile. "I'm not even sure how long it has been anymore. In my mind, I was here tending to him yesterday, but I suppose it has been quite a while longer."

"You could have just said the guy was dead instead of draggin' us all the way up here," Vince complained.

Axel crouched next to the distraught vargyr.

"I'm really sorry you lost yer mate. How did he die?"

"The last time I told anyone this, it cost me dearly." Derrick rose from the ground, dusting the sand from his fur. "No one wants to believe our *savior* was actually the cause of our damnation."

"I believe it," Cole said, his gaze shifting toward the ocean. "The moment I found out he was a demon, I guessed as much."

Sensing the anguish, Derrick rested his hand on the wilkyr's shoulder, giving him a gentle squeeze. "You're not long for the change, it seems. Being a vargyr isn't so bad; in fact, I prefer it to the wilkyr life."

"I was born human," Cole said softly.

Derrick jerked his hand away, and his ears folded against his head. "I apologize for my assumption." He stared back at the grave. "Xavier was also human-turned. Despite being eccentric, he was an incredible mind and one of the best lovers I'd ever had. You don't see deva'kohs much anymore, especially those that live long enough to end up in Varcross. He spent the majority of his human life in secret sects."

"It's not any better now," Cole said. "They don't even put them on trial anymore."

"For very good reason," Derrick continued. "I was so infatuated with Xavier because of his bizarre stories. He walked through the chaos, death, and endless pleasures of X'eeva—the Devah realm. He was fearless, always a knife's edge away from making that last journey."

"So that's where the demons come from?" I asked.

Derrick nodded. "We do not truly understand what they are. All we've learned from studying the deva'koh is they are a race of seemingly immortal beings from another realm. Though we call them demons, they aren't truly evil, but they do thrive in chaos. Atorien isn't known for being careless enough to reveal what he is. If you overheard him, he fully intended for that to happen."

The tall, black vargyr lowered himself to the grass before laying back with both hands behind his head. Though he'd regained his mind, he had no qualms with nudity. My face flushed as everything usually concealed became much more prominent in that position.

What he just said hadn't dawned on me when I was in that hall, listening to Gar talk to Josiah. I had forgotten he could smell me. Not only was he a vargyr, I was reeking at the time. How could I have been so stupid?

"I don't know how he ended up here, but the irony of it all is so delicious. The demon who started this curse is forced to live as a beast himself for however long the wards remain standing. He's either not as bright as ancient tomes make him out to be, or once again, this was all planned. Either way, it delights me to know he's miserable."

"How much do you know about him and this curse?" Cole asked, sitting next to Derrick on the grass. The bite of freezing air mixed with the warm briny mist from the ocean below created a unique perfume as gusts swirled over the bluffs. There were no trees here, just granite boulders scattered along the hillside with thick strands of golden grass. Beyond the hill into the bay, the noon sun shimmered on the surface of the choppy water before disappearing into frothy crests that slapped against the cliffside.

"Enough for him to do this to me. Xavier met a worse fate, but he was the first to know the secret. He always had his suspicions, of course. Years of talking to Devah gives a deva'koh a type of sixth sense. They can see through any visage, human or otherwise. As with his magic, his supernatural senses should have dulled in this world, but he was able to tap into something in town that brought them back."

Axel sat next to the black vargyr, fidgeting with a smooth stone as he listened.

"Xavier, as terrifyingly intelligent as he was, had one major flaw. He could drink any vargyr under the table, and being a human-turned, I couldn't fault him for trying to forget the events that led him to Varcross." Derrick sat upright and chucked a stone onto the pile. "The last night he was alive, he was so intoxicated he could barely keep himself standing on stage, and the other wilkyrs pulled him to the back room to recover. Gar wasn't happy, and he was on his way to scold Xavier, but not before Xavier revealed what he knew.

"Of course, no one believed him, rambling like a drunken idiot. Ten minutes later, Gar slithered into the room and handed Xavier an elixir to 'sober him up.' Whatever that concoction was, it did far more. I'll never forget the terror on his face after he imbibed it. He knew what Gar had done.

"The demon whispered, 'They're waiting for you,' and they were the last words he would ever hear. As he walked out on stage, he screamed. I'd never seen a transformation so violent, and he wasn't even supposed to make the full turn for another few years at least. His body was not prepared for that kind of trauma.

"Xavier ran from the town, likely losing his mind in the process. The next morning, I tracked his scent to the base of that cliff." He turned and pointed to the tallest bluff in the distance. "He was face-down in a blackened pool of his own blood, and the fall was high enough to kill him instantly. Whatever he drank took away the instinct to live."

Axel locked eyes with the vargyr, their expressions fragile. It seemed as though he wanted to comfort Derrick somehow, and after hesitating for a moment, he placed his hand on Derrick's.

The black vargyr smiled.

"I mourned him, rocking his broken body for hours before laying him to rest. That day was the worst day of my life, but I had to take it hour by hour; I didn't have a choice. I decided then to build a cabin close to his grave in secret during the day while working at the dungeon by night until my full turn. I wanted to disappear from the town after telling as many people as I could about what Gar was and what he did to Xavier.

"I knew the risks and was willing to take them, more so out of vengeance than anything. Nothing I said mattered, though. Gar's deception ran deep, and the town depended too much on him. Though they admonished me, I had done enough to sow some seeds of suspicion. However, as a full vargyr, my plan did not go smoothly. I didn't fully realize how difficult it was to live in solitude." He glanced at Axel and Vince. "You two probably know that feeling. We're social beasts, even more than when we were human."

"Yup," Axel said, clearing his throat. "I've left town a few times, and I thought I'd be able to stay away."

"I usually keep a steady head," Derrick continued, "but I'd never in my life felt that level of anxiety. I'd try to stay at my cabin for a few days, but it would become so unbearable, I'd come back. I would imbibe a few drinks before dragging myself to the dungeon, as a customer this time. I hated myself for doing it, but one can only ignore the curse for so long before it clouds the mind with lust. There were few I could call my friends in town, and I became so depressed that I would stay in my cabin alone for longer than I should have.

"This place was well-hidden, but eventually someone discovered it. I only ever had one visitor," he looked around at everyone and winked, "until now. Unfortunately, that was the last day I truly remember. Gar was disgustingly polite." Derrick's snarl made it harder for him to speak.

"You're a mage, aren't you?" Cole cut in, breaking the vargyr's train of thought. "And you're not just any mage, either. You're high-ranking."

His rage instantly turned to excitement. "I *was*, yes."

"I was taught that mages like you were immune to the curse."

Derrick rubbed the thick fur on his chin before letting out a howl of laughter.

"You were a student, yes?"

"I was for a little while."

"Then you heard the old fools and their stories. The archmages masquerade as teachers and the senators masquerade as leaders when really they are puppets of one another."

"Senators?" I asked. "Stellous is a representative democracy?"

Derrick scratched his head. "How do you not know that?"

"He's from a different world," Cole said.

"Ah, yes. I suppose that explains that. And 'representative democracy' is more than an oxymoron. It's often a veil hiding who this form of governance truly represents. The people in power tell lies that they themselves want to believe, and I discovered something in my studies that both the athenaeum and the senate wanted to keep secret.

"The purpose of the curse was to destroy Stellous from the inside out, and if the senate had tackled the problem from the start by getting international help, we wouldn't be sitting here, though, I'd have never been born, and that would be a shame." The black vargyr chuckled, his light-hearted nature bringing the mood back up. "Because I'm quite amazing. Did you know they once called me a savant? I'd have been the youngest archmage in history, had I not ended up here."

We all smiled at Derrick's proud gesture, except Cole, who was even more captivated by the vargyr mage.

"The senate in Stellous doesn't just hold influence over its territories, it's the most influential power in all of Eqiros. The last thing they wanted to do was expose a chink in the country's armor. You see, I wasn't the first vargyr born of a Stellous mage, nor was I the last. It was a surprise, though, because I was never told who or what my father was. When the change began, I understood why my mother abandoned me. It wasn't long before I was found out and torn from the only life I'd ever known, shackled and literally tossed to the wolves."

Derrick let out a disgusted groan. "I was forced out of a life of prestige into vile sexual servitude for the very beasts that sired me. To make matters worse, my own father was likely among my new *clients*. I hoped he had gone feral before my condemnation to this place—I choose to believe this anyway, for my own sanity."

"So how'd you end up like this?" Axel asked, looking Derrick over. "I mean, not like *this*, but you wasn't the same when I first saw you. Ain't never had anyone beat the crud outta me so hard before." He rubbed at the area on his chest Derrick had ripped open yesterday.

"Gar's handiwork," he said, his ears off to the side. "This world sits in a realm that obeys different natural laws, and the flow of magic ends at the wards that keep us bound to this place. Somehow, Gar is exempt from these laws, and he was able to overpower me with ease, locking me to the wall with Lo'rim. One-by-one he forced his potions down my throat, and that was when everything faded away. Whatever I was when I attacked was the result."

He paused and stared pensively at me.

"You healed unusually fast from whatever injury I gave you."

"We're just as confused as you are," Cole said, giving me a raised brow. "Unless you aren't telling us something, Leo."

"I did not have sex with Axel," I said, a little hesitant. "Does it spread through bites?"

"Highly unlikely," Derrick said dismissively. "The curse is entirely sexually transmitted. Hexes and curses take on the qualities of their creator. Had Atorien been a different type of demon, the curse would have a different effect and would be transmitted differently too.

Whatever deva'koh contracted him understood a demon like him was the most efficient way to spread such a devastating and virulent affliction."

"So he is a sex demon," I said.

"An incubus, yes. They gain their power and immortality through intercourse while slowly draining the life force from their victims, or they obtain it through powerful curses that involve their victims being forced to have sex with an innocent." He glanced at Vince and Axel. "Every time we satisfy the conditions of the curse, we extend his life and increase his power, even if he's just a shell of his former self in this place."

Derrick scooted closer until he was touching me. "You may be the biggest mystery here. Humans cannot travel past the wards. They were purposely designed that way to prevent abuse. You could see how easily it would be to get rid of political opponents or quell discourse if someone with power could simply cast troublemakers into a warded realm forever."

"I don't know how I got here, but I do know a mage named Josiah tricked me into passing through the wards." Derrick cocked his head as I continued. "Gar wants me cursed so I can somehow break him free."

Derrick's eyes widened. "You may have just revealed Gar's folly. He's not here by choice." Derrick's shock turned to a devious grin. "Now things have gotten interesting."

"What do you mean?" Cole asked. "Do you know how to vanquish him?"

The mage shook his head.

"There are still gaps in my knowledge. For example, I do not understand why Leo would be the key to freeing Gar or why he needs the curse to do so. However, the good news is Gar is looking for a way to break free. Remember what I said about how incubii gain power and extend their lives? One day, the supply of sane vargyrs will run dry, and since he's cut off from the aether stream of X'eeva, he will become mortal. He would have never willingly put himself in such peril, which means he was betrayed by his contract and tricked into coming here. I also do not know this *Josiah*, but from your description, he sounds like a chronomancer. How unfortunate for him."

"Is that bad?" I asked.

"Yes and no," Cole said. "Chronomancers are mages that can travel between realms and time, but that class of magic takes the lifeforce of the user as the only reagent."

"This Josiah must be desperate if he's using chronomancy to free a demon, and I could only assume his soul is on the line," Derrick said. "How far did you get in the athenaeum, Cole?"

The wilkyr looked away, embarrassed. "Level one."

"Don't be ashamed. I can see that spark of knowledge in your eyes, and I would love to have deeper conversations when time permits."

Cole smiled. "That would be amazing. One-on-one teaching from an archmage...no one gets that opportunity."

"I would gladly teach you what I know," he said, his tail swishing along the grass. "But first thing's first, what do you know about Josiah?"

"He's desperate," Cole said. "He's staking his life on a hypothesis, which means he must know more than I assume. From what Leo overheard, they haven't been successful, and Josiah probably won't survive another trip to that world if they fail."

This vargyr scholar brought out a part of Cole I hadn't seen. He spoke so passionately, as though he were trying to make a good impression, and Derrick was all too happy to stoke that fire in him.

"Another trip?" Derrick asked. "They have taken other humans from Leo's world?"

"Yeah," I said. "They did it once, I think, and that human went insane and had to be put down."

"I remember one of the vargyrs going bloodcrazed under suspicious circumstances long ago," Derrick said. "Coincidentally, this event coincided with the day Xavier's senses awoke."

"That's impossible," Cole said. "That human arrived about five years ago."

Derrick rubbed his chin again, pensively looking out at the bluffs. "This must have been another human. This means they've been bringing humans from Leo's realm to Varcross for decades, maybe longer. Josiah wouldn't have survived so many realm crossings. If humans from Leo's realm are the keys to breaking the wards, we need to learn why that is, but we should also keep Leo out of Gar's reach."

"We ain't got the time fer that, and we can't leave Gar," Vince said. "My mate's turning, and we don't know how he's gonna end up. I wanna know how to stop this bastard and get Cole his cure."

Derrick looked toward the grave again. "If either Xavier or I knew how to stop him, he wouldn't be dead, and I wouldn't be here talking to you. No one knows a Devah's curse better than a deva'koh, and Xavier was the only one. Once a curse is unleashed upon a world, no power that exists in either realm can break it. Not even the demon who created it."

"Then this really was a waste of time," Cole said, pushing himself from the ground. Derrick went to say something but stopped when the wilkyr took off down the hill with Vince trailing close behind.

Derrick stood and brushed the dead grass from his fur and tail. "He's so young. I wish I knew what to say, but there aren't any answers at the moment. There is something Xavier told me that might come in handy. Because demons have so little control over their own curses, they usually slip in a loophole in case things go awry. If Gar slipped one into his own curse, there might actually be a way to break it."

The black vargyr stretched and squinted as he stared up at the sky. "It will be dusk in a few hours, and I need to hunt. I am not sure if getting my sanity back was a blessing, but I intend to make the most of this second chance. I don't believe this was a coincidence, and you seem to be a wild card, Leo. Gar obviously wants to use whatever strange properties your otherworldly body possesses, and if Gar's interested, so am I. The key to his success or destruction may run through your veins. I am sorry that I do not have more answers."

Axel tossed an arm around the vargyr's neck and smiled. "It ain't nothin' to be sorry about, and this could be valuable info. Now that I know you're out here, ya ain't gotta be so lonely. I'll come visit ya, and we'll be huntin' buddies."

Derrick's tail wagged. "That would be thrilling! It's not every day I meet one of our kind that enjoys a fresh kill," he said before glancing at me. "You all are welcome here anytime, but keep my awakening secret. Gar wanted you to know what he is because he thinks you will despair and give in to his demands, but he did that not knowing you would find me."

"Your secret's safe with us," I said, extending a hand to shake his. "I'm glad we met you, Derrick."

"This was truly a pleasure," he replied, grabbing my hand before shaking twice. He gave us both a nod and dashed down the hill, disappearing into the trees.

Cole and Vince were still visible in the distance, but they weren't talking to one another. What could I do to console him now? Derrick may have mentioned a loophole, but unless we knew what it was—or if it existed—it was just more false hope.

"I don't want to lose him," I said, turning to Axel. "He's the best friend I've ever had."

"As long as we're all alive, there's a chance." Axel didn't smile this time; instead, he looked toward the woods Derrick dashed into. "I think he beat the curse. Gar's right to be afraid. He's losing control."

"I hope you're right about that. We'll have to test it out when we see him again."

A Different Kind Of Beast

"Let me go with you," I said, following Axel through the living room. It was well after dark by the time we got home, and I had been sluggish the entire hike. Vince and Cole kept ahead of us, and Axel wanted to check on them.

"You ain't feeling good." He knelt and leaned in, his thin lips lightly brushing my forehead. "I ain't gonna be away fer long."

"Okay, Mom," I joked before pressing my mouth into his for a quick kiss. "We did a lot of walking today, so I'm exhausted."

"You don't feel like you got a fever or nothin'." He stood upright again and gawked awkwardly.

"What's with that look?"

"Why don't you go on to bed, and I'll join ya soon. I wanna try somethin' tonight you might like—if yer up for it."

"Axel, I hope you're not suggesting what I think you are."

"Just trust me. I think you'll really like it." His voice had a slight pitchiness to it as he leaned over and licked my neck. The gesture would have been romantic if it hadn't been so forced.

"Is this a sex thing?"

Axel stammered. "It–it's a surprise," he said, stepping backward toward the door, fumbling for the knob. "It ain't gonna be dangerous or nothin'. I swear."

"Let me rephrase this. Is sex involved in any way?"

He said nothing as he turned and strutted outside, tripping on the slight step down. He deftly caught himself, pretending it was intentional.

"This is definitely a sex thing," I whispered to myself, shutting the door before securing the deadbolt.

Axel knew better than to take this too far. What we had was so delicate that one mistake could ruin everything, but if I couldn't get over my fear of him, then what chance would we have? I'd kissed him and slept up against him all night, and nothing happened, though I still couldn't help but wonder what the hell he had planned.

My feet creaked along the floor toward the bedroom, but I stopped and eyed the mattress Axel and I had shared only twice. There was still a lingering smell of feral Derrick clinging to my skin, but I was so tired. All I wanted to do was fall into bed, but I also didn't want to stink.

Or did I?

When Derrick was feral and when the other vargyrs came after me, they were drawn to my scent. Wolves and dogs liked scents that humans found off-putting, and vargyrs seemed to be more wolf than human at times.

Now I couldn't get the thought out of my head, which made it harder to picture myself going that far with him. Kissing him felt natural when I closed my eyes, but the moment I saw that huge monster face looking back at me, it got weird again. There was this tabooness, like I was breaking some kind of natural law by being even slightly intimate with him.

There was more than the superficial to consider, from the size difference to the anatomy. Since I had seen Derrick in the nude, and Axel wasn't that much taller, I kind of understood what I'd be getting into. Plus there were all the not-so-subtle hints Cole gave. Would my smaller human body even be able to accommodate him? I didn't have the rapid healing of a wilkyr.

It wasn't worth worrying about right now, and I wasn't even sure I'd be up for whatever Axel had planned. After grabbing one of my towels from the shelf, I removed my clothing and slipped into a hot shower, taking care not to turn the old, rusted lever too far to the left this time.

I grabbed the bottle of body wash and my loofah sponge. Even though I had the foresight to buy extra toiletries when I hit the road, I'd be running out of this soon and would need to ask Cole to get me some of the soap he'd gotten from Stellous. Wilkyrs rarely washed with soap, and vargyrs didn't bathe that much at all. When they did, they didn't use anything but water. Axel said it was because their fur was too thick. It took a long time and an entire expensive bottle just to get all the way clean. Most avoided this and simply swam in the rivers or lakes during the warmer seasons.

The soapy loofah glided down my arm, past the area Derrick had bitten. I still didn't understand how it healed so fast without Gar's medicine, and there wasn't a scar. Internally though, it had been alternating between numbness and pain every hour or so.

My left hand tingled, and this time there was a slight burning sensation in my upper arm. I turned away from the hot water and waited for the heat to dissipate, but instead of relief, the burning intensified and spread outward. There was a tightness in my chest as my pulse quickened, the burning now rippling through my entire body.

I slammed the water lever downward until the shower stopped, and I fell to my knees, groaning. The skin around the area of the bite darkened, and protruding veins snaked outward. As quickly as it began, the pain vanished, and the pigment of my skin lightened back to normal.

"What the fuck was that?" I whispered to myself.

I ran my fingers over the area, which was rough to the touch but otherwise appeared normal. After pulling myself up, I stepped out of the shower and wrapped the towel around my waist before wiping the condensation from the mirror. Glowing silver eyes peered back and startled me before dimming to a duller grayish blue, no longer the soupy green they were before. My facial hair had grown from stubble to a short, thick beard in just one day.

Feeling a wave of nausea, I gripped the sink while staring intensely at my reflection. Was everyone wrong? Could the curse actually spread through a vargyr's bite? I understood what Derrick said about the curse, but my reflection didn't lie. I didn't look wilkyr, and my mind wandered back to what Gar mentioned to Josiah about how unpredictable his potions were when taken by humans from Earth.

If this was the curse, I'd need to talk to Axel tonight and figure out what to do going forward.

※

I jerked awake, gasping as wet warmth enveloped me from below. I grabbed a handful of Axel's mane and pulled.

"What...are you doing?"

Axel's head was between my legs. He froze and pulled away, his eyes glowing blue for a moment.

"Uh oh," he whispered, placing a hand on my chest. "Was I wrong? I thought you knew what I was gonna do since you was just layin' here without any clothes on."

The last thing I remembered was drying off and sitting on the bed, worrying about every weird sensation, either real or imaginary. It was the first time I'd ever tired myself out so much that I fell asleep naked. Despite Axel seeing everything, his eyes remained blue. Knowing I wasn't in danger, I wouldn't object to him continuing what he was doing.

"That felt good," I said, spreading my legs further apart so we could both get more comfortable. I gave him a nervous nod but tensed when his stare turned hungry. He licked my shaft before wrapping his tongue all the way around, my dick quickly disappearing into his mouth.

His teeth grazed me, but the pulsating sensations of that long tongue made me forget just how sharp they were. The risk and danger only intensified the pleasure as I continued to experience the weirdest and most amazing blowjob I'd ever received. I never expected a vargyr to be so good at this, but this was Axel. He was unusually skilled at physical affection, it seemed.

His tongue continued to stroke and squeeze my cock, every taste bud rubbing the sensitive glans. There was a familiar ache coming from my muscles and hands, but the pain actually felt good in the moment. I wrapped my legs around his broad neck, moaning while gripping the sheets, barely noticing the tearing noises coming from them. He sped up, and I was getting closer, instinctively thrusting into his mouth as the sheets ripped. I arched my back, expecting to explode with pleasure, but instead, a boiling pain wracked my body. I instantly went from moaning in ecstasy to screaming in agony.

"Shit," Axel shouted, pulling away. "Did I bite ya?"

"No," I gasped out. "Something's wrong." I screamed again through gritted teeth before clustered cramps stabbed at my body like a murder of angry crows.

"Yer arm." Axel pushed himself to his knees and crawled beside me. I glanced over as thick, jet-black fur sprouted from where the bite was and spread outward like rippling tar. "This don't make no sense! I didn't do nothin' like that to you! I swear."

My gurgled cries distressed Axel even more as he tried to lift me from the bed. When he touched me, the sensation was like being wrapped in live electric wires, and I pushed him away.

"It hurts!"

The room resonated with what sounded like a bunch of knuckles cracking, and I could feel everything stretch. Becoming a full vargyr was supposed to take years, but as the palms of my massive hands turned black and hooked claws pushed their way from the nail beds, it appeared I'd skipped some crucial steps.

Axel could only stand and watch as I writhed, my body taking on everything at once, and I was reminded of what Derrick said about Xavier's violent transformation. The bed shrunk under me as my body continued to grow, new bone extending my spine in both directions. Though I couldn't see what was happening behind me, the feeling alone was enough to visualize as my tailbone jutted outwards.

Muscles I'd never seen before shook violently as they bulged, my arms tripling in size, pulling my skin taut under the fur.

Axel was saying words I couldn't understand as the room turned silver. The last thing I experienced before blacking out completely was intense pain in my skull and Gar's voice echoing in my thoughts.

"No one escapes…"

Where was I? It was supposed to be dark, but everything was bright and the colors were so vivid. Trees whipped by me as my feet raced along the fallen autumn leaves. There was no clarity as I pushed onward with no particular destination in mind, no logic to my actions, only intense emotions and sensations.

Footsteps frantically followed before catching up, Axel now running alongside me. Everything smelled so different, even the trees and dirt below. Scents from every direction hit me at once, each triggering a different emotional response.

"Where're you goin', buddy?" Axel asked, easily keeping up with my pace.

I could understand him, but I couldn't talk. It was as though that part of my brain was gone. As we left the trees and entered a clearing, I stopped and looked around at the hills and wind-swept grasses, the effulgence of the crescent moon covering everything it touched in a pale blue.

Axel slid to a stop next to me, and I looked at him, his eyes now level with mine, though he was still slightly taller. I looked down at my massive body, noting the thick, black mane on my chest narrowing to a thin line as it disappeared into the bushier fur of my groin. Then I noticed my feet, which were way different than any of the vargyrs I'd seen—except Gar. They were giant paws, my big toes half-visible as smaller dew claws near my ankles.

This wasn't my body, but I was still me. Every time I had any kind of higher thought process, it would last only a moment before more primal thoughts pushed them away. It was like being in a constant state of inebriation, but having incredible balance and coordination at the same time.

"Leo?" Axel asked while giving off a scent that distressed me. His ears folded downward and his eyes glistened. "Did I lose ya?" He grabbed my arms and stared with an intensity that made me want to run away from him. "If yer not feral, give me a nod or somethin'."

Was I feral? Axel said ferals never understood what he was saying, but his words were as clear as ever. I nodded as I dropped to my knees, holding my new wolf-like head in my hands. I wasn't feral, and I wasn't wilkyr. I was something alien.

Axel knelt in front of me and pulled me into his arms.

"I don't know what's going on, but we're gonna figure it out. You didn't go feral, and that's all that matters right now. Let's get you to Cole's, okay?"

Wild Times

"That's Leo?" Cole circled me before kneeling to poke at a dew claw. "Why the hell does he look like this?"

Vince hesitantly stepped closer, poking at my arms and chest with the hooked claw of his index finger. Being in this body and so much taller than both of them was almost dream-like, and the intense energy pulsing through my new muscles made me want to test boundaries. I should have been more upset about all of this, but that couldn't have been further from my thoughts. Was I losing my ability to think like a human?

Both Vince and Cole gave off two distinct scents: one made me want to give chase, and the other aroused me. It was easy to sense Cole's attraction, and the smell, though different, made me think of candy. I pressed my snout into his chest—then his neck. Every inhale seemed to dull my mind a little more, and before I could regain control of my faculties, I had buried my nose into his armpit, just as other vargyrs had done to me. I could now understand the appeal.

"Axel!" Cole scolded, pushing my head away. All my attention shifted to a snarling Vince. His ears pressed against his head, teeth bared. He was...scared of me. "You just couldn't help yourself, could you?"

"I didn't do nothin'! Well, maybe I did something, but we didn't do *that*. Plus, he'd be wilkyr, not a full vargyr."

"Is he feral?" Vince asked, whining as I ran over to him before shoving the smaller vargyr against the wall, my nose probing his upper body. He let out more distressed whimpers, but I didn't care; in fact, it sparked further aggression.

"I don't know. I'm around ferals all the time, and none of 'em look at me the way he does. He can definitely understand, but he ain't talkin' none."

"Get him the hell away from me," Vince shouted as I slammed him against the wall again, lifting him up slightly. He struggled to break free, going as far as snapping his jaws, but he was helpless.

Axel grabbed the nape of my neck and pulled me back toward the door.

"Alright, buddy. It ain't nice to be pickin' on Vince like that." As big as I was now, Axel was still a lot stronger. My body went limp against his as he held me in place.

"I'm so confused," Cole said, reaching a hand to my head so he could rub between my ears. The motion of his stroking made my eyes close and my tongue hang out. I felt a lot more drooly than any of the other vargyrs for some reason. "How in the world did he go from human to *that*?" He paused and eyed Axel again. "What was he doing before he turned?"

I grinned when Axel's eyes shifted downward. "Since he had such a hard day, I thought I'd put a smile on his face." The vargyr looked back up at Cole and shrugged. "All I did was use my mouth. That was it."

"Hmph. Would have been nice if you did that to me whenever we were together."

"Hey," Vince angrily cut in, slinking closer to us. "My tongue ain't good enough?" The smaller vargyr pushed me away and licked Cole's neck. "How 'bout I put a smile on yer face right now?"

Cole was still looking me over, and I could hear his pulse quicken. Vince took note of the wilkyr's unusual reaction.

"Stop lookin' at him!"

"I can't help it. He's so strange. He's not quite as weird as Gar, but I've never seen a vargyr like him. Maybe this is because he's from another world."

"It happened so fast," Axel said. "He was fine for a little while, but then he started screamin'. Cole, he went through it all in a couple minutes. It was awful."

Cole's hand slipped from my head and traced along my neck, but he pulled away when Vince snapped at him.

"Why you gotta touch him like that? There's other wilkyrs, so you ain't gotta fuck every vargyr in town, you know." Vince looked up at me, ears still folded back. "I don't like the way he's starin' at me. Why's he so fuckin' big?"

Cole walked away without saying a word before plopping down on the couch.

"Wait a minute," Vince said, stumbling after him. "I'm sorry, babe. I didn't mean it like that."

"Yeah, you did," Cole muttered as Vince sat next to him. The smaller vargyr went to open his mouth to reply, but Cole cut him off and looked back at Axel. "We need to figure out what happened to him. You said he can understand you, but he's acting like an animal."

"Maybe the potion did it," Axel said.

Cole shook his head. "If that were the case, don't you think Gar would have opened up with that move instead of trying to get every vargyr in town after him?"

They all went silent, save for the impatient tapping of my pawed foot against the floor. I'd never had so much pent-up energy, and all I wanted to do was start running.

Axel let go of me, and I followed a few interesting scent trails around the house, never venturing far from the living room. There were so many new sensations to explore, and I was bored, only half paying attention to whatever it was they were talking about.

"Maybe it was Derrick. You saw how sick he got after that nasty bite, then he just got better outta nowhere," Axel said.

"It can't spread that way," Cole said. "Before this place existed, feral vargyrs attacked and bit people all the time. The ones who survived never turned. They didn't even get sick."

"How do you know fer sure?" Axel asked. "That was hundreds of years ago, and Derrick said that the senate was hidin' things from the public."

"Okay, suppose a bite could change someone—which it doesn't—they'd still go through years of transformation. Leo went from human to vargyr in minutes." He pointed at me as I gnawed on the side of the table. Whatever wood Axel used to make this had a very pleasant, almost minty flavor.

"Derrick weren't a normal vargyr. You both didn't see him when he was a monster. It was like he was this demon-wolf hybrid, and he was so strong that he almost killed me. What if whatever Gar did to him made him pass the curse differently?"

The conversation faded in and out as my attention shifted from the table back to Vince, who was still sitting next to Cole. He snapped his head toward me, our eyes locking for a solid moment before his ears fell.

"Axel," Vince whispered, his head following me as I stalked through the house. "He's givin' me that look again."

The larger vargyr grabbed my arm and pulled me next to him.

Vince wrinkled his nose at me. "No use cryin'. May as well bring him to Gar and get Cole his treatment." He tried to nuzzle Cole's neck, but the wilkyr pushed him away.

"I know you don't like him, but I do. We don't know what Gar plans to do with Leo if he finds out about this."

"I don't give a shit what happens to him, and if it comes down to him or you, I'm gonna choose you." He took Cole's hand in his. "Look at him, Cole. His time's up, but you still got more."

Hearing him say that hurt worse than I expected, but I also understood how he was feeling. If it came down to saving some stranger I just met or the love of my life, I knew what I would choose.

"That's *my* mate yer talkin' about," Axel shouted. My attention snapped back to him. "I mean, potential mate."

"He's more like a pet now, don'tcha think?"

A loud huff of air raced through my nose as I turned toward the front door, pulling it open.

"He understands what yer saying, Vince."

The door slammed in the distance as I darted toward the woods, Axel following close. I knew he wouldn't leave me alone, but I just wanted some time to think—if I could still do that without some smell or noise distracting me. Being what I was made it so much harder to simply be me, but I couldn't hate it. I wanted to give in to it. Was this what Axel was talking about?

Even though Vince was an asshole about it, he was right. Gar would give Cole his treatment now that I had the curse. I vaguely remembered talking about this with Axel, but everything was so fuzzy. I pointed my snout to the wind blowing in from town, and the scent of vargyrs and smoke was heavy. My powerful legs pushed my pawed feet into the soft soil, kicking it up as I took off in that direction.

Axel grabbed my arm and pulled me to a reluctant stop.

"Why're you goin' there? Ain't nothing in town fer ya."

I could only respond with a growl while trying to tear away from his grip.

"Let's go home. Maybe if you get some sleep, this'll be better in the mornin'."

I shook my head and pointed to town, but then got an idea. A low-hanging limb supplied me with a small branch I could use to write with, and I knelt to the ground, clearing the leaves away. Axel got on one knee next to me.

The stick sunk into the dirt as I clumsily scribbled out what I wanted to say, but stopped mid-sentence when Axel tilted his head in confusion. I'd forgotten he couldn't read my letters, just as I couldn't read the runes he wrote with.

Axel stood and pulled me from the ground by my right arm. "It's what Vince said, isn't it?"

I nodded.

"Fuck Vince. Don't listen to him. I—" He paused, stumbling through a few grunts as he tried to find the words to say. "Maybe it's too soon to say it, but I just know yer the only one fer me in this world. Sure, you look different right now, but yer still Leo inside. We only just started, and I ain't lettin' you go do something stupid like give Gar what he wants."

Hearing those words made me smile. Though he was right about it being too soon, there was something to his words. Cole may have been my best friend, but Axel was a lot more than that. There was no point in playing coy, now that I was essentially a werewolf breathing in a scent that brought me more comfort than I'd felt in my entire life.

"I'm sorry this happened to ya," he said, pulling me into his arms. He licked the side of my face, and my backside started to shake. That's right. I had a tail now. "It's gonna take a lot of adjustment, but I ain't goin' nowhere."

I jerked awake as sunlight poured in from outside and sat up against the headboard, holding my bare, human arms in front of me. When did we get back to the house?

"Axel," I whispered, giving him a hard shake. "Wake up."

He snorted and sat upright, rubbing his eyes. "What's wrong? You okay?" He blinked twice as the realization hit him. "Yer human!"

I glanced down and was met with an unusual but welcome sight. Every muscle had doubled in size, and thick, fur-like hair blanketed my chest, narrowing to a trail that went lower. It was like looking at someone else.

"Is this normal?" I asked, throwing off the covers and jumping out of bed, the chill of the room nipping at my bare skin.

"Wilkyrs get thicker, yeah. Ain't none go all the way back to human, though."

I closed my eyes and took in a deep sniff as I stood in the middle of the room. My vargyr sense of smell remained strong, but it wasn't as information-heavy as last night. "Maybe the curse didn't stick."

Axel shifted to the edge of the bed, his broad, padded feet landing against the floor with a thud. He continued ogling me while wearing one of the dirtiest grins I'd ever seen him make.

"I dunno. Ya sure look different." When I knelt next to my bag to grab some clean clothes, he sighed.

"What's wrong?" I asked, grabbing the towel hanging on one of the two nails in the door.

"Nothin'. Don't worry 'bout it."

I walked back to the bed and kissed his wet nose before sitting naked on the mattress. "C'mon, tell me."

"I guess," he started, dithering his response. "I guess I'm glad you can talk again and all, but I was kinda excited. Had a dream last night that we was both huntin' and running through the woods together. It was so much fun."

"You really like hunting, don't you?" I folded my clothes and towel to the other side of me. "I don't know if I'd be into it."

"Ya never know. Everyone in town don't hunt either, and they's content eatin' the shit that comes in from Stellous. They really don't know what they're missing, and once you try it as a full vargyr, you'll understand. It's like I unlocked the best secret, but no one wants to know about it."

I rested my head against Axel's arm. "I couldn't tell you this yesterday, but thank you for stopping me. I don't know what I was thinking. I really couldn't think all that clearly."

"That's what friends is for."

"Friends?"

Axel averted his gaze.

"I don't remember a lot from last night, but I do remember some things."

"Oh," Axel whispered. "That stuff kinda slipped out in the heat of the moment."

"I think you're the only one for me, too."

He relaxed and put his arm around me. "I ain't rushin', but I can definitely see you sleeping next to me fer the rest of my life. It's comfortable."

He stared longingly, his tail gently swaying over the blanket, and I remembered having that same thought last night. The fur, teeth and claws weren't as off-putting anymore. He wasn't some ugly, malformed monster. He was handsome, and there was something more, something I couldn't see.

"The last thing I wanted to do when I left Colorado was rush into another relationship."

"Sorry. I shouldn't have said what I did."

I rubbed his head. "I didn't mean it like that. You're actually the best boyfriend I've ever had, and that's kind of sad considering it's been like, what? A couple days?"

"When I heard you was into guys that night in the pub, it got me wonderin' if I could put on the charms and get you to fall head-over-heels. Used to do it all the time when I was human. I might seem kinda simple, but I'm still a man, ya know? If I was human, you'd be the type I'd go fer."

"You were pretty obvious. I just had other things on my mind."

Axel smiled.

"I'm glad Cole had the sense to keep me in check. Nothin' much has changed since I was human, because I always found a way to prove people wrong about me. I wanted to beat the curse, it was just a matter of will, I thought." He paused and shook his head. "I didn't tell Cole the truth that day. I did more than think about it, and when you was in my bed, all vulnerable with nothin' to stop me, I paced for hours to the living room and back to the bed. I climbed on top of you, and my mouth wouldn't stop watering. It took so much to hold it back. I ain't never done hard drugs before, but if I did, you'd have been that drug." He went quiet, looking down at the floor. "Disappointed?"

"Impressed."

He smiled again. "I haven't felt that urge since the day the town went nuts. Last night was the biggest test, and I didn't think I'd be so good that I'd bring out the wolf in ya."

I gave him a playful shove.

"Shut up," I said, my face hot as I remembered how he made me feel before the pain of the transformation. "So this is it?"

He nodded. "I ain't gonna jinx it by saying I'm not cursed no more, but if havin' my nose buried in your crotch didn't bring it out, I don't think it's gonna happen."

I stood up from the bed, grabbing my clothes before wrapping the towel around my waist.

"Maybe Derrick was right about the loophole. Last night, I didn't have any kind of uncontrollable sexual need. Everything was completely different from what you described. Yeah, it was hard to think clearly, but I didn't feel compelled by anything more than my own impatience."

"What're you sayin'?"

"Maybe the curse is losing its potency."

"Or maybe yer just affected differently by it," he added. "You did have them paws instead of feet. That ain't normal either."

I hated getting my own hopes up, only to have a thought that dashed them all. We only had a few pieces of the puzzle, and getting the rest would take more time than we were given.

"I'm gonna get a shower," I said, turning toward the door before thinking of something that would take our minds off the situation, if only for a few moments. There was something eating at me that I had to confront. "If you want to join me, you can."

He jumped off of the bed, nearly tripping over his own feet as he skittered across the floor before prodding me impatiently into the hallway.

"I ain't gonna say no to that!"

⁂

I kept my eyes focused on the path while staring at Axel occasionally through my peripheral vision. We'd barely spoken three words to each other since we left the house, mostly because I wasn't sure how I felt after that experiment.

"You okay? Ya look kinda sick."

We trekked along the dirt road toward Cole's, but my mind lingered in that shower. I wanted to believe everything I'd heard about Axel was overly exaggerated, but when we started playing with each other, I wasn't prepared for that at all.

"I feel fine," I said quickly, giving him a reassuring smile. "Just got a lot on my mind."

While I was relieved that the one barrier stopping us from getting closer was gone, there was a new one now. I wanted to talk to Cole first about what I should do before bringing this up to Axel. Maybe this funny conversation would take his mind off of the crushing pressure Gar placed on him.

Axel cleared his throat, breaking the awkward silence again.

"I love it when it gets cold out. Fur's still a little damp, though. Always takes so long to dry off after a bath."

"You smell better, though, and you need to brush more. There's fur all over the house, and you clogged the drain three times. I'd never seen so many twigs and sandspurs in one tail before."

"I hate brushin'. Takes too damn long. Plus, I can't reach my back."

"Well, now you've got me. I'll brush you down better tonight when we get home."

Axel flashed me a half-grin as two vargyrs casually strolled by, one of them giving me a nod before grunting out a 'good morning.' I reciprocated the greeting and locked up.

"My lotion. I forgot to put it on," I whispered, looking back at the chatty pair as they continued along the road without giving me so much as a second glance. "Wait a minute."

"What's wrong?"

"That was the most normal interaction I've had here."

Axel gave me a few good sniffs before relaxing his posture. "You kinda smell like everyone else."

"Damn, really?" I gave myself a pit check.

"Not like that. There's a main smell, and a bunch of subtle ones. It's them that's changed."

"If I turn again, get me away from town."

His arm slipped around my waist. "Whatever happens, I ain't gonna leave ya, but you were pretty big, though. If you decide you really want to go somewhere, I don't know if I'll be strong enough to hold you back."

"Well, I wasn't completely stupid last night. But I have to wonder if there's a chance I'd end up like those vargyrs you had to put down."

"Come on, now," Axel said, giving me a slight shake. "I hate what-ifs. It don't happen that often, and you shouldn't spend yer time worrying about things that ain't even come to pass—and probably won't since this ain't normal."

"You don't know that." I pulled away from him and nervously crossed my arms over my stomach. "I haven't exactly been the luckiest so far."

"Really? You went full vargyr and turned human again. Yer probably the luckiest one here." His eyes narrowed on me. "Think about it: If I hadn't wandered away from Toby's to take a piss and a walk that night outside of town when you got here, things would have gone a lot different for ya."

"Axel, most of my life—"

"—don't matter here," Axel interrupted. "You ain't the same person you was last week, let alone years ago. You wanna spend yer life worrying about what you can't control, or do you wanna live in the moment?"

"I'm sorry."

Axel grabbed my hand and held it as we picked up the pace, Cole and Vince's house appearing through the trees in the distance.

"When yer with me, yer gonna live the right way. We'll do things that make us happy because we're lucky we can. When you start thinking those bad thoughts, talk to me. I may not know a lot, but I get that way sometimes too. Talkin' about it with someone always helps, and poor Toby always gets an earful when I get too drunk."

"Thanks, Axel. You know you can talk to me, too," I said as we walked up the porch steps. The front door opened before we could knock, and Cole stood on the other side with a ghostly complexion.

"Hey guys, I've got some company." He shuddered, his eyes flashing a silent warning I picked up on right away. Axel, however, didn't seem to notice.

"Aw shoot. We'll come back later when ya ain't busy."

"Nonsense." That voice made every hair on my body stand straight. "We were just talking about you."

Cole swallowed hard and turned to go back inside, revealing Gar planted on the sofa, his arms crossed while his pawed feet rested on the table. A sickening pang punched me in the gut as I suspected the worst. Did he force Cole to reveal the events of last night?

"Why are you here?" I asked, trying to avoid direct eye contact with him.

"I hadn't seen my most popular wilkyr in a while, and I wanted to see if anything was troubling him."

Axel growled, and I stealthily reached behind, pulling the fur on his mane to silence him.

"Usually those troubles go away with treatment, don't they?" I replied calmly.

The black vargyr kicked the table over and snarled, the sudden outburst startling all of us.

"Such a cocky tone in your position." He stood up and pulled a vial from his pocket. "You know what I'm here for." He tossed the small bottle of blue liquid onto the couch, and it rolled toward the armrest.

"What is that?"

"Cole's troubles," he replied with a sharp grin. As I rushed the couch, he put his arm in front of me, shoving me back. "Not yet. About the deal I made…" He sniffed the air, and I started to worry. I didn't smell human anymore. "I swear, I don't understand." He turned to Axel. "He's practically covered in your scent, and you still haven't been able to turn him."

I took another look at the bottle and gave Cole a silent signal. "I'm not doing it."

He snatched the vial from the couch and held it in front of Cole. "It's a shame you put your trust in someone so selfish, considering the lengths you went through to protect him. I'll save this for your replacement."

Axel leapt at Gar, but a ripple of white light threw him across the room before pinning the giant vargyr to the wall.

"I pretended last time, but we're not doing this again." He tossed a glance at Vince before his gaze settled on me. "You know about me already, and my patience has reached its breaking point. You all want to go back to your worlds, right?"

"Why do I have to be cursed for that to happen?"

Axel's strength was almost enough to break the flickering force holding him, but another bolt shot from below and pulled him downward.

"Animals belong on the floor, mongrel," Gar muttered, looking back at me. "What does it matter?"

"Maybe I'd be willing to change my mind if I knew."

"Change your mind?" He could barely catch his breath through the laughter. Now that he was smiling, I could see why he subdued his facial expressions in town. His mouth was huge, and he had way more sharp teeth than any other vargyr. "Oh, that's over now." He leaned in close and looked at my eyes. "Something's off about you."

The smell was one thing, but my eyes were a lot more telling.

"I don't feel any different," I lied.

His stare narrowed, but to my relief, he seemed to shrug it off.

"You don't need to know the details because they don't matter. You get the curse, and I'll do the rest. It's simple, and then you can go home, and everyone has their happy ending."

"If that's the case, what happened to the other humans from my world that ended up here?"

The demon grabbed my neck, pulling me close. "Enough with the questions." He shoved me toward the door, causing me to stumble forward. "Let's take a little trip to pleasure town. I have hungry customers waiting."

"Gar, please," Cole shouted, grabbing the demon's arm. "Don't do this to him. You gave him a choice, remember?"

I tried to run, but a crackling light pulled me back, binding my wrists together. It was painful, like low voltage shocks spreading tighter over my skin every time I struggled.

"The only choice I gave him was how he'd receive the curse, and even that was dangerously generous of me. Maybe I'm growing a little too soft." The demon glared at Axel before tossing the vial to the floor, shattering it. "There are no shortages of vargyrs in this town, and unlike you, they won't hesitate."

"You bastard!" Vince shouted, looking down at the shattered remains of the elixir. "Why?"

"Because it's no longer necessary."

"Ya can't do this to him," Axel said, struggling in vain to push himself from the floor. "He could get hurt."

"Oh, he will get hurt," Gar hissed. "But I won't let him die."

"Let Axel do it," Cole continued. "They can use our bedroom."

The demon pushed open the door and held it in place, the electrified shackles pulling me forward. "No." He pointed at Axel and Cole. "I won't have to worry about either of you for much longer, and Vince..." He turned and bared his teeth at the smaller vargyr. "No more dungeon for you."

He gave me another hard shove through the door, and I lost my balance. Expecting to hit the ground face-first, I closed my eyes and landed on something soft as everything around me went dark. I examined the empty, musty-smelling room as a single beam of pale light shined down from the ceiling, giving form to the stained mattress I was lying on. Gar's voice rang out from every direction, echoing from the bare stone walls.

"Make yourself comfortable. The show is about to start soon, and you're my star."

Breaking Free

Glowing red eyes leered at me from the panes of what looked like thick glass separating the room from a stone corridor. I wasn't sure how I ended up here, but this wasn't the same room I landed in earlier.

"I already have the curse," I shouted.

Cutting laughter echoed from above the empty room. "I am not sure what impresses me more: your stupidity or your boldness. You know what I am, and you know I created this curse."

"I'm telling the truth. Look at my eyes!"

"Iris discoloration could easily be a side-effect of the elixir I gave you, but please, tell me more. Can my curse make you fly, too? You know you're not the first from your world here, and I know how my curse would affect you if you had it."

"Give me time. I'll shift again," I pleaded, while trying to think vargyr thoughts, as if I had any clue what brought about the transformation to begin with, or if I even could shift back. Still, it couldn't hurt to try anything as Gar took his time mentally torturing me. I closed my eyes to concentrate; however, several flickers of blue flames erupted from the four corners of the room as torches roared to life, distracting me.

"It's almost time," Gar said, appearing next to me as a spectral image. "Look at them out there. They've been locked in this place for so long with no relief. They're feral and as virile and ravenous as they come. I wouldn't struggle if I were you."

"They'll kill me," I said, standing up from the bed.

"I can assure you, they will not. If there was any chance of that happening, you wouldn't be here."

"Why all of them?"

"Why not?" He rubbed his palms together, licking one of his sharp canines. "You've made an enemy of me when I could have been your friend. I'm going to enjoy watching them destroy you, but don't worry, you'll heal in time for more until the ritual is complete."

His image faded, and the only door clicked, bursting open as five feral vargyrs leapt toward me. I instinctively ran along the edge of the room toward the exit, but the rippling Lo'rim threw me back. One beast tackled me to the floor, and I let out a shriek when he raked at my pants with his claws, ripping them from the back.

Another vargyr let out a howl before lunging at me, or so I thought. As he tore into the other beast holding me down, Gar's translucent image faded back into the room. The crystal dangling from the stone ceiling dimmed as he slammed the tip of a metallic scepter into the floor, forming snakes of light that spread through the concrete before creeping up four of the vargyrs' legs. As the light enveloped the beasts, it pulled them apart, securing them against the walls while leaving one free.

Gar's image cackled. "My mistake. They might be a little *too* eager. I'll give them each a turn separately." The vision faded again, leaving me alone with the largest of the pack, and I recognized him. He was the one Axel called Loken, and the same vargyr who attacked me in the woods. There was no lucidity in his expression, no anger, just an emotionless thrall. Loken drooled, his eyes darting to the other restrained monsters before focusing directly on me. Seeing the others unable to move calmed him enough that he stalked languidly in my direction.

I tried to scramble to my feet, but he already had me in his grasp, flipping me onto my stomach before pulling me across the cold granite floor.

Trying in vain to kick loose, I soon understood what Gar meant earlier; the more I struggled, the more forceful the vargyr became.

He snapped his jaws, his mouth inches from my neck as he hovered over my back on his hands and knees. More fabric tore, and the chill of the room spread along my back before traveling lower. Both my shirt and pants parted as the beast lowered himself, the wet tip of his strange-looking cock slipping against my lower back.

The room darkened to a red tinge as a surge of strength coursed through me. With almost superhuman speed, I flipped over in time to see the vargyr's surprised expression when I pushed against him, my legs launching him across the room until he hit the wall with a thud. In another fluid movement, I went from lying on my back to standing upright. The vargyr I had thrown stumbled to his feet, momentarily dazed.

I glanced down at my body to see if I had made the transformation, there was nothing visually out of the ordinary. I was still human, but where had this strength come from?

"What was that?" Gar's voice echoed throughout the room. "What just happened?"

"I told you," I shouted at nothing above me. "I'm a vargyr!"

"I'm not blind, Leo," the demon hissed. "Has Cole been rifling through my elixirs again?"

The feral in front of me snarled, and the crystal lights in the ceiling flickered brighter as the four that were restrained fell loose from the walls. Before I could say anything more to Gar, all five of them attacked at once.

As if by instinct, my feet left the ground, and I was airborne for a second as I leaped over them, kicking off of a wall before landing hard on the other side, stumbling forward. One of the other vargyrs turned and lunged toward me, but my fist connected with the side of his head. He let out a loud yelp before falling to the floor, bleeding from the mouth. My fist caught some of the vargyr's sharp teeth, but there was no time to examine the wound as the other four surrounded me.

The one on the floor slowly pushed himself to his feet, shaking his head as his body rapidly healed. I wouldn't be able to hold them off forever, but what I did earlier made them think twice before coming at me again so carelessly. They had an unusual amount of awareness that affirmed Axel's description as they nodded and grunted at one another in an unspoken language.

The pack circled tightly around me like wolves around an injured deer, and the room dimmed again as light snaked through the floors toward my feet this time. Gar was going to restrain me like he did the other vargyrs earlier if I didn't do something now. Before the light could hold me in place, I looked up at the ceiling and found my temporary salvation. With all of my new lower body strength, I leapt from the floor toward the ceiling.

The only thing that looked secure enough to support my weight was the wooden rectangular fixture holding the crystal, so I grabbed onto the flattened sides of it, which had a gap just large enough for my fingers to hook through. I dangled there, waiting for what the vargyrs would do next as the light receded back into the floor. The light of the crystal brightened again, and so too did the rippling barrier blocking the exit.

"The game is over," Gar shouted from all directions. The demon must have been controlling the room using whatever this crystal was, and he may have finally discovered I was telling the truth. "There is nowhere to run. Your body will tire. Give up this pointless resistance."

The vargyrs began leaping up at me, and I used my core strength to lift my legs horizontally so they couldn't easily grab hold. I examined the crystal further while shifting away from sharp claws that swiped through the air like hooked knives. They weren't able to go as high as I did, perhaps because they were too heavy, but if I didn't dodge fast enough, they'd be able to get my feet.

I pounded the crystal with my fist while hanging with one other hand. It wouldn't budge. There was no way to use my full strength to dislodge the thing while performing evasion maneuvers at the same time, but I had an idea.

Grabbing the slenderer end of the crystal with my left hand, I quickly wrapped my right hand around the other side, now dangling from it instead of the solid frame to which it was attached. As expected, a pair of giant hands snatched my ankles, gripping them tight as the vargyr tried to pull me down with his weight. I could still keep my grip firm, but my palms were starting to sweat. The crystal made a cracking noise as I struggled to pull up not only my own weight, but that of a three-or-four-hundred-pound beast.

Another vargyr must have grabbed onto the one below me and pulled, because my enhanced strength was starting to give way. The crystal began to make pinging noises as light arced from it.

"Infuriating," Gar shouted as the Lo'rim engulfing the room faded. Where was he? Why did he use magical projections instead of capturing me in person? Whatever the reason, his absence from this place gave me a fighting chance. "You're a lot smarter than I thought you were."

"Just a hang on a little longer," I said to myself as I began to slip.

As the last of my strength vanished, the crystal shattered, sending me and the others falling to the floor as the room darkened. I landed on top of the vargyrs before kicking myself free. The Lo'rim sealing the door dissipated, and I leaped toward it, bracing myself in case the barrier was still there. I opened my eyes, and a black-stoned corridor appeared in front of me.

I couldn't believe it worked. Without a moment more of hesitation, I took off in a direction I hoped would lead me out of this place.

Snarls and scuffing of clawed feet reverberated behind me as I continued around a corner until a glowing doorway appeared. This would either be a dead end or an exit, and I crossed my fingers as my shaky legs carried me closer. I gripped the handle and threw open the door, freezing air enveloping me as I fell into light. With only a second to react, I glanced down and braced myself as I hit the ground, which sloped at a steep angle. Pine needles and branches scraped my naked body as I rolled downward, eventually crashing into a thick pine.

The force of the impact knocked the air out of me, and I blacked out for a moment before gasping and coughing. It hurt to move as branches and thorns dug into my skin, but I had to get away from the vargyrs. Luckily, I had enough energy left to stumble to my feet before limping the rest of the way down the hill.

No noise came from the direction of whatever building Gar held me in, so I stopped and turned to see if I was still being pursued. There was nothing: no vargyrs, no Gar—not even a building. As the adrenaline faded, I took a moment to catch my breath and examine my surroundings. Frigid gusts burned my bare skin, and the only landmarks that weren't shrouded in thick brush were enormous boulders scattered throughout the forest clearing.

Even though I had made my escape, there was a possibility I would freeze to death before finding shelter, especially since the sun was in a late afternoon position from what little I could see of the sky. Why was it so late? I was only in that prison for maybe an hour or more—or was I? Did time flow differently in whatever prison Gar had me in?

A sharp pain in my side made me groan, and I pressed against the source only to feel a warm dampness, the scent of blood catching my nose.

"I could really use some fur right about now," I whispered to myself, my lips trembling so violently I could barely speak. After being able to fend off those ferals, I knew the vargyr was still in me, somehow.

I had to keep moving; there wasn't a choice. Staying here meant I'd freeze—or be eaten by some predator. If I was going to die, I'd do it fighting to survive. The forest ahead had an unnatural darkness about it, the canopy so dense no sunlight could penetrate. Fear wasn't the only thing slowing me down as I approached the shadows that seemed to swallow the world; the ground was rocky here, and with the cold and no shoes, every step was agony.

Keeping as calm as I could, I crossed into the woods, and the daylight quickly retreated. At first, it was like walking through a cave with no headlamp, but as my eyes adjusted, the sheer beauty of nature glowed in a brilliant bioluminescence. Countless glowing fungi spread across the roots and up trees like a forest within a forest, each species giving off a different color. Ghostly reds, blues, oranges, and yellows of all different shapes and sizes lit different paths along the forest floor, and giant purple polypores spiraled up neon ivy-covered trunks as though they were leading to a fairy village overhead.

A sprawling web of roots blanketed the ground, but soft blue moss covered them, which made traversing the lumpy terrain slightly more comfortable. I didn't know where I was in relation to Varcross, but I recognized the giant baobab-like trees that usually made the woods so dark and imposing. It amazed me that trees so large could grow so close one another.

Warm steam seeped from the ground with every one of my clumsy footsteps. Since sunlight couldn't reach the forest floor, the same could be said for the bitter wind that lightly rustled through the leaves many hundreds of feet above me. It was still chilly, but at least I wouldn't die of hypothermia here.

Soft bird calls and the patter of little feet came from all directions, but the moment I could smell animals, my stomach tightened and complained. Everything about me seemed screwed up with vargyr abilities and senses manifesting and disappearing at random times. However, when I got a whiff of brine and chimney smoke gently wafting along the stale current of air, I knew I was heading in the right direction. I just had to hope my sense of smell didn't vanish like my strength did.

The scent trail intensified as the forest thinned and the night air grew colder. With a few more steps, I emerged from the glowing jungle of vines and mushrooms into a moonlit clearing. The stress of the day, combined with hours of walking sent my body into a hard crash. I was in a trance for the rest of the journey, letting my mind go blank while only focusing on putting one sore foot in front of the other.

Since I was still naked and now exposed to a northwesterly wind, maintaining a steady pace was nearly impossible. I ran my blue fingers along where the gash in my side had been, thinking it had scabbed over, but all that remained of the injury was a thick line of dried blood I easily wiped away. The rapid healing was still there, and it was probably the only reason I was still clinging to life.

Every step was like walking on dry ice, but soon my feet began to go numb—not a good sign, and I hoped any frostbite would heal as quickly as my side did. All I had to do was focus on that delicious smoke growing stronger. If I thought about nothing else, I could push through the pain.

Each tree along my path glowed an intense pale blue, almost as bright as evening. The scenery was familiar now, and though I couldn't place where I was, I continued trusting my nose and my gut. Sharp limbs of shrubbery clawed at my skin as I pushed through narrower paths, and I could hear the cheers of ocean waves close to where I was. My breath quickened when I cleared the brush. A mound of stones decorated one of the bluffs in the distance. Xavier's grave. Derrick's cabin wasn't far from this place.

Ten more agonizing minutes of limping across freezing ground took me to a cluster of trees hiding the cozy abode we'd stayed at the other day, smoke billowing from the chimney. It was a stone's throw away, but the closer I got, the harder it was to move my legs. The ground got higher as I dropped to my hands and knees, keeping my focus ahead despite my blurring vision. I crawled until I was at the door, and with the last of my strength, knocked three times before collapsing.

CHAPTER 18

The Lonely Scholar

A shadow in the shape of wolf ears danced along the log ceiling of the cabin, and flames crackled in the hearth. I groaned, pulling up the heavy fur blanket draped over me until it covered half of my face.

A huge, rough palm rested against my head.

"If you're going to come all the way out to visit me in this weather, you should probably wear clothing," Derrick said, giving me a pat as he knelt next to the bed, eye-level with me. He had a leather strip tied around the middle of his beard, and he was better groomed today. His silky black fur reflected a bit of the hearthlight, the mane on his head brushed and tied back. "Are you hungry?"

"Starving," I whispered. "Thanks for getting me warm."

Derrick stood and grabbed a bowl from one of the hand-made shelves nailed to the wall. "I take it you have quite the story," he said, ladling a thick brown stew from a medium-sized cauldron that hung from rusted chains.

"Gar made his move," I said, my stomach growling.

"I had a feeling something like this would happen." He smiled and held the bowl in front of me. I sat up, keeping the warm blanket draped around my lower half before taking the meal.

"Thanks." I shivered and held the bowl to my mouth, letting the steaming, savory broth coat my tongue with a thick, almost gravy-like texture. It was probably the most delicious thing I'd eaten since coming to Varcross. There were wild mushrooms and onions with potato-like root vegetables all mixed with tender chunks of meat that resembled stewed beef tips.

"You're quite welcome, of course. It's been a while since I've shared a meal with anyone," he said, pulling a wooden chair next to the hearth before grabbing a leather bag secured with a strap. He then reached for a curved pipe on another shelf next to him. "You mentioned he wanted you cursed, but I don't remember the gritty details. It was quite a day." He sprinkled some loose-leaf tobacco into the mouth of the pipe, packing it down with a small metal tamper. He repeated this a few times until the pipe was almost full.

"He told me that if I get the curse, everyone can go back to their worlds. That was really all he said before pushing me into some kind of interdimensional dungeon. I was almost gangbanged by five feral vargyrs."

Derrick lifted a flaming stick to the pipe and cocked an eyebrow. "You must have really angered him. My condolences." He lit the tobacco and drew in several long puffs.

"Somehow, I already have the curse, and I think you gave it to me."

Derrick coughed and sputtered, his eyes watering.

"I thought the only thing I did was bite you," he choked out, smacking his tongue and lips together. "This is quite embarrassing. I hope it wasn't too awful, though I wish I could remember what it felt like." He took another draw from his pipe

I sat the now empty bowl on my lap and shot him a disgusted stare, but he didn't react.

"That's not what happened. I think it was the bite. I went full vargyr that night after I got home."

Derrick took in another draw and wrinkled his nose. "This is awful."

"It's not all bad. I was able to turn back into a human."

"I was talking about the tobacco," he said, letting one ear fall forward as he tipped the pipe over the fire and emptied what remained. "Your story sounds absurd, though."

"Excuse me?"

"I wonder if hypothermia has any lasting effects on the brain," he muttered to himself. "Ah, I wish I still had access to the medical wing of the athenaeum." He coughed again and spat out the taste of what must have been decades-old tobacco. "Oh, how I miss the smell of old books."

"There's nothing wrong with my brain," I said. "Axel was there; he saw it happen. Cole and Vince saw me too."

Derrick sat his wooden pipe back on the shelf and dumped the sack of stale tobacco into the fire. "You were quite the sight when you showed up on my doorstep."

I tried to respond, but Derrick cut me off.

"You are obviously human, Leo. Not only that, but one doesn't just turn into a vargyr. You'd be a wilkyr right now."

"Gar said something about the curse and his potions affecting me differently because I'm from another world."

His ears perked up. "Ah, that's right. How fascinating." Derrick stood and walked over to a tall cabinet next to a small log table. He flipped the lock and opened it, revealing about a hundred thick, leather-bound tomes.

"Wow! That's a lot of books."

"This is a pathetic collection. The library in Stellous was a sight to behold. Endless text locked behind different levels of authority. I wasn't fortunate enough to make it to archmagi before the transformation."

After delicately grabbing a book, the black vargyr opened the dusty cover, licking a pointer finger before turning a few pages.

"There were so many books, one could never read them all in several thousand lifetimes. There were spells, histories, sciences— knowledge spanning many different worlds visited and studied extensively by chronomancers over the millennia. Their sacrifices in the name of progress shaped our world and culture far beyond what it would have been if we stayed in the dark ages hurling fireballs at one another with all the elegance of simians flinging feces." He flipped several more pages. "What was the name of that mage you mentioned?"

"Josiah," I said, placing the bowl on the floor before pulling up a chair next to him, the blanket still snugly wrapping my body. "Is he in this book?"

"Who's to say? Like the deva'koh, mages of his abilities are rare. Rarer still are the mages willing to risk their lives using that magic. However, if one wants to amass fame and fortune quickly, this is the way to do it. Knowledge from other worlds is worth more than an entire country's coffer—usually locked away on level four." He turned and gave me a look I could only describe as a professor's stare. "There were very few books I could bring with me before I was thrown here, but thankfully, we still trade with the home world. Wilkyrs earn a lot more money than vargyrs do, so I saved every bit of coin I made during my time working in the dungeon and created a tiny library of my own. During my free time, I developed an interest in chronomancy and the different worlds beyond ours. Most of my books are black market copies of originals that were stolen from athenaeum archives."

"How do you know if the information in that book is correct if you bought a forged copy? You just said this information was locked away."

"Level four isn't exactly maximum security, and there are mages with eidetic memories that can duplicate a book right down to the letter with a single spell. The archmagi in charge of the athenaeum know these mages exist, but the culprits aren't easily found out. It's one reason there are so many levels, each with their own security clearance. The higher up in level, the fewer people have access, which means higher risk of being discovered." Derrick continued to thumb through the book, occasionally glancing up at me. "I read this decades ago, and if memory serves, there are mentions of living, non-magical realms. Stumbling upon one in the cosmos is quite rare."

"I'd have thought it was the other way around," I said, looking over the vargyr's shoulder at the illegible runes and symbols scattered along the pages. Every so often, I'd see an elaborate sketch of a strange creature or two.

"A universe barren of magic rarely has life complex enough for interest, at least as far as we know. Chronomancers have the ability to feel the threads of life in any realm that manifests in their rituals.

Non-magic realms usually have no threads; therefore, that universe is abandoned. However, when a non-magic realm has them, a mage will jump at the opportunity to study it. Living, intelligent beings that inhabit such places are astronomically rare."

Derrick paused and gave me an awestruck smile as though he'd just figured something out.

"You're the rarest living creature in this entire realm. If Stellous knew you were here, they'd send an entire army just to collect you."

That actually kind of made me smile. Back on Earth, I was just another person, but here I was something rare—something special. The more thought I gave it, the more absurd it seemed.

"Good thing we're locked away then."

"Indeed," Derrick continued. "The humans of your world had to use cunning to evolve and survive, and considering you are human yourself, perhaps those of our realm once seeded yours eons ago. Every world like that never stays the same for long. You're always pushing further with every generation and can at times do the most impossible things, including developing technology that, while not as advanced as ours, is complex enough to study."

He paused for a moment, letting his finger trace along one particular page.

"I do not have a book categorized by world, but this one serves as an index. There are only summaries of cities or countries in the few notable non-magic worlds we've discovered. This isn't even close to the full archive, so hopefully there's something in here we can use. Tell me if any of these names sound familiar," he said, his eyes returning to the pages. "Albanon."

"No."

"Ciebus."

I shook my head, but he didn't look up. Instead, his ears pointed in my direction.

"You'll need to speak up."

"No, it's not familiar."

He continued rambling off names that got more bizarre by the moment. At one point, he was going through a list that sounded nothing like actual words, but were grunts and slurping noises. It was hard to contain my laughter as I watched the vargyr sputter and drool everywhere as he spoke.

"There are quite a lot of these," he said, wiping his mouth before flipping the page. "Not exactly the most graceful linguistics, admittedly."

"I'm pretty impressed you're able to pronounce these words," I said. "You'll probably want to stick to names that sound more human."

Derrick nodded. "My apologies. Sometimes I get carried away. I'll stick to less complicated names." He flipped a few more pages. "Loba'an. Xty'lyl. G'sholobasta—"

"Those are less complicated?" I interrupted, prompting him to look up for a moment before running his pointer finger to the center of the page.

"Tokyo, Cab—"

"That one," I shouted, startling Derrick. "Tokyo's a city in another country."

"That means we have the right book. There's mention of this city briefly, but the name of the chronomancer who discovered it was Magus Dolari, not Josiah. Now that I have records of the right planet, give me a name that may be of significance to Josiah. It could be an area he told you to go, or where he resided."

"What about Oregon?"

"Spell it."

"I can't," I muttered, looking downward. "This is kind of embarrassing."

"Are you illiterate?" Derrick asked bluntly, but without any sort of mockery behind his tone.

"No. It's just, your letters are different from mine."

The vargyr stood and grabbed a sheet of paper and an ink-laden fountain pen from his small desk next to the window.

"Here, write the letters. Let me see if I can read them."

I did as he told me and handed the paper back to him.

"Hmm. I can't read this," he said, looking up at me.

"Well, no shit. That's what I just said."

Derrick stroked his chin harder. "This is interesting. Spell out the letters."

"O-R-E-G-O-N."

"I understood that," he said, giving an *aha* expression. "A lingual enchantment was placed upon you at some point. You still think in your language, but what comes out of your mouth is something we can understand. This also works the other way, as what comes from my lips is interpreted by your brain as your language and whatever dialect fits the way we speak. Isn't that fun?"

"When the hell did that happen?"

"That is what we will eventually find out," he said, flipping through more pages, his eyes wildly scanning each line of text. "Oregon is not here."

I rubbed my forehead, trying to remember anything I could about my brief online encounters with the mage. Even in his profile, his location was Varcross, Oregon. However, the postmark on the letter he sent was different.

"Try Mount Shasta."

"A mountain?"

"A city near an active volcano."

"Thrilling," he said, flipping through a few more pages while scanning each one impressively fast. "Is this the mountain?" He held the book up, and there was an accurate sketch of the volcano in the center of the page.

"That's it."

He turned the book back and continued reading. "This is a surprising amount of information for a summary." He stopped and placed his finger on a line of strange text. "There are references here to five books, but I don't have them." He closed the tome and walked back to the cabinet, sliding it into the gap before running his finger along the spines of the other books. "But I do have *something*. Now where is it? Ah!" He grabbed a brown, cloth-bound book that was mostly bare except for a few runes in silver print. "This is the most fun I've had in decades!"

A tall, dapper monster getting so excited over figuring out a mystery was kind of adorable. Though he was on the opposite end of the spectrum intellectually, he was warm and charming like Axel.

"I suppose it is kind of fun, but I'm kind of worried about the others," I said with a warm smile, moving back to the bed.

"They can take care of themselves, and you can't make the journey back without clothing. For now, what we have is an opportunity to learn about your purpose here and our foe." Derrick sat back down on the groaning wooden chair, crossing one leg over his knee before cracking open the book. "Let's see what wonders we can find."

⁂

"Leo." Derrick shook me, his tail wildly swinging from side-to-side.

With one eye open, I sat up and yawned, noticing the pile of books surrounding Derrick's chair. "Damn. How long was I out? Did you find out anything?"

"You were quite exhausted, and I found a lot. There were so many references to generations of mages connected to Josiah's research, but get this: when I looked up those references, their names were redacted." He held up a ratty-looking book. "Xavier gave me this not long before he died, but I never had a chance to read it since things got so out of hand. I forgot I even had it, and this isn't some replica. This is an original!"

"Okay? Is that a good thing?"

"Very!" With intense enthusiasm, he pulled his chair next to the bed. "Josiah may have made some powerful enemies to have his entire bloodline stricken from records; either that, or his ancestors did. This book has hundreds of years of research in it from thirty different chronomancers, each one continuing the research of the last. I think Xavier got this book from Gar, somehow. That insane little bastard."

"Are you for real?"

He cocked his head to the side. "I'm not quite sure I understand the question."

"Never mind. What does it say?"

Derrick thumbed through the pages. "I've been skimming through what I can, though it would take months to fully understand the details. The first few sections date back over two hundred and fifty-eight years, a century after Varcross was repurposed to control the spread of the curse. Every section was written by the offspring of the previous, and the last portion was written by Josiah himself. It's a masterpiece! Generations of chronomancers from the same lineage working on the same research: how beings from non-magic worlds interact with our dimension."

"That sounds…promising," I said, trying to keep up with Derrick's enthusiasm. "And?"

"And? This is your very purpose for being here! The most recent notes were from three decades ago, but it stops there. In the last paragraph, he goes into extensive detail about an alchemical fusing process to combine deritium with a weakly radioactive substance from your world known as thorium. Apparently, both metals have the same atomic structure and instability, but the subatomic particles are different, yet are stable when fused. Apparently, merging the magic and non-magic metals was so powerful that it caused a brief short in both wards at the same time, but only when a living creature from a non-magic realm was sent through holding it. It's similar to how the mages put vargyrs and wilkyr into Varcross, but deritium alone doesn't pose a risk of overloading the wards, and it doesn't disable both at the same time."

"What does this have to do with me being cursed? Isn't that what you were supposed to find out?"

"Everything, Leo. This is where it gets really interesting. Instead of thorium and deritium, if a living creature from your realm is infused at the most basic level with something from a magical realm, they could theoretically hold enough energy to overload the wards, destroying them. However, you can't just fuse magic into living, non-magic creatures, otherwise they won't be living for very long. Josiah tried this with large and small animals, but the wards were never damaged. All that happened was they passed through, but like what happens with deritium, they disintegrated." Derrick scratched his head and flipped to the end of the tome. "What baffles me is that the research ends abruptly. The rest of the pages have been torn out, and the bottom two paragraphs on the last page have been scratched to the point of being completely illegible. There's more to it, but Gar wanted it removed for some reason."

He went silent and gave me an expectant nod, his tail fanning eagerly behind him.

"And how does this help? You still haven't explained where the curse comes into play here."

He sighed and patted my head. "I apologize. This is so exciting that I've gotten ahead of myself again. The curse is the only stable way to permanently infuse magic into non-magic creatures, and it only works with humans from your world. Gar and Josiah must have tried this and failed at some point. Given the restrictions and unstable nature of the curse in non-magic humans, it has to be spread to the right person. Male, young but not too young, healthy, light-eyed but dark-haired, and so-on... There's an entire list of physical specifications that you seem to meet, but even the most perfect specimen isn't a guarantee. This would explain why the curse was spread differently to you, and why it doesn't affect you in the same way it does us."

I jumped out of bed, still holding the blanket over me. "This is great! I can break the wards and free everyone!"

Derrick stood, his cheerful demeanor fading as he rested his hand on my shoulder. "A Lo'rim ritual is required to expose the wards first, and only Gar can do that. Plus, if you could break the wards on your own, there are several things to consider. First, the act of allowing vargyrs to return to Eqiros would be a death sentence. With no place to put the vargyrs when they are captured, well, you see where this is going."

"Genocide." I let out a defeated sigh and sat back down on the mattress.

"Second, the way the wards work would not bode well for you. There are two of them that require two different keys to open. The first lets in anything that is not human, a safeguard to prevent humans from ever going to Varcross again. However, it also lets those non-humans back out, so a second ward acts as a lock, keeping anything alive from passing through. Every vargyr and wilkyr thrown into Varcross wore collars of deritium which causes the second ward to short temporarily as it absorbs the metal. Once the vargyrs are in, the metal disintegrates, and the trip becomes one-way."

My eyes widened. "The metal key Josiah gave me turned to ash when I got to Varcross."

Derrick nodded, as though he had already known. "It was likely a fusion of both deritium and thorium, and since your atomic structure is different from the humans of Eqiros, the first ward probably did not recognize you as human. The thorium added enough potency to traverse worlds using Josiah's portal while the deritium shorted the ward." The vargyr paused and studied my face. "That means you likely passed through two portals to get here. Before you arrived to Varcross, you were on Eqiros for a short time, which was likely the moment you were enchanted with the ability to understand our language. You understand what this means, right?"

"We can't get back out without deritium."

"It's more than that," Derrick continued. "Remember when I said fusing non-magic creatures with magic has the same effect deritium has? Now that you are cursed, you are a living deritium rod, and potent enough to destroy the wards if they're exposed with Lo'rim. I am not entirely sure what your fate would be if this were to happen, but if this research is correct, you would not survive."

Silence fell upon the room, and I looked down at my hands. "Gar's not going to stop until he finds me. What am I going to do?"

"Well, you can't go back into town as a human, that's for sure, and the only ones that saw you as a vargyr were your friends, correct?"

I nodded.

"The answer may be to return to that form, gather what you can and leave before Gar finds out the truth."

"But I don't know how to go back to being a vargyr. It only happened once."

Derrick rubbed the pointed furry beard under his chin. "Do you remember what you were doing before you changed?"

Heat spread from my face as I broke eye contact and looked toward the window that was letting in a bit of moonlight from outside. "Uh, yeah."

"Try doing that."

I cleared my throat and slipped out of bed with the blanket still draped around me. "That's not gonna happen without Axel."

"What does Axel have to do with it?" Everything about my body language gave me away almost immediately. "OH!" He patted me on the back. "Good for you, finding a mate like that. Axel's a fine person from what I gathered. Sounds like my bite didn't curse you after all."

"No, he uh—" Why was I so embarrassed? Derrick was a vargyr, but he also seemed to have this primness about him that made me more self-conscious. "He used his mouth."

The vargyr cocked a grin, his eyes full of anticipation. "I see." He pointed to his muzzle. "Want me to give it a go?"

"Absolutely not! What the hell is wrong with you?"

Derrick burst into laughter. "Ah, that human shame. Once you're a vargyr for a while, that all goes away. Coitus between our kind is a lot different than it is with wilkyr or humans. It's not always romantic, but it can strengthen bonds of friendship and family."

"Yeah, that sounds really nice and all but...no."

"Well, you've got a hand; try using that."

"Right now? In here? I can't just turn it on."

"Why not? This is a great place for self-pleasure. I do it all the time, sometimes in that blanket you're wearing." My eyes shifted as I slowly let the covers fall to the bed. "And if you truly are a vargyr, you need not worry about 'turning it on.'"

I looked down at myself and then at the fur rug next to the hearth. "Alright," I said, looking at Derrick, who stood there staring at me. "Well?"

"Well what?"

"Are you going to leave?"

"I suppose it would be rather awkward for you if I watched." He chuckled to himself and walked toward the front door. "I will be around. Just give me a howl when you're done."

Live

I t actually worked. I didn't want to believe it, but as I sat there on the floor, panting, covered in black fur, my padded hand gripping a larger, more canine version of what I had as a human, I now knew the secret to my transformation.

It was humiliating.

I let go of the alien appendage, and it slipped into a thick, fur-covered sheath. I'd seen quite a few of these since I'd been in Varcross, but this was even weirder since it was now a part of my body. After playing a bit with Axel, there weren't many surprises, but the fist-sized bulge at the base still weirded me out.

The transformation wasn't as bad as the first, but it still hurt. There had to be a more efficient way to trigger the shift, but this was something new. No one else in town could do this, so it wasn't like anyone could teach me.

I stood on shaky foot-paws, nearly slipping on the wood floor where I'd finished moments ago. Derrick was right about being able to do this anywhere. Once I started, there was no stopping, and I was already in the mood for round two. However, I had to try to keep this animal mind focused and get back home to Axel.

After wiping my strange new feet on the rug, I made my way across the room to the door before pulling it open. Derrick stood in front of me, clapping slowly. He was eye-level with me now.

"Quite the impressive beast!" He looked down at my feet. "You certainly were right about the curse not affecting you the same way."

I was going to berate him for obviously watching, but as I went to speak, nothing came out. Being unable to talk in this form worried me, and I hoped this wouldn't become something permanent if one day I couldn't change back.

"You can't speak," he asked, patting me on the shoulder. I shook my head. "This happens to some wilkyrs when they shift for the first time. It's rare, but it usually goes away within the hour."

I shook my head again.

"It doesn't?" He looked me over once more before stepping back inside. "I shouldn't be surprised by what I don't know—which is apparently a lot. You should get back to town and let the others know you're okay. If you can, lead them back here so I can tell them everything."

I nodded and gave the vargyr a tight hug. If it weren't for him, an already terrible day would have ended much worse.

It didn't take long at full sprint to see Axel's house standing alone in the distance. Being able to run this fast and not tire was like being on the best drugs, and as the trees blurred by without me having to catch my breath, I wanted to see how much more I could do.

Thick, black fur insulated me from the painful blasts of icy wind, and there were so many smells...

I had to focus.

I couldn't let myself wander from the path again; I'd already done that four or five times already. As annoying as the poor attention span was, I now understood why Axel loved being a vargyr. If it weren't for the fact that I couldn't speak, I'd never want to get off this high. Nearly dying really put things into perspective, and I didn't want to go back to being fragile again, even at the cost of my humanity.

As I approached the darkened doorway of Axel's house, I turned the knob slowly and crept inside, sniffing the air. Nothing was fresh. No one had been back at the house since we left that morning. There was a risk of encountering Gar if I went to Cole's, if he was there at all. Even if he couldn't recognize me physically, there was always a chance he could smell who I really was.

I darted back to the dirt road and followed it until a flickering orange glow danced through the trees where Cole's house stood. The lights were off, but the hearth was lit. Carefully approaching, I peered through the window. Cole and Vince were sleeping, propped up against one another on the couch. Gar's scent was strong outside, but not recent. The demon had likely come by to look for me during the hours I was missing. What confounded me the most was if I was so important, why wasn't Gar at that dungeon in person? Why did no one chase me?

I opened the door and crept inside, startling Cole at first, but as his eyes adjusted, he lit up.

"Leo!" He jumped from the couch, and the sudden movement woke Vince. He threw his arms around me. "We thought you were dead or lost. Axel hasn't been back, and now we're worried about him too. Vince and I are too afraid to go back into town since Gar's on high alert."

After returning his hug, I tossed a quick glance at Vince, causing him to scramble to his feet and run into the dining room.

"Not again!"

I'd have given anything to speak to them, and I wondered how I would convey what Derrick told me. If only he had come with me, but I understood his trepidation when it came to this town, knowing what Gar did to him last time.

I let go of Cole and ran to the dining room table, pointing at it. The sudden movement startled Vince enough that he yelped and ran into the hallway. The poor guy really was scared of me, and after how I behaved the first time I shifted, I couldn't blame him. All of those weird feelings I had then didn't seem as strong now.

"What's wrong?" Cole asked. "What's with the table?"

I grabbed hold of the chair and flipped it upside-down, kneeling next to it while pretending to hold a hammer.

"Oh, I like this game," Vince said, racing back into the room.

"He's not playing, Vince." I looked up at Cole, nodding and smiling. "Wait, you are?"

I nodded again.

"Yer a carpenter," Vince said excitedly.

I nodded again and stood on my toes, grinning slyly while puffing my chest out.

"I remember this show when I was a kid. Thaddius Ritter," Vince said. I sighed, giving him a deflated look of confusion.

"How the hell would he know who that is?" Cole asked.

"Oh, that's right."

"He's Axel," Cole corrected, and I gave an enthusiastic thumbs up. "What about Axel?"

My hand acted as a visor against my forehead as I scanned the room.

"I don't know where he is right now, but if I had to guess, he's probably in town. The poor guy was beside himself after spending all day looking for you. We couldn't console him. If Toby let him back into the bar, that would be where he is."

I gave Cole a thumbs up and rubbed his head before turning away, but he caught me by the arm.

"I don't think this is a good idea. Let me go find him."

I shook my head.

"Gar ain't gonna recognize him like this. He even smells different."

Cole shoved his face into my chest fur. "Mmm, you're right."

"Hey!" Vince snapped, pulling Cole away.

"Wait, Leo," Cole said, glancing down at my pawed feet. "You're *too* different. If Gar see's you, he'll know."

I gave him a reassuring smile and backed my way out the door.

"Alright. Be careful."

With a nod, I took off in the direction of town.

Toby's tavern was busy as usual, and I slowed my pace to seem more inconspicuous. Maybe since everyone was so piss drunk, no one would notice how freaky I looked. Vargyrs that weren't passed out in the dirt around the pub stumbled aimlessly while gawking as I walked the path to the door. An inebriated, brown-furred patron tripped in front of me on his way out, but I caught him before he hit the ground.

"Thanks, buddy," he slurred, leaning against me as I helped him to a bench lining the deck against the wall. He plopped down and leaned his head back, his mouth hanging open as he snored.

The door swung open again, and another vargyr tumbled outside to the deck floor. I sighed and scooped him up before propping him next to the one that had fallen asleep. They were like toddlers trying to walk for the first time, each one needing to be supervised.

As another left the tavern, I caught the door with my foot and walked inside, scanning the room for Axel. The guy was usually hard to miss, but that wasn't the case tonight. He was slumped over, head down against the bar as Toby spoke to him while rubbing his head. The older barkeep always seemed prickly and unapproachable, but he obviously cared a lot about Axel.

Everyone in the bar stared at me. They were different reactions from when I was human. Some seemed shocked, others annoyed.

"Listen, buddy," Toby said, eying me with a grimace. "I know this isn't the classiest establishment, but how about putting some pants on while you're—" He froze and looked down. "What the hell?"

There wasn't much I could do but shrug and smile before resting my hand on Axel's back. He didn't acknowledge me at first, but when I rubbed my fingers through his mane, he finally looked up at me.

"Le—" I grabbed his snout before he finished saying my name, and I put a clawed pointer finger to my lips. Axel nodded in understanding before wrapping his arms tight around me, squeezing me so hard I thought my guts would come up my throat.

"Another weird *friend* of yours?" Toby muttered before quickly realizing the reason for Axel's sudden burst of happiness. "I'll be damned," he whispered. "You're gonna have to explain this."

"Can't right now," he said excitedly, his tail pounding against the stool. I grabbed his hand and pulled him toward the door. "G'night, Tobes. Thanks fer the drinks."

"Call me that one more damn time..."

Axel and I let out grunted laughter as I led him out of the bar. When we were clear of the others, he took his place at my side, losing his balance occasionally.

"I don't even wanna tell ya what I thought," he slurred. "Never felt so damn useless and scared in my whole life."

I let him lean against me, and he grinned, one ear falling to the side as he waited to see what I'd do.

"Still can't talk, huh?"

I shook my head.

"That ain't a problem. Who needs to talk all the time, anyway? I'm just glad yer okay. After Gar took you, I couldn't get off the floor for a while." He grabbed my hand. "I'm the strongest guy in town, but I can't do shit against magic, Leo. This is real scary. It's like when the mages were after me back on Eqiros."

He walked faster, and I sped up to match his footsteps.

"We're gettin' the hell out of here—all of us, the way Derrick did, except get to where Gar can't find us. Once Vince and Cole go feral, we'll say our goodbyes if they leave us. Maybe we'll go feral too, and we ain't gotta worry about nothin' then."

The possibility that I'd turn feral didn't scare me that much because the curse had no control over my thoughts. What terrified me was the possibility of losing everyone while out there in the undiscovered wilderness, living the rest of my life alone. Would Axel leave me if he went feral, or would he stay around? Either scenario was painful because he wouldn't be himself anymore.

As we approached the house, Axel pushed open the door, and I followed him inside.

"You guys need to pack."

"Why?" Vince asked, dazed at first, but that quickly devolved into anger. "Where the hell are we gonna go?"

Cole stood up from the couch without a word and dragged his feet along the floor toward the bedroom.

Axel pointed toward the window. "Out there."

"Here we go again with yer dumb ideas. There ain't nothin' out there—no booze, no games, no fuckin' nothing! What are we supposed to do?"

I sat next to Vince, but he scrambled to stand, trying to get away from me. However, I caught him by the tail and pulled him hard enough that he fell backward onto the cushions.

"Live," I grunted. The word took a lot longer to say, but Vince and Axel understood me. Derrick may have been right, but it was taking me much longer to recover my speech.

"That's the idea," Axel said with a gentle smile before focusing on Vince. "We're not living here, we're just existing. Out there we can be what we are."

"What we are is freaks." Vince growled at both of us and pulled away from me. "Cursed freaks. You make it sound like this is a natural thing, but all most of us wanna do is forget. If I'm gonna turn feral and lose Cole, I'm wanna be so piss drunk that nothin' matters."

"We're not gonna drink ourselves silly no more. We're wasting our lives when we should be makin' the most of what we have. Remember when we was kids, and we'd go out in the woods? There were new places to discover, and we'd build little huts out of sticks, dragon weed, and hangin' moss. Whenever I'd make you go out there with me, you always complained, but then I'd see that smile on yer face when we was away from that awful house. The world outside was ours."

"Yeah, it was fun times, but this ain't then, and we ain't kids no more. Even if it was terrible, we still had a place to go back to. We was fed and had a place to sleep. How are we going to survive out there?"

"Damn it, Vince, look in the mirror! Ya think we ain't designed to survive? I do it all the time, and I thrive out there. Everyone in town would be better off leavin' it behind because this world is more than a small, shitty town."

Vince pushed himself from the couch and crept closer to his friend, his nose wrinkled and teeth bared. "Not everyone loves bein' a monster, Axel. I hate it. I don't want to learn how to survive. I just want to go back to the way things were."

"That wouldn't happen even if we were still human," Cole muttered, walking back into the living room, holding two large bags by leather straps. "You can't go back, so I'm giving you a choice, because I'm not spending what little time I have left in this place. You can either stay here in a cold, empty house with no mate, no friends, and no quality of life while you pointlessly wish for things to go back to the way they were, or you can accept what you are and be with me. Either way, I'm not staying."

"Babe," Vince whined before embracing Cole. "Not you too. At least here we can be comfortable before the end."

"There's no comfort." Cole dropped one of the bags at Vince's feet before removing most of the gold necklaces lined with precious jewels he often wore, dropping them onto the table. All that remained were his piercings and a black choker. "All I've done for years is wear myself out, keeping everyone satisfied while losing more of who I am, and no one seems to care. I love you more than anyone, but I'm done. I can't watch you self-destruct anymore. I'm going to use the time I have left surrounded by friends who care about me. I want to see things I've never seen before."

The smaller vargyr said nothing for a moment, his eyes now wet.

"Then I'll follow you to hell," he whispered, touching Cole's forehead with his own. "I'm scared."

Cole dropped the other bag and took Vince's larger hand in two of his. "I know you are, and whatever happens out there, just know that I love you. I want you to be happy, even when I'm gone."

"I want you to live," Vince added, his tears dripping onto the floor as he embraced Cole. "Life ain't worth living if I don't have you. I wish I'd have been better."

Axel and I stared silently at one another, knowing we couldn't do anything. We were all powerless. In every relationship I'd been in, I was the one who willingly gave up control, relying on someone else's strength to pull me through. This time, I would meet Axel halfway and not let him shoulder this alone. It was funny, I felt more like a man as a beast than I had as a human.

A Long, Long Journey

When I was in college, I'd once heard a Yemeni student say that the worst part of being a refugee wasn't what he'd left behind; it was not knowing where he'd end up. My situation may have been different, but the sentiment held true. I would probably die if we didn't leave, but this world was uncharted. There were no borders to cross and no sanctuary. It was just us and an endless, unforgiving wilderness.

There was only so much I could carry in a duffel bag and backpack since Axel insisted on traveling light. I had some warm clothes in case I shifted back, two bottles of water, a lighter, and a pocket knife. I also brought my fully charged phone for pictures, but I'd need to keep it off most of the time to conserve the battery.

Axel was in his element. He wore a skimpy fur loincloth that I couldn't tear my eyes away from, his tooth necklace, and a leather harness with small sacks lined down the side straps. On his back, he carried our blanket, some knives, and a cooking pan.

The group kept wanting to go north, but I would veer away and follow the smell of smoke. I made several frantic gestures toward the direction of Derrick's cabin, and at first, no one understood.

Axel soon figured me out, and instead of stopping by, he planned on dragging the hermit vargyr along with us.

I doubted the ex-mage would want to leave his books to go on what could be a one-way adventure, but before Axel could knock on his door, Derrick threw it open, his sparkling green eyes wide and tail wagging in anticipation. The tall, black vargyr wore no clothing, as usual, but he did have a leather belt with sacks dangling from it, similar to Axel's harness. On his back was a faded green hiking bag stuffed full of supplies.

Axel started calling us a pack. If we were going to be a family, perhaps this time it would be a positive experience for me. Derrick's knowledge, combined with Axel's sheer strength and survival experience, made the rest of us more optimistic.

As we ventured further from town, I glanced at Vince, who was being unusually quiet. He wasn't complaining as much, and the hostile scent of his fear faded the further we got from town.

Cole clung to Axel's back, fast asleep, and Vince and I carried their bags. We were all tired, and we'd need to set up camp soon, but Axel wanted us to reach the plains before sunrise.

Instead of the shore, Axel and Derrick decided to follow one of the glacial streams since it was an ample supply of fresh water, and all rivers flowed from the northern peaks. Since we spent so much time shrouded in trees at night, it was easy to get turned around, even with a keen sense of smell. This gave us a solid direction.

Similar to that strange glowing forest I was in last night, fat tree trunks grew closer together here. Despite the freezing weather, many of them still had thick branches full of leaves that hadn't changed color or fallen. Most of the flora were alien, but every so often, we'd pass a more Earth-like birch or spruce.

Dawn cracked the midnight blue sky and shimmered through balding patches of canopy. The forest soon yielded to a meadow of frozen threads that stretched far into the distance, its advance halted by a phalanx of belching stratovolcanoes, their imposing peaks shrouded in billowing veils.

There were no breezes or bird calls here, only thick silence. Our crunchy footfalls disturbed the serenity, and every breath we took may as well have been gales compared to the icy stillness of the air.

Axel stopped, pointing his snout to the sky before inhaling long and deep. I did the same, closing my eyes as natural perfume tantalized my more sensitive nose. The scent got stronger as each step we took melted the frost, leaving a trail of damp, golden grass and beaded orange-colored buds.

"This is a good place to rest," Derrick said, letting out a yawn so contagious the rest of us joined in.

"About damn time." Vince scanned the area before running his hand along the grass. "Where the hell are we supposed to lay down?" he asked, wiping his hands on his faded blue shorts.

Axel lowered Cole before reaching into a larger bag for the thick, oversized blanket that used to be on our bed. He shook it out before spreading it over the ground.

"There's enough room fer all of us here if we sleep close. Leo, you got that other blanket?"

I nodded, unzipping one of Cole's duffel bags before grabbing the bedding he'd brought from his and Vince's bed.

Vince groaned and got down on all fours before crawling across the blanket. "This is hell," he muttered, over-exaggerating his discomfort as he shifted from his left side over to his right.

"As we get closer to the mountains, there may be caves," Derrick said excitedly, stepping onto the other side before lying down. "If we find one big enough, it would be a good place to call home until we build our own."

"Cozy," Vince muttered. "We can go from a cold, soggy ground to a cold, rocky one." He shifted again as Cole sat next to him. "I'm havin' a change of heart, babe. It wasn't perfect, but at least we had a bed. *Inside.*"

Cole shivered, scooting against Vince. "At least you have fur, so shut up and keep me warm."

"Alright, Leo," Axel rolled on his side up against Derrick before patting the space next to him. "This is kinda nice." Vince glared at Axel, but the larger vargyr didn't pay him any attention; instead, he looked up at me. "You like this, don't ya?"

Though I couldn't respond to his question, my tail answered him as I shook out the blanket and spread it over the group before crawling underneath. I poked my head out from under the covers, and Cole winked at me before he wrapped his arms around my chest.

"You both are so fluffy," he said, snuggling between Vince and I. "I wish you could talk. I miss talking to you."

"I sure as hell don't." Vince's muzzle rested over Cole's head as he glared at me. "Yer mouth ain't gotta be so close to his."

"Come on," Cole said, looking back at his mate. "Don't take your insecurities out on him."

"I—" The smaller vargyr choked on his words for a moment. "I ain't insecure about nothin'. At least I can talk."

"It is quite odd," Derrick interjected. "When he's human, he can form words again, so it's not permanent damage, thankfully. It might just be a matter of retraining that part of his brain while he's in this form. Unfortunately, that could take years."

"You know a lot about stuff," Axel said, turning to the other vargyr. "Wish I was smart like that. Growin' up in different foster homes meant no one really cared if ya learned anything. School was hard, and none of the other kids liked us much. We ended up just quittin'. It's always been something I regret."

"It's never too late to learn new things," Derrick said. "It is disgraceful how many children become lost in the system. The only reason I am considered *smart* is because I was born to a mage, which, despite its obvious downsides, is a life of privilege. I attended the best schools, and I lived in a palace that doubled as a library." He shuffled closer, patting Axel on the arm. "You're a lot more intelligent than you think you are. An open mind is a fresh slab of marble, and it can be carved into something impressive if you're willing to put in the effort."

"Ya think so?"

"No," Derrick said sharply, and Axel's ears fell. "I know it to be true because I've actually seen it happen. The only stupid people are the ones too complacent to recognize their own ignorance. This holds true for the pauper as well as the prince. Not even the archmagi and all of their decades of study have all the answers, and the very foundation of all knowledge starts with someone brave enough to ask what everyone else thinks are silly questions."

"Well, now he's gonna be pesterin' you with all them questions," Vince said.

"And I shall enjoy answering them, if I can."

The warmer light of the afternoon peeked through the top of the covers, which were now over my head. There was a slight draft coming from a gap at my feet, blowing upward over bare skin. I shivered and let out a sigh, slowly shimmying up the blanket before noticing Cole under the covers with me, wide awake. The last time I'd seen him smirk like that was when Axel was talking about making me furniture.

"What?" I whispered, trying not to wake the other snoring vargyrs.

"You're on my leg."

"No, I'm not."

Cole moved slightly, and my dick flopped to the side.

"Well, that was awkward," I said, turning to lie on my back.

"Glad you're human again."

I could only manage a grimace at that. "That makes one of us."

"Really?"

I nodded. "Everything was better. The world looks and smells so different, feelings feel...more intense? I can't explain it." When I turned to look at him, he seemed genuinely fascinated by my answer. "Plus, it's nice being bigger and stronger for once."

"You and Axel really are perfect for each other."

Howls broke out from the south, startling Cole and I first, but as more howls from the east joined in, Axel jolted awake. He threw off the covers and jumped from the bedding.

"Uh oh," Derrick said, rubbing his eyes as he took his place next to Axel. "How did that blasted demon figure it out so fast?"

I grabbed the blanket and pulled it over my lower half. "Could someone grab my bag, please?"

The three vargyrs gawked at me.

"How the hell do you keep turnin' back human?" Vince asked, frantically gathering his and Cole's belongings.

"You able to shift back?" Axel asked, grabbing my duffel bag before setting it next to me.

I shot Derrick a shifty stare as I slipped on some warm clothing under the blanket. "Not really. I don't know how to do it...*efficiently.*"

"Well, do it *un*-efficiently," Vince shouted. "We need our big, dumb pack mule."

"Why are you such an ass to me?" I asked while gathering the blankets.

Vince dashed to my front, his face a hair's width from mine as he snarled. This time, *he* was the bigger, stronger one. "What'd you just say to me?"

I cleared my throat and took a step back, rolling the blanket up. "Never mind."

"Vince, I ain't gonna tell you again," Axel snapped.

"That's right, he's yer mate now. Kinda nice how all that fell so perfectly into place. Always that dumb luck."

"That attitude's pissing me off." Axel threw three bags over his shoulders and one across his neck. "We ain't got time."

"You don't have to carry my bag, too," I said, taking a strap from his shoulder while picking up the one holding our blankets.

Axel put his hand on my back. "You'll be faster if you ain't got much to carry."

"You need to be able to carry Cole."

"Now, wait just a damn minute...*human,*" Cole cut in, snatching two bags off the ground. "I hadn't slept in two days, but I'm perfectly fit enough to walk and carry my own things."

"This is wonderful," Derrick said. "Now that you've both asserted how capable you are, perhaps we can use that enthusiasm to get far away from the angry Devah and his howling minions." While there was a certain bite to his words, they came across unusually cheerful. With Derrick, it was hard to determine whether he was being funny or serious.

"Right," Axel said as he walked, pointing north to the mountains. "Maybe we can get to them in a few days."

"Just a fair warning," Derrick said, looking out at the range. "Many of those are active stratovolcanoes. There may be more hazards going through them than around."

"Then we'll decide when we get there," Axel replied, making his way through the grassy meadow with us following behind.

Vince let out a huff through his snout, quickening his pace next to the larger vargyrs. "Ain't nobody told me the plan yet."

"What plan?" Axel asked.

"Yer serious? We're being hunted. Ya didn't just think he was gonna let the bait go without tryin' to get him back, did you?"

"Leo," Axel growled. "Start callin' him by his name."

"How 'bout I just keep callin' him bait, because as long as he's with us, they're gonna keep following."

"Then we keep goin' until we think of something."

"Damn it, Axel, yer always like this. When we was kids, you'd get all excited 'bout something you never thought all the way through, and you'd drag me along and get us both in trouble." He turned and squinted at me. "We should take you back."

Though his hackles were raised, Axel remained calm, keeping his focus ahead.

"What's the harm in letting Gar have him? He's already cursed. You heard what he said, once he breaks those wards, we all go home, even Leo."

"Then what?" I asked, prompting a moment of silence. "What's the plan after I break the wards?"

"Ain't talkin' to you, bait."

"Since when do you talk? All you do is bitch and complain."

The smaller vargyr threw down what he was carrying and ran up to me, his claws tearing into my shirt as he grabbed hold. With a jerk, he pulled me toward him, causing my bags to fall. Axel dashed over to us, but I looked at him and shook my head.

"What? You think you can take me now without Axel? Everyone's been fightin' yer battles for ya since you got here. You even got Cole mixed up in yer shit, and now look at us. Out here with nothin', getting chased by Gar. Cole ain't getting his treatments no more." He pushed me back until I lost my balance and fell. Vince folded his arms and stood over me.

"That's enough, Vince," Cole shouted, but the smaller vargyr kept his sharp focus on me.

"I had to move outta *my* house to make room fer you, and since you moved in on my mate, we ain't been the same. It's like I barely exist..." His voice cracked, and he backed away. "All he ever talks about is Leo this and Leo that."

"Now hold on," Cole said.

"Don't even try to deny it. You said he was an upgrade."

I pushed myself to my feet, wiping the grass and dirt from my pants. "He was mad at you, but he didn't mean that. We should have had this conversation a while ago," I said, picking up my bags. "Suppose I go back to Gar, and the wards fall. What then? What are you going to do?"

"You can't talk as a vargyr, and you ain't got no sense as a human. What do you think we're gonna do? We're goin' home!"

"But you're still cursed. Cole's going to turn, and there's going to be a bunch of vargyrs on the loose spreading the curse more because there's nowhere to put them. What do you think will happen then?"

Vince opened his mouth, but instead of arguing, he turned away and let out a frustrated growl.

"You know the answer, Vince. Right now, the vargyrs have an entire world to themselves, but if you all go back, they'll either cull you or put you in cages." I stepped back into his field of vision. "There is no going home because you don't belong there anymore. If you think being on the run from one demon is bad, just wait until you have an entire army of magic-wielding soldiers hunting you. It worked out so well for you all the last time, right?"

Without another word, he picked up his bags and continued walking.

I turned to Derrick who smiled and nodded.

"This was a one-way trip for Leo as well," he said. "If we hand him over to Gar, he dies."

Axel and Cole froze, looking back at me.

"I'm sorry I brought you all into this mess," I added, "but I'm lucky I found you guys. We've got to rely on one another now, and I want to be your friend, Vince." I tried to put my hand on his shoulder, but he jerked away. "It's not hopeless."

He remained quiet, and we continued walking in silence, each of us cooling our nerves while putting more distance between us and the occasional howling from the forest. Vince's frustration and animosity toward me were justifiable, and I knew a few encouraging words wouldn't do much, especially in our situation.

We needed a stress reliever, and once we put enough distance between us and Gar, I'd bring it up.

⁂

I whispered my idea into Axel's ear, and his mood shifted from dread to excitement in moments.

"Who's up fer some huntin'?" Axel asked, rubbing his hands together. After spending most of the day hiking through shoulder-high grasses along the plains, we'd finally come across a forested area.

"Splendid idea," Derrick said, jumping up from the fallen tree trunk he'd moved close to the campfire.

Axel tossed a glance at the smaller vargyr sitting on the ground next to Cole. "Vince?"

"No."

"C'mon. You gotta try it out before you shoot it down."

Vince lifted his knees to his chest and crossed his arms over them. "You freaks can go get yer jollies killin' defenseless animals without me."

"You eat those defenseless animals all the time, don't you?" Derrick asked, trying to sound non-confrontational.

"That's different. I ain't watchin' 'em die, knowing I caused them pain. I can't handle that."

Every time Vince opened his mouth, I learned something a little more endearing about him. He wore a vest of spikes, but under that, he was probably even more soft-hearted as Axel was.

"You really should give it a try," I said, tossing a broken branch on the fire.

"Just 'cause you made a good point earlier don't mean we're alright—me and you."

The frustrated scowl on my face lightened when I saw his tail sway. I was thankful for that oftentimes annoying appendage. It always gave a vargyr's true feelings away.

"Alright, whatever. I mean, given how small you are, you'd probably end up slowing them down, or scare everything away with your complaining." His nose wrinkled into a snarl, and I hoped this would work instead of starting another altercation. "We'd probably all starve to death because you're the shittiest vargyr here."

Cole gave me the side-eye, and Vince leapt to his feet, walking a few steps toward me before pointing his clawed finger at my face. "What the fuck do you know 'bout anything? I'm a shitty vargyr? You can't even keep yer form, and now yer useless. You been huntin' yet?" Before I could speak, he cut me off. "Don't even lie."

He really did a good job at knowing what to say to push my buttons, but I had to show some restraint or this wouldn't work.

"Okay, but I've done more as a vargyr in a day than you have six years of sitting on your ass playing video games." I turned to Cole and gave him a wink, hoping he'd play along. "Who's the better vargyr? Me or him?"

The wilkyr realized what I was doing and immediately broke into a sly smile. "Well, I know *you'd* go hunting for me, so I guess I'm going to have to go with the one who provides."

"F—" Vince seethed. "You—Fuck this!" He ran off, disappearing into the trees. "I'm the fastest vargyr in town, and I can catch anything. You ain't gettin' none of what I kill, Leo," he shouted back.

Axel gave me an excited thumbs up before chasing after Vince, with Derrick trailing behind.

"Reverse psychology," Cole said, stoking the glowing embers with a stick. "You know that's only going to work so much with him before he figures it out, right?"

"I can't believe he hasn't beaten the shit out of me yet." We both laughed, holding our hands next to the flames.

"Because he knows you'll probably pound him into the ground if you shift." Cole set the stick he was holding down next to him and rubbed his calves.

"You okay?"

"Yeah," he replied. "Just feeling achy and tired, but strangely—" He looked toward the west, squinting at the burnt-orange rays of the setting sun. "I've never felt so free."

"Today was kind of a wake-up call that we should probably stop making Vince jealous, even if it is effective at getting him off his ass," I said, changing the subject just as Cole's expression went somber.

"Well, sometimes you gotta stick with what works," he chuckled menacingly while tenting his fingers before letting his hands fall to his knees. "It's a little deeper than superficial jealousy. You and I have a connection that Vince and I don't have. Then, when you turned into this huge, sexy beast, it pushed him over the edge."

"A sexy beast, you say?" I shot him a half-cocked grin. "I really hope you didn't use those words to describe me in front of him."

"Oh, hell no. But I'm not gonna lie. You're a good-looking man and all, but wow. You might be the most attractive vargyr in town. If any of the other wilkyrs saw you, they'd be paying *you*."

"Okay, *that's* a lie."

"It was a half-lie," he added.

"What exactly makes a vargyr attractive?"

"When you're around them enough, you'll recognize what features are the most aesthetically pleasing. Vince, even though he's small, is very handsome. In my opinion, he's the perfect size for a vargyr. He always gets hung up on the size thing, but I like him better that way."

"Speaking of size," I said, wondering how I'd word this. "Let's talk about Axel."

Cole's face lit up. "There it is. I was wondering when you'd get around to seeing it."

"I'm serious. I don't know what to do or say to the guy. This is the first time in my life I've run into this problem. Usually, it's the opposite."

"Well, the first bit of advice I'll give is to stop overthinking. Axel's very patient—at least he is when the curse isn't making him crazy, and if you guys are right about that not affecting him anymore, he'll stay that way. He really likes you, Leo. Plus, who says he has to be the one on top?"

"I thought about that, but eventually, he's going to want to do what vargyrs apparently love to do."

"Which brings me to my second bit of advice: lots of lube and foreplay, and a high pain threshold."

"That's your advice?"

Cole shrugged. "Be resourceful. If anything, make sure you're a vargyr before you guys go that far. He won't seem that intimidating then. I've been with Axel a lot, and I survived. Plus, you've got rapid healing now."

"'*I survived*' is what you say when waking up in the hospital after falling from a roof. It's not exactly a pleasant thought in afterglow."

"Stop being such a baby, and just do it." Cole cupped his left hand before sending his right fist into it. "This is actually a rather accurate demonstration."

"You're a riot. Not everyone has a cavernous ass, Cole."

Cole's mouth dropped. "Excuse me. I am as tight as I was when I first met Vince."

I narrowed my eyes at that suspicious comment.

"Wilkyrs are stretchy," he continued. "And we heal really fast, so there's that."

We both let out lighthearted laughter as I tossed another limb on the fire.

"I know you've only had a little while together, but how are you guys doing?" Cole asked.

"I've never been with anyone like him before. It's like we've known each other forever. I can't believe how hard I'm falling for him."

"I can, and I'm glad you did. I've always wanted to see Axel happy, and since you're both my closest friends, it makes this even better. Of course, I doubted this would work out for obvious reasons, but there was always a part of me that really wanted you both together."

We went quiet for a moment, enjoying the serenity of the forest as the fire crackled and snapped. Hushed breezes rustled the leaves overhead, and the relaxing ambience made me realize how tired I was.

"I like this," I said, stifling a yawn.

"What?"

"*This.* I mean, I could do without the ever-present danger of being hunted down, but I love having us all together like this. I've just been thinking about what Axel said, about us being a family."

"You didn't have a family where you're from?"

"In name only," I replied, a little resentment hissing through my tone.

"You never talked to me about your family or your life much outside of your last relationship."

I sighed and tossed another branch into the fire. "Before I ended up here, I hadn't seen my family in nine years. I left home the moment I had enough money saved, which was the most terrifying thing I'd ever done, but it wasn't as scary as staying in that town with those people."

"Why were they so bad?"

"They were part of a crazy religious cult, and I'm pretty lucky I got out of it. I have a sister who's about twelve, and she's probably going to end up like them. Once you leave, you're considered worldly and irredeemable and aren't allowed back. My parents had pretty much disowned me for a while before then, anyway. Families never worked out for me in the past; neither have relationships. So, there's a part of me that thinks this is too good to be true."

Cole slipped his arm around me and laid his head against my shoulder. "You're my family, and even if Gar had the cure, I'd never trade you for it."

His words hit me right in the chest.

"And here I am, running away instead of doing the same for you."

"That's not the same. You sacrificing yourself negates everything we've given up to protect you. Those potions aren't going to keep working for me anyway. So don't even think like that."

I returned the embrace with my own, leaning into Cole. "You're like a brother."

"A sexy brother?"

My brows furrowed. "Great. You've just made it weird."

He burst into laughter, somehow managing to bring the mood back up again without even trying. I wished I could do that.

"I was thinking the same thing," Cole continued. "You've been through some really big changes, and for whatever reason, you haven't completely lost your mind. I had my doubts that you'd make it this far, but you're thriving. I hope I'll be able to get through this as well." He sighed, and the smile he wore faded. "This is pretty heavy."

"It hasn't happened yet. You said the blood craze is pretty rare, so it may not even happen at all."

"As strange as it is, I'm not so scared anymore. Whatever happens, at least my last memories will be us enjoying ourselves." He paused for a moment before looking up at me. "If you knew you could never return to this world, would you go back if you could escape?"

It really wasn't a hard question to answer. "I have a family, a guy who actually loves me, and a," I let out a reluctant sigh, "sexy brother. There's no way in hell I'd go back."

❦

Excited banter rang out in the distance before growing louder.

"Sounds like the hunt was a rousing success. I wonder how Vince fared," Cole said, looking toward the trees.

The three vargyrs bounded through the thick brush, and they were laughing. Even Vince wore a bloody grin. Axel and Derrick carried both ends of a large caribou buck, while Vince proudly held two smaller animals that resembled hare-sized pikas.

"Wow," Cole whispered, taken aback by the scene. "I haven't seen him smile like that in almost a decade."

"I had a feeling this would work," I said, standing up to brush the sand and dirt from my pants. "Even though I haven't been a vargyr for long, thinking about certain things makes me happier. When I ran to your house from Derrick's last night, all I wanted to do was chase something."

"Babe," Vince called out, now sprinting toward camp. "Look what I got us." He tossed the limp carcasses across the log next to the fire, flashing me a glare before looking back at Cole. "I got 'em all by myself. They was hard to catch, and Derrick and Axel was too slow. They couldn't get away from me, though."

"That was very impressive speed," Derrick said.

Cole jumped up from the ground and threw his arms around his mate before slipping into a wild kiss. As this happened, I reached into my bag and grabbed my phone so I could catch this moment. When they finished kissing, Cole turned to me, his mouth stained red. "My sexy hunter has returned with a bounty of..." He reached down and lifted one of the rodents' legs. "What the hell are these?"

"Delicious," Vince grunted, pulling Cole in closer. "See, now I wish we still had our bedroom."

"Hey, Leo," Axel called out, waving me over. Derrick tied a rope around the hind legs of the buck before tossing the other end over a sturdy branch, lifting the carcass in the air. I walked closer, and Axel grinned, thick, bloody saliva dripping from his mouth, his sharp canines tinged pink. "How's about a kiss for *yer* hunter?"

"How's about washin' yer face first," I replied, mimicking Axel's accent.

He cocked his head before rubbing some of the blood from his chin.

"Oh!" He dashed toward the stream close to camp, plunging his entire head into the rushing water, vigorously rubbing his face and head. He shook himself damp before trotting back over with his eager arms open.

"Well, now you're all wet."

His ears drooped, and his arms fell to his sides.

"Come here," I said with a laugh. His tail wagged as he embraced me. "I can't resist that face."

"I know," Axel said, his wet mouth connecting with mine. A flood of metallic saliva rushed over his tongue, but instead of grossing me out, I rather enjoyed the taste.

"I cannot wait to get this cooking," Derrick said, rubbing his hands together.

CHAPTER 21

Wandering The Wastes

By day four, everything took a turn for the worse. A strong headwind from a weather front blew our scents south toward our pursuers, giving away our locations faster than we could evade. They were relentless, howling from different directions most of the day while going silent when the wind would change. That was the only time we could rest. We weren't able to sleep through the night, and eating was a luxury for when we were too hungry to keep going. Since we were on the dry, wind-swept plains again, fires were out of the question, so everything we ate had to be raw.

It wasn't terrible, but I didn't have the teeth for it like everyone else. Even Cole's sharper canines and stronger jaw could shear through the toughest parts of the animal while it took me twice as long to get through one mouthful. I tried to force the shift during the rare moments I had to myself, but the results were always disappointing. I'd have killed for some predictability, but not even Derrick knew what was wrong.

My vargyr strength would return briefly after eating, but as quickly as it would come on, it would vanish. It was like being on some amazing steroid, only to have the effect wear off before a workout.

The rugged terrain and climbs in altitude pushed my endurance to its limits, and we were only approaching the much lower foothills.

"Hey, Derrick," I said, my breath quick and shallow as I spoke.

"Hmm?"

"Gar can use portals. He did it when he kidnapped me. Is he chasing us for fun or something? Why do they keep howling? They could have probably caught us by surprise by now if they had just been quiet."

The tall vargyr shook his head. "Oh, trust me, he is not finding this fun, and that's not exactly how portals work. One cannot be opened to a location the mage has not yet been to. There also needs to be some kind of strong network to draw magic from, or they collapse within seconds. Even if he could somehow manage to circumvent those limitations, he doesn't know our exact location, which means he can't use them to get to us. As for the howling? I'm not sure. We were too far ahead for them to catch us by surprise, and I think he means to exhaust and demoralize us so we'll give up faster."

He stopped briefly to catch his breath, but he grew increasingly frustrated.

"This altitude is making it hard to think clearly."

"At least now we know Gar can't get to us," Cole said.

Derrick shook his head. "That is not at all what I was implying. Judging by the four hours of reprieve we get, he's likely using portals, but in a clever way."

Cole leaned forward, panting. "I don't understand."

"If you were a mage with limitations on where you could use magic, how would you travel using portals?"

"Derrick, I can barely breathe. You're going to have to save the pop quizzes for later."

The older vargyr rubbed Cole's back. "Gar doesn't have to leave the dungeon to pursue us, because as long as he can see what the vargyrs see, the demon can open a portal anywhere they are. The vargyrs can come back to rest, and another squad could pick up exactly where he left off. It's why they're catching up to us so quickly. The good news is, it can take up to four hours to open a portal with no established network, and the further the distance, the longer it takes."

"So this is all pointless," Cole muttered, shoving his walking stick into the hard dirt before continuing up the hill where we were climbing. "We're not going to be able to keep this up."

"Then let's stop," Vince cut in, his right arm supporting Cole from behind. "I feel like I'm gonna throw up."

Axel kept quiet next to me, his snout facing forward. He had barely spoken since yesterday.

"Axel?" I said, tapping his shoulder. It was as though he couldn't hear me. I hooked my arm around his and pulled him to a stop. "Are you okay?"

"We gotta keep movin'." His voice was hoarse as he pulled me forward, but I broke away from him and turned south, letting the bags slip from my shoulders to the ground.

"We need to stop. Everyone's got altitude sickness."

"We ain't got time," Axel said, increasingly irritated.

I looked back and shook my head before sitting on the hillside. We were high enough to get a breath-taking view of the plains.

"We either come up with some kind of plan, or we go back. Otherwise, we're just prolonging the inevitable."

"Fer once, I agree with you," Vince muttered, sitting cross-legged on the grass.

Axel sauntered behind me and sat, sliding forward until I was between his legs. He then kissed the top of my head.

"Let's start by analyzing the problem," Derrick said, joining our circle. "There are two ways they are tracking us. The obvious is by scent, and they've been downwind of us since the weather cleared."

"What do you suggest?" I asked, my eyes narrowing on the smoke rising from the southwest. "They're starting to set up camps now."

"Probably because it's taking longer to open portals from this far."

"How about we go east?" Cole said, looking out at impossibly tall peaks that went on further than we could see. "At least we wouldn't be upwind anymore."

Derrick stroked his long beard and pointed to a strange mist in the distance. "This entire region is geothermically active. That smoke you see is likely coming from fumaroles. The gasses are toxic, but if we tread carefully, we could use them to our advantage. The sulfur would hide our scent, and this could put us days ahead of them."

"We went this way fer a reason, though. We can't carry much water with us, and I don't know if there'll be any drinkable rivers out that way," Axel said.

"That's a risk we will have to take," Derrick replied, sniffing the air before pointing to a herd of strange-looking herbivores grazing far in the distance. It was hard to make out what they were, as their gazelle-like heads would only occasionally poke from the tall grasses. "As long as we smell animals, there's bound to be potable water nearby. We will need to follow our noses and put more trust in our instincts." An exhausted smile pulled at the sides of his face as he looked at Axel. "You know we have what it takes."

Axel nodded, smiling back for the first time in days.

"The sulfur can't hide everything though, because they're also tracking what we're leaving behind. Everything we touch, every footprint, every disturbance leaves a trace they can follow. We've done a good job of minimizing our tracks, but we can't completely cover up the scents we leave behind."

"Wait a minute," I said, reaching into the front pocket of my backpack, my fingers grasping the smooth glass jar before I pulled it out. "Would this work on all of us?"

"What is this?" Derrick asked.

"Good thinking, Leo," Cole said, leaning in. "Gar's de-scenting lotion."

"That ain't gonna be enough fer all of us," Vince said.

"It's plenty." Cole grabbed the container and held it in front of Vince's face. "It only takes a few dabs in any place that produces a scent. It spreads through the skin in a few minutes and makes you practically invisible to vargyrs for hours."

Both Derrick and Axel's tails swished along the ground behind them.

"This, combined with a sudden change in direction, will throw them off for at least a week, maybe more." Derrick nodded to me. "Good job thinking ahead, Leo."

If only it had been intentional, but I had forgotten the jar was even in there after we got back from the beach after that encounter with feral Derrick.

"Only a week?" I asked, looking back out over the plains. "If they can't smell us, how would they still track us?"

Derrick continued staring pensively toward the east. "A demon's curse is more than magic, it's an imprint on our very souls. Since Gar is somehow able to use Lo'rim in this world, he could use divination rituals to track down the piece of himself in each of us. The good news is, it is a tedious ordeal that can take days, and it only tracks the location we were when the spell was cast, not where we currently are. If we keep moving, we'll never be in the same place, so he never finds us."

"What good is this?" Cole shouted. "This isn't a plan! We're back to square one."

"Not quite square one," Derrick said. "This buys us a lot of time, and we don't have to kill ourselves to stay ahead of them anymore."

"Why the fuck have we been killin' ourselves so far?" Vince asked, snatching the lotion from Cole's hand before baring his teeth at me. "You had this the whole time, and Mr. Bigbrain over there knew how we was bein' tracked, but ain't no one said nothin'!"

Derrick shrugged. "It is easy to lose sight of the bigger picture under extreme duress—" he drew in a deep, wheezy breath "—and extreme altitude. Leo had the right idea to stop and allow ourselves a moment of clarity."

"And uh," I muttered, finally coming clean. "I kind of forgot about the lotion until now. It's not like this has been a blast for me either, Vince."

"How do you forget somethin' like that? Useless." The smaller vargyr let out the usual annoyed hiss through his teeth before dipping a finger into the jar. "So where do I put this?"

"I can think of a place," I whispered to myself.

※

The blanket was a little cozier now that we weren't all on edge. Axel snored next to me, joining in the rumbling chorus of the others. Though I didn't want to leave the warmth, I wasn't able to sleep with all the noise.

Slowly, I pulled the blanket down and slipped out from the top, careful not to wake the others. The tall grasses that stretched endlessly across the high plains took on a pale shimmer as the night wind jostled them.

I thought about trying to turn into a vargyr again, but with how cold my hands were, it wasn't going to happen. I sat on a large granite boulder and looked around. These rocks were everywhere, which made me wonder when the mountain closest to us last erupted. Most of the volcanoes we'd seen were impossibly huge, and those that weren't spewing steam were still covered in glaciers.

"What are you up to?" Cole's voice startled me.

"I thought you were sleeping."

"Not without earplugs," he muttered, climbing up to sit next to me, his shoulder touching mine. "It just goes on and on, doesn't it?"

"I wonder if there are other civilizations living here."

Cole shrugged. "Probably not. Vargyrs have been in Varcross for centuries. We'd have seen someone by now."

"I'm surprised we haven't seen any ferals. With the way Axel was talking, they should have been all over the place."

"They're spread out, but they know how to stay hidden, especially with all the racket Gar's making."

Another breeze swept along the foothills, sending a fast-moving line down through the meadow. Cole's head rested against my shoulder.

"Hey," I whispered, shaking him awake. "Let's go back to bed."

"Just a little longer. I want to take it all in."

"You haven't looked well in days."

"I'll be fine," he said, lifting his foot up on the boulder before resting his arm on his knee. "Out here without work keeping my mind occupied, it's hard not to overthink things."

"Maybe running wasn't the right choice."

"It was the only choice."

"After all this, we deserve a happily ever after," I said, hoping to cheer him up a little.

"A happily ever after is just an unfinished story, Leo."

I glanced at Cole, who didn't look back at me. "That's kind of dark."

"That's life," he whispered, finally smiling, his glowing amber eyes watering. "There is no *happily ever after* because there is no ever after. The ones we love die—we'll die. Even the cosmos isn't forever. As much as I think I've made peace with this, I'm scared."

My arm slipped around Cole's shoulder. "It's okay to be scared of what you don't know. Everyone is. I guess, even if there are no happy endings in real life, we can still make the best of the story while we're alive."

"That's why I'm sitting here with you, breathing in clean air, trying to keep everything as happy as I can. I don't want my final human thoughts to be everything I've regretted. I want to feel okay leaving Vince to friends that care about him if the worst happens."

"I wish he didn't hate me so much." I squeezed Cole tighter. "But, *if* the worst did happen, which it won't, I'll do everything I can for him."

"He doesn't hate you. He just wants to blame someone. You're an easy target right now, and he'll probably be angry for a while, but be patient with him."

"I will," I said, trying to think of anything more helpful, but this was far beyond words. My best friend was struggling with his mortality, and I couldn't think of one thing to say to make him feel better. "We'll sit here a little longer, if you want. I could tell you a story."

"Oh! Is it an Earth story?"

"Yup. We call them fairy tales," I said, thinking of one that would lighten the mood. "This one has a happily ever after."

Cole chuckled.

"Once upon a time..."

Day five had been mostly uneventful until we crossed into a blackened wasteland as the sun lowered. The terrain was flatter here with steam and sulfuric gasses hissing from narrow fissures.

"Ow, hot," Derrick shouted, jumping back while rubbing his bare, padded foot. "We'll need to go the long way around this caldera." He covered his snout and coughed. "It's a little too active here."

"I bet there are hot springs close," Vince said, haphazardly jumping over one of the steam vents.

"Don't touch any water. It could scald you, or it could be a pool of acid. Those are common in these areas." Derrick coughed again. "That's if you don't suffocate first."

"This is a strange world," I said, following Derrick to the edge of the crater.

"Strange?"

"Yeah, I don't know how to explain it. Everything kind of seems out of place, somehow."

"Anything's gonna look strange when ya ain't seen it before," Axel chimed in from behind. "Eqiros has volcanoes; they just ain't as big."

A hot patch of ground crumbled under my foot, but Axel grabbed my arm and pulled me back.

"Thanks." I stared wide-eyed at the smoldering hole in the ground. "That was close."

"You are quite observant, Leo," Derrick continued. "And you're right. There's a reason everything appears kind of thrown together, because that's what this world is. Everything you see is a collection of different planets, created by powerful mages tens of thousands of years ago, though how much of that is true is up for debate. In fact, no one knew this place existed until an expedition uncovered small tablets from ruins under the north ocean."

"What kind of mages could create an entire planet?" Cole asked as we came upon a small pool of what looked like fresh water.

"Ones that were so advanced, they created records that could outlast their civilization to ensure their knowledge lived on in the future. When the tablets were discovered, those who touched them were given realistic visions of Eqiros as it was perhaps fifty to a hundred thousand years ago. There was so much information that it would take several lifetimes to get through even a fraction of it, and no one understood the language they spoke. Linguists were still trying to decode it when I was still in the athenaeum."

Vince knelt close to the steaming pool, but Derrick grabbed his shoulder before tossing a thin strip of leather into it. The *water* turned frothy as steam morphed to black smoke and the leather dissolved.

"You might not want to drink that."

The small vargyr backed away slowly.

"This place was never meant to be a prison," Derrick said. "It is a sister world that parallels our own, and regulated portals transported resources and people to and from it. Those portals still exist on the east side of town, and that's where the wards were set up. You can go around that road and never know they are there."

"I knew they were," I said, remembering that night. "They kept turning me back toward town."

"That's odd. Once the deritium-infused key disintegrated, they should have had no more effect on you." Derrick rubbed my head. "Yet another mystery about you we have yet to solve."

"Why did they create another world?" Cole asked, seemingly enthralled by the subject. He may not have had work to take his mind off of the dark thoughts, but conversations with Derrick seemed to do the trick.

"No one's been able to fully translate the records to know for sure. The archmage Johan Ettan discovered where the gateway to this world was several centuries ago after decades of research, and his successors worked tirelessly to open it. The senate poured all resources into the project. The mages knew from the visions the tablets granted that this world held vast resources that are rare on Eqiros. Stellous had many spies from other countries trying to learn the secrets as well. Every powerful nation wanted to be the first to open the portal to this world, but only Stellous had the knowledge and resources.

"Once they figured out how to access this world, the first and only town was built here. They named it Ettanward after the mage who first discovered the gateway. It was a time of peace and prosperity, and as Stellous reigned supreme, any lingering wars ceased. This control didn't go over well with the ambassadors from other nations who made up the senate, since their influence in matters of international law had been neutered.

"When the curse spread, the government originally planned to wipe out anyone suspected of being afflicted, but culling innocent civilians and male children sired by vargyrs would have been seen as barbaric and would have caused instability. After weeks of intense debate, the senate made the tough decision to temporarily repurpose this world in order to keep the vargyrs segregated from the rest of the population until a cure was found. They renamed the town Varcross, and when the mages discovered one vargyr could easily do in a day what twenty men could do in a week, we became a source of cheap labor. That meant finding a cure took a backseat to more *important* matters."

"They never taught any of this in school," Cole said. "It's as though everyone wants to forget this place exists."

"The curse's true origin is one of the nation's greatest embarrassments, and the only thing I know is that it was a betrayal from within the senate, likely an act of revenge from one of the foreign leaders or demonic corruption. The story changes because the truth is also kept locked away.

"How Atorien ended up trapped here will likely remain a mystery, but as hard as it is to believe, he must have been somehow deceived. Based on what you overheard, that connection with the outside world is the only hope for his freedom. He must keep the vargyrs working or risk the mages permanently closing the portal by cutting the stream of magic to both wards. It's an unlikely scenario, but he can't risk it. He's running out of time as Stellous continues gaining the upper hand against the curse. There are fewer wilkyrs trickling through the portal now, which means non-feral vargyrs are becoming rarer."

"If he's that desperate, he ain't never gonna stop," Axel said. "We can only do this for so long before we get tired."

"I don't want to keep piling on the bad news, but we can only stay a few steps ahead of the demon for so long before he figures out a better way. I also don't know enough about him to face him head-on, nor do I have any magic in this world to stand a fighting chance. Still, we must hold strong and continue to gather answers. I know he has a weakness, somewhere." Derrick's ears stood straight as he pointed to a patch of trees jutting from the surrounding barren landscape. "An oasis. That is a good sign."

"We need sleep. I'm about to fall over," I said, forcing myself to keep pace with the others.

"I hope there's water." Vince cleared his throat. "Ain't had nothin' to drink in a while."

"Here," I said, unzipping my bag to grab the full plastic bottle, handing it to him. "I filled it up back at the stream."

His usual glare softened as he held it to his mouth. "You thirsty too, babe?"

"A little," Cole replied.

Vince took a few more swallows before passing the water around. When we neared the oasis, pockets of steam rose from the ground.

"Well, crap," I muttered, staring down at another boiling pool.

"The trees here are thriving, so this isn't poisonous...I think," Derrick said, pointing to a flock of dog-sized water fowl with furry platypus-shaped heads. "They're not cooking, so it's probably cooler and drinkable."

We stepped through the island of evergreens, avoiding the small, steaming strips of mud and prickly palmettos. Thinking back on how Derrick explained this world's creation, it made more sense how we were able to cross so many biomes in just a few short days. We went from forest to the plains, then mountains and deserts, only to end up in a small jungle in the middle of a freezing volcanic wasteland.

There was a heavy splash behind me.

"Ow! Damn, that's hot," Vince shouted.

A vibration buzzed under my feet, growing more intense the longer I stood in place.

"Anyone else feel that?"

Everyone froze for a moment, listening to the strange rumbling coming from underground.

"Run!" Derrick shouted. "Run, run, run!" He pulled me away from a bubbling fissure, and we all dashed back out of the oasis as the vibrations turned to roars, like a pot about to boil. Thundering whooshes of steam launched from five of the fissures near where we had stood moments ago. The geysers shot high into the air for several minutes before settling into now filled, placid pools that slowly drained back into the ground.

We all stood there, watching in both horror and fascination.

"Alright, we're not fucking with this," I said, holding my chest as I led the way around the patch of jungle. Despite the distance being relatively short compared to the surrounding wasteland, it was still a trek, especially since I was reaching my limit.

After another twenty minutes of hiking, we came upon a tree next to the much larger pond. It resembled a broad acacia from the

African savannah burning a reddish-orange from the setting sun. Cole was the first to drop his bags before planting himself cross-legged in the shade.

"I am done," he said, leaning back against the trunk of the tree.

"I can't feel my feet anymore," I said, lying down on the soft, damp soil, unable to move. Tall grass grew in patches here, but the ground was mostly black, with sprawling ivy covering some of the dirt before entangling the much smaller palms and stubby pines.

"We need to go huntin'," Axel said, leaning against the tree to rest for a moment.

"I suppose we're all a bit peckish." Derrick got to one knee and tapped my chest. "Still no luck, I take it?"

"Huh?"

"You've been trying to shift during the night when you wander off alone. Is that method not working anymore?"

"You were watching me?"

Derrick grinned, not even bothering to contest the accusation. "I was more concerned than anything. You shouldn't be wandering away from the pack in your condition."

"I don't know what's wrong. Not being able to talk sucks, but I'd rather not be human out here. It'd be nice to hunt with you guys and not feel so tired all the time."

The black vargyr patted my abdomen. "I have a feeling you'll get your chance soon. You shifted twice, so it's in there. You'll just need to figure out how to bring it back out. Have you tried hurting yourself?"

"Unfortunately, yes." I sat up, reaching into my pocket before pulling out my foldable knife. "I tried small cuts at first to see if I still had quick healing before going deeper. But it's hard to push through the pain sometimes, so I always end up stopping before really hurting myself."

"You comin' Derrick?" Vince called out.

He turned and shouted back, "I'll catch up. You both go on ahead."

"I've even tried pretending to be a vargyr to see if that triggers anything, but whenever I do, Vince gives me weird looks."

"I was wondering what you were doing." He ran his fingers through his chin fur before pushing himself upright. "In my world, long ago, it was thought that only those born with innate abilities could become mages—that is, until a woman named Nomis Clavierre shattered that belief.

"Nomis wanted to become a mage more than anything, and despite not even being able to summon a spark from her hands, she studied for years. Scholars mocked her, and her parents cut her out of the estate since she refused to marry, as was a requirement for younger women in those times.

"Homeless, and using every silver coin she earned to further her research, she traveled the world, shifting her studies from magic to the few people who wielded it. She knew there must have been something about them, and she would only find her answer in a land far beyond the portal network.

"After visiting every shining magical city in Eqiros, she found herself wandering the forest outside of a monastery, hungry. She came upon a sect of monks sitting in a circle and wanted to ask them for succor, but she was about to witness something that would make her theory a reality.

"Their bodies were rigid and their eyes were closed as though they were locked in some kind of deep sleep. Orbs of pure energy flowed from one to the other as each monk held them in place, sensing where the magic was without looking. Fire then roared from the candles surrounding them, and the flames rose from their wicks, dancing in mid-air. The winds howled in a tempest with them in the eye. Vortices of water slithered through the air, turning to vapor before falling as snow.

"As the spectacle of this strange elemental magic came to a climax, it ended with that single ball of magic at the center. It disappeared when the monks opened their eyes and stared at the woman still awestruck by what they had done. These were simple monks, not mages. They had never studied the arcane arts, but through mindfulness, they chipped away at their limitations.

"She pleaded with them to teach her, and they were all too happy to share their enlightenment. She came to that monastery penniless, no closer to the answers she sought. However, she left a year later as one of the most powerful mages to have ever lived. When she learned true mindfulness, she knocked down the dam holding back the magic within her."

He went quiet, crossing his arms while giving me an expectant stare.

"That was a very long-winded way of telling me to try meditation."

"But it was a good story, was it not?"

My smile gave way to a bit of laughter.

"Yeah, it was."

Derrick vigorously rubbed the top of my head before running off to meet the others.

"What an amazing guy," Cole said, watching the vargyr disappear over a black dune in the distance. "Compared to him, I'm a complete moron."

"Oh, please. You guys play off of one another really well," I said, watching him scratching his arms and legs until they were red. "I'm really glad he came with us."

"I think he may be single-handedly keeping me sane with his constant rambling, but I wish I'd had him for a teacher back when I was younger."

"Meditation isn't such a bad idea, but I have no idea how to do it," I said, staring as Cole scratched his skin more. "Bug bites?"

"Maybe. It's been itching and burning since I sat down. I hope these ivy plants aren't poisonous."

I crawled next to him and took his arm, closely examining it. Aside from the heat of the irritated skin, the rest of his arm was colder to the touch.

"If you got into a poisonous plant, usually there'd be blisters or hives or something."

"I don't feel so good," he whispered, now trembling as he held his stomach. With the back of my hand, I touched his forehead. He was ice cold. This seemed all too familiar.

"You're gonna be okay. Probably just need to eat," I said, running over to the bag with one of the blankets. I shook it out before draping it over him. "Here."

"S—sit with me," he said, shaking so much he could barely speak. He was deteriorating a lot faster than I expected.

"I'll be right there." I cupped my hands around my mouth and pointed my head up, shouting Axel's name as loud as I could.

"I smell it, Leo." I looked back to see his eyes watering as his body locked up, and I ran over to him before slipping under the blanket.

"What do you smell?"

He fell silent and stopped shaking.

"Fear," he whispered, a low growl vibrating from his throat.

"Cole?" He didn't answer, so I scooted away from him.

A panicked scream tore from his throat as brown fur burst from his skin. I wanted to comfort him like Axel did me, but when his eyes turned crimson, I knew this was not going to end well for either of us.

He stopped screaming as his bones snapped and muscles bulged, his body morphing the way it did that day he saved me from that other vargyr, but his transformation was much more violent. I got to my feet and backed away from him as the final stage of his shift ended, now face to face with everything we feared.

"Are you still in there?"

My heart skipped when he snapped his jaws at me, a jagged grin crossing his face. He opened his mouth wide and growled out a word that answered my question.

"Hungry..."

Husk In The Sands

"It's me," I said, placing a hand over my chest as Cole stalked closer. His expression twisted into a snarl, and instead of the empty eyes that often accompanied the look of a vargyr falling under the influence of the curse, his stare sliced through me.

"Leeeeeooo," he said in a low rumble, taking another slow step forward. I grew hopeful when he said my name; perhaps he still recognized me as a friend.

That relief was short-lived when more saliva roped his mouth. Most vargyrs looked down when this happened, intending to strip me bare, but Cole kept his focus on my neck.

"You're my best friend," I stammered, backing away slowly. "Remember?"

He lowered to the ground, priming himself for a quick chase. "Run."

The Cole we all knew was gone, and I would be his first victim in this nightmarish, blood-crazed state. My legs propelled me from the oasis, my feet pushing hard against the solid black ground. I turned and glimpsed nothing following me, but I knew that would change. There was actual malevolence in his actions—he wasn't warning me to run to safety; he was giving me a head start because he wanted to play with his food.

"Axel," I screamed over and over, hoping he would hear. Running as fast as I could, I felt something stir within, a familiar strength that always seemed to manifest under stress. Would I be able to fend Cole off the way I did those vargyrs back in Gar's lair? They had no interest in eating me, so they could have been holding back. I was dealing with a creature that had no reason to use restraint.

Behind me, the thudding of rapid footfalls and panting clashed with my own heavy breathing. A brown figure dashed into the edge of my vision before lunging forward. I'd been so focused on his movements that I didn't see a rock jutting from the ground ahead. My foot hit, and I lost my balance, inertia sliding my tense body over the ground, kicking up fine, black dust. I turned in time to see his open jaws closing in.

The beast that was Cole bore all of his weight on top of me, and I instinctively pushed against his chest, keeping his teeth away from my neck. My face was warm with his spittle as he continued to snap and snarl. In a flash of red, sharp pain raked across my abdomen, but there was so much adrenaline, it only lasted a moment.

My right knee went full-force into the monster's ribs with a crack, causing him to whine and release me, but not before his claws tore through my shirt, slicing the skin on my chest. My blood seemed to come from everywhere as it soaked through ruined clothing. Was this it for me? I healed fast, but I wouldn't be able to survive another one of those—if he hadn't already hit a vital artery.

I had no other options. Despite my grave injuries, I had to take advantage of feeling little pain at the moment and fight. With increasing desperation, I jumped from the ground and landed on top of him, my hands holding two powerful arms with everything they had, trying to keep the rest of me away from those jaws. I screamed again for help, trying to buy more time for someone to hear.

In an instant, my strength disappeared, and I flew backward, the beast now on top of me, his jaws all I could see. Everything felt like slow motion, and I closed my eyes, waiting for the inevitable.

A breeze rushed over my skin as the weight bearing down disappeared, and scraping sounds to my left had me opening my eyes. Axel slid on all-fours after slamming Cole against a boulder. Two hands slid under my arms and pulled me back to safety.

"These injuries are deep," Derrick said, glancing at Vince, who was torn between watching the two vargyrs rip at each other and the gore seeping from me.

"That's Cole," I said with a gasp. "He's gone." Axel's hands wrapped around the helpless, brown vargyr's neck under him.

"Axel," Vince shouted, letting out an ear-piercing howl as he leapt toward the confrontation. "Don't kill 'im." His voice pitched upward as he fell to his knees. "Please don't kill my Cole."

"Cole?" A wail replaced the bestial roars, and his hands relaxed their grip. Cole snarled and bucked, struggling to free himself. "What do I do?" He looked up at Vince, tears welling in his eyes. "I can't make this choice."

"I don't wanna lose him." Vince crawled closer, trying to touch his blood-crazed mate. Cole's jaws latched onto Vince's hand. "C'mon babe, it's me." He whined low as tears poured down his face. "Can't ya see me no more?"

Derrick sat me up, but the pain in my gut left me breathless. More than the physical pain was the agony of watching something like this unfold. Vince and Axel crumbled as they held Cole down, frozen by indecision. We weren't in town anymore, so Axel didn't have to put him down. However, if they let him go, would he come back to finish what he started?

The struggling lupine released Vince's hand and took advantage of Axel's distraction to break free. Before either of them could react, he flipped on his hands and knees before leaping to his feet. Axel and Vince remained on the ground, dazed as their closest friend and mate vanished into the night. The sounds of struggle were replaced by deafening silence, broken by high-pitched dog whines as Vince fell forward on his hands.

Axel turned back to me, the fur on his face soaked with tears and blood as he stumbled to his feet and limped to my side. He knelt close, his hand lightly brushing over the open wounds on my chest and stomach.

"He will be okay. The bleeding has already stopped," Derrick said.

"Axel," I whispered, looking over at the small vargyr, staring heart-broken into the black void of the star-lit wasteland. "Cole told me not to leave Vince alone."

He took me into his arms, his sodden muzzle pressing into the side of my neck.

"I love you," he said before letting me go, wiping his face with the back of his arm.

He and I understood the significance of those words now more than ever as we watched Vince shudder while sobbing into the dirt. The last time those words are spoken may be the last time they're ever heard.

"I love you too."

He stood and dragged himself to his best friend, lifting the smaller vargyr from the ground. They embraced each other, and when Vince wailed, Derrick grimaced and looked away.

"This is hard to watch," he whispered. That was the first time I'd seen his usual cheerful face shatter. "Losing a mate is like dying. Part of you vanishes in the void and never returns. I would never wish this on anyone."

Everything was over in a flash, and it took me several minutes for the finality of it all to set in. I didn't want to come to terms with any of this. I would wake up tomorrow and Cole would be awake next to me with that enduring smile.

Tomorrow he'd be back, and we would have our happily ever after.

Axel's hand fell onto my arm, shaking me awake from the same nightmare that played in a loop.

"How're ya feelin'?"

I slipped my hand under the long-sleeved shirt I put on last night before running my fingers along smooth skin. The lacerations were gone. Maybe they were never there. The fantasy didn't last as I glimpsed the empty space where Cole and Vince usually slept.

"Where's Vince?"

Axel put his arm around me, and I leaned against his warmth.

"We might lose him," he whispered. "There ain't nothin' I can do."

"I guess it was too good to be true. Families never stay together." I choked out. "It was stupid to think Cole wouldn't be the rare case. We all kind of knew how this would end, and I gave him false hope."

Axel had been like steel since I met him, but even steel could only be stressed so much before it broke. He and Cole were friends a lot longer than we were, and if we were going to pull through, I needed this experience to harden me, not break me.

"I loved Cole for so many years—*really* loved him. I hate admitting this, but I was jealous of Vince. I never showed that ugly side of myself, though. Was awful being like that 'cause I loved Vince too. I have you now, and I love you more than anything, but I'll never forget them nights all three of us spent together. It was warm in so many ways." He sniffed, wiping his nose with the back of his arm. "I just wanted to be close to someone who cared about me. Now I've lost the two people who made life better when it wasn't. I hate this curse! I hate Gar, and I hate this life for always takin' from me!"

I had to pull him back.

"Remember that night in the dressing room?"

Axel nodded. "Ain't never gonna forget that."

"That was the night you changed me. You gave me hope in a hopeless situation. Even though the curse was there, there was something more." I forced a smile. "My gut told me—that you'd be my person." I crawled over his lap and wiped his tears away with both hands.

"Think about everything you've gone through and everything you've experienced. If any one thing had changed, you'd have never been on that road the night I drove into town. We may feel like life is punishing us when things go wrong, but it's actually the best teacher we'll ever have. We learn, and we get stronger. We don't have a choice." His eyes widened, and the tears stopped when I hugged him. "Every tragedy that happened in my life led me right into your arms. I'd never change what I went through, no matter how awful, because I'm right where I need to be. I don't know where we're going to end up after this, but we'll figure it out together."

Axel wrapped his arms around me and squeezed.

"I'm scared. I ain't scared of dyin' or turning feral. After seeing what I saw last night, I'm afraid of losin' what I have left. This life ain't gonna mean nothing if everyone in it disappears—and if something happens to you."

"Cole is still alive, and as long as he remains that way, we might be able to save him. There's got to be a way to bring him back. It happened for you and Derrick, and it can happen for him. We're going to find Vince and bring our family together again."

Axel lifted his nose to the air and sniffed, turning his head to the east. A small silhouette of a vargyr slowly sauntered toward camp, dragging his feet along the black sand.

"Thank God," I whispered, placing a hand on Axel's leg before standing. "If we don't want to lose him too, then we need to be there for him." I looked down at Derrick, who was still asleep, lying on his side. "We're going to need Derrick's experience. He's already gone through it, so he's the best person to talk to about dealing with this kind of grief."

Axel grunted in agreement before jumping to his feet, following me toward the lonely shadow in the distance. As we neared, the figure barely looked like Vince, just a wolfish husk shuffling slowly. Four days ago, I saw him light up for the first time, but that person might be gone forever now.

We stood on either side of him, our pace slowing to match his. Axel and I remained quiet, waiting to see what he would do.

"I couldn't find him." His voice was hoarse and hollow, his gaze never leaving the distance. "He was wearin' that lotion when he ran away, so I ain't able to get his scent."

"We'll find him," I said.

"Then what?" He turned and snarled at me. "What do we do with him when we find him? He almost killed you, and he'd probably try to kill any one of us now."

"Then why were you out there?" Axel asked.

"I want him to." Vince's shoulders slumped forward. "Him killing me would be exactly what I deserve fer doin' this to him."

"That's not what Cole wanted," I said, steeling myself as his glare grew hotter. "And it would kill Axel if you just gave up."

"Why the fuck would you care? Give me one reason why I should believe the shit that comes outta yer mouth?" he shouted, shoving me away. "This is yer fault. It's all yer fault!"

I clenched my teeth, remembering what Cole had told me the other night. I was the easiest target, the one he'd blame for his grief, but I also made a promise. There was a momentary surge of vargyr strength through my muscles, and I knew I needed to capitalize on it now before it vanished again.

"Vince," I said calmly, gripping his arms to turn him toward me. "When I first saw you, it was like looking at myself."

The small vargyr struggled to move, but I held him still. "I swear, if you don't let me go, I'm gonna bite."

"Then bite. I'll never know what your pain feels like, but that doesn't mean I don't understand it. You've built this wall so high that you can't see who I really am, and I guess I'm to blame for that as well." He leaned in and took my arm in his jaws, his sharp teeth struggling to penetrate my skin as he held back. "We all love you, and we've been to those dark places that we felt like we could never get out of. Don't push your family away."

His jaw trembled in place, but he never bit down. Instead, he let go, keeping his eyes fixed on the ground.

"We're gonna stick together, and we'll be your shoulders when you need to cry. Hell, I'll be your punching bag if you want that. May as well put the vargyr healing to good use." I chuckled while nervously wrapping my arms around his neck to pull him close. He tensed, pushing his hands against my chest in a weak protest before letting them fall limp at his side. "We're not going to give up on you, so please don't give up on yourself."

"I ain't got nothin'," he cried out, his forehead buried into my chest. "I ain't got nothin' no more. I felt like a kid in his arms, even though I was bigger and older. We got on each other's nerves, and I got nothin' but regrets for how bad I treated him." His voice got louder as he sobbed. "I hate myself for what I did, but I guess you were there to clean up my mess." He swallowed hard. "I...hate you because you did what I should have been doin' all along." He never looked up, and I kept my arms locked around him, his tears drenching my shirt. "I wasted so much time that I coulda been spending with him. How did I let it all get away from me?"

That familiar question hit me hard.

"That's what depression does. It keeps taking, eating years from your life until there's nothing left but regret. If you let it win, that's what's going to happen. You'll have nothing but regret." I pulled away and released my grip. "Cole's still out there, and there's a chance he can come back to us. We know the curse can be broken because it's already happened. I'll do anything I can to help him."

"If you was gonna do anything, you'd have turned yerself in. You'd have gotten him what he needed."

"That wasn't gonna solve nothin', Vince. You know exactly what Gar was gonna do once he had Leo. He wasn't gonna save Cole; he was gonna destroy the wards and leave," Axel said. "Stop blamin' him, because you know Cole wasn't gonna let him do it neither."

Vince folded his arms and sniffed, glancing at me a bit softer than before. His tail swayed languidly from side-to-side. "Yer too much of a fuckin' sap. I guess I can see why Cole liked you so much." He turned away and stomped off toward camp. "We ain't nothin' alike, Leo."

Axel and I exchanged a relieved glance before following Vince at a distance.

"Yer better at words than me," Axel whispered. "Ain't never been able to get through to him."

"We'll see. We've gotten him off the ledge for now, but this isn't going to be easy."

✺

Leaving camp was a quiet, somber experience, especially when it came time to gather Cole's belongings. Axel and Derrick took turns staying awake throughout the night in case he came back, but there was no sign of him—not even a scent. He was really gone, and we didn't have the luxury of time to search.

As we trekked the rest of the way around the giant caldera, the terrain shifted from black wasteland to a lush alpine forest. With how cold it was at this elevation, I was surprised that there was only a light dusting of snow on the trees. The scent of animals was strong in this area, and the only things I could hear were leaves rustling in the wind and complaining stomachs.

Vince remained mostly silent, occasionally giving a slight grunt or mumble when anyone spoke to him. Axel and I tried to lighten the mood as much as we could, but it was hard to pretend to be cheerful while mourning. Derrick proved to be the most valuable person on this journey yet again. His quirky sense of humor and levelheadedness kept the group emotionally grounded.

"I'd give anything to see his face again—like it was," Vince said. "Just wanna see his face."

Axel slipped his arm around his best friend, and an idea came to me.

"Why don't we stop for a while?" I asked, pointing to the small stream we'd been following for miles. "There's no reason to push ourselves."

Derrick nodded, wagging his tail. "I wholeheartedly agree. We could all use some rest and some good food." He tossed his bags at the base of a tree and shifted his attention back toward the direction we came, his ears pointing forward before turning off to the sides. "No fire, though. Sorry, Leo. You'll have to eat it raw again, or we risk sending out smoke signals to the enemy."

"It's okay. I've gotten used to it." I sat mine and Cole's bags next to his.

Derrick placed his hand on Vince's shoulder. "You stay with Leo, and we'll get the food."

"Fine," he muttered, planting himself on the ground next to the bags before leaning against the trunk of the pine.

Axel dropped his bags on top of the others and turned to the north, sniffing the air. "Howl if there's trouble," he said before he and Derrick disappeared into the woods.

Vince didn't reply, his stare blank as he looked out in the direction we'd come from.

"Can I sit with you?"

"Ain't like I can stop you," he said with more indifference than anger. Though his attitude toward me had improved since yesterday, there was still a deep animosity that would take a while to scab over.

I grabbed the phone from my bag and sat close to him, but he mostly ignored me, looking away while letting out annoyed huffs. After turning on the phone, I swiped through the pictures I'd taken at the start of our journey until I came across the one I was after. It was the best picture I'd ever taken—perfectly framed, the golden rays of light pouring in through the trees behind them as their lips joined.

"Hey," I whispered, gently patting Vince on the arm. "I want you to see something."

I handed him the phone, and he cocked his head.

"What do you want me to do with this?"

"Look at it," I replied, giving him a nod.

Vince's eyes turned to glass as he stared longingly at the screen, holding the phone closer.

"You said you wanted to see his face. Cole said he hadn't seen you smile in years, and when I watched you both, the world looked perfect for a moment."

Vince said nothing, sniffing while losing himself in the picture, tears soaking the fur of his face.

"Here," I said, touching the screen. "Take your finger and swipe to the left. There are a lot of pictures of Cole and everyone." As my finger slid, the image of a beaming Vince appeared. He was holding his first kills by the hind legs.

"I look different." He swiped again, and more pictures of him shuffled across the screen. "You sure got a lot of pictures of me."

"Because you're happy, and when you smile you're so handsome. That's what Cole loved."

We sat together like that for ten minutes, sliding through photo after photo. I wasn't sure if this was doing more harm than good, but I was about to get my answer as the vargyr handed the phone back to me.

"There ain't none of you in there."

"I guess I'd forgotten to have someone take a picture of me. I was so busy trying not to miss a moment that I kinda did."

He looked at me, his ears low. "What you said yesterday, 'bout knowing what I was goin' through. It sounded like you was full of shit at first, but when you said that thing about regrets—it was different. I ain't talked to anyone in town 'cause I ain't the only one suffering. They had their booze, and I had my games."

He shook his head and sighed. "You were right. I'm thirty-six years old, and all them years passed by so quick—years I coulda been spending with him, trying to make the most out of the time we had. The most fucked up part is, I knew I was hurting him, but I couldn't face reality no more."

He didn't pull away as my hand slipped over his.

"Cole loved you so much, and despite him trying to make you jealous, nothing ever happened between us. You were the only one for him, but he didn't know how to help you. Axel didn't either. I've had years in therapy, and while I'm not an expert on mental health, having the support and understanding of people who've been there is just as important. I've lost myself in video games too, trying to avoid reality." I shot him a smile. "But I didn't have anything as amazing as what you have. Holy shit."

"I know, right? You can get lost fer days, and it gets kinda dangerous. You forget to eat, and sometimes you piss all over yerself until you finally snap out of it." He let out a snuffled laugh. "Cole yelled at me a couple times 'cause I peed all over the couch. Man, thinkin' back on that. I was so pathetic I was actually peein' on couches."

"It could have been worse, right?" I said, trying to catch my breath.

"Well, I ain't tellin' you the whole story," he belted out, laughing harder.

"Oh, gross," I shouted, tears in my eyes. "Cole wrestled me and pushed my face into that couch!"

"They ain't the same cushions, dipshit." He drew in a gasp of air. "Done ruined a few sets of 'em."

After the laughter died, I turned to him and smiled. "I promised Cole I'd be here for you, so reach for me, okay? I don't care what time it is or what I'm doing. I'm not just saying that to make you feel better. I'm serious."

"Alright." His lips pinched upward, but the slight smile faded as quickly as it came. "I couldn't ever tell Cole about this 'cause he had to keep the town going and all. I'm sure he knew that I hated what he had to do, and his responsibilities made it hard to be with him. It ain't that I was disgusted or nothin', I just didn't want him to come home and me be another gross vargyr customer he had to fuck. Hell, I think Axel slept with him more than I did last year. Did he ever tell you why Gar wouldn't let him back in the dungeon?"

I shook my head. "He told me it was an embarrassing story."

Vince folded his arms and smirked. "Axel had a nasty habit of injuring every wilkyr he was with enough that they couldn't work the rest of the night. Eventually word got around, and everyone was scared to be with him, so Gar put his foot down. I don't know how he didn't go feral before he met Cole, but Cole always knew how to handle him. Havin' my best friend and my mate together like that hurt me more than I let on. It was hard to get in the mood with him after that. We never got to enjoy bein' with only each other."

"Did you ever tell them?"

"Not in words, but I guess I should've been more direct. There wasn't nothin' I could do, though. I didn't want Axel turnin' feral, but I also didn't want him with my mate. I had no right to complain because it was my fault Cole had to do what he did."

He shook his head and choked up.

"You okay?"

"The truth is...I knew there was a chance I'd attack him when I went full turn, but I only wanted one more night with him, just to hold him, nothin' more. I knew the mages was gonna catch me soon, but I was stupid to be alone with him." Vince's voice trembled. "He suffered, and it was my fault. He didn't get to enjoy none of his youth—didn't even get to follow his dreams of bein' a mage. Now he's out there, alone. I don't know if he's dead to the world or if he's still in there. The more I think about it, the more it would have been better to let Axel kill him than to let him suffer."

I hated seeing him so broken—so full of guilt. I just wanted to take it away, but this was going to take time. A lot of time.

"He ain't here to keep the curse away no more, and I can't go back to the dungeon. The only thing left is to go feral when my time comes."

"That doesn't have to happen," I said, looking away, hoping he'd understand what I was suggesting. This was a conversation I'd need to have with Axel later.

"Dumbass. Cole had to do it for the others, and I'll be damned if I let someone else go through it because of me. I ain't doin' that to Axel neither. You guys ain't even had yer first night together, so that needs to be special, not a mistake like mine was. He's yer mate now, and yer lucky to have each other. Can't think of a better guy for you to end up with."

I stared down at the frosty, brown grass, pondering the events of yesterday and the last few weeks. "I thought when Cole attacked me, he'd snap out of it like Axel and Derrick did, but he didn't. I actually believed there was something special about me that canceled the curse, but it may have been nothing more than wishful thinking."

Vince uncrossed his legs and stretched, his maw opening into a yawn. "You just wanted to help, and I don't blame ya for thinkin' that."

"It just doesn't make any sense. I was around Cole more than anyone, and the curse still got him."

Vince stopped stretching, looking strangely pensive. "Maybe you really did do something different, or maybe they did. What happened when Axel attacked you?"

"He was struggling to control himself, but he mostly kept off of me. It didn't really get physical at all. With Derrick, he almost killed me. If Axel hadn't been there, he would have probably ripped me to pieces. Luckily, he got my shoulder instead."

"Yeah, I can see why yer confused," Vince said. "If anything, I was gonna say that maybe yer blood had somethin' to do with it, but Axel didn't bite you."

My eyes widened. "I'm an idiot."

"What?"

"Vince—you're really fucking smart."

The smaller vargyr laughed. "Now that's somethin' I ain't ever heard anyone say." He paused and stared at me expectantly. "Why?"

"Because Cole didn't bite me."

Vince's ears fell flat against his head. "Yeah. We done established that."

"The constant here was my blood. One of the vargyrs tore my leg open, and Axel licked it. Derrick got a mouthful when he bit me, but Cole only used his claws because I had the strength to keep his mouth away from me."

"Well damn," Vince muttered.

"I need to test it," I said before crawling over to my bag. As I rifled through, I couldn't find my pocket knife. "Shit, I must have left it at one of the camps when I was cutting myself."

"Now why the hell are you doin' that?"

"It's not what you think." I crawled back beside him, holding my hand out. "I need you to cut me with a claw."

"They ain't that sharp. It's gonna hurt, you know."

"They're the only things sharp enough to cut me, or you can bite me. When I start bleeding, just lick up the blood."

"You sure?"

I nodded.

"Alright then. I'll make it fast so it won't hurt as much." He turned my hand until the palm was facing down, and he tapped his pointer claw against the back of my forearm. "Yer hand is gonna hurt too much. I'll do it here, and I'll count to three. Ready?"

I nodded again, and without the promised countdown, Vince's hooked claw sank into my flesh. In less than a second, there was a shallow gash in my arm, and sharp pain hit me after another second.

"Ow, God damn it!"

"Hey, now. You told me to do it. I just figured I'd make it easy by not giving you a chance to worry."

"It's fine." I lifted my arm to his snout, warm blood streaming around before dripping onto the grass.

Vince's thin, flexible tongue traced along the stream before lapping against the gash. He kept going until my healing kicked in and the bleeding stopped.

"Well?"

"You know, I wasn't all that hungry until now." He gave a wild stare. "What's the matter?"

"Hilarious, Vince," I muttered. "How do you feel?"

"Don't feel nothin'—" His irises reddened for a moment before fading to light-hazel, causing the vargyr to freeze before continuing as if nothing happened. "—out of the ordinary. Maybe it just takes a while to work."

"You didn't feel anything just now?"

Vince shook his head, his ears turning toward the trees. "Sounds like food's comin'," he said, his stomach growling again. "If it worked, I won't be getting them urges no more, and if it didn't, you gotta promise to let me go. Don't let me get my way."

"Let's be optimistic."

"You be optimistic, and I'll be realistic," Vince muttered, slipping his arm around my neck before pulling me into a rough hug. He quickly pushed me away. "Ugh. Okay enough of that."

A Delicate Undertaking

It was a three-day hike east through the forest before we found a pathway to the north, hidden between two different mountain ranges. The valley was like a gateway to a new world. On one side were the steep stratovolcanoes we'd kept our distance from, and on the other were broader ridges similar to what I'd seen throughout the Rockies. It was all so breathtaking and serene, the air crisp and clear with lower, wispy clouds rolling along the slopes.

There still wasn't a trace of Cole in the wind, but we'd also lost the vargyrs pursuing us. It wouldn't be long before Gar began his divinations for phase two of the chase, but we had a secret weapon of our own. Derrick may not have been a deva'koh, but his knowledge always kept us three steps ahead.

It was late afternoon, the sun now hiding behind the ranges. It was warmer in the valley, but still too chilly for a human to be comfortable without layers. Derrick tried teaching me how to meditate, but with everything going on, I could never clear my mind for more than a few minutes at most. I began to doubt I'd ever shift again.

"Is that what I think it is?" Vince asked, his voice containing an excitement we hadn't heard in almost a week. He pointed to steam rising from the pools of water, barely visible through the dense pines. "Better not be another one of them acid puddles."

"This might be it," Derrick said as he and Vince dropped their bags and raced toward the hot springs, disappearing into the brush.

Water splashed on the other side.

"Damn, that's nice and hot," Vince shouted.

"Don't just go jumping into things, you fool! That could have been boiling."

As the two splashed around, Axel and I took that rare moment of alone time to walk through the trees together.

"Couldn't have found these at a better time. Everyone's smelling pretty ripe," I said, maintaining a leisurely pace alongside Axel while holding his hand.

"It ain't so bad when yer half wolf. What you think stinks as human ends up smellin' kinda nice."

"I guess." We walked in view of the springs as Vince and Derrick wrestled in the water. Vince's frayed linen pants lay discarded in the dirt, so I dropped mine and Cole's bags to pick them up. With a few shakes, I folded and laid them next to Vince's things.

"You look flustered," Axel said.

"Obvious, huh?" I crossed my arms. "Nothing's working, and I'm slowing us down. Why can't I get my body to shift the way it did before?"

"I can't wait fer you to hit yer full turn. Ya love to be wild, just like me. If we could spend the rest of our lives living where we want, in a house we build, that would be my dream. Maybe we could build a town of our own out here with like-minded folks."

"It's beautiful out here, but the volcanoes make me nervous," I said, glimpsing the fast-moving clouds that were only partially concealing the glaciers. "I'd follow you anywhere, if I could work out my little problem first." I yawned, stretching my arms.

Axel sat next to one of the skinnier pines, parting his legs enough so I could sit in between them. We often relaxed like this, my back against his chest, wrapped in his arms. It always put me in a better mood. In fact, sitting like this often put me in *the* mood, and the triggers were a lot more subconscious than anything. Even though

I wasn't a vargyr, I still had a strong sense of smell, and when our scents intertwined, it fired off stranger feelings.

The emotions weren't human. I could always tell they weren't when I couldn't put my feelings into words. There were times I'd sit with him, and it got so overwhelming I'd have to move away.

"I've been thinkin'—" Axel's voice pulled me out of my thoughts. "We ain't really been with each other since the shower. We ain't never talked about it neither."

"There wasn't much to say. We took a shower together and played around."

"That ain't what I mean, and I think I know why you acted that way. I knew when I looked down at yer face."

Finally, the conversation I'd been dreading.

"I was surprised."

"You were scared."

"I guess I can't hide my feelings from anyone." I forced a smile, nervously picking at the dried dirt on my palms. "It's just not what I'm used to."

"When I was human, being blessed with size wasn't always a bad thing. Yeah, it scared away a few guys, but overall, no one seemed to mind it that much. That changed when I turned wilkyr and wouldn't stop growing. It happens with everyone who's cursed. Yer body gets a little bigger 'til yer full turn."

"Christ, how tall were you as a human?"

Axel grinned. "I was pretty tall, but when I went full vargyr, that was a surprise. You get so much bigger, and other things get a lot bigger too. Unfortunately for me, too much of a good thing wasn't all that good. It was hard to control myself enough not to hurt the wilkyrs, but I always did. When word got out about that, hardly any of 'em would take me on as a customer. Then one day, Gar told me I wasn't allowed back. If it weren't fer the curse, I'd have been gentler, but you know how that goes.

"I met Cole when he and Vince arrived in town. Vince was really protective, and when he found out what wilkyrs had to do, he blew his stack. Eventually Cole figured out how things worked, and like every wilkyr before him, he just adapted to it. It don't make much sense why he did it, but Cole saved me.

"I was close to turning feral, but I never told no one. It was there in my mind, and I prepared myself for it. One day, Vince was frustrated that Cole had to work in the dungeon again, and he didn't have no one. He invited me over, and I knew what he wanted. It was just like when we was younger, except he wasn't the same guy no more.

"He liked bein' behind me, and I didn't mind too much. When he was finished, I took my place behind him like we used to, but he growled and told me he wanted to go again. That was when Cole walked in and saw us together, my big ass in the air while little Vince was goin' to town."

I couldn't help but chuckle at the imagery.

"I remember that sly smile on his face, and once Vince was done, Cole invited me to be with him. I ended up hurting him, and Vince screamed that I wasn't welcomed back no more. But Cole didn't let me go because he knew what was happening. When we was in better spirits, we sat down with Vince and talked it out together, and that was when they brought me into their relationship." Axel rested his hands on my shoulders. "I talk too damn much, don't I?"

"Nah," I replied. "I'm glad you told me. It makes me feel better."

"I wanna be with you so bad. When we're like this and you smell the way you do, it's hard knowin' it's not gonna go nowhere. But I don't wanna hurt ya like I used to hurt Cole."

"I haven't asked in a while, but are you starting to feel the urges? Vince and I came up with a theory, and I'm almost certain we're right."

"Nope," he said, enthusiastically. "This ain't the curse. I'm just horny." He leaned over, his mouth next to mine, and I turned to kiss him. "I just wanna be with you. When you almost died, and when I saw Vince after losin' Cole—I don't wanna wait no more. We don't know what's gonna happen tomorrow, and I want us to be mates."

"Do you know what a side is?" I asked, remembering a conversation I'd had with an old friend of mine back home.

Axel shook his head.

"There are other ways to be intimate, you know. We don't have to go all the way like that."

His eager smile turned to a look of pure disappointment. "Never done just that before. Doesn't sound very romantic."

"Neither does being skewered."

"Fair point," he responded, looking away at the ground.

"How about this," I said, pulling at his chin fur. "Tonight, when Vince and Derrick are asleep, let's have a bath together and see where it goes."

"Ya mean it?" His tail pounded the ground behind us.

"Yes, but I need to lay down some rules though."

"Whatever you want."

"We can't rush. If we decide to take things further, I'm not going to be ready for you right away, and when I am ready, you need to go slow. I may have wilkyr healing, but that'll ruin the mood."

"Well I was gonna go slow anyw—"

"No, I mean *really* slow, and if I'm in too much pain, we're stopping."

He nodded.

"And second..." I paused, remembering what Cole suggested. "I get to go first."

"That sounds fun. Ain't had that done to me in a while—oh!" He pointed to the bags he sat next to the tree. "I thought somethin' like this would happen, so I brought a whole bag 'o stuff Cole gave me a while ago."

"A bag of what?"

He grinned. "You'll see."

"Okay, now I'm getting a little concerned."

He stood and dusted the dirt from his fur loincloth. "Ain't gonna tell ya. Don't wanna spoil the surprise."

"You two gonna bathe or what?" Vince asked before biting into a comically large caribou leg, his powerful jaws tearing the muscle and tendons from bone.

I swallowed the raw meat I'd been masticating for the past minute or so before answering.

"Why would I take a bath and eat something like this, only to have to take another bath to wash all the blood off?" I picked up another small chunk of the softer bit of the caribou Axel set aside for me. I wasn't sure what part of the animal this was, and I wasn't going to ask. We debated building a fire since no one could see the smoke at night; however, Derrick brought up a good point. If the wind suddenly changed direction, the stronger scent of cooking food might erase the lead we had. I used my flashlight as a lantern since I didn't have night vision like the others.

"Good idea. I'm definitely gettin' another bath when I'm done eatin'." Vince spoke with his cheeks stuffed full while sputtering pieces everywhere.

"Yer gonna take another bath?" Axel asked, his impatient stare shifting to me. "You've had a rough week and need to get some good sleep." He had been fidgety since he got back from the hunt, and he'd already horked down his dinner while waiting for the others to finish.

"We all had a rough week. What're you, my dad? I ain't tired at all," Vince muttered, swallowing down his bite.

We all fell silent save for the most annoying ambiance I'd ever experienced. Growls, grunts, wet smacking, crunching, belching—the way vargyrs ate wouldn't exactly pass a cotillion course at a finishing school. It would have annoyed me more had the first glimmer of moonlight not made it possible to see what was going on. I turned off the flashlight to conserve battery and shoved it into my bag, eying the thick patch of fur between Vince's legs.

"It's weird seeing you without pants on," I said, taking another bite.

"Why? Derrick ain't worn a pair of pants yet, and ya ain't said nothing to him."

"You can't really see too much," Derrick joined in. "For the most part, everything is neatly hidden away, and I enjoy being unburdened by clothing. We're covered in fur already, so wearing anything else is a ridiculous inconvenience." Derrick looked at me and flashed his brows. "Embrace the nudity, Leo."

"And die of hypothermia," I added.

"How's your meditation coming along?"

"About as well as the last time you asked. I never thought sitting and doing absolutely nothing would be so hard."

"It's a skill that takes time to master, but you have to keep at it."

"How much time are we talking? One? Two weeks?"

Derrick's overly stuffed, distended gut shook with laughter. "You'd have to be quite gifted to master it so quickly. It took Nomis nearly a year to reach a point where it actually made a difference."

"Damn it, Derrick," I yelled, snatching more raw meat sitting on the stump next to me. "You should have told me that. I wouldn't have wasted my time."

"*Someone* has no patience."

"*Someone* doesn't have time. I need a realistic solution."

Derrick rubbed his tied, pointy beard. "That *was* realistic. Your situation is unlike anything I've encountered before. It's as though you're trapped between all three states of being, which is why I suggested meditation. Think of the body as a stream, but instead of flowing with water, it's an unseen force. That force flows within all life.

"I'd wager those in your realm also have this, but a much weaker version. The curse is powerful magic, and it may be overwhelming the already weak flow of ethereal energy you had inside from the start, causing the flow to trickle. This dam of magic may be keeping you trapped between forms, and I'm not sure if that's dangerous or not. I'm not well-versed in knowledge of non-magic beings from other worlds, so I'm not entirely sure what will work—or if any of what I'm saying is right. In fact, most of what I just said may be utter nonsense, but if it's not, meditation is the only way I know to broaden the flow until the dam breaks."

I let out a heavy sigh, tossing the last piece of meat in my mouth before wiping my hands on a wet towel next to me.

"Don't be discouraged. We're bound to find an answer somewhere. You may even stumble across one when you least expect it."

"I'm getting a bath," Vince said, tossing a leg bone onto the ground as he stood. "Y'all wanna join?"

"I'm in," Derrick said, eying Axel and I. "Come on. The water is relaxing. It will be especially good for you, Axel. You've been quiet and antsy this evening."

"Just wantin' us all to go to bed soon," Axel replied through his teeth as he forced a smile.

I stood and rubbed Axel's head before following Vince to the steaming pools, now glowing a misty blue under the full moonlight. The poor guy was about to pop if we didn't get some real alone time.

"I'll be with ya in a bit," Axel said, grabbing Derrick's arm. "Can I talk to you fer a minute?"

I left the two alone and made my way to the spring before stripping to my underwear. When my toes hit the water, I recoiled. It was a lot hotter than I expected, and I'd need to take this slower than someone with fur would. It may not have even been safe for me to stay in for more than ten minutes.

"Lose the underwear," Vince muttered, glaring up at me from the water. "Ain't like you need to be shy no more. We're a pack, right? You wanna think like a vargyr or keep bein' human?"

That was an unexpected thing for Vince to say, but it made me feel a little less self-conscious.

"I guess this is a good test to see if what we did earlier worked," I said, cautiously pulling down my underwear while gauging Vince's reaction.

"Yup," the vargyr replied. "Yer literally bettin' yer ass right now."

"I'm sure Axel wouldn't let that happen," I said, hanging my boxers over a low-hanging branch. After sitting on the cold, smooth stones lining the edge of the springs, I slowly submerged, giving myself enough time to adjust to the extreme change in temperature.

A shimmer of drool from Vince's mouth immediately caught my attention.

"Vince?" My heart raced when I saw the blank, predacious stare; however, his eyes didn't change color. "Axel!"

Vince burst into a fit of manic laughter.

"That's not fucking funny!" I smacked the water, splashing it at the cackling vargyr. "God damn it."

"What's goin' on? What happened?" Axel asked, dashing up to the water.

I glared at Vince. "Nothing...yet. Stand by. You might have to kick Vince's ass."

Even if the prank took years off my life, it was good to see him laugh.

Derrick and Axel waded into the water, followed by me as I gritted my teeth and sank lower.

"We should hurry this along and get some sleep," Axel said with an even greater air of impatience.

"Why are you so hell-bent on going to bed?" Vince snapped. "Just shut up and relax. You gotta get some pleasure out here where you can, you know?"

"That was the plan, Vince," Axel muttered, his voice barely audible. "When you guys get to bed."

"Alright then. Sit back, relax, and enjoy it," Vince replied, clueless about what Axel was implying.

I leaned back against the stones, my legs floating along the surface as Derrick held his snout before sinking all the way into the water. Only his giant, black wolf head reemerged, bobbing along the surface while staring up at Vince.

"It might not be the best time to bring this up, but we haven't discussed it yet. If there's hope for Cole, we should search for him now that we've thrown Gar far off our trail."

Vince's ears fell, and he looked away. "How're we gonna find him? He's one person wanderin' around a whole lot of nothing. We're probably so far away from him, we ain't ever gonna see him again."

"I didn't mean to upset you."

The smaller vargyr sank into the water. "I hate—" he said, cutting his sentence short, pausing for a moment to compose himself. "I hate bein' reminded that he's out there. I already can't sleep at night, and I'm tryin' not to think about it too much."

"I understand, but we need to find him now that we know something Gar doesn't. If Leo's blood really is potent enough to undo the worst of the demon's curse, that means we can bring anyone back." Derrick swam over to Vince and gently stroked the smaller vargyr's head. "We will find him. Just one scent is all we'll need."

"I'm with you guys." Axel stood rigid in the water, and his voice went stern. "Tomorrow we'll start heading back south, but fer now, we should get to bed."

"What the hell is wrong with you?" Vince shouted. "You mad or somethin'?"

Axel let out a huff before grabbing tufts of his mane. "I ain't mad!"

Derrick eyed Axel and sniffed the air before his gaze landed squarely on me.

"Actually, I am feeling quite exhausted," he said.

"Well, I ain't."

"I think you are," Derrick said, his head nudging toward Axel and I. "We'll have more time in the spring tomorrow morning."

Vince narrowed his eyes. "What the hell's goin' on here?"

Axel let out a light groan, and I stealthily grabbed a handful of his left butt cheek, giving it a squeeze. I thought that would lighten his mood, but it sent him right over the edge.

"Go to bed, Vince!" The smaller vargyr's ears dropped, and Axel quickly walked back his tone. "Please?"

"Fine," Vince growled, jumping out of the water before vigorously shaking himself damp. Derrick followed close, whispering. The smaller vargyr turned to look back at us before his ears stood straight and tail wagged.

I needed to make sure to thank Derrick tomorrow.

CHAPTER 24

Letting The Monster Out

"You didn't have to snap at Vince," I said, turning to punch Axel in the arm. "That was mean."

"I'll apologize later," he whispered, cupping his hand under my chin. After a quick kiss, he wrapped his sopping arms around me, pulling my naked body into his. Though the rippling, moon-lit surface of the water obscured his lower half, his stiffness pressed into my abdomen. He crouched further into the water until we were face-to-face. "You nervous?"

I wanted to run screaming back to camp, but I wasn't about to admit it. As anxious as I was, being around him like this was also exciting. His eyes were wide, patient, and earnest. No one this close ever looked at me the way Axel did—like I was this rare piece of art instead just another piece of ass. With as much time as we'd spent together, I should have grown accustomed to that by now.

"A little," I replied, pausing to consider being more honest with him. "I'm more scared of messing this up."

His giant hand slid downward before gently squeezing my rear. Every sudden movement made me nervous, like he was struggling to control himself, but this was Axel. I had to let this go. Each breath he drew was deeper than the last as he leaned in, his long, thin tongue tracing the curve of my neck.

"You ain't gonna mess nothin' up," he whispered. "Ever since turnin', I never could make this part very romantic. Even without the curse, it's still hard. Vargyr's still a vargyr, even without the *losin' yer mind* part."

He licked my neck again, and the teeth that violently ripped prey apart tenderly grazed my skin. Axel seemed cool and controlled, but his grip on me tightened as he continued licking.

"Axel—" I could barely get enough air in my lungs to speak before he shifted his attention from my neck to my mouth. When his tongue slipped in, that was it for me. In a random surge of vargyr strength, I pinned Axel against the stones, attacking his tongue with my own.

His body went stiff, but the awkwardness didn't last when a growl of satisfaction rumbled from his throat, animal passion feeding off of my brief aggression. Saliva dipped from the sides of my mouth as he slid deeper, our breathing turning to gasps as neither of us wanted to break away.

Each time I inhaled through my nose, his scent would linger there, triggering more of the inhuman lust that threatened to rip from my chest. When he pulled away and sniffed me, his stare grew more intense.

Axel lifted me into his arms, and our tongues and lips fell into a steadier tempo. My legs hugged his waist, not able to wrap all the way around his body. I felt him, slick and rock hard, pushing up between the cleft of my ass. It swelled beneath me, teasing and terrifying me at the same time. I rocked my hips in time with him, our mouths still connected.

As I came to my senses a little more, the situation turned almost surreal. We were approaching the threshold that just a few weeks ago was too dangerous to cross. I was giving myself to a vargyr, willingly. No human would ever dare do this, but I wasn't human anymore.

My logical mind wanted to slow this down, but instead, the animal took control as I shook with anticipation, holding back the need to mount him for real. I was losing the battle. Why wasn't my body cooperating?

Axel growled again—or so I thought. Another vibration shook my throat, in an exciting and terrifying revelation. The change came out of nowhere, and I hadn't noticed at all. Thick, black hair blanketed my once smooth chest, and my teeth were much sharper than before, the canines almost twice as long. The odd sensation of my ears pulling upward to a point made me long to be a full vargyr again.

What little pain there was in this transformation melted into something more familiar as claws erupted from my fingers and toes, but that was where it ended.

I pulled away, panting. Axel beamed as he looked down at me, and there was a silvery reflection on his face from my glowing irises.

"Damn. Look at you," he whispered.

I went from elation to disappointment as I examined myself further. A wilkyr. That wasn't at all what I wanted to be; in fact, I had been glad when I thought I could skip this step entirely.

"We should slow down now," I replied, "or I won't be able to stop."

"Then don't stop." Axel's jagged, lustful grin widened as he leaned me back and orbited my sensitive, pierced nipple with his tongue before holding it gently between his teeth.

"Oh, fuck!" I shouted, forgetting about the other two vargyrs who were likely hearing everything from camp. My body quivered as he bit down enough that the pain felt good, but gentle enough not to draw blood. Between the biting and frotting, I wasn't sure how much more I could take. "It's gonna end early if you don't stop."

Axel nodded and sat my naked, hairy body on the cool stones that lined the edge of the spring.

"I just remembered somethin'." The vargyr jumped out of the water before running back to camp at full mast.

"Hey! Where the hell are you takin' that?" Vince's voice echoed angrily through the woods, but there was no reply.

As quickly as he left, Axel bounded back into the moonlight, dripping wet while holding a black leather bag in one hand and a balled-up blanket in the other.

"Uh oh," I said, examining the lumpy sack. "Is that the *bag 'o stuff*?"

Axel grinned. "Sure is. They get real creative over at the dungeon," he said enthusiastically, unfastening the straps holding the cover in place. "These'll help really enhance things." He pulled out a glass bottle of syrupy-looking liquid and a couple more bottles with questionable, multi-colored contents.

"Oh," I said, letting out an embarrassed laugh. "You had me thinking—" I paused and studied Axel's face as he squinted at me. "Never mind."

"What did you think was in here?"

My face boiled as I thought about my own secret bag of *toys* back at the house, lying forgotten and inconspicuous among my other belongings.

"Is this lube?" I asked, shifting the subject back to the bottles sitting upright along the blanket.

Axel scratched his head. "Kinda. I'm tryin' to remember what each of these did. It's been a while, though." He pointed to the bottle with blue liquid. "I know yer supposed to drink this, but then yer supposed to rub one of these thicker potions on either your privates... or yer hole. But it's supposed to be in the right combination, or...uh... it might not work like we want."

"Potions?" I asked, picking up a pinkish-looking bottle. "I don't think this is a good idea."

"They're harmless, and they're from Stellous, not Gar." He grabbed the bottle from my hand and examined it. "I think this one yer supposed to wet yer dick with." He picked up a yellow bottle and muttered something under his breath.

"You don't really know, do you?"

His ears fell back. "I do," he said, the confidence in his voice about as fragile as the glass he held. He dangled the yellow bottle in front of me. "Here. Rub this in yer ass."

I shoved the potion back into his hands. "How about you rub it in *your* ass first, and if you don't burst into flames, I'll consider it."

Axel gave me a nervous stare and nodded. "Alright," he said, uncorking the bottle before dabbing some of the slimy liquid onto his fingers. "Cole woulda said something if these was dangerous. I know you only need a little bit." He spread his legs and reached under himself, careful not to catch such a sensitive spot with his hooked claws. "There we go. Hmm."

"What?"

His eyes shifted to the side, and he gritted his teeth. "Uh oh."

"Oh no, what's going on? Are you okay?"

The huge vargyr whined like a puppy as he seemed to clench everything. He then lay on his back, writhing against the blanket. I couldn't tell if he was in pain or if he was about to come.

"Oh yeah," he moaned. "This was the right one." Axel pointed to the blue bottle. "Hand me that, and then you drink some. Just a sip."

I did as he said, now wanting to try out that yellow stuff as I watched him shudder while clasping the blanket hard in one hand. After Axel finished drinking, he gave it back to me. When I sipped, a very cool feeling passed from my lips and over my tongue. The flavor was hard to describe, a very earthy mint. As soon as it hit my stomach, my core temperature rose considerably, and it felt like every blood vessel in my body expanded at once. My limbs went slightly numb, and my eyes became a little more sensitive to the moonlight. The only other time I'd experienced a similar sensation was doing poppers with Ben, but this was on a completely different—and longer-lasting level.

"Alright, grab that pink one and rub it on yerself," Axel said with a slight moan. "The magic happens when the yellow and the pink mix."

I did as he instructed, uncorking the bottle before slathering a few fingers of the stuff on my sensitive erection. There was a slight burning sensation that only intensified as I corked the bottle with both hands, setting it off to the side.

"How do ya feel?" Axel asked, likely noticing my discomfort.

"I think this was a bad idea." A vibrating sensation tightened around my groin, and as I wrapped it with my fingers, the intensity of every nerve hit me at once. "Holy...shit," I shouted through gritted teeth. I hadn't even stroked myself before the most embarrassing thing happened. With a shaky and unusually low moan, I came, the force of it surprising even Axel.

"Got a little too excited, huh?" He let out a chuckle, and wiped his face with his hand. "Don't be embarrassed. That happens to everyone after drinkin' that stuff." He pointed at my lower half, and it was still throbbing and ready to go again. "The next part's even better."

It was easy to deduce what Axel was implying as he turned over, lying flat on his stomach with his tail up and off to the side. I crawled closer before steadying the wagging appendage with one hand while sinking one of my fingers into his tight, lubed-up hole. The vargyr gasped and jerked his head to the side, giving me a worried stare.

"What's wrong?" This was the first time I'd ever felt so dominant, and I cracked a grin. "Afraid of a few little fingers?"

Axel let out a whine. "Careful with them claws."

With a slight cringe, I slowly removed my eager digit and jerked my hand away. "Oh my God! I'm so sorry, Axel."

"Don't worry 'bout it. Yer doin' good, but why don't you try somethin' else?"

"What do you want me to do?"

Axel pointed to his mouth, sticking out his tongue while flashing his brows.

"Really? How am I going to do that? Unhinge my jaw?"

"Nah, not there," he said, pulling aside his tail.

I stared at his pert ass, which mostly looked human, aside from the fur and tail. This was something I occasionally did with Ben, but usually after a lot of coaxing and complaining from him. Axel and I were pretty clean, and the lube he used earlier had a very interesting berry scent to it, but I had obvious reservations.

"Maybe let's get the basics out of the way before we take that step," I said nervously, half-expecting him to pout or make me feel bad.

"Then you decide."

It didn't matter the situation; Axel knew me so much better than anyone else. I loved how different he was. Looking into those soft, eager eyes told me everything I needed to know. Despite not being accustomed to the physical difference, deep down, he was one hell of a good man.

"Alright," I said, crawling closer until the head of my cock pushed against his warm, slick opening. I could tell right away he hadn't done this in a while, and even though he was so much bigger, I was too much for him without a bit of preparation—especially since the transformation. I didn't really notice until then how much thicker I was as a wilkyr. "I'll go slow."

There was another startling sensation from below after I had come in contact with the lube Axel used on himself earlier. My shaft throbbed uncontrollably and my abdomen contracted as though I were doing planks. Axel let out a muffled whine as he loosened up before flipping onto his back. Though I'd seen it a few times, it was always shocking to see that monster appendage fully erect. Vargyr anatomy was both strange and familiar. There were obvious outlines where a human glans used to be, but the entire thing was an angry, veiny spire jutting from a wolf-like sheath. I remembered something else hidden below from when I was pleasuring myself in Derrick's cabin. This may have been new and scary, but that excited me even more.

I rubbed against him, and the slick sounds and sensations made it harder to not want to go straight in. Axel moaned before startling me with a snarl as he jerked back, tearing the blanket under his insane grip. Knowing what was about to happen, I wrapped both of my slippery hands around his cock and slid them from tip to base as fast as I could. He thrusted upward, howling as he came, his semen launching in ropey strands. It wasn't as though I hadn't expected there to be some volume to his release; after all, vargyrs were men, enhanced beyond anything natural.

The world around me slipped away as I pushed myself into Axel, forgetting that I needed to take my time. The wolf made uncompromising demands as a new sensation took over. Luckily, the mixture of lube made the vargyr under me even more receptive than before. I was glad Axel had had the foresight to bring that bag.

I wondered if the other wilkyrs felt exactly like this with their vargyr clients. If that were the case, it made sense that the few of them left had enough stamina to keep an entire town satisfied. This wasn't a normal desire. It was a need, as though my very survival depended on it.

After pulling out, I circled the area, slightly pushing in before pulling back out. Each time I teased him like this, Axel would whine and beg. It was unusual to have someone begging this way for a change. He wanted me the same way I wanted him, and he was so huge that all I could do was rock against him on my knees while he lay there on the blanket. I needed so badly to kiss him, but again, the size difference worked to our disadvantage.

As wet, pulsating warmth enveloped me, his eyes rolled upward, and he let out soft whimpers until I was all the way in. It only took a few more thrusts before it became too much. When his heady scent hit my nose, my body immediately responded, ready for another round.

"What the hell?" I said, breathless as my hips moved on their own, this time faster with much more stamina. "What was in that potion?"

Axel grunted, stroking himself in time with my movements.

"That ain't the potion."

I wanted to say something else, but my mind wasn't too keen on having a conversation at the moment. The thickening hair on the back of my neck stood straight as something began to happen. The feeling was akin to an internal pop, like I had broken free from a tiny cage. The stretchy hold around my cock tightened as I continued pounding into it, the warm feeling expanding as I got deeper. This animal haze...I knew this.

"Leo!" Axel gritted his teeth and let out a shriek. "Yer gettin' big." His eyes widened, and I tried to say something, but only managed a guttural warning from the back of my throat. "I think yer turnin'."

The forest faded to a point of light in front of me before my surroundings became unbearably bright, as though someone had turned on fluorescent lights in a dark closet. Though there was pain as muscles ripped and bones popped, it barely competed with the need to keep going.

Axel was really tight now as I sank even deeper into him, and he let out another yelp which shook me from the brief mindlessness of the greedy animal I'd become. I slowed and pulled back, the transformation finishing quickly. Warm fur blanketed my once cold flesh, and I towered over Axel, who lay back, relieved that I had stopped rutting him. I was almost as tall as he was, and I could now reach his mouth while still inside of him.

My thin lips graced his, and our mouths parted to let loose our restrained tongues. It was like lightning striking me over and over as the flexible muscles wrapped around each other, wildly lapping and drooling. My hips moved again—slower this time. The nerve endings that were once in my lips seemed to migrate to the rough taste buds along my new tongue which worked in tandem with my sensitive nose.

After a few stifled whines from the vargyr under me, the sounds of pain turned to something pleasant. I pulled back, wrapping my arms around him and lifting him from the ground. My new muscles made his heft negligible, especially since I could only focus on one thing, and that one thing sent my adrenaline into a surge of energy. Axel's thick legs wrapped around me as I stood straight while wildly fucking him at the same time. I was more beast at that moment than he was, my large paw-like feet sinking into the dirt as I lost my mind.

I supported him by grabbing each leg, my claws digging into his flesh. Axel threw his head back and snarled, snapping at me, and I retaliated by slamming his back against a broad tree, my lower body jackhammering him into submission. I leaned in to kiss him again, but the vargyr in me had a very different idea as my teeth caught the crook of his neck, my jaw locking into place.

What was I doing? Though it felt natural, this horrified the human part of my brain. There was no stopping me as everything went off-rhythm, my new cock so swollen, as instinct drove me to go even deeper.

Axel's feet hit the ground, halting my advance. My jaw locked tighter, but his hand slipped around the back of my neck, his hooked claws digging into the nape. We were both stalemated in that position, my cock still halfway inside of him as I tried thrusting more. He didn't release my neck as he held me back, preventing me from finishing inside of him.

There was an overwhelming need to get him back under me, but it was a bit too late. Now that I was mostly limp, I slipped out of Axel. This struggle had an unusual effect on both of us. He was enjoying this just as much as I was, and the scent of blood from both of us sent me into another form of sexual frenzy.

My tired jaws loosened enough for him to knock me away. There was a slight metallic tang lingering on my tongue, and I could feel my own blood wet on the back of my neck. The pain should have killed the mood, but I craved more of it. I honestly didn't care how we went about it; I just knew that I wanted this rough.

Axel's nose wrinkled as he bared his teeth.

"You sure got mean," he said, his grimace giving way to a challenging grin. "Just how I like it."

I grinned back at him, silently accepting the challenge.

"You're not gonna make it easy, are you?" I asked, my voice resonating much deeper in my throat.

Axel's ears pointed upward.

"Now yer talkin'!" He shifted into what looked like an attack stance, and I instinctively braced for what he might do. "You and I are pretty close in size." His grin widened. "How 'bout winner gets breedin' rights? What do ya say?"

"That's kinda hot," I said, a little breathless while crouching low as he stalked close. The more I tried to rationalize what was happening, the more it didn't make sense. I didn't care anymore. Axel's personality shifted with mine, and he turned from this gentle, patient lover, into a sex-crazed monster.

Axel lunged forward, knocking me back before pinning my arms to the ground. He was fast for his size, and the way he tried to force me into submission made me hard again. I pushed upward with all my strength, bucking him off before rolling around in the dead leaves and dirt. For a few seconds, I had the upper hand before my head hit the ground. Even though we were both about the same height, Axel was still much stronger. There was a reason he was so confident in his wager; he knew he would win.

In another surge of strength, I kicked him off, sending him flying through the air until he smashed against the trunk of a poplar tree, snapping it in half. He scrambled to his feet and tackled me against a huge pine which also relented in a cracking sound, toppling over with me falling with it.

As Axel overpowered me once more, I relaxed under him. It was as though someone had flipped a switch in my brain, and I went from wanting control to giving it away without any more of a fight.

"That's better," Axel said, still out of breath from our struggle. "Yer fun when yer mean, but this is nice too." He leaned in and kissed me again. "Ready?"

"No," I growled, remembering how amazing the pain felt earlier when his claws punctured the back of my neck. "Make it hurt."

"Now *that's* hot," he grunted, biting me hard on the crook of the neck, holding me in place as the slick, tapered end of his cock demanded I let it in. Not wanting to make it easy, I clenched as hard as I could, getting more turned on the more he struggled to penetrate me. His teeth broke skin, catching me off guard. As he clamped down harder, I relaxed enough that he was able to breach, opening me further than I'd ever experienced.

It was excruciating.

"Axel," I shouted, trying to catch my breath. He was barely in, and I was already whimpering like an injured animal. This was what I wanted, right? I regretted giving him that command earlier as he didn't relent, going deeper with each thrust.

His mouth silenced my complaining, that long, flexible tongue sliding around mine. Muffled moans and panicked cries left my nose, but the more anxious I got, the more of a turn-on it was. There was no telling what he would do to me next as he continued to wrangle me into full submission. His cock pushed deeper, hitting areas that no human would have ever been able to reach. My abdomen burned as he broke down another barrier within.

I cried out from my nose, and he leaned back, finally breaking away.

"How was that?" he asked, intensely studying my face. "You don't look so good. Maybe we need a safe word if we're gonna play rough like this."

"It's good," I said with a grimace. My face may have contorted into an expression of agony, but there was no longer a way for this vargyr brain to differentiate between pain and pleasure.

He smiled while grinding his hips, his eyes like two blue flames as he pulled me upright into his lap. Clawed hands caressed my ass as I rocked against him, his tongue soaking the fur around my mouth and neck.

The pain dulled the more I got used to him, but there was still discomfort. Axel lifted me over and over, sliding in and out, his powerful arms working like pistons as I moaned louder. His thrusts weren't as fast or as forceful as mine were earlier, but it wouldn't have felt as good if they were. He took his time with me, savoring the feeling.

"I'm gettin' close," he whispered, slightly winded. "Don't get freaked out."

Pangs rippled through my core as he quickened his pace. I didn't want this to end, but at the same time, we both were approaching the pinnacle, and each added moment would only diminish the feeling. This new body was everything I wanted, and that fear of intimacy may as well have never existed. I could be with Axel now, and there were no limitations. In that moment, the world was mine.

Even if I wanted to stop, I wouldn't have had the will. I wasn't sad about completely losing my humanity. I felt complete. Perhaps we were both overwhelmed by this as we stared into each other's eyes.

Axel laid me against the flat stones, the powerful momentum of his rutting making me gasp as he bared his teeth and leaned in as I had earlier. I closed my eyes as his jaws clamped down on my shoulder. There was no getting away from him now, and that feeling of helplessness under him made the experience all the more incredible.

After three final thrusts, the last one hit me the hardest as a sharp pop sent a searing pain shooting through me. Within seconds, he swelled bigger than before, pulsing inside of me.

His jaws loosened as he let me go. He then threw back his head and howled as a surge of heat spread through me. Another howl awoke an instinct as I lifted my head to join him, our powerful voices in near perfect pitch with one another as I finally approached my own climax. It was so different, and it seemed to go on forever. So this was what sex was like in this body. Why would anyone ever want to go back?

After all that buildup, it was over. Axel fell on top of me, our bodies still connected. Those painful memories I held onto from my old life no longer took on weight. This was my life in Varcross, and I didn't want to go back to that *normal*, touch-starved existence. Loneliness had become the norm for so long, I'd forgotten what this feeling was, but now that I had it, I never wanted to let it go.

Axel and I gazed at one another, his goofy grin making me laugh as I came down from that high. Fate had sure thrown me a curveball.

"I love you," I whispered, letting my head slowly fall back onto the stony ground.

Axel closed his eyes and leaned in close to my ear.

"Yer everything I ever wanted." He panted as he spoke. "I love you, Leo."

I tried to roll off to the side, but we were still awkwardly locked together.

"How long does this last?"

He maneuvered me on top of him while he fluffed the blanket to rest his head. "A while. We got all night to enjoy it."

Hostile Takeover

Waking up to a full body of warmth was something I hadn't experienced in a while. Even when Axel wrapped me in his arms at night, there was always a part of me that was left in the cold. Cole was right; vargyrs really could sleep anywhere.

Careful not to wake him, I scooted away from Axel before wobbling upright on shaky paws while balancing myself on the hocks that stood in place of once-human ankles. The sun was still low on the eastern horizon, painting the clouds above the mountains a soft pink while the rest of the sky tapered to a blackish-blue, a few specs of brighter starlight dotting the clear area beyond the evergreen canopy.

A light splattering of water from the spring caught my attention as two smirking vargyr heads poked from the water like furry crocodiles waiting for a thirsty gazelle.

"Well done, Leo. It looks like you unclogged your flow," Derrick said, dipping his face into the water as if stifling laughter.

"You both were so damn loud." Vince crossed his arms. "Didn't get much sleep last night with all the noise."

"Sorry," I said, stepping into the springs, which didn't feel as hot as they did when I was furless.

"Oh yeah, you can talk now. I forgot." Vince swam over to me and looked up. "I hate how big you are. I can't pick on you no more."

As I sunk into the water, my gaze narrowed on the smaller vargyr.

"I've never been able to speak as a vargyr before now. What do you mean you forgot?"

He slunk into the water and waded away from me. "What part of *yer too damn loud* didn't you understand?"

I raised an eyebrow at his suspicious reaction before turning to Derrick.

"Maybe all Nomis needed was a night of amazing sex instead of all that boring meditation," I said, slapping water at his face. "It would have saved her a year of frustration."

Instead of laughing, the older vargyr seemed to give my sarcasm actual consideration.

"She never sought out male or female companions. If they weren't books, they weren't worth her time." He paused, humming pensively. "You may be onto something. I have never heard of anyone unlocking the mysteries of advanced magic through—" he glanced over at the fallen trees "—disturbingly violent coitus before. I suppose there's always a first time, right?"

Vince eyed Axel, who was still asleep on the ground before turning back to me. "You really wore his ass out."

"I can't believe we did it."

"I can't believe yer still able to walk," Vince retorted with a snorty laugh. "I remember years ago he wanted to get behind me like he used to when we was human, and I took one look at that thing and told him he was out of his fuckin' mind. I could barely handle him when he *wasn't* a monster."

My face flushed with embarrassment.

"It wasn't bad."

"You handled him better than he handled you, the big baby."

Derrick backed away before jumping out of the pool. "Vince, you simple-minded..." He muttered the rest as he darted back toward camp.

I stood up, towering over the smaller vargyr.

"How would you know that?"

He shifted his stare toward Derrick, who had already disappeared through the trees.

"Derrick told me."

"You lying sack of shit. You're both dead," I snarled, grabbing the nape of his neck, pulling him up out of the water.

His ears snapped back. "Now hold on. Ya ain't gotta get violent. What else are we gonna do fer entertainment out here? You guys are the only ones havin' fun!"

I shook my head and dropped him back into the water.

"This is kind of embarrassing," I muttered, sitting with my back against the stone edge of the spring while not able to make eye contact. "That was a very personal moment, Vince."

"And ya shared it with the whole forest. Most of us ain't got no shame, anyway." Vince inched closer and elbowed my arm. "Hey, wanna hear somethin' that might make you feel better? Sometimes vargyrs just fuck in the middle of everyone, and if the rest ain't jerkin' to it, they just walk on by."

"Gross," I muttered.

Vince shrugged and looked down at the water. "We was just horny and bored, and it was kinda fun watching Axel get a dose of his own medicine."

A loud yawn made us turn toward a waking Axel who stumbled to his feet while rubbing his eyes.

"Mornin'," he said, smacking his jaws.

I turned all the way around and leaned against the edge, crossing my sopping arms over the stones. "You sleep okay?"

He walked into the spring and leaned into me before our mouths met.

"Slept real good," he whispered. He shot Vince a playful stare. "You two enjoy the show?"

"You knew?" I asked, eying a half-postured Derrick slinking back toward the water.

"You didn't? They was right there in the bushes when you threw me against that tree. Could see their eyes an' everything."

The tall black vargyr mage pursed his lips and shrugged.

"I have no defense," he said softly.

"Is this, like, a normal thing with you guys?"

"Don't be such a prude," Vince muttered, glaring as Derrick tiptoed back into the hot water.

"Alright, new rule," I shouted, scooting away from Axel. "No more watching us." Derrick disappeared into the water, his head poking up. "I mean it. This feels gross."

"After everything you did last night, this is what makes you feel gross?" Derrick asked without a hint of sarcasm in his tone. Sometimes I wondered if he was serious or just messing with me.

"After what you saw last night, you were right to run away when you did." I lunged at Derrick, but he dodged and hid behind Axel.

"Come now, Leo. It was a fascinating observation. You never see a human go through all three stages of transformation in one sexual encounter."

"C'mon. We're family," Axel said, ogling Vince and Derrick. "Since you guys liked it so much, why don't you join us next time?"

Both vargyrs scrambled out of the hot springs, vigorously shaking water from their fur. They nearly tripped over one another as they bolted toward camp.

"We should leave early today," Derrick said, stopping to look back at us before eyeing the glass bottles from last night. "I'll, uh, gather our belongings and get them ready." And with that, they both vanished.

Axel gave another smug laugh and leaned back, letting his feet float to the surface.

"Just so you know, we are not doing it with Vince and Derrick."

"Oh, I know that," he said. "But it was fun seein' 'em nearly pee themselves at the thought."

I floated next to him and grabbed his hand. "I thought they'd be into the idea."

"We're the weird ones, actually." He looked over at me, his eyes glowing blue. "I didn't think I'd ever find someone who likes it the way I do."

"I thought all vargyrs...but the instinct—"

"Vargyrs are rough," Axel said, "but you and I are on a different level. It's just one of the many reasons we're perfect fer each other." We floated in the spring, listening to the morning birds sing over the sounds of Vince and Derrick arguing in the distance. "What'cha thinkin' about?"

"A lot," I said, still looking at the brightening sky, the pine needles above us turning a rusty orange. "This is it. There's no going back now."

"You havin' regrets already? Did I do somethin' wrong?"

"That's not what I meant. It was just something I thought about last night, about never being able to go back to my world."

"Ah, I see," Axel replied. "Never had a real family, so I don't know exactly what yer feelin' right now. But I do know what it's like to get thrown into a world you don't know nothing about."

"I know you do, and it's not as though my family was ever there for me after I left home. My parents were terrible people, but I still kind of miss my little sister."

I turned to Axel as his face grew more concerned.

"It's not a big deal. There was never anyone in my life who really loved me. Before I met you guys, I didn't even have friends who had my back. Just a bunch of back-stabbing queens and an abusive boyfriend."

"You were friends with royalty?"

"Quite the opposite." I laughed while stroking the side of Axel's head. "I still can't believe you made an entire bed just to get my attention."

"Ya still ain't never got to use it."

"You barely knew me. Why'd you make something that elaborate?"

He held me against him. "You didn't pull away."

"Huh?"

"Gave ya a little test that night in the dressing room. You didn't pull yer hand away from mine. Ya didn't even hesitate. I couldn't stop thinkin' about it while I was carvin' the wood."

"You guys gonna start fuckin' again, or are we gonna leave before a demon catches us?" Vince shouted from the campsite.

"He sure knows how to set the mood, doesn't he?" I said, pushing myself up out of the spring. Axel followed, and we both shook ourselves as dry as we could.

"Do you really think we'll ever catch Cole?" Axel asked.

"I don't know." I knelt and gathered the blanket we slept on last night while Axel placed the jars back into his bag. "We might have to prepare Vince for the possibility that he won't ever see Cole alive again. If he went back to town, they'd probably kill him, and if he's further out in the wilds…" I paused and rubbed my head in frustration. "Like Vince said, it's a really big world."

"Been thinkin' a lot about Derrick."

"What about him?"

"Him and Vince been gettin' along really good lately. I know I don't wanna even think about replacing Cole, but if the worst does happen and the dust settles, Derrick could be good for him—even if they's just friends."

"Could you imagine those two? Derrick would literally talk Vince to death. I don't really like talking about this, though."

"Me neither," he said as we made our way through the trees, approaching camp. Derrick and Vince were holding their bags while engaged in what seemed like a serious conversation. "But now that yer a vargyr, you should watch the way they act around each other. Give 'em a good sniff, too. You'll see what I'm talkin' about. It ain't romance, but it ain't just friendship neither. They understand each other better than most."

Though I'd said it in my mind over and over, it was great to be a vargyr again, and now that I wasn't slowing us down, we could cover longer distances in a shorter amount of time. Instead of taking five days to get back into the grasslands to look for Cole, it took us two. It might have been faster if we didn't have to carry the bags or spend a lot of our time at higher altitudes.

Escaping into the wild gave us a much-needed head start, and now that Gar was good and confused, we could look for our missing friend without worrying as much. The situation we were in made us nomadic anyway, and if we were going to spend our lives on the run, we had to try the impossible.

"We're about a few hours away from where we lost Cole," I said, my energy waning as my stomach growled. "Should we keep going or rest?"

"It would make little sense to travel back to the wastelands," Derrick replied.

"But we gotta look for traces of Cole," Vince cut in, his tone growing more frustrated. "You said we was gonna look for him."

"Think about it." Derrick was always so calm, even when those around him got angry or anxious. "There is little prey and hardly any fresh water back at the caldera, but look around here." The black vargyr pointed down the hill at a herd of alien-looking animals we'd eaten before.

The others called them hyukans, and they were about the size of bull elk. Their fronts were broad and shaped like a bison's, but their rear flanks were leaner like a moose's. Their top-heavy gait made them surprisingly quick—and dangerous, but when Axel and Derrick caught them, they were the most delicious things I'd ever tasted. Apparently, the beasts were common livestock on Eqiros.

There were other strange herbivores on the plains, some of them Earth-like, while some were familiar to the others. We left most animals alone since no one knew what they were, or if they were even worth hunting.

"We also have to remember, Gar has likely been in this area, and if he knows we're here, he can portal directly to us," Derrick continued.

We all froze as the smell of death wafted through the breeze. This normally would have made me sick as a human, but my new brain knew how to handle the stronger, unpleasant odors.

"Smells a few days old," Axel said, turning toward the direction of the scent, us following close. As we approached, a vulture-picked skeleton lay before us, its limbs violently shorn away and strewn about the area. The dead hyukan's rib bones had been gnawed, some of them missing completely.

"Seems a bit excessive," Derrick said, kneeling to examine the corpse closer. After a few moments of picking through the carcass, he got on all fours and sniffed the surrounding area. "That's Cole's scent, but it has mostly faded. It's not enough to follow."

"Guys, over here," Vince shouted, his head poking up from the tall grasses. We ran toward him and were immediately hit with the scent of at least five different vargyrs. "Cole was here." He pointed to the dark splatters in the grass. It was too dark for our night vision to pick up the color, but the smell was unmistakable. "It don't smell like

Cole's blood, but I don't know." The smaller vargyr's voice pitched upward as tears welled in his eyes.

"It's not surprising they would be this close," Derrick said, rubbing Vince on the back before kneeling to examine the marks in the dirt where the grass had been kicked away. "The scene tells the story. Cole singled out one of the vargyrs and attacked him. He couldn't tell the difference between predator and prey, but it looks like they were evenly matched. Cole probably ran away before the others arrived."

Axel sat his bags down and stretched his arms, but Derrick stood in place, contemplating in silence while shaking his head.

"Something about this seems off. The claw marks where the struggle happened look haphazard. And that dead hyukan had been completely consumed in one sitting, the bones almost arranged."

"What are you thinking?" I asked, setting my bags next to Axel's. "Is this a trap?"

Derrick shrugged. "Or I could just be overly cautious. When dealing with demons, anything is possible."

"Well, we ain't goin' no further tonight, and there ain't no sense worrying about it for now. There's hyukan in the air, and we got us a new hunter." Axel playfully threw his arm around my neck.

"Oh yeah, now *you* can see what it's like." Vince's expression went from serious to a bit softer. "I bet yer gonna suck at it."

I hissed through my teeth. "I bet I'll, uh—" Though I tried to rebut Vince's teasing with confidence, I was nervous. What if he was right? I'd never live it down, especially after I berated him that day in front of Cole.

"Bet you'll what? Choke?" Vince let out a laugh and sat on the ground near a large boulder. "If you happen to spot one 'o them big rat things I caught last time, grab one for me—if you can catch it."

"You ain't coming?" Axel asked.

"Nah. Need to rest my feet. They been hurtin'."

"Are you okay? Do you want me to keep you company?" Derrick asked.

"Nah. Don't worry, just need some rest."

"Don't rest here, just in case this is a trap," Derrick insisted, pointing in the opposite direction. "We'll find you."

"We won't be gone too long," Axel said, scooping his best friend into his arms. "We know he's alive, so we'll find him."

Vince returned the hug before pushing Axel away.

"Between you and Leo, I swear." He gave a forced smile. "I'll be alright."

"You'll feel better once you got food in yer belly." There was a glimmer of excitement as Axel looked back at me. "You ready to embrace yer inner monster?"

A heavy feeling churned in my guts as I thought about how this would go. Would I be able to go through with it, or would I whimper and lose my nerve?

I nodded, but Axel could sense something was off.

"It's only first-time jitters. We all had 'em, but instinct will take over before you know it."

"I know why yer scared," Vince said eying me before walking away. "Yer afraid I'm a better hunter than you."

"No way in hell," I growled out, unintentionally falling for what Vince was doing. "Damn it."

He turned for a moment and cocked a grin. "Yer welcome."

"Take a long breath through yer nose and close yer eyes," Axel whispered while crouched beside me in the tall, moonlit grass. It didn't take long to track down the herd we saw close to the scene earlier, and I was surprised they hadn't traveled further away from us since they were downwind. As their scent grew stronger, our eyes went dark and our steps lightened.

I did as Axel said, closing my eyes while taking in two distinct streams of air into my nostrils, which contained more information than I could decipher. Low thuds of different pulses filled my ears, coming from us and the herd, and it was hard to tell them apart at first. As the ground got closer, my eyes snapped open. The prairie glowed a neon purple, and the sky became more vivid, the black, starry void turning a violet gradient around the moon. The herd should have been too far to see, especially through the grass, but my sense of smell combined with other acute senses gave the distant prey a wobbly white aura.

"You hit yer hunter's stance," Axel whispered. "You see 'em, and you know what to do. Derrick and I'll stay back here and let you have at it."

My snout never shifted as I stared straight ahead at the animals. There were eight—no—nine of them, seven adults and two calves. Saliva dribbled down the sides of my maw as I focused in on a large male hyukan who seemed less alert than the others as it wandered carelessly closer.

"I don't know." I could only speak in low grunts now. "I don't know if I'm ready for this."

"You are," Axel whispered. "Focus on yer mark and don't stop 'til you get it. Go fer the neck and don't let 'em catch you with them horns."

Giving one last nod, I inched forward. The animal lifted its head, likely hearing the nearly silent crunching under my padded paws. I kept low, my body concealed by the tall grass. It was then I could discern the heartbeats; the vargyrs were steady and calm while my prey's pulse quickened. Soon they would all either hear or smell me if I didn't make my move.

The claws on my toes gripped the ground as I primed my body to sprint. Strong pulses of blood rushed in my ears, my chest vibrating from the adrenaline high. It was time.

The white aura of my prey turned red as I pushed against the dirt, launching myself forward with an incredible burst of speed. The hyukans bellowed out alarm and scattered, but my target was too close to flee as I narrowed the gap. His eyes widened as he turned to run, his hind legs kicking up, striking me in the chest. I stumbled for just a moment, but regained my balance, shrugging off the pain.

"Watch them hooves too," Axel shouted from behind.

With a snapping snarl, my jaws latched onto its thick neck and clamped down. The panicked creature struggled for a few seconds before I bit harder, instinctively jerking my head from side-to-side, severing the beast's spine and arteries. It went limp in my mouth; a quick death, thankfully.

Flashbacks to that night when Cole lost his mind flickered into my thoughts. If I hadn't had the strength to hold him off, he would have done this to me. This was our true nature, and I wondered what would happen if I not only broke the curse but also the wards that held us here. Magic or no, would humans and vargyrs ever be able to coexist peacefully with such a vast imbalance of physical ability?

I opened my mouth, letting the lifeless animal fall to the ground with a thud as Derrick and Axel ran to me.

"Look'it that. Nice and big. Weren't nothin' fer you, was it?"

"Great hunting, Leo," Derrick said as he eyed me. "You don't look so well."

"Just thinking about stuff."

"You should try doin' less of that," Axel said with a deep laugh before hoisting the front of the heavy bull onto his shoulders, Derrick grabbing the other end. Even though we were all strong enough to carry it alone, sharing the load made walking easier. "You killed it, we carry it."

The mood as we searched for Vince turned dark. There was this lingering dread hanging over us, but hunting seemed to clear some of it away. Derrick cracked dirty jokes, and I held my sides as he would go into surprisingly explicit detail, using his typical sterile words. If I heard him say coitus one more time, I'd completely lose it.

As we followed Vince's scent back to where we left, a faint, high-pitched whining made my ears perk up. They were barely audible over the hissing breeze through the grass, and we all stopped to listen.

"Help." Vince's voice cracked as he cried out. My heart thudded as I sprinted in his direction, the other two dropping our dinner before following.

"Vince?" I called out, scanning the area for him. His scent took me from the campsite, further west.

"Over here," he shouted, a little louder than before. As I approached, he was sitting on the ground, his right foot caught in a green glowing trap. "Sorry I didn't listen. Was tryin' to get more of Cole's scent, and I stepped on this. I can't get out."

I knelt next to him, reaching for the device, which looked like a small bear trap, only the jaws of it oozed with neon energy, the teeth twisting like vine tendrils around his leg.

"Hold on! Don't touch th—" Vince's warning came too late as I tried to force the jaws open using my hands. A jolt of what felt like electricity pulsed from the trap, stunning both of us before throwing me back a few feet. "You think I ain't tried that, dumbass?" He looked up at me with a watery gaze. "This is a Gar trap fer sure. I might be done here."

"We will find a way to get you out," Derrick said calmly, kneeling to examine the device. After shoving one finger between a hinge, he smiled.

"You know how to free him?" I asked.

He shook his head. "Gar can use Lo'rim in this world, but it's quite limited. This can only stay charged for so long once it's activated. If there's no way to deactivate it manually, then we'll just simply wait it out."

"That's all the time he needs. He's going to open a portal to us," I said, dusting myself off before scanning the area around the camp. "If he's activated this trap, he knows where we are. He's probably going to be here any minute, and we need to be ready to fight."

"That won't be necessary," Vince said, his eyes glowing a nuclear green as Gar's voice melded with his.

"Motherfucker," I snarled, leaning in close to Vince's face.

"Who's this handsome fellow?" He looked like he was blind at first, but his vision seemed to sharpen, his stare falling onto me. "Look at what you've become. You're still sane, *and* you're not a wilkyr. It's not often I find myself surprised, but you've been full of them lately."

"Let go of Vince," Axel said, grabbing a handful of fur on the vargyr's chest.

"Careful now. This isn't *my* body." Vince's green eyes were devoid of pupils, and Gar's emotions were harder to discern. The puppet effect made everything about Vince's facial movements uncanny. "Way to go, Axel. Leo is perfect now. Absolutely perfect."

"I didn't—" My arm shoved into Axel's side.

"Wait a minute." Gar growled through Vince as he turned toward the black vargyr. "You! I wondered how Leo eluded my capture for so long, but it makes sense now. Spilling my secrets again, Derrick?"

"You spilled your own secrets. Intentionally, no doubt." Though Derrick chuckled to deflect and belittle the demon, there was a tension building in him. It was fear or anger, or both at the same time. "So how did you get trapped here, Atorien? Xavier didn't take your real name to his grave, and you know what one can do with such knowledge."

"And what will *you* do with it? What is an arcane user with no magic going to do with a demon's name?"

Derrick gritted his teeth.

"It seems we've all been reunited. Well, almost." He looked around camp and placed both hands on his face. "What happened to poor Cole?"

"I swear I'll kill you," Axel snarled, beating the ground with his fist.

"I liked Cole. The way he commanded the respect of the town, how he never turned anyone away—" He glared at Axel. "No matter how depraved." Gar sighed, seeming genuinely upset. "I knew how his end would come. Wilkyrs that go blood-crazed have a very distinct scarring on their souls, put there by the one they loved. Vargyrs who randomly choose their male victims won't do this, but those who have gotten a human to fall in love with them are quite rare.

"Vince's betrayal left one such scar. I prolonged Cole's wilkyr transformation because I truly felt sorry for the pathetic creature, and he did grow on me. I could have bought him another few years, but this was what you all chose. This little trip of yours was pointless in the end. Leo is cursed, and Cole is on death's door. Come back, destroy the wards, and you can all live the rest of your lives out here in the wild if you wish."

"Quick question, Atorien," Derrick said, his brows furrowed. "You wouldn't happen to be missing a very important tome, would you?"

Gar bared his teeth, his head snapping in Derrick's direction.

"I see now," Derrick continued. "We know how this will end, and we know your limitations."

"I should have killed you instead of showing you mercy."

"You call giving me a cocktail of poison that made me wander in mindless torment mercy? If we meet again, I will be better prepared to end you or die trying."

"By all means, I welcome you all back here to try your luck in vanquishing me."

"Why not just come here to us?" I asked, remembering what Derrick told me about Gar's portals. "Why drag it out, unless there's something wrong?"

There was a momentary flash of what I could only deduce was nervousness from the demon before he threw his head back and laughed. "There's no more point; you'll come to me." Vince's eyes dimmed and brightened again. "It seems I have little time left to extend my invitation, so I'll let someone else do it."

"Where's Vince?" Another voice melded with Vince's. I had only heard it for a moment when he turned, but I knew it was Cole. "Let me die."

"It's hard to bring a blood-crazed back temporarily. As you know, a demon's curse cannot be undone, so this is a very painful process." Gar no longer grinned; instead, he glared directly at me. "You *will* come, as I've now imprinted Cole's agony onto Vince's soul. They're connected now. He'll want to say goodbye, and I'll give him the chance. You'll not want to tarry for much longer."

Vince's eyes darkened, and he let out a horrible scream-like howl. The glow emanating from the trap dissipated, and the device broke open, releasing the vargyr's foot.

"Vince," I said, grabbing him by the arms to calm him, but that didn't help. His jaws clamped tightly around my arm, a reaction to whatever was happening to him. The episode continued for another couple of minutes before his breathing returned to normal and his jaws loosened. As soon as he let me go, he slumped forward and sobbed into my chest.

"He's hurtin'," Vince whimpered. "He torturin' Cole." His voice pitched more as his tears soaked the fur on my chest. "He's scared."

"He's won," I said blankly, looking up at Axel. "We've gotta go back."

"No," Axel said, his tone wavering. "We can't!"

"What are we gonna do then?" I asked, rocking a crying Vince in my arms. "I can't watch him suffer like this, and we can't go back without some kind of plan or it's pointless." I tossed a pleading glance at Derrick. "You're the only one who really knows him. What are our chances?"

"Even that knowledge is limited, Leo," Derrick said, kneeling next to Vince and I. He wiped the smaller vargyr's eye with his thumb. "This may be all or nothing."

"I don't wanna lose you," Axel said through tears. He scooped Vince and me into his arms. "We ain't even started our lives yet."

Elemental Stability

Vince finally calmed enough to slip into a restless sleep a few hours later. He couldn't eat anything without retching, and Derrick stayed by his side while Axel and I took a walk to clear our minds.

When I was a child, the very concept of eternity scared me more than others my age. Dying scared me. Hell scared me. I had been obsessed with both for most of my life. As physically tough as I was in this form, those thoughts made me feel like that scared little boy again. Gar knew how to make it impossible to run away, and I couldn't shake Vince's terror-stricken face and gurgled noises as he writhed and convulsed under that terrible spell. I'd have given anything to make it stop.

Axel walked without a word through the tall grass of the moonlit prairie. He kept his eyes straight ahead, as if he'd lost himself in the almost endless expanse of grass that stretched toward an inky starlit sea.

"I ain't letting ya go," he said, in a sterner tone than I'd heard before.

"Vince is like your brother."

He stopped, his eyes flashing as he grabbed my arm. "I can't do anything for him. I couldn't do anything for Cole, but I can save you. Yer not goin' back to that town."

"That's my choice, not yours."

"The hell it ain't!" He squeezed harder. "We're mates now, and I'll lose everything if you go." He whimpered, his ears drooping to the sides of his head. "I won't have nothin' left."

"Axel." Tears made his gorgeous blue eyes shimmer as I caressed his face with my rough, padded hand. "We have to do anything we can to save them. I feel like I want to throw up thinking about going back, but I'd feel just as sick if we abandon them. We're family, Axel. That's what you called us. I've had enough of my family abandoning one another."

"Don't you feel it, Leo? Think about if you was in my position and I was in yours. Really think about it."

"You've known Vince all your life, and Cole saved both of our lives. I wouldn't be here if it weren't for him—we wouldn't be together. Shouldn't they be worth the risk?"

"If it was my life to risk, then yes, but it ain't." He let go of me and snatched tufts of the unruly mane on his head. "It's like...everyone I love is hangin' off a cliff screamin' for help, and I gotta be the one to decide who to pull up and who to let fall. It's gonna hurt no matter what choice I make, but you heard Derrick. Losin' a mate is like dying."

I wrapped my arms around him. "I don't want to die and leave you, so we should fight like hell to make sure that doesn't happen."

"What are we gonna do against magic? He ain't even close to us and he's killin' Vince with it. He screwed up Derrick, and I couldn't even get off the floor to stop him from takin' you away that day. I'm the strongest damn vargyr in the whole town, and that skinny little snake pinned me like I was an ant. We can't *fight like hell* against that. All we can do is run."

"Look at me," I said, placing a hand on my chest. "I'm not helpless, and Gar isn't as limitless as everyone thinks. Derrick doesn't think so either. There was no reason for him to torture Vince and leave us out here. He didn't teleport to us because he couldn't for some reason, and the longer it takes us to get to him, the more time we have to plan. That puts him at a disadvantage. When he saw Derrick, he was afraid."

"Yer makin' a lot of assumptions right now."

"These aren't assumptions. These are observable facts. Even the traps he sets are limited. I still don't know how I escaped the place he took me to that day, but for some all-powerful being, he didn't seem to have a clue how to handle me. Why didn't he keep me restrained when he saw I was stronger? How did he let me escape so easily? It's all been bothering me for a while. If the stories about this demon are true, we wouldn't have gotten this far. He wants out of here now before his time is up, and we won't find out his weakness by running away."

Axel contemplated my words for only a moment before shaking his head and brushing past me.

"We can't do this without you," I said.

"We ain't gonna have to because you ain't going."

There was no getting through, no matter how much I tried to reason with him. So this was the bull-headed side of Axel.

"Give it more thought. We've gotta go back, and you know it."

He said nothing as he continued, his tail rigid as hackles along his neck and back gave him a wild, puffed-up look. I'd seen him use this tactic a few times, but this was the first time it was directed at me. It hurt to see him so out of his mind with panic, and I didn't know what I could do to not make it worse.

We arrived at camp, and Axel crawled into our blanket before staring up at me. The other two were dead asleep, Vince comfortably nestled in Derrick's arms. Axel was right about whatever was going on between those two, and they had grown so much closer as friends.

I lay next to Axel and pulled the blanket over us. There was this invisible wall of tension keeping us apart, though our bodies touched. So many powerful emotions swirled through both of us, and we couldn't deal with them the way we should have been able to. Our pack scraped through one trauma only to end up faced with another, but Gar still hadn't broken us—well he hadn't broken me.

I came into this world with luck on my side. Now I wanted to see how far it would take us all.

"He's staying?" Derrick whispered out of earshot of Vince, who was sitting on the ground, staring out into nothing.

"He said he wouldn't let me go, but now he's refusing to go with me."

Derrick raised a brow. "Interesting."

"What?"

"He knows you likely won't be able to leave without him."

"I'm sure he won't let us get far before changing his mind."

The black vargyr's inquisitive eyes lit up. "Oh boy! I have always wanted to see this kind of mate dynamic play out."

"Derrick," I said, rubbing my head. "I'm not a science experiment. What the hell are you talking about?"

"Vargyr mates share a powerful bond that goes well beyond simple instinct. It's quite fascinating! Unless you both part on willing terms, if either one of you doesn't want the other to leave...well, it's just a matter of who's more dominant at that point."

"Are you fucking serious?"

Derrick rubbed his hands together. "Shall we put it to the test?"

"How can you be so cheerful all the time?" I asked, picking up my and Cole's bags. "We could be walking to our deaths and you'd be excited to calculate the number of ways we'll die."

"Thirty-seven," Derrick said matter-of-factly.

"Excuse me?"

"There are thirty-seven ways Gar could kill us."

"Oh my God," I muttered, turning to Vince as Derrick broke into a light chuckle. "Are you ready to go, Vince?"

He slumped forward and wobbled to his feet before grabbing his bags, expressionless. "Where's Axel?"

"He'll catch up to us," I said, following Derrick down the hill.

"Y'all should just let me go back by myself," Vince muttered. "Axel knows I'm as good as dead. That's why he don't wanna come."

"He's scared," I said. "He doesn't know what to do."

"All I wanna do is die with my mate."

Derrick and I gave one another worried glances. With one spell, Gar undid an entire week's worth of positive mental health, and it felt like a punch in the gut. I was not going to let Vince fall back into despair, no matter what Axel did.

A howl cracked the air from further up the foothills, and my chest began to hurt. It was like every terrible emotion wanted to rip from me at once. I had to slow down to catch my breath.

"Oh, come now, Leo," Derrick said with a sly smile. "You were so dominant while mating, what happened?"

"Shut up, I'm fine," I growled, moving my shaky legs forward.

So this was what Derrick was talking about. I tried to fight it, but after another howl, my legs wouldn't move forward.

"He ain't gonna let you go," Vince said, stopping to look at me, his eyes glassy and face fur wet. "You know that, right? He loves ya too much to let you die."

"I'm not going to die! He's really gonna let you guys face him by yourselves."

"Derrick ain't gonna face nothin'."

The vargyr mage stepped in front of Vince. "You and I have been through this—"

"You ain't my mate," Vince interrupted. "I know we've been gettin' close, but you ain't throwing yer life away for my pathetic ass. No one's gonna do that for me no more! Get me close to town, and I'll see if Gar will let me say goodbye to Cole—if he ain't too pissed that Leo ain't there."

For a split second, Derrick seemed to shatter, but a usual sturdy countenance rebounded. "I understand."

"You ain't gotta be so nice to me."

"Kindness isn't an obligation, Vince." He grabbed one of Vince's bags and strapped it to his back before grabbing the smaller vargyr's hand. "I'll take you as far as you want me to." He turned back to me. "It may be better this way. If I make it through this without incurring Gar's wrath, perhaps we will meet again one day."

"Oh, come on, we're not going to be gone for long. I'll talk Axel down, and we'll catch up." I turned toward Derrick. "You're more brilliant than any of us, so I'm counting on you to come up with something that might give us a fighting chance. Gar's scared, and you know it. Try to think about why he wouldn't be able to portal to us when Vince got trapped."

"I've been mulling them over, and I may have some ideas—if indeed this is not goodbye."

"It's not—"

Vince threw his arms around me, squeezing as tight as he could.

"I can never repay you fer everything you did fer Cole," he said as he pulled away, and his ears fell off to the sides of his head, "and me. I love you like a brother."

I had to look away and take a few deep breaths through my nose to steel myself. After all the anger and resentment, to hear those words meant the world to me.

"Vince..."

"Don't be gettin' all soft like Axel," he said through his own tears as he lifted his bags again. "Maybe I'll see ya soon."

⁂

If Axel was going to show his ass, then I was prepared to meet him halfway. I said nothing to him as I walked by, and then I planted myself on the ground.

"I know yer upset," he said softly, picking my bags off the ground. "But I know in my gut this is right."

I remained silent, watching the two dots that were Vince and Derrick shrink until they were barely visible.

"I'm not moving, and you can't go very far." I looked up at Axel and smiled. "Derrick explained it."

He sighed heavily before plopping onto the ground next to me. "If we gotta stay here, then at least you'll be safe."

"For now." I squinted as the morning sun finally peeked over the eastern horizon. "Until Gar finds another way."

"You said last night he ain't got any other way. We'll go north and build us a home in the mountains."

"I know you're not stupid. Gar's a demon, and he's going to find me. It's only a matter of time before we fuck up and he's got us. We'll have sacrificed our family for a few more miserable months." I met his eyes. "Because that's what our last moments together are going to be like."

"I know yer makin' sense, but my gut's tellin' me to get you as far away as I can."

"Is that really what your gut's saying?"

He looked down at the ground. "It is."

"When you lie, you should look me in the eyes when you do it."

Axel shook his head and choked up.

"This is scary, I know," I said, laying my head against his shoulder. "But a life on the run while constantly looking behind us, expecting the worst...that's more terrifying than death."

Axel placed an arm behind my back. "I ain't strong enough to handle this. I can't even lead enough to get you to follow me."

"There's no leading without a destination. It's just wandering aimlessly at that point, with the other person just as lost. We're a team. Let me carry what you can't, and you do the same for me."

"I don't wanna lose you."

"You won't." I stood up and stretched before reaching down to help him up. "You know what my gut is telling me?"

Axel shook his head as I pulled him from the ground.

"There are no coincidences. We didn't get this far just to roll over and die, and we're not going to let Gar have his way." Just thinking about that horrible creature made me bare my teeth. I wasn't going to abide another monster in my life. There had been too many of those.

Axel's worried frown relaxed into a soft smile as his tail wagged.

"Yer kinda sexy when you snarl like that." He picked up our bags, handing me mine. "Sometimes I only know how to live in the moment. It's hard to think a few steps ahead, especially when things are really bad."

"I know," I said, walking alongside him to the southwest in the direction of the other two. "Just don't be so quick to brush me off, okay? Sometimes it takes a while, but if you give me a chance, I might be able to handle what you can't."

☙⚫❧

It took a half an hour at full-sprint to catch up to Derrick and Vince. They would have been further ahead if not for the randomly-timed episodes of torture that racked the smaller vargyr's body and mind. When we arrived, Vince was screaming in Derrick's arms, both of them lying on the ground. Gar wanted to emphasize how serious he was, reminding us that the clock was ticking and Vince would likely die when Cole's body finally gave out.

What a cruel creature. Was he even able to grasp the concept of empathy, or were we just a means to an end? He mentioned caring about Cole, and for a moment, I actually believed it. Gar's contradiction reminded me of something I often thought about when I was a child. We were God's children, but the Christian God randomly chose who had a good life and who lived a terrible one. If one was *blessed* enough to be born in a first-world country or in 'the right neighborhood', it meant they were one of God's chosen. It was easier to count blessings when one could dehumanize people in worse situations, as my parents often did—as Gar did.

Perhaps at its very core, cruelty was a fundamental part of existence, and higher beings like gods or demons didn't understand it. Then again, how could any immortal being truly understand the value of life since, in order to live, they must also die? In the same way, could one understand what being warm was like unless they've been cold at some point? A creator could create, but never truly understand his creations.

Philosophy aside, one thing was always certain—at least on Earth: there's only so much people can take before they rise to meet cruelty head-on. Those that don't rail against their tormentors die victims, and that wasn't going to be our death.

"So," Derrick said, as he lay Vince's head against a folded blanket. "I take it you two came to an understanding? That is good."

"How is he?" I asked, kneeling next to the two.

"About as well as to be expected, given the circumstances."

"I'm sorry," Axel said, kneeling next to his best friend. "I wasn't thinkin' right."

"Neither of you have anything to apologize for. We're charging into the unknown, and if the worst happens, I am proud to have been a part of this pack."

"Why do you keep talking like that?" I asked, slapping Derrick's back. "If we go into this already defeated, then that's exactly what's going to happen."

"I agree, but without a plan, we should say our goodbyes now," he retorted, returning my slap on the back with his own. "So, have you two made up your minds? Are we going to stick together and plan, or are we saying goodbye?"

"We ain't sayin' goodbye," Vince mumbled, waking from his brief bout of unconsciousness. "I trust you guys can figure this out." He sat up and gave me a nod. "Only you can cure Cole, and Gar don't know that. Maybe that might come in handy."

Derrick smiled at Vince and lifted the smaller vargyr to his feet. "It's good to hear some optimism in your voice."

I agreed with Derrick. Earlier, I thought the worst, but seeing that resolve on his face put how much he'd grown emotionally into perspective.

Vince rubbed his head. "This hurts, but at least if I feel his pain, I know he's still alive. And if he's still alive, Leo can stop him from sufferin'. I ain't givin' up if you guys ain't."

"We've got four days at most until we're back in town," Derrick said, stroking his chin fur. "In that time, we'll need to decide what to do. Cole cannot be our only focus because we need to have different courses of action depending on the situation we end up in."

"We should probably figure out where Cole is first." I turned to Vince. "Maybe we can go with your first suggestion. You can go into town alone and see if Gar will let you say goodbye."

"How the hell am I gonna convince him to let me see Cole? I didn't even think that far ahead; I just assumed the asshole would kill me right when he saw I wasn't with you."

"You could always pretend you broke away from the rest of us because we refused to help you, and perhaps feed Gar information about us in return for seeing Cole one last time." I unstrapped a bag and removed a vial I'd emptied and washed from the *bag 'o stuff*. "I'll fill this with my blood, and you'll hide it in your pocket. How convincing can you be when you lie?"

"Hmm," Vince said. "I see where yer goin' with this, and I have to admit, it's brilliant. Sorry I doubted ya."

"It's okay. I mean, it is kind of a long shot, but I think it'll work."

He pulled me into an unexpected hug. "Yer a really smart guy," Vince said before pulling away. The brown vargyr stared at me silently, as if expecting me to say something in return. "Well?"

"Well, what?"

"Was all that bullshit convincing enough?"

It was then that Vince, of all people, made me feel like a complete idiot.

"I think this bears repeating. You're an asshole."

The smaller vargyr took a bow before tugging at my arm. "You know I'm just kiddin'. So what is this information I'm supposed to trade with him?"

"Maybe you can tell him we're still heading north."

"Ah, that's good. I'll tell him what he already fuckin' knows."

"And it wouldn't work anyway," Derrick said. "He's seen every memory and heard every conversation Vince had the moment that trap was activated. There's actually nothing Vince could tell him that Gar wouldn't already know."

"Could he be listening to us through Vince? Why are you only just bringing this up now?" I asked, lowering my voice.

"The spell doesn't work that way. I mean, it could, but he'd have to tie his fate with Cole and Vince's, and he's not stupid or desperate enough to do something like that." He pulled at the fur on his chin while staring at Vince. "This gives me an idea, though. Vince, when you have your episodes, do you experience anything else?"

"Besides wishin' I was dead? No."

"Do you see or hear anything unusual?"

Vince paused, letting one ear fall to the side as he thought about the question. "Well, sometimes I see red. Other times I see a light shinin' down, but everything around me's too dark."

"Oh, this is too good," Derrick said through his teeth as he grinned.

"That ain't how I would describe it. Bastard," Vince muttered.

"No, this is good because his spell was unusually reckless. If he'd have known I was with you before you stepped into that trap, he'd have been more thorough."

"So that's why he looked worried when he saw you," I said excitedly. "Damn, I am so glad you're here."

"This has been the most fun I've had in years, aside from the possible excruciating death."

"There it is," I muttered. "So, how did he mess this up?"

"I know the spell he used, and there are different variations of it. It may be incomplete, which could mean one of two things: Gar is actually limited in what he can do, or he's not that good at magic. Considering he's a high-ranking demon, it's likely the former."

I turned to Axel. "I told you. I had a feeling he wasn't all that powerful."

Derrick held up his hands in protest. "Now, don't get me wrong, even weak magic can wreak havoc on all of us. But this means there are more chinks in his armor we can exploit. The curse Gar probably wanted to use was Uru-ti'ja, a combination of Uru, meaning pain, and ti'ja meaning to join the soul. The first part is important because it limits what the victim experiences through the other person. You can combine ti'ja with any number of experiences; however, if you don't specify a third limiter in the incantation, then the person will have a limitless soul connection. Vince isn't just experiencing Cole's pain. He's experiencing everything—every one of Cole's senses."

"I don't understand none of this shit. So, this is a good thing because...?" Vince asked, his glare narrowing. "Can you talk simple?"

Derrick nodded. "Tonight, we're going to try something to see if you can control the experience when you fall into another fit. You may be able to overhear or see something that will give his location away. If not, we've got a few more days to try something else." The mage looked at me and tilted his head. "You don't seem as excited as you were earlier."

"I'm just worried that we might be underestimating him a little too much. You said earlier he put that curse in the trap before he knew you were with us. Don't you think he's going to be extra careful now that he knows? He could cover Cole's head and ears."

Derrick nodded. "That is true, but you also may be overestimating him too. Desperation makes him unusually careless, and for now, it is worth trying. He may be careless again."

"And if he ain't?" Axel asked.

"Then we move on to the next plan."

"So how am I gonna control this?" Vince asked.

"Meditation."

"God damn it, Derrick," I snapped. The older vargyr crossed his arms and smirked. "We have four days, not a whole year. If it didn't work for me, what makes you think it'll work for him?"

"Well, for one, you're a terrible and impatient student. You also think too much." He draped his arm over Vince's shoulders. "Vince, on the other hand, would have no problem clearing his mind of all thoughts."

"Ha," the smaller vargyr scoffed, tossing me a smug stare. "Looks like I'm the better student."

"You realize he just implied you're stupid, right?"

Axel snorted.

Vince paused for a moment before his ears pressed against his head, and he pushed Derrick away.

"All of you can kiss my ass."

❧⦿⦿☙

"Alright, Vince. Tenth time's the charm," Derrick said, his tone exhausted as he sat behind the smaller vargyr, rubbing his shoulders.

"Guess my head ain't so empty after all, huh?"

"Ignore what Leo said, it is only distracting you. That's not at all what I meant. You are a brilliant young vargyr." Derrick looked up at me and winked. "You have more clarity and mental fortitude. Those are quite admirable." He scooted closer until his chest was flush against Vince's back. Derrick rubbed harder as the small brown vargyr closed his eyes.

"Alright. Let's try again. This time, focus only on my touch. Don't think about anything else except where I'm rubbing you. Think about how hard or soft each stroke is."

"If he starts stroking lower, we should give them some privacy," I whispered to Axel, prompting him to break into snorted laughter.

Derrick and Vince angrily snapped their heads over at us, and I cleared my throat before looking away.

"That feels pretty good," Vince said, closing his eyes again.

"Shh, don't talk. Just concentrate."

Axel yawned, having nodded off on my shoulder a few times earlier. It had already been three hours, and each session got us no closer to learning anything.

Another ten minutes passed, and Vince began to jerk slightly, grabbing our attention as we studied the vargyr before he went still again. Axel sighed and lay back on the grass while I continued to pick the briar thorns and twigs out of my tail that had been tangled in there since we left the forest. I could have done something more useful during this time, like come up with a Plan B in case Gar had anticipated what we'd try.

What was Gar's limitation? How could he use magic in a world where magic didn't work? Well—that wasn't completely true. Magic did work, but only when contained in things. The town supposedly ran on it; that was how the lights and other devices functioned. But where did that magic come from? Did every device have batteries in them, or was there something else?

Vince groaned and jerked again, and this time, his body went stiff. Derrick removed his hands and waited, wetting his lips in anticipation.

"This might be it," he whispered.

"What are you doing?" Vince mumbled in a monotone, his muscles loosening as he appeared to look around, his eyes still closed.

He said nothing for a few more minutes, but that changed when he let out a sharp yelp.

"They're going to find you, Gar...we'll die together. They will never let you have Leo."

Vince wailed again, and Derrick prepared to lay him on the ground so he wouldn't hurt himself; however, something about this episode was different. It was as though Cole had entered Vince's body.

"Don't hurt him anymore. Let me die."

Derrick caressed Vince's head in his lap as he continued mumbling incoherently, his body heaving upward with every jolt of pain. After several minutes of this, he went limp again.

"Is that you, Vince? I miss you," the small vargyr whispered in Cole's dialect.

"Cole?" Derrick said, prompting Vince to jerk in surprise. "Can you hear me?"

"Derrick? You're very quiet."

"Tell me where you are. What can you see?"

Another moment of silence.

"Nothing. He doesn't let me see anything anymore."

"Shit," I hissed. "Of course he's a step ahead of us."

"It was worth a try," Derrick said, gently stroking small circles behind Vince's ears. "We'll wait for Vince to come back to his senses and figure something else out."

Axel and I leaned against one another. It felt like every bit of energy I had drained away as the hours we wasted yielded nothing useful. There were only so many things we could try before time would eventually run out.

"He's gone for now, but it's hard to hear. There's a glowing forest, look east." I immediately looked up from the ground when Cole said it. "There's a hill."

Vince went limp again, and Derrick maneuvered out from under him before supporting the smaller vargyr's head with the folded blanket.

"That last part was strange," Derrick said. "It might be useful."

"Oh my God. I know where he is," I said, beaming from ear-to-ear.

"What?" Axel said, sitting upright.

"Cole must have been lucid enough to see where he was being taken. This means Gar probably couldn't use his portals to transport him. I walked through a glowing forest to get to Derrick's house that day I escaped. I headed west, but he mentioned looking east to a hill, probably back to the location I'd fallen out of a portal."

Derrick's eyes widened. "Do you remember exactly how to get back there?"

"Not really. I was going in and out of it while trying to follow chimney smoke, but I'm sure if I retraced my steps from your cabin, we'd find the forest. There were certain landmarks I remember clearly, and maybe once we get there, I'll remember more."

"The weather's been clear fer a while," Axel said, jumping to his feet before dusting the grass from his fur. "If them vargyrs we smelled yesterday were the ones that took Cole, we only have to pick up their scent. It won't even take much to know we're on the right trail, so we ain't exactly going in blind."

Derrick nodded, pointing his head to the sky. "I know I like to keep up the confident façade, but this is the first time I've truly felt like we have a chance. There's still more we need to figure out, but it is quite a leap forward for once." He looked down at Vince. "He reminds me a lot of Xavier. They both had the same accent, and he was a bit of a grouch when he wasn't drunk." He gave the vargyr a light pat on the stomach and shook his head. "I don't want him to go through what I did. Cole is the other half of him. He's warm, loving, loyal, and he makes Vince better."

I pushed myself from the cold ground and stretched my legs. "When this is over, and if somehow we all make it, you should find someone again."

Derrick laughed. "Perhaps if the desire to mate comes back with the right person, I'll consider it. There aren't exactly a lot of mates to choose from back in town."

"There's thousands of ferals out there in them woods. It might take a while, but we could cure 'em all. That'd be up to Leo, though. It's his blood, and we'd need a lot of it," Axel said.

"I like that plan," I replied. "With that many vargyrs, we could build the town even better. No one would have to drink themselves half to death because of the curse. Also, if you think about it, without the curse or Gar, Stellous has no leverage. We won't need to trade with them at all, and once they find out they may need us more than we need them, we hold all the cards. They won't be able to use the vargyrs for cheap labor anymore, and I doubt they'd seal away the portals and all of the valuable resources here. And if they do, who cares? If life on the run so far has taught me anything, we've got everything we need."

Derrick put up his hands. "Okay, let's not get ahead of ourselves. Ridding this world of the demon comes first, then you can tackle the impossibly huge task of reordering society while dealing with the winding labyrinth of Stellous politics at a later time."

"Too ambitious?" I asked. "It's something I've been thinking a lot about."

"It is quite ambitious, and if it's something you decide to pursue, you need to understand a few things. Dealing with Stellous is dangerous when you start making the wrong demands. Not only that, there are ferals out there who are hundreds of years old, and when they come back to their senses, they'll realize everyone they've ever known back on Eqiros has long since died. Many had families, children, and parents. Then you'll have to convince most of the population to follow you, and vargyrs naturally gravitate toward not only the strongest, but the most confident and charismatic. This will not be the cheerful utopia you think."

I slumped forward under the weight of Derrick's words. "I guess you're right."

"That wasn't meant to discourage you. We'll have to start somewhere, and we'll have to start small, but with time and smart decisions, this could fall into place. The more time everyone has to embrace what they are without fear, the better our society will be for it."

Axel stepped in between us. "Don't mean to change the subject or nothin', but I've been thinking."

"What's on your mind?" Derrick asked.

"Been goin' over how them wards work. You said that if Leo gets near 'em, he'll end up like that magic metal you was talkin' about."

"Deritium, yes. What about it?"

"Why's Leo the only one that can break the wards?"

"Because the curse has fused his non-magic body with magic from X'eeva, making him of two realms. According to Josiah's research, that makes him a powerful conduit that will destroy the wards."

"But ain't Gar from two different realms? You guys said that he's trapped as a vargyr, so ain't he cursed, too?"

"The vargyr curse was created in X'eeva, so even though he's allowed himself to take the vargyr form, he's still of one realm."

"So they got vargyrs in the demon realm?"

"They—" Derrick paused, speechless for the first time. "Xavier never mentioned anyone taking on this form in X'eeva. That would have been a rather important revelation."

"I remember something Gar let slip back when he gave me that potion," I interjected. "He said something about 'the part of the curse that affects the mind.' My blood obviously destroys that part of the curse. What if being a vargyr isn't a demonic curse?"

"You're right. It may not be a curse at all," Derrick said. "It may be a mutagenic disease that was infused with Gar's curse." He started breathing heavier. "This disease isn't of our realm...but it may still be of X'eeva." His look of revelation soon deflated.

"Suppose it ain't. Couldn't the same thing that would happen to Leo happen to Gar if he got close to the wards?" Axel asked.

"No. If the vargyr curse just infuses us with the affliction of the mind and a disease that turns us into another species from a different realm, then that would make everyone here of two worlds, and Gar wouldn't need Leo. Josiah's research clearly states that magic and non-magic elements need to be fused. Gar is from a magic realm. Also, if Gar's body could destroy the wards, that would have happened upon him entering Varcross."

"Derrick," I said, remembering something from the night we were at his cabin. "Did you bring that book with you?"

"Of course. I haven't finished memorizing it yet," he replied, reaching into his bag to pull out the old tome.

"You memorize these things?" Axel asked.

Derrick tapped the side of his head. "Eidetic memory, though what Gar did to me destroyed a lot of what I had memorized over the years. With all the illegal copies of books being made, I never told anyone while I was at the grand library."

"Can you go to the place that was ripped out?"

Derrick flipped to the back of the book, and before the redaction at the bottom and torn pages, there were familiar diagrams I remembered in chemistry.

"Do you think there could be anything else?" I asked. "You said you hadn't read it all, so maybe there's something you missed."

"I have read it all," Derrick corrected. "I just haven't committed it all to memory yet. We've already been over the only feasible way to break the wards."

"Only feasible way? There are others?" I asked.

"There's one other way, yes, but it is impossible."

I frowned, and looked down at the symbols and diagrams.

"This looks familiar," I said, pointing to the drawing of an atom.

"If you're interested, I suppose we have some time before Vince wakes up to delve into the fascinating world of Josiah's research."

"Do you have a short and sweet version of the other experiment?"

"Well, let's see. One could *theoretically* cause a catastrophic failure if something immensely powerful was sent through with a large amount of a non-magic stable material. That material doesn't exist here, and even if it did, we would either need a small amount of the rare stable isotope or we'd have to get at least a ton of the stuff through the wards at a high rate of speed with a very angry demon using a lot of magic at the same time. We would have better luck waiting for planetary alignment."

"Christ. I wonder why Josiah went through the trouble of writing that out."

"He is a scientist, and no matter how pointless a theory or experiment, the data can come in handy for something else. Some of our greatest inventions happened by accident."

I stared at the atomic structure for a little while longer. "What element is this?"

"This is an illustration of the most structurally and atomically stable element in your realm, iron fifty-six." My eyes went wide. "But with enough regular iron, we wouldn't need the isotope to have the same effect on the wards." He looked up at me. "You know something."

"You said we needed at least a ton of Iron. My car is made of steel, which is mostly iron, and it weighs more than we need."

The black vargyr tilted his head.

"It's a three-ton iron vehicle with wheels that can travel fast enough to get through the wards with Gar."

He stood still for a moment, and with a rush of exhilaration, the mage threw his arms around me.

"You're brilliant!" He pulled Axel in as well. "You're both brilliant. This is one hell of a speculation, but if the research is right, it can work."

Axel looked at me with a proud grin on his face. If it weren't for his questions, we'd have never gotten to this point.

"Josiah is a lot more cunning than I thought," Derrick added. "He may not truly be on Gar's side."

"Why do you think that? He's been workin' with him the entire time," Axel said.

The mage stroked his chin beard. "Of all the ways he could have gotten Leo through the wards, he allowed him to take a vehicle of iron alloy. He must know his research is no longer in Gar's possession, so he left it all to chance, giving the tools to anyone who could use them. Whether Leo dies or we succeed with this plan, the contract will be broken and Josiah's soul will be free. That doesn't mean the guilt won't weigh heavy on it. Josiah wants Leo to live."

"That's quite an assumption," I said.

"I know him well enough through his writing to make that assumption. His personal truth is hidden in symbolism that a heartless, immortal being like Gar would never understand. If we survive, I don't think Josiah truly deserves our ire, but that will be entirely up to you, Leo, since he risked your life for his."

To be honest, I hadn't thought much of Josiah lately, but could I really blame him? Perhaps one day if we were to finally meet face-to-face, I'd know more.

"Alright, so we've got a few days to take this information and come up with something. Should be easy, right? All we've got to do is lure a powerful demon to his destruction using my car...somehow. We also have to save Cole in the process," I said. "Oh, and Gar's probably got a bunch of vargyrs still on the lookout around the woods."

"Then we'll figure it out," Axel said with a starry-eyed smile, "'cause we're brilliant."

Desperation

Vince's deteriorating condition was the only constant on our journey, and it took over two days to make it to the forest's edge. It snowed at higher elevation and turned to rain as we got lower, but at least it finally stopped. Axel and I scouted ahead, watching as patrols meandered in pairs along the grasses closest to the trees. The other two stayed back in case Vince had another screaming episode. We were also running low on lotion, but at least the wind was on our side as it howled from the south, keeping us upwind from suspicious noses.

"What do you think?" I asked, lying low on the ground.

"They don't look right," he whispered, keeping his eyes forward. "There's a lot of 'em close."

"What do you mean they don't look right?"

He pointed to an auburn vargyr with a black mane. "That's Dreyfus. He was one of my drinkin' buddies, and he's one of the most lazy, laid-back guys you'd ever meet. He wouldn't be out here just walkin' around all stiff like that. Look at their eyes. None of 'em ain't said a word to each other the whole time we've been here."

"I wonder what Gar did to them." I eyed one of the vargyrs pointing his snout upward, sniffing feverishly before meandering again.

"I dunno, but we ain't gonna be able to get past them with Vince like he is."

"We expected this. We just have to find a way to get through this part of the woods to Derrick's cabin. Let's go back and tell the others."

Axel nodded, and we both stood away from the damp ground, still keeping low as we slipped back to camp.

⁂

"Sounds like we will need to wait for nightfall. We'll easily spot an ambush among the trees," Derrick said, chewing on one of the hare-like rodents Vince caught earlier. They were the only prey around here, and Vince was the only one fast enough to hunt them.

"Doesn't that go both ways?" I asked, a little frustrated by such a flawed suggestion, especially from Derrick. "What stops them from spotting us?"

"They ain't gonna be in hunting mode." Axel crunched on a small leg bone. "But we will, and we'll see 'em first."

"How do you turn it on without prey?"

"I'll teach you that later, so don't worry about it right now. Derrick and I got a lot of experience, so just follow us."

I glanced at Vince, who went about his meal, seemingly ignoring the conversation. "What if Vince starts screaming while we're trying to sneak by?"

"Then we won't have much choice but to pick him up and make a run for it," Derrick said, his eyes glowing a soft green as he scanned the plains. "We will likely need to add more time to our trip and head west to the coast before crossing into the forest. If the patrols reach the beach, we could at least swim far enough out that they wouldn't see us."

"If the wind shifts at all, we're fucked anyhow," Vince muttered, spitting a tiny, dismembered foot onto the ground.

"I wouldn't worry about that right now. The weather is warmer, and there's a system moving in from the southeast."

"So, westward it is," Axel said. "We should get some shuteye before tonight."

"That's a good idea." Derrick grabbed a bag with one blanket in it, and Vince grabbed the other. "We're hidden here, and as long as the wind holds, we'll be fine."

After Vince and Derrick set up the bedding, they rolled into it, Vince taking his spot in the middle now with Derrick on the other side. I lay next to Vince, and Axel took his place at the end.

"It's funny how the tables have turned," Vince muttered, now lying on his back as he tossed a quick glance around. "Guess I'm the new Leo."

I turned and glared at him.

"Oh, don't look at me like that. You know damn well what I'm talking about," he continued. "I'm already the smallest, and I was dumb enough to get my foot caught in that trap. Now I'm just a liability."

"There's nothing wrong with being small, Vince," Derrick said. "Your size makes you fast, and because of that, we were able to eat today."

"You don't gotta try to make me feel better. Always been small, even when I was human, and I didn't mind it much then. As a vargyr, it don't feel right." Vince kept his stare upward as the sun broke through a small gap in the clouds, his brown fur turning gold for a moment before the tumultuous sky swallowed the light. "If we get out of all this, I guess I'll be the one under Cole. Ain't like I took the lead in our relationship, anyway."

"Lead ain't the right word. One person can't shoulder all the responsibility, Vince," Axel said, nudging my arm. "Learned that the hard way."

I looked around at the three of them. "Is this how everyone thinks it's supposed to be?"

Derrick shrugged. "My relationship didn't last long enough for me to fully transform, so I can only go off of wilkyr mating behavior."

"You make it sound like we're animals," I said, my tone growing more frustrated.

"Habit, I suppose. There is no denying our instinct, no matter how intelligent we may be."

"I don't have this instinct," I said.

"You've been a vargyr's mate fer three seconds, and yer already an expert on how we're supposed to behave," Vince muttered under his breath.

"I'm not saying I'm an expert at anything," I whispered, quickly changing the subject. "I guess the point I was originally trying to make was just because you're smaller than Cole doesn't mean anything. You're just as capable as anyone else, and you're very handsome."

"This ugly dog-mug of mine ain't handsome."

"I didn't think much of it when I was human, but now that I'm like this, what Cole said makes sense," I said. "You just might be the perfect size for a vargyr."

Vince scoffed at that.

"Yer damn good-lookin'," Axel joined in. "There ain't no changin' being a vargyr, and now that Cole's done had his full turn, you gonna call him ugly, too?"

"That ain't what I mean."

"Then what do you mean?" I asked.

Vince stayed quiet for a few moments.

"I don't know, okay?" he said, calmer this time. "I used to be quite the looker when I was human, even though I was short. Even modeled underwear. Could have my share of men and women, and I did too. That all changed when I turned wilkyr, and I went from bein' everyone's beau to a half-monster everyone thought was gross—except for one."

He paused, staring intensely at the darkening clouds racing through the sky.

"When I first met Cole, I didn't know what to make of the kid. I was hidin' out in some old stables on his parents' estate while runnin' from the mages. He saw me sleepin' on the ground, and I woke up to a warm blanket and food on a plate next to me. I hadn't eaten anything in days.

"I was stuffing my face, and he stared at me through the gaps in the wood. He thought I didn't know he was there, but I was smelling him as I ate, wonderin' what he was thinking. He wasn't running away like everyone else did, so I growled at him and told him I knew he was there. I asked him what he wanted, and he stepped around the corner and looked at me. The way he held himself, the way he weren't afraid—I remember feeling like I could cry, but I didn't show that pussy side of myself. I never believed in bullshit like love at first sight until I saw him."

Vince smiled, his eyes watering. "He told me he ain't never seen a wilkyr before, and that he thought I looked handsome. Was actually kinda shocked by how forward he was with it, even though his face was as red as mata bisque. Still remember it like it happened just the other day. We got to talkin', and minutes turned to hours until it was dark again. He promised he'd give me food and company. On the weekends, we'd go out and cause all kinds of trouble. I was a bad influence on him.

"Then one night, we got a little too drunk, and I didn't have to say nothin'. We looked at each other, and I could smell he was ready. We fucked all night in them stables and into the day. Even the sex was good between us, and that was the first time it ever came with me falling in love. He loved everything about me, even what I was." He frowned and shook his head. "I can't lose him," he whispered, tears trailing his face as he closed his eyes. "He's my world, and he's been my world fer years, even through the fights. It's only been over a week without him, and it feels like years. I cover it up well, but I can't sleep through the night knowin' he's suffering."

Derrick placed his hand over Vince's chest, patting him.

"He's very lucky he found you, even though you may not think so with how things turned out." Vince bared his teeth, and Derrick grabbed his snout. "Don't look at me like that. You are so negative all the time, but for once, you told us something wonderful about your life." He licked Vince's nose before letting go. "I would bet my life Cole remembers that day just as vividly as you do, and when we rescue him, you will both have even better stories to tell. Vargyr lifespans are vast, so you're both going to make a lot more memories."

Vince's ears drooped.

"If only I knew then what I know now, I'd have never got him into this mess. I wouldn't have risked saying goodbye that night, and I'd let him forget about me. He coulda been happy. He'd have made one hell of a mage, I'm sure."

Derrick hummed contemplatively. "I don't think he would have been as happy as you think. Very few students become mages, Vince.

And those who do live lives of confinement and regret. I became a mage as a child, and I never had time for anything else. The pursuit of arcane knowledge was addictive, like any other drug. Once you start using magic, if you're not careful, you become a slave to it. Not only that, but you become the property of the state. The athenaeum becomes a home *and* a prison—like Varcross.

"When I was thrown into this place, my connection with magic was severed, and the hold it had over me vanished. My eyes opened for the first time, and what I once thought was bliss wasn't even close. The last time I had given any notice to myself, I was a child, and I still thought I was a child. So many years passed me by, and I went from being young and innocent to an adult in my early twenties in the blink of an eye.

"I can't even begin to put into words how terrifying it was to be thrust into adulthood with the mindset of one much younger. All magic comes at a price, remember that. Chronomancy takes your lifeforce; Lo'rim takes your sanity, and all other arcane practices keep you captive to them."

"At least he'd be alive," Vince said, his tone softer. "You said magic made you feel bliss. Maybe that's what he'd be feelin' now instead of pain."

"If Cole had continued down this path and succeeded, perhaps that would have been his life. He would never know love or life outside of magic." Derrick frowned. "But that's not much of a life. And that's only if Cole succeeded. He would have had to undergo harsh exams and sleepless nights for the first two years. If he made it that far, he would have to survive a gauntlet of seven trials. One mistake or forgotten incantation, and that would mean permanent disability or worse. He would be nothing at that point, worthless, expendable. You gave him more warmth and happiness in one night than he would have gotten in a lifetime as a mage."

Derrick kept rubbing the thicker mane on Vince's chest in a gentle back and forth motion.

"As much as I resented being a wilkyr, I met someone I fell in love with for the first time. Though I would end up losing him, I'll never forget the memories we created in that short time we were together. And now look at me. After decades of solitude as both human and beast, I have a family." He turned all the way over to stare at the smaller vargyr by his side. "I really like you, Vince. One day, perhaps I'll find a mate again, and I hope to find one that reminds me of you and Xavier. Every day I hear you put yourself down, but you don't see what we see. How could you? You've made it impossible to see the good in yourself.

"You merely pretend to be a stone, but no one close to you buys that act. You're sweet and empathetic to the extreme. You're someone who can melt glaciers with a grin. If you got your way and went back in time, you would have deprived Cole of everything that makes you wonderful—the person he fell in love with. This isn't going to last, and you'll look back on this moment twenty years from now and regret nothing."

"Why you gotta say them things?" Vince choked out, his tail wagging under the covers. "Y'all are too damn sappy." He sniffed and wiped his nose with the back of his arm. "I'm glad yer here, Derrick, and I'm glad I got you guys."

Vince buried his face in Derrick's chest mane, and I turned and wrapped one arm around the smaller vargyr. Axel spooned me from behind, his arm draping over me while rubbing Vince's head. The feeling that washed over me was nearly impossible to describe because I'd never experienced it as a human. The closeness we shared with one another made me want to fall asleep like that and never move again.

Forked lightning and thunder cracked the sky, the black, turbulent water pulling me under, tearing me from Axel's grip. My strength was useless against the violence that pulled me further out to sea, and when I'd finally get my head above water, another wave would drag me under. The brine burned my eyes as I frantically looked around for the others.

Choking on what little air I could fill my lungs with, I grabbed Axel, who was having a harder time than I was keeping to the surface. Before the furious ocean sucked us out again, I grasped his arm and pulled, kicking against the force of the current with every ounce of strength. He latched onto me and forced us up, allowing me a bit more buoyancy, but we were still no match for the towering crests.

Where were Vince and Derrick? So many terrible scenarios raced through my mind, and as I started to go under again, time slowed and survival instinct kicked in. It was time to put this body to the test.

Pulling myself and Axel above the water, I examined the waves in my precious seconds of supernatural clarity. As Axel struggled to paddle against the monstrous rip current, I pulled him back, leading him parallel to the shore. Another wave hit us from the side, pushing us closer to land, and we continued swimming before another crest brutally tossed us against the rocks.

Bruised and exhausted, I rolled to my stomach, coughing up the last of the water I'd aspirated, all the while trying not to breathe in the deluge of rain blowing sideways against my face. I rested my hand on Axel's back as he coughed and threw up.

"You okay?" I asked, scrambling all the way to my feet. He nodded and threw up again, and I scanned the rough ocean for any signs of Vince and Derrick in between lightning flashes. They were in the distance, and it seemed Derrick also understood how to handle the current, dragging Vince next to him while trying to keep both of their heads above water.

The waves carried them into the shallows, and they staggered to shore before falling to their knees. Axel and I ran over to see if they were okay as the rain started to let up.

"The seas—" Derrick choked out, retching as water poured from his mouth. "Are rather rough tonight. At least the storm is dying."

"Whose idiotic idea was this again?" Vince yelled, joining in the coughing fits.

"We had no choice," I said, helping Vince off the ground. "They were everywhere, so it was either this or get caught and outnumbered." I looked out over the ocean again. "It didn't look that bad twenty minutes ago."

"I didn't expect there to be so many patrolling this area. It makes me wonder if Gar knows our plan somehow, or if this was just a precaution to cover his flank. Either way, we need to go into this expecting the demon to be at least two steps ahead of us," Derrick said, shaking the seawater from his outer coat.

The rain lightened to a misty sprinkle, the thunder a little further away than before.

"That came out of nowhere," I said.

"I've lived near the coast long enough to see this happen. The seas are tepid and the air is often freezing during autumn and winter. This causes very severe and unpredictable weather," Derrick said.

Axel pulled a string of seaweed off of his arm, drawing in a deep breath before pulling me into a hug. "I woulda drowned out there without you pullin' me like you did."

"I'm just glad we're all okay," I said, wrapping my arms all the way around him. "Now that I think about it, we should have just used more lotion instead of risking our lives like this."

"They were close enough to see us if we continued. There aren't any trees along the shore to hide behind either," Derrick said, pointing to my backpack. "We'll still need to use it, though. The storm didn't allow us to get as far south as I would have wanted."

My legs shook as I followed the group, dragging my waterlogged body closer to the forest. The ocean seeped from my bag, dripping down my back. It was the only thing we could take with us, since everything else would have been too heavy to swim with. We'd left the rest of our belongings hidden in a craggy hollow further up north.

The ocean was calm when we waded out, and we had to get far enough away that we wouldn't be spotted or smelled. We had to take our chances with Vince, and we were very lucky he didn't seize up while in the water.

I unzipped my bag and pulled out the lotion, dabbing what I could in the right areas. Hopefully, it would hide our scents long enough to get far from this area before the patrols caught up to us. After the other three were done, I placed the almost empty container back into my bag before realizing my phone was still at the bottom.

"Oh crap," I said, shuffling through my soaked belongings before fishing it out. "Damn it. It's waterproof, but I don't know about salt water."

"All them pictures, eh?" Vince asked, shooting a look of concern at the device in my hands.

"It is what it is, I guess. The battery was going to die eventually, and there's no way to print anything out." I dropped the phone back into my bag. "It's the least of our worries."

"The cabin isn't too far from here if we're fast," Derrick said. "If Gar hasn't sent anyone to guard it, we'll rest and eat something, and you can try to retrace your steps, Leo. We've got one, maybe two more doses of the lotion, so we need to make this application count. This means that after we leave my cabin, we cannot rest until we are close."

"Alright," Axel said, stalking ahead of us, his hackles raised as he sniffed the air while keeping his body low. "I'll keep my eyes and nose out for anyone hiding in the trees."

Our trek came to an abrupt halt when Vince fell to the ground. He hadn't had an episode in a while, but Derrick could keep him somewhat quiet as he held the smaller vargyr in his arms. We had traveled for miles beyond Derrick's cabin, and I tried to spot anything that I may have been able to recognize. However, everything looked different. The only option we had was to continue going southeast until we either picked up on vargyr scents, or a landmark jarred my memory.

I walked with Axel, scouting the area around Vince and Derrick. We were never sure how long the fits would last. Sometimes they were a few minutes, other times they could last up to a half an hour. As we headed back to the others, Vince sat upright, calm and wiping his face.

"How are you feeling now?" I asked, kneeling next to him.

"Like shit, how do you think? I'll be good enough to walk in a little while." Vince bared his teeth, his ears hugging the sides of his head. "A quick death is too good. I wanna see Gar suffer."

"He knows," Derrick said, his eyes a little wider as I turned toward him.

"What?"

"He knows about your blood. I can't believe such a vital detail slipped my mind, but I've been wondering why so many vargyrs are after us, many not even showing signs of control. When he read

Vince's mind in the trap, he got our secrets, and he is placing his pieces on the board while waiting to see what our next move will be. He's even more dangerous now."

"Okay," I said, feeling slightly sick to my stomach. "It's not the end of the world."

"No, but the cure was our biggest card to play to get allies on our side. Gar has had time to poison the town against you. They know you can break the wards, and everyone wants to be free. He's likely told them all kinds of half-truths and lies, and if the town knew what you could do, what would they choose? A future where they would lose their minds to the curse, or a lifetime of peace knowing the curse has no control over them anymore? If they found out that you could be destroyed upon breaking the wards, we'd have the entire town against Gar. He knows he's not powerful enough to contain that kind of uprising."

"We can give them proof," I said, holding out my arm. "I'll go to town and demonstrate right there. They could spread the word."

Derrick shook his head. "He'll be expecting that. Gar is manipulative, and misinformation poisons desperate peoples' minds. Do you think they will believe you over his influence? We have to assume they mean to capture you by any means necessary. They will not be in the mood for a demonstration."

"But if they just drink the blood—"

Vince cut me off. "Ya can't feel it workin'. I'm cured, but it weren't no immediate effect. It might take a while before anyone realizes they ain't got the curse no more, and there's no ferals around here to give 'em a proper show."

"Do you still have that vial?" Derrick asked.

I nodded, reaching into my bag to pull it out.

"When we get closer to finding Cole, you'll need to fill it. In case we get separated, we need someone who could administer your blood. Having this in two places increases our odds, and now that Gar knows, I highly doubt he will give you an opportunity to get near Cole."

"We still ain't got a clue what we're gonna do when we get there. There're probably people at my house, so we can't get Leo's car. And even if we got it, how are we gonna shove that thing and Gar into the wards at the same time?" Axel asked, helping Vince off the ground.

Derrick's expression went blank as he shrugged. "We won't know until we find Cole. Gar still holds all the cards right now." He forced a light-hearted chuckle before slinging an arm around my neck. "We're going to need some of that supernaturally good luck of yours, Leo."

It's All Up Hill From Here

The weather went from cold to a death's touch in a matter of hours as we tracked scents along our route. My thick undercoat had thankfully dried earlier in front of Derrick's hearth, but the condensation beading around my nose turned to frozen shards of ice. Aside from the sting of subzero wind against my face, the rest of my body was well insulated.

"That's gotta be it," I said, pointing to a faint glow ahead.

We followed a rough trail to a smaller area of the glowing forest. It was much further east than I could recollect from my last trip through this place. As more recent vargyr scents marked the area, we decided it was best to go through the denser parts.

"Oooh," Axel said with excitement as he leapt onto one of the strong, table-sized polypores that spiraled up one of the taller trees. "Gonna see if I can get a better look of the area."

"Be careful," I shouted as he disappeared into the canopy.

"This place is fascinating," Derrick remarked as he reached for a knob-shaped blue mushroom, plucking it from a tangle of tree roots. "There's an entire ecosystem here that's different from anything else we've seen yet." He pointed to a shadowy, leopard-like creature watching us from a branch, its beady irises glowing a pale white. Though it kind of resembled a feline, its ears were short and rounded, and its tail was much longer and flexible, like a monkey's. "I wonder what sort of creature that is."

Axel landed on his feet in front of us. "Don't see no one," he said, baring his teeth at the curious creature watching us. It let out an annoyed hiss before climbing further away. "I bet we can eat those."

"Good luck catching it," Vince said, stumbling over the webbed system of roots that covered the forest floor. "Cause I ain't climbing no trees. It's hard enough walkin' around on this mess."

"If we succeed, I'll have to remember how to get back to this area. There're no telling what kinds of alchemical properties the flora here have," Derrick said, slicing into the mushroom with a claw, examining the bioluminescent ooze that seeped out before sniffing it.

"Everything looks weirder than usual, and that's saying something considering everything we've seen," I said, swatting a purple firefly away from my nose.

"I doubt this forest is a natural part of the world, seeing as how the fungi and plants seem to exhibit magical properties. There's been a Lo'rim-using demon living here for hundreds of years, experimenting with potions and reagents. This forest reminds me of Xavier's stories of X'eeva."

"You think Gar created this?" I asked.

"Without a doubt."

✦

We continued onward through the maze of trees for about an hour, and the root system along our path grew smoother as the woods became less dense. Beams of pale blue broke through the canopy, lighting the way forward, and the terrain took on a more familiar appearance. The bitter wind kicked up, and the temperature plummeted.

Derrick looked around and nodded. "That was a sudden transition," he said, turning back toward the woods. "Is any of this bringing back memories, Leo?"

"Kind of," I said, studying the area for any landmarks. "I was really shaken up when I escaped, so I didn't have a lot of time to take in the scenery."

"Understandable," Derrick replied as we continued through the smooth, frosty grasses. Axel left the group again to scout ahead, and Vince stayed mostly quiet, likely awaiting his next episode. Derrick placed his hand on my back. "How are you feeling?"

"Okay," I said, swallowing the pressure building in my throat. "A little worried."

"As are we all," he said with a smile that warmed even the coldest temperatures.

"You don't seem as concerned."

"I hide it well." The black vargyr breathed in deep through his nose, exhaling calmly through his mouth. "Atorien truly terrifies me; however, there is a part of me that wants to shut off every intelligent thought and allow the beast within to inflict as much damage as it can the moment I see him. At least then, I'll have given my life buying my friends some time, even if it ends up being an act of futility."

Vince pushed him forward.

"Don't even think about doin' that," Vince snapped. "I don't want any of you to die." He glared at me. "Even you."

Derrick draped his arm gently over Vince's shoulders. "It was just a thought." He leaned in and kissed Vince on the head before looking up at me. "And I don't want to lose any of you either, but I would sacrifice myself if I was sure it would end in your success."

"And the world would be worse off," I said with a grimace. "Even though you're older than all of us, you've only just started living. When I think about it, even though we've been running for our lives, I guess I could say the same for me, maybe for all of us."

"It's kinda fun, in a fucked-up way," Vince said. "It's like a video game, but the stakes are real."

"When you left my cabin that night, Leo, I packed what belongings I could carry, and sat close to the door, not really knowing if you all would return," Derrick said, taking in another shaky breath, but keeping up a fragile smile. "I have been very lonely for so long, and just having someone to read with was enough to rekindle that spark of companionship—" he let out another laugh, "even if you were asleep through most of it."

"I was exhausted," I said. "When all this is over, I'd really like to learn more from you. Especially more about Stellous."

"Are you still thinking of politics?"

"Unfortunately, yes."

"You helped me to be better," Vince said. "If you can do that, them old fucks in the senate shouldn't be a problem."

"Those that aren't corrupted beyond saving, perhaps." Derrick scanned the surrounding area as Axel came into view, standing close to a steep incline and a pine with snapped branches.

"I recognize this," I said, sprinting toward the tree. "I crashed into it when I fell through a portal." I pointed toward the top of the hill. "Up there."

Derrick hummed and stroked his tied-up chin beard. "Then let's hope the portal still exists." He reached behind Vince and pulled out an empty vial from my backpack, which he was wearing. "Before we go any further, you need to fill this so we have fresh blood. Go deep enough, or we won't be able to collect enough before you heal."

He handed the vial to me, and I hesitated. I wasn't good at injuring myself; in fact, even as a vargyr, thinking about slicing open a vein made me squeamish.

"Are you sure? What if I go too deep and bleed out?"

The three of them laughed, and I felt rather stupid for even asking.

"Your body is resilient to most injuries. If we could die so easily, the curse wouldn't have had time to be so virulent. Fusing humans with the essence of whatever wolf-like humanoid species we've become was admittedly a brilliant idea for a curse."

"That's what Cole said. Do you think there's an entire world full of vargyrs if they don't exist on X'eeva?" I asked, uncorking the vial.

Derrick shrugged. "Perhaps not physically the same as us, since we still have some of our human characteristics—except you, for some reason. However, if Gar collected the essence from elsewhere would make the most logical sense to assume such a world exists— or existed at one point, and such a world would have its own version of deva'koh." He looked down at my arm and tapped it with his claw. "Do you want to do this, or should I?"

"Sorry," I muttered, pushing my arm closer to him. "You do it. I'm too chicken."

"Chicken?" he asked, turning my wrist upward. "I've never heard that expression."

"It's a bird...never mind." As Derrick studied my arm, I thought more about the curse's origin. "I wonder if we could ever go to that world of vargyrs. Maybe everyone wouldn't feel like a monster if being a monster was normal." Derrick's claw sliced deep into my arm, and a sharp whine slipped out of my mouth.

"Sorry, Leo, but the pain will subside quickly." He tilted my arm, letting the blood stream into the vial as he pressed it against my arm so the fur wouldn't soak it up. "I'm not sure I'd want to go to that world."

"Why not?"

"Well, what if the creatures weren't all that intelligent, like our ferals? What if they are inherently violent like the blood-crazed? Or suppose they are intelligent with their own civilization and society. That doesn't mean we'd have anything in common with them. They may even think we're a threat and systematically kill us off."

Blood slowed to a trickle before stopping completely, and the pain faded. Derrick corked the top of the vial before placing it into the backpack still strapped to Vince.

"I think this world is perfect for us. It is vast, pristine, and full of food. Since I doubt the mages would create a world with sentient carnivorous monsters, we're also at the top of the food chain, as far as I know," Derrick continued. "If the outcome of our encounter with Gar goes in our favor, hopefully Stellous closes the portals for good so we can be left alone."

"But what happens to our society? We're just going to stay in this world with no way to reproduce? It's going to be boring."

"I agree with Leo," Axel said, having been strangely quiet for the last couple of hours. The stress was starting to get to him the more time passed. "Gotta be able to have kids."

"Kids are gross. Never liked 'em," Vince muttered while sitting cross-legged on the ground. "What Derrick described sounds like paradise. Was never much of a people person. Give me small-town livin' any day."

"Imagine if there were female vargyrs, and they gave birth to little vargyrs instead of humans. Think about how cute they'd be," I said.

"That'd be stinkin' adorable," Axel chimed in. "I'd definitely love to adopt a little shit of my own." He gave me a strange look that made my chest hurt. Both of us looked away from one another as we let out nervous laughter. "Always wanted to be a dad to a kid who ain't got one."

"Let's not get too ahead of ourselves," I said. Being a father was the furthest thing from my mind, but Axel was ten years older than me. "I don't even know if it's possible to have fully turned vargyr children."

"Fucking gross," Vince muttered. "You both are just gross. I like the world better without women. Less complicated."

"Not me," I said. "I miss going out with the girls. Plus, not everyone in town likes being with a male. I don't think I could ever truly be satisfied if I had to be with a woman for the rest of my life." I eyed the hillside where the invisible portal was. "Do you think Gar knows we're here?"

"If he did, this place would be guarded," Derrick replied. "This may all be a trap." He looked up toward the hill and swallowed hard, but said nothing more.

"I like us better this way." Axel said, quickly changing the subject. He plopped on the ground next to Vince and nuzzled him while the smaller vargyr struggled to push him away. "Look at how soft and warm we are."

"Get the hell off me," Vince shouted, laughing while kicking and struggling as Axel pinned him to the ground, tickling his stomach and play-biting his shoulder.

As the two wrestled, I stepped over to the more somber vargyr.

"We don't have much of a plan," Derrick whispered. "We're going in hoping Cole is alone, which is wishful thinking at best. It's also pretty safe to assume Gar knows we're here."

"What do you think we should do?"

"You're not going to like it."

"We're splitting up, aren't we?"

Derrick nodded.

"You're right, I don't like it, but it might actually be the safest option. You and Vince can cure Cole while Axel and I try to get my car as close to the wards as we can without being noticed."

"He won't kill us." Derrick looked down at Axel and Vince who were still rolling on the ground, biting and growling at one another. "He'll use us as leverage, though—I may not be as lucky. He will want revenge for what I've done."

"Maybe Axel and Vince can rescue Cole, and you and I can plan—"

"That may seem logical, but it would be catastrophic. You and Axel are mates now, and the demon can use that to his advantage."

The smell of fear emanated from us both, silencing the two on the ground.

"Leo?" Axel asked, brushing the grass and dirt from his fur.

"Let's just be together for a little while longer," I said, sitting at the base of the hill. "I don't know how this is going to turn out."

Axel sat next to me, and the other two sat cross-legged on the ground in front of us, Derrick's pensive stare appearing somewhat distant. I had to bring him back, though now everyone knew I was trying to put up a braver front.

"When we kill Gar and cure everyone, maybe we could convince Stellous to close the portals," I said, changing the subject. These little hypotheticals always seemed to put Derrick in a better mood, but that statement seemed to worry him more.

"Suppose we cleanse everyone of the curse, and the mages catch wind of it. I wonder if they would force us off of this world and back into ours so they can continue using this place for the resources."

"Yeah, but everyone wants to leave anyway, so who cares?" Vince said.

"That's what everyone thinks they want, but no one here has ever lived under the oppressive thumb of Stellous as I have—well, few of us have. There is little chance they will let us keep our freedom, and they may well use us as weapons. With an army of mages and uncursed vargyrs, what would the rest of the world do against that? Stellous could finally force every country under its banner like it has been trying to do since its founding."

"Well, this just turned depressing," I said, shoving Derrick's arm. "I was trying to cheer you up."

"I'm being realistic," he corrected. "And I'm not depressed. It's only depressing if you're apathetic. Being realistic gives you an opportunity to expect and plan for the worst while fighting for the best chance. The scenario I just described is not only possible, it's likely the outcome with the highest probability."

"You know what else is entirely possible in your world?" I asked.

Derrick hummed softly and shrugged.

"Vargyr mages. Anyone can learn magic, right? Imagine an army of vargyr mages. No one would mess with us."

"That is a truly terrifying prospect, yes, and I mean no disrespect in saying this, but you are being naive. Stellous mages are descendants of ancient beings who created an entire planet using knowledge gained over thousands of years from hundreds of worlds. Putting down a few magic vargyrs wouldn't take much effort."

"If they're so powerful, why haven't they conquered the entire world yet, like you mentioned earlier?" Derrick lifted his finger in protest but allowed me to finish. "Not only haven't they been able to conquer your world with all of their magic, but isn't all of their power centralized in one city?"

"One incredibly fortified city," Derrick corrected.

"I'm just saying, imagine vargyrs with magic."

Derrick scoffed at the idea for a moment, but his eyes widened. "Wait..." He trailed off, jumping to his feet before pacing. "I hadn't ever considered the possibility. Our longevity and healing grants us nearly unlimited life force. We may even be immune to demonic influence after you've cured us of the curse. Do you know what this means?"

"I think so," I said, smiling at him. "If each form of magic comes with a cost, what happens when the cost is negated?"

Derrick looked up at the moon.

"No limits," he whispered. "We could go to any world we wished. Nothing would stop us." His features darkened, and his arm fell limp. "But limits exist in nature for a reason that we would be fools to circumvent."

"But what about the good we could do?" Axel asked. "If we was careful—"

"You're talking about disturbing the balance of an entire universe with good intentions," Derrick interrupted, his tone becoming more heated. "We could be the destruction of everything—all the while being blinded by meaningless morals. All power corrupts, and seemingly limitless power is certainly no exception."

Axel's ears fell. "But if we're the good guys, then what have we got to worry about?"

"Maybe *we* are, but does this hold true for all vargyrs? And what exactly does it mean to be good?" Derrick asked, glaring down at the floundering vargyr. "Does Gar believe he's evil, or does he believe his intentions are lawful according to his realm? Every individual has their own opinion of what good is, and while society dictates a broader definition, such an abstract concept varies from culture to culture. Magic is not sentient. It does not care about good and evil, because both do not exist in nature. Chaos and order do, and magic can be both. Being a mage means never fully trusting the arcane, especially when it is pushed beyond what we know is possible." He paused and recomposed himself. "We should put this out of our thoughts."

Vince jumped to his feet, his eyes glazed over as he yawned and turned to the hill.

"Alright, you guys ain't makin' me feel any better," he shouted, picking up the backpack before stomping up the slope. "We've got a place to find, so let's—" Vince vanished mid-sentence.

"Vince?" Derrick called out, running up the hill before stopping inches away from where the smaller vargyr had disappeared. He picked up a large stone and chucked it in front of him. There was no thud, as if it simply ceased to be. "It seems we found the hidden portal." He turned back to us. "Like we agreed earlier, Leo, you two stay out here. I'd even recommend leaving now since Vince may have triggered a trap."

"Be careful," I said, backing away.

"I am always careful." No sooner had Derrick spoken, Vince popped back into existence several feet above the ground before falling on top of him, sending them both tumbling down the hill.

They rolled into the same tree that broke my fall weeks ago at the bottom, Derrick landing on top of poor Vince.

"You guys okay?" Axel called out as we ran over to help.

"Can't breathe," Vince squeaked while trying to push the larger vargyr off of him. We lifted a wobbling Derrick from the ground before helping Vince.

"What did you see in there?" I asked.

"Not much," Vince replied, picking the leaves and twigs out of his fur. "It was a dark stone hall. Didn't go far though 'cause it freaked the hell out of me. I turned back around and walked out the door, but then a damn rock hit me in the head, and I fell."

"Sounds like the place," I said, pacing nervously. "Cole's gotta be in here."

Derrick's forefinger slipped under my chin and lifted my face to meet his. "Have faith in the pack." The older vargyr slightly bowed his head. "This has been quite the journey, and it has certainly been the friendliest and most exhilarating experience."

Axel scooped Vince up into a hug, both of them clinging tightly to one another.

"Go get Cole, and you guys come back to us. Remember to listen to yer gut." There was this undertone none of us could ignore, though we tried. There was no sugar-coating the fact that they may not come back out if it was a trap; in fact, I think we all understood that deep down. The goal was to cure Cole and deal with whatever happened after. Chances were good that Gar would use all three as bait to lure me back in instead of killing them outright.

"Yeah," Vince said, pulling away.

Axel rubbed the top of Vince's head, and the smaller vargyr let out an annoyed sniff before turning toward the invisible portal, Derrick following him.

"We'll be back before you know it," Derrick said as they vanished together.

Axel and I stood silently, staring at an empty, moonlit hillside.

"How long you reckon we should wait?"

I sat cross-legged on the slope. "We need to get away from here and try to get the car."

Both of our noses pointed toward the west as the wind blew in a strong vargyr scent. We ran for the other side of the hill toward some brush, staying low; however, Axel pulled me to a stop.

"Look." He pointed at multicolored glowing dots in the trees below.

"Maybe we can go over the hill to the south," I whispered, pulling Axel in the other direction. As we got to the top, more eyes peeked from the tree shadows surrounding the hill.

"Shoot," Axel said as we crouched behind the shrubs. It wasn't much, but it kept us out of sight. "They're gonna smell us, if they haven't already. Let's get to the portal."

"We can't. If we go in there, he'll have all of us where he wants us." I let out a sigh. "Derrick mentioned this could be a possibility. They were all waiting." I slapped the side of my head as I remembered something important. "Shit."

"What's wrong?"

"I forgot to tell Derrick about the crystals. There are magic crystals in the ceiling that I think Gar feeds off of. I broke one last time, and all the magic and barriers went away. If it worked then, it'll work again—if he hasn't put any fail safes in place."

"If yer right, we have to get in there to tell them."

"You should do it. I need to get the car or this all falls apart." We looked around the hill, but there were no openings. They knew we were here, and they seemed to be waiting for something. "I don't know where to go."

"Then we stay together," Axel said, grabbing my hand. "All of us workin' together got us this far. There might be something in there that'll give us a chance, but we ain't got a chance out here."

"Alright," I said, following Axel close. "I guess we don't have a choice."

We dashed toward the spot Vince and Derrick had disappeared, and at that moment, the vargyrs emerged from hiding, darting at blazing speeds up the incline.

"The hall is narrow. They won't all be able to fit inside," I yelled. "But I don't know if there's another way out."

"It'll buy us time," Axel shouted, holding my hand tight as we leaped toward the portal. However, as Axel disappeared, I landed on the ground with a hard thud, losing my balance as I slid downward toward the vargyrs running up.

In an instant, I flipped over on my hands, my massive paws kicking off against the ground, back toward the portal. As I ran through, nothing happened. I realized too late just how elaborate Gar's trap was. He wanted to isolate me from the others. To be honest, none of this should have surprised any of us, but making any sort of plan fell to the back of my mind as instinct took over. Adrenaline pumped through my veins, and I darted forward.

As I approached the peak, two vargyrs jumped at me from the sides, and my paws left the ground. Time slowed to a near standstill as I soared above the trees, righting myself like a cat as I prepared for the hard landing.

I could hear my body falling against snapping branches, but I couldn't feel much of anything as my mind focused only on escape. I grabbed a limb before swinging off of it, softening the landing as my paws deftly sunk into dirt before I fled in a random direction.

The ground under me heaved upward, and I lost my balance, falling forward while sliding to a now painful stop. A familiar light streamed along the ground before the tingle of it pinned my arms and legs.

"I know you're eager to break those wards, but let's not get ahead of ourselves." I whimpered at the sound of his voice, and the demon knelt next to me, placing his hand on my chest. "It's not the end, Leo. Death is merely a transition to something better, and it will be over in an instant. You won't even feel it." He leaned in while keeping his voice low. "I won't be underestimating you this time," he said, standing up to look around at the vargyrs who gathered closer. "In a week, we're all going to be free," he shouted as the vargyrs erupted in cheers and howls.

"He's lying!" I shouted, struggling in vain to break free from the magic holding me down. "I can—" The light wrapped over my mouth, freezing it in place as a glowing animation of Axel and I played in front of everyone.

"Leo wanted the curse all along," Gar said as the surrounding crowd clamored. "How many of you would kill to be human again? To add insult, he and Axel would prefer you all stay here. They wanted to end my life, and Leo wanted to take control."

More of Vince's stolen memories played out in front of the crowd. It was all brilliantly taken out of context, making me look even more like a villain, but no one seemed to question how he was using magic. Instead, they were furious, hissing and snarling, some throwing rocks at me. A larger stone hit my ribs, the pain briefly taking my breath away. The Lo'rim slipped from over my mouth, allowing me to gasp.

"What happens after—" I took another labored breath. "You think the mages are going to let you all go? He's sending you to die!"

"If we die, then we die free," Gar shouted.

More cheers exploded from around me, and the demon leaned in close.

"I know about your blood. It must feel terrible to know Cole is so close, but you can't save him. It's frustrating, isn't it? Don't worry. I'll see that all of them get the best treatment before tossing you to the wards."

"There's no point in killing them, too."

"No point? There's plenty of reasons to end their lives, but how I do it depends on you. It will take at least a week to prepare the ritual to pull the wards into the physical realm, and in that time, maybe you can convince me to show mercy."

His eyes flashed white, and a blunt, electric pain spread from the back of my head. My ears rang as the world dimmed to static.

"How did they escape?" Gar's livid voice echoed from down the hall as I struggled to open my eyes. There wasn't any light where I was, and the back of my skull throbbed.

"I'm sorry." The familiar voice was so monotone and lifeless, it was hard to match who it belonged to. "They slipped through unnoticed, and the barriers failed."

A smile graced my dry lips as a stunned silence fell upon the place. Axel remembered what I said about the crystals, and it seemed Gar either hadn't had time to fix the vulnerability, or he couldn't.

The situation was still perilous, but the cracks in his veneer were showing through.

Rapidly approaching footfalls echoed through the hall before the metallic door slammed open, blinding crystal light searing my sensitive eyes.

"Wake up!" An iron chain slammed against the bars of the cage I was in, causing me to jump. "I've changed my mind about mercy." The vargyr that had been talking to Gar earlier loomed in the doorway as a silhouette. Gar turned to him. "I want everyone on alert. Gather the turned wilkyrs and track them down. Don't let anyone in town see or talk to Cole."

The figure bowed before turning to leave. "Yes, master."

"All dogs need masters," Gar whispered before pulling a stool up to the cage.

"More mind control?"

Gar didn't respond at first; instead, a smile slithered up his once emotionless face. "I always plan my moves far in advance, but that day you escaped threw everything into chaos."

"Good," I whispered, my eyes wide as I watched his erratic movements.

The demon leaned closer, baring his many, sharper teeth. "You don't need to pretend to be brave. If I had the time to study you, maybe I could find a way to unlock the wards without it leading to your destruction."

"You have the time," I said. "There could be a solution that benefits all of us, not just you."

"I've drained too much of the source to track you down, and time is no longer on my side." He stared at his hands and balled them into fists. "Something about you makes you immune to curses—maybe even more. No other human from your world lived long enough to do this. That was a careless oversight. The moment those wards go down, the whole damned city will fall to the vargyrs, and I'll be rid of this blasted contract."

"Those vargyrs are still people. They're not going to start a war."

The demon crossed his arms. "You seem pretty sure of that."

"I know enough about your curse."

"You know laughably little, but I will applaud Derrick for giving you a fighting chance."

My hands gripped the bars of the cage. "Why not just punish the mages? Why do you need to destroy an entire city?"

"City?" he sneered. "My contract is still active, and the deva'koh that forged it has long since died. The entire realm must be purged if I am to be allowed to ever return to X'eeva. Once the whole of humanity dies off, the contract will be void and my bonds broken."

I began to understand why the deva'kohs were executed. One person's greed could doom an entire world. How terrifying.

I needed to choose my words carefully now. "You and I are both the victims, so why not adapt and wait them out? Humanity won't last forever, but you're immortal. Waiting several thousand years is what? A few days to you?"

"Your appeal to my emotions is pointless. There is a vast difference between us that you will never understand. Do you take care not to step on insects when you walk, or are they so insignificant that you don't even notice the thousands of lives you extinguish simply by going from one place to another? You are like that to us."

"Vargyrs are more than that."

Gar raised an eyebrow.

"Have you ever considered what we're capable of, especially with magic? Derrick mentioned limitless power, and you'd throw all that away just because you're impatient? That's rather shortsighted, don't you think?"

"Limitless?" Gar sat back on his stool and smirked. "I know what you're doing. Derrick likely figured out my affliction, and you're trying to take advantage of my dwindling faculties."

That...was unexpected. I tried to hide my surprise so that maybe I could get more valuable information.

"I'm negotiating the lives of vargyrs, not taking advantage. Think about the possibilities, Gar. I'm the wild card. No one in Stellous knows what I may be capable of, and if we work together, we could probably find another way to break the wards and perhaps even solve your problem."

The demon said nothing for a moment before narrowing his eyes. "When you say limitless power, what do you mean?"

"My blood may negate all demonic curses, maybe more. Vargyrs have incredibly long lifespans and rapid healing, so any chronomancers among us would be able to manipulate time and space without dying."

"How does this benefit me?" Gar asked. "The magic I have access to is just enough to pull the wards from their hidden dimensions so that your unique physical properties can obliterate them. So what if vargyrs can use chonomancy? Such magic requires more than we have, and only I am capable of harnessing the source in this realm."

"How much time do you have left?" I asked, hearing the uncertainty in my own voice. "Before you succumb."

"This wretched form..." As if picking up on my ignorance, the demon squinted at me before standing. "You clever little ant. You almost had me convinced."

So Derrick was right. Gar was trapped in vargyr form against his will. That wasn't just speculation about him being careless. Gar was barely holding onto his mind, with more of it possibly fading the longer he remained a vargyr. Would this mean he wasn't immortal? What other tidbits of information could I get from him if I appealed to his superiority?

"I'm not a threat," I said, trying and failing to keep him there. Now I was the one that was sounding desperate. "I could be an ally to someone as powerful as you."

Gar said nothing more, but I could smell the fear wafting from him as he walked out of the room, leaving me alone in the dark.

The Rhythm Of Magic

AXEL

The cold floor hit me hard as I stumbled through, my eyes adjustin' to the dim light of a crystal high on the black stone wall.

"We need to get away from the portal," I shouted, turning back to an empty door. "Leo?"

I wanted to throw up when I didn't see him there, and I nearly tripped over my feet again scramblin' back out. It was too late when I saw that familiar Lo'rim light, and when I ran into it face first, the force of the magic flung me back 'til I hit the wall with a thud and slid to the floor.

A jumble of clawed footsteps ran toward me, and I took a moment to shake off the shock.

"Axel, what's wrong?" Derrick shouted.

This was my nightmare come true, and all I could think to do was pull on my mane while tryin' not to cry like a baby.

"I lost him."

Vince knelt next to me, giving me a hard shake. "Pull yerself together." He shoved my chin up. "How'd you lose him? What happened?"

"They was waitin' for us. When you guys went through, they started comin' out of the woods. We decided to make a run for the portal, and—he was right behind me. I don't know what happened."

"Portal memory," Derrick muttered, his ears pressed against his head. "I knew this was a possibility, which is why I told you both to stay out there. Leo had already gone through the portal once, and because of that, it was easy for Gar to keep him out while locking anyone else in. The moment Vince went into the portal, we got his attention."

"I don't know where they all came from," I said, looking down the black hall lit by pale crystals. "I got every vantage point covered, even climbed trees." I pulled my fur tighter. Why was I so stupid? "Didn't see nothin'! Maybe I didn't look hard enough."

"No use blamin' yerself. We all knew this was risky, and Gar's got portals."

Snarls came from the entrance of the hall behind us as vargyrs trickled in one by one until there were eight. I recognized the silver-black one.

"Tobes?" I said, backing away. He hated that nickname, but he didn't react. There weren't no emotion in his eyes.

"Toby," Derrick muttered. "It has been a while."

"Do I know you?" the vargyr grunted as the eight of 'em stepped closer. I didn't recognize them other vargyrs; never seen any of them in town before, but their eyes was just as dead as Toby's.

"Gar got him," I said, turning to Derrick. "There probably ain't no talkin' to 'em like this."

"Perhaps." Derrick was keeping his cool, somehow, even as everything was falling apart. "What is it you intend to do with us?"

Toby pointed us forward. "Move."

I opened my mouth to speak, but Derrick grabbed my shoulder, leaning in close.

"Even with your strength, we're outnumbered. We'll need to do as he says for now," Derrick whispered.

I nodded. Ol' Derrick may have been in the same situation, but he kept his head level, always thinking. He was someone who could probably think ahead two or three different scenarios second-by-second, even when things changed. I'd give anything to have a mind like his.

"Where's Cole?" Vince turned to ask but didn't get a response from Toby. "After everything he did fer you, can't you let me say goodbye?"

The old vargyr shuddered before grabbing at a metal pendant in the shape of a weird symbol hangin' from a thin chain he wore. Didn't look like nothin' we used in our language, and there weren't any friendly curves to that rune. The edges were jagged and evil, and the middle looked like a pair of sharp cat eyes. Toby's empty stare flashed blood orange before fading back to red.

"Master says he'll allow it," he said in a puppet-like tone of voice. "He's got what he needs, and none of you will leave this place alive when it's over."

"Master?" I asked, grabbing Toby's arms. The other vargyrs crouched into attack poses, and I backed away. "He ain't nobody's master."

"Move along," Toby growled, pointing forward. Derrick gave me a slight nudge with his elbow.

"Keep calm," he whispered. "Say nothing more, understand?"

I grimaced and nodded as we continued down the black hallway. It was like a real dungeon the further we got. The walls were made of thick, crooked blocks plastered together, and every twenty steps or so, there'd be another dim, white crystal above us, halos of magic rippling like a misty mornin'. They must have been what Leo was talkin' about before we were separated.

We approached a room before the bend, and Toby held the pendant to the wall, the crystals above us pulsing in a strange rhythm before a doorway materialized.

"This is where you will remain until the master returns."

"I see," Derrick said, his tone kinda uneasy, which made me worry. He reached for the knob and slowly pulled the door open. When we got inside, a sickly, dark brown vargyr huddled in the corner, his wrists and ankles chained to hoops secured to the floor by thick iron stakes. He had a linen bag tied over his head.

"Babe," Vince cried out as the door slammed shut and melded into the wall, with us trapped inside. He ran to Cole before dropping to his knees, throwing his arms around his mate. He loosened the leather and pulled the bag off of his head.

Derrick ignored all the commotion in the corner, and instead, he studied the wall, tapping out quiet beats with his claws in different areas. It kind of bothered me when Derrick got more interested in stuff that stoked his curiosity when his friends needed comforting, but this was his way. You could take the magic out of the mage, but you couldn't take the scholar out of the mage...or somethin' like that.

Cole snarled, droolin' blood. It was weird to see him without his jewelry or fancy piercings. "I want to die. Let me die."

"No," Vince said, unzipping Leo's backpack before pulling out the vial of blood. "I got somethin' from Leo that's gonna help you feel all better." He bit down on the cork, pulling it out of the bottle before holding it to Cole's blistered lips.

Never seen anyone so hungry for blood, but Cole was greedy as he gulped it down, lickin' the glass clean with his long, thin tongue. It was hard to watch. All I kept seein' in my head was him on top of Leo, so close to ripping him apart.

"More blood," Cole shouted before snapping at Vince's arm, clamping down tight. Vince howled in pain as Cole tore at him, shaking his head from side-to-side.

Derrick shifted his attention from the wall and lunged forward, grabbing Cole's neck while I pried open his mouth, allowing Vince a moment to pull back, blood squirtin' from the torn, hanging flesh on his arm.

"It ain't workin," Vince said, tears welling in his eyes, ignoring his own pain. "Why ain't it workin'?"

Maybe it didn't work for the blood-crazed, or maybe the blood wasn't fresh enough. A strange light streamed from the crystals in the ceiling, snaking through crooked lines in the wall to the floor, and they engulfed the chains before shattering them. Now, I had to hold Cole with all my strength or he would start attackin' us. Gar was gonna punish us in the worst way by making sure we'd be the ones to put our packmate down. Once we did that, Vince would die too.

"What do we do, Derrick?" I asked, keeping Cole still as he struggled violently against me. "He's sufferin', but if we kill 'im…"

"We wait," Derrick said sternly, taking command as he held Cole by the nape of the neck. "We wait, and we assess the situation calmly."

I took a deep breath and nodded, but Vince was on the verge of losing it.

"This will work," Derrick said. Vince sniffed, blinking the tears from his eyes, calmin' back down. "The curse may be different for Cole, but it's still the same curse. We will give it time, and if by some rare chance this doesn't work, we will figure something else out. Hysteria helps no one."

"Alright," Vince said, looking away from his struggling mate. "This is hard. He ain't Cole no more."

"I know." Derrick held tighter, forcing Cole to look at him. "He's merely having a dream he has no control over." He turned to me. "It took a while for me to come to my senses after I bit Leo, so if we have to hold him down for days, we'll do it."

Cole let out a whimper, and his body relaxed for the first time.

"Babe?" Vince crawled closer to his mate, keepin' his distance for now. "Open yer eyes."

Cole didn't respond. He slumped over, and we let him down gently onto the cold stone floor.

Vince trembled as he placed his hand over the wild vargyr's head. "Is he—"

"Sleeping," Derrick interrupted. "We'll keep a close eye on him to make sure he's not merely exhausted. If he shows any signs of aggression, we'll need to restrain him again."

"When he wakes up, we're gonna have another problem," I said, pointing to the wall. "There ain't no way out of here."

Derrick's ears fell to the sides of his head.

"One crisis at a time, Axel." He scratched his head while staring at the wall.

"What's wrong?"

"I'm thinking…"

"I know that look," Vince muttered. "Yer gonna start on and on about somethin', aren't you?"

"I actually wasn't, but since you insist on hearing about the history of Lo'rim magicks…" The older mage grinned wickedly at Vince.

Vince groaned, but I was kinda interested in hearing what he'd say.

"I jest," he said, his focus shifting to the bare walls and ceiling. "This place wasn't built."

I looked around, trying to understand what he was talkin' about.

"Looks pretty well built to me."

"Look closer," he said, running his fingers along something glossy.

A moment or two passed as I gawked at the stonework of irregular chunks of granite cemented together. At first, I thought the lines in the walls were mortar, but when I stepped closer, I noticed the jagged lines had a smooth, clear look to 'em.

"What in the world?" I said, tracing the lines with my pointer claw. "It looks like glass."

"Conduits," Derrick corrected, touching the same lines on the floor. "No one would have been able to physically build this. It was conjured using the natural material from the hills as reagents. Magic shaped the rock, interlacing it with geotirite. Those lines are not mortar holding the stones together. This structure is one giant stone melded together with a magic conducting crystal."

"Vince," Cole whispered, squirming against the floor. Even though his voice was much lower, it finally *sounded* like it belonged to my friend and not some monster.

Vince scrambled over to this mate, and with Derrick's help, they turned Cole onto his back.

"Babe," Vince said, on the verge of tears again. "How are you feeling?"

I hurried back to Cole's side and sat cross-legged next to him as he opened his familiar amber eyes which turned a lighter gold. There was life comin' from him, like he stepped back into his body again.

"How?" he asked, still weak. "I don't understand."

"It seems Leo is a lot more special than we thought," Derrick said, stroking the matted, bloody fur on Cole's stomach. "We're not entirely sure why his blood destroys the curse, but he's the key to everyone's salvation."

Cole sat up and groaned but didn't seem to be in as much pain as earlier. Vince wrapped his arms around his mate, holding him as tight as he could. Cole licked at Vince's face before their mouths met. It was strange seein' them kiss as full vargyrs, since Cole was usually smaller. Now the once-tiny wilkyr swallowed Vince in his longer arms.

"Yer still pretty thin," I said, rubbing Cole's head. "But a few hunts'll fix that."

Cole broke away from his mate and looked around. "Where is Leo?"

"Gar has him," Derrick said as he stood and stretched his arms. "And we're trapped in here."

Cole's expression darkened. "I don't want to seem ungrateful, but you guys shouldn't have come back! You sacrificed Leo!" He shook his head. "How could you do that after I told you all to let me go? Why did we even bother escaping if you were just going to hand deliver him to Gar?"

"Because if you die, Vince dies," Derrick said, as Cole looked down, his eyes wide. "You can scold Leo when we rescue him. Saving you both was ultimately his choice, and honestly, Cole...did you think for a moment we wouldn't come back for you? We're a pack, right?"

I couldn't help but smile at that as ol' Derrick gave me a wink.

Vince nodded in agreement. "Gar connected us with some kinda curse. He was torturing me with you. You don't remember?"

Cole looked down at the glass vial before picking it up. "I'll make his death slow." He threw it, and it shattered against the wall, causing a slight ripple Derrick turned toward.

Even though Cole was okay now, I couldn't enjoy it. "We don't know when Gar's gonna kill him."

"We've got time," Cole said, struggling to push himself to his feet. Vince helped him the rest of the way, and I stood as well.

"What did you find out?" Derrick asked, supporting Cole with his arm.

"That Gar's really damn confident." He took a few shaky steps and stopped. "Shit, I can barely move."

"Those injuries and the muscle fatigue will go away faster now that your body and mind aren't being poisoned," Derrick said, staying close by in case Cole tumbled.

"While he was torturing me, he put these visions in my head of the things he would do. He was trying to scare me, and it worked, but he also revealed the ritual he'd have to perform to pull the wards into this realm. There are two parts: the first will expose the wards, which could take up to a week...I think. I saw six sunsets, but knowing how angry we made him, he may try to rush things along."

"He won't. He's got one shot at this, and he'll take every precaution necessary," Derrick said. "But what you described in your vision is word for word what was in Josiah's book. The wards need to be pulled into this plane. Such a feat requires a lot of magic and time. The time, I understand, but the magic—"

"Is the second part," Cole interrupted. "As soon as the wards cracked and fell, magic poured into this world from Eqiros. Everyone in town and all the ferals instantly turned blood-crazed. He's going to use the magic to amplify his curse and force us to destroy Stellous. It seems the blood craze *was* the failsafe for him in case he was betrayed. I always wondered why this happened, since it seemed to contradict the very purpose of the curse, but now it's crystal clear. When it reaches the ends stage, it's not designed to spread. It's designed to destroy."

Despite being covered in fur, my skin got cold. The room was so quiet we could hear each other's racing heartbeats.

Derrick took a deep breath and nodded.

"The contract," he said, the confident grin he once wore now weighed down by panic. "It cannot be fulfilled. This is going to be much worse than you think."

"What does that mean, exactly?" Cole asked.

"Gar's ultimate goal is not only destroying Stellous. The deva'koh who made the contract died centuries ago, and the only way Gar can void it and return to his realm is by purging ours." He slammed his fist against the wall, and another brief light rippled through the conduits. "I always resented the archmages for their relentless hunting and purging of those who could speak to demons, but I never truly understood why they took such extreme and inhumane measures…until now."

"We saw what one blood-crazed can do. How many ferals do you reckon are out in them woods?" Vince asked.

"Over ten thousand," Derrick replied. "Maybe much more. These won't just be blood-crazed. Gar will likely infuse them with even more power once magic floods into this realm. They will have no rational thoughts or fears, and with a demon's magic and no valid contract to keep it restrained, they will wipe out everything. The mages of Stellous have the power to trap Gar, but not with an army like the one he's about to unleash upon them."

"We gotta rescue Leo," I said.

"We may have to wait for them to come back and create another entrance. No doubt Gar will want to see the result of this trap he's placed us in." Derrick scratched his head and stared at the ceiling. "He likely thinks we've already had to put Cole down, killing Vince in the process. He hasn't got a clue that Vince had a vial of Leo's blood. Perhaps if he was the one escorting us, he would have had the foresight to take the bag from Vince."

"Gar didn't bring you here?" Cole asked.

"No," I replied. "It was Toby and some others I didn't recognize. Gar's controlling 'em somehow."

Cole tilted his head and examined the wall. "How did Toby create the door? He can't use magic."

"That pendant he wore is likely the answer, since he was communicating directly to Gar using it earlier." Derrick tapped the glassy crystal lines with his claw. "This room has magic flowing through these conduits. It wouldn't surprise me if every room in this place could be made or unmade on the fly."

"Guys," I said, pointing to the two crystals in the ceiling. "Before we ran for the portal, Leo mentioned that he escaped last time by destroying them crystals. He said Gar feeds off of 'em."

"Feeds…" Derrick whispered to himself as he stared at the ceiling again.

"Alright, so let's get them things broken," Vince said, preparing to jump. Derrick grabbed him before his feet could leave the floor.

"Not so fast." The older mage rubbed the thicker fur on his chin. "If Leo did this to escape once, Gar would not repeat the same mistake. Remember when I said these rooms can be made or unmade?"

I nodded. "Yeah. So let's unmake this one."

"That could mean granite appearing out of nowhere the moment those crystals are destroyed, fusing us with this place. We wouldn't even know what hit us." Derrick continued to examine the crystal. "It's too risky."

"But Leo said when he did it, all them barriers went down."

"This room isn't sealed by barriers, Axel, and I don't know enough to start pulling random crystals out of the ceiling." He slammed his fist against the wall like he did earlier, and another white ripple snaked its way through the embedded crystal before disappearin'. He hummed to himself. "Gar's smarter than that, and we need to think like a demon."

"So, your plan is to just wait?" Cole asked.

Derrick slammed his fist against the wall again, higher this time. The magic rippled outward, lighting up the crystals. "Not exactly."

"What the hell are you doin'?" Vince asked.

"Observing." He moved his fist to the left, one block over, and pounded again in a series of rhythms. The light was a little brighter, and Derrick stopped. "So that's your secret, you crafty old snake."

Cole stepped closer to the wall. "You figured something out?"

"I've been torturing myself for a week, wondering how Gar is able to manipulate magic using Lo'rim in this world. It appears as though he needs only to will it, but I just realized by looking at this design that such a feat is impossible, as I thought."

"What does that matter at the moment?" Cole asked. "We should focus on finding a way out of here and figure out how Gar did it another time."

"Oh, the way out is rather straightforward. I just figured it out, actually," Derrick said, chuckling to himself, further annoying Cole.

"Well?" Cole pointed impatiently. "Why are we still here?"

"Impatience isn't going to make this work faster," Derrick muttered, banging different rhythms on the bricks. Each time his fist hit the wall, the light in lines between the stones would get brighter. "We're not going to save Leo without allowing ourselves time to understand his methods." He pounded out another set of rhythms in the shape of various runes, then another shape I couldn't figure out. A flash blinded us as a single white crystal appeared in the middle of the wall. "And behold: the *real* keystone." He pointed at the two crystals hanging from the ceiling. "Those were decoys, and I can almost guarantee that destroying either of them would have killed us."

With a yank, he tore the crystal from the stone, and it shattered in his hands. When the wall faded away, the dingy hallway we were in earlier appeared.

"This is quite the revelation, and I will need time to think on this more. I've been theorizing that Gar could conjure magic at will from some hidden source in this world, but there was always that missing piece of the puzzle." He broke another crystal in his hands that was attached to the stone in the hall. "Now I'm beginning to see the... cracks in that theory."

Cole and Vince groaned, but I chuckled a little bit. Never could resist a bad pun. Derrick and I followed both of them, us keeping quiet as we listened out for anyone close by.

"How'd you know how to get us out?" I asked.

His grin grew wide, and his tail wagged as we continued through the windin' black corridor. Derrick loved when I asked him questions, and he always had this excited look on his face whenever he'd answer.

"Magic and music share similar qualities, and each type of magic has a unique resonant frequency. I noticed earlier when I hit the wall that the tone sounded familiar."

"I didn't hear nothin'," I said, still confused.

"You wouldn't, unless you were the one striking it. I kept knocking on the stones, watching and listening. Imagine my surprise when what came back wasn't a Lo'rim tone. This place is infused with pure magic from Eqiros—a lot of it. The more I hit the stone, the more the geotirite conduits *sang*. The closer I got to the source, the louder and brighter the crystals got. All I had to do was create the runic pattern for Gi'ash, an arcane revelation spell. Isn't that incredible? Though it is a bit more of a pain than simply enunciating spells using vocalization, you can actually cast them by drumming the correct rhythm on a magical surface instead. With enough technique, one could cast any spell by simply using patterns as long as you can touch the magic using conduits."

"Is that what Gar's doing?" Cole asked. "He never made any noise while he was using magic."

Derrick nodded. "Now you understand why I am so baffled and impressed by this. Gar is manipulating magic by some other means; however, I do not believe he is a conduit himself. He is limited in the same way we are, but he has had centuries to hone his technique. He is somehow obtaining and storing magic from Eqiros while also converting it into demonic Lo'rim. He's also preserving large quantities in its pure form so he can perform the ritual—and create prisons like this that seem to exist in its own pocket realm." He reached up and grabbed another crystal from the wall, and it shattered in his hand. The lights of the crystals in that area flickered before wisps of magic puffed out and disappeared.

"So if we destroy all the geotirite crystals in whatever this place is, we could stop him from drawing magic," Cole said excitedly.

Derrick shook his head. "The only way to get into this place is by portal, which isolates this magic into its own source. It's probably why Gar isn't here and likely never would step foot into this place. Whatever magic can be used here cannot be used out there." He shattered another crystal, and the hall got a little darker than before. "The source here is too small to perform a ritual powerful enough to pull the wards into the Varcross. He's drawing from something massive."

We padded carefully through the hall, keeping our guards up in case Toby or the others were close by. I had a feeling that if they were, they'd have heard the racket we were makin' as we all pitched in and pulled out more crystals.

"He's gonna know when we leave, ain't he?" I asked.

"Most definitely." We approached the end of the hall. "In fact, we will need to make our escape quick. The portal remembers us; however, there is something working in our favor. To keep a portal locked requires concentration. Earlier, all Gar had to do was keep Leo out because his barriers would keep us in." He pulled the last crystal from the wall, and a flickering wave vanished as it passed over the exit. "This time, he has no barrier, and he's likely too focused on Leo to bother keeping the locks on." Derrick walked forward, stopping before the invisible portal. "On the count of three, we run like hell." He looked back at Cole and Vince and smiled. "I know we're running for our lives, but when we're out, you two should take some time alone."

"But what about Leo?" Cole said. "We don't have the time."

Derrick's watery green eyes glowed softly. "Make the time. You both escaped death. Some of us would give anything to have been granted such fortune. We're going head-first into the unknown, and frankly, this could be the last chance you get."

Cole looked down at Vince before pressing his forehead against his mate's.

"He's right, babe," Vince whispered. "I get to hold you again, and I'm never lettin' go."

LEO

Had it been seconds, hours, or days? The silence of the room gobbled my thoughts, and the darkness feasted on what remained. Deafening pulses of blood thudded in my inner ear, making it hard to think about anything else.

Gar must have done something to this room because the darkness seemed almost sentient, its formless tongues licking at my sanity. Though he didn't say it, I knew what the demon wanted me to experience—his despair. He was in mental anguish every day he was away from his world, and for a moment, I pitied him.

The room grew more unbearable by the second. Intense heat and humidity pressed on me from everywhere, clinging to the skin under my fur like a wool sweater dipped in swamp water. This made me think about the afterlife—of hell, if it truly existed. The idea of eternal torment shadowed me like the bogeyman, and heaven always seemed out of reach. Religion was something for miserable, simple people to grasp onto in lieu of rational thought, allowing them the illusion that someone was in control of their spiraling lives. The opium of the people...

Or so I thought.

This trip to another world, and my imprisonment by an *actual* demon had me second-guessing my arrogant stance on theism.

There was so much I didn't understand, as everything in this world should have been impossible by Earth's standards. Though the darkness of this place was eating my hope, one thing kept me grounded—the swinging, bladed pendulum of doom, inching ever lower as each agonizing second ticked by like hours.

The metal door cracked open, and a painful light split the blackness down the middle, melting it away like sunlight through fog. The cooler dankness flowing in may as well have been fresh air after what I'd been enduring. A silhouette of a muscly, stout vargyr padded into the room carrying something in his hands.

My eyes slowly adjusted as the figure held a tray in front of my cage.

"Eat."

"Toby?" The voice I'd heard earlier was his.

He knelt to one knee before meticulously sliding the tray of grayish meat through a short gap under the cell door. Toby stood back up and stared blankly, slobber roping from the corners of his mouth.

"What did he do to you?"

The vargyr said nothing as he continued watching me. I sighed and picked up the tray before carrying it back to the blanket on the floor. Despite my hunger, I set the food aside. The last time Gar gave me something to consume, I was nearly torn apart by half the town.

"We will all be feral soon," Toby mumbled. "The wilkyrs have shifted, and they now serve him as we all prepare to leave this place."

"What do you mean they shifted? Some of them had only just started transforming, and it takes years to turn."

"You say that as you sit before me fully turned."

I hadn't thought about that, and I didn't know how to explain my special circumstance to someone who was barely lucid enough to speak for himself. He somehow remembered I was human only a little while ago.

So the wilkyrs had all shifted—or more accurately, had been given something to make them shift faster. Of course he would. He had no use for them anymore, and without them, the town becomes more desperate to get back to Eqiros where only the humans can sate the curse.

"You do understand what will happen to you all when you go back, right?" I asked, vainly trying to get through. "The mages will kill you all."

"We would rather die than live as animals," Toby said, his voice dripping with what sounded like rehearsed passion. "We will follow Gar to the end, if it comes to that." He turned to the door to leave, but I jumped from the blanket and reached through the bars, catching his arm.

"Toby." He stopped and slowly turned his head, baring his teeth.

"Don't touch me."

"Will you do me a favor?" His brows furrowed. "Please. It would only take a second."

He turned all the way around and stepped up to the cage. "It depends on the favor."

"Bite my arm." I held out the limb, offering it to him. I didn't know how he would respond to such an odd request, but I had to try something.

Toby glared at me, his head tilting in annoyance. "Isolation has broken your mind already. Gar said you would say some crazy things that I should not believe."

I'd considered that, which was why I wasn't going to tell him I could break the curse.

"Please," I said, lifting my arm closer to his mouth. "Just one bite and you can leave. I need to feel something when I go back in the dark, even if it's pain. You'd be giving me relief."

His stare grew more suspicious.

"It costs you nothing. You've always hated me. Why not rip into my arm to relieve some of that frustration?"

"I feel nothing toward you." He looked down at my arm. "In fact, I feel little of anything, so such an act will do little to please me." Toby snatched me tightly, pulling my forearm closer to his sharp teeth.

"But, if you want to feel pain for a few seconds to ease your mind, then so be it, I will gladly allow you to suffer."

He opened his mouth and clamped down, his teeth sinking close to the bone. I wanted to scream, but I stood rigid, holding my breath, shaking and grimacing. It wasn't so much the feeling of teeth tearing into muscle that made me want to cry out in agony, it was the intense nerve pain, like I'd stuck my arm into an electric eel tank.

The dripping of my blood and his saliva pattered against the floor like a roof leak during a light rain. When he opened his mouth to release me, that was when I cried out. It was more painful when his teeth slid from my skin.

"Is that satisfactory?" he asked, his eyes still red and empty. I knew from when I cured Vince and Derrick that the effects likely wouldn't be immediate.

"It—it is. Thank you," I said with a sniffle as tears blurred my vision. The pain, fortunately, didn't last long thanks to the rapid healing, but that was something I didn't want to experience again.

"Good," Toby muttered before turning to the door. He grabbed the knob and walked out, leaving behind the darkness to swallow me again.

CHAPTER 30

Driver's Ed

AXEL

"We will need to assume we have less time than you saw in your vision," Derrick said as we stalked around the outskirts of town, bein' extra careful not to draw anyone's attention

"It's not like we can do much until we know where he's keeping Leo," Cole said, pulling the jar of lotion out of Leo's backpack, which was still strapped to Vince. He opened it and sighed. "There's hardly any left."

"Gar is likely keeping Leo in another pocket realm since he knows we're going to be looking for him, and we still don't know what source he's drawing his magic from." Derrick moved ahead of us. "Wait here," he whispered, disappearin' into the bushes close to the road. We stood there until he called out the all clear.

I ran toward the sound of Derrick's voice, tearing away the thick brush for the others until we were on the dirt path leading to Cole's. Even though we was in one hell of a pickle, it was nice to see something familiar.

"I doubt the source is in town," Cole said. "Something like that would have to be huge to store the amount of magic Gar needs for this, and we'd have noticed it."

"That is what baffles me. It's as though he's siphoning from ley lines, and I know for a fact that this world has no planetary source. There must be an artificial one, and it would need to be centralized so he could draw from it anywhere within a certain radius of town. But, like you mentioned, an artificial source to store that amount of magic would have to be colossal."

The clouds turned red as the sun was close to setting. Cole's house was just beyond the trees, and what surprised me was how miserable the old place looked. It was like opening my eyes for the first time to the awful way we lived. Vince must have felt the same since he wasn't speakin' much.

"I didn't think we'd be back," Cole said with a stifled laugh as we stepped onto the rickety porch. "There's no one around, so we should take some time to rest. We're going to be useless if we're exhausted."

Vince grunted in agreement as we filed through the front door. Cole closed the curtains before flipping the light switch on, but nothing happened. The house was ransacked, like the others was lookin' for us.

"Well, this blows," Cole muttered. "They might come back. We'll need to be on guard."

"It's just things," Vince said, collapsing onto the sofa before hugging one of the decorative pillows. "It's good to be back on my couch."

"Don't get too used to it," I said, while dragging one of the dining room chairs to the group. "When this is over, I don't know what's gonna happen to the town. Gar was the only one with any authority keepin' it together."

The lights flickered on for a second before going dark again, and we all looked up at the ceiling in unison.

"He's going to throw all of his cards on the table because he knows he's not going to be here much longer," Derrick said. "He also knows we're dangerous to his plan. I'm rather surprised he wasn't lying in wait for our return here, but with all he needs to do for that ritual, he's likely going on the defensive for once. I'm not sure if that's better or worse, but it gives us time to breathe."

I stared at the dead crystal on the ceiling. Light was somethin' we always took for granted, even though we didn't really need it. Hot water was another thing we got used to, but how it all worked was a mystery. I sometimes fixed thermal pipes, but I never understood how they got hot with none of them crystal batteries.

After standing again on my aching feet, I walked over to the kitchen and turned on the hot water, and as expected, only cold water came out.

"So the lights is connected to the hot water, too?"

"I believe so, yes," Derrick responded.

"How do we get our lights and hot water if there ain't no magic in this world? Where does it come from?"

"The town's energy infrastructure is a centuries-old conduit system, but it was built in such a way that it could last centuries more. It's not that great over long distances, but for a lonely town in a new world with no natural magic source, it was the only adequate solution—" Derrick froze and smacked his head. "That clever bastard."

He jumped off the couch and threw open the door before disappearing around the corner. We all looked at each other, Vince and I confused, but Cole ran after him with us following behind.

"I think I know what you're thinking," Cole said excitedly. "What are we looking for exactly?"

"I'm not sure. We don't have this type of dated technology in Stellous, so what we need to find is something that leads to an underground network. It would be relatively close to the house, I think." He looked around and shook his head. "I'd have expected to see something attached to the lower frame, but we may have to dig. Do you have a spade?"

"Yeah, we have a couple in the shed," Cole said as he ran around back.

"Axel," Derrick placed both hands on my shoulders, "keep asking questions. My mind is not as sharp as it used to be, and sometimes I need a fresh perspective."

I scratched my head. "I guess we just need to talk things through sometimes, huh?"

Cole returned with two shovels. He handed one to Derrick; the other he gave to Vince.

"What the hell am I supposed to do with this?"

"I'll start from this side and work around," Derrick said, pushing the spade into the dirt next to the foundation of the house. "If I'm right, there will be something shielding the conduit just below the surface. Keep digging around the perimeter until you strike something hard."

Vince sneered and handed the shovel back to Cole but stopped as his larger mate folded his arms and glared down at him.

"Just because we're back home doesn't mean I'm going to let you sit on that couch while we do all the work."

"Well, what about Axel?"

I rubbed my hands together, kinda excited about what I had to do. Leo never did let me drive his car, but I did watch him do it a few times.

Cole didn't say a word, and Vince slumped forward, his ears against his head as he moped to the other side, out of sight.

"You okay?" I asked Cole, keepin' my voice low.

"I love the guy, but I don't want him falling back into his old habits."

"You know he ain't like that no more." We both watched as Derrick continued digging, already halfway done with this side. "If we pull through this, maybe we should go back up in the mountains. It might be good fer all of us."

"That's not the answer to everything. It worked for you in the past, but we're not all cut out to leave everyone behind. It was fun for a little while, but Vince and I like stability and a permanent place to call home." He looked toward the window where his shower was. "And hot water."

"You know that feelin' yer havin' right now? You ain't glad that we're back here."

"What the hell do you know?" Cole snapped, the new, longer hackles on his neck raised. "There are other points of view that aren't yours. You'd be better off remembering that."

"I'm sorry," I said, tryin' to ease the tension between us. Cole hadn't been himself since he was cured, and I didn't feel it was the time to bring it up or argue. "Maybe I am bein' unreasonable."

"No." Cole took a moment to compose himself. "I didn't mean to say it like that."

A muffled metallic clank came from Derrick, who stabbed at the dirt a few more times in the same place. As the shovel sunk, it would stop with another clank.

"Oh boy," he said enthusiastically as he began digging around whatever that thing was, removing more of the dirt with his hands. Cole and I inched closer to examine what appeared to be a black container bolted to the cement foundation. Using the edge of the shovel, Derrick pried the box open, revealing a dark chunk of somethin'.

Confusion returned to Derrick's face.

"It seems I was wrong earlier when I said this was a conduit system. I'm not sure what this is."

"That's because it's relatively new," Cole said. "Stellous moved away from artificial conduits for territories outside of its network about thirty years ago. All magic flows through the ground in waves, but it's a lot weaker than natural ley lines. It's perfect for lighting and heating a house, but that's it."

"Waves?" Derrick knelt next to the box. "I've never seen this material before."

Cole knelt next to him, grabbing the solid chunk before giving it a firm tug. At first, I thought it wasn't attached to anything, but it turned out to be the end of a long, narrow rod that had been jammed into the dirt through a hole in its container.

"They really did keep you locked away, didn't they? With everything you've read, you never came across tanzonium links?"

"Infrastructure never interested me much. I was more fascinated with chronomancy, though I would never attempt such magic myself."

"It's magic storage. I think this is a tanzonium rod," Cole said, handing it to Derrick. "A fusion of deritium and talicite. The talicite draws in waves of underground magic to the rods like a magnet, and the deritium stores and condenses it into the top here, like a battery." He pointed to the metallic chunk. "That's all I know, which isn't a lot. Tanzonium is the only thing that makes sense, though."

Derrick leaned the spade handle against the wall. "This only leads to more questions. Unless Gar is a living tanzonium rod, this doesn't explain how he's able to draw from these *conduit-less* lay lines, especially with enough potency to cast such powerful spells."

"Honestly, I don't give a damn how he controls it." Cole pointed toward the woods. "If we destroy the source, that neuters him. No explanation necessary. We don't need a long, complicated answer for everything, Derrick."

The metal chunk at the end began to glow a pale yellow.

"Interesting," Derrick said, pointing to the edge of Cole's yard. "Shove it into the ground there."

Cole ran to where Derrick was pointing and pushed the rod into the soft soil. It glowed a little brighter, but faded a couple seconds later. Derrick walked over and knelt to the ground, lookin' at the device before pulling it out of the dirt.

"I know how we will find the source," Derrick said, playfully twirling the rod like a baton. "We will need a map, though."

"We don't know where to look, Derrick. What's a map going to—" As soon as the words came out, Cole's eyes widened, and Derrick's tail swayed from side-to-side. "You're going to use this as a divining rod for magic. Triangulation."

"It's so simple it almost pisses me off," Derrick added, glancing up at me. "You've been rather quiet."

"That's 'cause I don't understand none of this stuff."

Something snapped on the other side of the house.

"Fuckin' hell," Vince shouted.

"We forgot about Vince," Cole said before calling out to his mate. "We found it, babe. Come on back." Vince stomped into view, holding a broken shovel. "What happened?"

"Nothing." He looked at the empty box, then over at us. "How long ago'd you guys find this?"

Cole cleared his throat. "Just now."

"Mmhmm." Vince threw the broken spade to the ground and stomped over to us. "Anything else useless I can do for you guys?"

"It was useful," Cole said, wrapping his arm around Vince.

The smaller vargyr grunted before crossing his arms. "So, what are we doin'?"

"I'm gonna go get somethin', and I'll let you guys work out the details," I said before walking toward the road.

"Don't leave me here with them," Vince called out, walking close behind. "I'm too young to die of boredom."

⸙

Vince and I rounded the curve carefully, hopping into the trees just in case anyone was snooping around my house. Since Vince was smaller, he went on ahead, keeping low and quiet in the brush. I didn't say nothin'; instead, I waited for him to come back.

"All clear," he shouted, and I hurried toward the yard. It was good to see the old house again, and in front of it sat Leo's weird-looking car. The closer I got, the more I started to doubt I'd fit behind that steering device. It was hard enough to get in on the other side. "So this is the thing, huh?"

"Mmhmm," I replied, looking in through the side with the missing window. I had a brief flashback of me pullin' Leo out of there after he crashed into that tree. "I gotta remember where he put them keys to activate it."

"You ain't gonna fit in there, ya know." Vince followed me up onto the porch before we both stepped inside. The house was still pretty clean, and I looked down at the couch where Leo and I spent the night playing one of Vince's games. "You okay?"

"Yeah, just thinkin'," I said, looking around the tables. Something shiny caught my eye as I walked closer to the window. "Found 'em."

"He's gonna be okay." Vince sat down on the couch and looked over at his gaming console sitting under the LCR. Where Vince and I came from, we just called it a viewbox. "That guy rolled in like a fuckin' boulder and knocked everything around."

"I didn't think I'd ever get so lucky." I sat next to my best friend while holding the tiny keys in my hand. "What were the odds that the perfect man would come from another world?"

"He knows a lot about mental stuff," Vince said, staring out the window. "He's the first person that actually understood what I was goin' through." He pulled Leo's backpack into his lap and reached in before pulling out a familiar rectangular thing. "I don't know how to turn it on, or if it even still works, but when I look at his pictures, I see us the way he does. I hate how mean I was to him when all he wanted was to be my friend."

"You two got pretty chummy out there. He knows how you really feel about him. Hell, everyone can see right through ya."

Vince continued staring blankly at his own dark reflection on the glossy device before sighing.

"We all deserve to be happy," he said. "And we're the happiest when we're all together. I don't even want to play that damn game anymore. I just want us all to sleep under the same blanket again." He looked up at me with watery eyes. "Nothin' ever felt right here, and I want to feel what we felt out there again."

"Me too," I said, wrapping one arm around him as he leaned into me. "I miss this, you know? Why did we ever grow apart?"

"We wanted different things," he said, wiping his nose with the back of his forearm. "You wanted to see the world, and I got that modeling contract. The whole vargyr thing threw a wrench in all that, but I ain't upset no more when I think about it. If I hadn't turned wilkyr and lost everything, I'd have never met Cole. He's the one guy that makes me feel like a whole person."

"I want to see him smile again—really smile."

Vince nodded. "I don't think any of us will really smile until this is over. We're missing an important piece." He sat up and leaned forward. "Cole's really big now."

"That don't bother you, does it?"

"I don't care if he's a giant or pocket-sized, I'm just glad he's alive, but I get the feeling it bothers him. He looks like he's expecting me to take him into my arms like I used to, but I can't." Vince sighed again. "He's still the same Cole, but that hasn't caught up to him physically. How did you deal with Leo being so big now?"

"I dunno. He's still smaller than me, and he's got them cute paw feet—but there ain't really no roles between us. We just sorta fell onto this seesaw of dominance depending on the mood."

Vince stood and picked up Leo's backpack before dropping the phone back inside.

"You ready to get Leo's hunk of crap moving?"

"Not really," I said, rolling the keys around in my hand. "I was excited at first, but I'm starting to have second thoughts." I stood up and followed Vince outside. "And I don't think I'm gonna fit."

"Well, no shit," he said, pulling open the driver's side door. "But I can. How hard can it be?"

"You don't even know the first thing 'bout driving."

"And you do?"

He had a point. I shook my head and handed Vince the keys.

"Let me get in on the other side, and I'll tell you what I saw Leo do—if I can remember." I walked over to the door and tried to pull it open, but it wouldn't budge. "When did this break?"

"Hurry up and get in here," Vince called out as he shut the door.

Using a lot more force than I intended, I pulled the door open, but the frame made a snapping sound and the entire thing broke off.

"Don't be breakin' pieces of it off if we need it all to do the thing Derrick blabbed about," Vince said as I slid into the vehicle, dropping the detached door to the ground.

"This is a lot more comfortable, but I fucked up Leo's car."

"Wasn't that the end goal?" Vince asked, feeling around the console. "How do I turn it on?"

I pointed to the slit in the side of the steering device.

"Just stick the big black one in there and turn."

Vince shoved the key in and gave it a twist, but all that happened was some dings and the sound of static.

"Alright, now what?"

"I don't think it's on yet."

"How long do we have to wait?"

"I don't remember waiting," I said, examining the key. "Try turning it the other way, see what happens."

He turned the key again, and the car whirred and shuddered, which startled Vince enough that he let out a funny shriek and let go of the key.

"Is it supposed to do that?" he asked, as the car went dormant again.

"Yes, it's supposed to do that!" I reached over and turned the key, holding it in place until the car turned all the way on. "Alright, I think he moved this thing here," I said, grabbing the knob attached to a stick in the middle console. "I don't know what these symbols mean, but I do know that he put it here to back it up and here to make it move forward."

"What are these things on the floor for then?"

"I—I dunno. Try pressin' one with yer foot."

He pushed down on the fat left one.

"Nothing's happening," Vince said before pushing the other one hard. The car made an angry roar, and Vince shrieked again, this time throwing open the door and running into the yard.

"Get yer ass back in here."

"It obviously doesn't want me drivin' it."

"It's supposed to make that noise...I think."

Vince slowly stepped over toward the car again before sliding back into the seat.

"This was a bad idea. I don't wanna do this no more."

"C'mon now. I don't think yer supposed to press the pedal that hard. Try lightly tappin' it."

Vince gritted his teeth and slowly pressed down on the skinnier one. Instead of roaring, the car made a satisfied purr as it vibrated more.

"I think it liked that better," I said, patting Vince on the back. I tried moving the stick in the center to the backup position, but it wouldn't budge. "How the hell did he do this?"

"This is gonna take all damn day," Vince muttered, pressing the other pedal. When he did that, I was able to pull the lever down.

"Whoa, that did it."

The car began to slide backward as Vince lifted his foot.

"Hey, look at that," Vince said proudly as he pushed down on the other one. The car lurched backward, and Vince shrieked again. He pushed open the door, but I caught him by the arm before he could jump out.

"Don't you dare," I shouted. "Press the other pedal!"

He stomped down, and the car violently jerked to a stop right before we hit the fat trunk of a tree. Vince and I exhaled loudly at the same time.

"Alright, I'm gonna pull this thing here to make it go forward. When I do, *gently* let yer foot off that one and *gently* press the other. You gotta do that while turnin' the wheel in the direction you wanna go."

"I don't wanna do this. I don't wanna do this."

"You gotta." I started getting more frustrated, which wasn't really helpin' the situation. "You gotta do it for Leo, our missin' piece, remember?"

"I take it back. He ain't worth it."

I glared at him.

"Just do what I told ya."

Derrick and Cole ran over to the car, which was more or less in one piece. It started makin' one hell of a racket after we hit that fifth tree and ran into the ditch.

"What the hell did you guys do?" Cole shouted as I shifted the stick to the top, and Vince turned off the car.

The moment it shuddered to a stop, Vince threw open the door and fell to the dirt on his hands and knees.

"I hate cars," he shouted, shaking and sobbing. I kinda wanted to laugh at what a baby he was, but we did get pretty rattled. "I wanna eat whoever the hell invented this death trap."

"Well, it appears to still move, but I'm not sure how fast it will go anymore with that kind of damage," Derrick said. "And you both understand this thing needs to be moved close to where the wards are, right?"

"If I have to, I'll tie Gar to the front of it and throw the damn thing in myself," I said, rubbing my head from where it impacted the glass a few times.

"It looks like Vince is the only one who can fit in there, so he'll have to do it once we figure out where the source is," Derrick said.

With a hacking sound, Vince threw up in the dirt.

Cole rushed to his side.

"My poor ferocious mate," he said with a slight chuckle as Vince gagged again. "I'm proud of you."

"Ugh," he muttered with another dry heave. "Leo's fucked. I ain't gettin' back in that thing."

Derrick looked toward town, still holding that rod from earlier.

"Did you guys come up with an idea?" I asked.

"A solid one, thanks to Cole." Derrick looked back as Cole helped Vince off of the ground. "You probably would have made an excellent mage, you know?"

"I'm glad I didn't," Cole said, kissing Vince on the cheek. "I'd have been trapped in that boring old library, and I wouldn't have this guy."

Vince's tail wagged, and his ears pointed all the way up.

"We're going to use this rod to triangulate the source of the magic. As we get closer to the town, we'll measure the luminosity of the metal along the perimeter out of sight. We'll need to mark these points on a map so we can use simple math to calculate the source's approximate location," Derrick continued. "We only get one chance at this, so we need to know for sure what building it's hidden in—if it is, in fact, a building." He looked around at the group. "So, does anyone have any enchanted maps lying around?"

"That sounds like it's gonna take forever," I replied. "No tellin' what Gar's doin' to Leo right now. Can't we just sneak through town and use this thing to show if we're hot or cold? Not a lot of people know what Cole looks like as a vargyr."

"Don't you think me walking around town sticking a glowing rod into the dirt every few steps is going to look a little suspicious, Axel?" Cole's tone turned back to annoyance.

"Sorry, I guess that was a little stupid."

"You're not stupid," he said, his ears drooping downward. "Leo's your mate, and you're scared—and I didn't mean to snap like that." He gritted his teeth. "This new body irritates me."

Derrick patted my back. "If we're quick and really careful, this shouldn't take longer than a day. We have time, and we need to get this right." He started walking east toward town through the woods, and we followed. "I think I know where I can get a map, but I'll need to go into town by myself. We only have enough lotion for one person to make two trips. Not many of the townsfolk will know who I am, and I'm sure Gar is too busy preparing the ritual to be randomly wandering on patrol—unless I happen upon Tobias. As soon as I've procured the map, we'll find the location of the source, and I will destroy it."

"If we go head-to-head with him, even as a distraction, we're not going to last very long," Cole said. "We need to be able to protect ourselves from his magic long enough to give Derrick time."

"Unfortunately, since I don't understand how Gar uses magic, there's nothing I know of that can protect against it." He placed his hand on Cole's shoulder. "You're young, but you have a mind for this, and you know more about this technology than I do. If there's a way he's harnessing the magic using tanzonium, there must be a way for us to use it as well—or at the very least, ward against it."

"You really think I can come up with a solution?" Cole asked. "We're not even close to the same level of intellect. If I'm wrong, we all die."

"No pressure," Derrick said with a sly smile.

"That's not funny at all."

"Sometimes you have to find the humor in the darkness." Derrick let out a loud, forced laugh, which made Cole's grimace relax. "As dire as our situation may seem, don't let it crush your spirits, or failure will be a self-fulfilling prophecy."

There's the Derrick we could count on to make even the worst things seem okay.

"I'll sneak into town and try to find a map in the town hall basement. We'll use it to find the source before Gar completes his ritual. I'm going to need you three to work out a plan for a diversion, because once I get close to the source, Gar will know. You three will not only have to distract Gar, but you will need to draw every vargyr away from my location."

"Distract an all-powerful demon and a whole town full of pissed off vargyrs," Vince muttered. "That part's easy. Stayin' alive won't be."

"I'll figure something out," Cole said, glaring at Derrick. "If I can."

"We all believe in you, babe." Vince wrapped his arms around his larger mate. "I fell in love with that big brain of yers, after all—and that ass."

That made Cole laugh as he returned the hug.

We didn't say nothin' more to each other as we trotted through the woods toward town. It was a little further 'cause we had to take a longer route, and since we hadn't slept in over a day, we weren't able to run that fast.

"This is where I depart," Derrick said as he walked behind Vince and unzipped Leo's backpack. He pulled out the lotion and began dabbing it on himself.

"I was just thinkin'," Vince said, turning toward Cole, "I could make one hell of a distraction."

"You're actually volunteering for something?" I asked. "Something dangerous?"

"Ain't no one in town fast enough to catch me."

"Now you understand the advantages of your size," Derrick said, giving Vince a hard pat on the back.

"Well, I'm big where it counts, so I ain't stressin' about it no more."

I smiled at his enthusiasm.

"Why the hell are you lookin' at me like that? Ain't all of us got a hyukan-sized dick like you do." Vince turned away, hissing through his teeth. "Freak."

"That ain't what I—" Vince ignored me as he stomped off.

An Old Feud And A New Ally

LEO

Too much time had passed, and Toby hadn't returned. My blood had to have worked, right? Derrick, Axel, and Vince were proof of that. Toby mentioned that the others had escaped, but were they able to cure Cole? The difference between then and now was my body. If being a full vargyr somehow took my ability to cure the curse, then convincing Gar of anything would be impossible—if it wasn't already.

I sat in silence, trying to picture the outside world, but such thoughts were hard to conjure while whatever spell Gar cast over this room still lingered. A few more moments passed before the door slowly creaked open and the familiar stocky silhouette of a vargyr stumbled through.

"What the hell did you do to me?" Toby stood in front of my cell, clutching the bars with both hands before falling to his knees. I'd never been so happy to see him back to normal. "I'm gonna–" Pale-red colored vomit spewed from his mouth, some of it running through his nose as he gasped and wretched again. I jumped to the side as another rush of projectile vomit landed on the cell floor; this time it was blue, like one of Gar's potions.

"Are you okay?" I asked, stepping closer while avoiding the puddle on the floor. It didn't smell acidic like it should have. There was a strange, almost chemical scent to it with a trace of my blood. His body rejected whatever potions Gar had been giving him.

Toby pushed himself to his feet before stumbling backward onto a wooden stool and, with shaky hands, unclasped the strange necklace he wore.

"I just threw up for the first time in five decades. Do I look okay?" Toby snapped, holding his stomach while leaning forward. He studied me for a moment. "You look better as a vargyr."

"Uh, thanks," I said.

"It wasn't a compliment." He took in a deep breath and rubbed his forehead. "I can't believe that crazy deve'koh was right."

"Xavier?"

Toby glared up at me, one ear off to the side.

"What did you do to me?" he asked again, a bit more intrigued than annoyed. "The last thing I remember was biting you."

"I'm the cure."

"What?"

"For the curse," I said, sitting back on the blanket. "My blood nullifies the curse, and Gar knows this. He wants to leave this world, and he knows that if the other vargyrs get wind of what I can do, they won't let him sacrifice me to the wards."

Toby sat still, silently pondering while avoiding eye contact. He had that same sage-like stare Derrick often had when he was deep in thought.

"If you're the cure, why am I still a damned monster?"

"Derrick doesn't think our mutation is the curse. The drive to spread the curse is—or something like that."

"So the bastard's still alive?" Toby asked, looking down at the ground. "And he's lucid?"

I grabbed the cage bars with both hands. "We can talk about that later. You need to get me out of here."

"How the hell do you expect me to do that?" he replied, pointing to the door of the cell. "Gar uses Lo'rim somehow. Do you think he's going to put something so valuable in a place with an ordinary key?"

"Then could you at least find the others and tell them I'm okay? Maybe you could spread the word around town about what I can do."

Toby shifted the necklace around in his hands and smiled.

"We have some time," he whispered, looking back toward the hallway. "I don't know where they would be hiding, but I can try to get their scent. Axel always stinks to the heavens, so unless he's bathed recently, he shouldn't be too hard to track. It's hard for me to remember, but I think the others are probably hunting for them, and I don't think Vince and Axel have enough brain cells between them to evade. Or maybe they're just dumb enough to be lucky, but if Derrick is with them—" He wrinkled his nose.

"Did you see Cole? Was he cured?"

"I don't remember."

I glanced down at his hands. "What was that you put in your pocket?"

"Something I need to get rid of," he replied before standing. "The moment I came to my senses and saw it, I understood what Gar really is. I don't know as much about demonic magic, but I am familiar with X'eevolic symbols. This is a rune of zelab, which means 'two thoughts.' It's probably wise that I not have it around my neck while I'm talking to you."

Steady, clawed footsteps echoed through the hall, a meticulous, cocky stride I'd become all too familiar with.

"He's coming," I whispered.

Tobias shuddered and composed himself, letting all emotion slip from his face. As Gar entered the room, he cocked his head, his red eyes glowing as he examined what was happening.

"Tobias?" the demon asked slowly. "Why are you still here?"

"He refuses to eat," he said, his voice slipping effortlessly into monotone. "He threw up. Should I force the vomit down his throat?"

Good lord. He certainly was a convincing actor, though a part of me wondered if he would actually enjoy doing that.

Gar grinned and shook his head. "That won't be necessary. If our guest doesn't care for the meal, he can go hungry. It's not like a few days without eating will starve him to death." He narrowed his attention to Toby's chest. "Where is the nox-cirqet?"

"I apologize, master. During my tracking, it must have gotten caught on a branch and broke free. I am not sure where I lost it."

The demon's eyes went wide, and he grabbed Toby by the jaw, digging his claws in. "That was no simple trinket, mongrel. You are to search the area you lost it until you find it again, understood? I'll not have such a thing falling to the hands of that blasted mage." He shuddered after mentioning Derrick, and since Toby was lucid, he likely noticed it as well. The vargyr mage would probably know how to use it against him, which was all the more reason for Toby to find them. "Find it," he growled through his teeth, jerking his hand away.

"Yes, master," Toby said with a bow, remaining in his fake zombified state as he walked out of the room. His behavior looked pretty convincing to me, but I wasn't the one that he needed to fool.

Gar regained his composure.

"What a good boy." His toe claws tapped along the floor as he walked over to the stool in front of the cage. As soon as he saw the vomit, his cocky attitude shifted back to concern. "The food couldn't have been that bad."

I remained silent, hoping he wouldn't notice the chemical smell.

"Don't be so upset," he muttered, his red eyes glowing brighter before dimming again. "Mortal existence is excruciating, and though you don't realize it now, when I pluck your soul from the circle, you'll praise me for liberating you from this."

"What the hell are you talking about?"

"Our conversation. While you made a tempting offer, it's too much of a risk." He leaned back and folded his arms over his chest. "Do you know why my people exist?"

I shook my head.

"We are duty-bound beings. We exist because we need mortals of different realms to make pacts with us. It is why deva'kohs are a necessary nuisance. In exchange for their minds and souls, they can contract us to do anything their hearts desire. Nothing is off-limits— well, almost nothing. Though you have no choice, you are freeing me from a contract and a torment I cannot escape, and I want to bring you with me to the plains of X'eeva. That is where you will spend your immortal existence, as a Devah alongside me."

I had miscalculated before, but I may have still been able to salvage this.

"That's very generous of you," I said, fear knotting in my throat. "But why would my bargain be a risk?"

Gar sniffed the air and leaned forward. "Because you say one thing, but give off a different scent. There are some upsides to this body, one of them being my ability to determine if someone isn't quite as honest as they pretend to be. A little skill I picked up after a few centuries."

That was a bluff because I knew something he didn't. If he had been able to smell one's honesty, he would have caught Toby in his act right away. He also would have been able to smell his potion in the vomit. Something was wrong with his senses, but this dangerously high-stakes game of mental poker wasn't over yet.

"Fear doesn't necessarily belie my intentions. You locked me in this cage, put the entire room under some kind of spell while also intending to kill me. If this is a test, what did you think the outcome would be? I'm not immortal, so of course I'm scared, and I'm scared for my friends. Sure, you'd give me eternal life in your realm, but what about theirs? They're making a sacrifice as well."

Gar tapped a rhythm on one of the thicker bars of the cell and light arced from his claws. The door clicked and squealed open, but I didn't move from the floor. With the cell door ajar, Gar remained seated on the stool, studying my reaction.

"What you felt in this room," he said, closing his eyes, "is what I feel every day."

Knowing that, there was a small part of me that felt empathy, even though his plans were cold and careless. He wasn't just a demon, he was a person desperate to escape, his mind warped by centuries of being separated from his kind. That was a dangerous emotion. Gar wanted to kill us all to achieve his goal, and I was actually stupid enough to feel sorry for him.

"It doesn't have to be this way," I said, remembering his fear from earlier. Perhaps he would elaborate more on his affliction. "This is a big world, so why not adapt until humanity dies out, as I mentioned earlier?"

"Look at me, Leo," he said, his tone gentler. "In this body, time does not move the same way. A thousand years feels like a thousand years. That deva'koh knew once I took this form, I'd lose the ability to think like a demon. As Atorien, I could see countless paths one could take in life, and I could meticulously alter the fates of many in such a way to set a new course with an outcome only I knew. There was nothing anyone could do to circumvent what I had put into motion. As Gar, I can only think in terms of the present, the past, and the possible future. You couldn't possibly understand the torment of knowing you know everything while also being unable to know it."

"If you could see every outcome, how did you end up like this?"

Gar let out a weary sigh. "The deva'koh knew my X'eevolic name."

"A lot of people know your real name. Even Cole did," I said.

Gar chuckled and shook his head. "Gar, Atorien, those were names given to me, but a X'eevolic name does not easily linger on the tongues of mortals. Those that dare speak it are driven to madness in an instant. That human not only knew my true name, but how to speak it perfectly. The moment I heard it, there was a pang of betrayal. A human could never ward against such power—only another Devah."

"I guess it makes sense why Derrick was so confused by how you ended up here. Are you sure it was another demon?"

"Yes. And the longer I remain here, the longer whoever this was goes unpunished. There are reasons my kind abide by such strict rules. When you mentioned limitless power earlier, I knew you were either lying or completely ignorant. When you circumvent the laws of a given plane of existence, you hasten entropy—oblivion."

"Are you saying that whoever did this is trying to destroy everything?"

Gar swallowed before narrowing the fury in his eyes. "In this form, in this mind, I cannot answer that. I also do not divulge this information lightly, but since you will be dead soon and reincarnated as one of us, I see no harm. This recklessness could undo everything we've been working eons to achieve, and if I have to sacrifice billions of souls and countless worlds to stop it, I will. If I die here, this will happen to others of my realm until we fall. As you can see, I do not have the luxury of a bleeding heart."

This was way worse than I imagined, and part of me wished he had kept it secret. If we destroyed Gar, we'd be sealing our fates anyway.

"How long would it take for everything to end?"

The demon shrugged. "It could be a few decades or a few hundred thousand years." He lifted my chin with his forefinger, and his eyes traveled downward. "Your body has made unusual mutations, and my curse isn't present in you. I can't even sense the others you were traveling with anymore. Your physical appearance almost perfectly mimics the beings I created my curse from."

"So there really is another world with vargyrs?"

"Not vargyrs, but the creatures are somehow tied to humans, though no one knows why that is. Their disease has a fascinating effect on your kind, though." He stood up and turned toward the door.

"One more question before you go," I said, following him out of my cell. It was time for the checkmate, though that may have meant prolonging my torture. "If I don't have the curse, how do you know I'll break the wards?"

He locked up and looked down at the floor. "Just because I am limited in mind doesn't mean I haven't considered this." Gar turned back around. "It will work. Even if you aren't cursed."

"There aren't any wilkyrs anymore, are there?"

He remained silent, but I could feel his anger.

"You assumed I was cursed when you saw me through Vince's eyes, and you knew I'd be back once you bound Cole and Vince's fates together. You got complacent and turned your wilkyrs into full vargyrs, thereby increasing the fear and desperation of the town. Varcross would have maybe a month or two of stability, which was more than enough time to capture me and perform the ritual to expose the wards. What your now limited mind couldn't foresee was the fact that I wasn't cursed at all. Am I right?"

The demon bared his teeth.

"Without your curse, those wards stay up, and without my cure, the town turns feral and Stellous begins its campaign to purge

Varcross. You'll have used up all your magic here, which means no army. They will kill you because you're no longer immortal. Did I leave anything out, Gar?"

"The ritual will continue, and I will find a way."

"You're just being stubborn! Why not do things my way? You've backed yourself into a corner, and once you've exhausted your power, whatever happens—or doesn't happen, will determine your fate and the fate of your realm as well. Your guess is as good as mine at that point."

With a rhythmic click of his snake-like tongue, a bolt of Lo'rim threw me back into the cell, the barred door slamming shut with a deafening clank. My head hit metal, and my vision blurred until all I could see were two red eyes and a shadow.

"You're more dangerous than I thought," he said through his teeth. "I will figure out how to do things my way, but if by some small chance I fail, I'll use you in other ways. I will never allow you free reign in my thoughts, but you will make an excellent ally when I take you to my realm." His voice turned breathless as he ran his tongue along the rows of sharpened teeth. "I want you to spend a little more time sharing my torment." He walked through the door before stopping, not looking back. "It will be a bond we share."

The door gently came to a rest against the frame, and the sentient darkness seized me from all directions once again. What I said was a shot in the dark. Without the curse, the wards could still kill me, and even if they didn't, Gar could kill the others and lock me away. He could drain my blood to keep a couple hundred vargyrs from going feral in order to keep Varcross trading and ignorant until he found a way. Gar may have been limited, but he was still dangerously intelligent. I only hoped that if the others failed, the wards would kill me rather than suffer that fate.

AXEL

"Is it clear yet?" Vince asked for the twentieth time.

"When it's all clear, I'll tell ya," I said, tryin' to keep my voice quiet as I watched the back door of the town hall from my tall tree perch overlooking the buildings. "Now stop talkin' or someone's gonna hear us."

The vargyrs down there were like a bunch of angry hornets, ready to swarm at any moment. There wasn't nowhere I could see that didn't have someone watching close by.

"If the wind shifts, you will all need to run," Derrick whispered from below. "I'll slip into town hall. Hopefully, enough time has passed that no one recognizes me."

"You'd be wrong about that."

The harsh, familiar voice shook me, and my hands lost their grip. The ground came at me fast, and I didn't have time to position myself to land on my feet. With a hard thud, I landed on my side, which knocked a bit of the wind out of me.

"Toby," Vince said in a higher-pitched tone.

"Are you after us, too?" Cole asked.

"Yeah," the older vargyr said, crossing his arms. "Leo sent me to look for you. Have you idiots noticed the breeze has shifted?" His glare settled on me. "I've told you this before, but it bears repeating. You stink."

"You saw Leo?" I asked, feeling a race of relief for the first time in over a day. "Is he okay?"

"He's fine. Gar can't do anything until he's finished prepping the ritual." He started walking toward the woods before looking back. "Let me put this another way. Wind shifted. Vargyrs smell you. Stop standing there like morons!"

We scrambled close behind, Derrick dashing to Toby's side. "It's been too long, Tobias. I rather miss that piss-flavored cider of yours."

"Given your insatiable sexual depravity, it wouldn't surprise me that you would know what piss tastes like." Toby kept his eyes forward, not looking at our packmate. "I have refined the recipe since you've been gone. Added more bitters."

"As if your personality didn't add enough bitterness."

Cole and I looked at each other briefly as the tension between the two got worse.

"I guess you guys know each other pretty well?" I asked, thinkin' I could break the ice a little.

Toby gave me his usual side-eye. "I swear, between you and Leo, it amazes me that people can ask such dumb questions and still manage to walk while breathing at the same time."

Well, so much for breakin' the ice.

"What the hell are you guys doing here, anyway? I would have expected Vince or Axel to be dumb enough to charge head-first into town, but it's surprising to see you so eager to lead them, Derrick." He turned to get a better look at Cole. "I'm glad you're well."

"Thanks," Cole replied warmly. "Leo's blood cures the curse."

"I know. He tricked me into biting him." Toby shook his head. "After nearly a thousand years, the cure is right here, and Gar's going to destroy it."

"That's why we're here," Derrick said. "We need a map, and if you were with Leo, I'm guessing Gar still believes you're under his control."

"Brilliant deduction."

"This means you are likely to have access to areas Gar frequents. Perhaps you could search for an enchanted map among his possessions?"

"Absolutely not."

Derrick frowned. "Are you really going to continue this?"

"Do you have any idea how risky it is to return to him now? It was hard enough not giving away my awareness in the brief conversation I had with him before leaving. If I get caught, what use is any of this?" He reached into his pocket and grabbed the necklace he wore when escorted us. "He won't even let me return until I've *found* this, which I told him I lost."

Derrick looked down, letting out his usual hum of curiosity. "I didn't see it that well when it was around your neck." He snatched the item away. "Zelab," he said to himself. "You didn't wear this while you were talking to Leo, did you?"

"Did you not see me pull the thing from my pocket? I know what a nox-cirqet does."

Derrick smirked. "I see. I didn't expect a second-level mage to understand this tool. You must have been quite the studious custodian."

Toby clenched his fists while clearing his throat, but for the first time, he didn't have an insult ready.

"You don't actually know what this does, do you?" Derrick asked. Again, Toby didn't say nothin', and Derrick slapped the old vargyr's back. "Admitting when we're ignorant is a sign of intelligence. Maybe if you did that, I'd have a higher opinion of you."

"And any of your opinions are about as useful to me as a fistful of hyukan dung." He looked away. "I know enough about what it does, but not how it works. That's important enough."

"What does this do? Is it just for communication?" Cole asked, forcing his way into the argument.

"It is a lot more than that. They convey human—or vargyr—thoughts and senses as if the demon were living through the connected person. If his mind were that of an ordinary mortal, the intense pain of experiencing duality would be too much for him to bear."

Toby's eyes widened. "If that's the case, Gar knows I'm aware. He knows I lied about losing the necklace. Why would he let me go?"

"Relax," Derrick said. "He may not be an ordinary mortal, but he's still mortal in this realm. It's not on all the time, and these devices are activated when the wearer wishes to communicate. I'm not surprised Gar was able to get his hands on one, considering how often he and Josiah stay in contact with one another. The mage likely has generations' worth of forbidden trinkets squirreled away in hidden caches." He stroked his chin. "I wonder."

"What?" Toby asked.

"Demons do not use these because in order for it to work, they must willingly allow a part of themselves to be compromised. Even if they were designed solely for communication, these *nox-cirqets* are human-made without the intricacies of X'eevolic runecrafters embedding fail safes into their designs. There could be a weakness to exploit here, considering he can't take back the connection he has with this rune unless it is returned to him."

Toby stopped and opened his mouth, his expression turning to excitement, but he didn't say anything. Instead, he looked up at the sky and smiled.

"You know something," Derrick prodded.

"I know now why Gar was so terrified when I told him I lost it. It was only for a moment, but he lost his composure. It seems you have the ability to scare demons just as much as lovers."

Cole and I looked at one another again, and this time we started puttin' the pieces together.

Derrick rubbed his temples, ignoring Toby's jab. "We need more information, but unless we get it willingly from Gar, we'll have to proceed with what we were doing."

"Which was?"

"A map, Tobias. We need a map." He held up the tanzonium rod he carried. "We need to find the source of Gar's magic, and we don't have time to make guesses."

"What is that?"

"A tool for finding the source."

Toby rolled his eyes and turned away, but stopped when Derrick began to speak in a mocking tone.

"Curious. When I was gone, did you ever find a mate?"

"I don't want a mate," Toby growled.

"Of course. That's the reason," Derrick said sarcastically.

"You're not exactly a catch yourself. It's no wonder you and Xavier got along so well. He was the only one crazy enough to fuck you willingly."

Things between the two got heated again, but I'd never seen Cole and Vince more entertained, both of them staring at the two, eagerly waiting for the other to hurl another insult.

"I wonder, Tobias. When you're not at the dungeon, do you still enjoy your unfulfilling nights in bed alone with a full stein and a greased-up crank handle?"

"Damn," Vince whispered to Cole.

"Okay, I can't deal with this no more," I said, stepping between the two of them. "I don't know what this is between you two, but I ain't in the mood to hear it. Everyone's ass is on the line if we don't get this done soon, and if Derrick says we need a map, then we need a map." I turned to Toby. "So go get us a damn map."

He growled at me, but I didn't care. He was always hard-headed, but he didn't have a leg to stand on when it came to arguing my point.

"Fine," he muttered, turning back toward town. "But going back to Gar is out of the question. Where exactly were you hoping to find a map back there?"

"Town hall," Derrick replied. "There's an old archive in the basement that I've looked through a few times many years ago. There were hand-drawn maps on worn parchment down there among the records. They're likely not enchanted anymore, but if they hadn't been taken, they will at least have landmarks on them we can use."

Toby turned away and started back toward town. "You all stay here, but keep your eyes open. Some of them may have picked up on your scents."

Derrick looked a little more shaken up than he let on, his hackles raised like he was preparin' to fight. That didn't seem like something he would have done before, but Toby did insult his dead mate.

"What's the history here?" I asked. "You two hate each other?"

The older vargyr quickly calmed down, shaking his head.

"I never hated Toby, but he hated me for a long time. It was odd considering how close we were the first few years after I arrived in Varcross. After I met Xavier and fell in love, that was when things soured. He had a lot of prejudice against deva'kohs, like many other mages of Stellous. Perhaps I was filthy by association."

"I often forget he was a mage," Cole said. "He doesn't talk like one."

"I don't know much about his history of magic, only what he told me when we were friends. He left the athenaeum years before I got there, and since he wasn't a Stellous native or particularly interested in advancing, he took up looking after the lower levels of the tower." Derrick frowned. "When he told me this, I thought he was either lazy or just not smart enough, but what I really think happened was he fully understood the costs and had the common sense to eventually leave it behind. After somehow sneaking away, he took a portal to his town but was soon ambushed by vargyrs."

"He was human-turned?" Cole's eyes widened, and Derrick grew more solemn.

"He's one of the few human-turned in town that hadn't gone feral right after he became a vargyr. He's obviously got one hell of a resilient mind, but that also makes him a major prick."

"Well, hopefully that prick comes through fer us," I said, sitting on the ground against a tree to rest my legs. "I need some shut-eye. Derrick, can you keep watch?"

The older vargyr nodded. "Of course."

"I'm with ya on that," Vince said, curling up next to me.

"I can't wait 'til we're all together again, sleepin' under the stars whenever the mood hits us." Despite saying something so hopeful, all I could feel was hollow. "This'll be the first time in a while he hasn't been next to me sleepin'."

"Don't get used to it," Vince said. "He'll be back, and no one's gonna get a decent night's sleep with you two carryin' on."

Cole sat down on the other side of me. "He didn't leave me to die, and we're not going to leave him."

The two of them wrapped their arms around me, which brought a smile to my face. What a blessing it was to have a family like this.

Nox-Cirqet

LEO

The unnatural darkness of Gar's prison toyed with my perception of time, and the longer I was under its influence, the more of myself seemed to disappear. Perhaps Gar wanted me in a state of catatonic misery as a mercy before the sacrificial ritual. I had expected him to be more ruthless, but the more I thought about his *reward*, the more I wondered what his people were like.

Toby hadn't been back, and I assumed no news was good news. I was impressed with his collectedness in handling such a delicate situation with no time to plan. I hoped he found the others and was able to calm Axel's mind. He had awful anxiety, and I could only imagine how terrible it was for him to worry about me.

Sitting alone like this made me long to be with them. Even in this place, comfort came in remembering the warmth of everyone huddled together on our blanket, and of Axel holding me as I slept. I knew he would pull through one way or another, despite what he may be feeling in my absence.

We hadn't known each other for very long, but I loved him so much it hurt. I often imagined what he looked like as a human. I bet he was just as handsome then as he was as a vargyr, and I wanted more time with him—to do all those things he talked about.

The tears didn't stop, but I didn't feel like I was crying. Seeing Axel's smile in my mind took me to a place I wanted to be. With my eyes squeezed shut, my breath grew steady, and the air cooled, peppered with the scent of trees and wildflowers.

Deep breaths...

A clear mind...

Deep breaths...

My pulse slowed and morphed into a rushing stream after the snow thawed, and when I opened my eyes, the grand majesty of it all lay before me. The blackness was gone, replaced by giant stratovolcanoes and rolling, wavy meadows parted by the cleanest water. The wind tousled the trees as they danced and swayed in the distance.

My body tingled and grew lighter than it had in a while, as though gravity had relaxed enough to let me float from the ground, but something was off. There was an uncomfortable coldness to the air, and though I was formless in this vision, my bare skin pressed against the cool stones of the dungeon floor.

Darkness returned when I opened my eyes, and I ran my smooth smaller fingers over my now human face. The door to the room opened, sending a rush of icy air over me as I hurried back to the blanket, shivering.

"The ritual is proving more difficult—" Gar froze in the doorway, his red eyes piercing me from his blackened silhouette against the light from behind. "No." He rushed into the room and popped the magic seal keeping the cell door locked before kneeling next to me. "This is impossible."

"Obviously not," I said, still shivering. With no fur, what I once perceived as wet warmth was unbearably frigid. Was this it? Was it really over? Being a vargyr was exhilarating and comfortable, but now I was back to being fragile. "I guess it wasn't meant to be."

Gar leaned in closer to study my face.

"You're more upset than I am," Gar whispered.

"I just wanted to be happy for once." I looked into Gar's emotionless eyes, and I finally broke. Being human may have put the kibosh on the ritual for now, but the demon wasn't going to stop until he was free. Even the alternative was terrible. Sure, my life would be spared for now, but what did it matter if all of reality unraveled?

"I keep wanting to hate you, but I'm probably more like you than anyone here," I whispered, turning away. "I'm not interested in being a noble sacrifice or doing anything for the *greater good*, if such a concept really exists. All I care about is what I have left."

Gar pulled away and sat on the floor next to me.

"That was—unexpectedly honest."

"Unexpectedly?"

"Mortals lie," he said, sitting back against the bars of the cage before looking up. "And so do I. I've actually grown to enjoy living among my creations, and that is what terrifies me. My mind has become so weak that I am desperate. Keeping my curse from reaching the terminal state has gone from being a part of my plan to escape to being an assurance that I wouldn't be trapped here all alone if nothing worked. However, a curse is still a curse—uncontrollable and unstoppable, and all I can do was slow its progression."

"Well, it's a good thing my cure is a little more permanent," I said. "Would it really be so bad to remain here with us?"

"You're asking if I would choose exile from my world to live life as a mortal." The more he spoke, the more *human* he seemed. "You're asking if I would choose death."

"You look alive to me."

"Because I am alive, for now. Unlike what you believe, I cannot wait out human civilization, because if I die here—" he took a deep breath, but said nothing more.

"It's permanent, isn't it?"

"When mortals die, they go to the circle to begin life anew. When my kind dies, our essence feeds the ether, and we cease to exist." He stood and offered me his hand. "This unusual turn of events will require me to rethink my plan. You're obviously not completely immune to the lycanthropic disease."

I grabbed his rough hand, and he pulled me to my feet.

"But I am immune to your curse, Gar. If that was the stipulation for breaking the wards, then I'm sorry to break it to you—"

"The curse was just a vessel of Lo'rim you'd carry with you. An 'all-in-one' package so to speak. With enough Lo'rim surrounding you,

I could manage the same effect as the curse—but I have no way of knowing exactly how much would be required." He smiled and pulled me along the corridor, causing me to drop the blanket covering my naked body. "I will have a vargyr infect you with the disease again, and before your body can fight it, I will send you through the wards with every bit of Lo'rim I've collected over the centuries as insurance."

"You think you'll have much left after the ritual? That's reckless," I said, losing my composure again. I had expected Gar's desperation to give me the upper hand, but all it did was push him further into recklessness. "What if you're wrong? What if you don't break the wards, but kill me in the process? You'll lose everything."

"I still have Josiah, and there are bound to be others like you."

"How many trips has he taken to my world?" I asked as we approached a warm room ahead. Gar froze. "How do you know he'll survive the next trip? Derrick told me what that kind of magic costs."

He swallowed hard and continued onward toward the room. Inside was a hearth of fiery crystals, a bed, a desk with alchemical supplies, and a bookshelf with five heavy tomes.

"I'll let you choose who will infect you when I complete the ritual."

"Did you even listen to me?"

Gar pushed me onto the bed before pacing the floor. "You want me to go along with your plan to cure the vargyrs and live among them, giving up any hope of returning home. You called me short-sighted, but you fail to understand the risks to me. I don't have the luxury of time to study you or find another way. It took every bit of knowledge I had to concoct elixirs to stay my curse temporarily, but I've even forgotten that. I am losing the battle with this body, and while your proposition has its merits, I cannot take the gamble. My plan has the best chance of success."

"What about Derrick?"

Gar's eyes flashed red. "All the more reason to finish this now. That mage could undo everything I've worked hard to accomplish."

"Then why didn't you kill him?"

The demon once again seemed to hold back a response, as if ashamed.

"If Derrick is so detrimental to your plan, why did you keep him alive?"

"Because he was under my control. If everything I'd done had failed, he would have been my Josiah on this side. He would have had no choice but to find another way to break the wards or he'd go back to being a monster. That in itself was a huge risk, and I only kept him as a last resort."

"Do you really not feel anything for us?" I asked, trying to capitalize again on his moment of vulnerability. "You've had how many lifetimes of pleasure and happiness? All I want is this. Even if you are mortal now, vargyrs live a long time."

"I know your past, Leo. I'm offering you eternal pleasure. You'd be willing to give that up for a mediocre existence in a magicless world with Axel?"

"You'd understand if you would embrace it," I said softly, draping myself in the blanket on the bed. "I can't explain it to someone who's never felt it before."

"Likewise," Gar muttered as he stepped out into the stone corridor. "I also cannot explain eternity to someone who has only ever known weakness. When I pluck your soul from the circle, you will thank me."

"I don't want that future!" I shouted, fur sprouting from my skin.

Gar turned back in amazement, stepping closer to me as my transformation continued. It seemed I wasn't human after all, and while the thought was a relief, it was short-lived.

"Amazing." He knelt in front of me as my body finished the transformation. There was no pain, and the shift was unnaturally quick. Could I actually control what form I was in? "How did you do that?"

"I don't know," I lied, looking up at Gar. "Perhaps I require more study."

The demon gently lifted my head with his fingers, rubbing my maw with his thumb. "I—no."

For a brief moment, it almost seemed like he considered it.

"Look at me! I'm not normal. There's a chance I won't even be able to break the wards. You have the time. It's not like you're going to lose your mind in a couple days."

"Josiah's experiments were conclusive."

"What if Josiah is deceiving you?" I asked, noting his eyes shifting and tail lowering. "What if he chose me specifically because I *couldn't* break the wards?" In a final attempt to sway him, I gambled dangerous knowledge. "I know you can, though. So does Derrick. So did Josiah. It was written in the book Xavier stole from you."

He clenched his teeth and swallowed hard. "You expect me to trust you now? This whole time..." He paused, his voice growing tired as he turned to leave. "I'll take the chance. If you don't break the wards, I will find another way. I rescind my offer of bringing you into our fold."

"This is irrational!"

He looked back, slumping forward as if in defeat.

"This is what must be done."

AXEL

"Honestly, Tobias. The storage shed behind *your* bar?" Derrick stomped ahead of us, Toby trailing close behind while balling his fists.

"There is no *source* in that shack, you imbecile. I knew I should have drawn the points."

Derrick raised his right hand and waved dismissively. "It's simple trigonometry, not theoretical arcane mechanics. You can't mess up lines and angles, you old fool. That source must be in there. Don't you use that storage shed as a place for your stills?"

Both of them stared at one another, their hackles stickin' straight. Toby seemed to bring out the worst in Derrick, but he could bring out the worst in anyone. Cole and Vince couldn't get enough of their bickering though.

"Yes, I do," his voice grew louder, "which is why I'm telling you there is no source! I'd have noticed a giant hunk of tanzonium in the middle of the damn room. In fact, if this source does what you say, that shack wouldn't be nearly big enough to hold it, you impetuous brat."

The two went silent while Derrick continued to lead the way, slowing his pace before coming to a stop at a large tree. He closed his eyes and took in a deep breath before grabbing Vince and turning him around.

"Hey," Vince growled. "Just 'cuz yer all bigger than me doesn't mean you get to jerk me around."

Derrick ignored him and pulled the map out of the backpack Vince was still wearing.

Toby smirked and crossed his arms. "Double checking your work?"

Derrick tried to ignore him, but after studying the map, he folded it calmly, spun Vince around again and stuffed it back into the bag.

Vince snarled. "I swear, I'm gonna bite."

Derrick leaned back against the tree with a slight weariness about him. "What happened to us? We were the closest of friends."

"The fact that you even have to ask that pisses me off more. You were clueless back then just as you are now," Toby replied.

"My calculations are flawless and always have been. The source is in that storage shed...somehow."

"This is the hill you really intend to die on, isn't it?" Toby grabbed Vince, and spun him around to get to the backpack, but Vince snapped at him. Toby slapped him across the nose. "You bite me, boy, and you'll be eating all your food prechewed for a week."

Vince's ears lowered as Toby unfolded the map, examining the marks.

"You honestly believe I made a mistake?" Derrick asked.

Toby scanned each point again and again. "This doesn't make any sense."

"What if it's not above ground?" Cole asked, looking over Toby's shoulder.

"That—" Toby paused to consider it. "That would make a lot more sense."

"So there's a cellar in the shed," Derrick said, folding his arms. "Again I asked: really, Tobias?"

"Do you think I'm both stupid *and* blind?" The older vargyr bared his teeth. "I'd have noticed a cellar."

"Look at the map. It's there," Derrick prodded. "I don't know much about Varcross, but I do know magic sources. My mind may not be as sharp as it once was, but I am doing my best. I just want to save Leo and our world."

Toby's bushy, angry eyebrows softened.

"Fine." He held the map up again. "I've been in Varcross long enough to know the ins and outs. The only place I know of that has a cellar is town hall, and I was just there to get that map."

"What's this?" Reaching over Toby's arm, I pointed to a shaded squiggle over three of the buildings, passing over the shed. "You think this is something?"

"It looks like a stain," Derrick said, him and Toby taking a closer look. "This map is hundreds of years old. There are bound to be some imperfections."

Toby squinted and moved the map closer to this face.

"Perhaps it deserves more scrutiny," he said, shoving Vince off to the side before turnin' him around.

"Just take the damn thing," Vince shouted, shoving the bag into Toby's arms.

The older vargyr pulled out an intricate magnifying glass interlaced with golden symbols. The glass was tinted a greenish color, and the handle looked like that tanzonium metal on the rod we was usin'.

Derrick shot the old vargyr a judgmental stare.

"What? It looked fancy, and it's not like anyone was using it." He carried it into the sunlight and examined it closer. "Well damn."

"See something?" Derrick asked.

"Look at this." He handed over the map and magnifying glass. "I guess there was a reason this was in close proximity."

The other vargyr looked through the glass and grinned. "This is an enchanted map after all. I knew the original settlers had to have brought them."

"Put the glass over town hall," Toby said.

Derrick did as he said, while at the same time tracing his clawed finger over somethin' I couldn't see. "This goes everywhere, and there are several arteries that lead outside of town."

"That's kind of overkill, don't you think?" Cole remarked. "If they just needed a place for the source, they could have just made one underground location."

"I understand now why I got the town's magic infrastructure confused with the ancient conduit design. In text, Varcross's description was hundreds of years older than the curse. These were not part of the town's original design," Derrick said. "Everything you see under this glass is updating in real time as the tanzonium handle absorbs the faintest traces of magic that seep up through the ground while the glass reacts with the deritium dust in the parchment. It's redrawing the map based on what has changed since it was last activated. These tunnels were likely designed by Gar with the help of the first vargyrs centuries ago who have long since turned feral. It's the reason only Gar knows where the source is."

"So I was right about the smudge," I said, feelin' proud of myself again.

"Actually...that was just a stain," Derrick said, patting me on the back.

"Oh."

"Don't pout," Toby grumbled, dragging the glass over more sections of the map. "You had the right idea, which was more productive than our bickering."

A huge shadow crept along the ground, and we all looked up at a sharp sliver of blackness that parted the sky, growing wider. It was like someone sliced into the atmosphere, leaving nothin' but a starry void.

"He started the ritual early," Derrick said. "Have you found anything else, Toby?"

The older vargyr held up his hand, still following the lines snaking across the map.

"How long do you think we have?" Cole asked.

"It can take several hours or days to pull the wards into this realm. We have until the sky turns completely black."

Toby lifted his head and pointed to the north. "If this thing is actually correct, there's an entrance to the tunnels at the far end of town, where the wilkyrs lived."

"I'll search for it," Derrick said, reaching for the map, but Toby snatched it away.

"All you'll do is get caught going through town, and then we may as well just hand ourselves to Gar on a silver plate."

"Then what do you suggest? I'm the only one that knows how to dismantle the source...safely."

Toby grabbed the tanzonium rod from Derrick's other hand. "Well, I know how to dismantle it quickly."

"You're going to end up killing yourself while destroying half the town in the process."

Toby grunted. "Think of it as another distraction."

"Toby..." Derrick trailed off.

"We're screwed either way. If this thing isn't destroyed, everyone dies. If there's anyone remaining in that part of town, they're not going to look twice at me. You need to figure out how to hold Gar's attention and avoid dying because he will know what I'm doing the moment he senses my presence near the source."

"If it's gonna kill ya, then there's gotta be another way," I said, looking over at Derrick who seemed a lot more anxious than I thought he'd be.

"I'm not going to kill myself," Toby muttered. "I was working with deritium before Derrick was shitting in diapers. Tanzonium is even more stable than that, end of discussion."

Derrick stepped closer to Toby, reaching for the rod to no avail. "At least let me show you how to cause a chain reaction without making it fully self-destruct right away."

"We want it to self-destruct as quickly as possible," Toby snapped, turning away toward town, but stopped for a moment, standing a little taller. "We had a lot in common back then."

"We did," Derrick agreed. "We still do."

As Derrick opened his mouth to say more, Toby disappeared into the trees.

Something glimmered on the ground where Toby stood earlier, and I reached down to pick it up. "He left this necklace thing."

"I would call him careless, but dropping it on the ground was probably the wisest move."

"Gimme that," Vince said, snatching the chain out of my hand. "I think it would look good on me."

"Don't put that on." Cole slapped Vince on the back of the head. "Did you not hear Derrick earlier?"

"I ain't gonna wear it now, but once Gar bites it, I want a souvenir."

"Make sure I check it first before you do," Derrick added, turning to Vince. "I need you to do something for me."

"What?"

"Run back to your house and grab the spade. After that, I need you to go to the houses around the area and dig up more boxes. We're going to need more of those rods."

"You—you want me to do all that by myself?"

"You broke the other shovel," Cole said. "And you're the fastest."

"The boxes should all be on the right wall as you're facing the front, I think. All of the houses were designed roughly the same way." Derrick looked up at the sky which was growing darker. "This should work, but I want to be the first to try it."

"What are you thinkin'?" I asked, watching as Vince grew more annoyed.

"The plan to destroy the source gave me an idea. Tanzonium pulls and stores magic, but when connected to a conducting rod like the ones outside of the houses, they easily discharge it as well. This prevents the crystal from becoming overloaded and exploding if too much is absorbed and not used, since it wouldn't have time to naturally dissipate. I'm hoping if any Lo'rim is aimed at us, we can use these to redirect it." Derrick rubbed his head. "But I don't know if the crystals could handle the amount of magic he'll likely use, even if they are able to discharge. It could simply be too much, since we'll be practically on top of the source."

"Do you think he'll risk using that much magic?" Cole asked. "He'll already be using a ton to pull the wards into this realm."

"Never discount one's desperation. We've seen Gar make an unusual amount of irrational decisions, and I won't disregard that this time," Derrick replied.

"I'll go get them rods," Vince said, sounding a little more agreeable before sprinting off toward home.

"Alright," I said. "We've got eggs in two baskets, but I don't know if that's gonna be enough. If these things don't work, I ain't gonna be able to distract him for long before that magic has me on the ground. Plus, we gotta get that car close to where Gar is without him knowin' what we're doin'."

Derrick rubbed his chin before sitting on the ground under one of the trees close by. "I need rest." He leaned back and stretched. "I thought we'd have more time, but Gar rightly fears us."

"Well yeah. We know how to kill him, and he probably knows it by now," Cole said.

"Maybe." Derrick closed his eyes and went silent. Cole and I waited for him to say something until he started to snore.

"Poor guy," Cole said, turning to me. "When's the last time he slept?"

"It's been about two days," I said, giving him a smile. "You and I ain't had a chance to talk much. You been okay?"

Cole nodded. "Yeah. I haven't really come to terms with this new body yet, but I'm getting used to it."

"Miss bein' a wilkyr?"

"I miss being smaller." Cole looked down at his hands. "I miss being held."

"Vince is still gonna hold ya. I mean, when you guys first met, he was shorter than you."

"Yeah, but he was stronger. He could toss me around and hold me against him at night. He won't be able to do that anymore, and I don't like being this big."

"I was wonderin' why you was acting different. I didn't know this was bothering you so much. Never knew what it was like to be held like that. I've always been the one doin' the holding."

Cole looked up at the sky. "I hope Vince gets back soon."

"You guys'll figure somethin' out. Vince is still a pretty dominant guy; he just feels intimidated. Maybe try being more submissive around him and see what happens. It's a new vargyr thing you gotta get used to."

Cole let out a snort. "I want him to be rough with me again, like he was before he turned. Ever since that day, he's been too afraid."

"Leo's violent," I said, blurtin' that out without thinking.

"What?"

"When we mated, he got violent."

"You guys—" Cole's eyes lit up. "You guys actually did it? Did you enjoy it?"

"It was the best I ever had." I could feel myself getting hot under the fur. "We only did it once, though. He went full howler and tore my ass up. Never been more turned on in my life. We wrestled each other for dominance."

"Damn." He leaned back against the tree and folded his arms. "That's hot. Finally found someone who can dish it out, huh?"

"He's like me in a lot of ways, just smarter. I don't think I'll ever meet anyone else who gets me like he does."

"We're not going to lose him," Cole said, glancing down at a sleeping Derrick. "But we do need something more concrete than guesses. We're also going to need to confront Gar before Toby gets to the source. There's going to be traps everywhere down there."

"If he knows Toby's going fer the source, he's gonna activate all of 'em."

"That's why we need more distractions. Three of us dodging Lo'rim bolts while trying to get to Leo won't cut it. It might distract him enough from trapping Toby completely, but Gar's got supernatural concentration. He's on a different level than any one of us."

"Thinkin' about it makes me want to throw up," I said, holding my stomach. It wasn't just words. I'd never been more scared in my life. "If we screw this up—"

"Let's trust in Derrick's plan for now and hope for the best."

✺

We let Derrick sleep while waiting but became more alert when quick, shallow footsteps rustled closer. Vince sprinted along the path carrying six tanzonium rods in his arms.

"Why'd you get so many?" I asked. "You know we don't have a lot of time, right?"

"I figured the more of these things we have, the better. I ain't taking any damn chances." His foot nudged Derrick's knee. "I'm back."

Derrick snorted, shaking away the surprise.

"How long has it been?" He glanced up at the sky and sighed in relief.

"Not too long," Cole said, grabbing one rod from Vince. "How are we going to use these against Gar?"

"Well, we can't really use them *against* him, but if I'm right, we should be able to deflect his magic. The problem is, if Gar sends a fully charged attack at one of us, it will overload these since they're not designed to draw in so much at once."

"We're also forgetting something kind of important here," Cole said. "Gar's not going to be our only concern."

Derrick sighed. "We're not going to have the stamina to fight off the other vargyrs while also avoiding Gar. I'm not going to sugarcoat this; we're going to need some luck the moment Toby starts to dismantle the source."

"What if Gar traps him?" I asked.

"Traps would have been more of a concern for me, but he still believes Toby is under his control. The problem is, we have no way of knowing when Toby starts to destroy the source. Gar will definitely know what's going on the moment that happens."

"Well, shit," Vince hissed. "What are we gonna do, guess? Roll the dice? That's fuckin' stupid!"

"We ain't gonna have a choice but to try and hold Gar and the other vargyrs off for as long as it takes." I gritted my teeth. "You know what they say: a wild animal is more dangerous when you've got him cornered. We ain't even been at our full strength, and wolves ain't strong by themselves. Same is true fer us. We're a pack, and Gar's gonna have us cornered. We ain't gonna just roll over."

"Wait a minute." Vince pulled out the necklace he had in his pocket earlier. "You said this thing lets Gar hear thoughts, right?"

"It goes both ways, Vince. That's a very dangerous relic," Derrick said.

"It's still pretty fuckin' distracting, don't you think?"

"Vince that..." Derrick rubbed his chin. "That's actually not a bad idea."

"Of course it ain't," Vince said, cocking a half smile. "It's common sense."

"The nox-cirqet is a permanent line of communication to the demon's thoughts. Everything—emotions, feelings, physical pain—it all gets channeled to him if the wearer wills it. If Vince wears this mid-battle, the level of distraction goes up exponentially, and he will not have the ability to stop Toby. It may also hinder his ability to tap into the rhythm of Lo'rim to cast more powerful spells."

"That's dangerous though," Cole said. "The moment Vince puts it on, he's exposed. Gar will be able to predict every move he makes."

"Then we'll need to use it as a last resort." Derrick stood and stretched. "It's another tool in our arsenal, and it greatly improves our chances." He reached for Vince's hand, and ran his fingers over the rune. He then grabbed one of the rods Vince had placed on the ground earlier. "It needs to be unlocked if we're to use it in any detrimental way."

Derrick tapped out a rhythm on the tanzonium part of the rod.

"How the hell do you already know how to do that so seamlessly?" Cole asked.

Derrick smiled before defiantly shoving the rod into the ground, maintaining the rhythm. The crystal at the top glowed dimly at first, but soon brightened, turning all different colors. "Hand me the relic, Vince."

Vince dangled the necklace in front of Derrick, and the older vargyr clasped it tight, the beat of his fingers against the rod shifting as the crystal changed colors again.

"You really are an archmage," Cole said in amazement while watching Derrick's eyes pulse bright green with the rhythm.

"What is he doin'?" Vince asked.

"He's casting a spell to unlock the rune using rhythms instead of an incantation. He's unlocking the device, which means the moment it goes around anyone's neck, Gar will be inundated with that person's thoughts and emotions with no way to shut it down."

The necklace hummed in Derrick's left hand as he continued tapping with the other. When the rhythm slowed to a stop, Derrick opened his palm, revealing a pale, glowing rune. He handed it back to Vince.

"Remember, this is a last resort. If we become overwhelmed, I'll need you to put it on and hurl as many of those vulgar insults as only you can do."

"Ain't...nobody ever wanted me to do that before," Vince said gleefully as he shoved the amulet in his pocket.

"Let's go," I said, looking up at the sky, which was getting blacker by the minute. "We got a demon to kill."

Strength In The Pack

LEO

A sliver of light split the sky, and a death-like chill rushed over the town from the giant hole Gar had carved into the air using the crystal end of his staff. It looked like he had torn into a canvas, our reality rippling off to the sides, letting more of the void seep into the realm. The vargyrs watched on, some of them shaken by what they were witnessing. Deep down, they knew something wasn't right, but like Gar, they felt they had no other choice.

My arms and legs were bound to a metal post jammed into the ground, so close to the tear the vacuum pulled on me. The more I struggled, the tighter my bonds became until I could no longer move. All I could do was cry out for Axel as the final grains of sand in the hourglass of my life poured into oblivion.

No one cheered or threw things anymore as my cries reached them. Many shook their heads, their ears and tails low, the body language of distress. Even Gar, as heartless as he seemed, couldn't stop averting his gaze.

"Stop," Gar demanded, pulling his attention from his ritual to me. He had been drawing a strange light from the ground, and it wrapped like a serpent around his staff while also undulating over his arms and hands. "I promise you will not feel any pain."

"I don't want to die."

He placed a hand on my shoulder. "No mortal wishes for death because you cannot know what waits beyond. That fear of the unknown is instinct, but while in this shell, you cannot see the wonders. Don't think of it as dying. You're simply shedding a heavy coat in the summer heat."

"Gar," a familiar voice called out from the crowd. It was the vargyr who pointed the way to the dungeon on my first day in town. "This feels wrong."

"Ignore it, Mikael," Gar said, pointing at the smaller vargyr. "Do you realize that once the wards are down, you'll all have access to humans? There's hope for the ferals as well."

The vargyr's eyes widened before they wandered to the ground. "Killing an innocent to avoid our fate will mean a lifetime of guilt. And Leo had a point. What happens when we get over there? We'll be spreading misery again, and the relief we get will be temporary. We won't be free."

A shadowy figure with glowing red eyes maneuvered behind another vargyr close to Mikael while everyone else's attention was on Gar.

"There is no other option. We are losing more of the town to the curse." Gar gave a slight nod, and the figure jabbed something into the vargyr's arm before vanishing into the crowd. "Without access to wilkyrs, you will become mindless beasts. The mages will finish what they started, knowing everyone here is at a disadvantage. Do you want to be culled while you're unable to defend yourselves, or do you want to fight?"

The other vargyr howled, collapsing to the ground. The crowd put distance between themselves and the suffering beast, now writhing in the dirt. In moments, his eyes faded to red, and he 'stood' on his hands and feet like a wolf.

"Restrain him," Gar shouted. The vargyrs under his command surrounded the feral, securing him in a collar and metal chains. He snarled and whined, no longer able to form words. "Bring him to me."

They did as he commanded, and Gar looked out to the horrified crowd, many of whom had never witnessed this stage of the curse.

"Look at him. This will happen to all of you, and anyone could be next. It's a fate worse than death. Even if the mages don't cull you, imagine living for thousands of years trapped in a body you can't control. Your sentient mind will still be intact, but you can do nothing but watch on as the curse reaches its finale. You won't lose your minds; you will be imprisoned in them."

I tried to scream a warning, but as I moved my mouth, no words came out. The crowd clamored, and Gar leaned in close.

"No," he whispered. "This sacrifice is noble, Leo. If you truly care for them, then when you join me in X'eeva, gather their souls."

My salvation was right there, feet away, and I could do nothing. Gar turned back to the crowd and held up his staff while signaling for other vargyrs to come take the feral away.

"If anyone else wishes to voice concern, do so now." He gave Mikael a sympathetic look. "Are you still against this?"

The vargyr looked at me and let out a weeping whine, tears soaking the fur on his face. He bowed his head and stepped back.

"Then I shall continue," Gar said, turning to the void tear while holding the staff to the sky. Painfully cold wind raced from the hole like angry bees as the rip in our plane grew wider. Whatever light was left in the sky was gone, and the ground rumbled as massive, black obelisks slowly emerged, each perhaps two hundred feet or more in height and thicker than some of the smaller buildings in town. Both of them tapered to a point at the tops and bottoms, hovering a few feet above the ground. One by one, invisible runic symbols burst into violet light traveling up the spines of the pillars. "It worked," Gar whispered in relief.

"Demon!"

Vince? I turned toward the direction of the voice as a small brown vargyr rushed toward me holding what appeared to be some kind of crystal scepter.

"I was wondering when you'd finally turn up," Gar said, pointing his staff at Vince. "There's still plenty of magic left to deal with all of you." White light arced from the top, barely missing him as the smaller vargyr zipped in and out of the trees.

"Leo is the cure," Cole shouted from behind the crowd, catching the attention of several red-eyed vargyrs. "If he dies, you all die!" Before he could get away, they were upon him, throwing him to the ground. Lo'rim slithered in jagged lines along the dirt and gravel with Cole the main target, but Axel barreled in and threw him out of the way before it exploded upward, throwing a couple of the vargyrs into buildings. Now that they confronted Gar, he was even more dangerous. The vulnerable emotional state he was in moments earlier vanished as much colder demeanor took over.

Using the scepter he carried, Axel knocked one of the vargyrs unconscious, his limp body falling to the ground.

"You will die," Gar said calmly, pointing his staff at the huge vargyr; however, the light made a sharp turn, hitting Vince who had emerged from the trees for a second. He flew backward, his back and head striking one of the trunks hard.

There was no hiding from his magic, and Vince looked really injured. What were they doing? If just running at a demon was their only plan, they should have just left me.

"Leo," came a hushed voice from behind one of the wards. While I couldn't quite make out what he was doing, I could hear a faint rhythm tapping against the metal. Gar jerked toward the obelisk, but before he could react, violet lightning branched from Derrick, hitting Gar in the center of his chest. The demon fell backward, and Derrick ran to me, pressing the crystal end of his scepter into the bonds until the Lo'rim swirled into it, disappearing. "Run! The car is just west of the town near the tavern."

Light crackled through the ground, and Derrick pushed me out of the way, shoving the rod into the dirt as the light began to swell; however, instead of exploding, it rushed up the rod and into the crystal. An entire spectrum of colors burst from the once dull rod, and what sounded like cracking glass had Gar jumping for cover as Derrick pointed the rod at him. It exploded with such force that it threw Derrick and me several yards away.

"What just happened?" I asked, jumping to my feet.

"Get the car, please! Axel can't hold them off by himself. The rest of the town looks to be taking cover. Now's your chance."

I nodded and took off running toward the woods before Gar noticed what was happening.

"After him! Leave the others. I'll take care of them," the demon shouted.

Derrick tapped the end of the scepter, drawing light from the ground once again, forming a barrier between me and the rest.

"Hurry," he shouted. "I'm not strong enough to hold this."

TOBY

The once vibrant wilkyr longhouses now looked like three empty coffins in the unnatural twilight. I felt terrible knowing what Gar had done to them, but none of it would matter if we managed to pull through. It wouldn't matter if we lost either. This chapter of our lives was at an end.

I checked the map once more before looking around for any kind of entrance underground. Vargyrs were never allowed to stay long in this part of town for obvious reasons, but in all that time, no one had ever mentioned something like this. It must have been very well hidden.

A gravel path weaved along the abodes, circling a purple tree at the center, its massive branches providing shade from the slice of sunlight that had remained in the sky. I double checked the landmarks and knew this had to be the place.

One by one, I searched, kicking in doors, pulling up rugs, moving beds and sofas for any way down. The floors were solid, not making much noise as I stomped over them while listening for any hollow thuds. At first I was annoyed by the lack of progress, but as the darkness swallowed the last of the daylight, the countdown began.

The stars and distant galaxies were so vivid, as though our atmosphere had been ripped away. It was much colder now, my breath visible in the dim stellar light. A bright explosion lit the center of town in the distance followed by a deafening shockwave that nearly knocked me off my feet, shattering every window. The showdown had begun, and I was still at square one. Failure wasn't an option.

I wasn't half the mage Derrick was, and I knew he would have found his way to the source by now, but he wouldn't have gotten far into the tunnel before triggering something deadly. The demon had tendrils of Lo'rim everywhere, the entire town now likely an extension of his body. Nothing could slip by, but I could—at least until I got to the source.

Fueled by something much heavier than pride, I ran back and forth, retracing my steps. Now that it was much darker, everything looked different. The tanzonium rod in my hand began to brighten the closer I got to the trunk of the strange huge tree in the center of the village and dimmed when I walked away from it.

With the rod glowing brighter, I approached, touching the smooth bark with the crystal end. Part of it disappeared as though the entire thing was an illusion, but it would come back the moment I pulled away. The tiny chunk of tanzonium couldn't absorb the mirage fast enough before the trunk reappeared. Even though it wasn't real, the tree itself was quite real to me and anyone who would have passed by. When I tried to walk into it, my head hit solid matter.

I had an idea, but the sound of another explosion caught my attention as a rainbow of light shot up to the sky from the town. With the tapered end of the rod facing the trunk, I used all of my strength to jam it into one of the gnarled knot holes. The tanzonium crystal brightened as it sucked the magic away like a straw. As the tree disappeared, the rod fell to the ground.

The entrance that appeared was a hole so black I couldn't see the bottom. Using the now charged crystal rod as a torch, I stuck it into the hole and peered inside. The bottom wasn't too far down, and without wasting another second, I jumped in and followed the tunnel system, using the map as my guide.

VINCE

The pain took my breath away. That bastard hit me a lot harder than I expected, but I'd be damned if the rod didn't save my life. Derrick may have been an annoying egghead sometimes, but he sure came in clutch with his brilliant ideas. Even though I was pretty banged up, I kept hold of the rod and stumbled to my feet. Gar was preoccupied with the others to notice me limpin' away so I could hide behind one of the trees and wait for my body to heal. My abdomen was bleeding, but the wound wasn't nearly as bad as it could have been. I'd be fine in a minute or two, and I wasn't gonna let him catch me off guard again.

Derrick had managed to get Leo free, but it didn't take long before that barrier went down and twenty or so of them red-eyes were after him. The rest of the town didn't know what the hell was happening. Most of 'em scattered, trying to avoid the explosions, and the others looked torn between helping Cole or running after Leo to catch him. They still didn't understand what that guy could do, and they probably weren't in the right mind to listen to reason either. It didn't matter. The barrier was keeping those guys back, and Leo was really the only one that could drive that death trap he called a car. Axel could handle the few loyalists that remained to fight, even though Gar was looking at him as the next target.

The demon held his staff up, and I didn't have time to wait for my pain to go away. Axel was my brother, and it was my turn to protect him for a change. I pushed myself faster, swinging the rod at Gar's head before diving into the trees again.

I wasn't stupid. The best strategy I had was the *hit-and-hide*, even though he managed to duck out of the way in time. If he tried to aim again, I'd come at him from a different angle.

Derrick grabbed another rod from Leo's backpack, since the one he had earlier overloaded. I knew we'd need more. There wasn't a doubt in my mind that Derrick was right about being able to deflect his spells. We owed that guy everything, and if we got out of this, I'd make sure to repay him. Him and Leo both kept me from givin' up everything after I thought Cole was gone for good.

Dammit, I wasn't paying attention. Another light flashed from Gar's staff and angled toward me. Even though I was hidden, he knew exactly where I was. There wasn't time to dodge it, so I held up the staff just in time for the light to reach me. Instead of hitting my chest, it bent toward the crystal before discharging into the ground. This one wasn't as strong as the last one he sent at me.

"Clever, Derrick," Gar said with a snarl. Derrick held up the rod, expecting Gar to hit him with another beam, but the ground swelled out of sight near his feet.

"Derrick, behind you!" I shouted.

A force shot through my shoulder, throwing me back before another explosion rocked the town, blinding us. After my vision cleared, my heart sank as Derrick stumbled around, barely able to stand. His arm was twisted and broken, and the rod he held earlier had shattered. Light wrapped around his legs before engulfing his entire body, but he stood defiantly as Gar stepped closer. Axel threw another vargyr off of him before lunging at the demon, but that weird magic shot up from under the ground, spearing Axel through the chest.

"No! Damn you!"

My screams came out as an involuntary reaction as my best friend slumped forward, blood pouring from his mouth. Light appeared out of the corner of my eye, but I dodged it in time, dashing toward a building close by. There was a feral vargyr chained to a tree, left alone while cowering, trying desperately to run away from all the commotion and explosions.

I wanted to untie him so he could run, but I couldn't risk taking another bolt. Where was Cole? Did something happen to him too?

"I don't know what to do," I whimpered out as I watched us fall one-by-one. It was up to Toby and Leo now, but without a distraction, they weren't gonna make it.

Barely twenty minutes into the battle, and we couldn't even keep him distracted. I pulled out the necklace and held it in my hand. Sure felt braver earlier when I volunteered to do this, but now I was shakin' so bad I nearly dropped it. Still, I had to, and once I did, I really wouldn't be able to hide from him no more. Maybe if I could distract him enough, I could buy Toby and Leo a little more time.

"I love you, Cole," I whispered, about to fasten the chain around my neck, but I stopped when I looked at that feral again.

That's when I got an idea. If I put this thing around my neck, Gar would be distracted with my thoughts, but what would happen if he got a dose of whatever was racin' through that feral's mind? When I stepped out from behind the building, Gar saw me immediately. Another bolt arced in my direction and I had to duck back behind the wall.

"Toby, damn you," Gar shouted, sending a stream of light into the ground.

He'd figured it out.

I primed myself to go back while he was distracted, but that was when Cole tore from the trees and lunged at him, wrapping his arms tightly around Gar's arms and chest.

"Release me!"

"Not until your dead body goes limp in my arms," he screamed, squeezing tighter. Gar's bones popped under the strain. "Go ahead. Try to use magic with no hands. I know your game."

Nothing happened. Gar gasped for air, and wispy light wiggled up from the ground around him, struggling to take form.

"My game, huh?" Gar said harshly, clickin' his snake-like tongue.

The light took shape and sprouted like vines. I tried to run out again, but one of them shot at me, pinning me to the wall, but when the ground shook, I knew Toby succeeded.

The magic pulled away from Gar, and he stepped back from a strugglin' Cole. His staff levitated, allowing the demon to grab hold before aiming at the ground again, but an angry noise revved into town, and a pair of lights, as bright as the sun, caused him to redirect his magic. The Lo'rim fired into the car, causing it to stop right before it could ram into him. It was enough for the magic pinning me to the building to fade away.

LEO

"Shit!" I screamed, throwing open the door before leaping out as another jagged bolt caused the car to nearly catch fire. I managed to think those pleasant thoughts earlier to get back into my human form in order to fit behind the wheel, but survival instinct brought the vargyr back out mid-dodge. One more hit would probably cause the car to explode. This was a failure. Without it running, there was no way to push Gar into the wards.

As I waited for the next shot of Lo'rim, screams tore from Gar's direction, and I shot up in time to see the demon holding his head while mumbling incoherently.

"That's right fucker," Vince shouted, standing next to the feral from earlier, Toby's silver chain hanging from its neck. "I may not be wearin' it, but I'm still gonna call you a cunt-faced son of a whore!"

Vince continued a barrage of insults before a shockwave cracked through the air, the force of an intense blast sending sections of buildings flying in every direction. The light binding Cole and Derrick shattered, and they fell to the ground as a giant white vortex whirled in the distance, coming from the center of town.

A strong arm pulled me away from the car, and I turned toward a smiling Axel. Blood soaked his chest, but he was able to stand upright, shrugging off the pain.

"We're done sufferin'," Axel said, slowly walking toward the vehicle as Gar continued gripping his head in agony, stumbling back toward the void he'd ripped into existence. "You ain't strong."

As the magic vortex spread outward, it narrowed into a white ribbon, funneling itself into Gar.

"Strong?" Gar shouted, the air vibrating around us as his voice boomed. "I'll show you what strength is."

The demon's body swelled, his muscles tripling in size. He alternated between screaming out in pain and roaring with rage. The last of the magic trickled into him, and he stood two feet taller than Axel. Even his canines and claws had gotten longer, making him look more monster than ever.

Axel crouched into an attack stance, snarling defiantly at the impossible obstacle in front of him. With a burst of speed, I got to Axel's side as Gar held both of his gigantic hands off to the sides, preparing to strike.

"He's not strong like you," I whispered, grinning at him through tears. "Remember?"

"Damn right," he shouted through his teeth as Gar swiped, both of us catching his arm. The sheer force made us slide back, and it took both of us at full strength to stop just one arm. We both knew then how this would end.

"Away with you!" A crackle of light snaked around my body, sending me soaring toward the obelisks. "You've been a pest for too long, Axel. You're finished."

Gar's other arm connected with Axel's jaw while he was distracted by me, and the last thing I saw was him being lifted off the ground. The void came at me fast, and I landed hard on the other side of it.

The demon's rage turned to horror as I struggled to stand. I didn't know what was happening at first, but as I looked up at the intact wards while still drawing breath, it all made sense. Gar had made a grave miscalculation.

A roar shattered the silence as Axel barreled shoulder-first into Gar's stomach, causing him to lose his balance.

"I'll kill you!" he bellowed out before sending a fist into Gar's face. My struggle to stand caught Axel's eye enough for him to see I still lived, but the distraction proved disastrous as a giant hand snatched his throat.

"I will be free, and when that day comes, you will all experience pain beyond limits long after death." He stood, squeezing tighter before lifting Axel off the ground once again. There was nothing he could do but struggle, raking his claws over the demon's trunk-like arms.

Cole stepped behind them both, holding one of the crystal staves. With a howl, he shoved the end of it into Gar's back.

"All magic comes at a price, bastard." He twisted the rod in deeper, and Gar let out a deafening screech. It drew the magic inside of him out and into the crystal tip. "I want to hear you scream!"

Gar shuddered, letting Axel fall to the ground.

"I want my face to be the last thing you see."

The crystal quickly overloaded with a cracking sound before exploding, and Cole dodged it in time. The demon reached back, pulling the broken rod from his flesh before tossing it to the ground, the magic healing the wound in seconds.

"I hate to disappoint." With unnatural speed, he knocked Cole back before kicking him in the ribs. The vargyr let out a wheezy whine as Gar pressed his pawed foot into his chest.

"Fight me," Axel shouted, wrapping one arm around Gar's neck, pulling him back until he was all the way off of Cole.

The demon broke free, launching his fist into Axel's face again, but instead of flying backward, Axel dug his foot into the ground to keep himself upright and returned a punch just as strong. Gar stumbled backward and snarled.

"Looks like ya ain't so strong no more," Axel said, punching the demon's stomach. Gar grabbed hold of his arm, slamming his forehead into Axel's nose, his blood splattering my face.

I ran to his aid, but Axel held up his hand.

"This is personal," he shouted before deflecting another blow from Gar's fist, using the opening to put the demon into another choke hold. "It's my fight!"

"It didn't work last time, and it won't work now," Gar shouted.

"You sure about that?" He focused all of his strength, pushing Gar backward. When the demon lost his footing, Axel was able to pick up speed and momentum while lifting the demon off the ground like a runaway train. With a loud crash, he fell into my car as Axel let go, the force of the impact causing the steel to partially engulf his body.

Wasting no time, Axel jumped on top of him, pummeling his face with both fists over and over until the demon went limp. He pushed himself away, and with everything he had, he gripped the underside of the car, his arms trembling as he folded warped steel over the struggling demon. This was strength on a different level, something well beyond the limits of a normal vargyr. Like wrapping a potato in foil, Axel grabbed the other end, folding it over.

He knelt next to Gar. "I get my strength from my pack." He looked back at me and nodded before snapping his powerful jaws next to the demon's face. "You'll never know what that's like. I pity you."

Axel stood and lifted the car up over his head, his arms shaking as he bled from the nose.

"Go back to hell!" With a roar, he sent it flying into the obelisks before collapsing.

A deafening thunderclap mixed with the sound of snapping tree branches ripped through the air as the car disintegrated. Though I couldn't see him, I could just make out Gar's faint screams over the boom—then I heard nothing but an echo. The gentle wind carried with it a familiar black soot, but the peace would only last a few seconds.

The ground undulated, knocking me down as jagged fissures cracked the wards from side-to-side. One of them fell toward me, but I couldn't scramble to my feet fast enough. Axel grabbed my arm, pulling me out of the way in time as part of the obelisk hit the ground with such force that the shockwave sent us airborne. The dust cleared, and a massive, swirling violet portal stood where the void was moments ago. Twilight sucked away the inky cosmos as Gar's ritual came to an abrupt and violent end.

Axel's heart pounded as I lay against him on the ground. We both panted, shaking against one another for several minutes. Did we win? Was it over? If we were all still alive, we weren't coming unscathed.

"It's over," Axel whispered before pulling me into a weak hug. "I love you so much. When he threw you to the wards, I thought that was it." It was as though every emotion rushed from him like a broken dam. "But here you are. I love you, Leo."

I gently kissed the blood from his quivering lips.

"I love you too. I'm going to say it all the time. I promise."

The broken obelisks turned to black sand, revealing Cole lying on top of Derrick in the distance, neither of them moving.

"I need to check on them. Are you going to be okay?"

He nodded. "I overdid it and can't move. Need some time to heal."

After stumbling to my feet, I approached Cole, who looked up at me, shaking his head.

"He's barely got a pulse. Gar did something different to him." He pointed to the electric scars all over Derrick's body, his fur having been singed away.

Vince ran to us, sliding over the dirt as he stopped and knelt next to injured vargyr.

"He better not be dead."

"He's not," I said, placing two fingers under his jaw, trying to find a pulse. Cole was right; it was dangerously slow. "As long as he's still breathing, he can heal, right?"

"Maybe." Cole lifted Derrick's head into his lap. "He took a lot of Lo'rim though. We can heal physical wounds, but this is magic."

Slow and unsteady footsteps scraped along the path as Toby limped toward us. The fur on the right half of his body had been burned away, and he had several shards of crystal sticking out of his upper arm. He didn't display much emotion as he approached, though he did wince in pain as he knelt beside me.

"Bet you could use some cider," he said, his tone shaky. "You were always so clueless." He looked up at us, eyes watering. "What a pointless waste of time."

"What is?" I asked.

Toby leaned over, pressing his ear to Derrick's chest.

"I spent my life resenting him when I could have appreciated what we had." He let out a laugh. "It's fun when we argue." He carefully placed an arm under Derrick's neck and another under his legs before lifting him slowly from the ground.

"I should carry him," I said. "You're pretty banged up."

Toby ignored my offer as he dragged himself through the debris toward what was left of the town.

A Required Position

Buildings lay in smoldering shambles, save for the wilkyr village, the dungeon, and the houses sparsely spread around ground zero. I stayed with Axel as he lay unconscious on the grass, his body pushed to its very limits. Vince and Cole followed Toby as he carried Derrick far from the destruction, and the rest of the vargyrs wandered aimlessly through the splintered remains of places that once brought them a sense of normalcy.

Hours had passed, and the sun faded behind a black horizon. Crackles and hisses followed by arcs of what appeared to be electricity flashed through the swirling, violet hole in reality hovering in place of the fallen wards. It was like watching a coming storm, and as the lightning became more frequent, I thought it best to move Axel as far away as I could carry him.

Axel hung over my shoulder, limp while letting out the occasional groan. Though I tried to be gentle, there was only so much care I could take. I was much stronger now, but he was still huge and awkward to hold. There were a few times he slipped, and I had to hoist him back over my shoulder, causing him more pain.

I managed to get halfway home before his weight became too much, and I laid him carefully in the grass on the side of the road.

"Axel?" I whispered, but he didn't respond. Instead, he took in ragged breaths, and I pressed an ear to his chest. I'd been doing that obsessively whenever he'd start to breathe funny. Behind me, a blue flash exploded through the trees, coming from the direction of town. The starry night sky turned to day for about ten seconds before it faded back to darkness.

"That didn't look good," Axel whispered, his eyes half-open.

"I'm sure it's fine," I whispered calmly while running my fingers through his mane. Did that portal explode, or did something come through it? We couldn't handle another conflict right now.

"Leo." Axel's voice croaked when he tried to get out the words, and his ears pressed against the sides of his head. "I love you."

The phrase that once had me overjoyed now took on a melancholy tone, making my heart fall into my stomach.

"We're going to be fine," I said, still stroking his head.

"I ain't able to move." He took in a sharp breath. "Maybe you should get far away from here, just in case."

"I'm done with that. If we're fucked, we're fucked together. There's not much we can do, but at least we tried." He grimaced and I leaned in to kiss him. "I'm going to be optimistic, and you should too. Let's try to sleep. We've got a long day tomorrow, and it might be a sad one."

"You think Derrick ain't gonna make it?"

"He looked really bad," I said, lying next to Axel. Now that the conflict with Gar was over, I could finally cry a little.

"I really like him." Axel shifted slightly, trying to get closer to me. "We were good huntin' buddies, and wasn't nothin' that ever seemed to upset him. Don't know if I could ever get over it if we lost him."

"He's very strong-willed," I whispered, nuzzling his neck. "It's hard to kill a vargyr."

Axel sniffed and nodded, tears dampening the fur on his face.

Morning light poured over my face, and I opened my crust-covered eyes to a purple canopy overhead. I didn't feel Axel next to me, so I jerked the rest of the way awake, sitting all the way up.

"Anaste, the beast has come to," a human male voice called out from my side. As I turned to face him, my head slammed against bars of pure, white energy, stunning me for a few seconds before I fell back.

"Good morning." A human clad in black, flowing robes knelt next to the magic cage. A thin, silk-like hood covered his head, obscuring part of his face. "Are you well enough to answer some questions?"

"Who are you?"

"My apologies." The man lifted his hood, revealing a middle-aged, bearded face. His hair was short and dark brown with streaks of silver, and he had a medium-length, pointed brown beard similar to Derrick's. His expression was calm, yet exuded stern confidence, and when he smiled, deep crow's feet appeared along the corners of his eyes. Though it was hard to tell through the robe, he seemed to have a tall yet slender frame, typical of just about every mage I'd seen depicted in fantasy. "I am Archmage Anaste Torr, advisor to the senate of Stellous. You must be Leo."

"How did you know my name?" I asked, eying the other mages in similar robes as they studied me. "What happened?"

"I've heard quite a lot about you," the mage replied, using his staff as leverage to push himself back to his feet. "And you're in here as a precaution."

"Where's Axel?"

"All of the other vargyrs are safely contained." He pulled something out of his pocket. "You look famished. Would you like a treat?"

Having not eaten in days, I was drooling at the thought of anything going into my stomach. I nodded, and he tossed what looked like a dog biscuit through the bars.

"That's fucking hilarious."

Anaste let out a hearty chuckle. "Now don't give me that look." He wiped his eyes with his thumb. "Before I let you out of that cage, I want to be certain of the things that have come to light." He pointed to the bone-shaped biscuit. "It will force you to tell the truth."

"I've got nothing to hide, but fine," I said, picking the *treat* up from the ground before stuffing it into my mouth. Despite the stale aftertaste, I was so hungry it didn't matter.

"Let us begin." The mage pulled over a foldable stool before sitting with one leg over his knee. "Where do you come from?"

"Earth."

"How did you end up in Varcross?"

"A mage named Josiah gave me a key and tricked me into coming here."

He nodded, folding his hands in his lap.

"You already know all of this, don't you?" I asked.

The mage looked me over for a moment longer before continuing. "Are you still able to spread the curse?"

"No, and I can cure it."

"How?"

"My blood."

Anaste paused, turning to a mage behind him.

"Bring the beast."

They bowed and dispersed, each hovering above the ground toward some tents in the distance. They stopped at a huge cart surrounded by bars with the frightened feral vargyr from town. Using an invisible force, they effortlessly wheeled the cart in our direction.

"Are you going to let me out of here?"

The cart stopped in front of us, the feral running from end-to-end, pounding on the bars while howling. After the trauma he'd endured yesterday, and the terror on his face, I felt really sorry for him.

"After I see this cure for myself."

"Fine," I said, ready to slice into my arm with a claw.

The man grabbed my hand through the cage to stop me before running his fingers across the bend of my elbow. He let go of me and drew his other hand back slowly, whispering something in a low, rhythmic chant. My arm warmed before blood floated through the air in sanguine globules.

There was no pain. It was as though blood had been teleported out of my veins. My hackles stuck straight as I realized just how deadly archmages were. They could bleed a person to death by simply uttering a few words. After everything magic had done to me and my friends, I hoped we'd never have to experience it again. It seemed like an impossible dream.

Anaste threaded my blood through the air toward the other vargyr in sharp ribbons before they slithered into the reluctant beast's mouth and down his throat.

"It may take a while," I said, as the mages murmured quietly amongst themselves.

Anaste sat back down on the stool and crossed his legs.

"It's a shame what happened to you. Humans from your realm know nothing of magic and curses, but you're still as susceptible to lycanthropy as we are." He leaned forward, resting his cheek against his forefinger and thumb. "If you're immune to demonic curses, then this deformation of your body must not be a curse. This validates the theories that vargyrs are infected with a virulent disease that accompanies the curse."

"We've already figured that out," I said.

"What's going on?" a grunty voice whined. The vargyr leaned against the bars of his cage, his eyes wide as the humans surrounded him. "Mages..."

"After nearly eight hundred years," Anaste whispered, turning back to me. With a wave of his staff, the bars of light around me disappeared. "No one on Eqiros could find the cure. We'd given up, as curing demonic curses was thought to be impossible."

"I'm well aware of all of this. What I'm more interested in is why you're all here?" I asked, my nerves unraveling. As I looked around at the army of magic users, Derrick's warnings about Stellous became startlingly clear.

"An explosion shook the city, and an unregulated portal suddenly appeared in the place of some of the strongest wards ever created. As you can probably guess, that drew quite a lot of attention." He stopped talking for a moment and rubbed his forehead. "We now need to take alternative measures in regards to Varcross."

"What do you mean?"

"That's not important right now."

"The hell it isn't!" I looked past Anaste at the rows of tents along the forest clearing. "Are you forcing us out of Varcross?"

"On the contrary," he said, pointing at me. "You and the other vargyrs belong to Stellous. They can never return to their families as they are, but we can integrate them into our army. There have already been proposed plans."

"Absolutely not!" I shouted.

"We only want to maintain peace, and in order to do that, we need to bring all countries together under one banner. We have the most powerful army of mages on the planet, but it's not enough. However, a magic army combined with the brute power of nearly unkillable beasts would guarantee everyone lay down arms and join us."

"I don't want to be in the army," the vargyr in the cage said. "I want to be with my family."

Anaste nodded in agreement. "Perhaps they can come visit if you all prove your loyalty to the senate. What sounds more appealing to you: spending the rest of your days in this primitive world, or living a life of prestige?"

"I just want to see my family again. I miss my mother."

"How old are you?"

"I was seventeen when I went wilkyr. That was maybe a few years ago."

"So young," Anaste said, feigning compassion. Perhaps he was being genuine, but I had a hard time believing that. "I'm sure there are a lot of young men such as yourself who wish they could see their loved ones again. We can make that happen."

"What about me?" I asked. "I don't belong in your world."

"Your place is at the athenaeum where we can study your unique condition. We may even be able to finally solve some mysteries of X'eeva and put an end to the Devah threat."

"I'd rather stay here, thanks."

"That wasn't meant to sound like I was giving you a choice," Anaste said sharply. "You'll be well taken care of, as will your friends."

"I refuse to be a soldier," the vargyr in the cage shouted, rattling the bars. "I want to be with my family. If I am cured, then I want to go back home where I belong."

"You don't belong among humans. You may be cured of the demon's curse, but the disease you carry may still spread. Your temperaments are unpredictable, and you hold a significant physical advantage over the rest of the population. Allowing you all to intermingle would be an unregulated nightmare."

"Then you won't get loyalty from us," the vargyr warned, pointing his clawed finger through the bars at the archmage. "You'll get an uprising."

Anaste said nothing, his eyes rolling slightly to the side. He turned to one of the other hooded mages standing at attention next to the cage. "Take him back to the town."

"As you command," he said, nodding to the others as they held up their staves.

I dashed to the front, raising both hands. "If you want respect, you can start here by not treating us like animals. You know he's cured, so let him out."

Anaste let out an exasperated sigh. "Fine. Escort the *person* to town."

"Thank you," I said, trying to appear diplomatic, but deep down I wanted to punch this guy in the face.

The mages momentarily hesitated as one of them removed the lock from the cage. Before they could do anything more, the vargyr burst out, sending everyone scrambling out of the way.

"I'm not going to be a soldier," he shouted as he disappeared into the trees.

Anaste glared at me before sliding a small silver hand mirror out from under his robes. The *mirror* had beveled runic edges that glowed a pale blue.

"This is what happens when you treat a vargyr like a person, but no matter. Magic always finds you."

He stood still, his brows furrowed as he studied the device.

"Archmage?" one of the other humans asked.

Anaste glanced up at me. "It seems we can no longer track him."

"How tragic," I replied with a smug smile. "Did you forget he's no longer cursed? That's what you're tracking, right?"

"You don't seem to understand the implications of your cure. Vargyrs are too dangerous to live among us without a way to keep track of them." The mage rubbed his forehead again. "We can't bring cursed vargyrs to Stellous, and we can't let cured vargyrs roam a low security facility while being invisible to our methods of tracking. It will also be a drain on resources to keep every vargyr contained in smaller facilities, not to mention it won't be very humane."

"Well, *Anaste*. I've been giving our situation a lot of thought since my transformation, and I might have a solution."

"Doubtful, but let's hear it," he replied.

Biting my lower lip with a canine, I maintained a cool head.

"Does Stellous keep a record of all of the vargyrs they've kept here?"

"Of course. What a silly question."

"How many?"

Anaste narrowed his eyes. "Why?"

"I'll need to know how many to track down and cure. Give me time to do that at least, and in return, we'll continue trading the resources you need. More vargyrs means more trade, right?"

"And what guarantee do I have you'll keep your word? How do you know the others will continue to work after they're cured?"

"The town was destroyed when the wards fell, and we need this place to feel like home again. The vargyrs will want a functioning town and society, and they don't want to be cut off from their home world."

"The wards are down, and it could take generations to not only replace them but also repair the rip between both of our worlds," he replied. "I also want to know the cause of this destruction."

"There was a demon trapped in this world. If we hadn't destroyed him, he would have broken free and destroyed Eqiros."

Anaste laughed. "You can't be serious."

"He had a contract," I said, watching the smug look on his face turn serious. "A *dead* contract that couldn't be fulfilled. I think you know what that means."

The mage's eyes went wide as he stood in silence, and now it was time to embellish the truth a bit.

"Your entire planet was saved by us beasts. Stellous owes us because we could have just as easily let him escape."

"Though you make a compelling case, I cannot overlook the problem. We have no way of making sure the vargyrs remain here. We also have no way of regulating or stopping the flow of magic between worlds. I doubt we will ever be able to control the rift aside from sealing it completely, and no one in the senate will agree to that."

"You mean to tell me the most powerful city in the world can't guard one rift?"

"Not if thousands of vargyrs organize and come through at once. There are limits to magic, Leo. We'd be overwhelmed and powerless to stop an onslaught like that."

"If you're already scared of a revolt, that means you have no intention of treating us fairly. Free and happy people don't revolt, do they?" Neither of us broke eye contact with one another. "We're already off on the wrong foot."

"I didn't get to my position by being naïve," he said, walking toward the mage encampment with me at his side. "Stellous has been unchallenged for thousands of years. Just one vargyr could best fifty human soldiers or more. Your endurance, strength, speed, and rapid healing make you practically unstoppable if you organized a military. We're to just allow your kind to build a potentially hostile civilization on our doorstep?"

"Did the vargyr that ran away sound like he was eager to fight? If you take the time to talk to the town after I've cured them, you'll see that most are just civilians, not soldiers. They want to live normal lives, and if they can have that in exchange for a bit of fair labor, I don't think there will be much of an issue." I paused and turned toward the archmage. "It's a simple concept, Anaste. If you treat the people right, no one rebels. If you treat them like an expendable resource, then expect the worst."

The mage pondered as we continued toward Varcross.

"You seem to think the situation is binary, but there are so many more nuances you're not considering, but the senate will. If

I am to give this consideration, your kind must be willing to make compromises. As far as your request, I'll take it up with the senate—under the right stipulations."

"Like what?"

"Varcross again becomes a colony of Stellous—"

"Out of the question," I interrupted. "I don't know what history was like in your world, but colonies never worked out in mine."

The mage was growing more frustrated with my objections. "And what do you suggest? Do you wish to have an actual negotiation, or will this be one-sided?"

"How about we join Stellous but keep our statehood. We do something like that back in the country I come from, and it's worked for hundreds of years."

"Merely hundreds of years? We've had the same form of government for ten times that long, and it has stood the test of time. We only allow statehood for countries that have already been established, and they are represented in the senate. Varcross isn't its own country; it has always been a colony."

"You can't have an entire planet as a colony."

Anaste laughed. "Since it was our ancestors that created this planet, we can have whatever we desire."

"Would you rather us fight to claim this world?"

"I caution you to choose your words more carefully. You may unintentionally declare war.

"Only countries can declare war," I retorted. "Recognizing a declaration of war would force you to recognize us as our own country. So which is it?"

That was the moment I had the upper hand. There was a distinct smell of fear on him, and I was once again glad to be a vargyr.

"We have nothing to lose and everything to gain," I added. "So tell me: do you want a peaceful resolution, or would you rather we fight for our freedom? Either way, that's the outcome you'll get."

It was then I had an uncomfortable feeling and had to pull back my aggression. Gambling the lives of everyone in town without them knowing was wrong, not to mention we were still at a major disadvantage. Only seven people were cured, the town had about two hundred lucid vargyrs, and the rest were ferals spread across the wilderness.

"I could have you bound and taken back with us right now, and what could the rest of you do in your current state?"

Damn it. I had to remember this was a human very similar to Derrick, and I wasn't good at putting my thoughts before my mouth. "Then why didn't you do that when I was unconscious?"

The archmage went silent again, and another scent emanated from him. He was still afraid, though he didn't outwardly express it. I was missing something. In my mind, Stellous had the advantage, despite my posturing, but judging from Anaste's reaction, that may not have been the case.

"Name your conditions."

"Excuse me?"

"Your conditions for forming your own nation. I need something to bring to the senate floor, and whatever we come up with needs to be beneficial for both Stellous and Varcross."

"Uh—" I wasn't expecting to have to come up with something so important on the fly. This was something I'd need to discuss with Derrick and Toby, and I wasn't even sure Derrick was still alive. "I—I don't know enough about your world for this to be my call. Someone else from town is probably better suited."

"You'd better learn to handle these situations with more grace if you want to be a representative."

The skin under my fur went cold at that statement. "Did you not hear what I just said?"

"It has to be you," Anaste interrupted, lowering his voice. "I'll be blunt: the senate leader would reject this madness before it even came up for a vote. Your situation, however, is unique and gives you leverage that any other vargyr wouldn't have. Do you understand?"

"Why would you tell me this?" He wasn't making any attempts to hide the truth from me this time.

"Because I know potential when I see it," he said. "I work with senators as a liaison, but I wouldn't be against the idea of working closer with Varcross if you are its representative."

"So you want something." I shifted my gaze to him. "Do you think my inexperience would make me easier to manipulate?"

Anaste smiled. "Clever. Hold onto that way of thinking, and you'll never have to worry about being manipulated."

"And what if the senators reject the request?"

The archmage grabbed my thicker arm, pulling me toward the trees. He turned to a tall, elvish-looking woman with smooth, pale skin and flowing white hair, signaling her toward the direction we were heading earlier. "We're going to take the scenic route. Be sure the dome is reinforced. We can't have cursed vargyrs running around free." He pointed to another mage, a hooded male with a youthful black beard. "Head back to the encampment. Inform them to keep a close eye on the tramadar. There are feral vargyrs that may be close."

They both nodded in compliance before Anaste turned back to me.

"Tramadar?" I asked.

He held up the 'mirror' he used earlier. "We have larger ones that cover more area, but we've only seen a few indicators of vargyrs outside of town. I have a feeling that will change when they smell us and come running."

"Why are we alone?"

"Because I don't want what I have to say going back to the senate. If you want to ensure they accept, you need to cure as many vargyrs as you can find. You'll also need to find a way to unite them while building a proper capital city. The more support and unity you have here, the less likely you are to be laughed out of the building—or worse, betrayed. Right now, they could agree to the terms and, once you are in Stellous for study, lock you away. Since your people are scattered, there won't be any organized rebellion. However, if you earn the trust here and form a real nation, it will be impossible for them to betray you without serious consequences."

I felt even more afraid after that. I needed Derrick, now.

"We have a lot going for us," he continued. "Vargyrs can do the work of tens of men in a short amount of time, and it's hard to find humans that would leave Eqiros to mine a world with no real infrastructure, especially among those they consider monsters. Not only that, gathering every vargyr, keeping them contained while training them to be soldiers in Stellous would be an expensive and lengthy process—if it even works. Given the options, though I loathe to admit it, your way makes the most sense. Having Varcross stand on its own while still under Stellous control would be the most ideal outcome.”

“And what are they going to do with me?”

“The scholars and doctors will draw blood while testing certain spells and devices. It won’t be anything you can’t handle, and I’ll teach you how to navigate Stellous politics in private.”

We both took a moment, neither of us speaking as we continued trekking over fallen leaves.

“I need time to consult with my p—my advisors.”

Anaste cocked a brow. “Getting yourself accustomed to the role?”

“I can’t do this alone.”

“I wouldn’t take too long. The senate will need to be kept abreast of what’s happening here, and I’d prefer to go to the atheneum with something concrete.”

There was a nagging gut feeling that something was off. I’d been a nobody for most of my life, and now this mage wanted me to lead an entire country.

“I’ll let you know tomorrow,” I said, my confidence fading more as we neared the edge of town. There was an odd distortion in front of us, like heat rising from asphalt in the summer.

“Then I will await your decision on the northeast side of town tomorrow, where the wards fell.” He turned and hesitantly stretched out his hand to shake mine. As I closed my much larger hand around his, it only reinforced how fragile humanity was compared to us—at least, that was the illusion. If Gar’s hulking transformation mid-battle was anything to go by, magic in their hands made them terrifying. “I have a feeling we’ll be working a lot together in the future,” he said, lifting his staff. The distortion faded into a narrow opening.

“I don’t really have much of a choice.” I stepped through the opening, and the barrier closed behind me.

“There’s always a choice, Leo. Not all are wise, though.” Without another word, he turned and started back toward the encampment.

When he disappeared, so too did the anxiety I’d held onto for the last hour. We were both wary of one another, but I was likely a lot more intimidated by his presence than he was of mine.

Seeing the ruins of Varcross in the daylight gave more detail to the destruction we'd caused. The buildings of town were nothing more than cement slabs, wiped clean from their foundations. The destruction reminded me of news footage of Greensburg after a powerful tornado tore through when I was younger. The only difference was the black crater in the middle town where the source had exploded. How had Toby survived that?

No one walked around anymore, and Varcross was eerily silent save for a few birds in the distance where trees hadn't been flattened by the shockwaves. My nose caught the pungent scent of the vargyrs on the outskirts, many of them sifting through splintery debris for anything salvageable. They all looked so aimless, but they also didn't know they were going to be free from the curse soon.

I picked up the pace, my foot-paws pushing along the gravel road toward Cole's place. All the houses in the woods still stood, though those closest to town sustained significant damage, while the rest only had shattered windows. Cole's house stood out in the distance, smoke billowing from the chimney.

The front steps groaned as I climbed them toward the front door. Grabbing the pitted iron knob, I turned it slowly, keeping as quiet as I could while opening the door. Inside, Toby sat on the floor fast asleep, his back against the couch. Derrick lay behind him, his breathing still labored as he slept with his tongue hanging off to the side. His entire torso had been wrapped in bloody bandages.

Toby sniffed the air and opened his eyes, looking up at me expectantly.

"Well?"

"Well what?" I asked while shutting the door.

"What do they want?"

"I'll discuss that later," I whispered, sitting on the floor next to him in front of the fireplace. "How's he doing?"

"Stubbornly hanging in there." He placed his hand on the other vargyr's chest. "I'd expect no less from him."

"Did you love him?"

Toby shrugged.

"Maybe. A long time ago. We were close friends when he arrived in Varcross, and it was nice to talk to a fellow mage who understood that life. When Xavier came along, that was when things soured. He fell in love with a cruel mage who cohorts with demons, and I was demoted from a friend to a customer."

"Why didn't you tell him how you felt?"

"There was an unspoken rule every vargyr followed. We weren't allowed to choose wilkyr mates. The only reason Cole and Vince were allowed to cohabitate is because they were already mates before they came to Varcross. Before Xavier, when Derrick and I were together, it was always more than sex—at least to me."

Two sets of footsteps creaked from Cole and Vince's bedroom, thudding quickly across the floor.

"Great," Toby muttered, leaning back against the couch again, his hands folded over his stomach. "So much for peace and quiet."

Axel and Cole burst into the living room, Axel yanking me from the floor into a crushing hug.

"If it's not demons, it's mages," Cole said, joining Axel as he wrapped his arms around me from the back. "They carted Axel to town, but you weren't with him. We thought the mages had taken you to Stellous."

"I hate mages," Axel muttered, backing away. "We can't run away from them like we could with Gar."

"Speaking of Gar, what the hell happened to him before the explosion?"

"We can thank Vince for that," Cole said, glancing at the hallway. "He's still sleeping."

"He's less of an idiot than I thought," Toby said. "I still don't know what possessed him to latch the pendant to that feral, but it was..." He trailed off, shifting his eyes to the floor. "It was a brilliant move, and he saved my life." Toby smacked his tongue, wrinkling his nose. "If words had a taste, that would have made me ill."

"The pendant?" I asked.

"That necklace Vince used, the nox-cirqet. Gar can feel everything the wearer feels, and he hears all thoughts the wearer thinks. Derrick unlocked it, and Vince strapped it to a feral. It seems the chaotic thoughts and emotions are overwhelmingly painful. Or maybe he got a dose of what he put us through, and it was too much for him," Toby said.

"Good job Vince," I whispered to myself. "How's he been since he got back?"

"Insufferable," Toby muttered. "He's never going to shut up about it, and he didn't even land the killing blow." He looked at Cole. "Speaking of brilliant. Good job with that tanzonium rod. Axel would have never been able to overpower Gar if you hadn't drained him."

"I agree," Axel said, his tail wagging excitedly, hugging Cole again. "We should all pile on Vince to wake him up."

"That's going to really piss him off," Cole said. "Count me in!"

Compromises

"No," Axel shouted, sending his fist through our bedroom wall. "Why did you agree to somethin' like that without talkin' to me first?"

"I didn't agree to anything yet," I shouted back. "What do you want me to do?"

"You said yerself that they can't track us once we're cured. Let's get the hell out of here and do what we had planned."

"And leave everyone behind?"

"I don't care anymore! I'm tired, Leo. If it's not demons, it's mages, and I don't want anything to do with either. Let's just gather our pack and run one more time."

"I'm not doing that, and I don't think they'll agree either."

He grabbed my arms. "I'll drag you with me if I have to."

"I believe we've been through this already," I said, grabbing the nape of his neck.

He slipped from my grasp, throwing me back against the wall. I lunged forward, tackling him to the floor, snapping my jaws, my teeth catching his arm. Blood splattered on the wood floor, and he threw me back again. I was airborne for a second before he leapt at me, his full weight now bearing down as his teeth sunk into my shoulder.

We were both so pent-up that I knew where this *fight* was headed. My claws dug into his side, and he winced, pulling away. We froze, panting as we locked eyes with one another, our hackles raised and bloodied teeth bare. As our scents intertwined, the anger shifted to something a lot more primal. His arousal poked from his sheath as did mine, and I reared back, preparing for us to meet in another clash, only this time, it wouldn't be teeth going into each other.

It was startling how similar the feelings were as a vargyr—this razor-thin line between unbridled bestial rage and sexual passion. Axel and I hadn't actually been fighting to hurt each other, and we hadn't had a moment of intimacy since that first time. This was not only a struggle for dominance, but one hell of a stress reliever.

It had been roughly a week since the last time I woke up with a smile on my face. Axel held me close, his nose buried in the thick mane of my neck. Despite our argument turning physical last night, I wanted to wake up like this every day for the rest of my life.

I understood why he was upset. Axel had different plans for our future, plans that would take us far from the painful memories of this place. There was a vast world to explore, and without the curse looming over everyone, we could take that journey together untethered. Some of us belonged out there, and even though Vince would deny it, I'd catch him staring longingly at the trees. We'd gotten a taste of freedom and adventure, and now the wanderlust had permanently taken up residence in our thoughts.

But there was no running from duty, and the mages would keep me bound to both Varcross and Stellous for years to come. I tried to make Axel understand that until we came up with a realistic plan, I had no other choice. Despite him being so cheerful and patient, he had an obstinate side.

We were exhausted but satisfied, having had the most intense sex I'd ever experienced. Though I could heal quickly now, I was still sore all over, and judging from the missing fur on Axel's chest and neck, he was likely in the same boat. This was only our second time, but again, our love-making had turned bloody. It was something we both enjoyed. For whatever reason, the rage during our love-making enhanced the tenderness after it was over.

I looked around at the damage we caused. The mattress had been ripped in multiple places, and the sheets had bloody fur and finger stains. Deep claw marks pocked the headboard, and our pillows were torn on the floor, down stuffing surrounding them. Axel's large bed teetered unsteadily since one of the legs had broken off. Just thinking about what we did made me want to shake him awake so we could do it again, but the freshly healed wounds on my back and hips didn't work with that idea.

Axel stirred awake, and I stared at him, the new, silvery glow of my irises reflecting in his darker blue. It certainly didn't take much to get him on top of me; however, he let out a soft whine and rolled back over.

"Ow," he whispered. "We overdid it—again."

"You think?" I shifted my weight closer so I could kiss him, but the bed tilted upward before the remaining rear leg broke off causing the end of the bed to collapse. We were now lying at an angle, both of us trying not to slide off.

We broke into fits of laughter.

"We ruined the bed," I said, holding my sides.

"We still got yers over at Cole's. It's a little sturdier than this one."

I slid down the mattress until my rough, padded paws touched the floor.

"We're not destroying that beautiful bed." I grabbed a towel from the closet and draped it over my arm. "We'll probably have to have sex in the woods or on the floor from now on," I growled seductively at him. "Like animals."

Axel snorted, his eyes narrowing on me.

"I've been thinkin' about what that mage wants," he said, pushing himself up against the wobbly headboard. The two remaining legs snapped and the wooden frame fell all the way to the floor. "Damn it." He looked up and grinned. "At least it's level now."

I folded my arms. "What are you thinking?"

Axel's ears pulled back, and he looked down at the floor. "I'm sorry. I ain't mad at you; I just hate them mages 'cause they're gonna do them experiments on you. They might keep you locked away."

"I have a strategy to keep that from happening, and once Derrick pulls through, I'll need his help again. It's going to be hard walking into a room full of humans like this and be taken—" I paused and smirked.

"What's that look for?"

"Axel, I'm gonna try something again."

"I'm too sore right now, Leo. Maybe later," he said, covering his crotch with his hands.

"Not that," I said, tossing the towel on the broken bed. "But I'll take you up on that offer."

I closed my eyes, letting my mind wander to the thoughts that seemed to calm me the most. Everything appeared as it did before: the mountains, the streams, the trees. Was this meditation?

A familiar tingling sensation pulsed through my body, and the icy air of the room pricked at my now human skin.

"No freakin' way," Axel said, breathless as he struggled to stand. "How'd the hell you do that? Can anyone do it?"

"I don't know. Apparently being a vargyr isn't as permanent as we thought. I might even be able to go wilkyr too. This might come in handy for today's negotiation."

Axel traced his fingers along the stubble covering my cheek. "It don't matter if yer human or vargyr. Yer handsome, and yer mine."

The skin on my face grew warmer at his compliment. "I wonder if you could do it too. Maybe it was the curse that keeps everyone locked into one form."

He shook his head. "I'll pass. Don't wanna go back to bein' human. What if I get stuck that way?"

"You wouldn't. You'd be able to shift back." I smiled at him. "It would be nice to know what you look like."

Axel plopped back down on the lower bed, staring at the floor again.

"Alright, I guess I can try," he said. "How do you do it?"

"Meditation, I think," I said, trying to think of how to put feelings into words. "I think I owe Derrick an apology. You remember when we first met, and you had a technique you used to keep control?"

"I ain't done that in a while, but I can try." He closed his eyes, his brows wrinkling as he held his breath.

"Don't force it. It's not going to work if you do that. Just try to remember what you looked like as a human."

His face relaxed, and his ears drooped. After a minute, his breathing slowed, and the longer he sat there, the more anxious I got. As nice as it was making love in vargyr form, I really wanted to kiss his human lips.

"Am I supposed to feel somethin'?" he asked, cracking one eye open.

"Yeah," I replied, a little disappointed. "You don't have to do this if you don't want to."

"I'll try for you."

I smiled. "If it happens, it happens. I'm not sure anyone else can do this except me, anyway."

After a quick shower, I rushed back into the room to check on Axel, who had propped himself up against the headboard with his eyes closed. At first I thought he was still trying to meditate but realized after a gentle snore that he'd fallen back to sleep. Not wanting to disturb him, I rummaged through the closet for any warm clothing I'd left behind before our escape. All of our stuff was hopefully still in that crevice along the beach and hadn't been washed away by an unusually high tide. I also wondered if Vince still had my backpack. My phone was likely ruined by now, along with all of the pictures I'd taken. With the car gone, there was no longer a way to charge it anyway.

Sadness finally hit me now that I had a moment to recollect the confrontation with Gar. That reliable old Subaru got me to Varcross, and I had a lot of good memories driving it. I also thought of Gar and how desperate he was to escape. Had he been thinking clearer, I may have been able to get through to him and none of this would have happened. I wouldn't waste tears on him, though. He nearly killed us all.

I slipped into what I could find, but not before an old case up on one of the shelves caught my eye. It was bound in glossy, scratched-up leather with holes torn in it. I reached up and slid the case from the shelf before flipping the antique-looking latches. Inside were an assortment of odd items: rocks, a child's shoe, letters, torn cloth, and—something that resembled a black screen.

Holding the heavy plastic-like item in my hand, I turned it around. It was cream-colored on one side and completely black on the other. Since whatever it was didn't appear to work, I tossed it back into the box. A flash of light burst from the device, and an image faded into it. Two younger men appeared in the photograph in front of a huge lake or bay with a futuristic-looking and bright skyline in the distance. One of them was tall, broad-shouldered, but lean with unbrushed, short black hair and a fresh five-o'clock shadow. He was gorgeous, his jaw strong and his eyes deep blue. That starry look on his face and goofy smile was something being a vargyr thankfully hadn't erased. The clothes he wore were very similar to what people wore on Earth, but the style was more reminiscent of the mid-nineties. Loose-fitting jeans and a beige shirt with their odd runic letters printed on the front.

Next to him was a much shorter man, but no less handsome. He was more muscular, with light brown hair and darker stubble on his face. His eyes were an unnatural gold, and he wore a confident, yet mischievous grin. He looked like the kind of guy who could pick anyone up from a bar and leave them in a second. He wore similar clothing, though they were a bit tighter, and he crossed his arms, while at the same time flexing for the camera.

So this was what those two looked like. They had a lot of the same features as they did now, though Axel had gotten a lot thicker than Vince when he turned. They looked so happy when this was taken, but smiles often hide pain. I wondered how many years ago this was. I'd ask Axel later, but for now, I needed to get going.

I slipped the picture back into the case and placed it on the shelf where I got it. As I walked by Axel, I stared at him, imagining the man he was. It honestly didn't matter what form he was in, I loved him all the same.

It was hard to leave, but I eventually slipped out of the bedroom toward the front door. The angry bite of the wind had me missing my fur. Yes, there were obvious downsides to being a vargyr, especially the fleas and thorny briars that would cling to and mat up my coat, but when it was cold, there was nothing better than having a body covered in a natural warmth.

The sky was cloudless and a deep blue, the canopy along the sides of the road blocking most of the late-morning sunlight. Ahead of me, wandering along the road was a solid black vargyr, looking around at the trees. His skinny tail was tucked between his legs, his ears pulled back and eyes wide. When I was close enough to get a better look, I thought my mind was playing ticks. The vargyr's feet were paws, like mine were.

Instinct pulled at me to run, but as our eyes met, there was nothing familiar. Could this even be possible? The vargyr didn't look completely normal, but he also didn't have the demonic qualities to which I became familiar. For one, his maw was more slender, which would have never been able to fit the amount of teeth Gar had. His eyes were amber instead of red, but I couldn't ignore his fur, which was unusually short like Gar's, only there were random sprouts of mane on his head and chest that hadn't fully grown in. His face was also capable of more complex expressions, something Gar could never quite do, and his body was thicker, his shorter fur giving him more definition. He even had a different scent.

"Excuse me, human," he said with a slight tremble. It was deep, but had a strikingly familiar nuance. "Where am I?"

If he wasn't Gar, could he have been one of the ferals? If the demon who created the curse was now dead, would it have gone away on its own?

"This is Varcross," I replied, keeping my eyes locked with his.

His irises flashed as though the name brought about a deluge of memories, and a snarl wrinkled his snout.

"Leo..." The way he said my name made my hair stand on end. There was no more denying who he was.

"How the hell did you survive?" I asked, trying to hold back the transformation as fur covered my arms. When he started chanting a rhythm I had come to associate with Lo'rim, I nearly tripped over my feet trying to put distance between us. As I ducked into the trees, the bolt of energy I had expected to arc after me never came.

In either a moment of curiosity or stupidity, I crept closer to the road to see what had happened, but he was gone, his new scent trailing to the south through the woods. The demon was still alive, and he was running loose. If Gar still stalked around in this world, he could pose an even greater danger than the mages did—especially with magic flowing freely into the world.

A small opening in the barrier appeared in front of me, and I stepped through it. Anaste and ten other mages wrapped in a tight formation, each aiming their staves at my chest. I threw up my hands.

"Another warm welcome?"

"State your name and rank," Anaste said. "I demand to know what imbecile sent you in there alone. Are you cursed? You have five seconds to answer."

"It's me, Leo," I shouted, my heart racing. I knew they wouldn't recognize me, but I certainly didn't expect such aggression toward one of their own. It was the entire reason I shifted.

"Leo?" Anaste lowered his staff, and the rest of the mages whispered amongst themselves. "How—in the world?"

"I don't know," I said, lowering my hands. "I can shift at will." I looked around at the mages still in formation as well as the army of hundreds that stood at attention behind them. "I've already established I'm no threat. Why the show of force?"

"This changes a lot of things," he said, waving his hand, dispersing the guards. "And this isn't merely a show of force. Depending on our agreement, we'll be taking down the barrier, and we need security." His pale eyes shimmered in the sunlight as he stared at me. "You look much younger than I thought you were. What is your age?"

"Twenty-seven."

"Odd. I'd have guessed twenty," he said with a grin.

"About the agreement," I said as the archmage curiously ran his fingers along my face. "Everyone's going to be worried for the future, and I want to put that to rest. I still don't know if I can trust you." I slapped his hand away. "Stop that."

"Sorry," he said, his tone still breathy. "Just had to see if this was some kind of illusion. Magic flows here now, and there are mages among you. I can't be too careful." He recomposed himself. "About the future: you're going to need allies, young man. I'm not asking you to trust me completely, but know that our interests align—for now."

"If you really want me as an ally, you'll allow me some concessions." His expression darkened, and I walked back my tone. "If you'll actually listen."

"Lesson number one, Leo: never lower yourself in front of others. You are in a better position to bargain than you assume, but that is all I will say on the matter. What are these concessions you seek?"

"Well...I'll need time," I said. "You want me to represent Varcross, but practically no one knows me beyond what the demon led them to believe. I can't do anything if I don't have the time or resources to gain their trust. I also need time to not only cure the town but also find all of the ferals and cure them too. Did you ever find out how many there are?"

Anaste glanced down at the glowing parchment he carried. "Eleven thousand two hundred and eighty-six."

"Christ," I whispered, scratching my head. "That could take years."

"You don't have years, and a good leader knows how to delegate resources to make a process like this more efficient. When vargyrs pose a possible threat to Stellous, the senate won't think in terms of years."

"This is impossible," I said, clenching my fists. "Those ferals are so spread out all over that I haven't even come across one yet. It could take years just to find them."

Anaste handed me the rune-covered mirror he used yesterday. "You still think you're alone in this, but you have resources. You only need to ask."

I took in a relieved breath before grabbing the base of the device. It only showed white dots spread across glass, concentrating in an area I assumed was town. Its orientation shifted like a compass as I turned each direction.

"I'll give you three months to cure the town and one year to get everything rebuilt before your first trip to Stellous. Hundreds of strong, hearty beasts should have no problem with that, and there are scholars among you that can help with the planning. You'll also have enough time to prepare a detailed report of what happened here with the demon as well as what your plans are for Varcross. Thousands of scholars will be chomping at the bit to meet you."

The demon...

Gar was out there, but I couldn't divulge that information to Anaste, lest they keep their army here to search for him. Once Derrick healed, I'd need to discuss how we were going to deal with this problem.

"So, we have a deal then?" I extended my hand. "We'll be free citizens of Varcross, and in exchange, I'll become a representative and..." My voice trailed off as I tried to find the words without choking on them. "I'll allow the mages to study me. We'll also keep trade going."

He grabbed my hand enthusiastically, giving it a firm shake.

"We'll also need to discuss eventual integration and limits to magic usage."

I jerked my hand away. "Integration? Magic? Why are you adding more to this?"

"Welcome to politics," he said with a smirk that made me want to rip his face off.

"Explain. I don't want to agree to something I don't understand."

"Gladly," he said, folding his hands behind his back while walking along the trees with me next to him, staying close to the barrier. "Our mages have been studying the rift where the wards fell. Whatever ritual that demon performed stitched our worlds together. Magic flows freely from our source to your world and back again, like a grafted artery.

"This is not a terrible thing; in fact, when this world was created, the most complicated issue was the lack of a stable source in this world, so they built artificial sources to store magic. The flow was always one way, and it always found its way back to its original source, regardless of what plane of existence it was in. So magic had to be brought over here in storage units, and once it was used, some of it flowed back to the artificial source, but most vanished from this realm back to Eqiros. It's the reason only one town exists here. They couldn't connect the towns using a portal network because it was impossible to build an artificial source to store enough magic to keep such a network running with any reliability.

"Now, such networks are possible, but there's obvious concern about your kind practicing. I mentioned earlier that there are powerful mages among you, and one of them in particular will be a significant problem once he is cured. The threat of vargyrs is great enough, but your kind harnessing the arcane shifts the power startlingly in your favor."

"I can't exactly stop mages from using magic. That's sorta what they do."

"We'll likely need to gather the mages among you and bring them back to Stellous."

I shook my head. "No. All vargyrs stay in Varcross. I won't accept any other alternative to that."

"Then we will need your word that your mages will refrain from practicing magic, and they cannot teach other vargyrs the craft. We will not budge on this issue either. Mages are trained weapons, and aside from the savant who resides here, you have four others who were advanced enough to rival our most powerful and several hundred more that were lower-rank." Anaste gave a long pause. "A vargyr archmage. I can't even fathom such a nightmare."

He was obviously talking about Derrick, but he had been thrown into Varcross as a wilkyr. They wouldn't know what he looked like now, and I intended to keep him a guarded secret.

"Fine, we'll figure something out. What about the integration part?"

"Eventually, humans may want to settle here. We'll need to see how humans and vargyrs interact with one another in a post-curse world. We can only assume for the moment that lycanthropy can still be spread, even without the curse. It may not be as virulent, but it could be a concern. If a human understands the risks and decides to take a vargyr partner, that's a choice we'll give them. However, we're keeping cohabitation strictly male."

"Why? If I did decide integration was acceptable, we'd need women as well as men. I'm not just talking about relationships. Men and women have different perspectives that are important for a balanced society."

"I understand your concern, but we simply cannot allow it. Plus, vargyrs do not need female companionship and thrive perfectly well in same-sex bonds. You all have very long lives and are still be able to pass those genes along to offspring, even without the curse. Overpopulation is a concern. If the vargyrs are able to still get human females pregnant, then we will need to keep them away."

"Then how about no integration at all?" I said, the volume of my voice rising. "Humans can't even get along with other humans. I don't want a society marred by prejudice, especially if it means one group being oppressed to suit the needs of the majority."

Anaste nodded. "That's a valid concern, and I'll bring it before the senate for discussion."

I felt like I'd already failed at my first task because I was walking away from this without a lot to show for it. This wasn't my forte, and I was going to require proper counsel. There was no way I'd allow Stellous to cripple us. While I feared magic, there was no undoing what had been done, and if we had mages, we'd likely have very little limitations. Anaste must have suspected this as well, but if he didn't, I didn't want it getting out either.

Derrick would need to lead the way in magic research without Stellous knowing. Listening to how Anaste manipulated the conversation, there was a chance things could go south later on. We had to prepare now for anything Stellous might pull in the future. As long as we were connected to Eqiros, there was always the risk of falling victim to whatever they considered *progress*. If the senate made a decision to remove us from the world, or enslave us, we'd need to have the tools to fight a war on our terms or escape to another realm.

Both sides were going to distrust each other anyway, and I wasn't going to allow us to be caught unprepared. This was likely a prelude to a cold war of sorts, and it would be my job to keep things from escalating to the point of mutual assured destruction. My mouth went dry again.

"Fine," I relented.

"You don't seem as enthusiastic as you were earlier. It's hard to tell without the ears and tail."

"It's a lot to think about, and there's too much to do. Call off your mages and leave." I turned away, intending to make a confident but hasty exit, but that ended when my face smashed against the barrier, knocking me to the ground. A few of the mages that saw what happened giggled quietly. "Can you get rid of this thing?" I shouted, cupping my bleeding nose.

"As you wish." Anaste unlatched his staff from a strap across his back, shoving into the ground. The distortion around the town shattered from the bottom to the top before the magic dissipated into glittering sand-like particles. "We'll meet again in three months with the official paperwork and amended agreement."

My heart began to race again.

"What do you mean, amended?"

"Well, obviously the terms will need to be negotiated by the actual people in charge."

"That's ridiculous!"

"That's politics," the mage said with a crooked smile before turning away.

⁂

"Are you sure?" Cole whispered, keeping his voice low so he wouldn't disturb Derrick. Both of us took Toby's usual spot next to the couch.

"I don't know what I'm sure of anymore. Axel threw him and that car, and everything turned to ash."

Derrick snorted, and I paused, expecting him to wake up. When he fell back into a light snore, I continued, a little quieter.

"I survived when he threw me, so maybe Josiah's research was wrong. You know how Gar had that weird, snaky look to him?"

Cole nodded.

"Not anymore. He still has paws, but everything else is normal aside from his fur. He also seemed confused."

"This is bad," Cole said. "There's magic flowing into this world now. Gar might be even more dangerous now."

The sound of a throat clearing behind us took our attention.

"Doubtful."

"Derrick," I said, Cole and I sliding across the floor toward him. "When did you wake up?"

"Earlier this morning, but everyone was saying such interesting things, I figured I'd rest my eyes for another few more hours."

"I'm glad you're okay," Cole said, placing his palm against the mage's chest. "Whatever Gar did to you slowed down your healing."

"It's temporary, and magic flows through me again," Derrick said with his usual care-free smile. "Your description of Gar intrigues me. Did you happen to capture him? I need to have a…conversation."

"He ran into the woods," I replied as the mage's ears fell. "He was trying to chant a spell."

Derrick shook with laughter before groaning in pain. "Oh—oh goodness. That wasn't pleasant."

"Why did you laugh?" Cole asked.

"Because the fiend is not able to use Lo'rim anymore, and while this is just a theory, it makes the most plausible sense based on your description." He tried to sit up, but ended up turning his head instead. "He may be completely cut off from X'eeva, and he can't use normal magic without converting it."

Cole sat cross-legged next to Derrick's face. "Does that mean he's not a demon anymore?"

"Who's to say?" Derrick looked up at me. "Was I hallucinating from the pain, or were you human during the fight?"

I nodded. "You were right about meditation, and I am a terrible student."

"Fascinating."

"I'm going to get you some food and water," I said, gently stroking the side of Derrick's face. "We were all scared you wouldn't make it."

His eyes watered as he cast a glance at Cole and I. "Knowing I have a family that cares so deeply for my well-being is probably why I'm still alive. You all mean more to me than all the books and knowledge in the universe—and for me, that's saying something."

Cole grabbed Derrick's hand. "If it weren't for you, I can't even fathom where we'd be right now. Our lives wouldn't be the same." He leaned in and pressed his head against the mage's forehead. "Just so you know, we're never letting you leave."

"You couldn't get rid of me now if you wanted."

All Together

One Week Later...

"How are you feeling, Leo?" Cole asked, handing me another hunk of raw meat.

"About as well as anyone having the life literally sucked out of them." I balled my fist, squeezing tight as Derrick used the bloodletting spell. Red globules floated through the air before streaming into small standing vials lined along the table.

Derrick had mostly recovered, though he still walked around with a slight limp. The Lo'rim left lightning-like scars along his back and abdomen, and fur wouldn't grow to cover them. They would likely never fully heal, and the older vargyr seemed to prefer that, bragging about how rugged his battle scars made him look.

"Oh, don't be so dramatic. At least we know now that this will be more than enough to cure the town." Derrick looked over at Axel, who was guarding the door of what we used to call The Dungeon. "After I'm done with the last of these vials, only let twenty in at a time. We must keep the crowd from becoming too unruly."

"I got this," Axel boasted before peeking through the window. "They're getting real antsy out there."

The six of us had spent all of yesterday clearing out most of the tables so there'd be plenty of room for a queue. Everything in town bore the scars of the past, and this building was one of the worst reminders. We all agreed to tear it down eventually and replace it with a monument—something to actually be proud of.

"Are you all ready?" Derrick asked, looking up from the vials at all of us standing in a line along the old bar.

"Let's get this over with." Toby picked up his dropper and uncorked one of the tiny containers of my blood. Vince and Cole gave a thumbs up.

"Then let us bring this dreadful chapter of our lives to a satisfying end."

Evenings around the hearth became a nightly ritual at what used to be Cole's house. The wards had fallen over two weeks ago, and every day we were together, our pack bond strengthened. Toby was noticeably happier, despite losing everything in the explosion. I expected more bitterness than usual, but the opposite seemed true, especially as he and Derrick spent more time together.

With the help of one of the upholsters in town, Axel made us a mattress to go on the bed he made me a while ago. It wasn't as plush as the other one, but we needed to make do with what few resources we had available until trade opened back up between Stellous and Varcross. Most of our belongings were here now, and Axel's little house went to four others that had become homeless in the calamity. Everyone had to do what they could to help.

The six of us now lived together, which was both fun and frustrating, but when we laughed and talked around the warm fire, the frustration melted away.

"I can't believe I got it to work," I said, swiping through another picture on my phone. There was still about sixty percent battery left, and I wanted to get the most out of it before it was dead. "This one was the first picture I took here." The others passed the device around, looking at the image of Axel sitting patiently on the ground in the front yard. "He didn't want to wake us up."

Axel snorted and pulled me close. We were on the floor with our backs to the fire. Derrick and Toby were curled up in a blanket in front of us while Vince and Cole were on the couch. Some nights we would tell stories; others we'd play games. The most fun was charades, even when they'd reference things in their home world I didn't know.

"I was so excited to see you again. I couldn't even sleep." He gave my shoulder a light nip. "I knew I'd get ya."

"Are you guys sleeping well?" I asked, looking at Toby and Derrick. "I know the floor isn't the most comfortable place."

"Uh—quite well, yes," Derrick said, looking down at the floor.

Cole turned to Axel. "How's their bed coming?"

"I'm workin' on it. I told you both yer welcome in our bed 'til I'm done. We got plenty of room."

Derrick gritted his teeth, his eyes darting to Toby, who furrowed his brow before shaking his head. "It's actually quite nice out here in front of the fire. Our bedrolls are soft enough, and we wouldn't want to put a damper on your intimacy."

"Intimacy my ass," Toby cut in. "The walls in this place are thin as hell, and you both scared Derrick half to death. I found the whole thing disturbing myself."

"We really tried to be quiet," I said, glancing at Cole. "Did you guys hear us, too?"

Cole pursed his lips and hesitated, not making eye contact, but Vince was all too eager to rip into us.

"We ain't never heard noises like that comin' from a bedroom before. Sure sounded fun, though." He looked over at Cole and nudged his arm. "Now how come we don't almost kill each other while we're havin' sex?" He looked back at us again. "Oh, that's right. 'Cause it's fucked up!"

"I thought we was pretty tame." Axel threw another log on the fire. "We didn't break nothin' this time."

"There wasn't as much blood either," I added.

"Jesus Christ," Cole said under his breath. He seemed to enjoy using that phrase more, despite not knowing who Jesus was. It was mostly to irritate me. "You're both freaks."

"Oh?" I retorted with a half smile. "This house must be haunted, because I hear chains rattling at all hours of the night from down the hall."

Cole looked at the floor again and didn't reply.

I turned to Derrick. "So, you guys are doing well?"

"Not as well as the four of you, but…" He smirked at Toby and held his hand out, palm facing up as though he were about to catch something falling from the ceiling. He spoke indecipherable words in a rhythm as a cold, blue flame puffed into existence, hovering in the air. "Things aren't all vanilla between two mages; we're just a little more discrete." He paused and stared wide-eyed at me. "And less violent—a lot less violent."

Toby grabbed Derrick's hand, squeezing his palms shut.

"Only in the bedroom. We've discussed this."

"Old habits die hard," Derrick muttered. "I finally feel like me again, though."

"I've discussed this with Anaste, and we'll need to talk about magic use later." I turned to Derrick. "I'm going to need a lot of help in the coming months because I don't know what the hell I'm doing."

"Of course, my friend. I will always be here for you, for whatever you require of me."

"Thank you," I said. "I feel bad asking you to do more stuff."

"Nonsense! I love politics, and having the opportunity to advise a leader has always been a dream of mine—well, after being a mage, of course."

"A leader…" I trailed off as more disturbing thoughts raced through my head. "I don't even know where to begin."

"Think of it like cleanin' a really dirty house," Axel said. "You just take it one room at a time until yer done."

"I couldn't have said that better myself," Derrick said. "I have no doubt you can do this, and you're never alone in a pack."

"Speakin' of," Vince cut in, "yer a part of this pack, Leo, but there ain't no pictures of you with the rest of us in that phone thing."

"Oh yeah. I can set a timer and get us all in the frame."

"I will look up ways to pull images out of otherworldly devices so we can hold onto the memories for years to come," Derrick said. "It would be a shame to lose them all."

Anaste made good on his commitment to Varcross and convinced Stellous to supply the town with the necessary hardware to rebuild. Now that we were hard at work eradicating the curse, the dismay lifted a little more with every passing week. The new sawmill had been processing the surplus of lumber we'd been gathering from the surrounding forest, and I was putting the vargyr form to good use carrying lumber with Axel. There were over two hundred of us well enough to make quick work of this, and if I was going to gain enough trust, I needed to do more than bleed myself. I wanted to be involved in everything from planning to building, even if I didn't know what I was doing.

I hadn't yet made anything public about my upcoming role in establishing Varcross as more than a colony. There were still too many vargyrs without homes, and sometimes fights broke out. Despite the frustration, patience prevailed, and for the most part, everyone had come together with a common goal.

"You look tired," Axel said, breaking my focus as we carried bundles of logs on our backs. "I can carry yers if you need a rest."

"No way. I'll be as strong as you are if I keep this up." There weren't enough carts for everyone to push around wood, and Axel and I had volunteered to carry it by hand until enough were made.

"You can't be everything." He walked a little closer and gave me a playful shove. "You're messin' around with all this when you should be learnin' more smart stuff from Derrick."

"I am," I said, stopping to lay the lumber on the ground. Axel did the same and we sat on the grass together. "Right now, this is more important. Derrick's not going anywhere."

"I wonder how many more ferals they found."

"More than we have houses for."

"If we need to, we'll give up Cole's house and sleep outside. No one's gonna die if they gotta rough it for a while. We did just fine out in the mountains."

"They're going to be confused and really upset. The least we can do is make them feel like people again." We both looked at each other, and though we were smiling, I could tell he was just as exhausted as I was. "When this is over, we'll need to do something. Maybe make this into some kind of official holiday."

"I like that idea. It'll keep the morale up." Axel kissed me on the side of the face before jumping to his feet again. "I'm gonna carry both loads and be done for the day. You stay here and rest."

"Axel—"

"Rest. We'll do some huntin' tonight and you cook something good. How's that sound?"

"Are you sure you can carry all that?"

"Leo, I threw yer car and a swollen demon at the wards. I can carry a few sticks back to town."

With that, he gathered both bundles and carried them over his right shoulder. As strong as I thought I was, there was no way to match him. Every time I *won* our little foreplay battles for dominance, it was always a bit of a hollow victory because he'd let me win. It was still hot, though.

"Alright. I'll see you at home."

Axel nodded and disappeared through the trees, and I remained on the ground looking up at the cloudless sky. This world had a beauty unmatched by anything I'd seen on Earth, and the longer I was here, the more I wanted to protect it.

My hands were tied by Stellous for now, though. The country had grown to rely heavily on the precious ore we mined and the rare, black lumber we sent through the trade portals. The humans of Earth and those of Eqiros weren't that different. I often wondered if this was just human nature, or if all intelligent civilizations went through this phase. When I saw that picture of human Axel and Vince, the city skyline appeared far more advanced than Earth, but how advanced were they really?

The brush rustled behind me, but the wind was blowing toward the direction of the sound. I couldn't smell who was there, but I did have this feeling I was being watched for weeks. I'd pretend not to notice, and I'd wander the roads alone to see if I could prod him out of hiding, but he'd always disappear.

Slowly, Gar emerged from the trees, and instead of seeing someone I feared or hated, I saw something pathetic. I'd never seen him so defeated, so exhausted. Even though most of his fur was much shorter than normal, the bits of longer tufts in his little mane were tangled in twigs and caked with dirt. His ribs were showing, and his posture slumped forward as he took one painful step after the other.

I pushed myself to my feet, crossing my arms.

"I can't die," he whispered.

The words I'd been wanting to say to him couldn't come out. A part of me would have given anything to grant him that death. He could have made the right decision, but he chose wrong.

"Why not throw yourself off the bluff like Xavier?"

He stumbled before falling to the ground, and I sat next to him, watching him struggle to sit up. Again, I was caught in between murderous rage and feeling sorry for him.

"This body keeps me alive. It may as well be a curse in itself." He let out a weak, throaty laugh. "The irony."

"I know you've been watching me from the forest," I said, studying his movements carefully. "Why?"

Gar sighed and lowered his head. "I wanted to witness this society of beasts destroy itself and you."

"Disappointed that our nature is different from the savages of X'eeva?"

He snarled but dropped his head again in defeat. "I hated you—or rather, I hated that you were right. I expected them to turn on you since you damned them to a quality of life even worse than before."

"It won't be like that forever."

"I know," Gar said. His tone took on a lighter quality, as though he were relieved.

"What will you do now?" I asked, watching his body language grow more despondent.

"I am damned." He looked up at the sky and drew in a deep, shaky breath. "I failed so catastrophically that all of who I was is gone, and I will never again see my home." Tears welled in his eyes, and he blinked them away. "Such a dreadful feeling. Such a hopeless, painful, dreadful feeling."

"It's sadness," I said, finally placing a hand on his back, able to feel the vertebrae along his spine. "You've never felt it? The entire time you were locked in here, away from X'eeva, you never felt it?"

"Not once," he replied, wiping another tear with his finger before staring inquisitively at the dampness. "What a pathetic state."

"It doesn't last."

"Even being away for eight hundred years was enough to turn me reckless, but now…" He sniffed and wiped more tears away. "Now it is over. I only wanted to return home."

"I know," I whispered. "We both could have had what we wanted—"

"I didn't trust you," Gar interrupted. "With Derrick's help, you would have had time to conspire to stop me from breaking free and destroying Eqiros, and I would have never been rid of that contract."

"Maybe I didn't care if you destroyed it…"

Gar snapped his head toward me, his wide eyes glowing amber. "You mean to tell me that you would have been cold-hearted enough to sacrifice an entire world?"

I struggled to answer, but the truth was likely written on my face. "That's not my world. If it was us or them, what do you think I'd choose?"

The ragged vargyr gave me a crooked smile. "You really would have made one hell of a Devah."

"And I hate myself for that."

"Good and evil are relative, Leo. I see you working every day, building trust, building a community and a new town, but I also hear your concerns about the future. You are good in the sense that you would do anything to protect your own, but you are evil to those that would threaten all of it." Gar's hand fell onto *my* back this time. "Just like you were to me, and I was to you. You'll have no choice but to straddle that line over and over in the coming years."

"I can't trust myself to make the right decisions without becoming a real monster. Earth's history is full of so-called leaders who committed atrocities believing they were doing good." I let out a dispirited laugh. "And I here I am, justifying genocide. If Axel knew…"

"I am someone who has committed these atrocities, and the old me would not have not stopped to consider what you just did. You have two things that I did not: a history to learn from and close friends you would trust with your very life. Mortal leaders fail when they feel they're the only ones capable of making the *right* decisions."

"Are you actually giving me good advice?"

"Yes. And I hate myself for that."

We both let out quiet laughter, and Gar wobbled to his feet with me standing next to him.

"Maybe you don't have to die, but I honestly don't see you ever being allowed near town again."

"I'm already dead," Gar replied. "I'm just waiting for my body to catch up. My mortal soul will go to the circle, and Atorien's memories and legacy will fade to nothing. In a way, that would be the greatest mercy, more mercy than my people will grant you."

"What does that mean?"

He eyed me and smiled. "My actions have guaranteed my exile from both my homeland and from Varcross. When I became mortal, my contract was utterly destroyed. There will be consequences for this, but that is no longer my problem. When I'm ready to die, I'll seek Derrick."

"Be careful what you wish for. He really will kill you, and now that he can use magic, I don't think he'll make it quick, either."

The skinny vargyr slumped forward again, his ears lower. "I am experiencing pain, sadness, loss, and intense loneliness. These emotions made my curse powerful, but I never knew what they felt like through a mortal's eyes. If my kind experienced such things, we likely would have never been able to make the first contract."

"Empathy is one hell of an equalizer."

"I will not apologize for the things I did while I was Devah. That being died when he fell into the void."

"You can't exactly start over. You may look and smell different, but you can't hide those paws or that voice. Keeping a low profile in town won't work because Derrick will find you."

Gar looked out to the woods. "I have a tree shelter in my Lo'rim forest, far away from this place. You've been there."

I nodded.

"Perhaps I could use what I created as a Devah for the benefit of Varcross. If I'm to truly atone, it would need to be with actions, but the loneliness will be a problem."

"That comes with being what you are now," I said, aware of what he was hinting at. "How do I know I can trust you?"

"You don't," he replied. "But what do I have left to betray you with? I can no longer use magic. There's no contract to fulfill, no home to return to. All I have left is my knowledge of Devah culture, Lo'rim, and potions." He smirked at that, which made my spine tingle. "You'll need all of that knowledge sooner than you think, but I'm not foolish enough to give it all away right now. You need me, whether you like it or not."

"And you need me." The words dripped like bile from my mouth. "Perhaps I'll visit you in secret, if you aren't insufferable company."

"Oh, I *will* be insufferable, Leo. You're going to need more advisors than just Derrick. I have the years—the tens of thousands of years. Did I mention I was a leader as well?"

"Once or twice," I said sarcastically. "But a representative democracy is way different from whatever hellish dictatorship you're used to."

"You'd be surprised just how similar they are to one another. You'll understand that once you pull back the luscious, colorful rind to see that rotten flesh underneath." He chuckled to himself, his tail wagging for the first time.

As much as I hated him, he was right. He was also being intentionally nebulous about something else. This all reeked, but I'd be stupid not to listen.

"Alright, Gar. I won't tell Derrick where you are, but I'm not putting any trust in you."

"You don't have to trust me, just listen. Deal?"

I hesitated before turning back toward town. "You get one chance. *Only* one, and that's a hell of a lot more than you deserve."

The vargyr paused, the sound of his smooth, pitbull-like tail slapping his legs. "Then I'll try not to disappoint. Maybe."

Secrets And Sages

With all the manual labor, there hadn't been much time for Axel and me to be alone except in bed. I enjoyed the closeness of the pack, but that little house seemed to get smaller as the weeks passed. Vince fell back into the routine of making messes and not cleaning them, which would spark heated arguments between him and Cole.

Derrick and Toby would leave for a few days every week to search the wild with vials of my blood, taking the magic tool Anaste left behind. He'd figured out a way to enhance it beyond its original capabilities, which made searching vast distances a much simpler task. This week, they ventured further into the unexplored eastern plains, beyond the wastelands.

Then there was Gar. I'd been sneaking away during breaks to pay him visits, and he kept his word about offering me advice while also telling me stories of his home world—though, he still avoided my questions about what he mentioned earlier. The wounds he'd inflicted were still raw, and as much as I tried, I couldn't let go of the lingering animosity toward him, which only made him more cryptic in his responses. He opted to keep the conversations annoyingly light while giving the occasional back-handed compliment in place of the sarcastic insults he'd rather have hurled in my direction.

Today, I decided to take a break, walking hand-in-hand with Axel around the outskirts of town. Since the rest of the hauling carts were built, we'd changed up our routines. Instead of carrying wood, Axel put his carpentry skills to use, making basic furniture such as tables and chairs while also teaching eager apprentices. He'd come home so excited, skipping through the door before going on about his day.

"And that's how Loken nailed his hand to the cabinet," Axel finished, bursting into deep laughter. I'd only been half-paying attention, and it took me a moment to catch on before chuckling. His ears fell and he turned to me. "You okay?"

"Yeah," I said, forcing a smile. "I'm just thinking."

"What'cha thinkin' about?"

"I'm going to complain. Is that okay?"

Axel leaned into me. "It's what I'm here for."

"I don't feel useful anymore. All I can really do to help is carry wood. I tried my hand at building, but I messed up the frame in one room so badly that it tilted and they couldn't attach the ceiling. That set everyone back half a day, and I'm not allowed near the construction sites anymore." I sighed and looked out at the vast cleared land of skeletal structures and scaffolding. Most of the debris from the destruction had been cleared away, being either burned or repurposed. "Now half of Varcross thinks I'm incompetent, and the other half barely knows who I am."

"No one thinks you're incompetent," Axel said, slipping his arm around my back. "They just said construction ain't for you."

"What else have they been saying?"

He put up his hands. "Nothin'!"

I eyed him suspiciously.

"What they say don't matter none. You should go to the dungeon more and drink with the others. A little mingling would do you some good."

"We need to call that place something else," I said, facing forward again, changing the subject. "There's never enough time."

"That's cause you keep disappearin' whenever I turn around." His ears pointed straight before narrowing his eyes. "Been meaning to ask you about that."

"I've just been trying to find better hunting areas." Lying to Axel always felt wrong, but in this case, it was necessary. My visits with Gar would need to remain secret for now.

He slapped my back. "That's perfect! I'm sure there's a few in town that'd love to try it with you teachin' 'em. Why not do that?"

"Because it's just more gathering."

"No, it ain't. It's fun and it takes real skill to master," Axel said, pointing to the vargyrs hoisting planks and pounding nails. "Ain't many here that's the huntin' type, and there's no food coming from Stellous lately since trade stopped. The stores are almost empty now."

"You might be onto something," I said, my lower half shaking a bit as my tail sprung back to life. "Who do you think would want to help with this?"

He shrugged. "Dunno, but you can find out if you actually come to the pub once in a while." Axel smiled, leaning in to kiss me. "If you wanna be recognized as a leader, they gotta feel like yer one of 'em. Pretending work in Stellous, but it ain't gonna hold up here."

The shadow of the black building loomed over the town, half of it covered in colorful murals from those with any artistic ability. The vibrant golds, blues, purples and greens made the dungeon much more inviting.

"Speakin' of lies," Axel added, his tone a sterner. "Where have you really been disappearin' to? Ain't like you to go huntin' and not bring anything back."

Axel wasn't stupid, and I should have known he'd see the holes in my answer. Despite not being book smart, he was startlingly intuitive. What he often described as a gut feeling usually ended up being this ability to see the truth in just about anything. I'd need to put a lot more trust in Axel, especially since we were so close.

"I've been visiting Gar," I blurted, both relieved and worried as Axel's ears clung to the sides of his head, his eyes flashing blue. "I know what you're thinking, but don't."

"Don't what? Hunt him down? Rip him apart?" He snarled. "I've killed people I cared about because of him. If you think I wouldn't enjoy watchin' him suffer, you'd be wrong."

"I didn't want to tell you this."

"Why, Leo?" Axel asked, turning toward me before grabbing both of my shoulders, his claws digging in. "Why would you hide him from us? You know Derrick's been itchin' for vengeance, and you'd take that away from him? He's yer packmate."

"If you think I haven't been fighting urges to rip his throat out, you'd be wrong," I said, jerking away. "Don't make me feel like shit because I chose a much better way to deal with this than more violence."

Axel slumped forward. "I'm sorry. I didn't mean to snap at ya."

"Honestly, I expected you to react much worse, and you'd be justified. I'm definitely not telling Derrick, and you're not either. Derrick's got magic now, and he scares me sometimes."

"Derrick ain't nothin' to be scared of. He'd never hurt ya."

"That's not what I mean. He'd never hurt me, but that doesn't mean he wouldn't use magic to get anything he wants. Why would he listen to me? Why would someone so powerful listen to anyone?"

"Because he ain't human." Axel continued walking along the road with me next to him. "He vowed to be yer advisor, and he ain't the kind of vargyr who reneges."

"He seems like the kind who would lead from behind." I let out a sigh. "God, I'm already suspicious of those closest to me, and I owe Derrick my life. This is only going to get worse when I go to Stellous."

"Don't be paranoid of the people who love ya. Derrick lights up when he sees you, and you know he's got yer back. If you don't trust him enough to tell him about Gar, then you ain't gonna trust him when it really matters."

"It's not him I don't trust. It's the magic. He even admitted how much this shit alters the mind. Arcane made him forget who he was. It could happen again, and I don't know what to do. I can't make him stop using it, especially since I still don't know what Anaste's motives are." My thoughts wandered back to my own world. "Once both sides have a devastating weapon, it boils down to luck and the threat of mutually assured destruction to keep it in check."

"Sounds like you have experience with this."

"Experience? No. I have history," I responded, grabbing his hand. "Just because humans here can wield magic doesn't mean they are any different from humans where I come from. Even though we're not human anymore, we still have our humanity. That's not going to change, and this is why I need to keep Gar alive. Derrick is still human at heart. Gar never had any humanity, and I need his perspective as well as Derrick's if I have a snowball's chance in hell at not screwing everything up."

"You want the perspective of a demon?" Axel's eyes grew wide. "Leo, he'll turn ya into a weapon, not a leader."

"That's where Derrick comes in. Eventually, he will have to know Gar has been advising me, and that will deter any kind of manipulation. I may need a third advisor. Someone who keeps their distance from both and remains impartial. Someone who's aware of a mage's mental state and a demon's manipulation."

"A deva'koh?" Axel asked.

"Oh hell no. Plus, Gar's not a demon. He's something else now, but he still sort of thinks like one."

"Yer not gonna find anyone here who's impartial. We've all been fucked over by that monster."

I nodded. "We'll take it one day at a time. For now, I need to let enough time pass before telling Derrick, and I need to figure out a way to appeal to his sense of logic instead of his emotions."

We lived for the hunt out in the wild. The party only consisted of four, including me, but attitudes were changing as we brought back bounties of the freshest meat, resupplying the dwindling stores. Over the weeks, I managed to find vargyrs that had no qualms embracing the beast within, and we often spent our time together in silence, communicating through body language and expression. It was incredible how we adapted to one another so quickly in order to achieve a common goal. This was the very essence of being what we were. The bond we shared went beyond words.

The three of them had been wilkyrs when I arrived, including Feran. They were forced to undergo the transformation in an unnatural way, many of them on the verge of going feral before my cure.

Feran ended up being nearly as large as Cole, his unusual blonde fur allowing him to seamlessly blend in with the golden grasses of the meadow when we hunted hyukan. Calvin was auburn and on the shorter side, a little taller than Vince, which made him excellent at hunting faster and more agile game. Sebastian was ashy-gray, almost the color of Axel. He was medium build but had military experience before being thrown into Varcross. He was a master at setting up ambushes, learning every hill and cave, while also studying the migration habits of each animal. It still wasn't complete, but with every passing day, we got better at knowing where our prey would be and adapting to any changes due to our presence in the area.

Then there was me. My foot-paws and forward posture gave me an advantage of being able to sprint long distances on my hands and feet. It was strange at first, but I started getting used to running like that. My spine was perfectly adept at the position, even more so than standing upright, which often left me feeling a bit off-balance. Since Feran and I were the largest, we could overpower much larger animals.

"So, how do I join?" asked the black vargyr I'd encountered at Toby's bar the first night I arrived. His name was Jet, and despite his slight altercation with Axel a while ago, the two had become good friends.

It was late evening, and the town was starting to come alive after a day of hard work. There was such a different feeling I got from everyone, including myself. A sense of normalcy. The old tension and anxiety had long since been replaced by laughter and loud, drunken conversation.

"You gonna actually be useful for once?" Toby asked, comfortably serving drinks from behind the bar as though he'd never stopped. It was something he often did when he and Derrick returned to town.

"I'm plenty useful!" The vargyr slid his wooden stein toward Toby. "Now make yourself useful and refill this."

Toby snapped his head toward Jet, baring his teeth.

"Please," Jet said, his ears falling to the sides of his head. There was no denying Toby's imposing personality, which made him a pretty great leader. Could I ever become that?

"That's what I thought." Toby grabbed the stein and held it under the tap of a large wooden keg.

"Sebastian insisted on training new recruits," I said, giving Jet a pat on the back. "Talk to him, and he'll get you started."

The black vargyr nodded with a grin before downing his cider, made from real fruit this time. It was actually sweet instead of bitter.

"I'm so proud of you," Axel said with a slur, leaning into my arm. "Now I wanna join in the huntin'."

"I never thought these words would come out of my mouth, but we need you to make more stuff." Toby threw a stained towel over his shoulder. "I've got an order of bar stools you still haven't finished yet."

"I'm workin' on it." Axel gave Toby a cocky stare. "You might get yer order faster if you tell me how much you love what I make."

The barkeep huffed, turning back to the other patrons.

"He's never going to say that," I said, taking another drink of the delicious alcohol.

"Well, I love what you make," Derrick said from behind. "That new bed was just beautiful. The craftsmanship is impressive."

"Aw, shucks," Axel said, gulping down the rest of his drink. "You always know what to say."

"I wouldn't be much of an advisor if I didn't." Derrick walked up to Jet and tapped him on the shoulder. "Mind if I take your seat?"

"Y—yes sir," Jet said, stumbling to his feet. He often got that kind of response from most people in town. Derrick went from being a vargyr everyone despised decades ago to being almost a celebrity. It never went to his head, oddly enough.

The older vargyr took a seat beside me, his once jovial expression turning more serious. "I need to talk to you."

"This sounds bad."

"Not at all, but I'm not entirely sure how you will respond." His ears fell. "I've been seeing someone in secret, and I think you should know who it is."

My stomach knotted.

"How bad could it be?"

"It's Josiah." He turned to gauge my reaction. "He wants to meet you—in person this time."

I gripped the handle of my stein, taking another drink as I gave what he was saying more thought. This was a man who deceived me and nearly got me killed, but he was also responsible for me finding true happiness for the first time in my life. I didn't know how to feel.

"I am not good at deciphering emotions. Are you upset or indifferent?"

"Alright," I said, taking a deep breath. "I'll meet him. Just set up a time."

"Of course," Derrick said, pointing to a brown vargyr in a tattered robe, sitting in the corner while eying me. "How about now?"

"What?" I jumped off the stool. "I thought he was human!"

"He was." Derrick stood and followed me across the bar. "But he was also on the verge of death when he came to me, having sneaked through the portal a few weeks ago. His use of chonomancy had taken its toll."

"Did you..."

"Without a second though," Derrick responded in a disturbingly nonchalant manner. "He may have been weak, but he was still a human—and I am still a randy beast. He wanted to contract lycanthropy to stay alive, and I certainly didn't want such a valuable mind to disappear." We both slowly padded through the bar, approaching as Derrick whispered into my ear. "It seems the vargyr disease is quite potent, and can still be spread without the curse. I climaxed—"

"Thanks Derrick," I interrupted him before turning to the vargyr staring up at me with milky blue eyes. The top of his mane was swept into a neat part on both sides, and he wore his pointed chin beard tied with a leather strip like Derrick. His fur was very clean for a vargyr, almost silk-like in sheen. Though he appeared younger than I assumed, he certainly had that sage-like demeanor I'd grown accustomed to around Derrick and Toby.

"Leo," he said with a low grunt. "At last."

"Josiah," I responded, my tone hiding a growl. "You're brave."

"I'm a coward," he responded with a smirk. "I heard through the athenaeum a vargyr senator would soon be gracing Stellous."

"There are so many things I want to say to you, but—they don't mean anything anymore," I said, sitting next to him at the table. Derrick took his seat on the other side. "I take it you know our magical secret."

He nodded. "It's one of the main reasons I agreed to become a monster. I hope one day you'll forgive me, but that will likely take—"

"You're forgiven," I interrupted. "If I were in your position, I'd have probably done the same thing, and even though it was fucked up, you did save me."

Josiah smiled warmly. "I hoped you would find my research and would figure it out so that you wouldn't end up like the others, but I was also realistically preparing for a lifetime of more innocent blood on my hands. I did not expect Derrick to still be alive, but you were lucky he was. And you were lucky my research ended up in his capable hands." The mage rubbed his chin. "I'd give anything to see Atorien now."

"He's likely dead," Derrick said casually. "He's a vargyr all alone. It's pure torture, and with no one to turn to, he likely threw himself from one of the bluffs. Wouldn't that be poetic justice? I would not miss an opportunity to piss on his carcass."

I cleared my throat. "I uh...also have a confession to make."

Black Tobacco

"You what?" Derrick shouted, silencing the loud banter in the bar. His glare was like the desert sun, and I was an ant under a magnifying glass. "Where is he now?"

"Far from town," I said, trying to keep my tone calm. "He's harmless."

"You're a fool." I wasn't surprised that he was angry. I just didn't expect him to lash out at me this way. A flash of pale blue light arced from his eyes, his nose brushing against mine. "This is a violation of trust—of our friendship. Did our journey mean nothing? Did our sleepless nights and exhaustion and pain at the hands of that monster somehow slip your mind?"

"I didn't violate anything, Derrick. I hate him too, but we need to put our emotions aside and consider the benefits of having him in our arsenal."

"Arsenal? What good is an arsenal when it's friendly fire? You... you want *him* to advise you?"

"I want his knowledge," I lowered my voice to a whisper. "You know what I trust less than a neutered demon? A powerful nation with its sights set on us."

"You're letting fear cloud your judgment," he whispered back. "This is unbecoming of a leader. Listening to the poison that drips from that fiend's mouth will put us down a path we do not want to tread." He gave a nod to Josiah and grabbed my hand, pulling me toward the entrance of the dungeon with the other mage following. "I have caused enough of a scene."

"It's why I didn't want to tell you," I said as the cold night air stung my nose. "I'm not stupid enough to put my trust in Gar, but I'm also not stupid enough to let you kill him when Stellous is months away from marching through those wards with an army of mages."

"What possible answer do you think he has?" Derrick asked, the snarl on his face softening as he returned to the usual thoughtfulness. "And I wouldn't kill him," he held his claws out, and flames erupted from his palm, "not at first."

"Leo may be right," Josiah chimed in, surprising us both. "An ancient being with a new mortal perspective may work to your—our advantage." He looked down at his hands. "I'm still getting used to this."

Derrick stroked his chin fur, and his raised hackles disappeared under his mane. "You have insight we lack regarding the demon. Do you truly think it wise to listen to any advice he gives?"

"Listen, yes. Act upon it? That is to be determined. Atorien has been cut off from his precious Lo'rim, and he can now die. However, his contract was destroyed in such a devastating and unconventional way that it no doubt sent tremors through X'eeva. He may not be foolish enough to do anything to incur your wrath, but the Devah threat may not be over. We might have inadvertently triggered a coming reckoning."

"Gar said something about this, but he's been intentionally leaving out the details," I said.

Derrick froze before staring up at the sky. "I hadn't considered..." He choked on his words. "Atorien's absence and the contract's destruction likely altered how magic flows in their plane of existence. They will want to investigate what happened, and they will likely want vengeance. The bastard's won, hasn't he? I can't kill him, and he knows it."

"Let's not get ahead of ourselves. Their culture is one of constant struggles for power. I can guarantee no one will be seeking vengeance for Atorien, but any damage to the aether may have shaken the Devah ruling over X'eeva. This could be a weakness countless worlds have been trying to exploit, and having any knowledge of this could very well bring about our end.”

What I mentioned to Axel earlier was standing in front of me, and the remaining anger I had toward Josiah turned to intrigue.

“I’m going to suggest something that you might not like,” I said, turning to Derrick. “You can’t be my only advisor.”

“Nonsense, I—”

“Not after tonight. We’re all fallible, Derrick, especially when we’re too emotionally involved. Gar is your opposite, and I need him, but I also need someone intelligent and impartial.” I turned to Josiah. “You’ll be the third.”

“I have no interest in getting involved with Stellous politics.”

“I wasn’t asking,” I said with a snarl, gripping his shoulder tight with my claws. “It’s the least you can do. And you won’t have to be involved with Stellous at all.”

Derrick said nothing, but I felt the building rage radiating from him. The scent he gave off was familiar, and I only smelled it once before when we were fighting Gar. Part of me wanted to hold off on telling him, but the longer this went on, the harder it would be.

“You’re still my packmate, my friend, and my advisor, Derrick.”

“Yet you lack any trust in me.” He took a deep breath, his nostrils flaring.

“I don’t trust magic. You told me that arcane altered your state of mind. How do I know it won’t happen again?”

“Because I’m different now,” he shouted, snapping his jaws at me. “I feel nothing like I felt when I was human. I control the magic now, not the other way around.”

“I agree, you’re different now. You’re not the same Derrick you were before you got your magic back.”

“This disdain for magic needs to stop,” he said, turning away. “Magic is who I am—it’s all I am and ever was. When you reject it, you reject me.” He stopped, and his hackles raised again. “The glowing forest.”

“Derrick!” I grabbed his arm again, ignoring the shocks stinging the pads of my palms. “Please.”

"Don't be a fool," Josiah said calmly. "Confront him, and you will kill him in your state of mind. I'd rather not see the collapse of this world before I've even grown accustomed to being in it."

The black vargyr jerked away and disappeared into the trees, the only trace of him remaining was the fading blue electric footprints that crackled before dissipating.

"I didn't expect to ever be afraid of Derrick."

"Have a little more faith in him." Josiah placed his hand on my shoulder. "He saved my life when he could have just let me die for working with Gar."

"Yeah, knowing how horny Derrick is, that was probably more self-serving than altruistic."

Josiah sighed. "My point is, he may have a mind focused on vengeance, but Derrick was well known for his ability to place logic over emotion."

"You knew him before?"

He shook his head. "Knew *of* him, but I never knew him personally. The athenaeum kept him locked away in an arcane prison. What he remembers is what they wanted him to remember. As long as they could keep his mind occupied with books and an endless thirst for knowledge, they could keep his hold on magic contained until they figured out a way to control him. Derrick's skill with magic is on a level most cannot comprehend."

"Great," I muttered. "And he's got all of his magic back and then some. Why were they so afraid of him?"

"Stellous fears what it cannot control." Josiah walked with me down the path toward the houses. "Derrick wanted to free the knowledge locked away in the great library. He thought that all knowledge should be accessible to everyone, regardless of rank or magic ability. He was also very open about dangerous ideas in his youth that would challenge the senate's power. If there's one thing Stellous is good at, it's smothering the embers of rebellion before they can burn."

DERRICK

There were few times I could recall this place ever being warm. The air smelled so stale, time having covered everything I owned in several layers of moldering filth. Why did I keep coming back to the bitter memories and frigid loneliness?

I opened my locked cabinet of tomes, running a pointer claw over the spines. Such a pathetic collection. How was I to grow an army of advanced magic users with such trivial tools? We needed Gar. I could taste the vomit threatening to spew from the back of my throat at the thought, but the more I distanced myself from the rage, the more undeniable it became.

Leo used good judgment—as a good leader often does, and I had failed at my first task. Did he even need me? He certainly didn't need tumultuous emotions. He required an advisor who used logic. Perhaps that was what drove him to Gar.

The cabin door opened, and a rush of freezing air made the flames in the hearth dance.

"I had a feeling you'd be here." I turned toward Tobias as he shut the door. "Quite the show you put on tonight."

"It was shameful."

"It was human."

Hearing that was like a punch to the gut. "I suppose it was."

Tobias smiled warmly before sitting in front of the fire on the old caribou-skin rug. "There's a constant struggle between that human side of ourselves that we can't let go of and the beast that lives in the moment. I'd have probably reacted the same way if Gar had done to me what he did to you. You lost yourself to anger. I've always been an expert at that."

With my back to the wooden wall, I looked up at the dusty, rotting ceiling. "The worst is supposed to be over, but I fear that may no longer be the case."

"I brought you something." Tobias reached into a sack he carried and pulled out another, smaller leather satchel. "You still have your pipe?"

The cherry scent of fresh pipe tobacco immediately clashed with the miserable mustiness. It reminded me of when I was a wilkyr, Toby and I talking and making love well past the witching hour. The scent of sex and smoke lingered in my thoughts.

"I do," I said, reaching for the polished bog oak pipe and box of accessories before settling on the rug next to my old friend. "How did you get this?"

"Found it in the rubble of my old tavern. I ordered it from Stellous a while ago, when Leo and the other three came asking about you."

Using the metal tamper, I packed the pipe half full before lighting, impatiently inhaling the soothing smoke before letting it sail from my thin lips like a swirling schooner. "This is Calabrai leaf," I said, handing the pipe to Tobias. "Even after all these years, you still smoke it."

"Because it reminded me of the way things were between us."

"I never had the opportunity to appreciate the culture, and this will be as close as I will ever get."

"The most influential mage in history was Calabrai."

I nodded, thinking back on the towering murals of Nomis adorning the most looked-upon walls of the athenaeum. When she walked that place long ago, her pupils described her as a living statue of granite—black, beautiful, and hardened by decades of scouring Eqiros for knowledge that was at one time forbidden.

When I would look at my reflection as a young boy, I would see that same spark of curiosity that drove her into the unknown. My roots were written in more than melanin, though. Perhaps one day I would meet the Calabrai vargyr who sired me, and he could be more than just a painful reminder of the curse.

"Nomis is still my inspiration. She advocated for the freedom of anyone to pursue knowledge and magic, but she died before her movement could take root. I could have followed in her footsteps, but..." I glanced at the hooked claws jutting from my fingertips, faint jagged lines of electricity arcing from each one. "I would never be allowed back into the grand library like this. Maybe if I could control it like Leo—"

"Enough lamenting about that oppressive place. You can still accomplish what she set out to do, but you can do it right here in Varcross."

"I can feel Stellous breathing down my neck. They aren't yet aware of my lucidity, and I fear the day they figure it out."

Tobias paused, seeming to give what he would say next careful consideration. "Would you object to sealing the portal permanently if it meant you could no longer use magic?"

Such a thought made the hackles on my neck stand straight. "What am I without magic?"

"Everything." Tobias drew in a lungful of smoke before leaning in to lock lips with mine. His dominant behavior had me savoring the familiar taste of his saliva mixing deliciously with cherry notes of tobacco. "We haven't had much alone time since that first night."

"I miss this," I said, carefully grabbing the pipe from his rough, extended hand. "I miss you. Why did we grow apart? It couldn't have only been jealousy."

"You really don't remember?"

I shook my head.

"I hated Xavier," he said, his words clawing at my heart. "He had you so fooled that I couldn't break through. I couldn't stand seeing the bruises."

"He was never abusive," I said, trying to recall hazy memories. "He may have had a few drinks now than then, but he was still my mate."

"He treated you like shit when he was drunk, and that was all the time. You always made excuses because you were blindly in love with his insanity."

"He was intelligent beyond his years. The knowledge he possessed rivaled anything I had learned at the athenaeum—"

"And it all came from X'eeva," Toby interrupted, silencing me. "That kind of knowledge comes at a price, and I couldn't keep watching you fall. Do you know why you have trouble remembering the past?"

"I understood the risks."

"You didn't love him." Toby turned to me, his stare so intense it almost burned. "You loved me. He stole that memory, and that wound wouldn't easily heal. You loved me, Derrick."

I dropped the pipe on the floor, and I leaned in to touch his forehead with mine. "I'll always hurt for him," I whispered. "That wound won't easily heal, either."

"I know." He gently laid me onto the rug, his heftier body covering me in the warmth I craved earlier. We were both ready, the scent of our arousal making me lightheaded. "We've got all the time in the world to heal together."

⁂

We often didn't say much after mating, but this time was different. While lying next to one another, we locked eyes, and he knew what I was thinking. He also knew what I needed to hear.

"Leo needs your guidance, and I need a mate. You can fill both of those roles."

I smiled. "Will you wear the outfit I gave you?"

"Outfit? What outfit? You gave me three fang necklaces and a leather belt."

"Exactly. What more do you need?"

"Pants, Derrick! Pants!"

It was always a thrill to tease him. "Wear the outfit and walk around town with me, and I'll be your mate."

"Derrick," Tobias growled.

"That's the condition. I am trying to start a trend."

"You haven't changed at all, have you? The weird voyeurism is all coming back to me."

"And you still fell in love." It was so strange saying something like that, but this was a side of him I hadn't seen in so long.

Toby rolled his eyes and snorted. "I'm having second thoughts."

"Wear the outfit," I said, leaning in to whisper more. "Be a naked beast with me."

"I'm the only one normal in this pack, aren't I?"

"Give it time."

One Size Doesn't Fit All

COLE

The empty house put me in a state of emotional limbo. Derrick and Toby were staying at the cabin, and Axel dragged Leo out of the house to camp near the mountains. Vince had been at the bar drinking most nights, and as for me, I took the rare moment of peace to start on some of the books Derrick had loaned me, but my wandering thoughts had me re-reading the same paragraph for the past thirty minutes.

After Leo and Derrick's falling-out, I found the silence more disturbing than comforting, like the peace before the chaos of an earthquake. I also made matters worse when I took Derrick's side after Leo explained what happened. How could I not, and how could Leo keep something like that from the rest of us?

But the time alone allowed me the clarity to understand Leo's reasoning, especially given what we didn't know about the consequences of a shattered contract. Apparently, such a thing should have been impossible, but there we were, perhaps on the cusp of oblivion yet again. Could we have pissed off an entire world of powerful, immortal beings? If Gar was just posturing to buy himself time, then we'd likely be caught unawares.

With a heavy sigh, I closed the book before throwing it onto the living room table. As if by habit, I reached for the LCR remote before remembering it wasn't there. With the old source destroyed, and the wireless conduit system incompatible with the magic flowing in through Eqiros, few devices that we'd taken for granted actually worked. Only three places in town had hot water, so most of my showers were either freezing cold or a week apart.

There was nothing worse than feeling gross, and since I'd made the full transformation, I felt filthy all the time. The fleas were unbearable, and with six vargyrs under one little roof, I couldn't get away from them. I would have blamed Axel, but it was most likely Leo bringing them and every other manner of parasite home after hunts.

The door slammed open, and a drunken Vince stumbled in, his fur roughed up. He was bleeding from the nose and mouth, and when he went to speak, there was a gap where his right-front canine used to be.

"I'm goin' to bed."

"Really, Vince?" I asked, standing to inspect his injuries. "I swear, every night, you're missing teeth."

"Gotta defend my honor."

"Did you win?"

His ears drooped as he wiped the blood from his nose with his forearm.

"What do you think?"

I took his hand and led him to the couch before both of us collapsed into it.

"You might have been able to scrap against bigger guys when you were human, but you're at a physical disadvantage here."

"I hate bein' small," Vince whined out. "It ain't fair. Why ain't I big like you?"

"I'm not exactly having the time of my life either."

"I don't get it," Vince replied, scratching his head. "Yer huge. You won the lottery like Axel and Leo."

"I miss being held."

Vince slipped his arms around me. "I hold ya all the time."

"Yeah, but it's awkward now, and I always feel like I'm squishing you. I miss being the little spoon, and everyone treats me weird. I'm used to vargyrs being excited when they'd see me coming, but no one even makes eye contact anymore."

"Could be worse. Everyone could look down on ya."

"People look down on you because you act like a jerk when you're drunk. It has nothing to do with you being short." I stroked the top of his head. "You've always been so hot-headed."

"And you love it." He gave me another gappy grin. "It turns you on, don't it?"

That goofy, swollen look on his face made me laugh. "You're the only one for me," I said, leaning in for a quick kiss. "Stop pissing everyone off, though."

"Why don't you sit in my lap, like ya used to?"

"Are you serious?"

"Damn right I'm serious!" Vince confidently patted his leg. "C'mon. Move that ass over here."

My tail wagged at the thought. "Alright. If I'm too heavy, let me know, okay?"

"You ain't gonna be too heavy."

I gave him a smile and slid across the sofa until I was on his lap.

"I've been trying to get the conduits working with Varcross's new flow of magic. Maybe once I succeed, I'll get the LCR and your gaming system working again." I turned back to an unusually quiet Vince staring wide-eyed at me. "It's up in the air, though. The whole system is so outdated—are you okay?"

He nodded, but his eyes began to water.

"Vince?"

"Okay, ya might be too heavy," he cried out. "I can't feel my legs."

"Damn it. You should have said something." I crawled off of him and felt a slight pop from underneath. "Uh oh. What was that?"

"My bones," he squeaked out.

"I've been trying to do what Leo does when he shifts back to human, but it doesn't work for me."

"The guy's a freak. Nothin' he does makes sense," Vince said, rubbing both of his knees. "It don't matter what you look like or how big you are; yer still mine. We'll just have to adjust because it sure beats the alternative." He held my hand. "We spent so many years waitin' for the end. When I thought I'd have to live the rest of my life without you, I didn't wanna go on. That's how much I love you."

Moments like this were what I loved. He may have been brash, violent, and acted on impulse, but I was one of the few that got to see this side of him. Soft, sensitive, loving, protective and loyal to the end—all of those wonderful traits mental illness took from him for so long.

"I'm so lucky I have you," I whispered before leaning in to kiss his forehead. "I still remember the day we met like it was last week. I didn't know what it was then, but I fell for you hard. You were the most handsome man I'd ever met. You're still handsome."

"Even though I'm small?"

"You're the perfect size. I only wish I was."

"Yer fine. It's just different now, and I'm okay with it." Vince held up a finger, his eyes brightening. "I got an idea."

"Oh?"

"Yeah. I learned a thing or two from Derrick when we was out on the prairie durin' that time you were—you know. He taught me how to meditate, and maybe it can help you."

"It's not going to work."

"It ain't just for what Leo does. I still do it when I get all jittery, or when I'm angry—it doesn't work when I'm drunk, though." He patted his chest. "Just lean back into me this time."

"I'll be more careful." I leaned against his chest and he wrapped his arms around me while gently stroking my abdomen.

"When Derrick rubbed my shoulders, it was kinda weird how relaxed I got. Then I realized vargyrs like bein' petted—or at least I do. It's a little weird, but it works."

"That feels nice."

He whispered in my ear. "Close yer eyes, but don't go to sleep."

"Alright." I closed my eyes and melted into his touch. Every stroke of his hands made me let go of a little more until I remembered the ocean. High, exposed bluffs turned gold as the sun set, the waves slamming into them before exploding into mist.

It may have been a long walk, but I wanted to sit there again, staring up at the stars with Vince lying next to me. The sun disappeared, and I got lost in a shimmering sky as Vince's gentle petting rubbed away more tension until it all turned into long strands of silk.

The air grew cooler, and I floated into the sky. I was human again here, and though the icy wind felt like thousands of tiny ant bites, the fluffy warmth of Vince's embrace soothed it.

Gentle snoring pulled me out of the trance, and I turned toward Vince, who had fallen asleep. I was all the way in his lap, the feeling of it so familiar. My smooth fingers traced over...human skin for the first time in almost a decade. The shock left me breathless, but I would savor this moment, resting my head against his chest before drifting off into the most wonderful dreams.

Something stirred, jolting me awake as muffled yelps shattered the peace of midnight.

"Cole, yer crushin' me!"

I scrambled off of Vince, who lay still, almost imprinted into the couch. It seemed Leo was right about not being able to control the shift back, and I wasn't sure how long poor Vince had been pinned under me.

"I'm sorry...again." I knelt next to him and grinned. "I did it. I turned human."

Vince sat up and rubbed his head. "For real?"

"I think I remember the way I felt, but I don't know how I did it."

"Leo's gonna flip! He ain't that special after all."

"Don't tell him. If I can figure out how to shift more seamlessly, I want it to be a surprise."

LEO

The hot springs were just as cozy as I remembered. This time, the occasion was much less harrowing, and there were no more bottles of sex potions and lube. Axel and I sat next to each other in the steamy water, staring up at the fiery-orange canopy as the sun peeked from behind the eastern range. These last three days with him were exactly what I needed. It was like a honeymoon of sorts—though I wondered exactly what our relationship was.

"Are we married?" I asked, turning to study his expression which narrowed to confusion as one ear drooped down.

"We're...uh..." Axel scratched his head. "I don't really know what to call it. We sure as hell ain't friends, and we ain't just lovers."

"Now that we've had time to adjust, I've had so many weird feelings to sort out. I think differently now, and it's kind of scary. It's like I died and became someone else."

"That ain't true," Axel said, slipping his arm around my waist. "You didn't lose the Leo you were. You added to him."

"I feel like I've just been going with the motions for most of my life. I'm trying to learn how to live the way I want to live while finding new things I enjoy doing. That's a weird feeling." I turned to him again. "What do you find so interesting about me?"

"Yer smart, and you listen to yer gut. You like to be wild, and you know what to say to people to make 'em feel better. No one ever got through to Vince, not even Cole, but you did. You've got a strong sense of family 'cause you never had one. You're like me, just a younger, smarter version."

"You're smarter than you think. While everyone else drank themselves stupid, you taught yourself how to do things like craft and hunt. To be able to have patience to teach yourself new skills is a rare trait. I always used to just give up so easily after my first failure."

"Failure's the best teacher," Axel said softly. "You and me are gonna fail a lot, but we ain't alone no more. When we lean on each other, it makes failing a little easier."

"I really love you." I grabbed both of his hands, and we waded deeper into the spring. "Saying *I love you* was something I've always done out of fear. If I said it, it meant the relationship was still good. It meant I wasn't alone, but that was the delusion. They were just words."

He went to say something, but I pulled him close.

"When I say it to you, I feel it in my stomach and my chest like a fire that never goes out. It takes my breath away because I know you don't just hear it. You don't just hear things, Axel. You know things most people don't, especially things about me."

"And I wanna know more," Axel whispered as our mouths touched. "I wanna see how strong you get." His breath was hotter than the steam rising around us. "Yer gonna make a good leader, but don't ever forget that you got yer pack and you got me. Don't keep things to yerself."

I understood what he was implying, and I would need to confront Derrick now that things had cooled. Perhaps I'd even beg for his forgiveness if it came down to it, even if I knew it was the right decision. That look of betrayal on his face hurt worse than anything, but I had time to fix it, and I couldn't dwell on these thoughts now that the mood had shifted with our scents.

"Make it hurt," I growled before letting go of my humanity once more as my teeth sank into his shoulder.

Axel responded with a low growl before pinning me to the side of the hot spring. Being vargyr brought out the most intense passion and intimacy I'd never experience if I were still human. This was my life now, and I wanted to live it to the fullest.

A week later

Derrick and I locked eyes with one another as we both sat on the ground next to Xavier's grave. The others were playing in the ocean at the base of the bluffs, giving us a much-needed moment to talk.

"I'm sorry," I said, finally looking away from the intensity that made my hackles stand on end. "I never wanted to hurt you like that, and I was wrong not to trust you more."

He leaned in and rested his hand on my shoulder. "And I also apologize. I acted shamefully, letting my emotions overrule common sense. While I may reel at the thought of possibly working with that bastard, I understand the benefits. It was good that you did not tell me sooner." He gave a wicked grin. "I would have killed him."

"Is it wrong that I feel sorry for him?"

Derrick shook his head. "It means you have a good heart, and I should trust your judgment going forward. Having three advisors is very wise, though admittedly, it did sting."

"I didn't mean—"

"It wasn't your words," Derrick interrupted. "It was the realization that I can't do it alone. I wasn't taking my own advice, and I've always thought of myself as more infallible than I truly am. It was humbling, and I'm not accustomed to it."

I scooted from in front of him to beside him before draping my arm over his shoulders. "I'll never be able to thank you enough for everything you did, and I look to you for guidance more than anyone. I don't know Josiah, and I sure as hell don't really know Gar, but you and I have been through hell together. I would never trust them with my life, but I'd trust you."

"That's all I needed to hear," Derrick whispered before leaning into me. "Oh! Have you ever smoked?"

"Uh, no. Not really much of a cigarette person."

"What is a cigarette?" He reached into one of the sacks dangling from the leather belt he wore. Of course, that was the only thing he wore.

"Never mind. What's that?"

Derrick pulled out a worn wooden pipe and a little leather satchel of black cherry-scented herbs.

"Calabrai tobacco. It is the most sought-after due to its medicinal properties. When smoked alone, it doesn't do much for the mind, but—" He packed the tobacco, and with a blue flame from his fingers, he ignited it, drawing in the smoke before pointing his snout in the air and exhaling. "When smoked with friends, the mixture of their saliva with yours adds something almost magical." He licked the mouthpiece before handing the pipe to me. "Now you."

"Alright," I said, turning the warm, antique tool before sticking the end in my mouth, taking in the gentle smoke. It was like breathing fruity mist, barely a hint of burning. The effects were immediate as a smile inched up my face and a rush of calm enveloped me. "Wow."

Derrick stopped me before I could give the pipe back to him.

"Don't forget the saliva," he said, pointing to the mouthpiece.

"This actually does something?"

The mage nodded before taking back the pipe. He slid the end in his mouth and closed his eyes, drawing in even more smoke than before.

"What you feel only happens when you're with someone who truly cares. I care about you, Leo. I worry for you, and I will never let any harm come to you as long as I draw breath." He closed his eyes and smiled. "And I know you would do the same. There may be times when we are at odds, but let us never forget our bond. I certainly will not."

"Neither will I," I said, now so completely calm that I was starting to revert to human form. The problem was, I had no clothes on. "Well, damn it."

"Oh, it seems I had forgotten about that," Derrick said, ogling me with a sly grin.

"Sure you did." I stood, grabbing a blanket from my backpack before draping it over my body. "You're such a pervert."

"I suppose I'm guilty."

"And don't ever change," I said, giving him a firm hug.

A Forever Home

Sapphire flames in black metal street lamps lit the once dark gravel path leading into town. The light danced in time with the faint tribal drumbeat and cheerful howls in the distance, marking a well-deserved end of a painful era.

After only five months, the town had been rebuilt bigger and better than it had been before. Every feral we cured added more skills and legitimacy to Varcross. We had builders, welders, tailors, carpenters, musicians, scholars, mages—even older politicians, which may prove useful in the coming months.

"Sounds like the celebration's already in full swing," I said, picking up the pace as the six of us made our way to town. "Wish we could have gotten all of the ferals, though."

"There's not enough adequate housing," Derrick replied. "Once we get more longhouses, we'll finish what we started."

"How many are left?" Cole asked.

"Five thousand, seven hundred and fifty-two, but those are from Stellous's records. Though it's rare, there may be some who may have died out there."

"Imagine living hundreds of years with a curse only to die right before the cure." Cole's solemn statement had us all silently pondering for a few moments before Vince barked a usual complaint to change the subject.

"Hopefully all the good food ain't gone. What the hell took you so long, Derrick?"

"It's better to be fashionably late," the mage replied, adjusting the small satchels attached to his belt before leaning into Toby. "Speaking of fashion, it's good to see you wearing *the outfit*."

Toby let out a growled huff and rolled his eyes.

"I can't believe the entire town stopped wearing clothes for this," Cole said. "What the hell have you done, Derrick?"

"Liberation. We've finally cast off the shackles of humanity."

"You just wanted to see everyone naked," Toby muttered.

"You have to admit this is a lot more fun." Derrick slipped a finger under one of Toby's tooth necklaces. "You look so handsome wearing Vince's teeth."

"Glad to do my part." Vince grinned, showing off three small newly-grown canines, two on the top and one on the bottom. "Don't even have to brush 'em anymore. I just grow a new set every week once they're all knocked out."

"You don't brush your teeth?" I asked, turning back to the smaller vargyr.

"Do I need to?"

"Yes," the rest of us shouted in unison.

"I can usually tolerate smells, but yer breath makes my nose hairs shrivel up," Axel said. "I was tryin' to be polite by giving you all them mint leaves and tooth brushes, but you never did take a hint very well."

"My breath don't stink!" He huffed a few times into his hand before sniffing. "Don't smell a damn thing."

"Did someone break your nose, too?" Toby asked, wrinkling his snout. "Is that fish?"

"Sure is," Vince replied. "Caught and cooked it myself this afternoon."

"How's the collar, Leo?" Derrick asked, pointing to the stylish accessory he gave me a few weeks ago. Axel had the same one. They were made of shiny, treated leather with our names inscribed in silver runes on the fronts and polished tanzonium studs decorating the circumference.

"Haven't had one flea since putting it on." The moment the mages announced they'd finally found a solution to what plagued the town, everyone lined up for the opportunity to get an enchanted collar.

It grew from being a necessity to yet another fashion trend set by Derrick. "The designs are actually nice. I was expecting something so functional to be a lot plainer."

Cole's collar was burgundy with gold embroidery, which went well with the jewelry he often wore. Somehow, the piercings and jeweled necklaces suited him better in that form, and even though he was one of the larger vargyrs, he was also one of the cleanest and best groomed. He seemed happier now that he was turning heads again.

Vince's collar was pink with black runes embroidered on it. At first, he refused to put it on, but when Axel held him down and slipped it around his neck, the color somehow worked. It went from looking ridiculous to rather distinguished. It brought more attention to the light almond shade of his irises.

Toby's collar was brown with small silver stein-shaped studs, and Derrick's was deep purple with glowing white runes. No one but him knew how to read them, and the mage kept the inscription's meaning a secret.

"Yours and Axel's are special," he said as we neared the outskirts of town. "Perhaps one day you'll unlock what's hidden inside."

"Oh!" Axel shouted before grabbing my arm to stop me. "Leo and I made somethin' for ya. Was gonna give it to ya after the celebration, but you might want to use it before then." He pulled out a long, slender pipe he and I had designed, handing it to Derrick. "I hope you like it."

The mage let out a short gasp as he ran his fingers along the intricate carvings. I'd found an illustration of the pipes often used by archmages at the Athenaeum, and Axel was skillful enough to carve every detail, even going as far as adding Derrick's name at the end. He used the valuable black petrified wood from his secret spot, which was hidden in a volcanic ravine. The strange wood was completely resistant to fire and didn't need to be treated or polished.

"This is gorgeous," Derrick said, eagerly reaching into one of his small leather sacks for a pinch of tobacco. "I'm going to use it right now." He packed the dried leaves into the small opening at the end, pausing before looking at Axel and me. "I am truly at a loss for words. Thank you both."

"Derrick? At a loss for words?" Vince said with a chuckle. "I know I said this before, but I want you guys to know how much it meant to me—what you did when I thought I lost Cole. If I didn't have all of you, I'd have just given up." He turned to me and hooked his arm around my back. "You had every right to abandon me after the way I treated you. I thought you was my rival, but you ended up bein' a brother." Before I could reply, he pushed me away. "Alright, this is gross."

"We're all brothers in a way," Axel said, slapping Vince on the back so hard he nearly fell forward. "We all found each other for a reason."

Derrick rubbed his beard. "Though it defies logic, calling all of this mere coincidence would be insulting. There are things that probably can't even be explained by the Devah. If Atorian's predicament taught me anything, it's that they are just as susceptible to the threads of fate as we are."

The resolved way he mentioned that name made me feel a little more at peace with my decision.

"He still hasn't revealed much of what he knows. I think he's toying with me now," I said, catching a whiff of the delicious smoke now pouring from Derrick's new pipe.

"Probably," Derrick said, taking another deep toke. "Or perhaps he's keeping you in the dark because he's afraid of being abandoned once you have all you need from him. It does make me feel both vindicated and sorry to know he's experiencing a taste of what he put me through. That alone makes me glad he still draws breath. Death, even the slow and agonizing one I had planned for him, would have been too hollow." He smirked and passed the pipe to Toby. "He still remembers what it was like to be an all-powerful immortal being, but now he must live with the same torment he once put us through. One could not conceive of a better punishment."

"Would you have actually killed him like that?" Cole asked. "Even as much as I hate him, I wouldn't want to see him suffer."

Derrick sighed. "I don't know. When I think about it, it's easy to dole out such a punishment, but in reality? After everything I'd experienced, I developed a crippling sense of empathy."

"I wouldn't call it crippling," Toby cut in, passing the pipe to Cole. "Those feelings make you a person, not a weapon. Battle mages exist because their humanity was stripped from them. You were very lucky to get it back."

"Humanity…" Derrick breathed in deep and shook his head. "Humanity created mages as weapons of mass murder. We are more than that, and after tonight, everyone will see it."

Out of the corner of my eye, a naked human Cole stood shivering while clutching Derrick's pipe in his right hand.

"Holy shit!" I shouted as everyone turned back to see what was going on. "What the hell is really in that tobacco, Derrick?"

The mage shrugged. "I'm not entirely sure, but I think we've stumbled onto something rather useful."

"I did it before," he said, his teeth chattering. "I wanted to do it again, but I never could."

"The smoke can calm even the wildest beast," Derrick said, now ogling Cole with that same predatory expression he gave me when I was human. "If Cole can shift, it means any one of us can."

"This is great and all, but I'm about to freeze to death." Cole handed the pipe back to Derrick, and Vince wrapped him in his arms.

"It'll only last about ten minutes," I said, before turning to Derrick. "I meant to ask you something when I saw Josiah as a vargyr. How did that happen so fast? I thought I was the only one that could bypass the wilkyr phase."

"Wilkyr was a loophole of Gar's curse. It's not a natural state of being—which sounds a bit funny considering how unnatural our existence is. This disease we carry mutates humans quickly without the constraints of demonic magic. It's barcly a hypothesis, but it's the only explanation I can come up with."

"I see," I said, looking down at my padded hands and claws. "Maybe one day we can figure it out."

"The answer to what we are now likely won't come from this world. Those are details you could try to pull out of Gar if he ever decides to start feeding you useful information."

◈

Paper lanterns of all colors hung from draped cords on buildings, crossing over the cobblestone paths. The fatty flame-roasted haunches of meat my growing team of hunters brought back glistened with steam as they hung from hooks over booths. Giant kegs of every type of alcohol were staggered along the main street with crude wooden steins stacked around each one. It wasn't the most sanitary setup, but we didn't need it to be.

A band of musicians played their strange-looking instruments, many of them familiar to what we used on earth. A lanky vargyr with his mane cut into a narrow strip of fur pounded out a catchy beat on the drums while several others played what looked like skinny fiddles, guitars, and fat woodwinds. These were custom-made by artisans to fit the odd shape of muzzles while accounting for thinner lips. As expected, most everyone wore nothing more than their collars. Some were still rather shy, opting to keep their pants on, but sooner or later the alcohol would win the war on modesty—just as Derrick anticipated.

Something strange caught my eye. Propped against what used to be Gar's dungeon was a tall, black obelisk, similar to the wards we'd destroyed but smaller. Thick beams of wood kept the object from falling off to the sides.

"Hey, Leo, watch this," Cole said, tapping my shoulder before unleashing a swarm of neon butterflies from his hands. They fluttered around the town, each one exploding in a rainbow of arcane. "Pretty, isn't it?"

"I didn't know you were back to studying magic," I said, watching as some of the townsfolk swatted drunkenly at the colorful manifestations.

"I've had a lot of free time and ample access to Derrick and his books. He's a great teacher. Much better than the stuffy old geezers at the athenaeum."

"How does it feel? Are there any side-effects?"

"None," he replied, unleashing another swarm, but violet this time. Some of them rested on his head like a crown of flittering wings. He turned to me and cocked his head. "Are you okay?"

"I'm just concerned. If Stellous figures this out, we're screwed. Derrick was supposed to keep the magic on the down low, but it's everywhere."

"If Derrick's not worried, you shouldn't be either." He grabbed my arm and turned me toward him. "Did you ever imagine we'd end up like this when you first arrived?"

I marveled at all of the new buildings, the intricately arched designs similar to what I'd seen in fantasy movies. "What if it's all a dream and I wake up back in my old life?"

Cole pinched my left butt cheek just below my tail.

"Ow!"

"That takes care of the dream hypothesis." He leaned in and kissed the side of my face. "Derrick's been scheming."

"What do you mean?"

"He's been dropping hints about something he's going to do tonight."

"I wonder if it has anything to do with that." I pointed to the lifeless obelisk. "That wasn't there yesterday."

Cole hummed in contemplation while scratching his head.

"Do you know what it is?" I asked

"I'm not sure." He nodded toward Axel in the distance who was giving me a drunken grin. "You should go dance with your mate."

"It's so weird," I said, waving back. "He's my mate. One day I'll get used to saying that."

"I knew he was your match that first week you came to live with me. You both were disgustingly infatuated with one another."

"Well, there was chemistry," I said, padding along the road toward Axel. "You gonna stay here?"

"I need to check on Vince. He was supposed to be back with drinks, but I think he's probably getting into another fight."

"You may need to put his leash on him."

Cole reached into his bag, pulling out a long strip of leather with a latch at the end. "I know you were joking, but the gloves have come off."

With that, he disappeared into the crowd, and I made my way over to Axel, who was now stumbling along.

"How much did you drink?"

"Uhh," Axel rubbed his stomach, "five hard ciders, three shots of Toby's new stuff, a couple steins of wine, I think, and some cake that was soaked in somethin' strong."

"Dude, it's been like thirty minutes since we arrived. You've never heard the phrase, 'pace yourself,' have you?"

He smiled and locked lips with mine. His breath was so powerful, I was starting to get tipsy just inhaling the fumes.

"Wanna go have some fun behind the stands?"

"In public?"

"I'm in the mood, and we're already naked."

"No way," I whispered harshly.

He nudged me with his elbow while arching his brows. I had to admit, the possibility of getting caught was hotter than I thought.

"Maybe," I said, grabbing him by the hand, but froze when the lanterns all over town dimmed until all the light disappeared, save for the full moon overhead. The music stopped, and the once boisterous bantering lowered to a wave of hushed whispers.

"What an amazing night for a celebration," Derrick said, his voice coming from every direction. Thousands cheered, many looking around for any sign of the mage. "I can hardly believe how fast the day has come upon us."

A pale aura gradually flickered into existence, giving Derrick, Toby and four other mages an almost spectral appearance. The crowd quickly separated, granting them a clear path to a grassy mound where the old source used to be.

Derrick stepped in front of me and grabbed my hand, pulling me along. "None of this would be possible without the blood and ambition that gave us all a second chance at life."

I looked around before nervously inching away from Derrick. This unplanned speech put me on the spot, and I was never good in front of a crowd. His hand tightened, and he gave me a tug until I was back by his side.

"That second chance came from a man who knew nothing of magic or curses, who was forced to contend with beasts that saw him only as a way to relieve their affliction. He had every right to hate us, especially those who willingly abandoned common sense to follow an insane Devah."

Several hundred ears lowered at that biting remark, but Derrick held up his hand in protest.

"That wasn't intended to scold, but to remind us of how dangerous propaganda in the hands of self-serving evil can be. Had we listened to that fiend, we would have spread like a scourge across Eqiros, slaughtering, raping, and turning everyone until not a shred of civilization remained. Gar cared nothing for our well-being. He would sacrifice millions of worlds if it meant regaining his immortality and status, and it would behoove us to keep that lesson fresh. There are many powerful people like him who hide behind honeyed words and serpent-like smiles, those who leech off of a society they've distracted with manufactured discourse."

He placed his hand on my shoulder, his serious green gaze locking with mine.

"We may have vanquished one demon, but monsters in human skin still have greedy eyes trained on us. Stellous means to put us under its oppressive thumb because it fears us, but thanks to Leo and his blood, we have naught to fear from them. He dreams of a world where we can live as freely as we are now. The only reason we're not slaves at this very moment is because of his quick thinking with the archmages while the rest of us were indisposed."

He certainly embellished that, considering how clumsily I'd handled my negotiations with Anaste.

"It's time for you to lead, and I'll do what I can," he whispered, before turning back to the crowd. "I have been holding audiences with the elders and the mages of Varcross, and we have unanimously agreed that we must have someone who can lead our people."

"What are you doing?" I whispered. "I'm already going to be the senator."

"Senators are worthless," he replied with a grin. "I have a much better alternative."

Derrick held up his hand, and the loud talking died again.

"Rebuilding the town was the first step. Forming a functioning and fair system of government will prove much harder, but we've all faced impossible odds. However, we will not be able to do anything without protection. Many of us here called Stellous home, but we are now outcasts. We no longer belong to them, and I aim to keep it that way."

He nodded to Toby, who then raised his arms with the four other mages in a circle. The violet glow surrounding them intensified into an explosion of pastel. A strong beam of blinding light pierced through Derrick, the force of power knocking me away. As his feet slowly left the ground, he hovered, his eyes a solid purple as he chanted rhythmically in a language I couldn't understand.

The obelisk leaning against the old dungeon hummed, and the ground vibrated, arcane snaking like veins through the ground, spreading out rapidly into the distance until they disappeared into the dense brush of the surrounding wilds. The strange device began to hover, knocking away the thick planks of wood holding it upright.

The massive object floated weightlessly above the town until it settled above the mound Derrick and I were standing on moments ago, the runes carved into the sides slowly illuminating what looked like a warning.

"With this masterpiece of cooperation and knowledge, we will never need to worry about our neighbor's duplicity."

"Derrick, we can't—" My words were cut short by the mage's booming voice.

"You will not be our senator, Leo." His words cut through me, but what he would say next gave me relief for the first time since this all started. "We won't need one. We will be our own country in our own world. Stellous be damned!" The town stared wide-eyed, confused, some shaking their heads.

"You've cut them off," I whispered, trying to keep my voice from being heard. "They weren't ready for this."

"We don't have the luxury of time, nor could we chance any of what we had planned falling upon the wrong ears." As soon as the ward completely activated, all the excess magic disappeared from Derrick. He placed his hand on my shoulder. "Toby asked if I could give up magic if it meant protecting us all, and here's the answer. I truly apologize for not telling you, friend. I couldn't put you at risk with this knowledge before making sure this was possible."

"Will this be enough?" I asked, eying the now wary crowd, some of whom were starting to shout protests. "Because we're fucked if it's not."

"It will be enough." He turned back to the crowd. "I had anticipated discourse. There may never be a way to calm all of it, but I hoped you would have an idea."

"You expect me to be able to smooth everything over unprepared? What the hell did you expect me to do?"

He smiled as if he were completely unfazed. "Many are still suffering the after-effects of the curse. What would you say to Axel or Vince to put them at ease?"

"I don't have anything prepared."

Derrick shook his head. "Prepared speeches are tools for those used as tools. A leader worth listening to speaks from the heart."

"You and I are gonna have a long talk after this," I said with a slight snarl as Derrick stepped away, bowing as I stood in front of a symbol of either freedom or oppression—even I didn't know which at that moment. Glowing, multicolored wolf eyes fixated on me like prey.

"July twenty-sixth, nineteen ninety-four. That doesn't really make sense to any of you, but that was the day I was born." My voice carried the same way Derrick's did across a crowd of thousands without the need for a microphone. It seemed not all the magic was gone. I took a deep breath before Axel caught my attention. His soft stare calmed the erratic current of emotions stirring in my mind. "No one ever expected or encouraged me to do anything worthwhile, so I spent most of my life believing my worth and happiness were tied to the very people keeping me from realizing who I was. It wasn't until I came here that all of that changed.

"Stellous sees me as a tool. The deal I stumbled into would have likely made me a prisoner, and Derrick knows this. He knows a lot. You all may not agree with what he just did, but I trust his word. A lot of you have family and friends on the other side, but Anaste made it quite clear that none of us would ever walk Eqiros freely."

"They wanted to make us soldiers!" Everyone turned to the wide-eyed, young vargyr who the mages had in a cage that day I negotiated. "Leo talked them out of it, but I know they'd do it. They do it all the time. After everything they've put us through, I don't want to die for them, too."

"We should've had a say," another in the crowd shouted. "A representative democracy wasn't perfect, but it was still democracy! What have we got now? A dictatorship?"

The crowd began to shout again before I howled out an objection.

"Absolutely not! That will never happen, and something like this will never happen again." My intense stare fell upon Derrick, and his ears fell to the sides. "Though, I'm curious about your representative democracy. Did any of you ever feel like you were actually represented?"

The vargyr shouting protests stood in silence as the rest of the town whispered.

"In my world, only the interests of the few are actually represented because those with all the wealth are the only ones who can feasibly run for office. It's why we never saw people like ourselves in positions of power. But that doesn't have to be us. We may not be human anymore, but we're in a unique position to learn from humanity's mistakes."

Hushed voices echoed around me as my words either sparked encouragement or worry. I couldn't tell if anything I was saying actually mattered, but this was all I could do.

"I'm not going to promise a utopia because one could never exist, but look around at each other. You don't see strangers. You see brothers. We came together and built an entire town in record time because we had brothers who needed places to live. No one told any of you that you had to do it or you wouldn't get compensated. You all put your talents and skills to use, and came up with this." I lifted my arms, pointing at all the buildings.

"We don't always get along." I looked over at a beat-up Vince standing next to Cole with a leash attached to his collar. "We fight, we argue, we have different opinions. That's never going to change, but we'll still love one another. We're all we've got. We live a long time and can't reproduce, and humans won't be able to come through the portal anymore." I smiled at the overwhelming feeling I had just then. "Maybe I'm weird, but I find comfort in that."

There were fewer grimaces in the crowd as they listened.

"I never had a family that loved me before I ended up here, and now I have a family of several thousand and growing. That's what

I feel when I look at each of you. I'll never be homesick, and I hope that in time—after most of the painful memories of the curse have faded—you'll all feel like you've finally made it home as well."

Warm tears soaked my face as I looked at the people I loved—Toby, Derrick, Cole, Axel, and Vince. Living without any one of them would have left a void that could never be filled.

Toby held Derrick, and for the first time, I saw the hardened stone on his face crack, his eyes glassy and shimmering. He'd spent so much of his time with nothing, even if he seemed to have more than most. Now everything he ever really wanted was in his arms, and Derrick was able to move forward instead of dwelling on the past.

Cole squeezed Vince, and it was like seeing them again that day in the woods—that moment frozen in time when the rays of sunlight turned them into angels. Their eyes were closed as they breathed each other in. Both of them had come so close to losing it all, but by luck or grace, they still lived.

I'd never been spiritual, but when I locked eyes with Axel, I saw eternity. I saw the universe of countless worlds fuse into one singularity as if he were everything. The town at one point resumed their celebrations, though a little more somber this time, but it all faded away, except him—the person I loved more than anything. The one person I would cross hell for—again and again.

His hand took mine, and our noses touched.

"We both made it home," he said, his deep voice resonating through my ears

We held each other for a moment before more arms joined in the embrace. The combined scent of my family filled me with a comfort those back on Earth would likely never know. They surrounded me, and I was at the center, warmer than I'd ever been in my life.

My family.

I made it home.

If you enjoyed The Varcross Key, share it with friends, and most importantly, rate and review it.

ABOUT THE AUTHOR

Aeron Dusk was born in Florida but moved to Colorado in late 2022. Inspiration for his descriptions of scenery and natural beauty comes from living in one of the most beautiful places in the country. He has always had a love for magic, fantasy, adventure, and above all, happy endings.

Books make our wildest dreams reality.

To learn more about Aeron, visit: www.howlingdusk.com

www.ingramcontent.com/pod-product-compliance
Lightning Source LLC
Chambersburg PA
CBHW061047210726
48294CB00001B/50